P9-DBT-089

STRANGE HIGHWAYS

ALSO BY DEAN KOONTZ

Dark Rivers of the Heart
Mr. Murder
Dragon Tears
Hideaway
Cold Fire
The Bad Place
Midnight
Lightning
Watchers
Strangers
Twilight Eyes
Darkfall
Phantoms
Whispers
Night Chills
The Vision
The Mask
The Funhouse
The Face of Fear
Shattered
The Voice of the Night
The Servants of Twilight
The House of Thunder
Shadowfires
The Key to Midnight
Winter Moon
The Door to December
Icebound

STRANGE HIGHWAYS

DEAN KOONTZ

WARNER BOOKS

A Time Warner Company

A Brandon Tartikoff Book

"Strange Highways" copyright © 1995 by Dean R. Koontz

"The Black Pumpkin" copyright © 1986 by Nkui, Inc., originally appeared in *Twilight Zone Magazine*, December, 1986; reprinted by permission of Nkui, Inc.

"Miss Attila the Hun" copyright © 1987 by Nkui, Inc., originally appeared in *Night Visions 4*, published by Dark Harvest, Arlington Heights, Illinois; reprinted by permission of Nkui, Inc.

"Down in the Darkness" copyright © 1986 by Nkui, Inc., originally appeared in *The Horror Show*, Summer 1986, reprinted by permission of Nkui, Inc.

"Ollie's Hands" copyright © 1972 by Dean R. Koontz, originally appeared in *Infinity Four*, edited by Robert Hoskins, published by Lancer Books; revised version copyright © 1995 by Dean R. Koontz.

"Snatcher" copyright © 1986 by Nkui, Inc., originally appeared in *Night Cry*, Fall 1986; reprinted by permission of Nkui, Inc.

"Trapped" copyright © 1989 by Nkui, Inc., originally appeared in *Stalkers*, edited by Ed Gorman and Martin H. Greenberg, published by Dark Harvest, Arlington, Illinois; reprinted by permission of Nkui, Inc.

"Bruno" copyright © 1971 by Dean R. Koontz, originally appeared in *The Magazine of Fantasy and Science Fiction*, April, 1971; revised version copyright © 1995 by Dean R. Koontz.

"We Three" copyright © 1974 by Dean R. Koontz, originally appeared in *Final Stage*, edited by Edward L. Ferman and Barry N. Malzberg, published by Charterhouse, New York, New York; revised version copyright © 1995 by Dean R. Koontz.

"Hardshell" copyright © 1987 by Nkui, Inc., originally appeared in *Night Visions 4*, published by Dark Harvest, Arlington Heights, Illinois; reprinted by permission of Nkui, Inc.

"Kittens" copyright © 1966 by Dean R. Koontz, originally appeared in *The Reflector*, Shippensburg University, Shippensburg, Pennsylvania; revised version copyright © 1995 by Dean R. Koontz.

"The Night of the Storm" copyright © 1974 by Dean R. Koontz, originally appeared in *Continuum 1*, edited by Roger Elwood, published by G. P. Putnam's Sons, New York, New York; revised version copyright © 1995 by Dean R. Koontz.

"Twilight of the Dawn" copyright © 1987 by Nkui, Inc., originally appeared in *Night Visions 4*, published by Dark Harvest, Arlington Heights, Illinois; reprinted by permission of Nkui, Inc.

"Chase" copyright © 1972 by K. R. Dwyer (a pseudonym for Dean R. Koontz), published by Random House, New York, New York; revised version copyright © 1995 by Dean R. Koontz.

Copyright © 1995 by Dean Koontz
All rights reserved.

Warner Books, Inc., 1271 Avenue of the Americas, New York, NY 10020

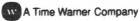 A Time Warner Company

Printed in the United States of America

ISBN 0-446-51974-X

This book is dedicated
with much affection to
Jerry and Mary Ann Crowe.
After all these years
of being your friends,
Gerda and I have learned
that we have infinite patience.
Thanks for the friendship,
for all the laughs
you've given us
(some of them intentional),
for buying the house
built over the gate to Hell,
and for pointing out to me
every error I make.
Every tiny error.
Every teeny-tiny error.
Every minute error that
no one else, not even God,
would notice.
Thank you. Thank you.
Thank you.

CONTENTS

STRANGE HIGHWAYS
1

THE BLACK PUMPKIN
156

MISS ATTILA THE HUN
175

DOWN IN THE DARKNESS
204

OLLIE'S HANDS
229

SNATCHER
245

TRAPPED
261

BRUNO
311

WE THREE
338

HARDSHELL
346

KITTENS
373

THE NIGHT OF THE STORM
379

TWILIGHT OF THE DAWN
402

CHASE
432

NOTES TO THE READER
553

STRANGE HIGHWAYS

STRANGE HIGHWAYS

1

O<small>N THAT AUTUMN AFTERNOON, WHEN HE DROVE THE RENTAL CAR</small> into Asherville, Joey Shannon broke out in an icy sweat. A sudden and intense hopelessness overcame him.

He almost hung a hard U-turn in the middle of the street. He resisted the urge to jam the accelerator to the floorboards, speed away, and never look back.

The town was as bleak as any in Pennsylvania coal country, where the mines had shut down and most good jobs had been lost decades ago. Nevertheless, it wasn't such a desperate place that the very sight of it should chill his heart and bring him instantly to the edge of despair. He was puzzled by his peculiar reaction to this long-delayed homecoming.

Sustained by fewer than a thousand local residents and perhaps two thousand more in several smaller outlying towns, the commercial district was just two blocks long. The two- and three-story stone buildings—erected in the 1850s and darkened by a century and a half of grime—were pretty much as he remembered them from his youth.

Evidently the merchants' association or the town council was engaged in a beautification project. All the doors, the window frames, the shutters, and the eaves appeared to have been freshly painted. Within the past few years, circular holes had been cut out of the sidewalks to allow the planting of young maple trees, which were now eight feet tall and still lashed to support poles.

The red and amber autumn foliage should have enlivened the

town, but Asherville was grim, huddled, and forbidding on the brink of twilight. Balanced on the highest ridges of the western mountains, the sun seemed strangely shrunken, shedding light that didn't fully illuminate anything it touched. In the sour-yellow glow, the rapidly lengthening shadows of the new trees reached like grasping hands onto the cracked blacktop.

Joey adjusted the car heater. The greater rush of hot air did not immediately warm him.

Above the spire of Our Lady of Sorrows, as the retiring sun began to cast off purple cloaks of twilight, an enormous black bird wheeled in circles through the sky. The winged creature might have been a dark angel seeking shelter in a sacred bower.

A few people were on the streets, others in cars, but he didn't recognize any of them. He'd been gone a long time. Over the years, of course, people changed, moved away. Died.

When he turned onto the gravel driveway at the old house on the east edge of town, his fear deepened. The clapboard siding needed fresh paint, and the asphalt-shingle roof could have used repair, but the place wasn't ominous by any measure, not even as vaguely Gothic as the buildings in the heart of town. Modest. Dreary. Shabby. Nothing worse. He'd had a happy childhood here in spite of deprivation. As a kid, he hadn't even realized that his family was poor; that truth hadn't occurred to him until he went away to college and was able to look back on their life in Asherville from a distance. Yet for a few minutes, he waited in the driveway, overcome by inexplicable dread, unwilling to get out of the car and go inside.

He switched off the engine and the headlights. Although the heater hadn't relieved his chill, he immediately grew even colder without the hot air from the vents.

The house waited.

Maybe he was afraid of facing up to his guilt and coming to terms with his grief. He hadn't been a good son. And now he would never have another opportunity to atone for all the pain that he had caused. Maybe he was frightened by the realization that he would have to live the rest of his life with the burden of what he'd done, with his remorse unexpressed and forgiveness forever beyond reach.

No. That was a fearful weight, but it wasn't what scared him. Neither guilt nor grief made his mouth go dry and his heart pound as he stared at the old homestead. Something else.

In its wake, the recessional twilight drew in a breeze from the northeast. A row of twenty-foot pines stood along the driveway, and their boughs began to stir with the onset of night.

At first Joey's mood seemed extraordinary: a portentous sense that he was on the brink of a supernatural encounter. It was akin to what he had sometimes felt as an altar boy a long time ago, when he'd stood at the priest's side and tried to sense the instant at which the ordinary wine in the chalice became the sacred blood of Christ.

After a while, however, he decided that he was being foolish. His anxiety was as irrational as any child's apprehension over an imaginary troll lurking in the darkness under his bed.

He got out of the car and went around to the back to retrieve his suitcase. As he unlocked the trunk, he suddenly had the crazy notion that something monstrous was waiting in there for him, and as the lid rose, his heart knocked explosively against his ribs. He actually stepped back in alarm.

The trunk contained only his scuffed and scarred suitcase, of course. After taking a deep breath to steady his nerves, he withdrew the single piece of luggage and slammed the trunk lid.

He needed a drink to settle his nerves. He always needed a drink. Whiskey was the only solution that he cared to apply to most problems. Sometimes, it even worked.

The front steps were swaybacked. The floorboards on the porch hadn't been painted in years, and they creaked and popped noisily under his feet. He wouldn't have been surprised if he had crashed through the rotting wood.

The house had deteriorated in the two decades since he had last seen it, which surprised him. For the past twelve years, on the first of each month, his brother had sent a generous check to their father, enough to allow the old man either to afford a better house or to renovate this place. What had Dad been doing with the money?

The key was under the rubber-backed hemp mat, where he'd been told that he would find it. Though Asherville might give him the heebie-jeebies, it was a town where a spare key could be kept in an obvious place or a house could even be left unlocked with virtually no risk of burglary.

The door opened directly into the living room. He put his bag at the foot of the stairs to the second floor.

He switched on the lights.

The sofa and the armchair recliner were not the same as those that had been there twenty years ago, but they were so similar as to be indistinguishable from the previous furniture. Nothing else appeared to have been changed at all—except the television, which was big enough to belong to God.

The rest of the first floor was occupied by the combined kitchen and dining area. The green Formica table with its wide chrome edge band was the one at which they had eaten meals throughout his childhood. The chairs were the same too, although the tie-on cushions had been changed.

He had the curious feeling that the house had been untenanted for an age, sealed tomb-tight, and that he was the first in centuries to invade its silent spaces. His mother had been dead sixteen years, his dad for only a day and a half, but both seemed to have been gone since time immemorial.

In one corner of the kitchen was the cellar door, on which hung a gift calendar from the First National Bank. The picture for October showed a pile of orange pumpkins in a drift of leaves. One had been carved into a jack-o'-lantern.

Joey went to the door but didn't open it right away.

He clearly remembered the cellar. It was divided into two rooms, each with its own outside entrance. One contained the furnace and the hot-water heater. The other had been his brother's room.

For a while he stood with his hand on the old cast-iron knob. It was icy under his palm, and his body heat didn't warm it.

The knob creaked softly when he finally turned it.

Two dim, dust-covered, bare bulbs came on when he flicked the switch: one halfway down the cellar stairs, the second in the furnace room below. But neither chased off all the darkness.

He didn't have to go into the cellar first thing, at night. The morning would be soon enough. In fact, he could think of no reason why he had to go down there at all.

The illuminated square of concrete floor at the foot of the steps was veined with cracks, just as he remembered it, and the surrounding shadows seemed to seep from those narrow fissures and rise along the walls.

"Hello?" he called.

He was surprised to hear himself speak, because he knew that he was alone in the house.

Nevertheless, he waited for a response. None came.

"Is someone there?" he asked.

Nothing.

At last he shut off the cellar lights and closed the door.

He carried his suitcase to the second floor. A short, narrow hallway with badly worn gray-and-yellow-flecked linoleum led from the head of the stairs to the bathroom at the back.

Beyond the single door on the right was his parents' room. Actually, for sixteen years, since his mother's death, his dad had slept there alone. And now it was nobody's room.

The single door on the left side of the hall led to his old bedroom, into which he had not set foot in twenty years.

The flesh prickled on the nape of his neck, and he turned to look down the stairs into the living room, half expecting to discover that someone was ascending after him. But who might have been there? Everyone was gone. Dead and gone. The stairs were deserted.

The house was so humble, small, narrow, plain—yet at the moment it felt vast, a place of unexpected dimensions and hidden rooms where unknown lives were lived, where secret dramas unfolded. The silence was not an ordinary quiet, and it cut through him as a woman's scream might have done.

He opened the door and went into his bedroom.

Home again.

He was scared. And he didn't know why. Or if he knew, the knowledge existed somewhere between instinct and recollection.

2

THAT NIGHT, AN AUTUMN STORM MOVED IN FROM THE NORTHWEST, AND all hope of stars was lost. Darkness congealed into clouds that pressed against the mountains and settled between the high slopes, until the heavens were devoid of light and as oppressive as a low vault of cold stone.

When he was a teenager, Joey Shannon had sometimes sat by the single window of his second-floor bedroom, gazing at the wedge of sky that the surrounding mountains permitted him. The stars and the brief transit of the moon across the gap between the ridges were a much-needed reminder that beyond Asherville, Pennsylvania, other worlds existed where possibilities were infinite and where even a boy from a poor coal-country family might change his luck and become anything that he wished to be, especially if he were a boy with big dreams and the passion to pursue them.

This night, at the age of forty, Joey sat at the same window, with the lights off, but the sight of stars was denied him. Instead, he had a bottle of Jack Daniel's.

Twenty years ago, in another October when the world had been a far better place, he'd come home for one of his quick, infrequent visits from Shippensburg State College, where with the help of a partial scholarship, he had been paying his way by working evenings and weekends as a supermarket stock clerk. His mom had cooked his favorite dinner—meatloaf with tomato gravy, mashed potatoes, baked corn—and he had played some two-hand pinochle with his dad.

His older brother, P.J. (for Paul John), also had been home that weekend, so there had been a lot of laughter, affection, a comforting sense of family. Any time spent with P.J. was always memorable. He was successful at everything that he tried—the valedictorian of his high-school and college graduating classes, a football hero, a shrewd poker player who seldom lost, a guy at whom all the prettiest girls looked with doe-eyed interest—but the best thing about him was his singular way with people and the upbeat atmosphere that he created wherever he went. P.J. had a natural gift for friendship, a sincere liking for most people, and an uncanny empathy that made it possible for him to understand what made a person tick virtually upon first meeting. Routinely and without apparent effort, P.J. became the center of every social circle that he entered. Highly intelligent yet self-effacing, handsome yet free of vanity, acerbically witty but never mean, P.J. had been a terrific big brother when they had been growing up. More than that, he'd been—and after all these years, still *was*—the standard by which Joey Shannon measured himself, the one person into whom he would have remade himself if that had been possible.

In the decades since, he had fallen far short of that standard.

Although P.J. moved from success to success, Joey had an unerring knack for failure.

Now he took a few ice cubes from the bowl on the floor beside his straight-backed chair and dropped them into his glass. He added two inches of Jack Daniel's.

One thing that Joey hadn't failed at was drinking. Although his bank account had seldom been above two thousand dollars in his entire adult life, he always managed to afford the best blended whiskey. No one could say that Joey Shannon was a *cheap* drunk.

On the most recent night that he'd spent at home—Saturday, October twenty-fifth, 1975—he had sat at this window with a bottle of RC Cola in his hand. He hadn't been a boozer back then. Diamond-bright stars had adorned the sky, and there had seemed to be an infinite number of possible lives waiting for him beyond the mountains.

Now he had the whiskey. He was grateful for it.

It was October twenty-first, 1995—another Saturday. Saturday was always the worst night of the week for him, although he didn't know why. Maybe he disliked Saturday because most people dressed up to go out to dinner or dancing or to a show to celebrate the passage of another workweek—while Joey found nothing to celebrate about having endured another seven days in the prison that was his life.

Shortly before eleven o'clock the storm broke. Brilliant chains of molten-silver lightning flashed and rattled across the wedge of sky, providing him with flickering, unwanted reflections of himself in the window. Rolling thunder shook the first fat raindrops from the clouds; they snapped and spattered against the glass, and the ghostly image of Joey's face dissolved before him.

At half past midnight he rose from the chair and went to the bed. The room was as black as a coal mine, but even after twenty years he could find his way around without light. In his mind's eye, he held a detailed image of the worn and cracked linoleum floor, the oval rag rug that his mother had made, the narrow bed with simple painted-iron headboard, the single nightstand with warped drawers. In one corner was the heavily scarred desk at which he had done his homework through twelve years of school and, when he was eight or nine, had written his first stories about magical kingdoms and monsters and trips to the moon.

As a boy, he had loved books and had wanted to grow up to be a writer. That was one of the few things at which he hadn't failed in the past twenty years—though only because he had never tried. After that October weekend in 1975, he'd broken his long habit of writing stories and abandoned his dream.

The bed was no longer covered by a chenille spread, as it had been in those days, and in fact it wasn't even fitted with sheets. Joey was too tired and fuzzy-headed to bother searching for linens.

He stretched out on his back on the bare mattress, still wearing his shirt and jeans, not bothering to kick off his shoes. The soft twang of the weak springs was a familiar sound in the darkness.

In spite of his weariness, Joey didn't want to sleep. Half a bottle of Jack Daniel's had failed to quiet his nerves or to diminish his apprehension. He felt vulnerable. Asleep, he'd be defenseless.

Nevertheless, he had to try to get some rest. In little more than twelve hours, he would bury his dad, and he needed to build up strength for the funeral, which wasn't going to be easy on him.

He carried the straight-backed chair to the hall door, tilted and wedged it under the knob: a simple but effective barricade.

His room was on the second floor. No intruder could easily reach the window from outside. Besides, it was locked.

Now, even if he was sound asleep, no one could get into the room without making enough noise to alert him. No one. Nothing.

In bed again, he listened for a while to the relentless roar of the rain on the roof. If someone was prowling the house at that very moment, Joey couldn't have heard him, for the gray noise of the storm provided perfect cover.

"Shannon," he mumbled, "you're getting weird in middle age."

Like the solemn drums of a funeral cortege, the rain marked Joey's procession into deeper darkness.

In his dream, he shared his bed with a dead woman who wore a strange transparent garment smeared with blood. Though lifeless, she suddenly became animated by demonic energy, and she pressed one pale hand to his face. *Do you want to make love to me?* she asked. *No one will ever know. Even I couldn't be a witness against you. I'm not just dead but blind.* Then she turned her face toward him, and he saw that her eyes were gone. In her empty sockets was the deepest darkness he had ever known. *I'm yours, Joey. I'm all yours.*

He woke not with a scream but with a cry of sheer misery. He sat on the edge of the bed, his face in his hands, sobbing softly.

Even dizzy and half nauseated from too much booze, he knew that his reaction to the nightmare was peculiar. Although his heart raced with fear, his grief was greater than his terror. Yet the dead woman was no one he had ever known, merely a hobgoblin born of too little sleep and too much Jack Daniel's. The previous night, still shaken by the news of his dad's death and dreading the trip to Asherville, he had dozed only fitfully. Now, because of weariness and whiskey, his dreams were bound to be populated with monsters. She was nothing more than the grotesque denizen of a nightmare. Nevertheless, the memory of that eyeless woman left him half crushed by an inexplicable sense of loss as heavy as the world itself.

According to the radiant dial of his watch, it was three-thirty in the morning. He had been asleep less than three hours.

Darkness still pressed against the window, and endless skeins of rain unraveled through the night.

He got up from the bed and went to the corner desk where he had left the half-finished bottle of Jack Daniel's. One more nip wouldn't hurt. He needed *something* to make it through to the dawn.

As Joey uncapped the whiskey, he was gripped by a peculiar urge to go to the window. He felt drawn as if by a magnetic force, but he resisted. Crazily, he was afraid that he might see the dead woman on the far side of the rain-washed glass, levitating one story above the ground: blond hair tangled and wet, empty eye sockets darker than the night, in a transparent gown, arms extended, wordlessly imploring him to fling up the window and plunge into the storm with her.

He became convinced that she *was* floating out there like a ghost. He dared not even glance toward the window or risk catching sight of it from the corner of his eye. If he saw her peripherally, even that minimal eye contact would be an invitation for her to come into his room. Like a vampire, she could tap at the window and plead to be let in, but she could not cross his threshold unless invited.

Edging back to the bed with the bottle in his hand, he kept his face averted from that framed rectangle of night.

He wondered if he was just unusually drunk or if he might be losing his mind.

To his surprise, he screwed the cap back on the bottle without taking a drink.

3

IN THE MORNING, THE RAIN STOPPED FALLING, BUT THE SKY REMAINED low and threatening.

Joey didn't have a hangover. He knew how to pace his drinking to minimize the painful results. And every day he took a megadose of vitamin-B complex to replace what had been destroyed by alcohol; extreme vitamin-B deficiency was the primary cause of hangovers. He knew all the tricks. His drinking was methodical and well organized; he approached it as though it were his profession.

He found the makings of breakfast in the kitchen: a piece of stale coffee cake, half a glass of orange juice.

After showering, he put on his only suit, a white shirt, and a dark red tie. He hadn't worn the suit in five years, and it hung loosely on him. The collar of the shirt was a size too large. He looked like a fifteen-year-old boy dressed in his father's clothes.

Perhaps because the endless intake of booze accelerated his metabolism, Joey burned off all that he ate and drank, and invariably he closed each December a pound lighter than he'd begun the previous January. In another hundred and sixty years, he would finally waste away into thin air.

At ten o'clock he went to the Devokowski Funeral Home on Main Street. It was closed, but he was admitted by Mr. Devokowski because he was expected.

Louis Devokowski had been Asherville's mortician for thirty-five years. He was not sallow and thin and stoop shouldered, as comic books and movies portrayed men of his trade, but stocky and ruddy faced, with dark hair untouched by gray—as though working with the dead was a prescription for long life and vitality.

"Joey."

"Mr. Devokowski."

"I'm so sorry."

"Me too."

"Half the town came to the viewing last night."

Joey said nothing.

"Everyone loved your father."

Joey didn't trust himself to speak.

Devokowski said, "I'll take you to him."

The front viewing room was a hushed space with burgundy carpet, burgundy drapes, beige walls, and subdued lighting. Arrangements of roses loomed in the shadows, and the air was sweet with their scent.

The casket was a handsome bronze model with polished-copper trim and handles. By phone, Joey had instructed Mr. Devokowski to provide the best. That was how P.J. would want it—and it would be his money paying for it.

Joey approached the bier with the hesitancy of a man in a dream who expects to peer into the coffin and see himself.

But it was Dan Shannon who rested in peace, in a dark-blue suit on a bed of cream-colored satin. The past twenty years had not been kind to him. He looked beaten by time, shrunken by care, and glad to be gone.

Mr. Devokowski had retreated from the room, leaving Joey alone with his dad.

"I'm sorry," he whispered to his father. "Sorry I never came back, never saw you or Mom again."

Hesitantly, he touched the old man's pale cheek. It was cold and dry.

He withdrew his hand, and now his whisper was shaky. "I just took the wrong road. A strange highway . . . and somehow . . . there was never any coming back. I can't say why, Dad. I don't understand it myself."

For a while he couldn't speak.

The scent of roses seemed to grow heavier.

Dan Shannon could have passed for a miner, though he had never worked the coal fields even as a boy. Broad, heavy features. Big shoulders. Strong, blunt-fingered hands cross-hatched with scars. He had been a car mechanic, a good one—although in a time and place that had never offered quite enough work.

"You deserved a loving son," Joey said at last. "Good thing you had two, huh?" He closed his eyes. "I'm sorry. Jesus, I'm so sorry."

His heart ached with remorse, as heavy as an iron anvil in his chest, but conversations with the dead couldn't provide absolution. Not even God could give him that now.

When Joey left the viewing room, Mr. Devokowski met him in the front hall of the mortuary. "Does P.J. know yet?"

Joey shook his head. "I haven't been able to track him down."

"How can you not be able to track him down? He's your brother," Devokowski said. For an instant before he regained the compassionate expression of a funeral director, his contempt was naked.

"He travels all over, Mr. Devokowski. You know about that. He's always traveling, on the move, researching. It's not my fault . . . being out of touch with him."

Reluctantly, Devokowski nodded. "I saw the piece about him in *People* a few months ago."

P.J. Shannon was the quintessential writer of life on the road, the most famous literary Gypsy since Jack Kerouac.

"He should come home for a while," Devokowski said, "maybe write another book about Asherville. I still think that was his best. When he hears about your dad, poor P.J., he's going to be broken up real bad. P.J. really loved your dad."

So did I, Joey thought, but he didn't say it. Given his actions over the past twenty years, he wouldn't be believed. But he *had* loved Dan Shannon. God, yes. And he'd loved his mother, Kathleen—whose funeral he had avoided and to whose deathbed he had never gone.

"P.J. visited just in August. Stayed about a week. Your dad took him all over, showing him off. He was so proud, your dad."

Devokowski's assistant, an intense young man in a dark suit, entered the far end of the hallway. He spoke in a practiced hush: "Sir, it's time to transport the deceased to Our Lady."

Devokowski checked his watch. To Joey, he said, "You're going to the Mass?"

"Yes, of course."

The funeral director nodded and turned away, conveying by body language that this particular son of Dan Shannon had not earned the right to add "of course" to his answer.

Outside, the sky looked burnt out, all black char and thick gray ashes, but it was heavy with rain.

Joey hoped that the lull in the storm would last through the Mass and the graveside service.

On the street, as he was approaching his parked car from behind, heading for the driver's door, the trunk popped open by itself and the lid eased up a few inches. From the dark interior, a slender hand reached feebly toward him, as if in desperation, beseechingly. A woman's hand. The thumb was broken and hanging at a queer angle, and blood dripped from the torn fingernails.

Around him, Asherville seemed to fall under a dark enchantment. The wind died. The clouds, which had been moving ceaselessly out of the northwest, were suddenly as unchanging as the vaulted ceiling of Hell. All was lifeless. Silence reigned. Joey was frozen by shock and cold fear. Only the hand moved, only the hand was alive, and only the hand's pathetic groping for salvation had any meaning or importance in a world turned to stone.

Joey couldn't bear the sight of the dangling thumb, the torn nails, the slow drip-drip of blood—but he felt powerfully compelled to stare. He knew that it was the woman in the transparent gown, come out of his dream from the night before, into the waking world, though such a thing was not possible.

Reaching out from the shadow of the trunk lid, the hand slowly turned palm up. In the center was a spot of blood and a puncture wound that might have been made by a nail.

Strangely, when Joey closed his eyes against the horror before him, he could see the sanctuary of Our Lady of Sorrows as clearly as if he were standing upon the altar platform at that very moment. A silvery ringing of sacred bells broke the silence, but it was not a real sound in that October afternoon; they rang out of his memory, from morning Masses in the distant past. *Through my fault, my fault, my most grievous fault.* He saw the chalice gleaming with the reflections of candle flames. The wafer of the host was held high in the priest's hands. Joey strained hard to detect the moment of transubstantiation. The moment when hope was fulfilled, faith rewarded. The split instant of perfect mystery: wine into blood. *Is there hope for the world, for lost men like me?*

The images in his mind became as unbearable as the sight of the blood-smeared hand, and he opened his eyes. The hand was gone. The trunk lid was closed. The wind was blowing again, and the dark clouds rolled out of the northwest, and in the distance a dog barked.

The trunk had never actually popped open, and the hand had never reached toward him. Hallucination.

He raised his own hands and gazed at them as though they were the hands of a stranger. They were trembling badly.

Delirium tremens. The shakes. Visions of things crawling out of the walls. In this case, out of a car trunk. All drunks had them from time to time—especially when they tried to give up the bottle.

In the car, he withdrew a flask from an inside pocket of his suit jacket. He stared at it for a long time. Finally he unscrewed the cap, took a whiff of the whiskey, and brought it to his lips.

Either he had stood half mesmerized by the car trunk far longer than he'd realized or he had sat for an awfully long time with the flask, struggling against the urge to open it, because the funeral-home hearse pulled out of the driveway and turned right, heading across town toward Our Lady of Sorrows. Enough time had passed for his father's casket to be transferred from the viewing room.

Joey wanted to be sober for the funeral Mass. He wanted that more than he had wanted anything in a long time.

Without taking a drink, he screwed the cap back onto the flask and returned the flask to his pocket.

He started the car, caught up with the hearse, and followed it to the church.

More than once during the drive, he imagined that he heard something moving in the trunk of the car. A muffled thump. A tapping. A faint, cold, hollow cry.

4

OUR LADY OF SORROWS WAS AS HE REMEMBERED IT: DARK WOOD lovingly polished to a satiny sheen; stained-glass windows waiting only for the appearance of the sun to paint bright images of compassion and salvation across the pews in the nave; groin vaults receding into blue shadows above; the air woven through with a tapestry of odors—lemon-oil furniture polish, incense, hot candle wax.

Joey sat in the last pew, hoping that no one would recognize him. He had no friends in Asherville any more. And without a long drink from his flask of whiskey, he wasn't prepared to endure the looks of scorn and disdain that he was sure to receive and that, in fact, he deserved.

More than two hundred people attended the service, and to Joey the mood seemed even more somber than could be expected at a funeral. Dan Shannon had been well and widely liked, and he would be missed.

Many of the women blotted their eyes with handkerchiefs, but the men were all dry eyed. In Asherville, the men never wept publicly—and rarely in private. Although none had worked the mines in more than twenty years, they came from generations of miners who had lived in constant expectation of tragedy, of friends and loved ones lost to cave-ins and explosions and early-onset black-lung disease. Theirs was a culture that not only valued stoicism but could never have existed without it.

Keep your feelings to yourself. Don't burden your friends and family with your own fear and anguish. Endure. That was the creed of Asherville, a guiding morality stronger even than that which was taught by the rector of Our Lady and the two-thousand-year-old faith that he served.

The Mass was the first that Joey had attended in twenty years. Evidently at the insistence of the parishioners, it was a classic Mass in Latin, with the grace and eloquence that had been lost when the Church had gone trendy back in the sixties.

The beauty of the Mass did not affect him, did not warm him. By his own actions and desire over the past twenty years, he had placed himself outside the art of faith, and now he could relate to it only in the manner of a man who studies a fine painting through the window of a gallery, his perception hampered by distorting reflections on the glass.

The Mass was beautiful, but it was a cold beauty. Like that of winter light on polished steel. An Arctic vista.

From the church, Joey drove to the cemetery. It was on a hill. The grass was still green, littered with crisp leaves that crunched under his shoes.

His father was to be buried beside his mother. No name had yet been cut into the blank half of the dual-plot headstone.

Being at his mother's graveside for the first time, seeing her name and the date of her passing carved in granite, Joey did not suddenly feel the reality of her death. The loss of her had been excruciatingly real to him for the past sixteen years.

In fact, he had lost her twenty years ago, when he had seen her for the last time.

The hearse was parked on the road near the grave site. Lou Devokowski and his assistant were organizing the pallbearers to unload the casket.

The open grave awaiting Dan Shannon was encircled by a three-foot-high black plastic curtain, not to provide a safety barrier but to shield the more sensitive mourners from the sight of the raw earth in the sheer walls of the pit, which might force them into too stark a confrontation with the grim realities of the service that they were attending. The undertaker had also been discreet enough to cover the mound of excavated earth with black plastic and to drape the plastic with bouquets of flowers and bunches of cut ferns.

In a mood to punish himself, Joey stepped to the yawning hole. He peered over the curtain to see *exactly* where his dad would be going.

At the bottom of the grave, only half buried in loose earth, lay a body wrapped in blood-smeared plastic. A naked woman. Face concealed. Ribbons of wet blond hair.

Joey stepped back, bumping into other mourners.

He was unable to breathe. His lungs seemed to be packed full of dirt from his father's grave.

As solemn as the sepulchral sky, the pallbearers arrived with the casket and carefully deposited it onto a motorized sling over the excavation.

Joey wanted to shout at them to move the casket and look, look below, look at the tarp-wrapped woman, look at the bottom of the pit.

He couldn't speak.

The priest had arrived, his black cassock and white surplice flapping in the wind. The interment service was about to begin.

When the casket was lowered into that seven-foot-deep abyss, atop the dead woman, when the grave was filled with earth, no one would ever know that she'd been there. To those in the world who loved her and sought her with such desperation, she would have vanished forever.

Again Joey tried to speak, but he was still unable to make a sound. He was shaking violently.

On one level, he knew that the body at the bottom of the grave was not really there. A phantom. Hallucination. *Delirium tremens.* Like the bugs that Ray Milland had seen crawling out of the walls in *Lost Weekend.*

Nevertheless, a scream swelled in him. He would have given voice to it if he could have broken the iron band of silence that tightened around him, would have shouted at them, would have demanded that they move the casket and look into the hole, even though he knew that they would find nothing and that everyone would think him deranged.

From the grave or from the mound beside it rose the fecund smell of damp earth and rotting vegetable matter, which called to mind all the small, teeming creatures that thrived below the sod—beetles, worms, and quick-moving things for which he had no names.

Joey turned away from the grave, pushed through the hundred or more mourners who had come from the church to the cemetery, and stumbled down the hill, through the ranks of tombstones. He took refuge in the rental car.

Suddenly he was able to breathe in great gasps, and he found his voice at last. "Oh, God, oh, God, oh, God."

He must be losing his mind. Twenty years of all-but-constant inebriation had screwed up his brain beyond repair. Too many cells of gray matter had died in the long bath of alcohol.

He was so far gone that only another taste of the same sin would give him surcease. He took the flask from his coat pocket.

Aware that a month's worth of gossip was in the making, the startled mourners at the grave site must have followed his stumbling flight with considerable interest. No doubt many, afraid of missing the next development, were still risking the disapproval of the priest by glancing downhill toward the rental car.

Joey didn't care what anyone thought. He didn't care about anything any more. Except whiskey.

But his dad still wasn't buried. He had promised himself that he would remain sober until the interment was complete. He had broken uncounted promises to himself over the years, but for reasons that he could not quite define, this one was more important than any of the others.

He didn't open the flask.

Uphill, under the half-bare limbs of the autumn-stripped trees, beneath a bruised sky, the casket slowly descended into the uncaring earth.

Soon the mourners began to leave, glancing toward Joey's car with unconcealed interest.

As the priest departed, several small whirlwinds full of dead leaves spun through the cemetery, exploding over headstones, as if angry spirits had awakened from an uneasy rest.

Thunder rolled across the heavens. It was the first peal in hours, and the remaining mourners hurried to their cars.

The undertaker and his assistant removed the motorized casket lift and the black plastic skirt from around the open grave.

As the storm resumed, a cemetery worker in a yellow rain slicker stripped the tarp and flowers from the mound of excavated dirt.

Another worker appeared behind the wheel of a compact little earth-moving machine called a Bobcat. It was painted the same shade of yellow as his raincoat.

Before the open grave could be flooded by the storm, it was filled—and then tamped down by the tread of the Bobcat.

"Goodbye," Joey said.

He should have had a sense of completion, of having reached the end of an important phase of his life. But he only felt empty and incomplete. He had not put an end to anything—if that was what he had been hoping to do.

5

BACK AT HIS FATHER'S HOUSE, HE WENT DOWN THE NARROW STEPS FROM the kitchen to the basement. Past the furnace. Past the small water heater.

The door to P.J.'s old room was warped by humidity and age. It squealed against the jamb and scraped across the sill as Joey forced it open.

Rain beat on the two narrow, horizontal casement windows that were set high in one basement wall, and the deep shadows were not dispersed by the meager storm light. He flicked the switch by the door, and a bare overhead bulb came on.

The small room was empty. Many years ago, the single bed and the other furniture must have been sold to raise a few dollars. For the past two decades, when P.J. came home, he had slept in Joey's room on the second floor, because there had been no chance that Joey would pay a visit and need it himself.

Dust. Cobwebs. Low on the walls: a few dark patches of mildew like Rorschach blots.

The only items of proof that remained of P.J.'s long-ago residence were a couple of movie posters for flicks so trashy that the advertising art had an unintentionally campy quality. They were thumbtacked to the walls, pus yellow with age, cracked, curling at the corners.

In high school, P.J.'s dream was to get out of Asherville, out of poverty, and become a filmmaker. "But I need these," he had once said to Joey, indicating the posters, "to remind me that success at any price isn't worth it. In Hollywood you can become rich and famous and celebrated even for making stupid, dehumanizing crap. If I can't make it by doing worthwhile work, I hope I've got the courage to give up the dream altogether instead of selling out."

Either fate had never given P.J. his shot at Hollywood or he had lost interest in filmmaking somewhere along the way. Ironically, he had achieved fame as a novelist, fulfilling Joey's dream after Joey had abandoned it.

P.J. was a critically acclaimed writer. Using his ceaseless rambles back and forth across the United States as material, he produced highly polished prose that had mysterious depths under a deceptively simple surface.

Joey envied his brother—but not with any malice. P.J. earned every line of the praise that he received and every dollar of his fortune, and Joey was proud of him.

Theirs had been an intense and special relationship when they were young, and it was still intense, though it was now conducted largely at great distances by phone, when P.J. called from Montana or Maine or Key West or a small dusty town on the high plains of Texas. They saw each other no more than once every three or four years, always when P.J. dropped in unannounced in the course of his travels—but even then he didn't stay long, never more than two days, usually one.

No one had ever meant more to Joey than P.J., and no one ever would. His feelings for his brother were rich and complex, and he would never be able to explain them adequately to anyone.

The rain hammered the lawn just beyond the ground-level windows of the basement. In a place so far above that it seemed to be another world, more thunder crashed.

He had come to the cellar for a jar. But the room was utterly empty except for the movie posters.

On the concrete floor near his shoe, a fat black spider seemed to materialize from thin air. It scurried past him.

He didn't step on it but watched it race for cover until it disappeared into a crack along the baseboard.

He switched off the light and went back into the furnace room, leaving the warped door open.

Climbing the stairs, almost to the kitchen, Joey said, "Jar? What jar?"

Puzzled, he stopped and looked down the steps to the cellar.

A jar *of* something? A jar *for* something?

He couldn't remember why he had needed a jar or what kind of jar he had been seeking.

Another sign of dementia.

He'd been too long without a drink.

Plagued by the persistent uneasiness and disorientation that he'd felt since first entering Asherville the previous day, he went upstairs. He turned off the cellar lights behind him.

His suitcase was packed and standing in the living room. He carried the bag onto the front porch, locked the door, and put the key back under the hemp mat where he had found it less than twenty-four hours ago.

Something growled behind him, and he turned to confront a mangy, rain-soaked black dog on the porch steps. Its eyes were as fiercely yellow as sulfurous coal fires, and it bared its teeth at him.

"Go away," he said, not threateningly but softly.

The dog growled again, lowered its head, and tensed as if it might spring at him.

"You don't belong here any more than I do," Joey said, standing his ground.

The hound looked uncertain, shivered, licked its chops, and at last retreated.

With his suitcase, Joey went to the head of the porch steps and watched the dog as it hunched away into the slanting sheets of gray rain, gradually fading as though it had been a mirage. When it moved around the corner and out of sight at the end of the block, he could easily have been convinced that it had been another hallucination.

6

THE LAWYER CONDUCTED BUSINESS FROM THE SECOND FLOOR OF A BRICK building on Main Street, above the Old Town Tavern. The barroom was closed on Sunday afternoons, but small neon signs for Rolling Rock and Pabst Blue Ribbon still glowed in its windows brightly enough to tint the rain green and blue as it fell past the glass.

The law offices of Henry Kadinska occupied two rooms off a dimly lighted hallway that also served a real-estate office and a dentist. The door stood open to the reception room.

Joey stepped inside and said, "Hello?"

The inner door was ajar, and from beyond it a man responded. "Please come in, Joey."

The second room was larger than the first, although still of modest proportions. Law books lined two walls; on another, a pair of diplomas hung crookedly. The windows were covered with wood-slat venetian blinds of a type that probably had not been manufactured in fifty years, revealing horizontal slices of the rainy day.

Identical mahogany desks stood at opposite ends of the room. At one time Henry Kadinska had shared the space with his father, Lev, who had been the town's only lawyer before him. Lev had died when Joey was a senior in high school. Unused but well polished, the desk remained as a monument.

Putting his pipe in a large cut-glass ashtray, Henry rose from his chair, reached across the desk, and shook Joey's hand. "I saw you at Mass, but I didn't want to intrude."

"I didn't notice . . . anyone," Joey said.

"How're you doing?"

"Okay. I'm okay."

They stood awkwardly for a moment, not sure what to say. Then Joey sat in one of the two commodious armchairs that faced the desk.

Kadinska settled back into his own chair and picked up his pipe. He was in his midfifties, slightly built, with a prominent Adam's apple. His head seemed somewhat too large for his body, and this disproportionateness was emphasized by a hairline that had receded four or five inches from his brow. Behind his thick glasses, his hazel eyes seemed to have a kindly aspect.

"You found the house key where I told you?"

Joey nodded.

"The place hasn't changed all that much, has it?" Henry Kadinska asked.

"Less than I expected. Not at all, really."

"Most of his life, your dad didn't have any money to spend—and when he finally got some, he didn't know *how* to spend it." He touched a match to his pipe and drew on the mouthpiece. "Drove P.J. crazy that Dan wouldn't use much of what he gave him."

Joey shifted uneasily in his chair. "Mr. Kadinska . . . I don't understand why I'm here. Why did you need to see me?"

"P.J. still doesn't know about your dad?"

"I've left messages on the answering machine in his New York apartment. But he doesn't really live there. Only for a month or so each year."

The pipe was fired up again. The air was redolent of cherry-scented tobacco.

In spite of the diplomas and books, the room wasn't much like an average law office. It was a cozy place—shabby-genteel but cozy. Slumped in his chair, Henry Kadinska seemed to be as comfortable in his profession as he might have been in a pair of pajamas.

"Sometimes," Joey said, "he doesn't call that number for days, even a week or two."

"Funny way to live—nearly always on the road. But I guess it's right for him."

"He seems to thrive on it."

"And it results in those wonderful books," said Kadinska.

"Yes."

"I dearly love P.J.'s books."

"Virtually everyone does."

"There's a marvelous sense of freedom in them, such a . . . such a *spirit.*"

"Mr. Kadinska, the weather being as bad as it is, I'd like to get started back to Scranton as soon as possible. I have to catch a commuter flight out of there early in the morning."

"Of course, yes," said Kadinska, with an unmistakable note of disappointment.

Now, he seemed to be a lonely little man who had hoped only for some friendly conversation.

While the lawyer opened a file drawer on his desk and searched for something, Joey noticed that one of the crookedly hung diplomas was from Harvard Law. That was a wildly unlikely alma mater for a small-town, coal-country lawyer.

Not all the shelves were filled with law books, either. Many were volumes of philosophy. Plato. Socrates. Aristotle. Kant. Augustine. Kierkegaarde. Bentham. Santayana. Schopenhauer. Empedocles, Heidegger, Hobbes, and Francis Bacon.

Perhaps Henry Kadinska wasn't comfortable being a small-town lawyer but was simply long resigned to it, trapped first in the orbit of his father and then by the gravity of habit.

Sometimes, especially in a whiskey haze, it was easy for Joey to forget that he himself wasn't the only person in the world whose dearest dreams had come to nothing.

"Your father's last will and testament," said Kadinska as he opened a file folder on his desk.

"A reading of the will?" Joey asked. "I think P.J. should be here for that, not me."

"On the contrary. The will has nothing to do with P.J. Your father left everything to you."

A sickening pang of guilt quivered through Joey. "Why would he do that?"

"You're his son. Why *wouldn't* he?"

Joey made a point of meeting the attorney's eyes. On this one day, even if never again, he wanted to be honest about these matters, to conduct himself with a dignity of which his father would have approved.

"We both know the hard answer to that, Mr. Kadinska. I broke his heart. Broke my mother's heart too. More than two years she withered from the cancer, but I never came. Never held her hand, never consoled my dad. Never saw him once in the last twenty years of his life. I called maybe six or eight times, no more than that. Half the time he didn't know how to reach me, because I didn't always give him my address or phone number. And when he did have my number, I always kept an answering machine switched on so I wouldn't have to pick up. I was a rotten son, Mr. Kadinska. I'm a drunk, a selfish shit, and a loser, and I don't deserve any inheritance, no matter how little it is."

Henry Kadinska appeared to be pained to hear any man criticize himself so mercilessly. "You're not drunk now, Joey. And the man I see before me isn't bad in his heart."

"I'll be drunk by tonight, sir, I assure you," Joey said quietly. "And if you can't see me the way I described myself, then you're a lousy judge of character. You don't know me at all—and you should count that as a blessing."

Kadinska put his pipe in the glass ashtray again. "Well, your father was a forgiving man. He wanted everything to go to you."

Getting to his feet, Joey said, "No. I can't take it. I don't want it." He started toward the door to the outer room.

"Wait, please," said the lawyer.

Joey stopped and turned to him. "The weather's miserable, and I've got a long drive out of these mountains to Scranton."

Still slumped in his chair, picking up his pipe again, Henry Kadinska said, "Where do you live, Joey?"

"You know. Las Vegas. That's where you got hold of me."

"I mean, where do you live in Las Vegas?"

"Why?"

"I'm a lawyer. I've spent my life asking questions, and it's hard to change this late in the game. Indulge me."

"I live in a trailer park."

"One of those upscale parks with a community swimming pool and tennis courts?"

"Old trailers," Joey said bluntly. "Mostly real old."

"No pool? No tennis?"

"Hell, not even any grass."

"What do you do for a living?"

"I'm a blackjack dealer. Run roulette wheels sometimes."

"You work regularly?"

"When I need to."

"When the drinking doesn't get in the way?"

"When I can," Joey amended, remembering his promise to himself to deal with all of this truthfully. "Pays well, with the tips from the players. I can save up for when . . . when I have to take some time off. I do okay."

"But with your work record, always moving on, you don't find jobs in the new, flashy casinos very often any more."

"Not often," Joey agreed.

"Each job is in a seedier place than the one before."

"For a man who sounded so compassionate a minute ago, you sure are showing a cruel streak all of a sudden."

Kadinska's face reddened with embarrassment. "I'm sorry, Joey, but I'm just trying to make the point that you're not exactly in a position to walk away from an inheritance."

Joey was quietly adamant. "I don't deserve it, don't want it, won't take it. That's flat final. Anyway, nobody would buy that old house, and I sure as hell won't move back here to live in it."

Tapping the documents in the open file folder, Kadinska said, "The house has little value. You're right. But the house and its contents aren't the meat of this inheritance, Joey. There's more than a quarter of a million dollars in liquid assets—certificates of deposit and money-market accounts."

Joey's mouth went punk dry. His heart began to pound fiercely. The lawyer's office harbored a terrible darkness of which he had been dangerously unaware, and now it was rising up around him.

"That's crazy. Dad was a poor man."

"But your brother has been a success for a long time now. For about fourteen years, he's been sending your father a check every month, just like clockwork. A thousand dollars. I told you how it drove P.J. crazy that your dad wouldn't spend more than a little of it. Dan pretty much just banked check after check, and through what bankers like to call the miracle of compound interest, the principal has grown."

Joey's voice was shaky: "That's not my money. That belongs to P.J. It came from him, it should go back to him."

"But your father left it to you. All to you. And his will is a legal document."

"Give it to P.J. when he shows up," Joey insisted, and he headed for the office door.

"I suspect P.J. will want whatever your dad wanted. He'll say you should keep it all."

"I won't, I won't," Joey said, raising his voice.

Kadinska caught up with him in the reception lounge, took him by the arm, and halted him. "Joey, it's not that easy."

"Sure it is."

"If you *really* don't want it, then you have to renounce the inheritance."

"I renounce it. I already did. Don't want it."

"A document has to be drawn, signed, notarized."

Although the day was cold and the office was on the chilly side, Joey had broken into a sweat. "How long will it take to put these papers together?"

"If you'll come back tomorrow afternoon—"

"No." Joey's heart was jackhammering almost hard enough to shatter the ribs and breastbone that caged it. "No, sir, I'm not staying here another night. I'm going to Scranton. A flight to Pittsburgh in the morning. Vegas from there. All the way out to Vegas. Mail me the papers."

"That's probably better anyway," Kadinska said. "It'll give you more time to think, to reconsider."

At first the lawyer had seemed to be a gentle, bookish man. Not now.

Joey no longer saw kindness in the man's eyes. Instead he perceived the slyness of a bargainer for souls, something with scales under the disguise of skin, with eyes that in a different light would be like the sulfur-yellow eyes of the dog that had confronted him on the front porch a while ago.

He wrenched loose of the attorney's hand, shoved him aside, and made for the outer door in a state close to panic.

Kadinska called after him: "Joey, what's wrong?"

The hallway. Past the real-estate office. The dentist. Toward the stairs. He wanted desperately to be out in the fresh air, to be washed clean by the rain.

"Joey, what's the matter with you?"

"Stay away from me!" he shouted.

When he reached the head of the stairs, he halted so abruptly that he almost pitched to the bottom. He grabbed the newel post to keep his balance.

At the foot of the steep stairs lay the dead blonde, bundled in a transparent tarp partly opaque with blood. The plastic was drawn tightly across her bare breasts, compressing them. Her nipples were visible but not her face.

One pale arm had slipped out of her shroud. Although she was dead, she reached out beseechingly.

He could not bear the sight of her mangled hand, the blood, the nail hole in her delicate palm. Most of all he was terrified that she would speak to him from behind her plastic veil and that he would be told things that he shouldn't know, mustn't know.

With a whimper like that of a cornered animal, he turned from her and started back the way he had come.

"Joey?"

Henry Kadinska stood in the dimly lighted hall ahead of him. Shadows seemed to be drawn to the attorney—except for his thick eyeglasses, which blazed with reflections of the yellow light overhead. He was blocking the way. Approaching. Eager to have another chance to offer his bargain.

Now *frantic* for fresh air and cleansing rain, Joey spun away from Kadinska and returned to the stairs.

The blonde still sprawled below, her arm extended, her hand open, silently pleading for something, perhaps for mercy.

"Joey?"

Kadinska's voice. Close behind him.

Joey descended the precipitous flight of stairs hesitantly at first, then faster, figuring that he would step over her if she was really there, kick at her if she tried to seize him, down two stairs at a time, not even holding on to the handrail, barely keeping his balance, a third of the way, halfway, and *still* she was there, now eight steps below, six, four, and she was reaching out to him, the red stigmata glistening in the center of her palm. He screamed as he reached the last step, and the dead woman vanished when he cried out. He plunged through the space that she had occupied, crashed through the door, and staggered onto the sidewalk in front of the Old Town Tavern.

He turned his face up into the Pabst-blue and Rolling Rock-green rain, which was so cold that it might soon turn to sleet. In seconds he was soaked—but he didn't feel entirely clean.

In the rental car again, he fumbled the flask out from under the driver's seat where he'd tucked it earlier.

The rain had not cleansed him *inside.* He had breathed in corruption, swallowed it. Blended whiskey offered considerable antiseptic power.

He unscrewed the cap from the flask and took a long swallow. Then another.

Choking on the spirits, gasping for breath, he replaced the cap, afraid that he would drop the flask and waste the precious ounces that it still contained.

Kadinska hadn't followed him out into the storm, but Joey didn't want to delay another moment. He started the car, pulled away from the curb, splashed through a flooded intersection, and drove along Main Street toward the end of town.

He didn't believe that he would be allowed to leave. Something would stop him. The car would sputter, stall, and refuse to start. Cross traffic would crash into him at an intersection, even though the streets seemed deserted. Lightning would strike a telephone pole and drop it across the road. *Something* would prevent him from getting out of town. He was in the grip of a superstition that he could not shake or explain.

In spite of his dire expectations, he reached the town line and crossed it. Main Street became the county road. Forests and fields replaced the huddled and depressing buildings of Asherville.

Still shuddering as much from fear as from having been soaked by the rain, he drove at least a mile before he began to realize how strangely he had reacted to the prospect of receiving a quarter of a million dollars. He had no idea why a sudden windfall should have terrified him, why a stroke of good fortune should instantly convince him that his soul was in peril.

After all, considering how he had lived his life thus far, he was doomed to Hell anyway, if it existed.

Three miles outside Asherville, Joey came to a three-way stop. Directly ahead of him, beyond the rural intersection, the county route continued: a glistening black ribbon dwindling down a long, gradual slope into the early twilight. To the left was Coal Valley Road, leading to the town of Coal Valley.

On that Sunday night twenty years ago, when he had been on his way back to college, he had planned to take Coal Valley Road twelve miles through the mountains, until it connected with the old state three-lane that the locals called Black Hollow Highway, then go west nine miles to the Pennsylvania Turnpike. He always went that way, because it was the shortest route.

But on *that* night, for reasons he had never since been able to recall, he had driven past Coal Valley Road. He'd followed the county route another nineteen miles to the interstate and had taken the interstate in a roundabout loop toward Black Hollow Highway and the turnpike. On the interstate he'd had the accident, and thereafter nothing had ever gone right for him again.

He had been driving his ten-year-old '65 Ford Mustang, which he had salvaged and restored—with his dad's help—from an auto junkyard after the original owner had rolled it. God, how he had loved that car. It had been the only thing of beauty he'd ever owned, and most important, his own hands had brought it back from ruin to glory.

Recalling the Mustang, he hesitantly touched the left side of his forehead just below the hairline. The scar was an inch long, barely visible but easily felt. He remembered the sickening slide, his car spinning on the rain-slick interstate, the collision with the signpost, the shattering window.

He remembered all the blood.

Now he sat at the three-way stop, staring down Coal Valley Road to his left, and he knew that if he took this route, as he should have taken it on that eventful night long ago, he would at last have a chance to put everything right. He would get his life back on track.

That was a crazy notion, perhaps as superstitious as his earlier certainty that fate would not allow him to drive out of Asherville—

but this time he was right. It was true. He had no doubt that he was being given another chance. He *knew* that some superhuman power was at work in the fading October twilight, *knew* that the meaning of his troubled life lay along that two-lane mountain route—because Coal Valley Road had been condemned and torn up more than nineteen years ago, yet now it waited to his left, exactly as it had been on that special night. It was magically restored.

7

JOEY EASED THE RENTAL CHEVY PAST THE STOP SIGN AND PARKED ON THE narrow shoulder, on the dead-end side of the three-way intersection, directly across from the entrance to Coal Valley Road. He switched off the headlights but left the engine running.

Overhung by autumnal trees, those two lanes of wet blacktop led out of the deepening twilight and vanished into shadows as black as the oncoming night. The pavement was littered with colorful leaves that glowed strangely in the gloom, as though irradiated.

His heart pounded, pounded.

He closed his eyes and listened to the rain.

When at last he opened his eyes, he half expected that Coal Valley Road wouldn't be there any more, that it had been just one more hallucination. But it hadn't vanished. The two lanes of blacktop glistened with silver rain. Scarlet and amber leaves glimmered like a scattering of jewels meant to lure him into the tunnel of trees and into the deeper darkness beyond.

Impossible.

But there it was.

Twenty-one years ago in Coal Valley, a six-year-old boy named Rudy DeMarco had tumbled into a sinkhole that abruptly opened under him while he was playing in his backyard. Rushing out of the house in response to her son's screams, Mrs. DeMarco had found him in an eight-foot-deep pit, with sulfurous smoke billowing from fissures in the bottom. She scrambled into the hole after him, into heat so intense that she seemed to have descended through the gates of Hell. The floor of the pit resembled a furnace grate; little Rudy's legs were trapped between thick bars of stone, dangling into whatever inferno was obscured by the rising smoke. Choking, dizzy, instantly disoriented, Mrs. DeMarco nevertheless wrenched her child from the gap in which he was wedged. As the unstable floor of the pit quaked and cracked and crumbled under her, she dragged Rudy to the sloped wall, clawed at the hot earth, and frantically struggled upward. The bottom dropped out altogether, the sinkhole rapidly widened, the treacherous slope slid away beneath her, but still she pulled her boy out of the seething smoke and onto the lawn. His clothes were ablaze. She covered him with her body, trying to smother the flames, and *her* clothes caught on fire. Clutching Rudy against her, she rolled with him in the grass, crying for help, and her screams seemed especially loud because her boy had fallen silent. More than his clothes had burned: Most of his hair was singed away, one side of his face was blistered, and his small body was charred. Three days later, in the Pittsburgh hospital to which he had been taken by air ambulance, Rudy DeMarco died of catastrophic burns.

For sixteen years prior to the boy's death, the people of Coal Valley had lived above a subterranean fire that churned relentlessly through a network of abandoned mines, eating away at untapped veins of anthracite, gradually widening those underground corridors and shafts. While state and federal officials debated whether the hidden conflagration would eventually burn itself out, while they argued about various strategies for extinguishing it, while they squandered fortunes on consultants and interminable hearings, while they strove indefatigably to shift the financial responsibility for the clean-up from one jurisdiction to another, Coal Valley's residents lived with carbon-monoxide monitors to avoid being gassed in the night by mine-fire fumes that seeped up through the foundations of their homes. Scattered across the town were vent pipes, tapping the tunnels below to release smoke from the fire and perhaps minimize the build-up of toxic gases in nearby houses; one even thrust up from the elementary-school playground.

With the tragic death of little Rudy DeMarco, the politicians and bureaucrats were at last compelled to take action. The federal government purchased the threatened properties, beginning with those houses directly over the most hotly burning tunnels, then those over secondary fires, then those that were still only adjacent to the deep, combustible rivers of coal. During the course of the following year, as homes were condemned and the residents moved away, the reasonably pleasant village of Coal Valley gradually became a ghost town.

By that rainy night in a long-ago October, when Joey had taken the wrong road back to college, only three families remained in Coal Valley. They had been scheduled to move out before Thanksgiving.

In the year that followed the departure of those last residents, bulldozers were to knock down every building in the village. Every scrap of the demolished structures was to be hauled away. The streets, cracked and hoved from the pressures of the hidden fires below, would be torn up. The hills and fields would be seeded with grass, restoring the land to something resembling a natural state, and the mine fires would be left to burn—some said for a hundred or two hundred years—until the veins of coal were at last exhausted.

Geologists, mining engineers, and officials from the Pennsylvania Department of Environmental Resources believed that the fire would eventually undermine four thousand acres—an area far greater than that encompassed by the abandoned village. Consequently, Coal Valley Road was likely to suffer sudden subsidence at numerous points along much of its length—a deadly danger to motorists. More than nineteen years ago, therefore, after the ghost town had been demolished and hauled away, Coal Valley Road had been torn up as well.

It had not been there when he had driven into Asherville the previous day. Now it waited. Leading out of the rain-slashed twilight into an unknown night. The road not taken.

Joey was holding the flask again. Although he had opened it, he had no memory of unscrewing the cap.

If he drank what remained of the Jack Daniel's, the road that led into the dark tunnel of trees might blur, fade, and finally vanish. Perhaps it was wise not to pin any hopes on miraculous second chances and supernatural redemption. For all he knew, if he put the Chevy in gear and followed that strange highway, he would be changing his life not for better but for worse.

He brought the flask to his lips.

Thunder rolled through a cold Heaven. The rataplan of rain swelled until he could not even hear the idling car engine.

The whiskey fumes smelled as sweet as salvation.

Rain, rain, torrential rain. It washed the last light out of the bleak day.

Although he was beyond the touch of the rain, the heavy pall of descending darkness was inescapable. Night entered the car: a familiar companion with whom he had passed uncountable lonely hours in troubled contemplation of a life gone wrong.

He and the night had finished many bottles of whiskey together, and eventually he had always been granted the surcease of sleep, if nothing else. All he had to do was put the flask against his lips, tip it, and drain the few ounces that it still contained, whereupon this dangerous temptation to embrace hope would surely pass. The mysterious highway would vanish, and then he could get on with a life that, although lacking hope, could be passed in a safe, blessed anesthetic haze.

He sat for a long time. Wanting a drink. Not drinking.

Joey wasn't aware of the car approaching along the county road behind him until its headlights suddenly shot through the back window of the Chevy. A virtual explosion of light shattered over him, as though from an onrushing locomotive with one giant, blazing Cyclopean eye. He glanced at the rearview mirror but winced and looked away as the bright reflection stung his eyes.

The car roared past him and hung a hard left onto Coal Valley Road. It cast up such a heavy plume of dirty water from the puddled pavement that it was impossible for Joey to see any details of it or get a glimpse of its driver.

As the spray washed down the side window of the Chevy and the glass cleared again, the other vehicle slowed. Its taillights dwindled until it had gone perhaps a hundred yards along the colonnade of trees, where it came to a full stop on the roadway.

"No," Joey said.

Out there on Coal Valley Road, the red brake lights were like the radiant eyes of a demon in a dream, frightening but compelling, alarming but mesmerizing.

"No."

He turned his head and stared at the night-cloaked county road in front of him, the route that he'd taken twenty years ago. It had been the wrong highway then, but it was the right one now. After all, he wasn't headed back to college as he had been that night; now he was forty years old and bound for Scranton, where he had to catch a commuter flight to Pittsburgh in the morning.

On Coal Valley Road, the taillights glowed. The strange car waited.

Scranton. Pittsburgh. Vegas. The trailer park. A shabby but safe little life. No hope . . . but no nasty surprises, either.

Red brake lights. Beacons. Shimmering in the deluge.

Joey capped the flask without drinking from it.

He switched on the headlights and put the Chevy in gear.

"Jesus, help me," he said.

He drove across the intersection and onto Coal Valley Road.

Ahead of him, the other car began to move again. It quickly picked up speed.

Joey Shannon followed the phantom driver through a veil between reality and some other place, toward a town that no longer existed, toward a fate beyond understanding.

8

THE WIND AND THE RAIN SHOOK LEAVES FROM THE OVERHANGING TREES and hurled them onto the pavement. They smacked the windshield and clung briefly, batlike shapes that furled their wings and fell away when the wipers swept over them.

Joey remained about a hundred yards behind the other car, not quite close enough to discern what make and model it was. He told himself that he still had time to turn around, drive to the county road, and go to Scranton as he had planned. But he might not have the option of turning back if he got a good look at the car ahead of him. Intuitively he understood that the more he learned about what was happening, the more thoroughly his fate would be sealed. Mile by mile he was driving farther away from the real world, into this otherworldly land of second chances, and eventually the intersection of the county route and Coal Valley Road would cease to exist in the night behind him.

When they had gone only three miles, they came upon a white, two-door Plymouth Valiant—a car that Joey had admired as a kid but hadn't seen in ages. It was stopped at the side of the road, broken down. Three sputtering red flares had been set out along the shoulder of the highway, and in their intense light, as if by a dark miracle of transubstantiation, the falling rain appeared to be a downpour of blood.

The vehicle that he was following slowed, almost halted beside the Valiant, then accelerated again.

Someone in a black, hooded raincoat stood beside the disabled Plymouth, holding a flashlight. The stranded motorist waved at him, imploring him to stop.

Joey glanced at the dwindling taillights of the car that he had been pursuing. It would soon pass around a bend, over a rise, out of sight.

Coasting past the Plymouth, he saw that the person in the raincoat was a woman. A girl, really. Arrestingly pretty. She appeared to be no older than sixteen or seventeen.

Under the hood of the coat, her flare-tinted face reminded him, curiously, of the haunting countenance on the statue of the Virgin Mother at Our Lady of Sorrows, back in Asherville. Sometimes the Virgin's serene ceramic face had just such a forlorn and spectral aspect in the crimson glow of the flickering votive candles arrayed in red glasses beneath it.

As Joey rolled slowly past this girl, she stared entreatingly, and in her porcelain features he saw something that alarmed him: a disturbing premonition, a vision of her lovely face without eyes, battered and bloody. Somehow he *knew* that if he didn't stop to help her, she would not live to see the dawn but would die violently in some black moment of the storm.

He parked on the shoulder ahead of the Valiant and got out of the rental car. He was still soaked from having stood in the cleansing downpour outside Henry Kadinska's office little more than twenty minutes ago, so the pounding rain didn't bother him, and the cold night air wasn't half as chilling as the fear that had filled him since he had learned of his inheritance.

He hurried along the pavement, and the girl came forward to meet him at the front of her disabled Valiant.

"Thank God, you stopped," she said. Rain streamed off her hood, a glistening veil in front of her face.

He said, "What happened?"

"It just failed."

"While you were rolling?"

"Yeah. Not the battery."

"How do you know?"

"I've still got power."

Her eyes were dark and huge. Her face glowed in the flare light, and on her cheeks, raindrops glistened like tears.

"Maybe the generator," he said.

"You know cars?"

"Yeah."

"I don't," she said. "I feel so helpless."

"We all do," Joey said.

She gave him a peculiar look.

She was just a girl, and at her age she was surely naive and not yet fully aware of the world's cruelty. Yet Joey Shannon saw more in her eyes than he could comprehend.

"I feel lost," she said, evidently still referring to her lack of knowledge about cars.

He unlatched and raised the hood. "Let me have your light."

At first she seemed not to know what he meant, but then she handed the flashlight to him. "I think it's hopeless."

While rain pounded against his back, he checked the distributor cap to be sure that it was seated securely, examined the spark-plug leads, scrutinized the battery cables.

"If you could just give me a ride home," she said, "my dad and I can come back here tomorrow."

"Let me try it first," he said, closing the hood.

"You don't even have a raincoat," she worried.

"Doesn't matter."

"You'll catch your death."

"It's only water—they baptize babies in it."

Overhead, the branches of the mountain laurels clattered in a bitter gust of wind, shaking loose a flock of dead leaves that whirled briefly but then settled to the ground as spiritlessly as lost hopes sifting down through the darkness of a troubled heart.

He opened the driver's door, got behind the steering wheel, and put the flashlight on the seat beside him. The keys were in the ignition. When he attempted to start the engine, there was no response whatsoever. He tried the headlights, and they came on at full power.

In front of the car, the girl was caught in the bright beams. She was no longer tinted red. Her black raincoat hung like a cowled robe, and in its folds, her face and hands were white and gloriously radiant.

He stared at her for a moment, wondering why he had been brought to her and where they would find themselves by the time this strange night had ended. Then he switched off the headlights.

The girl stood once more in the lambent light of the flares, lashed by crimson rain.

After leaning across the seat to lock the passenger door, Joey got out of the Valiant, taking the flashlight and the keys with him. "Whatever's wrong, I don't have what's needed to fix it." He slammed the driver's door and locked it as well. "You're right—the best I can do is give you a lift. Where do you live?"

"Coal Valley. I was on my way home when the trouble started."

"Hardly anyone lives there any more."

"Yeah. We're one of the last three families. It's almost like a ghost town."

Thoroughly soaked and cold to the bone, he was eager to get back to the rental car and switch the heater to its highest setting. But when he met her dark eyes again, he felt more strongly than ever that *she* was the reason that he had been given another chance to take the road to Coal Valley, as he should have done twenty years ago. Rather than run with her to the shelter of the Chevy, he hesitated, afraid that whatever he did—even taking her home—might be the *wrong* thing to do, and that in choosing a course of action, he would be throwing away this last, miraculous chance at redemption.

"What's wrong?" she asked.

Joey had been staring at her, half mesmerized, contemplating the possible consequences of his actions. His empty gaze must have disconcerted her every bit as much as the concept of consequences disconcerted *him.*

Speaking without thinking, surprised to hear these particular words issuing from himself, he said, "Show me your hands."

"My hands?"

"Show me your hands."

The wind sang epithalamion in the trees above, and the night was a chapel in which they stood alone.

With a look of puzzlement, she held out her delicate hands for his inspection.

"Palms up," he said.

She did as he asked, and her posture made her resemble more than ever the Mother of Heaven entreating all to come unto her, into the bosom of everlasting peace.

The girl's hands cupped the darkness, and he couldn't read her palms.

Trembling, he raised the flashlight.

At first her hands were unblemished. Then a faint bruise slowly appeared in the center of each rain-pooled palm.

He closed his eyes and held his breath. When he looked again, the bruises had darkened.

"You're scaring me," she said.

"We *should* be scared."

"You never seemed strange."

"Look at your hands," he said.

She lowered her eyes.

"What do you see?" he asked.

"See? Just my hands."

The storm wind crying in the trees was the voice of a million victims, and the night was filled with their pathetic pleas for mercy.

He would have been shaking uncontrollably if he had not been paralyzed by fear. "You don't see the bruises?"

"What bruises?"

Her gaze rose from her hands, and her eyes met his again.

"You don't see?" he asked.

"No."

"You don't feel?"

In fact, the bruises were not merely bruises any more but had ripened into wounds from which blood began to ooze.

"I'm not seeing what is," Joey told her, overcome by dread. "I'm seeing what *will be.*"

"You're scaring me," she said again.

She wasn't the dead blonde in the bloodstained plastic shroud. Under her hood, her face was framed by raven-black hair.

"But you might end up like her," he said more to himself than to the girl.

"Like who?"

"I don't know her name. But she wasn't just an hallucination. I see that now. Not a drunk's delirium. More than that. She was something . . . else. I don't know."

The grievous stigmata in the girl's hands became more terrible by the second, though she continued to be unaware of them and seemed to feel no pain.

Suddenly Joey understood that the increasing grisliness of his paranormal vision meant that this girl was in growing danger. The fate for which she had been destined—the fate that he had postponed by taking Coal Valley Road and stopping to assist her—was grimly reasserting itself. Delaying by the side of the road was apparently the wrong thing to do.

"Maybe he's coming back," Joey said.

She closed her hands, as if shamed by the intensity with which he stared at them. "Who?"

"I don't know," he said, and he looked into the distance along Coal Valley Road, into the impenetrable gloom that swallowed the two rain-swept lanes of blacktop.

"You mean that other car?" she asked.

"Yeah. Did you get a glimpse of whoever was in it?"

"No. A man. But I didn't see him clearly. A shadow, a shape. Why does it matter?"

"I'm not sure." He took her by the arm. "Come on. Let's get out of here."

As they hurried toward the Chevy, she said, "You sure aren't anything like I thought you'd be."

That struck him as a peculiar statement. Before he could ask her what she meant, however, they reached the Chevy—and he stumbled to a halt, stunned by what stood before him, her words forgotten.

"Joey?" she said.

The Chevy was gone. In its place was a Ford. A 1965 Mustang. *His* 1965 Mustang. The wreck that, as a teenager, he had lovingly restored with his dad's help. Midnight blue with white-wall tires.

"What's wrong?" she asked.

He had been driving the Mustang *that* night twenty years ago. It had sustained major body damage when he had spun out on the interstate and collided with a signpost.

There was no body damage now. The side window, which had shattered when his head hit it, was intact. The Mustang was as cherry as it had ever been.

The wind picked up, shrieking, so the night itself seemed mad. Silvery whips of rain lashed around them and snapped against the pavement.

"Where's the Chevy?" he asked shakily.

"What?"

"The Chevy," he repeated, raising his voice above the storm.

"What Chevy?"

"The rental car. The one I was driving."

"But . . . you were driving this," she said.

He looked at her in disbelief.

As before, he was aware of mysteries in her eyes, but he had no sense that she was trying to deceive him.

He let go of her arm and walked to the front of the Mustang, trailing one hand along the rear fender, the driver's door, the front fender. The metal was cold, smooth, slick with rain, as solid as the road on which he stood, as real as the heart that knocked in his chest.

Twenty years ago, after he'd hit the signpost, the Mustang had been badly scraped and dented, but it had been drivable. He had returned to college in it. He remembered how it had rattled and ticked all the way to Shippensburg—the sound of his young life falling apart.

He remembered all the blood.

Now, when he hesitantly opened the driver's door, the light came on inside. It was bright enough to reveal that the upholstery was free of bloodstains. The cut that he'd suffered in his forehead had bled heavily until he'd driven to a hospital and had it stitched, and by that time the bucket seat had been well spattered. But this upholstery was pristine.

The girl had gone around to the other side of the car. She slipped into the passenger seat and slammed the door.

With her inside, the night seemed as utterly empty of life as a pharaoh's crypt undiscovered beneath the sands of Egypt. All the world might have been dead, with only Joey Shannon left to hear the sound and know the fury of the storm.

He was reluctant to get behind the steering wheel. It was all too strange. He felt as though he had surrendered entirely to a drunkard's delirium—although he knew that he was stone sober.

Then he remembered the wounds that he'd foreseen in her delicate hands, the premonition that the danger to her was increasing with every second they remained at the roadside. He got in behind the wheel, closed the door, and gave her the flashlight.

"Heat," she said. "I'm freezing."

He was barely aware of being sodden and cold himself. For the moment, numb with wonder, he was sensitive only to the deepening mystery, to the shapes and textures and sounds and smells of the mystical Mustang.

The keys were in the ignition.

He started the engine. It had a singular pitch, as familiar to him as his own voice. The sweet, strong sound had such nostalgic power that it lifted his spirits at once. In spite of the flat-out *weirdness* of what was happening to him, in spite of the fear that had dogged him ever since he'd driven into Asherville the previous day, he was filled with a wild elation.

The years seemed to have fallen away from him. All the bad choices that he'd made were sloughed off. For the moment, at least, the future was as filled with promise as it had been when he was seventeen.

The girl fiddled with the heater controls, and hot air blasted from the vents.

He released the emergency brake and put the car in gear, but before he pulled onto the highway, he turned to her and said, "Show me your hands."

Clearly uneasy, regarding him with understandable wariness, she responded to his request.

The nail wounds remained in her palms, visible only to him, but he thought that they had closed somewhat. The flow of blood had diminished.

"We're doing the right thing now, getting out of here," he said, although he knew that he was making little—if any—sense to her.

He switched on the windshield wipers and drove onto the two-lane blacktop, heading toward the town of Coal Valley. The car handled like the fine-tuned masterpiece that he remembered, and his exhilaration intensified.

For a minute or two he was entirely possessed by the thrill of driving—just *driving*—that he had known as a teenager but never since. Deep in the thrall of the Mustang. A boy and his car. Lost to the romance of the road.

Then he remembered something that she had said when he had first seen the Mustang and had halted before it in shock. *Joey?* She had called him by his name. *Joey? What's wrong?* Yet he was certain that he had never introduced himself.

"Some music?" she asked with a nervous tremor in her voice, as though his silent, rapturous involvement with the unrolling road was more disturbing to her than anything he'd previously said or done.

He glanced at her as she leaned forward to switch on the radio. She had pushed back the hood of her raincoat. Her hair was thick and silky and darker than the night.

Something else she'd said, which had struck him as peculiar, now came back to him: *You sure aren't anything like I thought you'd be.* And before that: *You never seemed strange.*

The girl twisted the tuning knob on the radio until she found a station playing Bruce Springsteen's "Thunder Road."

"What's your name?" he asked.

"Celeste. Celeste Baker."

"How did you know my name?"

The question made her self-conscious, and she was able to meet his eyes only briefly. Even in the dim backwash of light from the instrument panel, he could see that she was blushing.

"You never noticed me, I know."

He frowned. "Noticed you?"

"You were two years ahead of me at County High."

Joey shifted his attention from the dangerously slick roadway longer than he should have, mystified by what she'd said. "What're you talking about?"

Staring at the lighted face of the radio, she said, "I was a sophomore when you were a senior. I had a terrible crush on you. I was in despair when you graduated and went off to college."

He was barely able to look away from her.

Sweeping around a curve, the road passed an abandoned mine head and a broken-down tipple that loomed out of the darkness like the half-shattered skeleton of a prehistoric beast. Generations had toiled in its shadow to bring forth coal, but they were now gone to bones or to city work. As he followed the curve, Joey braked gently, slowing from fifty to forty, so badly rattled by what the girl had said that he no longer trusted himself to drive safely at the higher speed.

"We never spoke," she said. "I never could get up the nerve. I just . . . you know . . . admired you from afar. God. Sounds so stupid." She glanced at him from under her brow to see if, in fact, he was amused at her expense.

"You're not making any sense," he said.

"Me?"

"How old are you? Sixteen?"

"Seventeen, almost eighteen. My dad's Carl Baker, and being the principal's daughter makes everything worse. I'm a social outcast to begin with, so I have a hard time striking up a conversation with a boy who's even . . . well, who's even *half* as good-looking as you."

He felt as if he were in a chamber of fun-house mirrors where everything, including conversation, was distorted until nothing quite made sense. "What's the joke here?"

"Joke?"

He slowed to thirty miles an hour, then slowed further still, until he was not quite keeping pace with the racing water that nearly overflowed the wide drainage ditch along the right shoulder of the highway. The surging torrents cast back leaping silvery reflections of the headlights.

"Celeste, damn it, I'm forty years old. How could I be just two years ahead of you in high school?"

Her expression was somewhere between astonishment and alarm, but then it swiftly gave way to anger. "Why're you being like this? Are you *trying* to spook me?"

"No, no. I just—"

"Trying to give the principal's kid a real scare, make a fool of her?"

"No, listen—"

"You've been away to college all this time, and you're *still* that immature? Maybe I should be glad I never had the guts to talk to you before."

Tears shimmered in her eyes.

Nonplussed, he returned his attention to the highway ahead—just as the Springsteen song ended.

The deejay said, "That's 'Thunder Road,' from *Born to Run*, the new album by Bruce Springsteen."

"*New* album?" Joey said.

The deejay said, "Is that *hot* or not? Man, that guy is gonna be *huge.*"

"It's not a new album," Joey said.

Celeste was blotting her eyes with a Kleenex.

"Let's spin one more by the Boss," said the deejay. "Here's 'She's the One,' off the same album."

Pure, passionate, exhilarating rock-'n'-roll exploded from the radio. "She's the One" was as fresh, as powerful, as joyful as it had been when Joey had first heard it twenty years ago.

He said, "What's this guy talking about? It's not new. *Born to Run* is twenty years old."

"Stop it," she said in a voice colored half by anger and half by hurt. "Just stop it, okay?"

"It was all over the radio back then. He knocked the whole world on its ass. The real stuff. *Born to Run.*"

"Give it up," she said fiercely. "You're not scaring me any more. You're not going to make the principal's nerdy kid cry."

She had fought back her tears. Her jaw was clenched, and her lips were tightly compressed.

"*Born to Run,*" he insisted, "is twenty years old."

"Creep."

"Twenty years old."

Celeste huddled against the passenger door, pulling as far away from him as she could.

Springsteen rocked.

Joey's mind spun.

Answers occurred to him. He dared not consider them, for fear that they would be wrong and that his sudden rush of hope would prove unfounded.

They were traveling through a narrow passage carved from the mountain. Walls of rock crowded the blacktop and rose forty feet into the night, reducing their options to the road ahead and the road behind.

Barrages of cold rain snapped with bullet-hard ferocity against the Mustang.

The windshield wipers throbbed—*lubdub, lubdub*—as though the car were a great heart pumping time and fate instead of blood.

At last he dared to look at the rearview mirror.

In the dim light from the instrument panel, he could see little, but what little he *could* see was enough to fill him with wonder, with awe, with wild exhilaration, with fear and with delight simultaneously, with respect for just how very strange the night and the highway had become. In the mirror, his eyes were clear, and the whites of them were *luminescent* white: They were no longer bleary and bloodshot from twenty years of heavy drinking. Above his eyes, his brow was smooth and unlined, untouched by two decades of worry and bitterness and self-loathing.

He jammed his foot on the brake pedal, the tires shrieked, and the Mustang fishtailed.

Celeste squealed and put out her hands to brace herself against the dashboard. If they had been going fast, she would have been thrown out of her seat.

The car skidded across the double yellow line into the other lane, toward the far rock wall, but then slid into a hundred-eighty-degree turn, back into the lane where they'd begun, and came to a stop on the roadway, facing the wrong direction.

Joey grabbed the rearview mirror, tilted it up to reveal a hairline that had not receded, tilted it down past his eyes, left, right.

"What are you doing?" she demanded.

Though his hand was shaking uncontrollably, he found the switch for the dome light.

"Joey, we could be hit head-on!" she said frantically, though there were no headlights approaching.

He leaned closer to the small mirror, turned it this way and that, craned his neck, trying to capture every possible aspect of his face in that narrow rectangle.

"Joey, damn it, we can't just *sit* here!"

"Oh, my God, my God."

"Are you crazy?"

"Am I crazy?" he asked his youthful reflection.

"Get us off the road!"

"What year is it?"

"Drop the stupid act, you moron."

"What year is it?"

"It isn't funny."

"What *year* is it?" he demanded.

She started to open her door.

"No," Joey said, "wait, wait, all right, you're right, got to get off the road, just wait."

He swung the Mustang around, back in the direction they had been heading before he'd slammed on the brakes, and he pulled to a stop on the side of the road.

Turning to her, pleading with her, he said, "Celeste, don't be angry with me, don't be afraid, be patient, just tell me what year it is. Please. Please. I need to hear you say it, then I'll know it's real. Tell me what year it is, and then I'll explain everything—as much as I *can* explain it."

Celeste's schoolgirl crush on him was still strong enough to overcome her fear and anger. Her expression softened.

"What year?" he repeated.

"It's 1975," she said.

On the radio, "She's the One" rocked to its glorious end.

Springsteen was followed by a commercial for the current big hit in the movie theaters: Al Pacino in *Dog Day Afternoon.*

The past summer it had been *Jaws.* Steven Spielberg was just starting to become a household name.

The previous spring, Vietnam had fallen.

Nixon had left office the year before.

Amiable Gerald Ford was in the White House, caretaker president of a troubled country. Twice in September, attempts had been made on his life. Lynnette Fromme had taken a shot at him in Sacramento. Sara Jane Moore had gone after him in San Francisco.

Elizabeth Seton had become the first American to be canonized by the Roman Catholic Church.

The Cincinnati Reds had won the World Series in seven games.

Jimmy Hoffa had disappeared.

Muhammad Ali was world heavyweight champion.

Doctorow's novel *Ragtime.* Judith Rossner's *Looking for Mr. Goodbar.*

Disco. Donna Summers. The Bee Gees.

Now, although still soaked, he realized that he wasn't wearing the suit in which he had attended the funeral and which he had been wearing when he'd fled Henry Kadinska's law office. He was in boots and blue jeans. Hunter's-plaid flannel shirt. Blue-denim jacket with sheepskin lining.

"I'm twenty years old," Joey whispered as reverentially as he once would have spoken to God in the hush of a church.

Celeste reached out and touched his face. Her hand was warm against his cold cheek, and it trembled not with fear but with the pleasure of touching him, a difference that he was able to sense only because he was young again and acutely sensitive to the currents of a young girl's heart.

"Definitely not forty," she said.

On the car radio, Linda Ronstadt launched into the title song from her current hit album: "Heart Like a Wheel."

"Twenty years old," he repeated, and his vision blurred with gratitude to whatever power had brought him to this place, this time, this miraculous passage.

He wasn't merely being given a second chance. This was a shot at a whole new beginning.

"All I've got to do is the right thing," he said. "But how will I know what it is?"

Rain beat, beat, beat on the car with all the fury of Judgment drums.

Moving her hand from his cheek, smoothing his rain-soaked hair back from his forehead, Celeste said, "Your turn."

"What?"

"I told you what year it is. Now you're supposed to explain everything."

"Where do I start? How do I . . . make you believe?"

"I'll believe," she softly assured him.

"One thing I know for sure: Whatever I've been brought back here to do, whatever I'm supposed to change, you're at the center of it. You're the heart of it. You're the reason that I have hope for a new life, and any better future I might have hinges on you."

As he'd spoken, her comforting hand had withdrawn from him. Now she held it over her heart.

For a moment the girl seemed unable to breathe, but then she sighed and said, "You get stranger by the minute . . . but I'm starting to like it."

"Let me see your hand."

She took her right hand from her heart and turned it palm up.

The dome light was still on, but even that didn't provide enough light for him to read the meaning of the stigmata.

"Give me the flashlight," he said.

Celeste handed it to him.

He switched on the beam and studied both her palms. The wounds had been fading when last he'd looked. Now they were deep again and oozing blood.

Reading the reawakened fear in his face, she said, "What do you see, Joey?"

"Nail holes."

"There's nothing."

"Bleeding."

"There's nothing in my hands."

"You can't see, but you've got to believe."

Hesitantly, he touched her palm. When he raised his finger, the tip of it glistened with her blood.

"I can see it. I can feel it," he said. "It's so frighteningly real to me."

When he looked at her, she was staring wide-eyed at his crimson fingertip. Her mouth was an oval of surprise. "You . . . you must've cut yourself."

"You can see it?"

"On your finger," she confirmed, a tremor in her voice.

"In your hand?"

She shook her head. "There's nothing on my hands."

He touched another finger to her palm. It came away wet with her blood.

"I see it," she said tremulously. "Two fingers."

Transubstantiation. The precognitive vision of blood in her hand had been transformed by his touch—and by some miracle—into the real blood of her body.

She touched the fingers of her left hand to the palm of her right, but they found no blood.

On the radio, Jim Croce—not yet dead in a plane crash—was singing "Time in a Bottle."

"Maybe you can't see your own fate by looking at yourself," Joey said. "Who of us can? But somehow . . . through me . . . through my touch, you're being . . . I don't know . . . being given a sign."

He gently pressed a third finger to her palm, and it too came away slick with blood.

"A sign," she said, not fully grasping what was happening.

"So you'll believe me," he said. "A sign to make you believe. Because if you don't believe me, then I might not be able to help you. And if I can't help you, I can't help myself."

"Your touch," she whispered, taking his left hand in both of hers. "Your touch." She met his eyes. "Joey . . . what's going to happen to me . . . what *would* have happened if you hadn't come along?"

"Raped," he said with total conviction, although he didn't understand how he knew. "Raped. Beaten. Tortured. Killed."

"The man in the other car," she said, gazing out at the dark highway, and the tremor in her voice became a shudder that shook her whole body.

"I think so," Joey said. "I think . . . he's done it before. The blonde wrapped in plastic."

"I'm scared."

"We have a chance."

"You still haven't explained. You haven't told me. What about the Chevy you thought you were driving . . . your being forty years old?"

She released his hand, leaving it covered with her blood.

He wiped the blood on his jeans. With his right hand he focused the flashlight on her palms. "The wounds are getting worse. Fate, your destiny, whatever you want to call it—it's reasserting itself."

"He's coming back?"

"I don't know. Maybe. Somehow . . . when we keep moving, you're safer. The wounds close up and start to fade. As long as we're moving, change can happen, there's hope."

He switched off the flashlight and gave it to her. He popped the hand brake and drove back onto Coal Valley Road.

"Maybe we shouldn't go the way he went," she said. "Maybe we should go back to the county route, to Asherville or somewhere else, anywhere else, away from him."

"I think that would be the end of us. If we run . . . if we take the wrong highway like I did before . . . then there's not going to be any mercy in Heaven."

"Maybe we should get help."

"Who's going to believe this?"

"Maybe they'll see . . . my hands. The blood on your fingers when you touch me."

"I don't think so. It's you and me. Only you and me against everything."

"Everything," she said wonderingly.

"Against this man, against the fate you would have met if I hadn't taken the turn onto Coal Valley Road—the fate you *did* meet on that other night when I took the county route instead. You and me against time and the future and the whole great weight of it all coming down like an avalanche."

"What can we do?"

"I don't know. Find him? Face him? We just have to play it as it lays . . . do what seems right, minute by minute, hour by hour."

"How long do we have to . . . to do the right thing, whatever it is, to do the thing that'll make the change permanent?"

"I don't know. Maybe until dawn. The thing that happened on *that* night happened in darkness. Maybe the only thing I have to set right is what happened to you, and if we keep you alive, if we just make it through to sunrise, maybe then everything's changed forever."

The tires cut through puddles on the rural lane, and plumes of white water rose like angels' wings on both sides of the car.

"What's this 'other night' you keep talking about?" she asked.

She gripped the extinguished flashlight in both hands in her lap, as though afraid that something monstrous might fly at the Mustang from out of the darkness, a creature that could be repelled and banished by a withering beam of light.

As they drove through the deep mountain night toward the nearly abandoned town of Coal Valley, Joey Shannon said, "This morning when I got out of bed, I was forty years old, a drunk with a rotting liver and no future anyone would want. And this afternoon I stood at my father's graveside, knowing I'd broken his heart, broken my mom's heart too. . . ."

Celeste listened raptly, able to believe, because she had been given a sign that proved to her that the world had dimensions beyond those she could see and touch.

9

OUT OF THE RADIO CAME "ONE OF THESE NIGHTS" BY THE EAGLES, "Pick Up the Pieces" by the Average White Band, Ronstadt singing "When Will I Be Loved," Springsteen pounding out "Rosalita," "Black Water" by the Doobie Brothers—and all of them were new songs, the big hits of the day, although Joey had been listening to them on other radios in far places for twenty years.

By the time he had recounted his recent experiences to the point at which he had seen her disabled Valiant, they had reached the top of the long slope above Coal Valley. He coasted to a stop in gravel at the side of the road, beside a lush stand of mountain laurels, though he knew that they couldn't linger for long without risking a reassertion of the pattern of fate that would result in her murder and in his return to living damnation.

Coal Valley was more a village than it was a town. Even before the insatiable mine fire had eaten a maze of tunnels under the place, Coal Valley had been home to fewer than five hundred people. Simple frame houses with tar-shingle roofs. Yards full of peonies and lush huckleberry bushes in the summer, hidden under deep blankets of snow in the winter. Dogwood trees that blazed white and pink and purple in the spring. A small branch of County First National Bank. A one-truck volunteer fire station. Polanski's Tavern, where mixed drinks were rarely requested and most orders were for beer or for beer with shooters of whiskey on the side, where huge jars of pickled eggs and hot sausages in spicy broth stood on the bar. A general store, one service station, a small elementary school.

The village wasn't big enough to have streetlights, but before the government had finally begun condemning properties and offering compensation to the dispossessed, Coal Valley had produced a respectable warm glow in its snug berth among the surrounding night-clad hills. Now all the small businesses were shuttered and dark. The beacon of faith in the church belfry had been extinguished. Lights shone at only three houses, and those would be switched off forever when the final residents departed before Thanksgiving.

On the far side of town, an orange glow rose from a pit where the fire in one branch of the mine maze had burned close enough to the surface to precipitate a sudden subsidence. There the seething subterranean inferno was exposed, where otherwise it remained hidden under the untenanted houses and the heat-cracked streets.

"Is he down there?" Celeste asked, as though Joey might be able to sense clairvoyantly the presence of their faceless enemy.

The fitful precognitive flashes he had experienced thus far were beyond his control, however, and far too enigmatic to serve as a map to the lair of the killer. Besides, he suspected that the whole point of his being allowed to replay this night was to give him the chance to succeed or fail, to do right or do wrong, drawing only on the depth of his own wisdom, judgment, and courage. Coal Valley was his testing ground. No guardian angel was going to whisper instructions in his ear—or step between him and a razor-sharp knife flashing out of shadows.

"He could've driven straight through town without stopping," Joey said. "Could've gone to Black Hollow Highway and maybe from there to the turnpike. That's the route I usually took back to college. But . . . I think he's down there, somewhere down there. Waiting."

"For us?"

"He waited for me after he turned off the county route onto Coal Valley Road. Just stopped on the roadway and waited to see if I was going to follow him."

"Why would he do that?"

Joey suspected that he knew the answer. He sensed suppressed, sharp-toothed knowledge swimming like a shark in the lightless sea of his subconscious, but he couldn't entice it to surface. It would soar out of the murky depths and come for him when he was least expecting it.

"Sooner or later we'll find out," he said.

He knew in his bones that confrontation was inevitable. They were captured by the fierce gravity of a black hole, pulled toward an inescapable and crushing truth.

On the far side of Coal Valley, the glow at the open pit pulsed brighter than before. Streams of white and red sparks spewed out of the earth, like great swarms of fireflies, expelled with such force that they rose at least a hundred feet into the heavy rain before being quenched.

Fearful that a fluttering in his belly could quickly grow into a paralyzing weakness, Joey switched off the dome light, steered the Mustang back onto Coal Valley Road, and drove toward the desolate village below.

"We'll go straight to my house," Celeste said.

"I don't know if we should."

"Why not?"

"It might not be a good idea."

"We'll be safe there with my folks."

"The idea isn't just to get safe."

"What *is* the idea?"

"To keep you alive."

"Same thing."

"And to stop him."

"Stop him? The killer?"

"It makes sense. I mean, how can there be any redemption if I knowingly turn my back on evil and walk away from it? Saving you has to be only half of what I need to do. Stopping him is the other half."

"This is getting too mystical again. When do we call in the exorcist, start spritzing holy water?"

"It is what it is. I can't help that."

"Listen, Joey, here's what makes sense. My dad has a gun cabinet full of hunting rifles, a shotgun. That's what we need."

"But what if going to your house draws him there? Otherwise maybe your parents wouldn't be in danger from him, wouldn't ever encounter him."

"Shit, this is deeply crazy," she said. "And you better believe, I don't use the word 'shit' often or lightly."

"Principal's daughter," he said.

"Exactly."

"By the way, a little while ago, what you said about yourself—it isn't true."

"Huh? What did I say?"

"You're not nerdy."

"Well."

"You're beautiful."

"I'm a regular Olivia Newton-John," she said self-mockingly.

"And you've got a good heart—too good to want to change your own fate and ensure your future at the cost of your parents' lives."

For a moment she was silent in the roar of the sanctifying rain. Then she said, "No. God, no, I don't want that. But it would take so little time to get into the house, open the gun cabinet in the den, and load up."

"Everything we do tonight, every decision we make, has heavy consequences. The same thing would be true if this was an ordinary night, without all this weirdness. That's something I once forgot—that there are always moral consequences—and I paid a heavy price for forgetting. Tonight it's truer than ever."

As they descended the last of the long slope and drew near the edge of town, Celeste said, "So what are we supposed to do—just cruise around, stay on the move, wait for that avalanche you talked about to hit us?"

"Play it as it lays."

"But how does it lay?" she asked with considerable frustration.

"We'll see. Show me your hands."

She switched on the flashlight and revealed one palm, then the other.

"They're only dark bruises now," he told her. "No bleeding. We're doing something right."

The car hit a narrow band of subsidence in the pavement, not a deep pit with flames at the bottom, just a shallow swale about two yards wide, although it was rough enough to jolt them, make the car springs creak, scrape the muffler, and spring open the door on the glove box, which evidently had not been closed tightly.

The flapping door startled Celeste, and she swung the flashlight toward it. The beam flared off a curve of clear glass in that small compartment. A jar. Four or five inches tall, three to four inches in diameter. Once it might have contained pickles or peanut butter.

The label had been removed. It was filled with a liquid now, which was made opaque by the glimmering reflections of the flashlight beam, and in the liquid floated something peculiar, not quite identifiable, but nevertheless alarming.

"What's this?" she asked, reaching into the glove box without hesitation but with a palpable dread, compelled against her better judgment, just as Joey was, to have a closer look.

She withdrew the jar.

Held it up.

Floating in pink-tinted fluid was a pair of blue eyes.

10

GRAVEL RATTLED AGAINST THE UNDERCARRIAGE, THE MUSTANG THUMPED across a depression, and Joey tore his gaze from the jar in time to see a mailbox disintegrate on contact with the front bumper. The car churned across the lawn of the first house in Coal Valley and came to a stop just inches before plowing into the front porch.

Instantly he was cast into a memory from the first time that he had lived through this night, when he had failed to take the turnoff to Coal Valley:

. . . *driving the Mustang recklessly fast on the interstate, in a night full of rain and sleet, in a frenzy to escape, as though a demon were in pursuit of him, torn up about something, alternately cursing God and praying to Him. His stomach is acidic, churning. There's a roll of Tums in the glove box. Holding the wheel with one hand, he leans to the right, punches the latch release, and the door in the dashboard drops open. He reaches into that small compartment, feeling for the roll of antacid—and he finds the jar. Smooth and cool. He can't figure what it is. He doesn't keep a jar of anything in there. He takes it out, The headlights of an oncoming big rig, on the far side of the divided highway, throw enough light into the car for him to see the contents of the jar. Eyes. Either he jerks the wheel reflexively or the tires hydroplane on the slick pavement, because suddenly the Mustang is totally out of control, sliding, spinning. The signpost. A terrible crash. His head smacks against the window, safety glass shattering into a gummy mass but cutting him nonetheless. Rebounding from the steel signpost, slamming into the guardrail. Stopped. He forces open the damaged door and scrambles out into the storm. He has to get rid of the jar, dear Jesus, get rid of it before someone stops to help him. Not much traffic in this killing weather, but surely someone will be a good Samaritan when that is the last thing he needs. He's lost the jar. No. He can't have lost the jar. He feels around frantically in the car: the floor in front of the driver's seat. Cool glass. Intact. The lid still screwed on tight. Thank God, thank God. He runs with it past the front of the car to the guardrail. Beyond is wild land, an open field full of tall weeds. With all the strength he can muster, he hurls the jar far into the darkness. And then time passes and he finds himself still standing on the verge of the highway, not sure what he's doing there, confused. Sleet stings his exposed face and hands. He's got a fierce headache. He touches his forehead, finds the cut. He needs medical attention. Maybe stitches. There's an exit one mile ahead. He knows the town. He can find the hospital. No Samaritan has stopped. It's that kind of world these days. When he gets back into the battered Mustang, he is relieved to discover that it's still operable and that the damaged fender isn't binding against the front tire. He's going to be all right. He's going to be all right.*

Sitting in front of the Coal Valley house, with pieces of the mangled mailbox scattered across the lawn behind him, Joey realized that when he'd driven away from the crash scene on the interstate twenty years ago, he had forgotten about the jar and the eyes. Either the head injury had resulted in selective amnesia—or he'd *willed* himself to forget. He was overcome by the sick feeling that the explanation involved more of the latter than the former, that his moral courage—not his physiology—had failed him.

In that alternate reality, the jar lay hidden in a weedy field, but here it was in Celeste's grip. She had dropped the flashlight and held fast to the jar with both hands, perhaps because she was afraid that the lid would come loose and the contents would spill into her lap. She shoved the container into the glove box and slammed the small door shut.

Gasping, half sobbing, she hugged herself and bent forward in her seat. "Oh, shit, oh, shit, oh, shit," she chanted, using the word no more lightly now than before.

Gripping the steering wheel so tightly that he wouldn't have been surprised if it had broken apart in his hands, Joey was filled with an inner turmoil more violent than the hard shatters of wind-driven rain that broke over the Mustang. He was on the brink of understanding the jar: where it had come from, whose eyes it contained, what it meant, why he had blocked it from memory all these years. But he couldn't quite bring himself to step off that brink into the cold void of truth, perhaps because he knew that he didn't yet possess the strength to face what he would discover at the bottom of the fall.

"I didn't," he said miserably.

Celeste was rocking in her seat, hugging herself, huddled over her crossed arms, making a low, tortured sound.

"I didn't," he repeated.

Slowly she raised her head.

Her eyes were as appealing as ever, suggesting unusual depths of character and knowledge beyond her years, but a new quality informed them as well, something disturbing. Perhaps it was an unsought and unwanted awareness of the human capacity for evil. She still looked like the girl he had picked up only eight or ten miles back along the road—but in a fundamental sense she was *not* that girl any more, and she could never return to the state of innocence in which she had entered the night. She was not a schoolgirl now, not the shy doe who had blushed when revealing the crush she had on him—and that was unspeakably sad.

He said, "I didn't put the jar there. I didn't put the eyes in the jar. It wasn't me."

"I know," she said simply and with a firm conviction for which he loved her. She glanced at the glove box, then back at him. "You couldn't have. Not you. Not you, Joey, not ever. You aren't capable of anything like that."

Again he teetered on a precipice of revelation, but a tide of anguish washed him back from it rather than over the edge. "They've got to be her eyes."

"The blonde in the plastic tarp."

"Yeah. And I think somehow . . . somehow I know who she is,

know how she wound up dead with her eyes cut out. But I just can't quite remember."

"Earlier you said that she was more than a vision, more than a drunk's hallucination."

"Yeah. For sure. She's a memory. I saw her for real somewhere, sometime." He put one hand to his forehead, gripping his skull so tightly that his hand shook with the effort and the muscles twitched the length of his arm, as if he could *pull* the forgotten knowledge out of himself.

"Who could have gotten in your car to leave the jar?" she asked.

"I don't know."

"Where were you early in the evening, before you set out to go to college?"

"Home. Asherville. My folks' house. I didn't stop anywhere between there and your Valiant."

"Was the Mustang in the garage?"

"We don't have a garage. It's not . . . that kind of house."

"Was it locked?"

"No."

"Then anybody could have gotten into your car."

"Yeah. Maybe."

No one had come out of the house in front of them, because it was one of the first properties condemned in Coal Valley, abandoned for months. On the white aluminum siding, someone had spray-painted a big "4" and drawn a circle around it. As red as fresh blood in the Mustang's headlights, the number was not graffiti but an official designation: It meant that the house would be the fourth structure to be torn down when the last citizens of Coal Valley moved out and the demolition crew came in with its bulldozers.

The state and federal bureaucracies had been so inefficient and slow in dealing with the mine fire that it had been allowed to spread relentlessly until its white-hot tributaries lay under the entire valley, whereupon it had grown too far-reaching to be extinguished by anything other than time and nature. With the destruction of the village, however, the authorities clearly intended to be as orderly and speedy as a clockwork military operation.

"We're sitting ducks here," he said.

Without checking Celeste's hands, certain that this immobility had already resulted in a resurgence of the stigmata, he shifted the Mustang into reverse and backed across the lawn to the street. So much rain had fallen that he was worried about getting bogged down in the soft sod, but they reached the blacktop without trouble.

"Where now?" she asked.

"We'll look around town."

"For what?"

"Anything out of the ordinary."

"It's *all* out of the ordinary."

"We'll know it when we see it."

He cruised slowly along Coal Valley Road, which was the main thoroughfare through town.

At the first intersection, Celeste pointed to a narrow street on the left. "Our house is over there."

A block away, through beaded curtains of rain and past a few screening pines, several windows were filled with a welcoming amber light. No other house in that direction appeared to be occupied.

"All the neighbors are gone, moved out," Celeste confirmed. "Mom and Dad are alone over there."

"And they may be safer alone," he reminded her, crossing the intersection, driving slowly past her street, studying both sides of the main drag.

Even though Coal Valley Road led to destinations beyond the town of Coal Valley itself, they had encountered no pass-through traffic, and Joey figured that they weren't likely to encounter any. Numerous experts and officials had assured the public that the highway was fundamentally safe and that there was no danger of sudden subsidence swallowing unwary motorists. Following the demolition of the village, however, the road was scheduled for condemnation and removal, and the residents of those mountain towns had long ago become skeptical about *anything* the experts had to say about the mine fire. Alternate routes had become popular.

Ahead of them, on the left, was St. Thomas's Catholic Church, where services had once been conducted every Saturday and Sunday by the rector and the curate of Our Lady of Sorrows in Asherville, who were circuit priests covering two other small churches in that part of the county. It was not a grand house of worship, but a wooden structure with plain rather than stained-glass windows.

Joey's attention was drawn to St. Thomas's by flickering light at the windows. A flashlight. Inside, each time the beam moved, shadows spun and leaped like tormented spirits.

He angled across the street and coasted to a stop in front of the church. He switched off the headlights and the engine.

At the top of the concrete steps, the double doors stood open.

"It's an invitation," Joey said.

"You think he's in there?"

"It's a pretty good bet."

Inside the church, the light blinked off.

"Stay here," Joey said, opening his door.

"Like hell."

"I wish you would."

"No," she said adamantly.

"Anything could happen in there."

"Anything could happen out *here* too."

He couldn't argue with the truth of that.

When he got out and went around to the back of the car, Celeste followed him, pulling up the hood of her raincoat.

The rain was now mixed with sleet, as when he'd lived through this night the first time and crashed on the interstate. It ticked against the Mustang with a sound like scrabbling claws.

When he opened the trunk, he more than half expected to find the dead blonde.

She wasn't there.

He removed the combination crowbar and lug wrench from the side well that contained the jack. It was made of cast iron, comfortingly heavy in his hand.

In the faint glow of the trunk light, Celeste saw the toolbox and opened it even as Joey was hefting the crowbar. She extracted a large screwdriver.

"It's not a knife," she said, "but it's something."

Joey wished that she would stay behind in the car with the doors locked. If anyone showed up, she could blow the horn, and he would be at her side in seconds.

Although he had met her hardly an hour ago, he already knew her well enough to recognize the futility of trying to dissuade her from accompanying him. In spite of her delicate beauty, she was uncommonly tough and resilient. Any lingering uncertainties of youth, which might have inhibited her, had been burned away forever with the realization that she'd been marked for rape and murder—and with the discovery of the eyes in the jar. The world as she knew it had abruptly become a far darker and more disturbing place than it had been when the day began, but she had absorbed that change and adapted to it with surprising and admirable courage.

Joey didn't bother to close the trunk quietly. The open doors of the church made it clear that the man who had led him onto Coal Valley Road was expecting him to follow here as well.

"Stay close," he said.

She nodded grimly. "Guaranteed."

In the front yard of St. Thomas's, a one-foot-diameter vent pipe rose six feet above the ground. It was surrounded by an hourglass construction of chain-link, which served as a safety barrier. Plumes of mine-fire smoke rose from deep underground and wafted from the top of the pipe, lessening the likelihood that toxic fumes would build to dangerous levels in the church and in nearby homes. During the past twenty years, as all efforts to extinguish—or even to contain—the subterranean inferno had proved inadequate, almost two thousand such vents had been installed.

In spite of the continuous scrubbing by the rain, the air around the entrance to St. Thomas's had a sulfurous stench, as if some rough beast, slouching toward Bethlehem to be born, had taken a detour to Coal Valley.

Painted in red on the front of the church was a large "13" with a red circle around it.

Curiously, Joey thought of Judas. The thirteenth apostle. The betrayer of Jesus.

The number on the wall merely indicated that the building had been the thirteenth property in Coal Valley to be condemned and added to the master demolition list, but he couldn't shake the notion that it was significant for other reasons. In his heart he knew that it was a warning to guard against betrayal. But betrayal from what source?

He hadn't gone to Mass in two decades, until the funeral this morning. He had called himself an agnostic—and sometimes an atheist—for many years, yet suddenly everything he saw and everything that happened seemed to have a religious association for him. Of course, in one sense, he wasn't a cynical and faithless man of forty any more but a young man of twenty who had still been an altar boy less than two years ago. Perhaps this strange fall backward in time had brought him closer to the faith of his youth.

Thirteen.

Judas.

Betrayal.

Rather than dismiss that train of thought as superstition, he took it seriously and decided to be more cautious than ever.

Sleet had not yet mantled the sidewalk in ice, and the scattered pellets crunched under their feet.

At the top of the steps, at the open doors, Celeste clicked on the small flashlight that she had brought from the car, dispelling some of the darkness inside.

They crossed the threshold side by side. She slashed left and right with the beam, quickly revealing that no one was waiting for them in the narthex.

A white marble holy-water font stood at the entrance to the nave. Joey discovered that it was empty, slid his fingers along the dry bottom of the bowl, and crossed himself anyway.

He advanced into the church with the crowbar raised and ready, holding it firmly in both hands. He wasn't willing to trust to the grace of God.

Celeste handled the flashlight expertly, probing quickly to all sides, as though accustomed to conducting searches for homicidal maniacs.

Although no Masses had been said in St. Thomas's for the past five or six months, Joey suspected that the electrical service had not been disconnected. For safety reasons, the power might have been left on, because all the dangers inherent in an abandoned building were greater in darkness. Now that official indifference and incompetence had resulted in the loss of the entire town to the hidden, hungry fire below, the authorities were uniformly enthusiastic proponents of safety measures.

A faint scent of incense lingered from past Masses, but it was largely masked by the smell of damp wood and mildew. A trace of sulfurous fumes laced the air as well, and that stink gradually grew stronger till it drowned the spicy aroma from all the old ceremonies of innocence.

Although volleys of sleet rattled against the roof and the windows, the nave was filled with the familiar hush of all churches and with a sense of quiet expectation. Usually it was an expectation of the subtle visitation of a divine presence, but now it was the apprehension of a hateful intrusion into that once-consecrated space.

Holding the crowbar in one fist, he slid his other hand along the wall to the left of the narthex arch. He couldn't locate any switches.

Encouraging Celeste to move to the right of the arch, he felt along that wall until he found a panel of four switches. He snapped them all up with one sweep of his hand.

From overhead, cone-shaped fixtures cast dim, chrome-yellow light on the ranks of pews. Along the walls, hooded sconces directed soft light down across the fourteen stations of the cross and onto the dusty wood floor.

The front of the church beyond the sanctuary railing remained shrouded in shadows. Nevertheless, Joey could see that everything sacred had been removed, including all the statuary and the great crucifix that had graced the wall behind the altar.

Occasionally, as a boy, he had traveled with the priest from Asherville to Coal Valley, to serve when the local altar boys were ill or were for some other reason unavailable, so he was familiar with the appearance of St. Thomas's prior to its deconsecration. Carved by a villager in the latter part of the previous century, the twelve-foot-high crucifix had been a rough piece of work, but Joey had been fascinated by it, for it had possessed a power that he'd never seen in more professionally carved and polished versions.

When his gaze settled from the blank wall where the crucifix had been, he saw a pale and shapeless mound on the elevated altar platform. A soft radiance seemed to issue from it, but he knew that was only a trick of reflection—and his imagination.

They walked cautiously along the center aisle, checking the pews to the left and right, where someone could have been crouching out of sight, waiting to spring at them. The church was small, capable of seating approximately two hundred people, but this night there was neither a single worshiper nor a beast among the pews.

When Joey opened the gate in the sanctuary railing, the hinges squealed.

Celeste hesitated, then preceded him into the sanctuary. She was riveted by the pale mound on the altar platform, but she didn't direct the flashlight at it, evidently preferring, as he did, to delay the inevitable revelation.

As the low gate creaked shut behind him, Joey glanced back into the nave. No one had entered behind them.

Directly ahead was the choir enclosure. The chairs, the music stands, and the organ had all been hauled away.

They followed the ambulatory to the left, around the choir. Though they tried to tread lightly, their footfalls on the oak floor echoed hollowly through the empty church.

On the wall beside the door to the sacristy were more switches. Joey flicked them, and the sanctuary filled with sour light no brighter than that in the nave.

He motioned for Celeste to slip past the closed door, and when she was out of the way, he kicked it open as he had seen cops do in countless movies, rushed across the threshold, and swung the crowbar with all his might, right to left and back again, on the assumption that someone was waiting for him there. He hoped to surprise and cripple the bastard with a preemptive blow, but the length of iron cut the empty air with a *whoosh.*

Enough light spilled past him from the sanctuary to confirm that the sacristy was deserted. The outer door was standing open when he entered, but a gust of cold wind threw it shut.

"He's already gone," Joey told Celeste, who stood rigid with fear in the inner doorway.

They returned to the sanctuary, followed the ambulatory to the presbytery, and stopped at the foot of the three altar steps.

Joey's heart slammed in his breast.

Beside him, Celeste made a soft, plaintive sound—not a gasp of horror but a murmur of compassion, regret, despair. "Ah, no."

The high altar, with its hand-carved antependium, was gone.

Only the altar platform remained.

The mound that they had seen from the nave was neither as pale nor as shapeless as it had appeared to be when the sanctuary lights had been off. Portions of the fetally curled corpse were visible through the heavy-gauge, rumpled plastic. Her face was concealed, but a limp flag of blond hair trailed out of a gap in the folds of the tarp.

This was no precognitive vision.

Not an hallucination either.

Not merely a memory.

This time the body was real.

Nevertheless, the events of the past twenty-four hours had left Joey in doubt about what was real and what was not. He distrusted his own senses enough to seek confirmation from Celeste: "You see it too, don't you?"

"Yes."

"The body?"

"Yes."

He touched the thick plastic. It crackled under his fingers.

One slender, alabaster arm was exposed. The hand was cupped, and a nail hole marked the center. The fingernails were torn and caked with blood.

Although he *knew* that the blonde was dead, in his heart Joey harbored a fragile and irrational hope that the eyes in the jar were not hers, that a thread of life still sewed her to this world, and that she might yet be resuscitated. He dropped to his knees on the top altar step and put his fingertips against her wrist, seeking at least a feeble pulse.

He found no pulse, but the contact with her cold flesh jolted him as if he'd grasped a live electrical wire, and he was shocked into another memory that had been long suppressed:

. . . only wanting to help, carrying the two suitcases through the icy rain to the back of the car, putting them down on the gravel driveway to unlock the trunk. He raises the lid, and the small bulb inside the trunk is as dim as a half-melted votive candle in a ruby-dark glass. The light is tinted red, in fact, because the bulb is smeared with blood. The hot-copper stench of fresh blood virtually steams from that cramped space, making him gag. She is there. She is there. She is completely and totally there—so utterly unexpected that she might have been mistaken for an hallucination, but instead she is more solid than granite, more real than a punch in the face. Naked but swaddled in a semitransparent tarp. Face hidden by her long blond hair and by smears of blood on the inner surface of the plastic. One bare arm is free of the shroud, and the delicate hand is turned with the palm up, revealing a cruel wound. She seems to reach out beseechingly to him, seeking the mercy that she has found nowhere else in the night. His heart swells so terribly with each apocalyptic

beat that it cramps his lungs and prevents him from drawing a breath. As the iron treads of thunder roll across the mountains, he hopes that lightning will strike him, that he will join the blonde in death, because trying to carry on with life after this discovery will be too hard, too painful, joyless, and pointless. Then someone speaks behind him, barely louder than the susurrant song of the rain and wind: "Joey." If he's not permitted to die here, right now, in this storm, then he prays to God to be struck deaf, to be blinded, to be freed from the obligations of a witness. "Joey, Joey." Such sadness in the voice. He turns from the battered corpse. In the nebulous blood-tinted light, he faces tragedy, faces the ruination of four lives in addition to that of the woman in the car trunk—his own, his mother's, his father's, his brother's. "I only wanted to help," he tells P.J. "I only wanted to help."

Joey exhaled explosively, then inhaled with a shudder. "It's my brother. He killed her."

11

THERE WERE RATS IN THE CHURCH. TWO FAT ONES SCUTTLED ALONG THE back of the sanctuary, squeaking, briefly casting elongated shadows, vanishing into a hole in the wall.

"Your brother? P.J.?" Celeste said in disbelief.

Although she had been *five* years behind P.J. in school, she knew who he was. Everyone in Asherville and all the surrounding villages had known P.J. Shannon even before he'd become a world-famous author. As a sophomore at County High, he had become the youngest quarterback in the history of the football team, a star player who had led his teammates to the divisional championship—and then he had done it twice again, in his junior and senior years. He was a straight-A student, valedictorian of his graduating class, humble in spite of his natural gifts and achievements, a real people-loving guy, handsome, charming, funny.

And the most difficult thing to reconcile with the body in the trunk: P.J. was kind. He gave a lot of time to charitable activities at Our Lady of Sorrows. When a friend was ill, P.J. was always first in attendance with a small gift and get-well wishes. If a friend was in trouble, P.J. was at his side to provide whatever help he could. Unlike many other jocks, P.J. wasn't cliquish; he was as likely to be found hanging out with the skinny, myopic president of the chess club as with members of the varsity team, and he had no tolerance for the nerd baiting and other cruelties in which popular, good-looking kids sometimes indulged.

P.J. had been the best brother in the world.

But he was also a brutal killer.

Joey couldn't reconcile those two facts. It would've been easy to go mad trying.

Remaining on his knees on the top altar step, Joey released the dead woman's cold wrist. From the touch of her flesh, in a manner almost mystical, he'd received a dreadful and shattering revelation. He could have been no more profoundly affected if he had, instead, just now *seen* a Eucharist transformed from a wafer of unleavened bread into the sacred flesh of God.

"P.J. was home on a visit from New York City that weekend," he told Celeste. "After college he'd landed a job as an editorial assistant at a major publishing house, figuring to work there until he could get a foot in the door of the film business. We'd had a lot of fun together on Saturday, the whole family. But after Mass on Sunday morning, P.J. was out all day, seeing old friends from high school to talk about the glory days, and driving around a little to enjoy the fall foliage. 'Taking a long, lazy nostalgia bath,' he called it. At least that was what he said he'd been doing."

Celeste turned her back to the altar platform and stood facing the nave, either because she could no longer tolerate the sight of the dead woman or because she feared that P.J. would creep back into the church and take them unaware.

"We usually had Sunday supper at five o'clock, but Mom held it up for him, and he didn't get home till six," Joey said, "well after dark. He apologized, shamefaced, said he'd been having so much fun with his old friends, he'd lost track of time. All through dinner he was so *on*, spinning out jokes, full of energy, as if being in his old stomping grounds had given him a big kick and revitalized him."

Joey folded the loose flap of the plastic tarp over the dead woman's bare arm. There was something obscene about her punctured hand being exposed on the altar, even if St. Thomas's had been deconsecrated.

Celeste waited silently for him to continue.

"Looking back on it," he said, "maybe there was a weird manic quality about him that evening . . . a *dark* energy. Right after dinner, he rushed down to his room in the basement to finish packing, then brought up his suitcases and put them by the back door. He was eager to get going, because the weather was bad and he had a long drive back to New York, wasn't likely to get there until two in the morning at the earliest. But Dad didn't want to see him leave. God, he loved P.J. so much. Dad brought out his scrapbooks about all those high-school and college football triumphs, wanted to reminisce. And P.J. gives me this wink, like to say, *Hell, what's another half hour matter if it makes him happy?* He and Dad went into the living room to sit on the sofa and look through the scrapbooks, and I decided I could save P.J. some time later by putting his suitcases in the trunk of his car. His keys were right there on the kitchen counter."

Celeste said, "I'm so sorry, Joey. I'm so, so sorry."

He hadn't become desensitized to the sight of the murdered woman in the bloodstained plastic tarp. The thought of what she'd suffered was enough to make him sick to his stomach, weigh down his heart with anguish, and thicken his voice with grief, even though he didn't know who she was. But he could not get up and turn his back on her. For the moment he felt that his rightful place was on his knees at her side, that she deserved no less than his attention and his tears. Tonight, he needed to be the witness for her that he had failed to be twenty years ago.

How strange that he had repressed all memory of her for two decades—yet now, in this replay of that worst night of his life, she had been dead only a few hours.

Whether by twenty years or by a few hours, however, he was too late to save her.

"The rain had let up a little," he continued, "so I didn't even bother to put on my hooded windbreaker. Just snatched the keys off the counter, grabbed both suitcases, and took them out to his car. It was parked behind mine at the end of the driveway, in back of the house. I guess maybe Mom must've said something to P.J., I don't know, but somehow he realized what was happening, what I was doing, and he left Dad with the scrapbooks to come after me, stop me. But he didn't get to me in time."

... a thin but bitterly cold rain, the blood-filtered light from the trunk bulb, and P.J. standing there as if the whole world hasn't just fallen apart, and Joey saying again, "I only wanted to help."

P.J. is wide-eyed, and for an instant Joey wants desperately to believe that his brother is also seeing the woman in the trunk for the first time, that he is shocked and has no idea how she got in there. But P.J. says, "Joey, listen, it isn't what you think. I know it looks bad, but it isn't what you think."

"Oh, Jesus, P.J. Oh, God!"

P.J. glances toward the house, which is only fifty or sixty feet away, to be sure that neither of their parents has come out onto the back porch. "I can explain this, Joey. Give me a chance here, don't go bugshit on me, give me a chance."

"She's dead, she's dead."

"I know."

"All cut up."

"Easy, easy. It's okay."

"What've you done? Mother of God, P.J., what've you done?"

P.J. crowds close, corners him against the back of the car. "I haven't done anything. Not anything I should rot in jail for."

"Why, P.J.? No. Don't even try. You can't ... there can't be a why, there can't be a reason that makes any sense. She's dead in there, dead and all bloody in there."

"Keep your voice down, kid. Get hold of yourself." P.J. grips his brother by the shoulders, and amazingly Joey isn't repelled by the contact. "I didn't do it. I didn't touch her."

"She's there, P.J., you can't say she isn't there."

Joey is crying. The cold rain beats on his face and conceals his tears, but he is crying nonetheless.

P.J. shakes him lightly by the shoulders. "Who do you think I am, Joey? For Christ's sake, who do you think I am? I'm your big brother, aren't I? Still your big brother, aren't I? You think I went away to New York City and changed into someone else, something else, some monster?"

"She's in there," is all Joey can say.

"Yeah, all right, she's in there, and I put her in there, but I didn't do it to her, didn't hurt her."

Joey tries to pull away.

P.J. grips him tightly, presses him against the rear bumper, nearly forcing him backward into the open trunk with the dead woman. "Don't go off half-cocked, kid. Don't ruin everything, everything for all of us. Am I your big brother? Don't you know me any more? Haven't I always been there for you? I've always been there for you, and now I need you to be there for me, just this once."

Half sobbing, Joey says, "Not this, P.J. I can't be there for this. Are you crazy?"

P.J. speaks urgently, with a passion that rivets Joey: "I've always taken care of you, always loved you, my little brother, the two of us against the world. You hear me? I love you, Joey. Don't you know I love you?" He lets go of Joey's shoulders and grabs his head. P.J.'s hands are like the jaws of a vise, one pressed against each of Joey's temples. His eyes seem to be full of pain more than fear. He kisses Joey on the forehead. The fierce power with which P.J. speaks and the repetition of what he says are hypnotic, and Joey feels as though he's half in a trance, so deeply in P.J.'s thrall that he can't move. He's having difficulty thinking clearly. "Joey, listen, Joey, Joey, you're my brother—my brother!—and that means every- thing to me, you're my blood, you're a part of me. Don't you know I love you? Don't you know? Don't you know I love you? Don't you love me?"

"Yes, yes."

"We love each other, we're brothers."

Joey is sobbing now. "That's what makes it so hard."

P.J. still holds him by the head, eye to eye with him in the cold rain, their noses almost touching. "So if you love me, kid, if you really love your big brother, just listen. Just listen and understand how it was, Joey. Okay? Okay? Here's how it was. Here's what happened. I was driving out on Pine Ridge, the old back road, cruising like we used to cruise in high school, going nowhere for no reason. You know the old road, how it winds all over, one damn twist and turn after another, so I'm coming around a turn, and there she is, there she is, running out of the woods, down a little weedy slope, onto the road. I hit the brakes, but there's no time. Even if it hadn't been rainy, there wouldn't have been time to stop. She's right in front of me, and I hit her, she goes down, goes under the car, and I drive right over her before I get stopped."

"She's naked, P.J. I saw her, part of her, in the trunk there, and she's naked."

"That's what I'm telling you, if you'll listen. She's naked when she comes out of the woods, naked as the day she was born, and this guy is chasing her."

"What guy?"

"I don't know who he was. Never saw him before. But the reason she doesn't see the car, Joey, the reason is because just then she's glancing back at this guy, running for all she's worth and glancing back to see how close he is, and she runs right in front of the car, looks up and screams just as I hit her. Jesus, it was awful. It was the worst thing I hope I ever see, ever happens to me my whole life. Hit her so hard I knew I must've killed her."

"Where's this guy that was chasing her?"

"He stops when I hit her, and he's stunned, standing there on the slope. When I get out of the car, he turns and runs back to the trees, into the trees, and I realize I gotta try to nail the bastard, so I go after him, but he knows the woods around there and I don't. He's gone by the time I make it up the slope and into the trees. I go in after him, ten yards, maybe twenty, along this deer trail, but then the trail branches off, becomes three paths, and he could've followed any of them, no way for me to know which. With the storm, the light was bad, and in the woods it's like dusk. With the rain and the wind, I can't hear him running, can't follow him by sound. So I go back to the road, and she's dead, just like I knew she'd be." P.J. shudders at the memory and closes his eyes. He presses his forehead to Joey's. "Oh, Jesus, it was terrible, Joey, it was terrible—what the car did to her and what he'd done to her before I ever came along. I was sick, threw up in the road, puked my guts out."

"What's she doing in the trunk?"

"I had the tarp. I couldn't leave her there."

"You should've gone for the sheriff."

"I couldn't leave her there alone on the road. I was scared, Joey, confused and scared. Even your big brother can get scared." P.J. raises his head from Joey's, lets go of him, gives him a little space for the first time. Looking worriedly toward the house, P.J. says, "Dad's at the window, watching us. We stand here like this much longer, he's going to come out to see what's wrong."

"So maybe you couldn't leave her there on the road, but after you put her in the trunk and came back to town, why didn't you go to the sheriff's office?"

"I'll explain it all, tell you the whole thing," P.J. promises. "Let's just get in the car. It looks strange, us standing here in the rain so long. We get in the car, turn on the engine, the radio, then he'll think we're just having a private chat, a brother thing."

He puts one suitcase in the trunk with the dead woman. Then the other. He slams the trunk lid.

Joey can't stop shaking. He wants to run. Not to the house. Into the night. He wants to sprint into the night, through Asherville and across the whole county, on to places he's never been, to towns where no one knows him, on and on into the night. But he loves P.J., and P.J. has always been there for him, so he's obligated at least to listen. And maybe it'll all make sense. Maybe it isn't as bad as it looks. Maybe there's hope for a good brother who will take the time to listen. He's only being asked for time, to listen.

P.J. locks the trunk and takes the keys out of it. He puts his hand against the back of Joey's neck and squeezes lightly, partly as a gesture of affection, partly to urge him to move. "Come on, kid. Let me tell you about it, all about it, and then we'll try to figure out what's the right thing to do. Come on, in the car. It's just me, just me, and I need you, Joey."

So they get in the car.

Joey takes the passenger seat.

The car is cold, and the air is damp.

P.J. starts the engine. Turns on the heater.

The rain begins to fall harder than before, a real downpour, and the world dissolves beyond the windows. The interior of the car seems to shrink around them, humid and intimate. They are in a steel cocoon, waiting to metamorphose into new people and be reborn into an unguessable future.

P.J. tunes the radio until he finds a station that is coming in clear and strong.

Bruce Springsteen. Singing about loss and the difficulty of redemption.

P.J. turns down the volume, but the music and the words are as melancholy when played softly as they are when played louder.

"I figure the sonofabitch must've kidnapped her," P.J. says, "been

holding her somewhere in the woods, in a shack or a hole somewhere,
raping her, torturing her. You read about that sort of thing. Year by
year there's more of it. But who'd ever think it would happen here,
in a place like Asherville? She must've gotten away from him some-
how when he let his guard down."

"What did he look like?"

"Rough."

"What's that mean?"

"Dangerous. He looked dangerous, a little crazed. He was a big
guy, maybe six four, a good two hundred forty pounds. Maybe it's
a good thing I didn't catch up with him. He could've creamed me,
Joey, that's how big he was. I'd probably be dead now if I'd caught
up with him. But I had to try, couldn't just let him run away without
trying to bring him down. Big guy with a beard, long greasy hair,
wearing dirty jeans, a blue flannel shirt with the tail hanging out."

"You have to take her body to the sheriff, P.J. You have to do that
right now."

"I can't, Joey. Don't you see? It's too late now. She's in my trunk.
It could look like I was hiding her there until you found her by
accident. All sorts of interpretations could be put on it—and none
of them good. And I don't have any proof that I saw the guy chasing
her."

"They'll find proof. His footprints, for one thing. They'll search
the woods out there, find the place where he was keeping her."

P.J. shakes his head. "In this weather, the footprints have all been
washed away. And maybe they won't find where he was keeping her,
either. There's no guarantee. I just can't take the chance. If they
don't turn up any proof, then all they have is me."

"If you didn't kill her, they can't do anything to you."

"Get serious, kid. I wouldn't be the first guy to be railroaded for
something he never did."

"That's ridiculous! P.J., everyone around here knows you, likes
you. They know what kind of guy you are. They'll all give you the
benefit of the doubt."

"People can turn on you for no reason, even people you've been
good to all your life. Wait till you've been away at college longer,
Joey. Wait until you've lived awhile in a place like New York City.
Then you'll see how hateful people can be, how they can turn on
you for little or no reason."

"Folks around here will give you the benefit of the doubt," Joey insists.

"You didn't."

Those two words are like a pair of body blows, a one-two punch of truth that leaves Joey deeply shaken and more confused than ever. *"God, P.J., if only you'd left her back there on the road."*

P.J. slumps in the driver's seat and covers his face with his hands. He's weeping. Joey has never seen him weep before. For a while P.J. can't speak, nor can Joey. When at last P.J. finds his voice, he says, *"I couldn't leave her. It was so awful—you didn't see, you can't know how awful. She's not just a body, Joey. She's somebody's daughter, somebody's sister. I thought about—what if some other guy had hit her and I was her brother, what would I want him to do in my place. And I'd have wanted him to take care of her, to cover her nakedness. I'd never want him to just leave her there like a piece of meat. Now I see . . . maybe it was a mistake. But at the time I was rattled. I should have handled it differently. But it's too late now, Joey."*

"If you don't take her to the sheriff's office and tell them what happened, then the guy with the beard, the long hair—he's going to get away. Then he'll do to some other girl the same as he did to this one."

P.J. lowers his hands from his face. His eyes are pools of tears. *"They'll never catch him anyway, Joey. Don't you see that? He's long gone by now. He knows I saw him, can describe him. He wouldn't have hung around these parts ten minutes. He's out of the county by now, running fast as he can for the state line, headed for someplace as far away from here as he can get. You better believe it. Probably already shaved off his beard, hacked at his long hair, looks totally different now. What little I can tell the cops won't help them find him, and I sure as hell can't testify to anything that would convict the bastard."*

"It's still the right thing to do—going to the sheriff."

"Is it? You're not thinking about Mom and Dad. Maybe if you thought about them, it wouldn't be such a right thing."

"What do you mean?"

"I'm telling you, kid, when the cops don't have anybody else to pin this on, they'll try to pin it on me. They'll try real hard. Imagine the stories in the paper. The star football player, the local boy who

*made good and won a full scholarship to a big-time university, gets
caught with a naked woman in the trunk of his car, tortured to death.
Think about it, for God's sake! The trial's going to be a circus.
Biggest circus in the history of the county, maybe the state."*

Joey feels as though he is repeatedly throwing himself against a
giant, furiously spinning grindstone. He is being worn down by
his brother's logic, by the sheer power of his personality, by his
unprecedented tears. The longer Joey struggles to discern the truth,
the more confused and anguished he becomes.

P.J. switches off the radio, turns sideways in his seat, leans toward
his brother, and his gaze is unwavering. It's just the two of them
and the sound of the rain, nothing to distract Joey from the fiercely
persuasive rhythms of P.J.'s voice. "Please, please, listen to me, kid.
Please, for Mom's sake, for Dad's, think hard about this and don't
ruin their lives just because you can't grow up and shake loose of
some altar-boy idea of what's right and wrong. I didn't hurt this
girl in the trunk, so why should I risk my whole future to prove it?
And suppose I come out all right, the jury does the right thing and
finds me innocent. Even then there'll be people around here, lots of
people, who'll continue to believe I did it, believe I killed her. All
right, I'm young and educated, so I get out of here, go anywhere,
start a new life where no one knows that I was once tried for murder.
But Mom and Dad are middle-aged and dirt poor, and what they
have now is pretty much all they're ever going to have. They don't
have the resources to pull up stakes and move. They don't have the
options that you and I have, and they never will. This four-room
shack they call a house—it isn't much, but it's a roof over their
heads. They almost don't have a pot to piss in, but at least they've
always had a lot of friends, neighbors they care about and who care
about them. But that'll change even if I'm cleared in a courtroom."
The arguments rolled from him, a persuasive tide of words. "The
suspicion is going to come between them and their friends. They'll
be aware of the whispering . . . the unceasing gossip. They won't
be able to move away, because they won't be able to sell this dump,
and even if they could sell it, they don't have any equity to speak
of. So here they'll stay, trapped, gradually withdrawing from friends
and neighbors, more and more isolated. How can we let that happen,
Joey? How can we let their lives be ruined when I'm innocent in
the first place? Jesus, kid, okay, I made a mistake not leaving her*

back there and not taking her to the cops after I wrapped her up and put her in the trunk, so go get a gun and shoot me if you have to, but don't kill Mom and Dad. Because that's what you'll be doing, Joey. You'll be killing them. Slowly."

Joey cannot speak.

"It's so easy to destroy them, me. But it's even easier to do the right thing, Joey, even easier just to believe."

Pressure. Crushing pressure. Joey might as well be in a deep-sea submersible instead of a car, at the bottom of a trench four miles under the ocean. Thousands upon thousands of pounds of pressure per square inch. Testing the integrity of the car. Bearing down on him until he feels as though he will implode.

At last, when he finds his voice, it sounds younger than his years and dismayingly equivocal: "I don't know, P.J. I don't know."

"You hold my life in your hands, Joey."

"I'm all mixed up."

"Mom and Dad. In your hands."

"But she's dead, P.J. A girl is dead."

"That's right. Dead. And we're alive."

"But . . . what will you do with the body?"

When he hears himself ask that question, Joey knows that P.J. has won. He feels suddenly weak, as if he is a small child again, and he is ashamed of his weakness. Bitter remorse floods him, as corrosively painful as an acid, and he can deal with the agony only by shutting down a part of his mind, switching off his emotions. A grayness, like a fall of ashes from a great fire, sifts down through his soul.

P.J. says, "Easy. I could dump the body somewhere it'll never be found."

"You can't do that to her family. They can't spend the rest of their lives wondering what happened to her. They won't ever have any hope of peace if they think she's . . . somewhere in pain, lost."

"You're right. Okay. I'm not myself. Obviously, I should leave her where she can be found."

The internal grayness—sifting, sifting—gradually anesthetizes Joey. Minute by minute he feels less, thinks less. This strange detachment is vaguely disturbing on one level, but it is also a great blessing, and he embraces it.

Aware of a new flatness in his voice, Joey says, "But then the cops might find your fingerprints on the tarp. Or find something else, like some of your hair. Lots of ways they might connect you to her."

"Don't worry about fingerprints. There aren't any to find. I've been careful. There's no other evidence either, none, no connections except . . ."

Joey waits with bleak resignation for his brother—his only and much-loved brother—to finish that thought, because he senses that it will be the worst thing with which he has to deal, the hardest thing he will have to accept, other than the discovery of the brutalized body itself.

". . . except I knew her," says P.J.

"You knew her?"

"I dated her."

"When?" Joey asks numbly, but he is almost beyond caring. Soon the deepening grayness in him will soften all the sharp edges of his curiosity and his conscience.

"My senior year in high school."

"What's her name?"

"A girl from Coal Valley. You didn't know her."

The rain seems as if it might never end, and Joey has no doubt that the night will go on forever.

P.J. says, "I only dated her twice. We didn't hit it off. But you can see, Joey, how this will look to the cops. I take her body to the sheriff, they find out I knew her . . . they'll use that against me. It'll be that much harder to prove I'm innocent, that much worse for Mom and Dad and all of us. I'm between a rock and hard place, Joey."

"Yes."

"You see what I mean."

"Yes."

"You see how it is."

"Yes."

"I love you, little brother."

"I know."

"I was sure you'd be there for me when it counted."

"All right."

Deep grayness.

Soothing grayness.

"You and me, kid. Nothing in the world is stronger than you and me if we stick together. We have this bond, brothers, and it's stronger than steel. You know? Stronger than anything. It's the most important thing in the world to me—what we have together, how we've always hung in there, brothers."

They sit in silence for a while.

Beyond the streaming windows of the car, the mountain darkness is deeper than it has ever been before, as if the highest ridges have tilted toward one another, fusing together, blocking out the narrow band of sky and any hope of stars, as if he and P.J. and Mom and Dad now exist in a stone vault without doors or windows.

"You've got to be getting back to college soon," P.J. says. "You've got a long drive tonight."

"Yeah."

"I've got a long one too."

Joey nods.

"You'll have to come visit me in New York."

Joey nods.

"The Big Apple," P.J. says.

"Yeah."

"We'll have some fun."

"Yeah."

"Here, I want you to have this," P.J. says, taking Joey's hand, trying to push something into it.

"What?"

"A little extra spending money."

"I don't want it," Joey says, trying to pull away.

P.J. grips his hand tightly, forcing a wad of bills between his reluctant fingers. "No, I want you to have it. I know how it is in college, you can always use a little extra."

Joey finally wrenches away without accepting the bills.

P.J. is relentless. He tries to shove the money into Joey's coat pocket. "Come on, kid, it's only thirty bucks, it's not a fortune, it's nothing. Humor me, let me play the big shot. I never get to do anything for you, it'll make me feel good."

Resistance is so difficult and seems so pointless—only thirty dollars, an insignificant sum—that Joey finally lets his brother put the money in his pocket. He is worn out. He hasn't the energy to resist.

P.J. pats him on the shoulder affectionately. "Better go inside, get you packed up and off to school."

They return to the house.

Their folks are curious.

Dad says, "Hey, did I raise a couple of sons who're too dumb to come in out of the rain?"

Putting an arm around Joey's shoulders, P.J. says, "Just some brother talk, Dad. Big-brother–little-brother stuff. Meaning of life, all that."

With a smile, Mom teasingly says, "Deep, dark secrets."

Joey's love for her at the moment is so intense, so powerful, that the force of it almost drives him to his knees.

In desperation, he retreats deeper into the internal grayness, and all the bright hurts of the world are dimmed, all the sharpness dulled.

He packs quickly and leaves a few minutes before P.J. Of all the goodbye hugs that he receives, the one from his brother is the most all-encompassing, the most fierce.

A couple of miles outside of Asherville, he becomes aware of a car closing rapidly behind him. By the time he reaches the stop sign at the intersection of the county route and Coal Valley Road, the other vehicle has caught up with him. The driver doesn't stop behind Joey but swings around him, casting up great sheets of dirty water, and takes the turn onto Coal Valley Road at too high a speed. When the tire-thrown water washes off the windshield, Joey sees that the car has stopped after traveling a hundred yards onto the other highway.

He knows it is P.J.

Waiting.

It isn't too late.

There is still world enough, and time.

Everything hinges on making a left turn.

That is the route he had intended to take anyway.

Just turn left, as planned, and do what must be done.

Red taillights, beacons in the dismal rain. Waiting.

Joey drives through the intersection, straight ahead, passing the turnoff to Coal Valley, taking the county route all the way to the interstate.

And on the interstate, although he still invites the devil of detachment into his heart, he can't prevent himself from recalling certain things that P.J. said, statements that have a more profound meaning now than they'd had earlier: "It's so easy to destroy me, Joey ... but ... even easier just to believe." As if truth were not an objective view of the facts, as if it could be whatever a person chose to believe. And: "Don't worry about fingerprints. There aren't any to be found. I've been careful." Caution implied intent. A frightened, confused, innocent man wasn't rational enough to be cautious; he didn't take steps to ensure that he'd eradicated all the evidence linking him to a crime.

Had there been any bearded man with greasy hair—or had that been a Charles Manson–inspired convenience? If he'd hit the woman up on Pine Ridge, hit her hard enough to kill her instantly, why wasn't his car damaged?

Southbound in the night, Joey becomes increasingly distraught, and he drives faster, faster, faster, as though he believes that he can outrun all the facts and their dark implications. Then he finds the jar, loses control of the Mustang, spins out, crashes ...

... and finds himself standing by the guardrail, staring out at a field full of knee-high grass and taller weeds, not quite sure what he's doing there. Wind howling down the interstate with a sound like legions of phantom trucks hauling strange cargo.

Sleet stings his face, his hands.

Blood. A cut above his right eye.

A head injury. He touches the wound, and a brightness spirals behind his eyes, brief hot fireworks of pain.

A head injury, even one as small as this, provides infinite possibilities, not the least of which is amnesia. Memory can be a curse and a guarantee against happiness. On the other hand, forgetfulness can be a blessing, and it can even be mistaken for that most admirable of all virtues—forgiveness.

He returns to the car. He drives to the nearest hospital to have his bleeding wound stitched.

He is going to be all right.

He is going to be all right.

At college again, he attends classes for two days, but he finds no value in following the narrow highways of formal education. He is a natural autodidact anyway and will never find a teacher as demanding of him as he is of himself. Besides, if he is going to be a writer, a novelist, then he needs to acquire a fund of real-world experiences from which to draw on for the creation of his art. The stultifying atmosphere of classrooms and the outdated wisdom of textbooks will only inhibit development of his talent and stifle his creativity. He needs to venture far and wide, leave academia behind, and plunge into the turbulent river of life.

He packs his things and leaves college forever. Two days later, somewhere in Ohio, he sells the damaged Mustang to a used-car dealer, and thereafter he hitchhikes west.

Ten days after leaving college, from a desert truck stop in Utah, he drops a postcard to his parents, explaining his decision to begin the experience-gathering process that will give him the material he needs to be a writer. He tells them that they should not worry about him, that he knows what he's doing, that he'll keep in touch.

He's going to be all right. He's going to be all right.

"Of course," Joey said, still kneeling beside the dead woman in the deconsecrated church, "I was never all right again."

The rain on the roof was a mournful sound, like a dirge for her, the doubly dead, in that she died so young.

Joey said, "I drifted from place to place, job to job. Fell out of touch with everyone . . . even with the dream of becoming a writer. I was too busy for dreams. Too busy playing the game of amnesia. Didn't dare see Mom and Dad . . . and risk coming apart, spilling the truth."

Turning away from the deserted nave over which she had been keeping watch, returning to his side, Celeste said, "Maybe you're being too hard on yourself. Maybe the amnesia wasn't just self-delusion. The head injury *could* explain it."

"I wish I was able to believe that," Joey said. "But the truth *is* objective, not just what we'd like to make it."

"Two things I don't understand."

"If there're only two, then you're way ahead of me."

"In the car with P.J. that night—"

"Tonight. It was twenty years ago . . . but also just tonight."

"—he'd already convinced you to believe him, or at least to go along and get along. Then, after he had you in the palm of his hand, he told you he knew the dead girl. Why would he make a revelation like that when he'd already won? Why would he risk raising your suspicions again and losing you?"

"You had to know P.J. well to understand. There was always this . . . dangerous quality about him. Not recklessness, not anything that anyone found truly scary in any way. Just the opposite. It added to his allure. It was a wonderful, romantic sort of dangerousness, a thing that people admired. He liked to take chances. It was most obvious on the football field. His maneuvers were often so bold and unorthodox—but they worked."

"They always said he liked to play on the edge."

"Yeah. And he enjoyed driving fast, really fast—but he could handle a car about as well as anyone in the Indy 500, never had an accident or traffic ticket. In a poker game, he'd bet everything he had on a single hand, even a bad one if the timing felt right to him— and he nearly always won. You can live dangerously, almost to any extreme, and as long as you win, as long as the risks you take pay off—then people admire you for it."

Standing over him, she put her hand on his shoulder. "I guess that also explains the other thing I didn't understand."

"The jar in the glove box," he guessed.

"Yeah. I'm assuming he put it there while you were packing your bags to go back to college."

"He must've cut out her eyes earlier in the day, kept them as a memento, for God's sake. I'm sure he thought it would be funny to put them in my car and let me find them later. Test the strength of our bond."

"After he'd convinced you he was innocent, persuaded you to let him dispose of the body, he was *crazy* ever to let you see the eyes— let alone give them to you."

"He couldn't resist the thrill. The danger. Walking that thin line along the edge of disaster. And you see—he pulled it off again. He got away with it. I let him win."

"He acts like he thinks he's blessed."

"Maybe he is," Joey said.

"By what god?"

"There's no god involved."

Celeste stepped past him onto the altar platform, moved to the far side of the dead woman, pocketed the screwdriver and flashlight, and knelt. Facing him across the body, she said, "We have to look at her face."

Joey grimaced. "Why?"

"P.J. didn't tell you her name, but he said she's from here in Coal Valley. I probably know her."

"That'll make it even harder on you."

"There's no choice but to look, Joey," she persisted. "If we know who she is, we might have a clue about what he's up to, where he's gone."

They found it necessary to roll the body on its side to pull free a loose end of the plastic tarp. They eased the dead woman onto her back again before uncovering her face.

A thick fall of blood-spotted blond hair mercifully veiled her ravaged features.

With one hand Celeste carefully pushed the hair aside with a tenderness that Joey found deeply touching. Simultaneously, with her other hand, she crossed herself and said, "In the name of the Father, Son, and Holy Ghost, amen."

Joey tilted his head back and stared at the sanctuary ceiling, not because he hoped to get a glimpse of the Trinity, whose names she had intoned, but because he couldn't bear to look into the empty sockets.

"There's a gag in her mouth," Celeste told him. "One of those things you wash a car with—chamois. I think . . . yes, her ankles are tied with wire. She wasn't running from any crazed mountain man."

Joey shuddered.

"Her name's Beverly Korshak," Celeste said. "She was a few years older than me. A nice girl. Friendly. She still lived with her folks, but they sold out to the government here and moved into a house in Asherville last month. Beverly had a secretarial job there, at the electric-company office. Her folks are good friends with my folks. Known them a long, long time. Phil and Sylvie Korshak. This is going to be hard on them, real hard."

Joey still stared at the ceiling. "P.J. must've seen her in Asherville earlier today. Stopped to chat her up. She wouldn't have hesitated to get in the car with him. He wasn't a stranger. At least . . . not apparently."

"Let's cover her," Celeste said.

"You do it."

He wasn't squeamish about what her eyeless face might look like. He was afraid, instead, that in her empty sockets he would somehow be able to see her blue eyes, still intact, as they had been in the last moments of her terrible agony, when she had screamed for help through the wadded rag in her mouth and had *known* that no savior would answer her pleas.

The plastic rustled.

"You amaze me," he said.

"Why?"

"Your strength."

"I'm here to help you, that's all."

"I thought *I* was here to help *you.*"

"Maybe it's both ways."

The rustling stopped.

"Okay," Celeste assured him.

He lowered his head and saw what he first thought was blood on the floor of the altar platform. It had been revealed when they shifted the position of the corpse.

On second look, however, Joey realized that it was not blood but paint from a spray can. Someone had written the number 1 and drawn a circle around it.

"You see this?" he asked Celeste, as she rose to her feet on the other side of the dead woman.

"Yeah. Something to do with the demolition plans."

"I don't think so."

"Sure. Must be. Or maybe just kids vandalizing the place. They painted more of them back there," she said, gesturing in the general direction of the nave.

He got up, turned, and frowned at the dimly lighted church. "Where?"

"The first row of pews," she said.

Against the dark wood backs of the benches, the red paint was difficult to read from a distance.

After picking up the crowbar, Joey swung his legs over the presbytery balustrade, dropped into the three-sided choir enclosure, and went to the sanctuary railing.

He heard Celeste following him, but by way of the ambulatory.

On the front pew to the left of the center aisle, a series of sequential numbers, circled in red, had been painted side by side. They were spaced approximately as people would have been if any had been sitting there. Farthest to the left was the number 2, and the last number, nearest the center aisle, was 6.

Joey felt as though spiders were crawling on the back of his neck, but his hand found none there.

On the pew to the right of the center aisle, the red numbers continued in sequence—7, 8, 9, 10, 11, 12—to the far side of the church.

"Twelve," he brooded.

Joining him at the sanctuary railing, Celeste said softly, "What's wrong?"

"The woman on the altar . . ."

"Beverly."

He stared intently at the red numbers on the pews, which now seemed as radiant as signs of the Apocalypse.

"Joey? What about her? What is it?"

Joey was still puzzling it out, standing in the shadow of truth but not quite able to see the whole icy structure of it. "He painted the number one and then put her on top of it."

"P.J. did?"

"Yeah."

"Why?"

A hard blast of wind battered the old church, and a draft swept through the nave. The faintly lingering scent of stale incense and the stronger smell of mildew were swept away, and the draft brought with it the stink of sulfur.

Joey said, "Do you have any brothers or sisters?"

Clearly puzzled by the question, she shook her head. "No."

"Does anyone else live with you and your folks, like maybe a grandparent, anyone?"

"No. Just the three of us."

"Beverly's one of twelve."

"Twelve what?"

He pointed at Celeste, and his hand shook. "Then your family— two, three, four. Who else still lives in Coal Valley?"

"The Dolans."

"How many of them?"

"Five in their family."

"Who else?"

"John and Beth Bimmer. John's mother, Hannah, lives with them."

"Three. Three Bimmers, five Dolans, plus you and your folks. Eleven. Plus her, there on the altar." With a sweep of his hand, he indicated the numbers on the pews. "Twelve."

"Oh, God."

"I don't need any psychic flash to see where he's going with this one. The number twelve must appeal to him for the obvious reason. Twelve apostles, all dead and lined up in a deconsecrated church. All of them paying silent homage not to God but to the *thirteenth* apostle. That's how P.J. sees himself, I think—as the thirteenth apostle, Judas. The Betrayer."

Still holding the crowbar, he pushed open the sacristy gate and returned to the nave.

He touched one of the numbers on the left-hand pew. In places, the paint was still tacky.

"Judas. Betraying his family," Joey said, "betraying the faith he was raised in, with reverence for nothing, loyal to nothing, to no one. Fearing nothing, not even God. Walking the most dangerous line of them all, taking the biggest imaginable risk to get the greatest of all thrills: risking his soul for a . . . for a dance along the edge of damnation."

Celeste moved close to Joey, pressed against his side, needing the comfort of contact. "He's setting up . . . some sort of a symbolic tableau?"

"With corpses," Joey said. "He intends to kill everyone who still lives in Coal Valley before the night is through and bring their bodies here."

She paled. "Did that come to pass?"

He didn't understand. "Come to pass?"

"In the future that you've already lived—were all the people in Coal Valley killed?"

With a shock, Joey realized that he didn't know the answer to her question.

"After *that* night, I pretty much stopped reading newspapers, news magazines. Avoided TV news. Changed stations on the radio every time a news report came on. Told myself that I was burnt out on news, that it was all just airplane crashes and floods and fires and earthquakes. But what it really must have been . . . I didn't want to read about or hear about any women being mutilated, murdered. Didn't want to risk some detail of a crime—eyes cut out, anything like that—making a subconscious connection for me and maybe blowing away my 'amnesia.' "

"So for all you know—it happened. For all you know—they found twelve dead people in this church, lined up on the front pews, one of them on the altar platform."

"If it did come to pass—if that's what they found—no one ever nailed P.J. for it. Because in my future, he's still on the loose."

"Jesus. Mom and Dad." She pushed away from him and ran down the center aisle toward the back of the nave.

He rushed after her, through the narthex, through the open front doors, into the sleety night.

She slipped on the icy walkway, fell to one knee, scrambled up, and hurried on, rounding the car to the passenger side.

As he reached the driver's door of the Mustang, Joey heard a rumble that first seemed to be thunder—but then he realized that the sound was coming from beneath him, from under the street.

Celeste looked worriedly at him across the roof of the car. "Subsidence."

The rumble built, the street trembled as though a freight train were passing through a tunnel under them, and then both the shaking and the ominous sound faded away.

A section of a burning mine tunnel had collapsed.

Glancing around them, seeing no disturbance of the ground, Joey said, "Where?"

"Must be somewhere else in town. Come on, come on, hurry," she urged, getting into the car.

Behind the wheel, starting the engine, afraid that a sudden fissure in the street might swallow the Mustang and drop them into fire, Joey said, "Subsidence, huh?"

"I've never felt it that bad. Could be right under us but very deep, so far down that it didn't affect the surface."

"Yet."

12

EVEN THOUGH THE TIRES HAD WINTER TREAD, THEY SPUN USELESSLY A couple of times on the way to Celeste's place, but Joey concluded the short trip without sliding into anything. The Baker house was white with green trim and had two dormer windows on the second floor.

He and Celeste ran clumsily across the lawn to the front-porch steps, avoiding the walkway, which was far more treacherous than the frozen grass.

Lights glowed throughout the downstairs, glittering in laces of ice that filigreed some of the windows. The porch lamp was on as well.

They should have entered with caution, because P.J. might have gotten there ahead of them. They had no way of knowing which of the three families he intended to visit first.

But Celeste was in a panic about her folks, so she unlocked the door and plunged heedlessly into the short front hall, calling out to them as she entered. "Mom! Daddy! Where are you? *Mom!*"

No one answered.

Aware that any attempt to restrain the girl would prove futile, brandishing the crowbar at every shadow and imagined movement, Joey followed close behind her as she burst through doorways and flung open those doors that were closed, shouting for her mother and father with increasing terror. Four rooms downstairs and four up. One and a half bathrooms. The place wasn't a mansion by any definition, but it was better than any home that Joey had ever known, and everywhere there were books.

Celeste checked her own bedroom last, but her parents weren't there, either. "He's got them," she said frantically.

"No. I don't think so. Look around you—there aren't any signs of violence here, no indications of a struggle. And I don't think they would have gone out with him anywhere willingly, not in this weather."

"Then where *are* they?"

"If they'd had to go somewhere unexpectedly, would they leave a note for you?"

Without answering, she spun around, dashed into the hall, and descended the stairs two at a time to the ground floor.

Joey caught up with her in the kitchen, where she was reading a message that was pinned to a corkboard beside the refrigerator.

Celeste,
Bev didn't come home from Mass this morning.
No one knows where she is. The sheriff is
looking for her. We've gone over to Asherville
to sit with Phil and Sylvie. They're half out
of their minds with worry. I'm sure it's all
going to turn out fine. Whatever happens,
we'll be home before midnight. Hope you had
a nice time at Linda's place. Keep the doors
locked. Don't worry. Bev will turn up. God
won't let anything happen to her. Love, Mom

Turning from the corkboard, Celeste glanced at the wall clock—only 9:02—and said, "Thank God, he can't get his hands on them."

"Hands." Joey suddenly remembered. "Let me see your hands."

She held them out to him.

The previously frightful stigmata in her palms had faded to vague bruises.

"We must be making right decisions," he said with a shiver of relief. "We're changing fate—your fate, at least. We've just got to keep on keeping on."

When he looked up from her hands to her face, he saw her eyes widen at the sight of something over his shoulder. Heart leaping, he swung toward the danger, raising the iron crowbar.

"No," she said, "just the telephone." She stepped to the wall phone. "We can call for help. The sheriff's office. Let them know where they can find Bev, get them looking for P.J."

The telephone was an old-fashioned rotary model. Joey hadn't seen one of those in a long time. Curiously, more than anything else, it convinced him that he was, indeed, twenty years in the past.

Celeste dialed the operator, then jiggled the cradle in which the handset had been hanging. "No dial tone."

"All this wind, ice—the lines might be down."

"No. It's him. He cut the lines."

Joey knew that she was right.

She slammed down the phone and headed out of the kitchen. "Come on. We can do better than the crowbar."

In the den, she went to the oak desk and took the gun-cabinet key from the center drawer.

Two walls were lined with books. Running one hand over their brightly colored spines, Joey said, "Just tonight, I finally realized . . . when P.J. conned me into letting him . . . letting him get away with murder, he stole my future."

Opening the glass door of the gun cabinet, she said, "What do you mean?"

"I wanted to be a writer. That's all I ever wanted to be. But what a novelist is always trying to do . . . if he's any good, he's trying to get at the truth of things. How could I hope to get at the truth of things, be a writer, when I couldn't even face up to the truth about my brother? He left me with nowhere to go, no future. And *he* became the writer."

She removed a shotgun from the rack in the cabinet and put it on the desk. "Remington. Twenty-gauge. Pump action. Nice gun. So tell me something—how could he be a writer if it's supposed to be all about dealing with truth? He's only about lies and deceit. Is he a good writer?"

"Everyone says he is."

She took another shotgun from the cabinet and put it on the desk beside the first weapon. "Remington too. My dad's partial to the brand. Twelve-gauge. Pretty walnut stock, isn't it? I didn't ask you what everyone else says. What do *you* think? Is he any good as a novelist—in this future of yours?"

"He's successful."

"So what. Doesn't necessarily mean he's good."

"He's won a lot of awards, and I've always pretended to think he's good. But . . . I've really never felt he was much good at all."

Crouching, pulling open a drawer in the bottom of the cabinet, quickly pawing through the contents, she said, "So tonight you take your future back—and you *will* be good."

In one corner stood a gray metal box the size of a briefcase. It was ticking.

"What's that thing in the corner?" Joey asked.

"It monitors carbon monoxide and other toxic gases seeping up from the mine fires. There's one in the basement. This room isn't over the basement, it's an add-on, so it has a monitor of its own."

"An alarm goes off?"

"Yeah, if there's too many fumes." In the drawer she found two boxes of ammunition. She put them on the desk. "Every house in Coal Valley was equipped with them years ago."

"It's like living on a bomb."

"Yeah. But with a long, slow fuse."

"Why haven't you moved out?"

"Bureaucrats. Paperwork. Processing delays. If you move out *before* the government has the papers ready to sign, then they declare the house abandoned, a public danger, and they aren't willing to pay as much for it. You have to live here, take the risk, let it happen at *their* pace if you want to get a halfway fair price."

Opening one of the boxes of shells as Celeste opened the other, Joey said, "You know how to use these guns?"

"I've been going skeet-shooting and hunting with my dad since I was thirteen."

"You don't seem like a hunter to me," he said as he loaded the 20-gauge.

"Never killed anything. Always aim to miss."

"Your dad never noticed that?"

"Funny thing is—whether it's shotguns or rifles, whether it's small game or deer, he always aims to miss too. Though he doesn't think I know it."

"Then what's the point?"

As she finished loading the 12-gauge, she smiled with affection at the thought of her father. "He likes just being in the woods, walking in the woods on a crisp morning, the clean smell of the pines—and having some private time with me. He's never said, but I've always sensed he would've liked a son. Mom had complications with me, couldn't carry another baby. So I've always tried to give Dad a little of the son stuff. He thinks I'm a real tomboy."

"You're amazing," he said.

Hastily dropping spare shells into the various pockets of her black raincoat, she said, "I'm only what I'm here to be."

The strangeness of that statement harked back to other enigmatic things that she had said earlier in the night. He met her eyes, and once again he saw those mysterious depths, which seemed too profound for her years, too deep to be plumbed. She was the most interesting girl that he had ever known, and he hoped that she saw something appealing in *his* eyes.

As Joey finished stuffing spare shells into the pockets of his sheepskin-lined denim jacket, Celeste said, "Do you think Beverly is the first?"

"The first?"

"That he's ever killed."

"I hope so . . . but I don't know."

"I think there've been others," she said solemnly.

"*After* that night, after Beverly, when I let him go . . . I know there must've been others. That's why he was a gypsy. Poet of the highway, my ass. He liked the life of a drifter 'cause he could keep moving through one police jurisdiction after another. Hell, I never realized it before, didn't *want* to realize it, but it's the classic sociopathic pattern—the loner on the road, the outsider, a stranger everywhere he goes, the next thing to invisible. Easier for a man like that to get caught if the bodies keep piling up in the same place. P.J.'s brilliance was to make a profession out of drifting, to become rich and famous for it, to have the unstructured lifestyle of a rootless serial killer but with the perfect cover—a respectable occupation that all but required rootlessness, and a reputation for writing uplifting stories about love and courage and compassion."

"But all that's in the future, as far as I'm concerned," Celeste said. "Maybe my future, our future. Or maybe only one possible future. I don't know how that works—or that it'll even help to think about it."

Joey had a bitter taste in his mouth—as though biting into a hard truth could produce a flavor as acrid as chewing on dry aspirin. "Whether it was one possible future or the *only* future, I still have to carry some of the guilt for all those he killed after Beverly, because I could've put an end to it that night."

"Which is why you're here now, tonight, with me. To undo it all. Not just to save *me* but everyone who came after . . . and to save yourself." She picked up the 12-gauge and chambered a shell. "But what I meant was that I think he's killed *before* Beverly. He was just too cool with you, Joey, too smooth with that story about her running in front of his car up on Pine Ridge. If she'd been his first, he'd have been easily rattled. When you opened that trunk and found her, he'd have been more shaken. The way he handled you—he's used to carting dead women around in his car, looking for a safe place to dump them. He's had a lot of time to think about what he'd do if anyone ever caught him with a body before he was able to dispose of it."

Joey suspected that she was right about this, just as she was right about the weather not being responsible for the dead telephone.

No wonder he had reacted with blind panic in Henry Kadinska's office when the attorney revealed the terms of his father's last will and testament. The money in the estate had originally come from P.J. It was blood money in more ways than one, as tainted as Judas's thirty pieces of silver. Cash accepted from the devil himself could have been no less clean.

He chambered a shell in his shotgun. "Let's go."

13

OUTSIDE, THE SLEET STORM HAD PASSED, AND RAIN WAS FALLING ONCE more. The brittle ice on the sidewalks and in the streets was swiftly melting into slush.

Joey had been wet and cold all night. In fact, he had lived in a perpetual chill for twenty years. He was used to it.

Halfway along the front walk, he saw that the hood was standing open on the Mustang. By the time he got to the car, Celeste was shining the flashlight into the engine compartment. The distributor cap was gone.

"P.J.," Joey said. "Having his fun."

"Fun."

"To him it's all fun."

"I think he's watching us right now."

Joey surveyed the nearby abandoned houses, the wind-stirred trees between them: south to the end of the next block where the street terminated and the forested hills began, north one block to the main drag through town.

"He's right here somewhere," she said uneasily.

Joey agreed, but in the tumult of wind and rain, his brother's presence was even less easily detected than a reluctant spirit at a seance.

"Okay," he said, "so we're on foot. No big deal. It's a small town anyway. Who's closer—the Dolans or the Bimmers?"

"John and Beth Bimmer."

"And his mother."

She nodded. "Hannah. Sweet old lady."

"Let's hope we're not too late," Joey said.

"P.J. can't have had time to come here from the church ahead of us, cut the phone line, wait around to disable the car, and still go after anyone."

Nevertheless, they hurried through the slush in the street. On that treacherous pavement, however, they didn't dare to run as fast as they would have liked.

They had gone only half a block when the subterranean rumble began again, markedly louder than before, building swiftly until the ground quivered under them—as though no boats plied the River Styx any more, leaving the transport of all souls to deep-running, clamorous railroads. As before, the noise lasted no more than half a minute, with no catastrophic surface eruption of the seething fires below.

The Bimmers lived on North Avenue, which wasn't half grand enough to be called an avenue. The pavement was severely cracked and buckled, as though from a great and incessant pressure below. Even in the gloom, the once-white houses appeared too drab—as if they were not merely in need of a fresh coat of paint but were all heavily mottled with soot. Some of the evergreens were deformed, stunted; others were dead. At least North Avenue *was* on the north side of town: across Coal Valley Road from the Baker house and one block farther east.

Six-foot-tall vent pipes, spaced about sixty feet on center and encircled by high chain-link safety barriers, lined one side of the street. From those flues, out of realms below, arose gray plumes of smoke like processions of fugitive ghosts, which were torn into rags by the wind and exorcised by the rain, leaving behind only a stink like that of hot tar.

The two-story Bimmer residence was curiously narrow for its lot, built to the compressed horizontal dimensions of a row house in a downtown neighborhood in some industrial city like Altoona or Johnstown. It appeared taller than it actually was—and forbidding.

Lights were on downstairs.

As he and Celeste climbed the porch steps, Joey heard music inside, and a tinny laugh track. Television.

He pulled open the aluminum-and-glass storm door and knocked on the wood door behind it.

In the house, the phantom studio audience laughed uproariously, and a lighthearted tinkle of piano music further cued the folks at home that they were supposed to be amused.

After the briefest hesitation, Joey knocked again, harder and longer.

"Hold your horses," someone called from inside.

Relieved, Celeste exhaled explosively. "They're okay."

The man who opened the door—evidently John Bimmer—was about fifty-five, shiny bald on top with a Friar Tuck fringe of hair. His beer belly overhung his pants. The bags under his eyes, his drooping jowls, and his rubbery features made him appear as friendly and comfortable as an old hound dog.

Joey was holding the shotgun down at his side, safely aimed at the porch floor, and Bimmer didn't immediately see it. "You're an impatient young fella, ain't you?" he said affably. Then he spotted Celeste and broke into a wide smile. "Hey, missy, that lemon meringue pie you brought by yesterday was every bit of a first-rate job."

Celeste said, "Mr. Bimmer, we—"

"First rate," he repeated, interrupting her. He was wearing an unbuttoned flannel shirt, a white T-shirt, and tan pants held up by suspenders, and he patted the bulge of his belly to emphasize how good the pie had been. "Why, I even let Beth and Ma take a smell of that beauty before I ate it all myself!"

The night echoed with a hard *crack*, as if the wind had snapped off a big tree branch somewhere nearby, but it was not a branch and had nothing to do with the wind, because simultaneously with the sound, arterial blood brightened the front of John Bimmer's T-shirt. His engaging smile turned strange as he was half lifted off his feet and thrown backward by the power of the shot.

Joey shoved Celeste through the open doorway and to the living-room floor. He scrambled after her, dropped beside her, rolled onto his back, and kicked the front door shut hard enough to rattle a pair of pictures—John Kennedy, Pope John XXIII—and a bronze crucifix on the wall above the sofa.

Bimmer had been thrown backward with such force that he wasn't even lying in their way, which meant that the caliber of the weapon was big, damn big, a deer rifle, maybe even bigger than that, a lot of punch. Probably hollow-point cartridges too.

In a blue bathrobe and a crown of pink hair curlers, Bimmer's wife rose from an armchair in front of the television, even as the door was slamming shut, stunned into silence but only for an instant. When she saw her husband's vest of blood and the two shotguns, she reached the logical but incorrect conclusion. Screaming, she turned away from them.

"Get *down!*" Joey shouted, and Celeste cried out, "Beth, stay down!"

Unheeding, in a blind panic, heading toward the back of the house, Beth Bimmer crossed in front of a window. It imploded with an incongruously merry, bell-like ringing of shattering glass. She took a shot in the temple, which snapped her head to the side so hard that it might also have broken her neck, and as the phantom audience on the television laughed uproariously, she crashed to the living-room floor in front of a birdlike elderly woman in a yellow sweatsuit, who was sitting on the sofa.

The older woman had to be Hannah, Bimmer's mother, but she had no time to grieve for her son and daughter-in-law, because two of the next three shots were generous destiny's gifts for her, pumped through the same window but delivered without the merry-bell music of breaking glass, killing her where she sat, as she reached for her hickory cane with one palsied hand, before either Joey or Celeste could even cry out to her.

It was late October of 1975, and the Vietnam War had ended back in April, but Joey felt as if he were in one of those Asian battle zones that had filled the television news when he was growing up. The sudden, senseless death might have shocked him into immobility and fatal indecision—except that he was actually a forty-year-old man in a twenty-year-old body, and those additional twenty years of experience had been gained during a time when sudden, senseless violence had grown commonplace. As a product of the latter decades of the millennium, he could cope reasonably well in the midst of gunfire and random slaughter.

The living room was filled with light, making easy targets of him and Celeste, so he rolled onto his side and fired the 20-gauge Remington at a brass floor lamp with a fringed shade. The roar of the shotgun in that confined space was deafening, but he pumped a fresh shell into the breech and fired at one of the end-table lamps flanking the sofa, then pumped it again and took out the lamp on the other end table.

Understanding Joey's intent, Celeste fired one round into the television screen, silencing the sitcom. The burnt-powder stench of gunfire was immediately overlaid with the hot, astringent odor of ruined electronics.

"Stay low, under the windows," Joey instructed. In the ear-stunning aftermath of the shotgun fire, he sounded as though he were speaking through a woolen winter scarf, but even though his voice was muffled, he could hear the tremor of fear in it. He was a child of the premillennium follies, steeled to the savagery of his fellow human beings, but he nevertheless felt as though he might wet his pants. "Follow the walls to a doorway, any doorway, just get out of the room."

Crawling frantically along the floor in the darkness, dragging the shotgun by its strap, Joey wondered what role he was supposed to serve in his brother's nightmare tableau. If Celeste's parents returned to town and stepped into P.J.'s gun sights, locals would provide all twelve bodies needed for the creation of his demented bit of theater. But he must have a use in mind for Joey too. After all, he had raced to catch up with the Mustang on the county route, swung onto Coal

Valley Road, and paused tauntingly, daring Joey to follow. Although he perpetrated atrocities that any normal person would call acts of madness, P.J. didn't otherwise behave irrationally. Even within his homicidal fantasies, he operated with an appreciation for structure and purpose, however grotesque they might be.

In the Bimmers' kitchen, the light in the oven clock cast a soft green glow that barely illuminated the room—but even that was bright enough to make most of the details visible and to keep Joey close to the floor.

Two windows. One over the sink. The other beside the breakfast table. Both had side-panel curtains and, better yet, vinyl roll-up blinds that were drawn halfway down.

Cautiously rising to his feet at the side of the breakfast table, with his back pressed to the wall, he reached out and pulled that blind all the way over the glass.

Breathing hard, both from exertion and fear, he was bizarrely convinced that P.J. had circled the house and was now directly behind him, outside, with only the wall between them. In spite of the wind and rain, maybe P.J. could track him by his loud breathing and would shoot him *through* the wall to which his back was pressed. The moment passed, and the shot in the spine didn't come, and his terror abated somewhat.

Although he would have preferred that Celeste remain on the floor, below any possible line of fire, she risked a bullet in the arm by drawing the blind at the sink window.

"You okay?" he asked, when they eased back to the floor and met again in the center of the kitchen, staying on their knees in spite of having secured the two windows.

"They're all dead, aren't they?" she whispered bleakly.

"Yeah."

"All three."

"Yeah."

"No chance—"

"No. Dead."

"I've known them all my life."

"I'm sorry."

"Beth used to baby-sit me when I was little."

The eerie green glow from the oven clock made the Bimmer

kitchen shimmer as though it were underwater or had passed through a veil into an unnatural realm outside the flow of real time and ordinary events. But the quality of the light alone could not provide him with blessed detachment, and his gut remained knotted with tension; his throat was so constricted that he could barely swallow.

Fumbling spare shells from his pockets, dropping them through his shaky fingers, Joey said softly, "It's my fault."

"No, it's not. He knew where they were, where to find them. He knows who's still left in town and where they live. We didn't lead him here. He'd have come on his own anyway."

The dropped shells rolled away from him as he tried to recover them. His fingers were half numb, and his hands were shaking so badly that he gave up trying to reload until he calmed down.

Joey was surprised that his heart could still beat. It felt like cold iron in his chest.

They listened to the deadly night, alert for the stealthy sound of a door slowly easing open or the telltale clink of broken glass underfoot.

Eventually he said, "Back home, earlier, when I found the body in the trunk of his car, if I'd called the sheriff then and there, none of these people would be dead now."

"You can't blame yourself for that."

"Who the hell *else* should I blame?" He was instantly ashamed that he had responded so harshly. When he spoke again, his voice was bitter and remorseful, but his anger was directed at himself, not at her. "I knew the right thing to do, and I didn't do it."

"Listen," she said, finding one of his hands in the green gloom, holding it tightly, "that's not what I meant when I said you couldn't blame yourself. Think about it, Joey. Not calling the sheriff—you made *that* mistake twenty years ago, but you didn't make it tonight because your second chance didn't begin with P.J. at the house today, didn't begin with the finding of the body. It began only when you reached Coal Valley Road. Right?"

"Well . . ."

"You weren't *given* a second chance to turn him in to the sheriff earlier."

"But twenty years ago I should've—"

"That's history. Terrible history, and you'll have to live with that part of it. But now all that matters is what happens from here on. Nothing counts except how you chose—and continue to choose— to handle things *after* you took the right highway tonight."

"Haven't handled them well so far, have I? Three people dead."

"Three people who would've died anyway," she argued, "who probably *did* die the first time you lived through this night. It's horrible, it's painful, but it looks as if that part of it was meant to be, and there's no changing it."

Sinking deeper into anguish, Joey said, "Then what's the point of being given a second chance if it isn't to save these people?"

"You might be able to save others before the night is through."

"But why not all of them? I'm screwing up again."

"Stop beating yourself up. It's not for you to decide how many people you can save, how much you can change destiny. In fact, maybe the purpose of being given a second chance wasn't to save *anyone* in Coal Valley."

"Except you."

"Maybe not even me. Maybe I can't be saved either."

Her words left him speechless. She sounded as though she could accept the possibility of her own death with equanimity—while for Joey, the thought of failing her was like a hammer blow to the heart.

She said, "It may turn out that the only thing you can really accomplish tonight is to stop P.J. from *going on from here.* Stop him from committing twenty *more* years of murder. Maybe that's the only thing expected of you, Joey. Not saving me. Not saving anyone. Just stopping P.J. from doing even worse than what he'll do tonight. Maybe that's all God wants from you."

"There's no God here. No God in Coal Valley tonight."

She squeezed his hand, digging her fingernails into his flesh. "How can you say that?"

"Go look at the people in the living room."

"That's stupid."

"How can a god of mercy let people die like that?"

"Smarter people than us have tried to answer the same question."

"And can't."

"But that doesn't mean there *isn't* an answer," she said with rising anger and impatience. "Joey, if God didn't give you the chance to relive this night, then who did?"

"I don't know," he said miserably.

"You think maybe it was Rod Serling, and now you're stuck in the Twilight Zone?" she asked scornfully.

"No, of course not."

"Then who?"

"Maybe it was just . . . just an anomaly of physics. A random fold in time. An energy wave. Inexplicable and meaningless. I don't know. How the hell could I know?"

"Oh. I see. Just some mechanical breakdown in the great cosmic machinery," she said sarcastically, letting go of his hand.

"Seems to make more sense than God."

"So we're not in the Twilight Zone, huh? Now we're aboard the starship Enterprise with Captain Kirk, assaulted by energy waves, catapulted into time warps."

He didn't reply.

She said, "You remember *Star Trek*? Anyone still remember it up there in 1995?"

"Remember? Hell, I think maybe it's a bigger industry than General Motors."

"Let's bring a little cool Vulcan logic to the problem, okay? If this amazing thing that happened to you is meaningless and random, then why didn't you get folded back in time to some boring day when you were eight years old and had the puking flu? Or why not to some night a month ago, when you were just sitting in your trailer out in Vegas, half drunk, watching old Road Runner cartoons or something? You think some random anomaly of physics would just by purest chance bring you back to the most important night of your life, this night of all nights, to the very moment it all went wrong beyond any hope of recovery?"

Just listening to her had calmed him, although his spirits had not been lifted. At least he was able to pick up the spilled shells and reload his shotgun.

"Maybe," she said, "you're living this night again not because there's something you have to *do*, not to save lives and bring down P.J. and be a hero. Maybe you're living this night again only so you'll have one last chance to believe."

"In what?"

"In a world with meaning, in life with some greater purpose."

At times she seemed able to read his mind. More than anything,

Joey wanted to believe in something again—as he had when he'd been an altar boy, so many years ago. But he vacillated between hope and despair. He remembered how filled with wonder he'd been a short while ago when he'd realized that he was twenty again, how grateful he had been to something-someone for this second chance. But already it was easier to believe in the Twilight Zone or in a fluke of quantum mechanics than in God.

"Believe," he said. "That's what P.J. wanted me to do. Just believe in him, believe in his innocence, without one shred of proof. And I did. I believed in him. And look where that got me."

"Maybe it wasn't believing in P.J. that ruined your life."

"It sure didn't help," he said sourly.

"Maybe the main problem was that you didn't believe in anything *else.*"

"I was an altar boy once," he said. "But then I grew up. I got an education."

"Having gone to college a little, you've surely heard the word 'sophomoric,'" Celeste suggested. "It describes the kind of thinking you're still indulging in."

"You're really wise, huh? You know it all?"

"Nope. I'm not wise at all, not me. But my dad says—admitting you don't know everything is the *beginning* of wisdom."

"Your dad the jerkwater high-school principal—suddenly he's a famous philosopher?"

"Now you're just being mean," she said.

After a while, he said, "Sorry."

"Don't forget the sign I was given. My blood on your fingertips. How can I not believe? More important, how can *you* not believe after that? You called it a 'sign' yourself."

"I wasn't thinking. I was all . . . emotional. When you take time to think about it, apply just a little of that cool Vulcan logic you mentioned—"

"If you think hard enough about *anything*, you won't be able to believe in it. If you saw a bird fly across the sky—the moment it's out of sight, there's no way to prove it existed. How do you even know Paris exists—have you ever been there?"

"Other people have seen Paris. I believe them."

"Other people have seen God."

"Not the way they've seen Paris."

"There are a lot of ways to see," she said. "And maybe neither your eyes nor a Kodak is the *best* way."

"How can anyone believe in any god so cruel that he'd let three people die like that, three innocent people?"

"If death isn't permanent," she said without hesitation, "if it's only a transition from one world to the next, then it isn't necessarily cruel."

"It's so easy for you," he said enviously. "So easy just to believe."

"It can be easy for you too."

"No."

"Just accept."

"Not easy for me," he insisted.

"Then why even bother to believe that you're living this night again? Why not write it off as just a silly dream, roll over, go on sleeping, and wait to wake up in the morning?"

He didn't answer. He couldn't.

Although he knew it was pointless to try, he crawled to the wall phone, reached up, and pulled the receiver off the cradle. No dial tone.

"Can't possibly work," Celeste said with an edge of sarcasm.

"Huh?"

"Can't work because you've had time to think about it, and now you realize—there's no way to prove there's anyone else in the world to call. And if there's no way to prove beyond a doubt, right here, right now, that other people exist—then they *don't* exist. You must have learned the word for that in college. 'Solipsism.' The theory that nothing can be proven except your own awareness, that there is nothing real beyond yourself."

Letting the telephone handset dangle on its springy cord, Joey leaned back against the kitchen cabinet and listened to the wind, to the rain, to the special hush of the dead.

Eventually Celeste said, "I don't think P.J.'s going to come in after us."

Joey had arrived at the same conclusion. P.J. wasn't going to kill them. Not yet. Later. If P.J. had wanted to waste them, he could have nailed them easily when they were on the front porch, standing in the light with their backs to him. Instead, he had carefully placed his first shot in the narrow gap between their heads, taking out John Bimmer with a perfectly placed bullet in the heart.

For his own twisted reasons, P.J. evidently wanted them to bear witness to the murders of everyone in Coal Valley, *then* waste them. Apparently he intended that Celeste should be the twelfth and final apostle in the freeze-frame drama that he was creating at the church.

And me? Joey wondered. *What do you have in mind for me, big brother?*

14

THE BIMMER KITCHEN WAS PURGATORY WITH LINOLEUM FLOORS AND Formica countertops. Joey waited to be propelled from that place either by events or by inspiration. There must be something that he could *do* to stop P.J.

Nevertheless, merely proceeding to the Dolan house with the intention of preventing those five pending murders would be sheer folly. He and Celeste would only serve as witnesses to the deaths.

Maybe they could slip into the Dolan place without anyone being shot down at the front door or at the windows. Maybe they could even convince the Dolans of the danger and conspire with them to turn the house into a fortress. But then P.J. could easily set a fire to kill them where they hid or to drive them out into the night where he could shoot them down.

If the Dolan house had an attached garage, and if the Dolans could get in their car and make a run for it, P.J. would shoot out the tires as they tried to flee. Then he would kill them with a spray of gunfire while they were helpless in the disabled vehicle.

Joey had never met the Dolan family. At that moment, convincing himself that they actually existed was, in fact, harder than he would have thought. How easy it would be to sit there in the kitchen and do nothing, let the Dolans—if they existed—look out for themselves, and believe only in the bottle-green shadows around him, the faint smell of cinnamon, the strong aroma of fresh coffee warming in the pot, the hard wood against his back, the floor beneath him, and the hum of the refrigerator motor.

Twenty years ago, when he turned his back on the grisly proof of what his brother had done, he had been equally unable to believe in all the victims to come. Without their bloodied faces before him, without their battered bodies piled high, they had been as unreal to him as the citizens of Paris were unreal to a man convinced of the wisdom of solipsism. How many people had P.J. killed in those twenty years following the first passage of this night? Two per year, forty in all? No. Too low. Killing that infrequently would be too little challenge, too little thrill. More than one a month for twenty years? Two hundred fifty victims: tortured, mutilated, dumped along back roads from one end of the country to the other or buried in secret graves? P.J. seemed more than sufficiently energetic to handle that. By refusing to believe in future horrors, Joey had ensured that they would come to pass.

For the first time he was aware of the true size of his burden of responsibility, which was far greater than he wanted to believe. His acquiescence to P.J. on that long-ago night had resulted in a triumph of evil so enormous that now he was half crushed by the belated recognition of its weight, under which his soul was pinned.

The ultimate consequences of inaction could be greater than the consequences of action.

"He wants us to go to the Dolans' place, so I can see them being murdered," Joey said thickly. "If we don't go right away . . . we'll be buying them a little time at least."

"We can't just sit here," she said.

"No. Because sooner or later, he'll go kill them anyway."

"Sooner," she predicted.

"While he's still watching us here, waiting for us to come out, we have to do something he's not expecting, something that'll make him curious and keep him close to us, away from the Dolans, something that'll surprise and unsettle him."

"Like what?"

The refrigerator motor. The rain. Coffee, cinnamon. The oven clock: ticking, ticking.

"Joey?" she prodded.

"It's so hard to think of something that might rattle him," he said miserably. "He's so sure of what he's doing, so bold."

"That's because he has something to believe in."

"P.J.? Something to believe in?"

"Himself. The sick creep believes in himself, in his cleverness and charm and intelligence. In his destiny. It's not much in the way of a religion, but he believes in himself with a real *passion*, which gives him a whole lot more than confidence. It gives him power."

Celeste's words electrified Joey, but at first he didn't quite understand why.

Then, with sudden excitement, he said, "You're right. He does believe in something. But he doesn't believe *only* in himself. He believes in something else all right. It's clear, isn't it? All the evidence is there, easy to see, but I didn't want to admit it. He believes, he's a *true* believer, and if we play into that belief, then we might be able to rattle him and get an advantage."

"I'm not following you," Celeste said worriedly.

"I'll explain later. Right now we don't have much time. You have to search the kitchen, see if you can find candles, matches. Get an empty bottle or jar and fill it with water."

"Why?"

Scrambling to his feet but staying in a crouch, he said, "Just find it if you can. I'll have to take the flashlight with me, so open the refrigerator door for more light if you need it. Don't turn on the overhead fluorescents. They're too bright. You'll throw a shadow on one of the blinds just when he's tired of waiting for us and ready to take a shot after all."

As Joey headed toward the open door to the dining room, leaving Celeste alone in the green gloom, she said, "Where're you going?"

"The living room. And upstairs. There's some stuff I need."

"What stuff?"

"You'll see."

In the living room, he used the flashlight judiciously, twice flicking it on and immediately off, to orient himself and avoid the three dead bodies. The second burst of light revealed Beth Bimmer's wide eyes as she stared at something beyond the ceiling of the room, beyond the confines of the house, far above the storm clouds outside, somewhere past the North Star.

To take down the crucifix, he had to climb onto the sofa and stand beside the body of the old woman. The long, affixing nail was driven not simply into plaster or dry wall but into a stud, and the head of it was larger than the brass loop through which it was driven, so he had to work hard to remove the stubborn cross from the wall. As he struggled in the darkness, he was afraid that Hannah's body would tip on its side and slump against his legs, but he managed to pry loose the prize and get down on the floor again without coming into contact with her.

A third flick of the light, a fourth, and he was at the stairs.

The second floor offered three small rooms and a bath, each revealed with a quick sweep of the flashlight.

If P.J. was watching outside, perhaps his curiosity had begun to be pricked by Joey's exploration of the house.

In spite of her advanced years and her cane, Hannah had slept on the second floor, and in her bedroom Joey found what he needed. A shrine to the Holy Mother stood in one corner, on a three-legged table in the shape of a pie slice: a ten-inch-tall ceramic statuette with a built-in three-watt bulb at the base, which cast a fan of light over the Virgin. Also on the table were three small ruby-red glasses containing votive candles—all extinguished.

Using the flashlight, he confirmed that the sheets on the bed were white, and then he pulled them off. He carefully bundled the statuette and other items in the sheets.

He went down to the living room again.

The wind was pushing through the broken window, tossing the drapes. He stood tensely at the foot of the stairs for a moment, until he was certain that, in fact, nothing else was moving at the window besides those streaming panels of fabric.

The dead remained dead, and in spite of the inrushing night air, the room stank like the car trunk in which the tarp-wrapped blonde had been kept.

In the kitchen, the refrigerator door was open a few inches, and by that cold light, Celeste was still searching the cabinets. "Found a half-gallon plastic jug, filled it with water," she said. "Got some matches too, but no candles yet."

"Keep looking," Joey said as he put down the sheet-wrapped articles from Hannah's room.

In addition to the entrance to the dining room and the exit to the back porch, the kitchen contained a third door. He cracked it open. The influx of freezing air, bringing the faint scent of gasoline and motor oil, told him that he'd found the attached garage.

"Be right back," he said.

The flashlight revealed that the only window in the garage was in the back wall and covered with a flap of oilcloth. He switched on the overhead light.

An old but well-maintained Pontiac with a toothy chrome grin stood in the single stall.

Beside a rough workbench was an unlocked cabinet that proved to be full of tools. After choosing the heftiest of three hammers, he searched through boxes of nails until he found the size that he needed.

By the time Joey returned to the kitchen, Celeste had located six candles. Beth Bimmer evidently had bought them to decorate the house or the dining table at Christmas. They were about six inches tall, three to four inches in diameter: three red, three green, all scented with bayberry.

Joey had been hoping for simple, tall, white candles. "These will have to do."

He opened the sack that he'd made by gathering the bed sheets, and he added the candles, matches, hammer, and nails to the items that he had collected earlier.

"What is all this?" she asked.

"We're going to play into his fantasy."

"What fantasy?"

"No time to explain. You'll see. Come on."

She carried her shotgun and the half-gallon jug of water. He carried the makeshift sack in one hand and his shotgun in the other. Thus encumbered, if they were threatened, they wouldn't be able to raise a weapon and fire with any accuracy or quickly enough to save themselves.

Joey was counting on his brother's desire to play games with them for a while yet. P.J. was enjoying their fear, feeding on it.

They left by the front door—boldly, without hesitation. The point was not to give P.J. the slip but to draw his attention and engage his curiosity. Joey's gut was clenched in dread anticipation of a rifle shot—not so much one aimed at him but one that might smash the porcelain beauty of Celeste's face.

They descended the porch steps into the rain, went to the end of the front walk, and turned left. They headed back toward Coal Valley Road.

The series of mine vents along North Avenue, set sixty feet on center, suddenly *whooshed* like a row of gas-stove burners being ignited all at once. Columns of baleful yellow fire, shot through with tongues of blue, erupted from the top of every pipe along the street.

Celeste cried out in surprise.

Joey dropped the bed-sheet sack, grabbed the shotgun with both hands, spun to the left, swung to the right. He was so jumpy that he half thought P.J. was somehow responsible for the spontaneous venting of the fires under the town.

If he was nearby, however, P.J. did not reveal himself.

Fire didn't merely flap like bright banners at the tops of the vent pipes and dissolve in the storm wind. Instead, it shot four or five feet above the iron rims, under considerable pressure, like flames from the nozzles of blowtorches.

The ground didn't rumble, as it had done earlier, but the fierce rush of gases escaping up those metal shafts from far below produced a great roar that vibrated in Joey's bones. Strangely, the sound had a disturbing quality of *rage* about it, as though it had been produced not by natural forces but by some colossus trapped in the inferno and less pained than infuriated by it.

"What's happening?" he asked, raising his voice though Celeste was close beside him.

"I don't know."

"Ever see anything like this before?"

"No!" she said, looking around in fearful wonder.

As though they were the pipes of a gargantuan carnival calliope, the vents pumped forth a midnight music of roars and growls and huffs and whistles and occasional mad shrieks. Echoes ricocheted off the smoke-mottled walls of the abandoned houses, off windows as dark as blind eyes.

In the backwash of spectral light from the ferocious gushes of fire, pterodactyl silhouettes swooped through the rain-shattered night. Mammoth shadows lurched across North Avenue as if thrown by an army of giants marching through the street one block to the east.

Joey picked up the bundle that he had dropped. With a sense that time was swiftly running out, he said, "Come on. Hurry."

While he and Celeste sprinted along the deeply puddled street toward Coal Valley Road, the burn-off of subterranean gases ended as abruptly as it had begun. The queer light throbbed once, then again, and was gone. The flying-lurching shadows vanished into an immobilizing darkness.

Rain turned to steam when it struck the fiercely hot iron pipes, and even above the sounds of the storm there arose a hissing as if Coal Valley had been invaded by thousands upon thousands of serpents.

15

THE DOORS OF THE CHURCH STILL STOOD OPEN. THE LIGHTS GLOWED softly inside, as Joey had left them.

After following Celeste into the narthex, he pulled the double doors shut behind them. The big hinges rasped noisily—as he had expected. Now, if P.J. followed them by that route, he would not be able to enter quietly.

At the archway between the narthex and the nave, Joey indicated the marble font, which was as white as an ancient skull and every bit as dry. "Empty the jug."

"Why?"

"Just do it," he said urgently.

Celeste propped her shotgun against the wall and unscrewed the cap from the half-gallon container. The water splashed and gurgled into the bowl.

"Bring the empty jug," Joey said. "Don't leave it where he can see it."

He led her down the center aisle, through the low gate in the sanctuary railing, along the ambulatory that curved around the choir enclosure.

The body of Beverly Korshak, swaddled in heavy plastic, still lay on the altar platform. A pale mound.

"What now?" Celeste asked, following him along the presbytery to the altar platform.

Joey put down the white bundle behind the dead woman. "Help me move her."

Grimacing in disgust at the prospect of that task, Celeste said, "Move her where?"

"Out of the sanctuary into the sacristy. She shouldn't be here like this. It's a desecration of the church."

"This isn't a church any more," she reminded him.

"It will be again soon."

"What are you talking about?"

"When we're done with it."

"We don't have the power to make it a church again. That takes a bishop or something, doesn't it?"

"We don't have the authority officially, no, but maybe that's not necessary to play into P.J.'s twisted fantasy. Maybe all we need is a little stage setting. Celeste, please, *help me.*"

Reluctantly she obliged, and together they moved the corpse out of the sanctuary and put it down gently in a corner of the sacristy, that small room where priests had once prepared themselves for Mass.

On the first visit to St. Thomas's, Joey had found the exterior sacristy door open. He had closed and locked it. When he checked it now, he found that the door was still securely locked.

Another door opened onto a set of descending stairs. Gazing into that darkness, Joey said, "You've gone to church here for most of your life, right? Is there an outside entrance to the basement?"

"No. Not even windows. It's all below ground."

P.J. wouldn't be able to get into the church that way either, which left only the front doors.

Returning with Celeste to the sanctuary, Joey wished that they had been able to bring a card table or other small piece of furniture to serve as an altar. But the low, bare platform itself would have to suffice.

He unfolded the twisted ends of the sheets, with which he had formed the sack, and he set aside the hammer, box of nails, red and green candles, votive candles, matches, crucifix, and statuette of the Holy Mother.

At Joey's instruction, Celeste helped him cover the platform with the two white sheets.

"Maybe he nailed her to a floor while he . . . did what he wanted," he said as they worked. "But he wasn't just torturing her. It meant more to him than that. It was a sacrilegious act, blasphemy. More likely than not, the whole rape and murder was part of a ceremony."

"Ceremony?" she asked with a shudder.

"You said that he's strong and difficult to rattle because he believes in something. Himself, you said. But I think he believes in more than that. He believes in the dark side."

"Satanism?" she asked doubtfully. "P.J. Shannon, football hero, Mr. Nice Guy?"

"We both already know that person doesn't exist any more—if he ever did. Beverly Korshak's body tells us that much."

"But he got a scholarship to Notre Dame, Joey, and I don't think they encourage Black Masses out there in South Bend."

"Maybe it all began right here, before he ever went away to the university or eventually to New York."

"It's so far out," she said.

"Here in 1975, okay, it's a little far out," he agreed as he finished straightening the sheets. "But by 1995, a troubled high-school kid getting into Satanism—it's not so unusual. Believe me. And it *was* happening in the sixties and seventies too—just not as often."

"I don't think I'd much like this 1995 of yours."

"You're not the only one."

"Did P.J. seem troubled in high school?"

"No. But sometimes the most deeply disturbed ones don't much show it."

The cloth was pulled taut across the altar platform. Most of the wrinkles had been smoothed. The white cotton seemed to be whiter now than when they had first unfolded the sheets—radiant.

"Earlier," Joey reminded her, "you said he behaves recklessly, so arrogantly it's as if he thinks he's blessed. Well, maybe that's *exactly* what he thinks. Maybe he thinks he's made a bargain that protects him, and now he can get away with just about anything."

"You're saying he sold his soul?"

"No. I'm not saying there *is* a soul or that it could be sold even if it existed. I'm only telling you what he might *think* he's done and why that ugly little fantasy gives him such extraordinary self-confidence."

"We do have souls," she said quietly, firmly.

Picking up the hammer and the box of nails, Joey said, "Bring the crucifix."

He went to the back of the sanctuary where a twelve-foot-high carving of Christ in blessed agony had once hung. No overhead spots were focused on the wall; instead, the plaster was washed with light from a pair of floor-mounted lamps. The rising light had been meant to lead the eye upward to the contemplation of the divine. He drove a nail into the plaster slightly above eye level.

Celeste slipped the brass loop over the nail, and once more St. Thomas's had a crucifix behind and above its altar platform.

Glancing at the rain-streaked windows and the unrelieved night beyond, Joey wondered if P.J. was watching them. What interpretation might he put upon their actions? Did he find these developments laughable—or alarming?

Joey said, "The tableau that he seems to want to create here—a mockery of the twelve apostles, arranged in a deconsecrated church, at the expense of twelve lives—it's not just an act of madness. It's almost . . . an offering."

"A while ago, you said he thinks he's like Judas."

"The Betrayer. Betraying his community, his family, his faith, even God. And passing along the corruption wherever he can. Pushing thirty dollars into my pocket in his car that night before sending me back to school."

"Thirty dollars—thirty pieces of silver."

Returning to the altar platform and putting aside the hammer, he grouped the six Christmas candles at one end of the white sheet. "Thirty dollars. Just a little symbolic gesture to amuse himself. Payment for my cooperation in letting him get away with her murder, making a little Judas out of me."

Frowning as she picked up the pack of matches and began to light the candles, Celeste said, "So he sees Judas Iscariot as—what?—like his patron saint on the dark side?"

"Something like that, I think."

"Did Judas go to Hell for betraying Christ?" she wondered.

"If you believe there's a Hell, then I guess he has one of the deepest rooms there," Joey said.

"You, of course, don't believe in Hell."

"Look, it doesn't really matter what *I* believe in, only what P.J. believes in."

"You're wrong about that."

Ignoring her comment, he said, "I don't pretend to know all the twists and turns of his delusions—just maybe the overall design of it. I think even a first-rate psychiatrist would have trouble mapping the weird landscape in my big brother's head."

As she finished lighting the six bayberry candles, Celeste said, "So P.J. comes home from New York, takes a ride around the county, and he sees how weird things have gotten here in Coal Valley. All the abandoned houses. The subsidence everywhere. More vent pipes than ever. The open pit of fire out on the edge of town. The church deconsecrated, condemned. It's as if the whole town's sliding into Hell. Sliding pretty fast, in fact, and right before his eyes. And it excites him. Is that what you think?"

"Yeah. A lot of psychotics are very susceptible to symbolism. They live in a different reality from ours. In their world, everyone and everything has secret meanings. There are no coincidences."

"You sound like you've crammed the subject for a test."

"Over the years I read lots of books about aberrant psychology. At first I told myself it was all research for novels I'd write. Then, when I admitted I'd never be a writer, I kept reading—as a hobby."

"But subconsciously, you were trying to understand P.J."

"A homicidal sociopath with religious delusions, of the sort that P.J. seems to have, might see demons and angels masquerading as ordinary people. He believes cosmic forces are at work in the simplest events. His world is a place of constant high drama and immense conspiracies."

Celeste nodded. She was the principal's daughter, after all, raised in a house full of books. "He's a citizen of Paranoialand. Yeah, okay, so maybe he's been killing for years, since he went away to college if not before, one girl here, one there, little offerings from time to time. But the situation in Coal Valley *really* gets his juices up, makes him want to do something special, something big."

Joey placed the ceramic statuette of the Holy Mother at the far end of the white sheets from the candles and plugged the cord into a socket on the side of the altar platform. "So now we'll screw up his plans by opening the door to God and inviting Him back into the church. We'll step straight into P.J.'s fantasy and fight symbolism with symbolism, counter superstition with superstition."

"And how will that stop him?" she asked, moving to Joey's end of the altar to light the three votive candles in the ruby glasses, which he had carefully arranged in front of the statuette of the Virgin.

"It'll rattle him, I think. That's the first thing we have to do—rattle him, shake his confidence, and get him to come in out of the darkness, where we have a chance at him."

"He's like a wolf out there," she agreed, "just circling beyond the campfire light."

"He's promised this offering—twelve sacrifices, twelve innocent people—and now he feels he's got to deliver. But he's committed to setting up his tableau of corpses in a church from which God's been driven out."

"You seem so sure . . . as if you're in tune with him."

"He's my brother."

"It's a little scary," she said.

"For me too. But I sense that he needs St. Thomas's. He has no chance of finding another place like it, not tonight. And now that he's started all this, he feels compelled to finish it. Tonight. If he's watching us right now, he'll see what we're doing, and it'll rattle him, and he'll come in here to make us *un*do it all."

"Why won't he just shoot us through the windows, then come in and undo it all himself?"

"He might have handled it that way—if he'd realized soon enough what we were up to. But the moment we hung the crucifix, it was too late. Even if I'm only half right about his delusions, even if he's only half as deeply lost in his fantasy as I think he is . . . I don't believe he'll be able to touch a crucifix on a sanctuary wall any more easily than a vampire could."

Celeste lit the last of the three votive candles.

The altar should have looked absurd—like a playhouse vignette arranged by children engaged in a game of church. Even with their makeshift stage furnishings, however, they had created a surprisingly convincing illusion of a sacred space. Whether it was a function of the lighting or arose by contrast with the starkness of the stripped, deconsecrated, dusty church, an unnatural *glow* seemed to emanate from the bed sheets on the altar platform, as though they had been treated with phosphorescent dye; they were whiter than the whitest linens that Joey had ever seen. The crucifix, lighted from below and at an extreme angle, cast an absurdly large shadow across the back wall of the sanctuary, so it almost appeared as though the massive, hand-carved icon that had been removed during deconsecration had now been brought back and lovingly rehung. The flames on the fat Christmas candles all burned strong and steady in spite of myriad cross drafts in the church; not one guttered or threatened to go out; curiously, the bayberry-scented wax smelled not at all like bayberry but quite like incense. By some fluke of positioning and trick of reflection, one of the votive candles in the ruby-red glasses cast a shimmering spot of crimson light on the breast of the small bronze crucifix.

"We're ready," Joey said.

He put the two shotguns on the floor of the narrow presbytery, out of sight but within easy reach.

"He saw us with the guns earlier," Celeste said. "He knows we have them. He won't come close enough to let us use them."

"Maybe not. It depends on how deeply he believes in his fantasy, how invincible he feels."

Turning his back to the altar steps, Joey dropped to one knee behind the presbytery balustrade that overlooked the choir enclosure. The heavy handrail and the chunky balusters offered some protection from gunfire, but he wasn't under the illusion that they provided ideal cover. The gaps between the balusters were two to three inches wide. Besides, the wood was old and dry; hollow-point rounds from a high-caliber rifle would chop it into kindling pretty quickly, and some of the splinters would make deadly shrapnel.

Kneeling beside him, as if reading his mind, Celeste said, "It won't be decided with guns, anyway."

"It won't?"

"It's not a question of force. It's a question of faith."

As on more than one previous occasion, Joey saw mysteries in her dark eyes. Her expression was unreadable—and strangely serene, considering their circumstances.

He said, "What do you know that I don't know?"

After meeting his gaze for a long beat, she looked out at the nave and said, "Many things."

"Sometimes you seem . . ."

"How do I seem?"

"Different."

"From what?"

"From everyone."

A shadow of a smile drew her lips into a suggestion of a curve. "I'm not just the principal's daughter."

"Oh? What else?"

"I'm a woman."

"More than that," he insisted.

"Is there more than that?"

"Sometimes you seem . . . much older than you are."

"There are things I know."

"Tell me."

"Certain things."

"I should know them too."

"They can't be told," she said enigmatically, and her pale smile faded.

"Aren't we in this together?" he asked sharply.

She looked at him again, eyes widening. "Oh, yes."

"Then if there's anything you know that can help—"

"Deeper than you think," she whispered.

"What?"

"We're in it together deeper than you think."

Either she was choosing to be inscrutable or there was less mystery in the moment than Joey imagined.

She returned her attention to the nave.

They were silent.

Like the frantic wings of trapped birds struggling to break free, rain and wind beat against the church.

After a while he said, "I feel warm."

"It's been heating up in here for some time," Celeste confirmed.

"How can that be? We didn't turn on any furnace."

"It's coming up through the floor. Don't you feel it? Through every chink, every crack in the boards."

He put his hand on the presbytery floor and discovered that the wood was actually warm to the touch.

Celeste said, "Rising from the ground under the church, from the fires far below."

"Maybe not so far any more." Remembering the ticking metal

box in the corner of the study at her house, Joey said, "Should we be worried about toxic gases?"

"No."

"Why not?"

"There's worse tonight."

Within only a minute or two, a fine dew of perspiration formed on his brow.

Searching his jacket pockets for a handkerchief, Joey found a wad of money instead. Two ten-dollar bills. Two fives. Thirty bucks.

He kept forgetting that what had happened twenty years in the past had also, in another sense, happened only hours ago.

Staring in horror at the folded currency, Joey recalled the persistence with which P.J. had forced it upon him back there in the humid closeness of the parked car. The body hidden in the trunk. The smell of rain heavy in the night. The odor of blood heavier in his memory.

He shuddered violently and dropped the money.

As they fell out of his hand, the rumpled bills became coins and rang against the wooden floor, making a music like altar bells. Glittering, spinning, clinking, wobbling, rattling, they quickly settled into a silent heap beside him.

"What's that?" Celeste asked.

He glanced at her. She hadn't seen. He was between her and the coins.

"Silver," he said.

But when he looked again, the coins were gone. Only a wad of paper currency lay on the floor.

The church was hot. The window glass, streaming with rain, appeared to be melting.

His heart was suddenly racing. Pounding like a penitent fist upon the wrong side of his breast.

"He's coming," Joey said.

"Where?"

Rising slightly, Joey pointed across the balustrade and along the center aisle to the archway at the back of the nave, to the dimly lighted narthex beyond the arch, to the front doors of the church, which were barely visible in the shadows. "He's coming."

16

WITH A FORTHRIGHT SHRIEK OF UNOILED HINGES, THE CHURCH DOORS opened out of darkness into shadow, out of the cold night into the strange heat, out of the blustering storm into a quiet one, and a man entered the narthex. He didn't proceed stealthily or even with any noticeable caution, but walked directly to the nave arch, and with him came the rotten-egg fumes from the vent pipe outside.

It was P.J. He was wearing the same black boots, beige cords, and red cable-knit sweater that he had been wearing earlier in the evening, back at the house, at dinner, and later in the car when he had argued the merits of forgetfulness and brotherly bonds. Since then he had put on a black ski jacket.

This was not the P.J. Shannon whose novels always found a home on the best-seller lists, not the New-Age Kerouac who had crossed the country uncounted times in various vans, motor homes, and cars. This P.J. was still shy of his twenty-fourth birthday, a recent graduate of Notre Dame, home from his new job in New York publishing.

He wasn't carrying the rifle with which he'd shot the Bimmers, and he didn't seem to think he needed it. He stood in the archway, feet planted wide, hands empty at his sides, smiling.

Until now, Joey had forgotten the *extreme* confidence of P.J. at that age, the tremendous power that he radiated, the sheer *intensity* of his presence. The word "charismatic" had been overused even in 1975; by 1995, it was employed by journalists and critics to describe every new politician who had not yet been caught stealing, every new rap singer who thought "hate" rhymed with "rape," every young actor with more smoldering in his eyes than in his brain. But whether in 1995 or 1975, the word seemed to have been invented for P.J. Shannon. He had all the charisma of an Old Testament prophet without the beard and robes, commanding attention sheerly by his presence, so magnetic that he seemed to exert an influence upon even inanimate objects, realigning all things around him until even the lines of the church's architecture subtly focused attention toward him.

Meeting Joey's eyes across the length of the church, P.J. said, "Joey, you surprise me."

With one sleeve, Joey blotted the sweat on his face, but he didn't reply.

"I thought we had a bargain," said P.J.

Joey put one hand on his shotgun, which lay on the presbytery floor beside him. But he didn't pick it up. P.J. could dodge out of the archway and back into the narthex before Joey would be able to raise the gun and pump off a round. Besides, at that distance, mortal damage probably couldn't be done with a shotgun even if P.J. failed to get out of the line of fire fast enough.

"All you had to do was go back to college like a good boy, back to your job at the supermarket, lose yourself in the daily struggle of life, the gray grinding boredom that you were born for. But you had to stick your nose in this."

"You *wanted* me to follow you here," Joey said.

"Well, true enough, little brother. But I was never sure you'd actually *do* it. You're just a little priest-loving, rosary-kissing altar boy. Why should I expect *you* to have any guts? I thought you might even go back to college and make yourself accept my cockamamie story about the mountain man up on Pine Ridge."

"I did."

"What?"

"Once," Joey said. "But not this time."

P.J. was clearly baffled. This was the first and only time that *he* would ever live through this strange night. Joey had been through a variation of it once before, and only Joey had been given a second chance to do it right.

From the floor beside him, Joey scooped up the thirty dollars and, still half sheltered behind the balustrade, threw it at P.J. Although wadded in a ball, the paper currency sailed only as far as the end of the choir enclosure and fell short of the sanctuary railing. "Take back your silver."

For a moment P.J. seemed stunned, but then he said, "What an odd thing to say, little brother."

"When did you make your bargain?" Joey asked, hoping that he was right about P.J.'s psychotic fantasy and was playing into it in a way that would shake him out of his smug complacency.

"Bargain?" P.J. asked.

"When did you sell your soul?"

Shifting his attention to Celeste, P.J. said, "You must have helped him puzzle it out. His mind doesn't have a dark bent that would let him see the truth on his own. Certainly not in the couple of hours since he opened my car trunk. You're an interesting young lady. Who are you?"

Celeste didn't answer him.

"The girl by the road," P.J. said. "I know that much. I would have had you by now if Joey hadn't interfered. But who *else* are you?"

Secret identities. Dual identities. Conspiracies. P.J. was indeed operating in the complex and melodramatic world of a paranoid psychotic with religious delusions, and he evidently believed that he saw in Celeste some otherworldly presence.

She remained silent. Crouching by the balustrade. One hand on her shotgun, which lay on the presbytery floor.

Joey hoped she wouldn't use the weapon. They needed either to lure P.J. farther into the church, within range—or they needed to convince him that they didn't need guns at all and felt confident about trusting in the power of the holy ground on which they stood.

"Know where the thirty bucks came from, Joey?" P.J. asked. "From Beverly Korshak's purse. Now I'll have to gather it up and put it in your pocket again later. Preserve the evidence."

At last Joey understood what role P.J. had in mind for him. He was expected to take the fall for everything his brother had done—and would do—this night. No doubt his own murder would have been made to look like suicide: Priest-loving, rosary-kissing altar boy flips out, kills twelve in Satanic ceremony, takes own life, film at eleven.

He had escaped that fate twenty years ago when he had failed to follow P.J. onto Coal Valley Road—but he'd taken a turn into another destiny that had been nearly as bad. This time, he had to avoid both those options.

"You asked when I sold my soul," P.J. said, still lingering in the narthex archway. "I was thirteen, you were ten. I got hold of these books about Satanism, the Black Mass—neat stuff. I was *ripe* for them, Joey. Held my funny little ceremonies in the woods. Small animals on my little altar in the woods. I was ready to slit *your* throat, kiddo, and cut your heart out if nothing else had worked. But it didn't come to that. It was so much easier than that. I'm not even sure the ceremonies were necessary, you know? I think all that was necessary was to *want* it badly enough. Wanting it with every fiber of my being, with all my heart, wanting it so badly that I *hurt* with wanting it—that's what opened the door and let him in."

"Him?" Joey said.

"Satan, Scratch, the devil, spooky old Beelzebub," said P.J. in a jokey and theatrical tone of voice. "Boy, he's not at all like that, Joey. He's actually a warm, fuzzy old beast—at least to those who embrace him."

Though Celeste remained crouched behind the balustrade, Joey rose to his full height.

"That's right, kiddo," P.J. encouraged. "Don't be afraid. Your big brother won't spout green fire out his nose or sprout leathery wings."

Desert-dry heat was still coming through the floor.

Like ectoplasmic faces pressed to the glass, condensation began to form on some of the windows.

"Why did you do it, P.J.?" Joey asked, pretending to believe in such things as souls and bargains with the devil.

"Oh, kiddo, even then I was sick to death of being poor, afraid of growing up to be a useless piece of shit like our old man. Wanted money in my pocket, cool cars when I got old enough for them, my pick of the girls. And there was no way that was ever going to happen to me like I was, not when I was just one of the Shannon boys, living in a room next to the furnace. But *after* I made the deal—well, look what happened. Football star. Top grades in my class. Most popular boy in school. Girls couldn't wait to spread their legs for me—and even after I'd dump one of them, she'd still love me, moon over me, never say a word against me. Then a full scholarship to a *Catholic* university, and how's that for irony?"

Joey shook his head in denial. "You were always a good athlete, even as a kid. And real smart. And everyone always liked you. You always *had* those things, P.J."

"The *hell* I did," P.J. said, raising his voice for the first time. "God gave me nothing when I came into this world, nothing, nothing but crosses to bear. He's a great advocate of suffering, God is. A real sadist. I had *nothing* until I made a deal for it."

Reason and logic would have no effect on him, especially not if his psychosis had taken root when he'd been a child. He was a long time gone into madness. The only hope of manipulating him into a disadvantageous position was to play into his fantasy, encourage him.

P.J. said, "Why don't you try it, Joey? You won't have to learn a lot of chants, conduct ceremonies in the woods, none of that. Just *want* it, open your heart to it, and you can have your own companion."

"Companion?"

"Like I have Judas. A rider on the soul. I invited him into me. I let him out of Hell for a while, and in return he takes good care of me. He has big plans for me, Joey. Wealth, fame. He wants me to satisfy every desire I have, because he experiences everything through me—feels the girls through me, tastes the champagne, shares the sense of power, the glorious power, when it's time to kill. He wants only the very best for me, Joey, and he makes sure that I get it. You could have a companion of your own, kiddo. I can make it happen, I really can."

Joey was rendered speechless by the astonishing complexity of P.J.'s twisted fantasy of Faustian bargains, negotiated damnation, and possession. If he had not spent twenty years reading the most exotic cases of aberrant psychology ever published, he could not have begun to grasp the nature of the human monster with whom he was dealing. He could not possibly have understood P.J. the *first* time that he'd lived through this night, because then he had lacked the special knowledge that allowed him to comprehend.

P.J. said, "You just have to *want* it, Joey. Then we kill this bitch here. One of the Dolan boys is sixteen. Big kid. We can make it look like he did it all, then killed himself. You and me—we walk away, and from now on we're together, tighter than brothers, together like we've *never* been before."

"What do you *really* need me for, P.J.?"

"Hey, I don't need you, Joey. I'm not out to *use* you for any reason. I just love you. Don't you think I love you? I do. You're my baby brother. Aren't you my one and only little baby brother?

Why shouldn't I want to have you at my side, share my good fortune with you?"

Joey's mouth was dry, and not just from the sudden heat. For the first time since turning off the county route onto Coal Valley Road, he longed for a double shot of Jack Daniel's. "I think you just need me to take down the crucifix for you. Maybe hang it upside down instead of the way it is."

P.J. didn't respond.

"I think you're desperate to finish the little tableau that you started to set up here, but now you're afraid to come into the church since we've restored things."

"You haven't restored anything," P.J. said scornfully.

"I bet if I took down the crucifix, blew out the candles, tore up the altar, if I just made the place safe for you again—then you'd kill both of us, just like you planned all along."

"Hey, kiddo, don't you see who you're talking to? This is your brother here. What's wrong with you? Am I your brother, the one who always fought all your fights with you, took good care of you? Am I ever going to hurt you? Hurt you? Does that make any sense at all?"

Celeste rose from her knees to stand beside Joey, as though she sensed that any small show of courage on her part would help convince P.J. that she and Joey were confident about the protection provided by the symbols with which they had surrounded themselves. Their confidence might feed his apprehension.

"If you're not afraid of the church, why won't you come farther in?" Joey asked.

"Why's it so warm in here?" P.J. tried to sound as self-assured as always, but doubt tainted his voice. "What's there to be afraid of? Nothing."

"Then come on in."

"There's nothing sacred here."

"Prove it. Put your fingers in the holy water."

P.J. turned his attention to the marble font at his right side. "It was dry before. You put the water there yourself."

"Did we?"

"It hasn't been blessed," P.J. said. "You're not a damn priest. It's just ordinary water."

"Then put your fingers in it."

Joey had read of psychotics who, swept away by delusions that they possessed Satanic power, were capable of literally blistering when they put their fingers into holy water or touched a crucifix. The injuries they suffered were real, although induced entirely by their own powers of suggestion, by the depth of their belief in their own sick fantasies.

When P.J. continued to regard the shallow pool of holy water with trepidation, Joey said, "Go on, touch it, go on—or are you afraid it'll eat into your hand, burn like an acid?"

P.J. reached hesitantly toward the marble bowl. Like a nervous dragonfly, his spread fingers hovered over the water. Then he pulled his hand back.

"Jesus," Celeste said softly.

They had found a way to use P.J.'s madness to protect themselves from him.

The first time that he had lived through this night, Joey had been little more than a boy, just out of his teens, up against not merely an older brother but a psychopath of extreme cunning and high intelligence. Now, he had twenty years of experience on P.J., which gave him the psychological advantage this time.

"You can't touch us," Joey said. "Not here in this sacred place. You can't do anything that you planned to do here, P.J. Not now, not since we've let God back inside these walls. All you can do now is run for it. Morning will roll around eventually, and we'll just wait here until someone comes looking for us or until someone finds the Bimmers."

P.J. tried again to put his hand in the water, but he couldn't do it. Crying out wordlessly in fear and frustration, he kicked the font.

The wide marble bowl crashed off the fluted pedestal, and P.J. took sufficient courage from that destruction to rush forward into the nave while the font was still toppling.

Joey stooped and reached for the 20-gauge.

Even as the contents of the bowl spilled onto the floor, P.J. stepped into the spreading puddle, and a cloud of sulfurous steam erupted around his feet, as if the water had, indeed, been blessed and had reacted with fierce corrosive power upon encountering the shoe of a demon-ridden man.

Joey realized that the floor must have been much hotter at the back of the nave than in the sanctuary, fearfully hot.

Having noticed the extreme and increasing heat in the church,

P.J. should have realized as much himself; however, in his dementia, he reacted not with reason but with superstitious panic. The gush of steam from the "holy" water reinforced his bizarre delusion, and he screamed as if he'd actually been burned. In fact, he surely *was* suffering, because to anyone afflicted with psychosomatic pain, it seemed as genuine as the real thing. P.J. let out a shriek of abject misery, slipped and fell in the water, into more steam, landing hard on his hands and knees, wailing, squealing. He raised his hands, fingers smoking, and then put them to his face but tore them away at once, as though the beads of water on them were indeed the tears of Christ and were searing his lips, his cheeks, half blinding him. He thrashed to his feet, stumbled out of the nave into the narthex, to the front doors, into the night, alternately shouting in rage and bleating in purest anguish, like neither a man nor a man possessed but like a wild beast in excruciating torment.

Joey had only half raised the Remington. P.J. had never come close enough to warrant the use of the gun.

"My God," Celeste said shakily.

"That was amazing luck," Joey agreed.

But they were talking about different things.

She said, "What luck?"

"The hot floor."

"It's not that hot," she said.

He frowned. "Well, it must be a lot hotter back there than at this end of the building. In fact, I'm wondering how long we'll even be safe here."

"It wasn't the floor."

"You saw—"

"It was *him.*"

"Him?"

She was as deathly pale as one of the distorted, ghostly faces of condensation on the church windows. Staring at the shallow puddle that was still lightly steaming at the far end of the center aisle, she said, "He couldn't touch it. Wasn't worthy."

"No. Nonsense. It was just the hot floor meeting the cool water, steam—"

She shook her head vigorously. "Corrupt. Couldn't touch something holy."

"Celeste—"

"Corrupt, foul, tainted."

Worried that she was on the brink of hysteria, he said, "Have you forgotten?"

Celeste met his eyes, and he saw such an acute awareness in her that he dismissed all concerns about panic attacks and hysteria. In fact, there was a curiously humbling quality about her piercing stare. She'd forgotten nothing. Nothing. And he sensed that her perception was, in fact, clearer than his.

Nevertheless, he said, "We put the water in the font."

"So?"

"Not a priest."

"So?"

"*We* put it there, and it's just ordinary water."

"I saw what it did to him."

"Just steam—"

"No, Joey. No, no." She spoke rapidly, running sentences together, frantic to convince him: "I got a glimpse of his hands, part of his face, his skin was blistered, red and peeling, the steam can't have been *that* hot, not off a wooden floor."

"Psychosomatic injury," he assured her.

"No."

"The power of the mind, autohypnosis."

"There's not much time," she said urgently, looking around at the crucifix and then at the candles, as if to make sure that their stage setting was still in order.

"I don't think he'll be back," Joey said.

"He will."

"But when we played straight into his fantasy, we scared the bejesus—"

"No. He can't be frightened. Nothing can scare him."

Even in her urgency, she seemed mildly dazed, in shock. But Joey was overcome by the odd certainty that she was not distracted, as she seemed, but was functioning at a level of awareness and with a degree of insight that he had never known. Heightened perceptions.

She crossed herself. "*. . . in nomine Patris, et Filii, et Spiritus Sancti . . .*" She was spooking Joey worse than P.J. had done.

"A homicidal psychotic," Joey said nervously, "is full of rage, sure, but he can be as susceptible to fear as any sane person. Many of them—"

"No. He's the father of fear—"

"—many of them live in constant terror—"

"—the father of lies, such inhuman fury—"

"—even when they're on power fantasies like he is, they live in fear of—"

"—fury driving him for eternity." Her expressive eyes were glazed, haunted. "He never gives up, never will, nothing to lose, in a perpetual state of hatred and rage ever since the Fall. . . ."

Joey glanced toward the spilled water in which P.J. had slipped. The church was hotter than ever, sweltering, but steam had stopped rising from the puddle. Anyway, that wasn't the fall she meant.

After a hesitation, he said, "Who're we talking about, Celeste?"

She appeared to be listening to voices that only she could hear. "He's coming," she whispered tremulously.

"You're not talking about P.J., are you?"

"He's coming."

"What? Who?"

"The companion."

"Judas? There's no Judas. That's fantasy."

"Beyond Judas."

"Celeste, be serious, the devil himself isn't *really* in P.J."

As alarmed by his insistence on reason as he was alarmed by her sudden descent into full-blown mysticism, she gripped him by the lapels of his denim jacket. "You're running out of time, Joey. Not much time left to believe."

"I believe—"

"Not in what matters."

She let go of him, vaulted over the presbytery balustrade into the choir enclosure, landing solidly on both feet.

"Celeste!"

Rushing to the sanctuary gate, she shouted, "Come touch the floor, Joey, touch where the water spilled, see whether it's hot enough for steam, hurry!"

Frightened for her, frightened by her, Joey also vaulted the balustrade. "Wait!"

She shoved through the sanctuary gate.

Over the incessant drumming of the rain on the roof, another sound arose. An escalating roar. Not from under them. Outside.

She hurried into the center aisle.

He looked toward the windows on the left. Toward the windows on the right. Darkness on both sides.

"Celeste!" he shouted as he pushed through the sanctuary gate. "Show me your hands!"

She was halfway down the aisle. She turned toward him. Her face was slick with sweat. Like a ceramic glaze. Glistening with candlelight. The face of a saint. A martyr.

The roar swelled. An engine. Accelerating.

"Your hands!" Joey shouted desperately.

She raised her hands.

In her delicate palms were hideous wounds. Black holes thick with blood.

From out of the west, shattering windows, smashing through clapboard and wall studs and old wood paneling and stations of the cross, the Mustang exploded into the church, headlights unlit but engine screaming, horn suddenly blaring, tires popping like balloons as the floor splintered under them, driving forward with tremendous power, plowing into the pews, unstoppable. Those benches cracked free of their moorings, tilted up, slammed into one another—pews and kneelers erupting and crashing together and piling one atop the next in a cresting wave of wood, in a geometry of penitence—and still the Mustang surged forward, engine racing, gears grinding, trumpeting as it came.

Joey fell to the floor in the center aisle and shielded his head with his folded arms, certain that he was going to die in the tsunami of pews. He was even more certain that Celeste would die, whether crushed to death now or, later, after being nailed to the floor or to the wall by P.J. Joey had utterly failed her, failed himself. Following the storm of broken glass, the hail of plaster, the avalanche of wood, there would be a rain of blood. Over the roar of the Mustang, over the banshee horn, over the crack-split-shatter of wood, over the ringing of falling glass, over the ominous creak of sagging ceiling beams, he heard one special sound separate and eerily distinct from all others, and instantly he knew what it was: the bronze clatter and thud of the crucifix dropping off the back wall of the sanctuary.

17

THE COLD WIND WAS IN THE CHURCH NOW, SNIFFING AND PANTING LIKE a pack of dogs through the ruins.

Joey lay facedown under a stack of tumbled pews and shattered wall beams, and although he felt no pain, he was afraid that his legs were crushed. When he dared to move, however, he discovered that he was neither injured nor pinned in place.

The rubble was a multitiered, three-dimensional maze. Joey was forced to crawl, writhe, and squirm through it as though he were a rat-seeking ferret exploring the depths of an ancient timberfall.

Shingles, laths, and chunks of other debris still dropped out of the demolished wall and from the damaged ceiling, clattering into the wreckage. The wind played the narrow twisting passages in the destruction as though they were flutes, piping an eerie, tuneless music. But the car engine had died.

After wriggling through an especially cramped space between slabs of prayer-polished oak, Joey came to the front wheel of the Mustang. The tire was flat, and the fender had crumpled around it like paper.

From the undercarriage, greenish antifreeze drizzled like dragon's blood. The radiator had burst.

He squeezed farther along the side of the car. Just past the driver's door, he reached a place where he was able to stand up between the vehicle and the surrounding rubble.

He hoped to see his brother dead in the Mustang, the shaft of the steering wheel driven through his chest by the impact or his body pitched halfway through the windshield. But the driver's door was open just wide enough to allow escape, and P.J. was gone.

"Celeste!" Joey shouted.

No answer.

P.J. would be looking for her.

"Celeste!"

He smelled gasoline. The fuel tank had burst.

The surrounding pews and slabs of wood paneling and sheared-off two-by-fours had tilted up higher than the car. He couldn't see much of the church.

Joey levered himself onto the roof of the Mustang. He rose to his feet, turning his back to the damaged wall and the rain-slashed night.

St. Thomas's was filled with strange light and swarming shadows. Some ceiling bulbs were still on, but others were out. Toward the rear of the church, showers of white-gold-blue sparks cascaded from a damaged overhead fixture.

In the sanctuary, the candles had toppled when the building had been shaken by the impact of the hurtling car. The sheets on the altar platform were afire.

Shuttling, weaving shadows made a fabric of confusion, but one among them moved with a linear purpose that snapped Joey's attention to it. Coming off the ambulatory onto the presbytery was P.J. He was carrying Celeste. She was unconscious, cradled in his arms, head tilted back, tender throat exposed, black hair trailing almost to the floor.

Christ, no!

For an instant, Joey couldn't breathe.

Then he was gasping.

He plunged off the roof of the Mustang onto the crumpled hood and clambered up from the car onto the surrounding jumble of pews and beams and buckled wallboard. The wreckage shifted under him, threatening to open and swallow him in a maw of wickedly splintered boards and twisted nails, but he kept moving, wobbling and lurching, arms spread like those of a lumberjack trying to maintain his balance in a log-rolling contest.

At the three altar steps, P.J. ascended.

The back wall of the sanctuary, without crucifix, crawled with images of fire.

Joey jumped down from the pile of rubble into an open space in front of the sanctuary railing.

On the altar, P.J. dropped Celeste onto the burning sheets, as though she were not a person—a special and needed person—but only an armful of trash.

"No!" Joey shouted, leaping across the sanctuary railing, stumbling into the curving ambulatory that would take him around the choir and up to the high altar.

Her raincoat caught fire. He saw the flames leap hungrily from that new fuel.

Her hair. *Her hair!*

Stung by the flames, she regained consciousness and screamed.

Rounding the ambulatory, reaching the presbytery walkway, Joey saw P.J. standing over Celeste, on the burning sheets, oblivious of the fire around his feet, hunched like some round-backed beast, the hammer in one hand and raised high to strike.

With his heart knocking as loud as Death's fist on a door, Joey crossed the presbytery, toward the altar steps.

The hammer arced down.

Her cry of terror. Heart piercing. Cut off by the sound of the steel hammer crushing her skull.

A bleat of misery tore free of Joey as he reached the foot of the altar steps.

P.J. whipped around. "Little brother." He was grinning. Eyes adance with reflections of fire. Face blistered by water burns. He triumphantly raised the blood-wet hammer. "Now let's nail her down."

"Noooooooo!"

Something fluttered across Joey's vision. No. Not across. The flutter wasn't anything in the church, nothing real. Behind his eyes. Like a darting shadow of wings on rippled, sun-spangled water.

Everything had changed.

The fire was gone.

So was P.J.

The crucifix hung on the back wall again. The candles were all upright, the makeshift altar cloth unburned.

Celeste grabbed him by the shoulder, spun him, seized the lapels of his denim jacket.

He gasped in surprise.

She said, "You're running out of time, Joey. Not much time left to believe."

He heard himself say, "I believe—"

"Not in what matters," she interrupted.

She let go of him and vaulted over the presbytery balustrade into the choir enclosure, landing solidly on both feet.

There was as yet no ragged breach in the west wall. The Mustang had not yet exploded into the church.

Replay.

Joey had been thrown back in time again. Not twenty years as before. Only a minute. Two minutes at most.

A chance to save her.

He's coming.

"Celeste!"

Running to the sanctuary gate, she shouted, "Come touch the floor, Joey, touch where the water spilled, see whether it's hot enough for steam, hurry!"

Joey put a hand on the balustrade, ready to vault across it and go after her.

No. Do it right this time. Last chance. Do it right.

Celeste shoved through the sanctuary gate.

Over the incessant drumming of the rain on the roof, another sound arose. An escalating roar. The Mustang.

He's coming.

With a terrifying conviction that he was wasting precious seconds and that this replay was running faster than the original event, Joey snatched the 20-gauge shotgun from the presbytery floor.

Celeste hurried into the center aisle.

He shouted frantically—"Get out of the way! The car!"—as he hurtled over the balustrade with the shotgun in one hand.

She was halfway down the aisle, as she had been the first time. She turned, as before. Her face was slick with sweat. Like a ceramic glaze. Glistening with candlelight. The face of a saint. A martyr.

The roar of the Mustang swelled.

Puzzled, she half turned toward the windows, raising her hands.

In her delicate palms were hideous wounds. Black holes thick with blood.

"Run!" he shouted, but she froze where she was.

This time he didn't even reach the sanctuary railing before the Mustang slammed through the west wall of the church. A tidal wave of glass and wood and plaster and broken pews crested before the running-horse hood ornament, washed back along both fenders, until the car was all but hidden in the debris.

A length of board, spinning like a martial-arts weapon, whistled through the air, hit Celeste, and knocked her to the floor more than halfway down the center aisle—which was something that Joey hadn't been able to see from his previous vantage point, the first time that he had lived through the crash.

With a double *bang* of blowing tires, the car came to a halt in steepled rubble, and even above the clatter of the last tumbling pews, Joey heard the curiously separate and distinct *clank* of the bronze crucifix falling off the back wall of the sanctuary.

Instead of lying half trapped under the destruction in the nave, as before, he was still in the sanctuary, untouched by anything other than the cloud of pale dust that the incoming wind swept out of the ruins. And this time he was armed.

Chambering a shell in the 20-gauge Remington, he kicked through the sanctuary gate.

The wreckage was still settling, and debris was falling from the corner of the roof that had sagged inward when the supports had been knocked from under it. The amount of residual noise was greater than it had seemed to Joey when he had been lying under the ruins, but then he had been half dazed.

As far as he was able to discern, the destruction had fallen into precisely the same patterns as before. The Mustang still could not be approached easily or directly. He could see only sections of it through gaps in the ruins.

He had to do it right this time. No mistakes. Finish him off.

Toting the gun, Joey climbed onto the precariously stacked pews. They creaked and groaned, wobbled and shuddered, treacherous beneath him. Wary of protruding nails and glass daggers, he nevertheless clambered quickly across upturned benches, splintered window frames, cracked two-by-fours, and slabs of wallboard, reaching the car much faster than when he'd had to snake his way to it from the bottom of the rubble.

Even as he jumped down from a pew onto the Mustang's hood, he fired a round from the shotgun into the pitch-dark interior of the car. He wasn't well balanced, and the recoil nearly knocked him off his feet, but he stayed upright, pumped the Remington, fired again, and a third time, filled with savage judgmental glee, confident that P.J. could not have lived through that storm of buckshot.

The three shots were thunderous, and in the fading echo of the third, he heard a movement behind him that didn't sound like merely another settling noise, that seemed to be more purposeful. It was impossible that P.J. could have gotten out of the car before Joey had arrived this time, impossible that he could have both gotten out *and* circled around behind. Joey started to turn, looking back and up—and beheld the impossible from the corner of his eye. P.J. was *right there*, coming down on him, descending the precarious woodpile with daunting agility, swinging a length of two-by-four.

The flat of the heavy club struck Joey hard along the right temple. He fell onto the car hood, losing his grip on the shotgun, instinctively rolling away from his assailant, drawing his knees up and tucking his head down in the fetal position. The second blow smashed the ribs along his left side and drove all the breath out of him. Wheezing for air, getting none, he rolled again. The third blow landed on his back, and a scintillant pain coruscated along his spine. He rolled through the shot-out windshield, over the dashboard, into the front seat of the dark Mustang, and from there dropped into a far deeper, more profound blackness.

When he came around, rising out of a cloistered inner space of softly scurrying midnight spiders, he was certain that he'd been unconscious for only a few seconds, surely less than a minute. He was still struggling mightily to breathe. Sharp pain in his ribs. The taste of his own blood.

Celeste.

Sliding through gummy safety glass and buckshot, Joey pulled himself behind the steering wheel. He pushed the door open as far as the embracing rubble would allow, but that was far enough to get out into the October wind and the flickering light.

Toward the narthex and the overturned holy-water font, sparks cascaded from a ceiling fixture.

In the other direction, orange reflections of fire and shadows of flames slithered up the back wall of the sacristy, but he couldn't see the blaze itself through the encircling ruins.

Having taken the first blow from the two-by-four on the right side of his head, he had little vision in that eye. Blurred shapes throbbed and swarmed among twinkling phantom lights.

He smelled gasoline.

He dragged-levered-kicked himself onto the roof of the Mustang. He was too dizzy to get all the way to his feet. On his knees, he surveyed the church.

With his left eye, he could see P.J. ascending the altar steps with Celeste unconscious in his arms.

The candles had toppled. The altar cloth was afire.

Joey heard someone cursing, then realized that he was listening to his own voice. He was cursing himself.

Cruelly dropping Celeste onto the seething altar platform, P.J. snatched up the hammer.

Joey heard sobbing where there had been cursing, and devastating pain detonated along his left side, through his broken ribs.

The hammer. Raised high.

Stung to wakefulness by the fire, Celeste screamed.

From the altar platform, P.J. peered across the church, toward the Mustang, toward Joey, and his eyes were filled with jack-o'-lantern light.

The hammer crashed down.

A flutter. Behind Joey's eyes. Like a darting shadow of wings on rippled, sun-spangled water. Like the flight of angels half seen at the periphery of vision.

Everything had changed.

His ribs were no longer broken.

His vision was clear.

He had not yet been beaten by his brother.

Rewind. Replay.

Oh, Jesus.

Another replay.

One more chance.

Surely it would be the last.

And he hadn't been cast backward in time as far as he had been before. His window of opportunity was narrower than ever, giving him less time to think; his chances of altering their fate were poor, because now he didn't have leeway for even a small error in judgment. The Mustang had *already* rammed into the church, the high altar was burning, and Joey was already scrambling across the steepled rubble, jumping down onto the hood of the car, squeezing the trigger on the Remington.

He checked himself just in time to avoid his previous mistake, whirled, and instead fired up at the jumbled pews behind him, from which P.J. had attacked him with the two-by-four. The buckshot shredded empty air. P.J. wasn't there.

Confused, Joey turned to the car and blasted out the windshield, as he had done before, but no scream came from inside, so he whipped around to cover his back again. P.J. still wasn't coming at him with the two-by-four.

Jesus! Screwing up again, screwing up, doing the wrong thing again. Think. Think!

Celeste. She was all that mattered.

Forget about taking P.J. Just get to Celeste before he does.

Carrying the shotgun with him even though it inhibited movement, Joey scrambled up the tilted pews and kneelers, across the rubble, toward the rear of the nave, down again into the center aisle where he'd seen Celeste knocked unconscious by the spinning chunk of wood. She wasn't there.

"Celeste!"

In the sanctuary at the front of the church, a slouching figure hunched along the ambulatory, through the dervish reflections of the altar fire above. It was P.J. He was carrying Celeste.

The center aisle was blocked. Joey ran between two rows of pews to the side aisle along the east wall of the church, and then raced forward along the unbroken panes of rain-beaten glass toward the sanctuary railing.

Rather than proceed to the altar as before, P.J. disappeared with Celeste through the door to the sacristy.

Joey leaped over the sanctuary railing, as though too eager to accept a proffered sacrament, and edged swiftly but warily along the wall to the sacristy. He hesitated at the doorway, fearful of stepping face-first into a hard-swung two-by-four or a gun blast, but then he did what must be done—the right thing—and stepped up to the threshold.

The sacristy door was closed, locked.

He stepped back, aimed the shotgun. One round trashed the lock and blew the door open.

The sacristy was deserted—except for Beverly Korshak's body, which lay in a corner, a pale mound in a plastic shroud.

Joey went to the exterior door. It was secured with a deadbolt from the inside, as he had left it.

The cellar door. He opened it.

In the moon-yellow light below, a serpentine shadow slithered into a coil and rolled out of sight around a corner.

The stairs were unpainted wood, and in spite of every effort he made at stealth, his boots met every tread with a hollow knock like the deliberative countdown of a doomsday clock.

Heat rose in parching currents, in torrid waves, in scorching tides, and by the time he reached the basement floor, he felt as if he had descended into a primal furnace. The air was redolent of superheated wood ceiling beams on the brink of charring, hot stone from the masonry walls, hot lime from the concrete floor—and a trace of sulfur from the mine fires below.

When he stepped off the final wooden tread, Joey would not have been surprised if the rubber heels of his boots had melted on contact with the cellar floor. Sweat streamed from him, and his hair fell across his face in lank, dripping strands.

The cellar appeared to be divided into several chambers that were separated by deep, offset archways, so it was impossible to see into one room from another. The first was illuminated only by a single, bare, dust-caked bulb seated in a coffer between two beams that severely limited the spread of the light.

A fat black spider, as if driven mad by the heat and sulfurous fumes, circled frenziedly around and around and around the crystal-glittering strands of its enormous web, in the same coffer as the lightbulb. Its exaggerated shadow jittered and stilted across the floor in a spiral that made Joey nauseous and dizzied him when he trod upon it as he headed toward the archway to the next room.

Aboveground, the structure had been a plain coal-country church, but its masonry underpinnings were more formidable, seemed older than the Commonwealth of Pennsylvania itself, and had a Gothic weight that imprisoned his heart. Joey felt as though he had descended not only into St. Thomas's basement but into haunted catacombs beneath Rome itself—one sea, one continent, one millennium away from Coal Valley.

He paused long enough to reload the Remington with shells from his jacket pockets.

As Joey entered the second room, the serpentine shadow shimmered away from him across the floor again, as though it were a stream of black mercury. It darkled out of the bile-yellow light and around the corner of another archway into the next crypt.

Because the slippery shade was P.J.'s shadow and bore with it the precious shadow of Celeste, Joey swallowed his fear and followed into a third vault, a fourth. Although none of those low-ceilinged spaces was immense, the subterranean portion of the church began to seem vast, immeasurably larger than the humble realm above. Even if the basement architecture proved to be supernaturally extensive, however, he would arrive eventually at a final chamber where brother could come face to face with brother and the right thing at last could be done.

The cellar had no windows.

No outside doors.

Confrontation was inevitable.

Sooner rather than later, holding the shotgun at the ready, Joey edged cautiously through a final archway with carved-scroll keystone, into a bleak hold that measured approximately forty feet from left to right and eighteen from the archway to the back wall. He figured that it lay under the narthex. Here, the floor wasn't concrete but stone, like the walls, either black by its nature or grime-coated by time.

Celeste lay in the middle of the room, in a drizzle of yolk-yellow light from the lone overhead bulb. Wispy beards of dust and tattered spider silk hung from the fixture, casting a faint faux lace over her pale face. Her raincoat was spread like a cape around her, and her silken hair spilled black-on-black across the floor. She was unconscious but, judging by appearances, otherwise unharmed.

P.J. had vanished.

In a socket between two massive beams, the single light didn't reach to every end of the chamber, but even in the farthest corners the gloom was not deep enough to conceal a door. Except for the entrance archway, the stone walls were featureless.

The heat was so intense that Joey felt as though his clothes—if not his body—might spontaneously combust, and he worried that his fevered brain was boiling up hallucinations. No one, not even the soul-mortgaged companion of Judas, could have walked through those walls.

He wondered if the walls were, in fact, as solid as they seemed and if exploration might reveal a panel of masonry cleverly hinged to swing open into an extension of the cellar. But even half roasted in that stone oven, confused and beginning to be disoriented, he couldn't bring himself to believe that there were secret passages, keeps, and dungeons under ramshackle old St. Thomas's. Who would have built them—legions of demented monks in some clandestine and evil brotherhood?

Nonsense.

Yet P.J. was gone.

Heart pounding like a blacksmith's hammer, the anvil ring of it filling his ears, Joey eased across the room to Celeste. She seemed to be sleeping peacefully.

He spun in a crouch and swept the room with the shotgun, finger taut on the trigger, certain that P.J. was looming behind him, having materialized out of thin air.

Nothing.

He needed to wake Celeste, if possible, and quickly lead her out of there—or carry her out as she had been carried in. If she had to be carried, however, he would need to set aside the shotgun, which he was loath to do.

Gazing down at her, at the fine filigree of dust-web shadows that trembled like a veil on her face, Joey recalled the frenzied spider pointlessly circling its web in the first room at the foot of the basement stairs.

Shocked by a sudden dreadful thought, he sucked hot breath between clenched teeth, producing a brief, thin whistle of alarm.

He stepped back from under the coffer that contained the light fixture. He squinted up into the unlighted three-foot-wide, foot-deep recess between the next pair of beams.

P.J. was *there*, a cunning shadow among shadows, not simply wedged in place and waiting to drop upon his prey, but scuttling straight at Joey from the right side of the chamber with all the horrid grace of a spider, diabolically nimble and impossibly silent, upside down, clinging to the ceiling by means unknowable, softly ricocheting back and forth between the timbers, defying gravity, defying reason, his eyes gleaming like polished coal, teeth bared—and there could no longer be any doubt that he was something other than merely a man.

Joey started to raise the 20-gauge, which felt like a ton weight in his arms. Too late and far too slow, he knew the despair of defeat even as he reacted, felt himself in the cold and paralyzing grip of nightmare though he was awake.

Like a bat erupting from its roost, P.J. sprang out of the well between the rough-hewn beams, swooped down, and knocked Joey off his feet. The shotgun spun away across the concrete, out of reach.

As boys, they had occasionally wrestled and roughhoused, but they had never actually fought each other with serious intention. They had always been too tight for that—the Shannon brothers against the world. But now twenty years of pent-up rage flashed through Joey with atomic heat, instantly purging him of all lingering affection and compassion for P.J., leaving only an energizing remorse-regret-resentment. He was determined not to be a victim any more. He had a *passion* for justice. He punched and clawed and kicked, fighting for his life and for Celeste's, tapping a wrath that was Biblical in its power, a righteous and frightening fury that freed a savage avenger within him.

But even driven by rage and desperation, Joey was no match for whomever and whatever his brother had become. P.J.'s stone-hard fists landed an avalanche of punches, and no blocking arm or turned head seemed able to deflect the power of a single blow. *His* fury was inhuman, his strength superhuman. As Joey's resistance collapsed, P.J. grabbed him, lifted him half off the floor, slammed him down, slammed him down, slammed him down again, bouncing the back of his skull off the stone.

P.J. rose from him, stood, loomed over him, looking down with scorching contempt. *"Fucking altar boy!"* The angry, sneering voice was P.J.'s but *changed*, deeper than it had ever been before, fierce and reverberant, like a raging voice out of an abysmal stone place, out of iron walls and inescapable prisons, shivering with icy hatred, each word echoing as hollowly as if it were a dropped stone that had found the impossible bottom of eternity. *"Fucking altar boy!"* With the repetition of those words came the first kick, delivered with incredibly vicious power, landing in Joey's right side, cracking his ribs, as if P.J. was wearing steel-toed boots. *"Rosary-kissing little bastard!"* Another kick, another, and Joey tried to curl up defensively, as though he were a pill bug turning its armor to the world. But each furious kick found a vulnerable spot—ribs, kidneys, the base of his spine—and seemed to have been meted out not by a man but by a pile driver, a mindless robotic torture machine.

Then the kicking stopped.

With one throttling hand clamped on Joey's throat and the other hand on the belt of his blue jeans, P.J. snatched him off the floor as a world champion power lifter might clean-and-jerk a barbell that carried only light-workout weights. He hoisted him overhead, turned, and threw him.

Joey bounced off the wall beside the archway and crashed to the floor in a broken-marionette heap. Mouth full of cracked teeth. Choking on blood. Chest tight. Lungs painfully compressed, maybe even punctured by a splintered rib. Inhaling with a consumptive wheeze, exhaling with a thick wet rattle. His heart was stuttering arrhythmically. Precariously balanced on a high wire of consciousness over a bottomless dark, he blinked through scalding tears and saw P.J. turn away from him and toward Celeste.

He also saw the shotgun. Within reach.

He could not control his extremities. He strove determinedly to reach out to the Remington, but his muscles spasmed. His arm merely twitched, and his right hand flopped uselessly on the floor.

A menacing rumble rose under him. Vibrations in the hot stone.

P.J. crouched over Celeste, turning his back to Joey, giving him up for dead.

The Remington.

So close. Tantalizingly close.

Joey focused all his attention on the shotgun, marshaled all his remaining strength for the task of getting hold of it, put all his faith in the power of the weapon, and *willed* himself to ignore the ungodly pain that crippled him, to overcome the paralyzing shock of the brutal beating that he had endured. *Come on, come on, you fucking altar boy, come on, do it, do it, do the right thing for once in your sorry damn life!*

His arm responded shakily. His hand clenched into a fist, then sprang open, then reached out. His trembling fingers touched the walnut stock of the Remington.

Hunched over Celeste, P.J. reached into a pocket of his ski jacket and withdrew a knife. At the touch of a button, the six-inch spring-loaded blade snapped out of the handle, and the yellow light lovingly caressed the razor-sharp edge.

Smooth walnut. Hot, smooth steel. Joey curled his fingers. They palsied, weak. Not good. He had to get a firm grip. Tight. Tighter. Try to lift. Quietly, quietly.

P.J. was talking—not to Joey, not to Celeste, either to himself or to someone whom he imagined to be present. His voice was low and guttural, still disturbing and strange, and now he seemed to be speaking a foreign language. Or gibberish. Rough and rhythmic, full of hard punctuation and low animal sounds.

The rumble grew louder.

Good. A blessing, that rumble—fearful but welcome. Together, the subterranean disturbance and P.J.'s queer muttering provided some cover for any sounds that Joey made.

He had one chance, and he needed to execute his plan—his feeble, pathetic plan—smoothly, quickly, confidently, before P.J. realized what was happening.

He hesitated. Didn't want to act precipitously, before he was sure that he had summoned all his depleted resources. Wait. Wait. Be sure. Wait forever? The ultimate consequences of inaction could be greater than the consequences of action. Now or never. Do or die. Do *and* die, but at least, for God's sake, *do* something!

In one fluid movement, clenching his broken teeth against the explosion of pain that he knew would come—that came—Joey rolled up from his side into a sitting position, pulling the shotgun with him, bracing his back against the wall.

Even over his muttering and the persistent rumbling in the earth under the church, P.J. heard and reacted, simultaneously rising from his crouch and turning.

Joey had both hands on the Remington. The butt of the stock was jammed against his shoulder.

The baleful light that glimmered on the switchblade also leaped in P.J.'s eyes.

Pointblank. Joey squeezed the trigger.

The *boom* seemed loud enough to shatter the stone around them, and echoes of the shot crashed back and forth from one end of the room to the other, from ceiling to floor, with a volume that seemed to swell rather than diminish.

The recoil from the Remington struck lightning bolts of pain through Joey's entire body, and the shotgun fell out of his hands, clattering to the floor beside him.

The powerful blast took P.J. in the belly and chest, lifted him off his feet, spun him all the way around. He stumbled and went to his knees still facing Joey, folding his arms around his torso, bending forward, hugging himself as though to prevent his buckshot-riddled intestines from spilling out.

If Joey could have lifted his arms, he would have picked up the shotgun and fired again. He would have emptied the magazine. But his muscles would no longer even so much as twitch. His hands wouldn't even flop convulsively at his sides. He suspected that he was paralyzed from the neck down.

The rumble under the church grew louder.

Thin exhalations of sulfurous steam rose through cracks in the mortar between the flooring stones.

P.J. slowly raised his head, revealing a face that was hideously contorted in agony, eyes wide with shock, mouth stretched in a silent scream. He gagged, retched, choked rackingly. A phlegmy gurgle in his throat suddenly became a violent series of disgorging spasms. From his mouth gushed not rich arterial blood but a grotesque silver vomit, a stream of small glittering coins that rang onto the floor, as though he were a human slot machine.

Repulsed, astonished, stone-cold terrified, Joey looked up from the silver hoard as P.J. spat out one last coin and broke into a grin that could have been no more malevolent if it had been on the bare-bone face of Death himself. He unfolded his arms from his blasted torso and held his pale hands out in the manner of a magician saying *Presto!*, and although his clothes had been torn by the buckshot, he seemed to have suffered no wounds at all.

Joey knew that he must be dying, hallucinating, more than halfway to the Other Side and out of his head with pain. The delirium tremens of death made the crawling walls of a drunkard's nightmares seem amusing by contrast.

He screamed at Celeste to wake up, to run, but the warnings were only whispers that even he could barely hear.

The quaking, steaming floor abruptly cracked the width of the room. Along that jagged line, thin spears of fierce orange light stabbed up from the realm below. Mortar crumbled into the burning mine. Stones broke loose and tumbled out of sight. The overhead timbers cracked, and the cellar walls shook. The fissure in the floor rapidly widened to an inch, two inches, six inches, a foot, two feet, filling the room with blinding light, providing a glimpse of white-hot mine walls below, separating Joey from P.J. and Celeste.

Over the groans and *skreeks* of the shaken church, over the roar of the fire below and the thunder of subsidence, P.J. said, "Better say goodbye to the bitch, altar boy." He shoved Celeste into the blaze beneath Coal Valley, into volcanic heat and molten anthracite and instant death.

Ah, no! No! Please, God, no, no, please, no, not her, not her. Me, but not her. I'm self-pitying, arrogant, weak, blind to the truth, too ignorant to know what a second chance means, and I deserve whatever happens to me, but not her, not her in all her beauty, not her in all her kindness, not her!

A flutter. Behind Joey's eyes.

A flutter like the feathery shadows of many wings taking flight across a mysterious, great sphere of light.

Everything had changed.

He was uninjured. Free of pain. On his feet.

He was upstairs in the church.

Replay.

The Mustang had already crashed through the wall. P.J. already had Celeste.

Time had been wound backward but not far enough to give him an opportunity to think through his predicament. Only a couple of minutes remained until the subsidence would hit, not a second to waste.

Joey knew beyond doubt that this was his last chance, that the next spiral of events would not be rewound to bring him back to any moment of fatal error. The next damnation he earned would be his to keep. So there must be no errors this time, no mistakes, no failure to believe.

He was running between two rows of pews toward the side aisle along the east wall of the nave.

In the sanctuary at the front of the church, a slouching figure hunched along the ambulatory, through the dervish reflections of the altar fire above. It was P.J. He was carrying Celeste.

Joey reached the side aisle and raced forward along the unbroken panes of rain-beaten glass toward the sanctuary railing. He threw down the shotgun. He had no faith in it any more.

P.J. disappeared with Celeste through the door to the sacristy, slamming it behind him.

Joey vaulted over the sanctuary railing, followed the ambulatory to the sacristy door, but didn't stop there. He continued to the presbytery, to the altar stairs, to the altar platform, sidled around the overturned candles and the burning sheets, and went to the back wall of the sanctuary.

The crucifix had been shaken off its nail when the Mustang had crashed into the church. It lay facedown on the floor.

Joey picked up the bronze figure on the wooden cross and rushed back to the sacristy door. Locked.

The previous time, he'd blown it open with one round from the Remington. Now he considered returning to the nave to retrieve the discarded weapon.

Instead, he reared back and kicked the door as hard as he could, kicked it again, kicked, kicked. The stop molding cracked on the other side, a little play came into the door, he kicked it again, and yet again, was rewarded by a *twang* of metal, by splintering wood. He kicked it once more. The lock sprang, the stop molding shattered, the door flew open, and he went into the sacristy.

The cellar door.

The wooden stairs.

Because he'd had to batter down the door, Joey was now behind schedule. He was arriving at this point later in the replay than he had the first time. His brother's serpentine shadow had already slithered out of the moon-yellow light below and was nowhere to be seen. P.J. was farther into the labyrinthine cellar than before. With Celeste.

Joey started to descend the stairs two at a time, then realized that caution was still required. By discarding the gun and taking up the crucifix, he had altered the future that would unfold from this point on. Previously, he had reached the final chamber in the cellar before encountering P.J., but this time his brother might be waiting elsewhere along the way. He clutched the stair railing with one hand and continued downward with circumspection.

Such heat. An oven.

The smell of hot lime from the concrete. Hot stone baking in the walls.

In the first room, the jittering shadow of the frenzied spider spiraled ceaselessly on the floor.

Warily crossing toward the archway, Joey searched the long, deep coffers between the ceiling timbers for something other than spiders.

By the time he reached the second room, a railroad rumble had arisen under St. Thomas's.

As he stepped into the third chamber, the ominous sound swelled and was accompanied by tremors in the floor.

No time for caution.

No time for mistakes either.

He gripped the crucifix tightly in his right hand, held it out in front of him: Professor Von Helsing in the castle of the count.

Overhead. Shadows. Only shadows.

Room by room to the final archway.

Celeste lay unconscious under the single lightbulb.

The village-rocking subsidence hit, the church shook, and Joey was *thrown* through the archway into the final chamber just as the stone floor cracked open. Blades of orange light slashed out of the tunnel below. The fault in the floor widened as mortar disintegrated and stones broke loose, creating a more formidable gap between him and Celeste.

P.J. seemed to have vanished.

Stepping under the ceiling coffer that lay just this side of the fissure, standing with the brink of the raging mine fire to his right, Joey peered up expectantly into the recess between the rough timbers. P.J. was there as before, scuttling toward him, spider quick and spider agile, defying gravity, weirder than ever in the seething firelight. He shrieked, twitched with an arachnid spasm, and flung himself down at his prey.

Joey had no more Twilight Zone explanations to fall back upon, no more quirks of quantum physics, no more Star Trek time warps or energy waves, no more relatively polite monsters from the *X-Files* that might be taken out with a shotgun, not even any more complex Freudian analyses. There was only the real thing now, the foul and ancient thing, purest evil, the greatest fear of so many other centuries, millennia, here now swooping at him, shrieking hatred, reeking of sulfur, dark devourer of souls, eater of hope: only the fundamentals now, only a beast so primal that believing in it was difficult even when face to face with it. Joey cast out all doubt, however, overcame all cynicism, shed the supposed sophistication of the postmodern age, raised the crucifix in both hands, and thrust it out in front of him.

The top of the crucifix was blunt, not pointed, but it impaled P.J. when he slammed into it. Impaled, however, he was not stopped. He fell into Joey and drove him backward. They staggered, stumbled, stayed on their feet, but teetered on the edge of the fiery gulf.

P.J. got one hand around Joey's throat. His fingers were as powerful as the jaws of a motorized vise, as shiny and hard as the carapace of a dung beetle. His yellow eyes reminded Joey of the mongrel dog that he'd seen only that morning on the front porch of his dad's house.

When P.J. spoke, black blood bubbled on his lips: *"Altar boy."*

In the inferno below, an expansive pocket of toxic gases burst from confinement and exploded, shimmering incandescently. A white ball of flame spun out of the cellar floor, engulfed them, igniting P.J.'s clothes and hair, scorching away his skin in an instant. He released Joey, lost his balance, and with the crucifix embedded in his chest, he dropped through the steadily widening fissure into the old mine tunnel, folding the cape of fire around his body and taking it with him.

Although Joey had been immersed in the flames, he was unharmed. His clothes were not even singed.

He didn't need to ask Rod Serling or Captain Kirk or the ever logical Mr. Spock or anyone else to explain his miraculous escape from injury.

The merciless subterranean light blazed so fiercely that he couldn't see much even when he squinted, but he was sure that his brother fell an immeasurably greater distance than merely to the floor of an old tunnel, farther even than any vertical shaft in any coal mine could have possibly bored into the earth. His body was a frenzied spiky darkness that spiraled down like a spider's shadow, jittering down and around, jittering around and down, around and down and away.

Joey leaped across the fissure in the floor as it cracked wider, and he knelt at Celeste's side.

He lifted her right hand and turned the palm up, then her left hand. No wounds. Not even faint bruises.

When he tried to wake her, she murmured and stirred but didn't regain consciousness.

Substrata of coal, eaten away by years of hidden fires, had left layered cavities under Coal Valley. The weight of the surface world, with all its iron sorrows, at last became too great to be supported by the impaired structures that had once served as its foundations. This section of the valley, if no other, suffered a catastrophic subsidence in which the empty veins of fire-stripped coal imploded, collapsed into one another. The cellar shook, the floor heaved, and the fissure widened in an instant from three to five feet. The upper portion of St. Thomas's was tweaked from a rectangle into a rhomboid; and the wooden walls began to tear loose of the stone substructure to which they had been so long anchored.

As the ceiling sagged dangerously, as plaster fell and beams cracked, Joey scooped Celeste off the floor.

Gasping for breath in the furnace-hot air, blinking through rivers of eye-stinging sweat, he turned to the fissure. It was now six feet across, far too wide to be jumped with the girl in his arms.

Even if he could get across the abyss somehow, he knew that he wouldn't be able to make it all the way back through the cellar chambers to the steps, up to the sacristy, and out of the place before it collapsed.

His heart slammed against his caging ribs. His knees shook not under the weight of the girl but with the hard realization of his own mortality.

They couldn't die like this.

They had come too far, survived too much.

He had done the right thing, and that was what mattered. He had done the right thing, and now, whatever happened, he would not be afraid, not even here in the valley of the shadow of death.

I will fear no evil.

Abruptly the splintering ceiling stopped sagging toward him and pulled up instead, increasing his head room, as the building's superstructure noisily uprooted itself and tipped away from this end of the cellar.

Cold wind howled at his back.

Joey turned to the end wall of the basement and was astonished to see the sill plate wrenching loose of the anchor bolts that had held it to the stone. Jack studs snapped, the sole plate buckled, and all of it rose in an arc through the night as the church slowly tilted up and away from Joey. A wedge-shaped gap had opened between the foundation and the receding wall, through which the storm wind surged down into the exposed cellar. The gap was growing wider as the building tipped backward from him.

A way out.

The cellar wall was still eight feet high. He saw no easy way to scale it. Especially not with Celeste in his arms.

With a thunder of falling stone, the pit widened at his back, and the firestorm raged closer to his heels. Inblown rain steamed off the floor.

His heart raced but not in fear now, only in wonder, as he waited for his destiny to unfold.

Before him, wide cracks opened in the cellar wall, zigzagging along the mortar lines. The shaking ground jarred loose a stone that clattered to the floor, bounced, and knocked painfully against his shin. Here, another stone; there, a third; and a little higher, a fourth, a fifth. The foundation wall retained its integrity, but now it offered handholds.

Joey shifted Celeste, slung her over his left shoulder in a fireman's carry. He climbed out of the suffocating heat into the rain-filled night as the building tilted away, away, away like a giant clipper ship tacking in a strong wind.

He dragged her through sodden grass and thick mud, past the vent pipe from which flames spouted like blood from an arterial tap. Onto the sidewalk. Into the street.

Sitting on the blacktop with Celeste in his arms, holding her tightly while she began to regain consciousness, Joey watched as the Church of St. Thomas was torn asunder, as the ruins ignited, and as the burning walls collapsed into a bright chasm, into far deeper grottoes, and finally into unknown kingdoms of fire.

Subsidence.

18

LONG PAST MIDNIGHT, AFTER GIVING THEIR STATEMENTS TO DEPUTIES from the county sheriff's department and to the Pennsylvania State Police, Joey and Celeste were driven back to Asherville.

The police had issued a condemnation order for the village of Coal Valley. Saved from P.J. without ever knowing that they had been in danger, the Dolan family had been evacuated.

The bodies of John, Beth, and Hannah Bimmer would be taken to the Devokowski Funeral Home, where Joey's father had so recently rested.

Celeste's parents, waiting in Asherville with the Korshaks for word of poor Beverly's fate, had not only been given the bad news about the murder but had already been informed that they would not be permitted to return to Coal Valley this night and that their daughter would be brought to them. In addition to the church, subsidence had suddenly claimed half a block of homes in another part of town, and the ground was too unstable to risk continued habitation.

Joey and Celeste sat in the back of the sheriff's-department patrol car, holding hands. After making a few attempts to draw them out, the young deputy left them to their shared silence.

By the time they turned off Coal Valley Road onto the county route, the rain had stopped falling.

Celeste persuaded the deputy to drop them in the center of Asherville and to allow Joey to walk her from there to the Korshaks' place.

Joey didn't know why she preferred not to be driven all the way, but he sensed that she had a reason and that it was important.

He was not unhappy about delaying his own arrival home. By now his mom and dad had no doubt been awakened by the police, who would want to search P.J.'s old basement room. They had been told about the monstrous things their older son had done to Beverly Korshak, to the Bimmers—and to God knew how many others. Even as Joey's world had been rebuilt by making good use of the second

chance that he'd been given, their world had been forever changed
for the worse. He dreaded seeing the sorrow in his mother's eyes,
the torment and grief in his father's.

He wondered if, by changing his own fate, he had somehow freed
his mother from the cancer that would otherwise kill her just four
years hence. He dared to hope. Things had changed. In his heart,
however, he knew that his actions had only made the world better
in one small way; paradise on earth was not pending.

As the patrol car drove away, Celeste took his hand and said,
"Something I need to tell you."

"Tell me."

"Show you, actually."

"Then show me."

She led him along the damp street, across a carpet of sodden
leaves, to the municipal building. All county government except the
sheriff's department maintained offices there.

The library was in the annex, toward the back. They entered an
unlighted courtyard through an archway in a brick wall, passed under
dripping larches, and went to the front door.

In the wake of the storm, the night town was as silent as any
cemetery.

"Don't be surprised," she said.

"About what?"

The lower part of the library door was solid, but the upper portion
featured four eight-inch-square panes of glass. Celeste rammed her
elbow into the pane nearest the lock, shattering it.

Startled, Joey looked around the courtyard and out toward the
street beyond the wall. The breaking glass had been a fragile, short-
lived sound. He doubted that anyone had heard it at that late hour.
Furthermore, theirs was a small town, and this was 1975, so there
was no burglar alarm.

Reaching through the broken pane, she unlocked the door from
inside. "You have to promise to believe."

She withdrew the small flashlight from her raincoat pocket and
led him past the librarian's desk into the stacks.

Because the county was poor, the library was small. Finding any
particular volume would not have taken long. In fact, she took no
time at all to search, because she knew what she wanted.

They stopped in the fiction aisle, a narrow space with books shelved eight feet high on both sides. She directed the beam of light at the floor, and the colorful spines of the books seemed magically luminescent in the backwash.

"Promise to believe," she said, and her beautiful eyes were huge and solemn.

"Believe what?"

"Promise."

"All right."

"Promise to believe."

"I'll believe."

She hesitated, took a deep breath, and began. "In the spring of '73, when you were graduating from County High, I was at the end of my sophomore year. I'd never had the nerve to approach you. I knew you'd never noticed me—and now you never would. You were going away to college, you'd probably find a girl there, and I'd never even see you again."

The fine hairs on the nape of Joey's neck prickled, but he did not yet know why.

She said, "I was depressed, feeling like the nerd of nerds, so I lost myself in books, which is what I always do when I have the blues. I was here in the library, in this very aisle, looking for a new novel . . . when I found your book."

"My book?"

"I saw your name on the spine. Joseph Shannon."

"What book?" Puzzled, he scanned the shelves.

"I thought it was someone else, a writer with your name. But when I took it off the shelf and checked the back of the jacket, there was a picture of you."

He met her eyes again. Those mysterious depths.

She said, "It wasn't a picture of you as you are now, tonight—but as you will be in about fifteen years. Still . . . it was recognizably you."

"I don't understand," he said, but he was beginning to think that he did.

"I looked at the copyright page, and the book was published in 1991."

He blinked. "Sixteen years from now?"

"This was in the spring of '73," she reminded him. "So at that time I was holding a book that wouldn't yet be published for eighteen years. On the jacket it said that you'd written eight previous novels and that six of them had been best-sellers."

The not unpleasant prickling sensation on the nape of his neck increased.

"I took the book to the checkout desk. When I passed it to the librarian with my card, when she took it into her hands . . . it wasn't your book any more. Then it was a novel by someone else, one that I'd read before, published in '69."

She raised the flashlight, directing the beam at the shelves behind him.

"I don't know if it's too much to ask," she said, "but maybe it's here again tonight, here again for just one moment on this night of all nights."

Overcome by a growing sense of wonder, Joey turned to look at the stacks where the flashlight focused. He followed the beam as it slipped along one of the shelves.

A small gasp of delight escaped Celeste, and the beam came to a halt on a book with a red spine.

Joey saw his name turned on edge, in silver-foil letters. Above his name was a title in more silver foil: *Strange Highways.*

Trembling, Celeste slid the book out from between two other volumes. She showed him the cover, and his name was in big letters at the top, above the title. Then she turned the book over.

He stared in awe at the photo of himself on the dust jacket. He was older in the photograph, in his middle thirties.

He was familiar with his appearance at that age, for he had already lived five years past it in his other life. But he looked better in this photograph than he had really looked when he'd been thirty-five: not prematurely aged, not dissipated by booze, not dead in the eyes. He appeared to be prosperous too—and best of all, he looked like a happy man.

His appearance in the photograph, however, was not a fraction as important as who was shown with him. It was a group portrait. Celeste was at his side, also fifteen years older than she was now—and two children, a beautiful girl of perhaps six and a handsome boy who might have been eight.

Unexpectedly filled with tears that he could barely repress, heart hammering with a wild joy that he had never known before, Joey took the book from her.

She pointed to the words under the photograph, and he had to blink furiously to clear his vision enough to read them:

> *Joseph Shannon is the author of eight other acclaimed novels about the joys and rewards of love and family, six of which have been national best-sellers. His wife, Celeste, is an award-winning poet. They live with their children, Josh and Laura, in Southern California.*

As he read, he followed the words with his trembling fingers, in precisely the way that he had done, as a child, when following the text in the missal at Mass.

"And so," she said softly, "ever since the spring of '73, I've known that you would come."

Some of the mysteries in her eyes were gone, but by no means all. He knew that regardless of how long a life they shared, she would be to some degree forever mysterious to him.

"I want to take this," he said of the book.

She shook her head. "You know you can't. Besides, you don't need the book to be able to write it. You only need to believe that you will."

He let her take the novel out of his hands.

As she returned the volume to the shelf, he suspected that he had been given a second chance not so much to stop P.J. as to meet Celeste Baker. While resistance to evil was essential, there could be no hope for the world without love.

"Promise me you'll believe," she said, putting one hand to his face, tenderly tracing the line of his cheek.

"I promise."

"Then all things," she said, "are possible."

Around them, the library was filled with lives that had been lived, with hopes that had been realized, with ambitions that had been achieved, with dreams for the taking.

THE BLACK PUMPKIN

1

T HE PUMPKINS WERE CREEPY, BUT THE MAN WHO CARVED THEM WAS far stranger than his creations. He appeared to have baked for ages in the California sun, until all the juices had been cooked out of his flesh. He was stringy, bony, and leather skinned. His head resembled a squash, not pleasingly round like a pumpkin, yet not shaped like an ordinary head, either: slightly narrower at the top and wider at the chin than was natural. His amber eyes glowed with a sullen, smoky, weak—but dangerous—light.

Tommy Sutzmann was uneasy the moment that he saw the old pumpkin carver. He told himself that he was foolish, overreacting again. He had a tendency to be alarmed by the mildest signs of anger in others, to panic at the first vague perception of a threat. Some families taught their twelve-year-old boys honesty, integrity, decency, and faith in God. By their actions, however, Tommy's parents and his brother, Frank, had taught him to be cautious, suspicious, and even paranoid. In the best of times, his mother and father treated him as an outsider; in the worst of times, they enjoyed punishing him as a means of releasing their anger and frustration at the rest of the world. To Frank, Tommy was simply—and always—a target. Consequently, deep and abiding uneasiness was Tommy Sutzmann's natural condition.

Every December this vacant lot was full of Christmas trees, and during the summer, itinerant merchants used the space to exhibit Day-Glo stuffed animals or paintings on velvet. As Halloween approached, the half-acre property, tucked between a supermarket and a bank on the outskirts of Santa Ana, was an orange montage of pumpkins: all sizes and shapes, lined in rows and stacked in neat low pyramids and tumbled in piles, maybe two thousand of them, three thousand, the raw material of pies and jack-o'-lanterns.

The carver was in a back corner of the lot, sitting on a tube-metal chair. The vinyl-upholstered pads on the back and seat of the chair were darkly mottled, webbed with cracks—not unlike the carver's face. He sat with a pumpkin on his lap, whittling with a sharp knife and other tools that lay on the dusty ground beside him.

Tommy Sutzmann did not remember crossing the field of pumpkins. He recalled getting out of the car as soon as his father had parked at the curb—and the next thing he knew, he was in the back of the lot just a few feet from the strange sculptor.

A score of finished jack-o'-lanterns were propped atop mounds of other pumpkins. This artist did not merely hack crude eye holes and mouths. He carefully cut the skin and the rind of the squash in layers, producing features with great definition and surprising subtlety. He also used paint to give each creation its own demonic personality: Four cans, each containing a brush, stood on the ground beside his chair—red, white, green, and black.

The jack-o'-lanterns grinned and frowned and scowled and leered. They seemed to be staring at Tommy. Every one of them.

Their mouths were agape, little pointy teeth bared. None had the blunt, goofy dental work of ordinary jack-o'-lanterns. Some were equipped with long fangs.

Staring, staring. And Tommy had the peculiar feeling that they could *see* him.

When he looked up from the pumpkins, he discovered that the old man was also watching him intently. Those amber eyes, full of smoky light, seemed to brighten as they held Tommy's own gaze.

"Would you like one of my pumpkins?" the carver asked. In his cold, dry voice, each word was as crisp as October leaves wind-blown along a stone walk.

Tommy could not speak. He tried to say, *No, sir, thank you, no,* but the words stuck in his throat as if he were trying to swallow the cloying pulp of a pumpkin.

"Pick a favorite," the carver said, gesturing with one withered hand toward his gallery of grotesques—but never taking his eyes off Tommy.

"No, uh . . . . no, thank you." Tommy was dismayed to hear that his voice had a tremor and a slightly shrill edge.

What's wrong with me? he wondered. *Why am I hyping myself into a fit like this? He's just an old guy who carves pumpkins.*

"Is it the price you're worried about?" the carver asked.

"No."

"Because you pay the man out front for the pumpkin, same price as any other on the lot, and you just give me whatever you feel my work is worth."

When he smiled, every aspect of his squash-shaped head changed. Not for the better.

The day was mild. Sunshine found its way through holes in the overcast, brightly illuminating some orange mounds of pumpkins while leaving others deep in cloud shadows. In spite of the warm weather, a chill gripped Tommy and would not release him.

Leaning forward with the half-sculpted pumpkin in his lap, the carver said, "You just give me whatever amount you wish . . . although I'm duty-bound to say that you get what you give."

Another smile. Worse than the first one.

Tommy said, "Uh . . ."

"You get what you give," the carver repeated.

"No shit?" brother Frank said, stepping up to the row of leering jack-o'-lanterns. Evidently he had overheard everything. He was two years older than Tommy, muscular where Tommy was slight, with a self-confidence that Tommy had never known. Frank hefted the most macabre of all the old guy's creations. "So how much is this one?"

The carver was reluctant to shift his gaze from Tommy to Frank, and Tommy was unable to break the contact first. In the man's eyes Tommy saw something he could not define or understand, something that filled his mind's eye with images of disfigured children, deformed creatures that he could not name, and dead things.

"How much is this one, gramps?" Frank repeated.

At last, the carver looked at Frank—and smiled. He lifted the half-carved pumpkin off his lap, put it on the ground, but did not get up. "As I said, you pay me what you wish, and you get what you give."

Frank had chosen the most disturbing jack-o'-lantern in the eerie collection. It was big, not pleasingly round but lumpy and misshapen, narrower at the top than at the bottom, with ugly crusted nodules like ligneous fungus on a diseased oak tree. The old man had compounded the unsettling effect of the pumpkin's natural deformities by giving it an immense mouth with three upper and three lower fangs. Its nose was an irregular hole that made Tommy think of campfire tales about lepers. The slanted eyes were as large as lemons but were not cut all the way through the rind except for a pupil—an evil elliptical slit—in the center of each. The stem in the head was dark and knotted as Tommy imagined a cancerous growth might be. The maker of jack-o'-lanterns had painted this one black, letting the natural orange color blaze through in only a few places to create character lines around the eyes and mouth as well as to add emphasis to the tumorous growths.

Frank was bound to like *that* pumpkin. His favorite movies were *The Texas Chainsaw Massacre* and all the *Friday the 13th* sagas of the mad, murderous Jason. When Tommy and Frank watched a movie of that kind on the VCR, Tommy always pulled for the victims, while Frank cheered the killer. Watching *Poltergeist*, Frank was disappointed that the whole family survived: He kept hoping that the little boy would be eaten by some creepazoid in the closet and that his stripped bones would be spit out like watermelon seeds. "Hell," Frank had said, "they could've at least ripped the guts out of the stupid dog."

Now, Frank held the black pumpkin, grinning as he studied its malevolent features. He squinted into the thing's slitted pupils as if the jack-o'-lantern's eyes were real, as if there were thoughts to be read in those depths—and for a moment he seemed to be mesmerized by the pumpkin's gaze.

Put it down, Tommy thought urgently. *For God's sake, Frank, put it down and let's get out of here.*

The carver watched Frank intently. The old man was still, like a predator preparing to pounce.

Clouds moved, blocking the sun.

Tommy shivered.

Finally breaking the staring contest with the jack-o'-lantern, Frank said to the carver, "I give you whatever I like?"

"You get what you give."

"But no matter what I give, I get the jack-o'-lantern?"

"Yes, but you get what you give," the old man said cryptically.

Frank put the black pumpkin aside and pulled some change from his pocket. Grinning, he approached the old man, holding a nickel.

The carver reached for the coin.

"No!" Tommy protested too explosively.

Both Frank and the carver regarded him with surprise.

Tommy said, "No, Frank, it's a bad thing. Don't buy it. Don't bring it home, Frank."

For a moment Frank stared at him in astonishment, then laughed. "You've always been a wimp, but are you telling me now you're scared of a *pumpkin?*"

"It's a bad thing," Tommy insisted.

"Scared of the dark, scared of high places, scared of what's in your bedroom closet at night, scared of half the other kids you meet—and now scared of a stupid damn pumpkin," Frank said. He laughed again, and his laugh was rich with scorn and disgust as well as with amusement.

The carver took his cue from Frank, but the old man's dry laugh contained no amusement at all.

Tommy was pierced by an icy needle of fear that he could not explain, and he wondered if he might be a wimp after all, afraid of his shadow, maybe even unbalanced. The counselor at school said he was "too sensitive." His mother said he was "too imaginative," and his father said he was "impractical, a dreamer, self-involved." Maybe he was all those things, and perhaps he would wind up in a sanitarium someday, in a boobyhatch with rubber walls, talking to imaginary people, eating flies. But, damn it, he *knew* the black pumpkin was a bad thing.

"Here, gramps," Frank said, "here's a nickel. Will you really sell it for that?"

"I'll take a nickel for my carving, but you still have to pay the usual price of the pumpkin to the fella who operates the lot."

"Deal," Frank said.

The carver plucked the nickel out of Frank's hand.

Tommy shuddered.

Frank turned from the old man and picked up the pumpkin again.

Just then, the sun broke through the clouds. A shaft of light fell on their corner of the lot.

Only Tommy saw what happened in that radiant moment. The

sun brightened the orange of the pumpkins, imparted a gold sheen to the dusty ground, gleamed on the metal frame of the chair—but did not touch the carver himself. The light parted around him as if it were a curtain, leaving him in the shade. It was an incredible sight, as though the sunshine shunned the carver, as though he were composed of an unearthly substance that *repelled* light.

Tommy gasped.

The old man fixed Tommy with a wild look, as though he were not a man at all but a storm spirit passing as a man, as though he would at any second erupt into tornadoes of wind, furies of rain, crashes of thunder, lightning. His amber eyes were aglow with promises of pain and terror.

Abruptly the clouds covered the sun again.

The old man winked.

We're dead, Tommy thought miserably.

Having lifted the pumpkin again, Frank looked craftily at the old man as if expecting to be told that the nickel sale was a joke. "I can really just take it away?"

"I keep telling you," the carver said.

"How long did you work on this?" Frank asked.

"About an hour."

"And you're willing to settle for a nickel an hour?"

"I work for the love of it. For the sheer love of it." The carver winked at Tommy again.

"What are you, senile?" Frank asked in his usual charming manner.

"Maybe. Maybe."

Frank stared at the old man, perhaps sensing some of what Tommy felt, but he finally shrugged and turned away, carrying the jack-o'-lantern toward the front of the lot where their father was buying a score of uncarved pumpkins for the big party the following night.

Tommy wanted to run after his brother, beg Frank to return the black pumpkin and get his nickel back.

"Listen here," the carver said fiercely, leaning forward once more.

The old man was so thin and angular that Tommy was convinced he'd heard ancient bones scraping together within the inadequate padding of the desiccated body.

"Listen to me, boy. . . ."

No, Tommy thought. *No, I won't listen, I'll run, I'll run.*

The old man's power was like solder, however, fusing Tommy to that piece of ground, rendering him incapable of movement.

"In the night," the carver said, his amber eyes darkening, "your brother's jack-o'-lantern will grow into something other than what it is now. Its jaws will work. Its teeth will sharpen. When everyone is asleep, it'll creep through your house . . . and give what's deserved. It'll come for you last of all. What do you think you deserve, Tommy? You see, I know your name, though your brother never used it. What do you think the black pumpkin will do to you, Tommy? Hmmm? What do you deserve?"

"What *are* you?" Tommy asked.

The carver smiled. "Dangerous."

Suddenly Tommy's feet tore loose of the earth to which they had been stuck, and he ran.

When he caught up with Frank, he tried to persuade his brother to return the black pumpkin, but his explanation of the danger came out as nothing more than hysterical babbling, and Frank laughed at him. Tommy tried to knock the hateful thing out of Frank's hands. Frank held on to the jack-o'-lantern and gave Tommy a hard shove that sent him sprawling backward over a pile of pumpkins. Frank laughed again, purposefully tramped hard on Tommy's right foot as the younger boy struggled to get up, and moved away.

Through the involuntary tears wrung from him by the pain in his foot, Tommy looked toward the back of the lot and saw that the carver was watching.

The old man waved.

Heart beating double time, Tommy limped out to the front of the lot, searching for a way to convince Frank of the danger. But Frank was already putting his purchase on the backseat of the Cadillac. Their father was paying for the jack-o'-lantern and for a score of uncarved pumpkins. Tommy was too late.

2

AT HOME, FRANK TOOK THE BLACK PUMPKIN INTO HIS BEDROOM AND
stood it on the desk in the corner, under the poster of Michael
Berryman as the demented killer in *The Hills Have Eyes*.

From the open doorway, Tommy watched.

Frank had found a fat, scented decorative candle in the kitchen
pantry; now he put it inside the pumpkin. It was big enough to burn
steadily for at least two days. Dreading the appearance of light in
the jack-o'-lantern's eyes, Tommy watched as Frank lit the candle
and put the pumpkin's stem-centered lid in place.

The slitted pupils glowed-flickered-shimmered with a convincing
imitation of demonic life and malevolent intellect. The serrated grin
blazed bright, and the fluttering light was like a tongue ceaselessly
licking the cold-rind lips. The most disgusting part of the illusion
of life was the leprous pit of a nose, which appeared to fill with
moist, yellowish mucus.

"Incredible!" Frank said. "That old fart is a real genius at this
stuff."

The scented candle emitted the fragrance of roses.

Although he could not remember where he had read of such a
thing, Tommy recalled that the sudden, unexplained scent of roses
supposedly indicated the presence of spirits of the dead. Of course,
the source of this odor was no mystery.

"What the hell?" Frank said, wrinkling his nose. He lifted the lid
of the jack-o'-lantern and peered inside. The inconstant orange light
played across his face, queerly distorting his features. "This is supposed to be a *lemon*-scented candle. Not roses, not girlie
crap."

◁ ▲ ▷

In the big airy kitchen, Lois and Kyle Sutzmann, Tommy's mother and father, were standing at the table with the caterer, Mr. Howser. They were studying the menu for the flashy Halloween party that they were throwing the following night—and loudly reminding Mr. Howser that the food was to be prepared with the finest ingredients.

Tommy circled behind them, hoping to remain invisible. He took a can of Coke from the refrigerator.

Now his mother and father were hammering the caterer about the need for everything to be "impressive." Hors d'oeuvres, flowers, the bar, the waiters' uniforms, and the buffet dinner must be so elegant and exquisite and drop-dead perfect that every guest would feel himself to be in the home of true California aristocracy.

This was not a party for kids. In fact, Tommy and Frank would be required to remain in their rooms tomorrow evening, permitted to engage only in the quietest activities: no television, no stereo, no slightest peep to draw attention to themselves.

This party was strictly for the movers and shakers on whom Kyle Sutzmann's political career depended. He was now a California State Senator, but in next week's election he was running for the United States Congress. This was a thank-you party for his most generous financial backers and for the power brokers who had pulled strings to ensure his nomination the previous spring. Kids verboten.

Tommy's parents seemed to want him around only at major campaign rallies, media photography sessions, and for a few minutes at the start of election-night victory parties. That was okay with Tommy. He preferred to remain invisible. On those rare occasions when his folks took notice of him, they invariably disapproved of everything he said and did, every movement he made, every innocent expression that crossed his face.

Lois said, "Mr. Howser, I hope we understand that large shrimp do *not* qualify as finger lobster."

As the nervous caterer reassured Lois of the quality of his operation, Tommy sidled silently away from the refrigerator and quietly extracted two Milanos from the cookie jar.

"These are important people," Kyle informed the caterer for the tenth time, "substantial and sophisticated people, and they are accustomed to the very best."

In school, Tommy had been taught that politics was the means by which many enlightened people chose to serve their fellow men.

He knew that was baloney. His parents spent long evenings plotting his father's political career, and Tommy never once overheard either of them talk about serving the people or improving society. Oh, sure, in public, on campaign platforms, that was what they talked about—"the rights of the masses, the hungry, the homeless"—but never in private. Beyond the public eye, they endlessly discussed "forming power bases" and "crushing the opposition" and "shoving this new law down their throats." To them and to all the people with whom they associated, politics was a way to gain respect, make some money, and—most important—acquire power.

Tommy understood why people liked to be respected, because he received no respect at all. He could see why having a lot of money was desirable. But he did not understand this power thing. He could not figure why anyone would waste a lot of time and energy trying to acquire power over other people. What fun could be gotten from ordering people around, telling them what to do? What if you told them to do the wrong thing, and then what if, because of your orders, people were hurt or wound up broke or something worse? And how could you expect people to like you if you had power over them? After all, Frank had power over Tommy—complete power, total control—and Tommy *loathed* him.

Sometimes he thought he was the only sane person in the family. At other times, he wondered if they were all sane and if he was mad. Whatever the case, crazy or sane, Tommy always felt that he did not belong in the same house with his own family.

As he slipped stealthily out of the kitchen with his can of Coke and two Milanos wrapped in a paper napkin, his parents were querying Mr. Howser about the champagne.

In the back hallway, Frank's door was open, and Tommy paused for a glimpse of the pumpkin. It was still there, fire in every aperture.

"What you got there?" Frank asked, stepping into the doorway. He grabbed Tommy by the shirt, yanked him into the room, slammed the door, and confiscated the cookies and Coke. "Thanks, snotface. I was just thinking I could use a snack." He went to the desk and put the booty beside the glowing jack-o'-lantern.

Taking a deep breath, steeling himself for what resistance would mean, Tommy said, "Those are mine."

Frank pretended shock. "Is my little brother a greedy glutton who doesn't know how to share?"

"Give me back my Coke and cookies."

Frank's grin seemed filled with shark's teeth. "Good heavens, dear brother, I think you need to be taught a lesson. Greedy little gluttons have to be shown the path of enlightenment."

Tommy would have preferred to walk away, to let Frank win, to go back to the kitchen and fetch another Coke and more cookies. But he knew that his life, already intolerable, would get far worse if he didn't make an effort, no matter how futile, to stand up to this stranger who was supposedly his brother. Total, willing capitulation would inflame Frank and encourage him to be even more of a bully than he already was.

"I want my cookies and my Coke," Tommy insisted, wondering if *any* cookies, even Milanos, were worth dying for.

Frank rushed him.

They fell to the floor, pummeling each other, rolling, kicking, but producing little noise. They didn't want to draw their folks' attention. Tommy was reluctant to let his parents know what was happening because they would invariably blame the ruckus on him. Athletic, well-tanned Frank was their dream child, their favorite son, and he could do no wrong. Frank probably wanted to keep the battle secret because their father would put a stop to it, thereby spoiling the fun.

Throughout the tussle, Tommy had brief glimpses of the glowing jack-o'-lantern, which gazed down on them, and he was sure that its grin grew steadily wider, wider.

At last Tommy was driven into a corner, beaten and exhausted. Straddling him, Frank slapped him once, hard, rattling his senses, then tore at Tommy's clothes, pulling them off.

"No!" Tommy whispered when he realized that in addition to being beaten, he was to be humiliated. "No, no."

He struggled with what little strength he still possessed, but his shirt was stripped off; his jeans and underwear were yanked down. With his pants tangled around his sneakers, he was pulled to his feet and half carried across the room.

Frank threw open the door, pitched Tommy into the hallway, and called out, "Oh, Maria! Maria, can you come here a moment, please?"

Maria was the twice-a-week maid who came in to clean and do the ironing. This was one of her days.

"Maria!"

Naked, terrified of being humiliated in front of the maid, Tommy scrambled to his feet, grabbed his pants, tried to run and pull up his jeans at the same time, stumbled, fell, and sprang up again.

"Maria, can you come here, please?" Frank asked, barely able to get the words out between gales of laughter.

Gasping, whimpering, Tommy somehow reached his room and got out of sight before Maria appeared. For a while he leaned against the closed door, holding up his jeans with both hands, shivering.

3

WITH THEIR PARENTS OFF AT A CAMPAIGN APPEARANCE, TOMMY AND Frank ate dinner together, after heating up a casserole that Maria had left in the refrigerator. Ordinarily, dinner with Frank was an ordeal, but this time it proved to be uneventful. As he ate, Frank was engrossed in a magazine that reported on the latest horror movies, with heavy emphasis on slice-and-dice films and with lots of color photographs of mutilated and blood-soaked bodies; he seemed oblivious of Tommy.

Later, when Frank was in the bathroom preparing for bed, Tommy sneaked into his older brother's room and stood at the desk, studying the jack-o'-lantern. The wicked mouth glowed. The narrow pupils were alive with fire.

The scent of roses filled the room, but underlying that odor was another more subtle and less appealing fragrance that he could not quite identify.

Tommy was aware of a malevolent presence—something even worse than the malevolence that he could *always* sense in Frank's room. A cold current raced through his blood.

Suddenly he was certain that the potential murderous power of the black pumpkin was enhanced by the candle within it. Somehow, the presence of light inside its shell was dangerous, a triggering factor. Tommy did not know how he knew this, but he was convinced that if he was to have the slightest chance of surviving the coming night, he must extinguish the flame.

He grasped the gnarled stem and removed the lid from the top of the jack-o'-lantern's skull.

Light did not merely rise from inside the pumpkin but seemed to be *flung* at him, hot on his face, stinging his eyes.

He blew out the flame.

The jack-o'-lantern went dark.

Immediately, Tommy felt better.

He put the lid in place.

As he let go of the stem, the candle relit spontaneously.

Stunned, he jumped back.

Light shone from the carved eyes, the nose, the mouth.

"No," he said softly.

He removed the lid and blew out the candle once more.

A moment of darkness within the pumpkin. Then, before his eyes, the flame reappeared.

Reluctantly, issuing a thin involuntary sound of distress, Tommy reached into the jack-o'-lantern to snuff the stubborn candle with his thumb and finger. He was convinced that the pumpkin shell would suddenly snap shut around his wrist, severing his hand, leaving him with a bloody stump. Or perhaps it would hold him fast while swiftly dissolving the flesh from his fingers and then release him with an arm that terminated in a skeletal hand. Driven toward the brink of hysteria by these fears, he pinched the wick, extinguished the flame, and snatched his hand back with a sob of relief, grateful to have escaped mutilation.

He jammed the lid in place and, hearing the toilet flush in the adjacent bath, hurried out of the room. He dared not let Frank catch him there. As he stepped into the hallway, he glanced back at the jack-o'-lantern, and, of course, it was full of candlelight again.

He went straight to the kitchen and got a butcher's knife, which he took back to his own room and hid beneath his pillow. He was sure that he would need it sooner or later in the dead hours before dawn.

4

HIS PARENTS CAME HOME SHORTLY BEFORE MIDNIGHT.

Tommy was sitting in bed, his room illuminated only by the pale bulb of the low-wattage night-light. The butcher's knife was at his side, under the covers, and his hand was resting on the haft.

For twenty minutes, Tommy could hear his folks talking, running water, flushing toilets, closing doors. Their bedroom and bath were at the opposite end of the house from his and Frank's rooms, so the noises they made were muffled but nonetheless reassuring. These were the ordinary noises of daily life, and as long as the house was filled with them, no weird lantern-eyed predator could be stalking anyone.

Soon, however, quiet returned.

In the postmidnight stillness, Tommy waited for the first scream.

He was determined not to fall asleep. But he was only twelve years old, and he was exhausted after a long day and drained by the sustained terror that had gripped him ever since he had seen the mummy-faced pumpkin carver. Propped against a pile of pillows, he dozed off long before one o'clock—

—and something thumped, waking him.

He was instantly alert. He sat straight up in bed, clutching the butcher's knife.

For a moment he was certain that the sound had originated within his own room. Then he heard it again, a solid thump, and he knew that it had come from Frank's room across the hall.

He threw aside the covers and sat on the edge of the bed, tense. Waiting. Listening.

Once, he thought he heard Frank calling his name— "Tooommmmyy"—a desperate and frightened and barely audible cry that seemed to come from the far rim of a vast canyon. Perhaps he imagined it.

Silence.

His hands were slick with sweat. He put the big knife aside and blotted his palms on his pajamas.

Silence.

He picked up the knife again. He reached under his bed and found the flashlight that he kept there, but he did not switch it on. He eased cautiously to the door and listened for movement in the hallway beyond.

Nothing.

An inner voice urged him to return to bed, pull the covers over his head, and forget what he had heard. Better yet, he could crawl under the bed and hope that he would not be found. But he knew this was the voice of the wimp within, and he dared not hope for salvation in cowardice. If the black pumpkin *had* grown into something else, and if it was now loose in the house, it would respond to timidity with no less savage glee than Frank would have shown.

God, he thought fervently, *there's a boy down here who believes in you, and he'd be very disappointed if you happened to be looking the other way right now when he really, really, really needs you.*

Tommy quietly turned the knob and opened the door. The hallway, illuminated only by the moonlight that streamed through the window at the end, was deserted.

Directly across the hall, the door to Frank's room stood open.

Still not switching on the flashlight, desperately hoping that his presence would go undetected if he was mantled in darkness, he stepped to Frank's doorway and listened. Frank usually snored, but no snoring could be heard tonight. If the jack-o'-lantern was in there, the candle had been extinguished at last, for no flickering paraffin light was visible.

Tommy crossed the threshold.

Moonlight silvered the window, and the palm-frond shadows of a wind-stirred tree danced on the glass. In the room, no object was clearly outlined. Mysterious shapes loomed in shades of dark gray and black.

He took one step. Two. Three.

His heart pounded so hard that it shattered his resolve to cloak himself in darkness. He snapped on the Eveready and was startled by the way the butcher's knife in his right hand reflected the light.

He swept the beam around the room and, to his relief, saw no crouching monstrosity. The sheets and blankets were tumbled in a pile on the mattress, and he had to take another step toward the bed before he was able to ascertain that Frank was not there.

The severed hand was on the floor by the nightstand. Tommy saw it in the penumbra of the flashlight, and he brought the beam to bear directly on it. He stared in shock. Frank's hand. No doubt about its identity, because Frank's treasured silver skull-and-crossbones ring gleamed brightly on one slug-white finger. It was curled into a tight fist.

Perhaps powered by a postmortem nerve spasm, perhaps energized by darker forces, the fisted hand suddenly opened, fingers unfolding like the spreading petals of a flower. In the palm was a single, shiny nickel.

Tommy stifled a wild shriek but could not repress a series of violent shudders.

As he frantically tried to decide which escape route might be safest, he heard his mother scream from the far end of the house. Her shrill cry was abruptly cut off. Something crashed.

Tommy turned toward the doorway of Frank's room. He knew that he should run before it was too late, but he was as welded to this spot as he had been to that bit of dusty ground in the pumpkin lot when the carver had insisted on telling him what the jack-o'-lantern would become during the lonely hours of the night.

He heard his father shout.

A gunshot.

His father screamed.

This scream also was cut short.

Silence again.

Tommy tried to lift one foot, just one, just an inch off the floor, but it would not be lifted. He sensed that more than fear was holding him down, that some malevolent spell prevented him from escaping the black pumpkin.

A door slammed at the other end of the house.

Footsteps sounded in the hall. Heavy, scraping footsteps.

Tears slipped out of Tommy's eyes and down his cheeks.

In the hall, the floorboards creaked and groaned as if under a great weight.

Staring at the open door with no less terror than if he had been gazing into the entrance of Hell, Tommy saw flickering orange light in the corridor. The glow grew brighter as the source—no doubt a candle—drew nearer from the left, from the direction of his parents' bedroom.

Amorphous shadows and eerie snakes of light crawled on the hall carpet.

The heavy footsteps slowed. Stopped.

Judging by the light, the thing was only a foot or two from the doorway.

Tommy swallowed hard and worked up enough spit to say, *Who's there?* but was surprised to hear himself say instead, "Okay, damn you, let's get it over with."

Perhaps his years in the Sutzmann house had toughened him more thoroughly and had made him more fatalistic than he had previously realized.

The creature lurched into view, filling the doorway.

Its head was formed by the jack-o'-lantern, which had undergone hideous mutations. That peculiar pate had retained its black and orange coloring and its gourdlike shape, narrower at the top than at the bottom, and all the tumorous nodules were as crusted and disgusting as ever. However, though it had been as large as any pumpkin that Tommy had ever seen, it was now only about the size of a basketball, shriveled. The eyes had sagged, although the slitted pupils were still narrow and mean. The nose was bubbling with some vile mucus. The immense mouth stretched from ear to ear, for it had remained large while the rest of the face had shrunk around it. In the orange light that streamed out between them, the hooked fangs appeared to have been transformed from points of pumpkin rind into hard, sharp protuberances of bone.

The body under the head was vaguely humanoid, although it seemed to be composed of thick gnarled roots and tangled vines. The beast appeared to be immensely strong, a colossus, a fierce juggernaut if it wished to be. Even in his terror, Tommy was filled with awe. He wondered if the creature's body had grown from the substance in its previously enormous pumpkin head and, more pointedly, from the flesh of Frank, Lois, and Kyle Sutzmann.

Worst of all was the orange light within the skull. The candle still burned in there. Its leaping flames emphasized the impossible emptiness of the head—How could the thing move and think without a brain?—and invested a savage and demonic awareness in its eyes.

The nightmarish vision raised one thick, twisted, powerful, vine-like arm and thrust a rootlike finger at Tommy. *"You,"* it said in a deep whispery voice that called to mind the sound of wet slush pouring down a drain.

Tommy was now less surprised by his inability to move than by his ability to stand erect. His legs felt like rags. He was sure that he was going to collapse in a helpless heap while the thing descended upon him, but somehow he remained on his feet with the flashlight in one hand and the butcher's knife in the other.

The knife. Useless. The sharpest blade in the world could never harm this adversary, so Tommy let the knife slip out of his sweaty fingers. It clattered to the floor.

"You," the black pumpkin repeated, and its voice reverberated moistly throughout the room. "Your vicious brother got what he gave. Your mother got what she gave. Your father got what he gave. I fed on them, sucked the brains out of their heads, chewed up their flesh, dissolved their bones. Now what do *you* deserve?"

Tommy could not speak. He was shaking and weeping silently and dragging each breath into his lungs only with tremendous effort.

The black pumpkin lurched out of the doorway and into the room, looming over him, eyes blazing.

It stood nearly seven feet tall and had to tilt its lantern head to peer down at him. Curls of sooty black smoke from the candle wick escaped between its fangs and from its leprous nose.

Speaking in a rough whisper, yet with such force that its words vibrated the windowpanes, the thing said, "Unfortunately, you are a good boy, and I've no right or license to feed on you. So . . . What you deserve is what you've got from now on—freedom."

Tommy stared up into the Halloween face, striving hard to grasp what he had been told.

"Freedom," the demonic beast repeated. "Freedom from Frank and Lois and Kyle. Freedom to grow up without their heels pressing down on you. Freedom to be the best that you can be—which means I'll most likely *never* get a chance to feed on you."

For a long time they stood face to face, boy and beast, and gradually Tommy achieved complete understanding. In the morning, his parents and his brother would be missing. Never to be found. A great and enduring mystery. Tommy would have to live with his grandparents. You get what you give.

"But maybe," the black pumpkin said, putting one cold hand upon Tommy's shoulder, "maybe there's some rottenness in you too, and maybe someday you'll surrender to it, and maybe in time I'll still have my chance with you. Dessert." Its wide grin grew even wider. "Now get back to your bed and sleep. Sleep."

Simultaneously horrified and filled with strange delight, Tommy crossed the room to the doorway, moving as if in a dream. He looked back and saw that the black pumpkin was still watching him with interest.

Tommy said, "You missed a bit," and pointed to the floor beside his brother's nightstand.

The beast looked at Frank's severed hand.

"Ahhhh," said the black pumpkin, snatching up the hand and stuffing that grisly morsel into its mouth.

The flame within the squashy skull suddenly burned very bright, a hundred times brighter than before, then was extinguished.

MISS ATTILA THE HUN

1

THROUGH FROST AND THAW, THROUGH WET AND DRY SEASONS, THE thing on the forest floor had waited many hundreds of years for a chance to live again. Not that it was dead. It was alive, aware, always alert to the passage of warm-blooded creatures in the dense woods around it. But only a small portion of its mind was required to monitor nearby animals for a possible host, while for the most part it was occupied with vivid dreams of previous, ancient lives that it had led on other worlds.

Deer, bears, badgers, squirrels, chipmunks, rabbits, possums, wolves, mice, foxes, raccoons, cougars, quail that had strayed in from the fields, dogs, toads, chameleons, snakes, worms, beetles, spiders, and centipedes had passed near enough to the thing to have been seized if they had been suitable. Some, of course, were not warm-blooded, which was one of the creature's primary requirements of a host. Those that did have warm blood—the mammals and the birds—did not meet the other important requirement: a high order of intelligence.

The thing did not grow impatient. It had found hosts in one form or another for millions upon millions of years. It was confident that it would eventually have an opportunity to ascend from its cold dreams and experience this new world, as it had experienced—and conquered—many others.

2

JAMIE WATLEY WAS IN LOVE WITH MRS. CASWELL. HE HAD CONSIDER-
able artistic talent, so he filled a tablet with drawings of his dream
woman: Mrs. Caswell riding a wild horse; Mrs. Caswell taming a
lion; Mrs. Caswell shooting a charging rhinoceros that was as big
as a Mack truck; Mrs. Caswell as the Statue of Liberty, holding a
torch high. He had not seen her ride a horse, tame a lion, or shoot
a rhino; neither had he ever heard of her having performed any of
those feats. And she certainly did not look like the Statue of Liberty
(she was much prettier), but it seemed to Jamie that these imaginary
scenes nevertheless portrayed the real Mrs. Caswell.

He wanted to ask Mrs. Caswell to marry him, although he was
not confident about his chances. For one thing, she was well-educated, and he was not. She was beautiful, and he was homely. She
was funny and outgoing, but he was shy. She was so *sure* of herself,
in command of any situation—Remember the school fire back in
September, when she single-handedly saved the building from burning to the ground?—while Jamie had difficulty coping with even
minor crises. She was already married too, and Jamie felt guilty
about wishing her husband dead. But if he were to have any hope
at all of marrying Mrs. Caswell, the worst problem to be overcome
was the difference in their ages; she was seventeen years older than
Jamie, who was only eleven.

That Sunday night in late October, Jamie sat at the plank-topped,
makeshift desk in his small bedroom, creating a new pencil drawing
of Mrs. Caswell, his sixth-grade teacher. He depicted her in their
classroom, standing beside her desk, dressed in the white robes of
an angel. A wonderful light radiated from her, and all the kids—
Jamie's classmates—were smiling at her. Jamie put himself into the
picture—second row from the door, first desk—and, after some
thought, he drew streams of small hearts rising from him the way
fog rose from a block of Dry Ice.

Jamie Watley—whose mother was an alcoholic slattern and whose father was an alcoholic, frequently unemployed mechanic—had never much cared for school until this year, when he had fallen under the spell of Mrs. Laura Caswell. Now, Sunday night was always the slowest night of the week because he was impatient for the start of school.

Downstairs, his mean-spirited, drunken father was arguing with his equally drunken mother. The subject was money, but the argument could as easily have been about the inedible dinner she had prepared, his eye for other women, her sloppy appearance, his poker losses, her constant whining, the lack of snack foods in the house, or which TV program they were going to watch. The thin walls of the decrepit house did little to muffle their voices, but Jamie was usually able to tune them out.

He started a new drawing. In this one, Mrs. Caswell was standing on a rocky landscape, wearing futuristic clothing, and battling an alien monster with a laser sword.

3

BEFORE DAWN, TEEL PLEEVER DROVE HIS BATTERED, DIRTY, EIGHT-YEAR-old Jeep station wagon into the hills. He parked along an abandoned logging road deep in the forest. As dawn was breaking, he set out on foot with his deer rifle. The gun was a bolt-action Winchester Model 70 in .270 caliber, restocked in fine European walnut, with a four-power scope on Stith Streamline mounts, incorporating windage.

Teel loved the woods at dawn: the velvety softness of the shadows, the clear early light spearing down through the branches, the lingering smell of night dampness. He took great satisfaction from the feel of the rifle in his hand and from the thrill of the hunt, but most of all he enjoyed poaching.

Although he was the most successful real-estate wheeler and dealer in the county, a man of position and modest wealth, Teel was loath to spend a dollar when the same item could be had elsewhere for ninety-eight cents, and he refused to spend a penny when he could get what he wanted for free. He had owned a farm on the northeast edge of Pineridge, the county seat, where the state had decided to put the new turnpike interchange, and he'd made better than six hundred thousand dollars in profit by selling off pieces to motel and fast-food chains. That was the biggest of his deals but far from the only one; he would have been a rich man without it. Yet he bought a new Jeep wagon only every ten years, owned one suit, and was notorious at Pineridge's Acme Supermarket for spending as much as three hours comparison shopping to save eighty cents on one order of groceries.

He never bought beef. Why pay for meat when the woods were full of it, on the hoof, free for the taking? Teel was fifty-three. He had been shooting deer out of season since he was seventeen, and he had never been caught. He had never particularly *liked* the taste of venison, and after having eaten uncounted thousands of pounds of the stuff over the past three and a half decades, he sometimes didn't look forward to dinner; however, his appetite always improved when he thought of all the money that he had kept in his pocket and out of the hands of cattle farmers, beef brokers, and members of the butchers' union.

After forty minutes of climbing the gently sloped, forested foothills without spotting deer spoor, Teel paused for a rest on a large flat rock between two big-cone pines. After he sat on the edge of the rock and put his rifle aside, he noticed something odd in the ground between his booted feet.

The object was half buried in the soft, moist, black soil. It was also partly covered by decaying, brown pine needles. He reached down with one hand and brushed the needles away. The thing was the shape of a football but appeared to be about twice as large. The surface was highly polished, as glossy as a ceramic glaze, and Teel knew the object must be man-made because no amount of wind and water abrasion could produce such a sheen. The thing was darkly mottled blue and black and green, and it had a strange beauty.

He was about to get off the rock, drop to his hands and knees, and dig the mysterious object out of the soil, when holes opened in several places across its surface. In the same instant, black and glossy plantlike tendrils exploded toward him. Some whipped around his head and neck, others around his arms, still others around his feet. In three seconds he was snared.

Seed, he thought frantically. *Some crazy damn kind of seed no one's seen before.*

He struggled violently, but he could not pull free of the black tendrils or break them. He could not even get up from the rock or move an inch to one side or the other.

He tried to scream, but the thing had clamped his mouth shut.

Because Teel was still looking straight down between his legs at the nightmarish seed, he saw a new, larger hole dilate in the center of it. A much thicker tendril—a stalk, really—rose swiftly out of the opening and came toward his face as if it were a cobra swaying up from a snake charmer's basket. Black with irregular midnight-blue spots, tapered at the top, it terminated in nine thin, writhing tendrils. Those feelers explored his face with a spider-soft touch, and he shuddered in revulsion. Then the stalk moved away from his face, curved toward his chest, and with horror he felt it growing with amazing rapidity through his clothes, through his skin, through his breastbone, and into his body cavity. He felt the nine tendrils spreading through him, and then he fainted before he could go insane.

4

ON THIS WORLD, ITS NAME WAS SEED. AT LEAST THAT WAS WHAT IT SAW in the mind of its first host. It was not actually a plant—nor an animal, in fact—but it accepted the name that Teel Pleever gave it.

Seed extruded itself entirely from the pod in which it had waited for hundreds of years and inserted all of its mass into the body of the host. Then it closed up the bloodless wounds by which it had entered Pleever.

It required ten minutes of exploration to learn more about human physiology than humans knew. For one thing, humans apparently didn't understand that they had the ability to hcal themselves and to daily repair the effects of aging. They lived short lives, oddly unaware of their potential for immortality. Something had happened during the species' evolution to create a mind-body barrier that prevented them from consciously controlling their own physical being.

Strange.

Sitting on the rock between the pine trees, in the body of Teel Pleever, Seed took an additional eighteen minutes to acquire a full understanding of the depth, breadth, and workings of the human mind. It was one of the most interesting minds that Seed had encountered anywhere in the universe: complex, powerful—distinctly psychotic.

This was going to be an interesting incarnation.

Seed rose from the rock, picked up the rifle that belonged to its host, and headed down the forested hills toward the place where Teel Pleever had parked the Jeep wagon. Seed had no interest in deer poaching.

5

JACK CASWELL SAT AT THE KITCHEN TABLE, WATCHING HIS WIFE AS SHE got ready for school that Monday morning, and he knew beyond a doubt that he was the luckiest man in the world. Laura was so lovely, slender, long limbed, and shapely that Jack sometimes felt as if he were dreaming his life rather than actually living it, for surely in the real world he would not have merited a woman like Laura.

She took her brown-plaid scarf from one of the hooks by the back door and wrapped it around her neck, crossing the fringed ends over her breasts. Peering through the half-steamed window in the door, she read the outside temperature on the big thermometer mounted on the porch. "Thirty-eight degrees, and it's only the end of October."

Her thick, soft, shiny, chestnut-brown hair framed a perfectly proportioned face reminiscent of the old movie star Veronica Lake. She had enormous, expressive eyes so dark brown that they were almost black; they were the clearest, most direct eyes that Jack had ever seen. He doubted that anyone could look into those eyes and lie—or fail to love the woman behind them.

Removing her old brown cloth coat from another hook, slipping into it, closing the buttons, she said, "We'll have snow well before Thanksgiving this year, I'll bet, and the whitest Christmas in ages, and we'll be snowbound by January."

"Wouldn't mind being snowbound with you for maybe six or eight months," he said. "Just the two of us, snow up to the roof, so we'd have to stay in bed, under the covers, sharing body heat to survive."

Grinning, she came to him, bent, and kissed him on the cheek. "Jackson," she said, using her pet name for him, "the way you turn me on, we'd generate so darn much body heat that it wouldn't matter if the snow was a *mile* higher than the roof. Regardless of how cold it was outside, it'd be sweltering in here, temperature and humidity over a hundred degrees, jungle plants growing out of the floorboards, vines crawling up the walls, tropical molds in all the corners."

She went into the living room to get the briefcase that was on the desk at which she planned her school lessons.

Jack got up from the table. A little stiffer than usual this morning but still in good enough shape to shuffle around without his cane, he gathered up the dirty breakfast dishes. He was still thinking about what a lucky man he was.

She could have had any guy she wanted, yet she had chosen a husband with no better than average looks and with two bum legs that wouldn't hold him up if he didn't clamp them in metal braces every morning. With her looks, personality, and intelligence, she could have married rich or could have gone off to the big city to make her own fortune. Instead she had settled for the simple life of a teacher and the wife of a struggling writer, passing up mansions for this small house at the edge of the woods, forgoing limousines for a three-year-old Toyota.

When she bustled into the kitchen with her briefcase, Jack was putting the dishes in the sink. "Do you miss the limousines?"

She blinked at him. "What're you talking about?"

He sighed and leaned against the counter. "Sometimes I worry that maybe . . ."

She came to him. "That maybe what?"

"Well, that you don't have much in life, certainly not as much as you ought to have. Laura, you were born for limousines, mansions, ski chalets in Switzerland. You *deserve* them."

She smiled. "You sweet, silly man. I'd be bored in a limousine. I like to drive. It's *fun* to drive. Heck, if I lived in a mansion, I'd rattle around like a pea in a barrel. I like *cozy* places. Since I don't ski, chalets aren't any use to me. And though I like their clocks and chocolates, I can't abide the way the Swiss yodel all the time."

He put his hands on her shoulders. "Are you really happy?"

She looked directly into his eyes. "You're serious about this, aren't you?"

"I worry that I can't give you enough."

"Listen, Jackson, you love me with all your heart, and I know you do. I *feel* it all the time, and it's a love that most women will never experience. I'm happier with you than I ever thought I could be. And I enjoy my work too. Teaching is immensely satisfying if you really try to jam knowledge into those little demons. Besides, you'll be famous someday, the most famous writer of detective novels since Raymond Chandler. I just know it. Now, if you don't stop being a total booby, I'm going to be late for work."

She kissed him again, went to the door, blew him another kiss, went outside, and descended the porch steps to the Toyota parked in the gravel driveway.

He grabbed his cane from the back of one of the kitchen chairs and used it to move more quickly to the door than he could have with only the assistance of his leg braces. Wiping the steam from the cold pane of glass, he watched her start the car and race the engine until, warmed up, it stopped knocking. Clouds of vapor plumed from the exhaust pipe. She drove out to the county road and off toward the elementary school three miles away. Jack stayed at the window until the white Toyota had dwindled to a speck and vanished.

Though Laura was the strongest and most self-assured person Jack had ever known, he worried about her. The world was hard, full of nasty surprises, even here in the rural peace of Pine County. And people, including the toughest of them, could get ground up suddenly by the wheels of fate, crushed and broken in the blink of an eye.

"You take care of yourself," he said softly. "You take care and come back to me."

6

SEED DROVE TEEL PLEEVER'S BATTERED OLD JEEP WAGON TO THE END of the abandoned logging road and turned right onto a narrow blacktop lane. In a mile the hills descended into flatter land, and the forest gave way to open fields.

At the first dwelling, Seed stopped and got out of the Jeep. Drawing upon its host's store of knowledge, Seed discovered this was "the Halliwell place." At the front door, it knocked sharply.

Mrs. Halliwell, a thirtyish woman with amiable features, answered the knock. She was drying her hands on her blue-and-white-checkered apron. "Why, Mr. Pleever, isn't it?"

Seed extruded tendrils from its host's fingertips. The swift, black lashes whipped around the woman, pinning her. As Mrs. Halliwell screamed, a much thicker stalk burst from Pleever's open mouth, shot straight to the woman, and bloodlessly pierced her chest, fusing with her flesh as it entered her.

She never finished her first scream.

Seed took control of her in seconds. The tendrils and stalks linking the two hosts parted in the middle, and the glistening, blue-spotted black alien substance flowed partly back into Teel Pleever and partly into Jane Halliwell.

Seed was growing.

Searching Jane Halliwell's mind, Seed learned that her two young children had gone to school and that her husband had taken the pickup into Pineridge to make a few purchases at the hardware store. She had been alone in the house.

Eager to acquire new hosts and expand its empire, Seed took Jane and Teel out to the Jeep wagon and drove back onto the narrow lane, heading toward the county road that led into Pineridge.

7

MRS. CASWELL ALWAYS BEGAN THE MORNING WITH A HISTORY LESSON. Until he had landed in her sixth-grade class, Jamie Watley had thought that he didn't like history, that it was dull. When Mrs. Caswell taught history, however, it wasn't only interesting but fun.

Sometimes she made them act out roles in great historical events, and each of them got to wear a funny hat suitable to the character he was portraying. Mrs. Caswell had the most amazing collection of funny hats. Once, when teaching a lesson about the Vikings, she had walked into the room wearing a horned helmet, and everyone had busted a gut laughing. At first Jamie had been a bit embarrassed for her; she was *his* Mrs. Caswell, after all, the woman he loved, and he couldn't bear to see her behaving foolishly. But then she showed them paintings of Viking longboats with intricately carved dragons on the prows, and she began to describe what it was like to be a Viking sailing unknown misty seas in the ancient days before there were maps, heading out into unknown waters where—as far as people of that time knew—you might actually meet up with dragons or even fall off the edge of the earth, and as she talked her voice grew softer, softer, until everyone was leaning forward, until it seemed as if they were transported from their classroom onto the deck of a small ship, with storm waves crashing all around them and a mysterious dark shore looming out of the wind and rain ahead. Now Jamie had ten drawings of Mrs. Caswell as a Viking, and they were among his favorites in his secret gallery.

Last week a teaching evaluator named Mr. Enright had monitored a day of Mrs. Caswell's classes. He was a neat little man in a dark suit, white shirt, and red bow tie. After the history lesson, which had been about life in medieval times, Mr. Enright wanted to question the kids to see how much they grasped of what they had been taught. Jamie and the others were eager to answer, and Enright was impressed. "But, Mrs. Caswell," he said, "you're not exactly teaching them the six-grade level, are you? This seems more like about eighth-grade material to me."

Ordinarily, the class would have reacted positively to Enright's statement, seizing on the implied compliment. They would have sat up straight at their desks, puffed our their chests, and smiled smugly. But they had been coached to react differently if this situation arose, so they slumped in their chairs and tried to look exhausted.

Mrs. Caswell said, "Class, what Mr. Enright means is that he's afraid I'm pushing you too fast, too hard. You don't think that I demand too much of you?"

The entire class answered with one voice: *"Yes!"*

Mrs. Caswell pretended to look startled. "Oh, now, I don't overwork you."

Melissa Fedder, who had the enviable ability to cry on cue, burst into tears, as if the strain of being one of Mrs. Caswell's students were just too much to bear.

Jamie stood, shaking in make-believe terror, and delivered his one speech with practiced emotion: "Mr. En-Enright, we can't t-t-take it any more. She never lets up on us. N-n-never. We c-c-call her Miss Attila the Hun."

Other kids began to voice rehearsed complaints to Mr. Enright:

"—never gives us a recess—"

"—four hours of homework every night—"

"—too much—"

"—only sixth-graders—"

Mr. Enright was genuinely appalled.

Mrs. Caswell stepped toward the class, scowling, and made a short chopping motion with her hand.

Everyone instantly fell silent, as if afraid of her. Melissa Fedder was still crying, and Jamie worked hard at making his lower lip tremble.

"Mrs. Caswell," Mr. Enright said uneasily, "uh, well, perhaps you should consider sticking closer to the sixth-grade texts. The stress created by—"

"Oh!" Mrs. Caswell said, feigning horror. "I'm afraid it's too late, Mr. Enright. Look at the poor dears! I'm afraid I've worked them to death."

At this cue, all the kids in the class fell forward on their desks, as if they had collapsed and died.

Mr. Enright stood in startled silence for a moment, then broke into laughter, and all the kids laughed too, and Mr. Enright said, "Mrs. Caswell, you set me up! This was *staged.*"

"I confess," she said, and the kids laughed harder.

"But how did you know I'd be concerned about your pushing them past sixth-grade material?"

"Because everyone *always* underestimates kids," Mrs. Caswell said. "The approved curriculum never challenges them. Everyone worries so much about psychological stress, the problems associated with being an overachiever, and the result is that kids are actually encouraged to be *under*achievers. But I know kids, Mr. Enright, and I tell you they're a much tougher, smarter bunch than anyone gives them credit for being. Am I right?"

The class loudly assured her that she was right.

Mr. Enright surveyed the class, pausing to study each child's face, and it was the first time all morning that he had really *looked* at them. At last he smiled. "Mrs. Caswell, this is a wonderful thing you've got going here."

"Thank you," said Mrs. Caswell.

Mr. Enright shook his head, smiled more broadly, and winked. "Miss Attila the Hun indeed."

At that moment Jamie was so proud of Mrs. Caswell and so in love with her that he had to struggle valiantly to repress tears far more genuine than those of Melissa Fedder.

Now, on the last Monday morning in October, Jamie listened to Miss Attila the Hun as she told them what medical science was like in the Middle Ages (crude) and what alchemy was (lead into gold and all sorts of crazy-fascinating stuff), and in a while he could no longer smell the chalk dust and child scents of the classroom but could *almost* smell the terrible, reeking, sewage-spattered streets of medieval Europe.

8

IN HIS TEN-FOOT-SQUARE OFFICE AT THE FRONT OF THE HOUSE, JACK
Caswell sat at an ancient pine desk, sipping coffee and rereading
the chapter he'd written the previous day. He made a lot of pencil
corrections and then switched on his computer to enter the changes.

In the three years since his accident, unable to return to work as
a game warden for the department of forestry, he had struggled to
fulfill his lifelong desire to be a writer. (Sometimes, in his dreams,
he could still see the big truck starting to slide on the ice-covered
road, and he felt his own car entering a sickening spin too, and the
bright headlights were bearing down on him, and he pumped the
brake pedal, turned the wheel into the slide, but he was always too
late. Even in the dreams, he was always too late.) He had written
four fast-paced detective novels in the last three years, two of which
had sold to New York publishers, and he had also placed eight short
stories in magazines.

Until Laura came along, his two great loves had been the outdoors
and books. Before the accident, he had often hiked miles up into
the mountains, to places remote and serene, with his backpack half
filled with food, half with paperbacks. Augmenting his supplies with
berries and nuts and edible roots, he had remained for days in the
wilderness, alternately studying the wildlife and reading. He was
equally a man of nature and civilization; though it was difficult to
bring nature into town, it was easy to carry civilization—in the form
of books—into the wild heart of the forest, allowing him to satisfy
both halves of his cleft soul.

These days, cursed with legs that would never again support him
on a journey into the hills, he had to be content with the pleasures
of civilization—and, damn it, he soon had to make a better living
with his writing than he had managed thus far. From the sales of
eight stories and two well-reviewed novels spread over three years,
he had not earned a third as much as Laura's modest teaching salary.
He was a long way from reaching the best-seller lists, and life at

the lower end of the publishing business was far from glamorous. Without his small disability pension from the department of forestry, he and Laura would have had serious difficulty keeping themselves housed, clothed, and fed.

When he remembered the worn brown cloth coat in which Laura had gone off to school that morning, he grew sad. But the thought of her in that drab coat also made him more determined than ever to write a breakthrough book, earn a fortune, and buy her the luxuries that she deserved.

The strange thing was that if he had not been in the accident, he would not have met Laura, would not have married her. She'd been at the hospital visiting a sick student, and on the way out she had seen Jack in the hall. He was in a wheelchair, sullenly roaming the corridors. Laura was incapable of passing an obviously depressed man in a wheelchair without attempting to cheer him. Filled with self-pity and anger, he rebuffed her; however, rejection only made Laura try harder. He didn't know what a bulldog she was, but he learned. Two days later, when she returned to visit her student, she paid a call on Jack as well, and soon she was coming every day just to see him. When he resigned himself to life in a wheelchair, Laura insisted that he work longer and harder with a therapist every day and that he at least *try* to learn to walk with braces and a cane. After some time, when the therapist had only moderate success with him, Laura wheeled him, protesting, into the therapy room every day and put him through the exercises a second time. Before long, her indomitable spirit and optimism infected Jack. He became determined to walk again, and then he *did* walk, and somehow learning to walk led to love and marriage. So the worst thing that had ever happened to him—the leg-crushing collision—had brought him to Laura, and she was far and away the *best* thing that had ever happened to him.

Screwy. Life sure was screwy.

In the new novel on which he was working, he was trying to write about that screwiness: the bizarre way that bad things could lead to blessings while blessings sometimes ended in tragedy. If he could thread that observation through a detective story in such a way as to explore the more profound aspects of it, he might be able to write not only a big-money book but also a book of which he could be proud.

He poured another cup of coffee and was about to start a new chapter when he looked out the window to the left of his desk and saw a dirty, dented Jeep station wagon pull off the county road into his driveway.

Wondering who could be calling, he immediately levered himself up from the chair and grabbed his cane. He needed time to get to the front door, and he hated to keep people waiting.

He saw the Jeep stop in front of the house. Both doors flew open, and a man and a woman got out.

Jack recognized the man, Teel Pleever, whom he knew slightly. Just about everyone in Pine County knew Pleever, but Jack figured that, like him, most folks didn't really know the man well.

The woman was vaguely familiar to him. She was about thirty, attractive, and he thought perhaps she had a child in Laura's class and that he had seen her at a school function. In only a housedress and an apron, she was not properly clothed for the chilly October morning.

By the time Jack caned halfway across the office, his visitors had begun to knock on the front door.

9

SEED PULLED OFF THE HIGHWAY AS SOON AS IT SAW THE NEXT DWELLING. After centuries of dreamy half-life, it was eager to expand into more hosts. From Pleever, it knew that five thousand people lived in the town of Pineridge, in which Seed intended to arrive by noon. Within two days, three at most, it would assume control of every one of the town's citizens and then would spread throughout Pine County, until it seized the bodies and imprisoned the minds of all twenty thousand residents in that entire rural area.

Although spread among many hosts, Seed remained a single entity with a single consciousness. It could live simultaneously in tens of millions or even billions of hosts, absorbing sensory input from billions of eyes and billions of ears and billions of noses, mouths, and hands, without risking confusion or information overload. In its countless millions of years of drifting through the galaxies, on the more than one hundred planets where it had thrived, Seed had never encountered another creature with its unique talent for physical schizophrenia.

Now it took its two captives out of the Jeep and marched them across the lawn to the front-porch steps of the small white house.

From Pine County it would send its hosts outward, fanning across this continent, then to others, until every human being on the face of the earth had been claimed. Throughout this period, it would destroy neither the mind nor the individual personality of any host but would imprison each while it used the host's body and store of knowledge to facilitate its conquest of the world. Teel Pleever, Jane Halliwell, and all the others would be horribly aware during their months of total enslavement: aware of the world around them, aware of the monstrous acts they were committing, and aware of Seed nesting within them.

It walked its two hosts up the porch steps and used Pleever to knock loudly on the front door.

When no man, woman, or child on earth remained free, Seed would advance to the next stage, the Day of Release, abruptly allowing its hosts to resume control of their bodies, though in each of them would remain an aspect of the puppetmaster, always gazing out through their eyes and monitoring their thoughts. By the Day of Release, of course, at least half of the hosts would be insane. Others, having held on to sanity in hope of eventual release from torment, would be rocked by the realization that even after regaining control of themselves, they must endure the cold, parasitic presence of the intruder forever; they too would then go slowly mad. That was what always happened. A smaller group would inevitably seek solace in religion, forming a socially disruptive cult that would worship Seed. And the smallest group of all, the tough ones, would remain sane and either adapt to Seed's presence or seek ways to evict it, a crusade that would not prove successful.

Seed rapped on the door again. Perhaps no one was at home.

"Coming, coming," a man called from inside.

Ah, good.

Following the Day of Release, the fate of this sorry world would conform to the usual pattern: mass suicides, millions of homicides committed by psychopaths, complete and bloody social collapse, and an irreversible slide into anarchy, barbarism.

Chaos.

Creating chaos, spreading chaos, nurturing chaos, observing and relishing chaos were Seed's only purposes. The thing had been born in the genesis explosion at the start of time. Before that, it had been part of the supreme chaos of supercondensed matter in the time before time began. When that great undifferentiated ball of genesis matter exploded, the universe was formed; unprecedented order arose in the void, but Seed was not part of that order. It was a remnant of precreation chaos; protected by an invincible shell, it drifted forth into the blossoming galaxies, in the service of entropy.

A man opened the door. He was leaning on a cane.

"Mr. Pleever, isn't it?" he said.

From Jane Halliwell, Seed extruded black tendrils.

The man with the cane cried out as he was seized.

A blue-spotted black stalk burst from Jane Halliwell's mouth, pierced the crippled man's chest, and in seconds Seed had its third host: Jack Caswell.

The man's legs had been so badly damaged in an accident that he wore metal braces. Because Seed did not want to be slowed down by a crippled host, it healed Caswell's body and shucked off the braces.

Drawing upon Caswell's knowledge, Seed discovered that no one else was at home. It also learned that Caswell's wife taught at an elementary school and that this school, containing at least a hundred and sixty children and their teachers, was only three miles away. Rather than stop at every dwelling on the road into Pineridge, Seed could more effectively go to the school, seize control of everyone, and then spread out with all those hosts in every direction.

Jack Caswell, though imprisoned by Seed, was privy to his alien master's thoughts, because they shared the same cerebral tissue and neural pathways. Upon realizing that the school was to be attacked, Caswell's trapped mind squirmed violently, trying to slip free of its shackles.

Seed was surprised by the vigor and persistence with which the man resisted. With Pleever and the Halliwell woman, it had noticed that human beings—as they called themselves—possessed a far more powerful will than any species with which it had previously enjoyed contact. Now Caswell proved to have a considerably stronger will than either Pleever or Halliwell. Here was a species that obviously struggled relentlessly to create order out of chaos, that tried to make sense of existence, and that was determined to *impose* order on the natural world by the sheer power of its will. Seed was going to take special pleasure in leading humanity into chaos, degeneration, and ultimately into devolution.

Seed shoved the man's mind into an even darker, tighter corner than that to which it first confined him, chained him more securely. Then, in the form of its three hosts, it set out for the elementary school.

10

JAMIE WATLEY WAS EMBARRASSED TO ASK MRS. CASWELL FOR PERMIS-
sion to go to the bathroom. He wanted her to think that he was special,
wanted her to notice him in a way that she did not notice the other
kids, wanted her to love him as much as he loved her—but how could
she think that he was special if she knew that he had to pee like any
other boy? He was being silly, of course. Having to go to the bathroom
was nothing to be ashamed about. Everyone peed. Even Mrs. Caswell—

No! He wouldn't think about that. Impossible.

But all through the history lesson he did keep thinking about his
own need to pee, and by the time they were finished with history
and halfway through math, he could no longer contain himself.

"Yes, Jamie?"

"May I have a lavatory pass, Mrs. Caswell?"

"Certainly."

The lavatory passes were on a corner of her desk, and he had to
walk by her to reach them. He hung his head and refused to look
at her because he didn't want her to see that he was blushing brightly.
He snatched the pass off the desk and hurried into the hall.

Unlike other boys, he did not dawdle in the restroom. He was
eager to get back to class so he could listen to Mrs. Caswell's musical
voice and watch her move back and forth through the room.

When he came out of the lav, three people were entering the end
of the corridor through the outside door to the parking lot: a man
dressed in hunting clothes, a woman in a housedress, and a guy in
khaki pants and a maroon sweatshirt. They were an odd trio.

Jamie waited for them to pass because they looked as if they were
in a hurry about something and might knock him down if he got in
their way. Besides, he suspected that they might ask where to find
the principal or the school nurse or somebody important, and Jamie
enjoyed being helpful. As they drew abreast of him, they turned
toward him, as one.

He was snared.

11

SEED WAS NOW FOUR.

By nightfall it would be thousands.

In its four parts, it walked down the hall toward the classroom to which Jamie Watley had been returning.

A year or two hence, after the entire population of the world had become part of Seed, when bloodshed and chaos were then initiated with the Day of Release, the entity would remain entirely on-planet only a few weeks to witness firsthand the beginning of the human decline. Then it would form a new shell, fill that vessel with part of itself, and break free of the earth's gravity. Returning to the void, it would drift for tens of thousands or even millions of years until it found another likely world, where it would descend and await contact with a member of the dominant species.

During its long cosmic journeying, Seed would remain in contact with the billions of parts of itself that it left behind on earth, although only as long as those fragments had hosts to inhabit. In a way, therefore, it would never really leave this planet until the last human being was destroyed centuries hence in one terminal act of chaotic violence, whereupon the remaining bit of earthbound Seed would die with that final host.

Seed reached the door of Laura Caswell's classroom.

The minds of Jack Caswell and Jamie Watley, hot with anger and fear, tried to melt through the shackles in which Seed bound them, and it paused briefly to cool them down and establish full control. Their bodies twitched, and they made gurgling sounds as they strove to scream a warning. Seed was shocked by the rebellion; while having no slightest chance of success, their resistance was nevertheless greater than any it had ever before encountered.

Exploring the minds of Jack and Jamie, Seed discovered that their impressive, stubborn exercise of will had been powered not by fear for themselves but by fear for Laura Caswell, teacher of one and wife of the other. They were angry about their own enslavement, yes, but they were even angrier about the possibility of Laura being possessed. They were both in love with her, and the purity of that love gave them the strength to resist the horror that had engulfed them.

Interesting.

Seed had encountered the concept of love among half of the species that it had destroyed on other worlds, but nowhere had it perceived the force of love as strongly as in these human beings. Now it realized for the first time that the will of an intelligent creature wasn't the only important power in the employ of universal order; love also fulfilled that function. And in a species that had both a strong will and an unusually well-developed ability to love, Seed had found the most formidable enemy of chaos.

Not formidable enough, of course. Seed was unstoppable, and within twenty-four hours all of Pineridge would be absorbed.

Seed opened the classroom door. The four of it went inside.

12

LAURA CASWELL WAS SURPRISED TO SEE HER HUSBAND ENTER THE ROOM with Richie Halliwell's mother, that old scoundrel Teel Pleever, and Jamie. She couldn't imagine what any of them, other than Jamie, was doing there. Then she realized that Jack was walking, actually *walking*, not shuffling, not dragging himself along stiff legged but walking easily like any man.

Before the wonder of Jack's recovery could sink in, before Laura could ask him what was happening, even as her students were turning in their seats, terror struck. Jamie Watley held his hands toward a classmate, Tommy Albertson, and hideous, black, wormlike tendrils erupted from his fingertips. They lashed around Tommy, and as the snared boy cried out, a repulsive snakelike thing burst from Jamie's breastbone and pierced Tommy's chest, linking them obscenely.

The children screamed and pushed up from their desks to flee, but with astonishing speed they were attacked and silenced. Hateful, glossy worms and thicker snakes spewed forth from Mrs. Halliwell,

Pleever, and Jack. Three more of Laura's nineteen students were seized. Suddenly Tommy Albertson and the other contaminated children joined in the attack; worms and snakes erupted from them toward new victims only seconds after they themselves had first been pierced.

Miss Garner, the teacher in the next room, stepped through the door to see what the shouting was about. She was taken before she could cry out.

In a single minute all but four thoroughly terrorized children had been taken firmly under the control of some nightmare organism. The four survivors—including Jane Halliwell's son, Richie—gathered around Laura; two were stunned into silence and two were crying. She pushed the kids behind her, into a corner by the chalkboard, and stood between them and the monstrosity that wanted them.

Fifteen possessed children, Pleever, Mrs. Halliwell, Miss Garner, and Jack gathered before her, staring with predatory intensity. For a moment all were still and silent. In their eyes she saw not merely reflections of their own tortured souls but the inhuman hunger of the thing that had taken control of them.

Laura was scared and sick at heart to think of that glistening black *thing* curled inside her Jack, but she was not hobbled by either confusion or disbelief, because she had seen her share of the movies that, for decades, had been preparing the world for precisely this nightmare. *Invaders from Mars. Invasion of the Body Snatchers. The War of the Worlds.* She knew immediately that something from beyond the stars had at last found the earth.

The question was: Could it be stopped—and how?

She realized that she was holding her chalkboard pointer as if it were a mighty sword and as if the nineteen alien-infected people in front of her would be kept at bay by that useless weapon. Silly. Nevertheless, she did not cast the pointer aside but thrust it forward challengingly.

She was dismayed to see her hand shaking. She hoped that the four children crouching behind her were not aware that she was in the grip of terror.

From the possessed group that confronted her, three moved slowly forward: Jane Halliwell, Jamie Watley, and Jack.

"Stay back," she warned.

They took another step toward her.

A bead of perspiration trickled down Laura's right temple.

Mrs. Halliwell, Jack, and Jamie advanced another step.

Suddenly they didn't seem to be as well controlled as the others, because they began to twitch and jerk with muscle spasms. Jack said, "Noooo," in a horrible, low, agonized voice. And Jane Halliwell said, "Please, please," and shook her head as if to deny the orders that she had been given. Jamie was trembling violently and holding his hands to his head as though trying to get at the thing inside him and wrench it out.

Why were these three being forced to complete the subjugation of the classroom? Why not others?

Laura's mind worked feverishly, sensing an advantage, searching for it, but not sure if she would recognize it when she found it. Perhaps the thing in Jane Halliwell wanted her to infect her own son, Richie, who hid behind Laura's skirts, as a test of its control over the woman. And for the same reason it might want Jack to experience the horror of inducting his wife into this colony of the damned. As for poor Jamie . . . well, Laura was aware of the boy's fierce crush on her, so maybe he was being tested as well, to see if he could be made to attack the person he loved.

But if they had to be tested, their master was not yet entirely certain of its dominance. And where it had doubt, surely its intended victims had hope.

13

SEED WAS IMPRESSED WITH THE RESISTANCE EXHIBITED BY THREE OF ITS hosts when the moment came to infect their loved ones.

The mother was furious at the thought of her son being brought into the fold. She pried at the restraints on her mind and struggled fiercely to regain her body. She posed a mildly difficult problem of control, but Seed squeezed her consciousness into an even tighter, darker place than that to which it had at first condemned her. It pushed her mind down, down, as if it were thrusting her into a pool of water, and then it weighted her in that deep place as if stacking heavy stones upon her.

Jamie Watley was equally troublesome, motivated as he was by pure, clean puppy love. But Seed reasserted authority over Jamie as well, stopped the boy's muscle spasms, and forced him forward toward the woman and children in the corner of the room.

The husband, Jack Caswell, was the most difficult of the three, for his will was the strongest; and his love was the most powerful. He raged against confinement, actually bent the bars of his mental prison, and would have gladly killed himself before taking Seed to Laura Caswell. For more than a minute he resisted his master's orders, and for one startling moment he seemed about to break free of control, but at last Seed squeezed him into full if grudging compliance.

The fourteen other captured children in Mrs. Caswell's sixth-grade class were easily seized and controlled, although they also exhibited signs of rebellion. As the teacher backed into the corner, as the three chosen hosts approached her, a hot wave of rage went through every child in the room, for they all loved her and could not bear the thought of her possessed. Seed clamped down on them at once, hard, and their brief exertions of will faded like sparks on an arctic wind.

Under the guidance of Seed, Jack Caswell stepped in front of his wife. He tore the pointer out of her hand and threw it aside.

Seed burst from Jack's fingertips, seized Laura, and held her, although she struggled fiercely to pull free. Opening the mouth of its host, Seed shot forth a thick stalk, pierced the woman's breast, and surged into her, triumphant.

14

No!

Laura felt it slithering along her nervous system, questing coldly in her brain, and she denied it. With the iron determination that she had brought to her campaign to make Jack walk, with the unlimited patience that she always brought to the instruction of her students, with the unshakable sense of self-worth and individuality with which she faced every day of her life, she fought the thing at every turn. When it cast restraining bands of psychic energy around her mind, she snapped them and threw them off. When it tried to drag her into a dark place and imprison her there under psychic stones, she threw off those weights as well and soared to the surface. She sensed the thing's surprise, and she took advantage of its confusion, delving into *its* mind, learning about it. In an instant she realized that it dwelled in all the minds of its hosts simultaneously, so she reached out to Jack and found him—

—I love you, Jack, I love you more than life itself—

—and she tore at his mental bonds with all the enthusiasm that she had shown when assisting him in therapeutic exercises for his ruined legs. Questing outward across the psychic net by which Seed linked its hosts, she found Jamie Watley—

—You're a sweet kid, Jamie, the sweetest, and I've always wanted to tell you that it doesn't matter what kind of people your parents are, doesn't matter if they're selfish mean-spirited drunks; what matters is that you have the capacity to be far better than they are; you have the capacity to love and to learn and to know the joy of a fulfilling life—

—and Seed swarmed over her, trying to draw her consciousness back into her own body, out of the minds of the others. However, in spite of its billions of years of experience and its vast knowledge acquired from hundreds of doomed species, it found itself unequal to the task. Laura examined it and judged it inferior because it did not need love, could not give love. Its will was weaker than human will because humans could love, and in their love they found a reason to strive, a reason to seek order out of chaos, to make better lives for those whom they cherished. Love gave purpose to will and made it infinitely stronger. To some species, Seed might be a welcome master, offering the false security of a single purpose, a single law. But to humankind, Seed was anathema—

—Tommy, you can tear loose if you'll think of your sister Edna, because I know you love Edna more than anything; and you, Melissa, you must think of your father and mother because they love you so much, because they almost lost you when you were a baby (did you know that?) and losing you would have broken them; and you, Helen,

you're one heck of a little girl, and I couldn't love you more if you were my own, you have such a sweet concern for others, and I know you can throw this damn thing off because you're all love from head to toe; and you, Jane Halliwell, I know you love your son and your husband because your love for Richie is so evident in the self-confidence you've given him and in the manners and courtesy you've taught him; you, Jimmy Corman, oh, yes, you talk tough and you act tough, but I know how much you love your brother Harry and how sad it makes you that Harry was born with a deformed hand, and I know that if someone made fun of poor Harry's twisted hand, you'd fight him with every bit of strength you have, so turn that love for Harry against this thing, this Seed, and destroy it, don't let it have you because if it gets you then it'll get Harry too—

—and Laura walked into the room, among the possessed, touching them, hugging this one, lovingly squeezing the hand of the next one, looking into their eyes and using the power of love to bring them to her, out of their darkness and into the light with her.

15

AS HE SHATTERED THE BONDS THAT HELD HIM, AS HE CAST OFF SEED, Jamie Watley experienced a wave of dizziness and actually blacked out for an instant, not even long enough to collapse to the floor. Blackness flickered through him, and he swayed, but he came to his senses as his knees were buckling. He grabbed the edge of Mrs. Caswell's desk and steadied himself.

When he looked around the classroom, he saw the adults and the other children in similar shaky postures. Many were looking down in disgust, and Jamie saw that they were staring at the slick, mucus-wet black substance of Seed, which had been expelled from them and which writhed in pieces on the classroom floor.

Most of the alien tissue seemed to be dying, and a few pieces were actually decomposing with an awful stench. But suddenly one lump coalesced into the shape of a football. In seconds it formed a mottled blue-green-black shell, and as if bazooka-shot, it exploded through the ceiling of the room, showering them with plaster and bits of lath. It smashed through the roof of the one-story schoolhouse and disappeared straight up into the blue October sky.

16

TEACHERS AND KIDS CAME FROM ALL OVER THE BUILDING TO FIND OUT what had happened, and later the police arrived. The following day, both uniformed air-force officers and plainclothes government men visited the Caswell house among others. Throughout, Jack would not move far from Laura. He preferred to hold her—or at least her hand—and when they had to separate for a few minutes, he held fast to a mental picture of her, as if that image were a psychic totem that guaranteed her safe return.

Eventually the furor subsided, and the reporters went away, and life returned to normal—or as close to normal as it would ever be. By Christmas, Jack's nightmares began to diminish in both frequency and vividness, though he knew that he would need years to scrub out the residue of fear that was left from Seed's possession of him.

On Christmas Eve, sitting on the floor in front of the tree, sipping wine and eating walnuts, he and Laura exchanged gifts, for Christmas Day itself was always reserved for visiting their families. When the packages had been opened, they moved to a pair of armchairs in front of the fireplace.

After sitting quietly for a while, sipping at a final glass of wine and watching the flames, Laura said, "I've got one more gift that will have to be opened soon."

"One more? But I've nothing more for you."

"This is a gift for everyone," she said.

Her smile was so enigmatic that Jack was instantly intrigued. He leaned sideways in his chair and reached for her hand. "What're you being so mysterious about?"

"The thing healed you," she said.

His legs were propped on a hassock, as healthy and useful as they had been before his accident.

"At least some good came of it," he said.

"More than you know," she said. "During those awful moments when I was trying to expel the thing from my mind and body, while I was trying to get the kids to expel it from theirs, I was acutely aware of the creature's own mind. Heck, I was *within* its mind. And since I'd noticed that you were healed and figured the creature must have been responsible for knitting up your legs, I poked around in its thoughts to see how it had worked that miracle."

"You don't mean—"

"Wait," she said, pulling her hand from his. She slipped off her chair, dropped to her knees, leaned toward the fireplace, and thrust her right hand into the leaping flames.

Jack cried out, grabbed her, and pulled her back.

Grinning, Laura held up blistered fingers as raw as butchered beef, but even as Jack gasped in horror, he saw that her flesh was healing. In moments the blisters faded, the skin re-formed, and her hand was undamaged.

"The power's within all of us," she said. "We just have to learn how to use it. I've spent the past two months learning, and now I'm ready to teach others. You first, then my kids at school, then the whole darn world."

Jack stared at her in astonishment.

She laughed with delight and threw herself into his arms. "It's not easy to learn, Jackson. Oh, no! It's hard. It's hard. You don't know how many nights I've sat up while you slept, working at it, trying to apply what I learned from Seed. There were times when my head felt as if it would burst with the effort, and trying to master the healing talent leaves you physically exhausted in a way I've never been before. It hurts all the way down in your bones. There were times when I despaired. But I learned. And others can learn. No matter how hard it is, I know I can teach them. I know I can, Jack."

Regarding her with love but also with a new sense of wonder, Jack said, "Yeah, I know you can too. I know you can teach anything to anyone. You may be the greatest teacher who ever lived."

"Miss Attila the Hun," she said, and she kissed him.

DOWN IN THE DARKNESS

1

DARKNESS DWELLS WITHIN EVEN THE BEST OF US. IN THE WORST OF us, darkness not only dwells but reigns.

Although occasionally providing darkness with a habitat, I have never provided it with a kingdom. That's what I prefer to believe. I think of myself as a basically good man: a hard worker, a loving and faithful husband, a stern but doting father.

If I use the cellar again, however, I will no longer be able to pretend that I can suppress my own potential for evil. If I use the cellar again, I will exist in eternal moral eclipse and will never thereafter walk in the light.

But the temptation is great.

⊿ ▲ ⊧

I first discovered the cellar door two hours after we signed the final papers, delivered a cashier's check to the escrow company to pay for the house, and received the keys. It was in the kitchen, in the corner beyond the refrigerator: a raised-panel door, stained dark like all the others in the house, with a burnished-brass lever-action handle instead of a conventional knob. I stared in disbelief, for I was certain that the door had not been there before.

Initially, I thought I had found a pantry. When I opened it, I was startled to see steps leading down through deepening shadows into pitch blackness. A windowless basement.

In Southern California, nearly all houses—virtually everything from the cheaper tract crackerboxes to those in the multimillion-dollar range—are built on concrete slabs. They have no basements. For decades this has been considered prudent design. The land is frequently sandy, with little bedrock near the surface. In country subject to earthquakes and mudslides, a basement with concrete-block walls can be a point of structural weakness into which all rooms above might collapse if the giants in the earth wake and stretch.

Our new home was neither crackerbox nor mansion, but it had a cellar. The real-estate agent never mentioned it. Until now, we had never noticed it.

Peering down the steps, I was at first curious—then uneasy. A wall switch was set just inside the doorway. I clicked it up, down, up again. No light came on below.

Leaving the door open, I went looking for Carmen. She was in the master bathroom, hugging herself, grinning, admiring the handmade emerald-green ceramic tiles and the Sherle Wagner sinks with their gold-plated fixtures.

"Oh, Jess, isn't it beautiful? Isn't it grand? When I was a little girl, I never dreamed I'd live in a house like this. My best hope was for one of those cute bungalows from the forties. But this is a palace, and I'm not sure I know how to act like a queen."

"It's no palace," I said, putting an arm around her. "You've got to be a Rockefeller to afford a palace in Orange County. Anyway, so what if it was a palace—you've always had the style and bearing of a queen."

She stopped hugging herself and hugged me. "We've come a long way, haven't we?"

"And we're going even further, kid."

"I'm a little scared, you know?"

"Don't be silly."

"Jess, honey, I'm just a cook, a dishwasher, a pot scrubber, only one generation removed from a shack on the outskirts of Mexico City. We worked hard for this, sure, and a lot of years . . . but now that we're here, it seems to have happened overnight."

"Trust me, kid—you could hold your own in any gathering of society ladies from Newport Beach. You have natural-born class."

I thought: *God, I love her. Seventeen years of marriage, and she is still a girl to me, still fresh and surprising and sweet.*

"Hey," I said, "almost forgot. You know we have a cellar?"

She blinked at me.

"It's true," I said.

Smiling, waiting for the punch line, she said, "Yeah? And what's down there? The royal vaults with all the jewels? Maybe a dungeon?"

"Come see."

She followed me into the kitchen.

The door was gone.

Staring at the blank wall, I was for a moment icebound.

"Well?" she said. "What's the joke?"

I thawed enough to say, "No joke. There was . . . a door."

She pointed to the image of a kitchen window that was etched on the blank wall by the sun streaming through the glass. "You probably saw that. The square of sunlight coming through the window, falling on the wall. It's more or less in the shape of a door."

"No. No . . . there was . . ." Shaking my head, I put one hand on the sun-warmed plaster and lightly traced its contours, as if the seams of the door would be more apparent to the touch than to the eye.

Carmen frowned. "Jess, what's wrong?"

I looked at her and realized what she was thinking. This lovely house seemed too good to be true, and she was superstitious enough to wonder if such a great blessing could be enjoyed for long without fate throwing us a heavy weight of tragedy to balance the scales. An overworked husband, suffering from stress—or perhaps afflicted by a small brain tumor—beginning to see things that were not there, talking excitedly of nonexistent cellars . . . That was just the sort of nasty turn of events with which fate too frequently evened things out.

"You're right," I said. I forced a laugh but made it sound natural. "I saw the rectangle of light on the wall and thought it was a door. Didn't even look close. Just came running for you. Now, has this new-house business got me about as crazy as a monkey or what?"

She looked at me somberly, then matched my smile. "Crazy as a monkey. But then . . . you always were."

"Is that so?"

"My monkey," she said.

I said, "Ook, ook," and scratched under one arm.

I was glad I had not told her that I'd opened the door. Or that I had seen the steps beyond.

◁ ∧ ▷

The house in Laguna Beach had five large bedrooms, four baths, and a family room with a massive stone fireplace. It also had what they call an "entertainer's kitchen," which didn't mean that either Siegfried and Roy or Barbra Streisand performed there between Vegas engagements, but referred instead to the high quality and number of appliances: double ovens, two microwaves, a warming oven for muffins and rolls, a Jenn Air cooking center, two dishwashers, and a pair of Sub Zero refrigerators of sufficient size to serve a restaurant. Lots of immense windows let in the warm California sun and framed views of the lush landscaping—bougainvillea in shades of yellow and coral, red azaleas, impatiens, palms, two imposing Indian laurels—and the rolling hills beyond. In the distance, the sun-dappled water of the Pacific glimmered enticingly, like a great treasure of silver coins.

Though not a mansion, it was unquestionably a house that said, *The Gonzalez family has done well, has made a fine place for itself.* My folks would have been very proud.

Maria and Ramon, my parents, were Mexican immigrants who had scratched out a new life in *El Norte*, the promised land. They had given me, my brothers, and my sister everything that hard work and sacrifice could provide, and we four had all earned university scholarships. Now, one of my brothers was an attorney, the other a doctor, and my sister was chairperson of the Department of English at UCLA.

I had chosen a career in business. Carmen and I owned a restaurant, for which I provided the business expertise, for which she provided the exquisite and authentic Mexican recipes, and where we both worked twelve hours a day, seven days a week. As our three children reached adolescence, they took jobs with us as waiters. It was a family affair, and every year we became more prosperous, but it was never easy. America does not promise easy wealth, only opportunity. We seized the machine of opportunity and lubricated it with oceans of perspiration, and by the time we bought the house in Laguna Beach, we were able to pay cash. Jokingly, we gave the house a name: *Casa Sudor*—House of Sweat.

It was a huge home. And beautiful.

It had every amenity. Even a basement with a disappearing door.

The previous owner was one Mr. Nguyen Quang Phu. Our realtor—a sturdy, garrulous, middle-aged woman named Nancy Keefer—said Phu was a Vietnamese refugee, one of the courageous boat people who had fled months after the fall of Saigon. He was one of the fortunate who had survived the storms, the gunboats, and the pirates.

"He arrived in the U.S. with only three thousand dollars in gold coins and the will to make something of himself," Nancy Keefer told us when we first toured the house. "A charming man and a fabulous success. Really fabulous. He's pyramided that small bankroll into so many business interests, you wouldn't believe it, all in fourteen years! Fabulous story. He's built a new house, fourteen thousand square feet on two acres in North Tustin, it's just fabulous, really, it is, you should see it, you really should."

Carmen and I made an offer for Phu's old house, which was less than half the size of the one he had recently built, but which was a dream home to us. We dickered a bit but finally agreed on terms, and the closing was achieved in just ten days because we were paying cash, taking no mortgage.

The transfer of ownership was arranged without Nguyen Quang Phu and me coming face to face. This is not an unusual situation. Unlike some states, California does not require a formal closing ceremony with seller, buyer, and their attorneys gathered in one room.

Nevertheless, it was Nancy Keefer's policy to arrange a meeting between the buyer and seller at the house, within a day or two of the close of escrow. Although our new home was beautiful and in splendid repair, even the finest houses have quirks. Nancy believed it was always a good idea for the seller to walk the buyer through the place to point out which closet doors tended to slide off their tracks and which windows wept in a rainstorm. She arranged for Phu to meet me at the house on Wednesday, May fourteenth.

Monday, May twelfth, was the day we closed the deal. And that was the afternoon when, strolling through the empty house, I first saw the cellar door.

Tuesday morning, I returned to the house alone. I didn't tell Carmen where I was really going. She thought that I was at Horace Dalcoe's office, politely wrangling with that extortionist over his latest greedy demands.

Dalcoe owned the small open-air shopping center in which our restaurant was located, and he was surely the very man for whom the word "sleazeball" had been coined. Our lease, signed when Carmen and I were poorer and naive, gave him the right to approve even every minor change we made inside the premises. Therefore, six years after we opened, when we wanted to remodel the restaurant at a cost of two hundred thousand dollars—which would have been an improvement to *his* property—we were required to give Dalcoe ten thousand in tax-free cash, under the table, for his okay. When I bought out the lease of the stationery store next door to expand into their quarters, Dalcoe insisted upon a steep cash payment for his approval. He was interested not only in large lumps of sugar but in tiny grains of it as well; when I put a new and more attractive set of front doors on the place, Dalcoe wanted a lousy two hundred bucks under the table to sign off on that small job.

Now, we wished to replace our old sign with a new and better one, and I was negotiating a bribe with Dalcoe. He was unaware that I had discovered that he didn't own the land on which his own little shopping center stood; he had taken a ninety-nine-year lease on the parcel twenty years ago, and he felt secure. At the same time that I was working out a new bribe with him, I was secretly negotiating a purchase of the land, after which Dalcoe would discover that, while he might have a stranglehold on me by virtue of my lease, I would have a stranglehold on him because of *his* lease. He still thought of me as an ignorant Mex, maybe second generation but Mex just the same; he thought I'd had a little luck in the restaurant business, luck and nothing more, and he gave me no credit for intelligence or savvy. It was not going to be exactly a case of the little fish swallowing the big one, but I expected to arrange a satisfactory stalemate that would leave him furious and impotent.

These complex machinations, which had been continuing for some time, gave me a believable excuse for my absence from the restaurant Tuesday morning. I'd be bargaining with Dalcoe at his office, I told Carmen. In fact, I went directly to the new house, feeling guilty about having lied to her.

When I stepped into the kitchen, the door was where I had seen it the previous day. No rectangle of sunlight. No mere illusion. A real door.

I worked the lever-action handle.

Beyond the threshold, steps led down into deepening shadows.

"What the hell?" I said. My voice echoed back to me as if it had bounced off a wall a thousand miles away.

The switch still did not work.

I had brought a flashlight. I snapped it on.

I crossed the threshold.

The wooden landing creaked loudly, because the boards were old, unpainted, scarred. Mottled with gray and yellow stains, webbed with hairline cracks, the plaster walls looked as if they were much older than the rest of the house. The cellar clearly did not belong in this structure, was not an integral part of it.

I moved off the landing onto the first step.

A frightening possibility occurred to me. What if a draft pushed the door shut behind me—and then the door vanished as it had done yesterday, leaving me trapped in the cellar?

I retreated in search of something with which to brace the door. The house contained no furniture, but in the garage I found a length of two-by-four that did the job.

Standing on the top step once more, I shone the flashlight down, but the beam did not reach nearly as far as it should have. I could not see the cellar floor. The tar-black murk below was unnaturally deep. This darkness was not merely an absence of light but seemed to possess substance, texture, and weight, as if the lower chamber was filled with a pool of oil. Like a sponge, the darkness absorbed the light, and only twelve steps were revealed in the pale beam before it faded into the gloom.

I descended two steps, and two more steps appeared at the far reach of the light. I eased down four additional steps, and four more came into view below.

Six steps behind, one under my feet, and twelve ahead—nineteen so far.

How many steps would I expect to find in an ordinary basement? Ten? Twelve?

Not this many, surely.

Quickly, quietly, I descended six steps. When I stopped, twelve steps were illuminated ahead of me. Dry, aged boards. Nailheads gleamed here and there. The same mottled walls.

Unnerved, I looked back up at the door, which was thirteen steps and one landing above me. The sunlight in the kitchen looked warm, inviting—and more distant than it should have been.

My hands had begun to sweat. I switched the flashlight from one hand to the other, blotting my palms on my slacks.

The air had a vague lime odor and an even fainter underlying scent of mold and corruption.

I hurriedly and noisily descended six more steps, then eight more, then another eight, then six. Now forty-one rose at my back—and twelve were still illuminated below me.

Each of the steep steps was about ten inches high, which meant that I had gone approximately three stories underground. No ordinary basement had such a long flight of stairs.

I told myself that this might be a bomb shelter, but I knew that it was not.

As yet, I had no thought of turning back. This was our house, damn it, for which we had paid a small fortune in money and a larger fortune in time and sweat, and we could not live in it with such a mystery beneath our feet, unexplored. Besides, when I was twenty-two and twenty-three, far from home and in the hands of enemies, I had known two years of terror so constant and intense that my tolerance for fear was higher than that of most men.

One hundred steps farther, I stopped again because I figured I was ten stories below ground level, which was a milestone requiring some contemplation. Turning and peering up, I saw the light at the open kitchen door far above me, an opalescent rectangle that appeared to be one-quarter the size of a postage stamp.

Looking down, I studied the eight bare wooden steps illuminated ahead of me—eight, not the usual twelve. As I had gone deeper, the flashlight had become less effective. The batteries were not growing weak; the problem was nothing as simple or explicable as that. Where it passed through the lens, the beam was as crisp and bright as ever. But the darkness ahead was somehow thicker, *hun-*

grier, and it absorbed the light in a shorter distance than it had done farther up.

The air still smelled vaguely of lime, though the scent of decay was now nearly the equal of that more pleasant odor.

This subterranean world had been preternaturally quiet except for my own footsteps and increasingly heavier breathing. Pausing at the ten-story point, however, I thought I heard something below. I held my breath, stood motionless, and listened. I was half sure that I detected strange, furtive sounds a long way off—whispering and oily squelching noises—but I could not be certain. They were faint and short-lived. I could have been imagining them.

After descending ten more steps, I came to a landing at last, where I discovered opposing archways in the walls of the stairwell. Both openings were doorless and unornamented, and my light revealed a short stone corridor beyond each. Stepping through the arch on my left, I followed the narrow passage for perhaps fifteen feet, where it ended at the head of another staircase, which went down at a right angle to the stairs that I had just left.

Here, the odor of decay was stronger. It was reminiscent of the pungent fumes of rotting vegetable matter.

The stink was like a spade, turning up long-buried memories. I had encountered precisely this stench before, in the place where I had been imprisoned during my twenty-second and twenty-third years. There, they had sometimes served meals largely composed of rotting vegetables—mostly turnips, sweet potatoes, and other tubers. Worse, the garbage that we wouldn't eat was thrown into the sweatbox, a tin-roofed pit in the ground where recalcitrant prisoners were punished with solitary confinement. In that filthy hole, I was forced to sit in foot-deep slime reeking so strongly of decay that, in heat-induced delusion, I sometimes became convinced that I was dead already and that what I smelled was the relentlessly progressing corruption of my own lifeless flesh.

"What's going on?" I asked, expecting and receiving no answer.

Returning to the main stairs, I passed through the archway on the right. At the end of that passage, a second set of branching stairs also led down. From tenebrous depths, a different rancidity arose, and I recognized this one as well: decomposing fish heads.

Not just decomposing fish but, specifically, fish *heads*—like those that the guards had sometimes put in our soup. Grinning, they stood and watched us as we greedily sucked up the broth. We gagged on it but were often too hungry to pour it on the ground in protest. Sometimes, starving, we choked down the repulsive fish heads as well, which was what the guards most wanted to see. They were unfailingly amused by our disgust—and especially by our self-disgust.

I hurriedly returned to the main stairwell. I stood on the ten-story-deep landing, shuddering uncontrollably, trying to shake off those unbidden memories.

By now, I was half convinced that I was dreaming or that I did, indeed, have a brain tumor which, by exerting pressure on surrounding cerebral tissue, was the cause of these hallucinations.

I continued downward and noticed that step by step the range of my flashlight was decreasing. Now I could see only seven steps ahead . . . six . . . five . . . four. . . .

Suddenly, the impenetrable darkness was only two feet in front of me, a black mass that seemed to throb in expectation of my final advance into its embrace. It seemed *alive*.

Yet I hadn't reached the foot of the stairs, for I heard those whisperings again, far below, and the oily, oozing sound that brought gooseflesh to my arms.

I reached forward with one trembling hand. It disappeared into the darkness, which was bitterly cold.

My heart hammered and my mouth was suddenly dry and sour. I let out a childlike cry, and I fled back to the kitchen and the light.

2

THAT EVENING AT THE RESTAURANT, I GREETED THE GUESTS AND SEATED them. Even after all these years, I spend most nights at the front door, meeting people, playing the host. Usually, I enjoy it. Many customers have been coming to us for a decade; they are honorary members of the family, old friends. But that night, my heart was not in it, and several people asked me if I was feeling well.

Tom Gatlin, my accountant, stopped by for dinner with his wife.

He said, "Jess, you're *gray*, for God's sake. You're three years overdue for a vacation, my friend. What's the point of piling up the money if you never take time to enjoy it?"

Fortunately, the restaurant staff we have assembled is first-rate. In addition to Carmen and me and our kids—Stacy, Heather, and young Joe—there are twenty-two employees, and every one of them knows his job and performs it well. Although I was not at my best, there were others to take up the slack.

Stacy, Heather, and Joe. Very *American* names. Funny. My mother and father, being immigrants, clung to the world they left by giving all their children traditional Mexican names. Carmen's folks were the same way: Her two brothers are Juan and José, and her sister's name is Evalina. My name actually was Jesus Gonzalez. Jesus is a common name in Mexico, but I had it changed to Jess years ago, though by doing so I hurt my parents. (The Spanish pronunciation is "Hay-seuss," although most North Americans pronounce it as if referring to the Christian savior. There's just no way you can be regarded as either one of the guys or a serious businessman when burdened with such an exotic moniker.) It's interesting how the children of immigrants, second-generation Americans like Carmen and me, usually give their own kids the most popular current American names, as if trying to conceal how recently our ancestors got off the boat— or in this case, crossed the Rio Grande. Stacy, Heather, and Joe.

Just as there are no more fervent Christians than those recently converted to the faith, there are no more ardent Americans than those whose claim to citizenship begins with themselves or their parents. We want so desperately to be part of this great, huge, crazy country. Unlike some whose roots go back generations, we understand what a blessing it is to live beneath the stars and stripes. We also know that a price must be paid for the blessing, and that sometimes it's high. Partly, the cost is in leaving behind everything we once were. Sometimes, however, there is a more painful price inflicted, as I well know.

I served in Vietnam.

I was under fire. I killed the enemy.

And I was a prisoner of war.

That was where I ate soup with rotting fish heads.

That was part of the price I paid.

Now, thinking about the impossible cellar beneath our new house, remembering the smells of the prison camp that had wafted out of the darkness at the bottom of those stairs, I began to wonder if I was still paying the price. I had come home sixteen years ago— gaunt, half my teeth rotten. I'd been starved and tortured but not broken. There had been nightmares for years, but I hadn't needed therapy. I had come through all right, as had many of the guys in those North Vietnamese hellholes. Badly bent, scarred, splintered— but, damn it, not broken. Somewhere, I had lost my Catholicism, but that had seemed a negligible loss at the time. Year by year, I had put the experience behind me. Part of the price. Part of what we pay for being where we are. Forget it. Over. Done. And it *had* seemed behind me. Until now. The cellar could not possibly be real, which meant that I must be having vivid hallucinations. Could it be that, after so long a time, the fiercely repressed emotional trauma of imprisonment and torture were working profound changes in me, that I had been ignoring the problem rather than dealing with it, and that now it was going to drive me mad?

If that was the case, I wondered what had suddenly triggered my mental collapse. Was it that we had bought a house from a Vietnamese refugee? That seemed too small a thing to have been the trigger. I couldn't see how the seller's original nationality alone could have caused wires to cross in my subconscious, shorting out the system, blowing fuses. On the other hand, if my peace with the memories of Vietnam and my sanity were only as stable as a house of cards, the barest breath might demolish me.

Damn it, I didn't *feel* insane. I felt stable—frightened but firmly in control. The most reasonable explanation for the cellar was hallucination. But I was largely convinced that the impossible subterranean staircases were real and that the disconnection from reality was external rather than internal.

At eight o'clock, Horace Dalcoe arrived for dinner with a party of seven, which almost took my mind off the cellar. As holder of our lease, he believes that he should never pay a cent for dinner in our establishment. If we didn't comp him and his friends, he would find ways to make us miserable, so we oblige. He never says thank you, and he usually finds something to complain about.

That Tuesday night, he complained about the margaritas—not enough tequila, he said. He fussed about the corn chips—not crisp enough, he said. And he groused about the albondigas soup—not nearly enough meatballs, he said.

I wanted to throttle the bastard. Instead, I brought margaritas with more tequila—enough to burn an alarming number of brain cells per minute—and new corn chips, and a bowl of meatballs to supplement the already meat-rich soup.

That night, in bed, thinking about Dalcoe, I wondered what would happen to him if I invited him to our new house, pushed him into the cellar, closed and latched the door, and left him down there for a while. I had the bizarre but unshakable feeling that something lived deep in the basement . . . something that had been only a few feet from me in the impenetrable darkness that had devoured the flashlight beam. If something *was* down there, it would climb the stairs to get Dalcoe. Then he would be no more trouble to us.

I did not sleep well that night.

3

WEDNESDAY MORNING, MAY FOURTEENTH, I RETURNED TO THE HOUSE to walk through it with the former owner, Nguyen Quang Phu. I arrived an hour ahead of our appointment, in case the cellar door was visible again.

It was.

Suddenly I felt that I should turn my back on the door, walk away, ignore it. I sensed that I could make it go away forever if only I refused to open it. And I knew—without knowing *how* I knew—that not only my body but my soul was at risk if I couldn't resist the temptation to explore those lower realms.

I braced the door open with the two-by-four.

I went down into the darkness with the flashlight.

More than ten stories underground, I stopped on the landing with the flanking archways. The stink of rotting vegetables came from the branching stairwell to the left; the foul aroma of rancid fish heads arose from the right.

I pressed on and found that the peculiarly substantive darkness did not thicken as quickly as it had done yesterday. I was able to go deeper than before, as if the darkness knew me better now and welcomed me into more intimate regions of its domain.

After an additional fifty or sixty steps, I came to another landing. As at the landing above, on each side an archway offered a change of direction.

On the left, I found another short hall leading to another set of stairs that descended into pulsing, shifting, malignant blackness as impervious to light as a pool of oil. Indeed, the beam of my flash did not fade into that dense gloom but actually terminated in a circle of reflected light, as if it had fallen on a wall, and the churning blackness glistened slightly like molten tar. It was a thing of great power, enormously repulsive. Yet I knew that it was not merely oil or any other liquid, but was instead the essence of all darkness: a syrupy distillation of a million nights, a billion shadows. Darkness is a condition, not a substance, and therefore cannot be distilled. Yet here was that impossible extract, ancient and pure: concentrate of night, the vast blackness of interstellar space decocted until it had been rendered into an oozing sludge. And it was evil.

I backed away and returned to the main stairwell. I did not inspect the branching stairs beyond the archway on the right, because I knew that I would find the same malevolent distillate waiting down there, slowly churning, churning.

In the main stairwell, I descended only a little farther before encountering the same foul presence. It rose like a wall in front of me, or like a frozen tide. I stood two steps from it, shaking uncontrollably with fear.

I reached forward.

I put a hand against the pulsing mass of blackness.

It was cold.

I reached forward a bit farther. My hand disappeared to the wrist. The darkness was so solid, so clearly defined, that my wrist looked like an amputee's stump; a sharp line marked the point at which my hand vanished into the tar-dense mass.

Panicked, I jerked back. My hand had not been amputated after all. It was still attached to my arm. I wiggled my fingers.

Looking up from my hand, straight into the gelid darkness before me, I suddenly knew that it was *aware* of me. I had sensed that it was evil, yet somehow I had not thought of it as *conscious*. Staring into its featureless countenance, I felt that it was welcoming me to the cellar that I had not yet quite reached, to the chambers below, which were still countless steps beneath me. I was being invited to embrace darkness, to step entirely across the threshold into the gloom where my hand had gone, and for a moment I was overcome with a longing to do precisely that, to move out of the light, down, down.

Then I thought of Carmen. And my daughters—Heather and Stacy. My son, Joe. All of the people I loved and who loved me. The spell was instantly broken. The mesmeric attraction of the darkness lost its hold on me, and I turned and ran up to the bright kitchen, my footsteps booming in the narrow stairwell.

Sun streamed through the big windows.

I pulled the two-by-four out of the way, slammed the cellar door. I willed it to vanish, but it remained.

"I'm nuts," I said aloud. "Stark raving crazy."

But I knew that I was sane.

It was the world that had gone mad, not I.

Twenty minutes later, Nguyen Quang Phu arrived, as scheduled, to explain all the peculiarities of the house that we had bought from him. I met him at the front door, and the moment that I saw him, I knew why the impossible cellar had appeared and what purpose it was meant to serve.

"Mr. Gonzalez?" he asked.

"Yes."

"I am Nguyen Quang Phu."

He was not merely Nguyen Quang Phu. He was also the torture master.

In Vietnam, he had ordered me strapped to a bench and had, for more than an hour, beaten the soles of my feet with a wooden baton—until each blow jarred through the bones of my legs and hips, through my rib cage, up my spine, to the top of my skull, which felt as if it might explode. He had ordered me bound hand and foot and submerged me in a tank of water fouled with urine from other prisoners who had been subjected to the ordeal before me; just when I thought I could hold my breath no longer, when my lungs were burning, when my ears were ringing, when my heart was thundering, when every fiber of my being strained toward death, I was hoisted into the air and allowed a few breaths before being plunged beneath the surface again. He had ordered that wires be attached to my genitals, and he had given me countless jolts of electricity. Helpless, I had watched him beat a friend of mine to death, and I'd seen him tear out another friend's eye with a stiletto merely for cursing the soldier who had served him yet another bowl of weevil-infested rice.

I had absolutely no doubt of his identity. The memory of the torture master's face was branded forever in my mind, burned into the very tissue of my brain by the worst heat of all—hatred. And he had aged much better than I had. He looked only two or three years older than when I'd last seen him.

"Pleased to meet you," I said.

"Likewise," he said as I ushered him into the house.

His voice was as memorable as his face: soft, low, and somehow cold—the voice a snake might have if serpents could speak.

We shook hands.

He was five ten, tall for a Vietnamese. He had a long face with prominent cheekbones, a sharp nose, a thin mouth, and a delicate jaw. His eyes were deeply set—and as strange as they had been in Nam.

In that prison camp, I had not known his name. Perhaps it had been Nguyen Quang Phu. Or perhaps that was a false identity that he had assumed when he sought asylum in the United States.

"You have bought a wonderful house," he said.

"We like it very much," I said.

"I was happy here," he said, smiling, nodding, looking around at the empty living room. "Very happy."

Why had he left Nam? He had been on the winning side. Well, maybe he'd fallen out with some of his comrades. Or perhaps the state had assigned him to hard farm labor or to the mines or to some other task that he knew would destroy his health and kill him before his time. Perhaps he had gone to sea in a small boat when the state no longer chose to give him a position of high authority.

The reason for his emigration was of no importance to me. All that mattered was that he was here.

The moment I saw him and realized who he was, I knew that he would not leave the house alive. I would never permit his escape.

"There's not much to point out," he said. "There's one drawer in the master-bathroom cabinets that runs off the track now and then.

And the pull-down attic stairs in the closet have a small problem sometimes, but that's easily remedied. I'll show you."

"I'd appreciate that."

He did not recognize me.

I suppose he'd tortured too many men to be able to recall any single victim of his sadistic urges. All prisoners who suffered and died at his hands had probably blurred into one faceless target. The torturer had cared nothing about the *individual* to whom he'd given an advance taste of Hell. To Nguyen Quang Phu, each man on the rack was the same as the one before, prized not for his unique qualities but for his ability to scream and bleed, for his eagerness to grovel at the feet of his tormentor.

As he led me through the house, he also gave me the names of reliable plumbers and electricians and air-conditioner repairmen in the neighborhood, plus the name of the artisan who had created the stained-glass windows in two rooms. "If one should be badly damaged, you'll want it repaired by the man who made it."

I will never know how I restrained myself from attacking him with my bare hands. More incredible still: Neither my face nor my voice revealed my inner tension. He was utterly unaware of the danger into which he had stepped.

In the kitchen, after he had shown me the unusual placement of the restart switch on the garbage disposal beneath the sink, I asked him if, during rainstorms, there was a problem with seepage in the cellar.

He blinked at me. His soft, cold voice rose slightly: "Cellar? Oh, but there is no cellar."

Pretending surprise, I said, "Well, there sure enough is. Right over there's the door."

He stared in disbelief.

He saw it too.

I interpreted his ability to see the door as a sign that destiny was being served here and that I would be doing nothing wrong if I simply assisted fate.

Retrieving the flashlight from the counter, I opened the door.

Protesting that no such door had existed while he had lived in the house, the torture master moved past me in a state of high astonishment and curiosity. He went through the door, onto the upper landing.

"Light switch doesn't work," I said, crowding in behind him, pointing the flashlight down past him. "But we'll see well enough with this."

"But . . . where . . . how . . . ?"

"You don't really mean you never noticed the cellar?" I said, forcing a laugh. "Come now. Are you joking with me or what?"

As if weightless with amazement, he drifted downward from one step to the next.

I followed close behind.

Soon, he knew that something was terribly wrong, for the steps went on too far without any sign of the cellar floor. He stopped, began to turn, and said, "This is strange. What's going on here? What on earth are you—"

"Go on," I said harshly. "Down. Go down, you bastard."

He tried to push past me toward the open door above.

I knocked him backward down the stairs. Screaming, he tumbled all the way to the first landing and the flanking archways. When I reached him, I saw that he was dazed and suffering considerable pain. He keened in misery. His lower lip had split; blood trickled down his chin. He'd skinned the palm of his right hand. I think his arm was broken.

Weeping, cradling his arm, he looked up at me—pain racked, afraid, confused.

I hated myself for what I was doing.

But I hated him more.

"In the camp," I said, "we called you The Snake. I know you. Oh, yes, I know you. You were the torture master."

"Oh, God," he said.

He neither asked what I was talking about nor attempted to deny it. He knew who he was, what he was, and he knew what would become of him.

"Those eyes," I said, shaking with fury now. "That voice. The Snake. A repulsive, belly-crawling snake. Contemptible. But very, very dangerous."

Briefly we were silent. In my case, at least, I was temporarily speechless, because I stood in awe of the profound machinery of fate which, in its slow-working and laborious fashion, had brought us together at this time and place.

From down in the darkness, a noise arose: sibilant whispers, a wet oozing sound that made me shudder. Millennial darkness was on the move, surging upward, the embodiment of endless night, cold and deep—and hungry.

The torture master, reduced to the role of victim, gazed around in fear and bewilderment, through one archway and the other, then down the stairs that continued from the landing on which he sprawled. His anxiety was so great that it drove out his pain; he no longer wept or made the keening noise. "What . . . what *is* this place?"

"It's where you belong," I said.

I turned from him and climbed the steps. I did not stop or look back. I left the flashlight with him because I wanted him to see the thing that came for him.

(Darkness dwells within us all.)

"Wait!" he called after me.

I did not pause.

"What's that sound?" he asked.

I kept climbing.

"What's going to happen to me?"

"I don't know," I told him. "But whatever it is . . . it'll be what you deserve."

Anger finally stirred in him. "You're not my judge!"

"Oh yes I am."

At the top, I stepped into the kitchen and closed the door behind me. It had no lock. I leaned against it, trembling.

Apparently Phu saw something ascending from the stairwell below him, for he wailed in terror and clambered up the steps.

Hearing him approach, I leaned hard against the door.

He pounded on the other side. "Please. Please, no. Please, for God's sake, no, for God's sake, please!"

I had heard my army buddies begging with that same desperation when the merciless torture master had forced rusty needles under their fingernails. I dwelt on those images of horror, which once I had thought I'd put behind me, and they gave me the will to resist Phu's pathetic pleas.

In addition to his voice, I heard the sludge-thick darkness rising behind him, cold lava flowing uphill: wet sounds, and that sinister whispering.

The torture master stopped pounding on the door and let out a scream that told me the darkness had seized him.

A great weight fell against the door for a moment, then was withdrawn.

The torture master's shrill cries rose and fell and rose again, and with each bloodcurdling cycle of screams, his terror was more acute. From the sound of his voice, from the hollow booming of his feet striking the steps and kicking the walls, I could tell that he was being dragged down.

I had broken into a sweat.

I could not get my breath.

Suddenly I tore open the door and plunged across the threshold, onto the landing. I think that I genuinely intended to pull him into the kitchen and save him after all. I can't say for sure. What I saw in the stairwell, only a few steps below, was so shocking that I froze—and did nothing.

The torture master hadn't been seized by the darkness itself but by two skeletally thin men who reached out of that ceaselessly churning mass of blackness. Dead men. I recognized them. They were American soldiers who had died in the camp at the hands of the torture master while I had been there. Neither of them had been friends of mine, and in fact they had both been hard cases themselves, bad men who had *enjoyed* the war before they had been captured and imprisoned by the Vietcong, the rare and hateful kind who liked killing and who engaged in black-market profiteering during their off-duty hours. Their eyes were icy, opaque. When they opened their mouths to speak to me, no words came forth, only a soft hissing and a faraway whimpering that led me to believe that those noises were coming not from their bodies but from their souls—souls chained in the cellar far below. They were straining out of the oozing distillate of darkness, unable to escape it entirely, revealed only to the extent required to grasp Nguyen Quang Phu by both arms and legs.

As I watched, they drew him screaming into that thick decoction of night that had become their eternal home. When the three of them vanished into the throbbing gloom, that rippling tarry mass flowed backward, away from me. Steps came into sight like swards of a beach appearing as the tide withdraws.

I stumbled out of the stairwell, across the kitchen to the sink. I hung my head and vomited. Ran the water. Splashed my face. Rinsed my mouth. Leaned against the counter, gasping.

When at last I turned, I saw that the cellar door had vanished. The darkness had wanted the torture master. That's why the door had appeared, why a way had opened into . . . into the place below. It had wanted the torture master so badly that it couldn't wait to claim him in the natural course of events, upon his predestined death, so it had opened a door into this world and had swallowed him. Now it had him, and my encounter with the supernatural was surely at an end.

That's what I thought.

I simply did not understand.

God help me, I did not understand.

4

NGUYEN QUANG PHU'S CAR—A NEW WHITE MERCEDES—WAS PARKED in the driveway, which is rather secluded. I got in without being observed and drove the car away, abandoning it in a parking lot that served a public beach. I walked the few miles back to the house, and later, when Phu's disappearance became a matter for the police, I claimed that he had never kept our appointment. I was believed. They were not suspicious of me, for I am a leading citizen, a man of some accomplishment, and in possession of a fine reputation.

During the next three weeks, the cellar door did not reappear. I didn't expect ever to be entirely comfortable in our new dream house, but gradually the worst of my dread faded and I no longer avoided entering the kitchen.

I'd had a head-on collision with the supernatural, but there was little or no chance of another encounter. A lot of people see one ghost sometime in their lives, are caught up in one paranormal event that leaves them shaken and in doubt about the true nature of reality, but they have no further occult experiences. I was sure that I would never see the cellar door again.

Then, Horace Dalcoe, holder of our restaurant's lease and loud complainer about albondigas soup, discovered that I was negotiating secretly to buy the property that *he* had leased for his shopping center, and he struck back. Hard. He has political connections. I suppose he encountered little difficulty getting the health inspector to slap us with citations for nonexistent violations of the public code. We have always run an immaculate restaurant; our own standards for food handling and cleanliness have always exceeded those of the health department. Therefore, Carmen and I decided to take the matter to court rather than pay the fines—which was when we got hit with a citation for fire-code violations. And when we announced our intention of seeking a retraction of *those* unjust charges, someone broke in to the restaurant at three o'clock on a Thursday morning and vandalized the place, doing over fifty thousand dollars worth of damage.

I realized that I might win one or all of these battles but still lose the war. If I had been able to adopt Horace Dalcoe's scurrilous tactics, if I had been able to resort to bribing public officials and hiring thugs, I could have fought back in a way that he would have understood, and he might have called a truce. Though I wasn't without the stain of sin on my soul, I was nonetheless unable to lower myself to Dalcoe's level.

Maybe my reluctance to play rough and dirty was more a matter of pride than of genuine honesty or honor, though I would prefer to believe better of myself.

Yesterday morning (as I write this in the diary of damnation that I have begun to keep), I went to see Dalcoe at his plush office. I humbled myself before him and agreed to abandon my efforts to buy the leased property on which his small shopping center stands. I also agreed to pay him three thousand in cash, under the table, for being permitted to erect a larger, more attractive sign for the restaurant.

He was smug, condescending, infuriating. He kept me there for more than an hour, though our business could have been concluded in ten minutes, because he relished my humiliation.

Last night, I could not sleep. The bed was comfortable, and the house was silent, and the air was pleasantly cool—all conditions for easy, deep sleep—but I could not stop brooding about Horace Dalcoe. The thought of being under his thumb for the foreseeable future was more than I could bear. I repeatedly turned the situation over in my mind, searching for a handle, for a way to obtain an advantage over him before he realized what I was doing, but no brilliant ploys occurred to me.

Finally, I slipped out of bed without waking Carmen, and I went downstairs to get a glass of milk, hopeful that a calcium fix would sedate me. When I entered the kitchen, still thinking of Dalcoe, the cellar door was there again.

Staring at it, I was very afraid, for I knew what its timely reappearance meant. I needed to deal with Horace Dalcoe, and I was being provided with a final solution to the problem. Invite Dalcoe to the house on one pretext or another. Show him the cellar. And let the darkness have him.

I opened the door.

I peered down the steps at the blackness below.

Long-dead prisoners, victims of torture, had been waiting for Nguyen Quang Phu. What would be waiting down there to seize Dalcoe?

I shuddered.

Not for Dalcoe.

I shuddered for me.

Suddenly I understood that the darkness below wanted *me* more than it wanted Phu the torture master or Horace Dalcoe. Neither of those men was much of a prize. They were destined for Hell anyway. If I had not escorted Phu into the cellar, the darkness would have had him sooner or later, when at last death visited him. Likewise, Dalcoe would wind up in the depths of Gehenna upon his own death. But by hurrying them along to their ultimate destination, I would be surrendering to the dark impulses within me and would, thereby, be putting my own soul in jeopardy.

Staring down the cellar stairs, I heard the darkness calling my name, welcoming me, offering me eternal communion. Its whispery voice was seductive. Its promises were sweet. The fate of my soul was still undecided, and the darkness saw the possibility of a small triumph in claiming me.

I sensed that I was not yet sufficiently corrupted to *belong* down in the darkness. What I had done to Phu might be seen as the mere enactment of long-overdue justice, for he was a man who deserved no rewards in either this world or the next. And allowing Dalcoe to proceed to his predestined doom ahead of schedule would probably not condemn me to Perdition.

But whom might I be tempted to lure to the cellar after Horace Dalcoe? How many and how often? Each time, the option would get easier to take. Sooner or later, I would find myself using the cellar to rid myself of people who were only minor nuisances. Some of them might be borderline cases, people deserving of Hell but with a chance of salvation, and by hurrying them along, I would be denying them the opportunity to mend their ways and remake their lives. Their damnation would be partly my responsibility. Then I too would be lost . . . and the darkness would rise up the stairs and come into the house and take me when it wished.

Below, that sludge-thick distillation of a billion moonless nights whispered to me, whispered.

I stepped back and closed the door.

It did not vanish.

Dalcoe, I thought desperately, *why have you been such a bastard? Why have you made me hate you?*

Darkness dwells within even the best of us. In the worst of us, darkness not only dwells but reigns.

I am a good man. A hard worker. A loving and faithful husband. A stern but doting father. A good man.

Yet I have human failings—not the least of which is a taste for vengeance. Part of the price that I have paid is the death of my innocence in Vietnam. There, I learned that great evil exists in the world, not in the abstract but in the flesh, and when evil men tortured me, I was contaminated by the contact. I developed a thirst for vengeance.

I tell myself that I dare not succumb to the easy solutions offered by the cellar. Where would it stop? Someday, after sending a score of men and women into the lightless chamber below, I would be so thoroughly corrupted that it would be easy to use the cellar for what had previously seemed unthinkable. For instance, what if Carmen and I had an argument? Would I devolve to the point where I could ask her to explore those lower regions with me? What if my children displeased me as, God knows, children frequently do? Where would I draw the line? And would the line be constantly redrawn?

I am a good man.

Although occasionally providing darkness with a habitat, I have never provided it with a kingdom.

I am a good man.

But the temptation is great.

I have begun to prepare a list of people who have, at one time or another, made my life difficult. I don't intend to do anything about them, of course. The list is merely a game. I will make it and then tear it to pieces and flush the pieces down the toilet.

I am a good man.

This list means nothing.

The cellar door will stay closed forever.

I will not open it again.

I swear by all that's holy.

I am a good man.

The list is longer than I had expected.

OLLIE'S HANDS

THE JULY NIGHT WAS HOT. THE AIR AGAINST OLLIE'S PALMS MADE HIM aware of the discomfort of the city's sweltering residents: millions of people wishing for winter.

Even in the cruelest weather, however, even on a bitterly cold night filled with dry January wind, Ollie's hands would have been soft, moist, warm—and sensitive. His thin fingers were tapered in an extraordinary manner. When he gripped anything, his fingers seemed to fuse with the surface of the object. When he let it go, the release was like a sigh.

Every night, regardless of the season, Ollie visited the unlighted alleyway behind Staznik's Restaurant, where he searched for the accidentally discarded silverware in the three large overflowing garbage bins. Because Staznik himself believed in quality, and because his prices were high, the tableware was expensive enough to make Ollie's undignified rooting worthwhile. Every two weeks, he managed to sense out enough pieces to constitute a matched set, which he sold to one of several used-furniture stores in exchange for wine money.

Recovered tableware was only one source of his funds. In his own way, Ollie was a clever man.

On that Tuesday night early in July, his cleverness was tested to its limits. When he made his nightly trip into the alley to sense out the knives, forks, and spoons, he found instead the unconscious girl.

She was lying against the last Dumpster, face toward the brick wall, eyes closed, hands drawn across her small breasts as if she were a sleeping child. Her cheap, tight, short dress revealed that she was no child; her pale flesh glimmered like a soft flame viewed through smoked glass. Otherwise, Ollie could not see much of her.

"Miss?" he asked, leaning toward her.

She didn't respond. She didn't move.

He knelt beside her, shook her, but was unable to wake her. When he rolled her onto her back to look at her face, something rattled. Striking a match, he discovered that she had been curled against the paraphernalia of a junkie's habit: syringe, charred spoon, metal cup, half-used candle, several packets of white powder wrapped in plastic and then in foil.

He might have left her and continued searching for spoons—he didn't like or understand snowbirds, being strictly a man of spirits himself—but the match flame revealed her face and thereby ensured his concern. She had a broad forehead, well-set eyes, a pert and freckled nose, full lips that somehow promised both erotic pleasure and childlike innocence. When the match went out and the darkness rushed in again, Ollie knew that he could not leave her there, for she was the most beautiful person he had ever seen.

"Miss?" he asked, shaking her shoulder again.

She did not respond.

He looked toward both ends of the alleyway, but he did not see anyone who might misinterpret his intentions. Thus assured, he bent close to her and felt for a heartbeat, found a weak one, held his moist palm close to her nostrils, and detected the barest exhalation of warm breath. She was alive.

He stood and wiped his palms on his rumpled, dirty trousers, cast one mournful glance at the unplumbed bins of waste, then lifted her. She weighed little, and he carried her in his arms like a groom crossing the threshold with his bride, although he gave no thought to the carnal aspect of the ritual. Heart pounding with the unaccustomed exertion, he took her to the far end of the alley, hurried across the deserted avenue, and disappeared into the mouth of another unlighted backstreet.

Ten minutes later he unlocked the door of his basement room and carried her inside. He put her on the bed, locked the door, and switched on a low-watt bulb in a newspaper-shaded junk lamp beside the bed. She was still breathing.

He gazed at her, wondering what to do next. Thus far, he had been purposeful; now, he was confused.

Frustrated by his inability to think clearly, he went outside again, locked the door after himself, and retraced his course to the rear of the restaurant. He located her purse and filled it with the skag and other items. Possessed by a strange anxiety that he could not understand at all, he returned to his basement room.

He had utterly forgotten the tableware in Staznik's garbage.

Sitting beside the bed in a straight-backed chair, Ollie pored through the contents of the purse. He removed the syringe and candle, destroyed them, and threw them into the waste can. In the bathroom, he ripped open the packets of heroin and flushed the contents down the toilet. She had used the metal cup to hold the candle with which she cooked each batch of dope; he placed the cup on the floor and methodically stamped it flat. He washed his hands, dried them on a tattered hotel towel, and felt much better.

The girl's breathing had grown shallower and less rhythmic. Her face was gray, and drops of perspiration were strung like bright beads across her forehead. Standing over her, Ollie realized that she was dying, and he was frightened.

He folded his arms so his long-fingered hands were hidden in his armpits. The fleshy pads of his fingertips were excessively moist. Dimly, he was aware that his hands could perform more useful tricks than locating silverware buried in mounds of garbage, but he did not want to admit to their capabilities: That way lay danger. . . .

He retrieved a gallon of wine from the rickety cardboard clothes cupboard and drank straight from the jug. It tasted like water.

He knew that he was not going to find release in wine—not with the girl lying on his bed. Not with his hands trembling as they were.

He put the wine away.

Ollie despised using his hands for anything but earning wine money, but now he had no choice. Other, more basic motivations drove him to act. The girl was beautiful. The smooth clear lines of her face were so symmetrical that even the hue of sickness could not much detract from them. Like a delicate web, her beauty caught

him, held him. He followed his hands to the bed as if he were a
blind man feeling for obstacles in a strange room.

For his hands to perform properly, he needed to undress her. She
wore no underclothes. Her breasts were small, firm, high; her waist
was too small, and the bones in her hips were sharp, though even
malnutrition hardly detracted from the sublime beauty of her legs.
Ollie appreciated her only as an objet d'art, not as a source of
physical gratification. He was a man ignorant of women. Until now,
he had lived in a sexless world, driven there by hands that any lover
would instantly have recognized as more than ordinary.

He placed his hands at her temples, smoothed her hair, and traced
his fleshy fingertips across her forehead, cheeks, jawline, chin. He
felt the pulse at her neck, gently pressed her breasts, stomach, and
legs, seeking the cause of her illness. In a moment he knew: She
had overdosed. He also perceived a truth that he did not want to
believe: The overdose had been intentional.

His hands ached.

He touched her again, moved his open palms in lazy circles until
he was not sure where his hands ended and her fair skin began, until
they seemed to have melted together. They might have been two
clouds of smoke, blending into one.

Half an hour later, she was no longer comatose, merely sleeping.

Gently, he turned her onto her stomach and worked his hands
along her back, shoulders, buttocks, thighs, finishing what he had
begun. He traced her spinal cord, massaged her scalp, blanked from
his mind all appreciation of her form, the better to let the power
seep out of him and into her.

Fifteen minutes later, he had not only remedied her current condition but had permanently cured her of her desire for drugs. If she
even thought of shooting up again, she would become violently ill.
He had seen to that. With his hands.

Then he leaned back in his chair and slept.

He bolted out of his chair an hour later, pursued by nightmares
that he could not identify. He went quickly to the door, found it still
locked, and peered through the curtains. He had expected to see
someone lurking there, but he found only the night. No one had
seen him use his hands.

The girl was still asleep.

As he pulled the sheets over her, he realized that he didn't even know her name. In her purse, he found identification: Annie Grice, twenty-six, unmarried. Nothing more, no address or relatives' names.

He lifted a glass-bead necklace but received no images from those small smooth spheres. He decided that the necklace was a recent purchase, imbued with none of her aura, and he put it aside.

In her well-worn wallet, he discovered a wealth of impressions, a fiercely compressed picture of the last several years of Annie's life: her first cocaine purchase, first use, subsequent dependence; her first time with skag, dependence, addiction; theft to maintain the habit; jobs in less reputable bars, hustling drinks; prostitution that she called something else to satisfy her troubled conscience; prostitution that she called prostitution; finally, irrevocably, a disassociation from life and society, a solidified loneliness that welcomed the release of death.

He put down the wallet.

He was drenched with perspiration.

He wanted wine but knew that it would not give him surcease. Not this time.

Besides, his curiosity had not been fully satisfied. How had Annie Grice become the woman that the seven-year-old wallet testified she was?

He found an old ring—family heirloom?—in her purse, held it, and let the images push into him. At first they did not concern Annie. When he saw that he was sensing back to the earliest history of the ring, to previous owners of it, he let his mind slide forward in time until Annie appeared. She was seven; the orphanage official had just given her what few artifacts remained of her heritage after a fire had destroyed her home and parents six months before. After that, her life was a string of depressing events: She was shy and became the target of malicious playmates; her bashfulness compounded her loneliness and kept her friendless through her formative years; her first love affair was a disaster that left her afraid of human contact more than ever before; with no money for college, she went from one clerking job to another, unhappy, confined, alone; in time, she tried to overcome her timidity with a brash aggressiveness, which achieved nothing but the acquaintance of a morally bankrupt young man named Benny, with whom she lived for a year and with whom she first snorted coke; after that, her addiction—a desperate attempt to escape from loneliness and lovelessness—followed the relentless pattern that Ollie had seen when sensing the images that permeated her tattered wallet.

He dropped the ring and got his jug of wine. He drank until he mercifully escaped the depression that was not really his but Annie's. He slept.

The girl woke him. She sat up in bed, stared at him where he slumped against the wall, and cried out in alarm.

Ollie got up and swayed toward her, blinking stupidly, sleepily, drunkenly.

"What am I doing here?" she demanded, clearly frightened. "What did you do to me?"

Ollie said nothing. Silence was his savior. He found it quite impossible to speak to anyone. He may have been mute, or he may have been afraid of words. His hands were trembling, moist, and pink. He shook his head and smiled nervously, hoping that she understood that he wanted only to help her.

Apparently she grasped the innocence of his intentions, for she looked less frightened. Frowning, she pulled the sheets to her neck to cover her nakedness. "I'm not dead, even though I overdosed."

Ollie smiled, nodded, and wiped his hands on his shirt.

Her eyes widened with an awful terror as she inspected her needle-tracked arms. Hers was a terror of life, a fear of existence. Despairing that her attempt at suicide had failed, she began to sob and wail, head thrown back, hair a golden frame about her white face.

He reached her quickly, touched her, and put her to sleep. Sobered, he went to the door, peered out at the early morning light that touched the shabby concrete steps, and closed the curtains again, satisfied that her cries had not alerted anyone.

In the bathroom, he splashed cold water on his face and wondered what to do next. He even considered carrying her back to the alleyway where he'd found her, to abandon her to her own devices. But he could not do that. He didn't know why he couldn't, and he didn't attempt to reason it out—because he was afraid of the answer that he might discover.

Drying his face on a filthy hand towel, Ollie realized that he was a sorry sight. He bathed, shaved, and dressed in clean clothes. He still looked like a vagrant, but a vagrant by choice rather than chance. A disillusioned artist, perhaps. Or, as in certain old movies, a rich man escaping from the boring responsibilities of wealth and position.

He was surprised by this fanciful turn of thought. He considered himself a man of routine and restricted vision.

Unsettled, he turned from his reflection in the bathroom mirror and went into the main room to check on the girl. Sleeping, she was serene, pure. He would let her sleep awhile yet.

Three hours later, after cleaning the two small rooms, Ollie changed her sheets while she slept. Even while admitting the impossibility of the notion, he toyed with the prospect of keeping her asleep and tending to her for years, as if he were a nurse and she were his comatose patient. He would be happy doing that—perhaps happier than he had ever been in his life to date.

But now he was hungry, and he knew that she would be hungry, too, when she woke. He left the apartment, locking the door behind him. Two blocks away, at a small grocery, he bought more food in one order than he had ever done before.

"Thirty-eight dollars, twelve cents," the cashier said. He did not conceal his disdain. Clearly, he felt that Ollie could not pay.

Ollie raised a hand, touched his forehead, and stared hard at the cashier.

The cashier blinked, smiled tentatively, and folded his hand over empty air. "Out of forty dollars," he said. He carefully placed the nonexistent currency in the cash register, handed Ollie the proper change, and bagged the food.

On his way home, Ollie was uneasy, because he had never before used his power to cheat anyone. If the girl hadn't come along, he would have finished his previous night's work at the garbage bins, perhaps completing another set of flatware, and would have gone on to other tasks like sensing out dropped coins in subway stations, earning a buck here and there. Therefore, the responsibility for this deceit was not entirely his. Nevertheless, dark portents of judgmental disaster plagued him.

At home he prepared dinner—stew, salad, fresh fruit—and woke Annie. She regarded him strangely as he pointed at the laden table. He sensed her blooming terror, a red flower. He swept his hand to take in the cleaned and ordered room, and he smiled encouragingly.

The girl sat up, propelled into her nightmare again—the cruel nightmare of being alive—and she shrieked in misery.

Ollie raised his hands imploringly, tried to speak, couldn't.

Blood rushed to her face as she sucked a deeper breath and tried to pull herself out of the bed.

He was forced to lay hands on her and put her to sleep again.

Tucking her in, he knew that he had been naive to imagine that she would be a different girl, with fewer fears and more composure, simply because he had bathed himself, shaved, cleaned the apartment, and cooked dinner. She would be different only if he helped her, which would take time, hard work—and sacrifice.

He threw the food away. He was no longer hungry.

Throughout the long night, he sat by the bed, elbows propped on his knees, his head held between his hands. The tips of his fingers seemed to merge with his temples while his palms lay against his cheeks. He sensed into her, sensed her despair, her hope, her dreams, her ambition, her limitations, her joys, her hard-won knowledge, her persistent misconceptions, and her moments of intellectual surety. He dwelt in the center of her soul—which was, by turns, beautifully in bloom and withered.

In the morning he used the bathroom, drank two glasses of water, and helped her to drink even while keeping her more than half asleep. Then he settled into the chiaroscuro world of her mind and remained there, except for brief rest periods, all through that day and night, diligently searching, learning, and making cautious adjustments to her psyche.

He never wondered why he made this expenditure of time, energy, and emotion, perhaps because he didn't dare risk the realization that his ultimate motive was loneliness. He merged with her, touched her, changed her, and gave no consideration to the consequences. By dawn of the next day, he was done.

Once more he partially awakened her and made her drink to keep from dehydrating; then he put her into deep sleep and lay beside her on the bed. He took her hand in his. Exhausted, he slept, dreaming that he floated in a vast ocean, a mere speck, about to be consumed by something prehistoric swimming in the gloom below him. Curiously, the dream did not frighten him. He had expected to be swallowed up by one thing or another all his troubled life.

Twelve hours later, Ollie woke, showered, shaved, dressed, and prepared another dinner. When he woke the girl, she sat straight up again, bewildered. But she did not scream. She said, "Where am I?"

Ollie worked his dry lips, instantly unsure of himself again, but finally he managed to sweep his hand around to indicate the room that by now must be at least somewhat familiar to her.

She appeared curious, ill at ease, but no longer possessed by that crippling fear of life itself. He had cured her of that.

She said, "Yeah, you've got a cozy place. But—how'd I get here?"

He licked his lips, searched for words, found none, pointed at himself, and smiled.

"Can't you speak?" she asked. "Are you mute?"

He thought a moment, opted for the out that she had offered, and nodded.

"I'm sorry," she said. She examined her bruised arm, staring at the hundreds of needle marks, doubtlessly remembering the overdose that she had carefully prepared and booted into her bloodstream.

Ollie cleared his throat and pointed to the table.

She instructed him to turn his back. She got out of the bed, stripped off the top sheet, and twisted it about herself as though it were a toga. As she sat at the table, she grinned at him. "I'm starving."

Such a waif. She charmed him.

He grinned back at her. What could have been the worst moment had passed without much strain. He put the food on the table and made a disparaging gesture to indicate his lack of culinary finesse.

"Everything looks delicious," she assured him. She reached for the main serving dish and began to heap food onto her plate. She did not speak again until she had finished eating.

She tried to help with the dishes, although she soon tired and had to retreat to the bed. When he had finished and sat in the straight-backed chair beside her, she said, "What do you do?"

He shrugged.

"For a living, I mean."

He thought of his hands, wondered how he possibly could have told her about them even if he had been able to talk. He shrugged as if to say, *Nothing much.*

She looked around the shabby room. "Panhandling?" When he did not respond, she decided that she'd hit on it. "How long can I stay here?"

By gesture, expression, and pantomime, Ollie made her understand that she could stay as long as she liked.

When this was clear, she studied him a long moment and finally said, "Could we have less light?"

He got up and switched off two of the three lamps. When he turned to her again, she was lying nude on top of the covers, her legs slightly spread to receive him.

"Look," she said, "I figure you didn't bring me here and nurse me back to health for nothing. You know? You expect a . . . reward. And you have a right to expect one."

Confused, frustrated, he got clean sheets from a stack in the corner and, ignoring her offer, proceeded to change the bed under her without once touching her. She stared at him in disbelief, and when he was done, she said that she didn't want to sleep. He insisted. He touched her and put her out for the night.

In the morning, she ate breakfast with the greedy efficiency that she had shown at dinner the night before, wasting nothing, then asked if she could take a bath. He washed dishes while her sweet voice came through the bathroom door, singing a lovely melodic song that he had never heard before.

She came out of her bath with clean hair as dark as burnt honey, stood nude at the foot of the bed, and beckoned to him. Already she seemed sleeker, healthier than when he had found her, though she was still leaner than she needed to be.

She said, "I was so stupid last night. My hair was a dirty mess and my body odor would've turned off a bull. Now I'm soapy-smelling."

Ollie turned away from her and stared at the few dishes that he still had to dry.

"What's the matter?" she asked.

He had no reply.

"You don't want me?"

He shook his head—*No.*

She drew a sudden deep breath.

Something struck him painfully on the hip. Turning, he saw that the girl was wielding a heavy glass ashtray. Drawing her lips back from her teeth, she hissed at him as though she were an angry cat. She pounded his shoulders with the ashtray, struck him repeatedly with one tiny balled fist, kicked, and screeched. Then she lost her grip on the ashtray and sagged against him, exhausted, crying.

He put his arm around her to comfort her, but she had enough energy to twist violently away. She turned, tried to reach the bed, stumbled, fell, and passed out.

He lifted her and put her to bed.

He pulled the covers around her, tucked her in, and sat down in his chair to wait for her to regain consciousness.

When she awakened half an hour later, she was trembling and dizzy. He soothed her, smoothing her hair away from her face, wiping her teary eyes, placing cold compresses on her brow.

In time, when she could speak, she asked, "Are you impotent or something?"

He shook his head.

"Then why? I wanted to repay you. That's how I repay men. I don't have anything else to give."

He touched her. Held her. With his expression and with his clumsy pantomime he tried to make her understand that she had a great deal to give. She was giving just by being here. Just by being here.

That afternoon, he went out to buy her pajamas, street clothes, and a newspaper. She was amused by his chaste choice of pajamas: full-sleeved, long-legged flannels. She put them on, then read the newspaper to him—comics and human-interest stories. She seemed to think that he couldn't read, and he was willing to play along with the misconception, since his illiteracy tended to reinforce his cover: Winos didn't collect books.

Besides, he liked to listen to her read. Her voice was sweet.

The following morning, Annie dressed in her new blue jeans and sweater to accompany Ollie to the corner grocery store, although he tried to dissuade her. At the register, when he handed a nonexistent twenty-dollar bill to the cashier and collected change, he thought that Annie was looking elsewhere.

Outside, however, as they walked home, she said, "How'd you do that?"

He feigned perplexity. *Do what?*

"Don't try to fool Annie," she said. "I almost croaked when he grabbed a handful of air and gave change."

He said nothing.

"Hypnotism?" she pressed.

Relieved, he nodded—*Yes.*

"You'll have to teach me."

He didn't reply.

But she was not going to be put off. "You have to teach me how you conned that guy. With that little trick I wouldn't need to hustle my body any more, you know? Christ, he *smiled* at that handful of air! How? How? Teach me! You've got to!"

Finally, at home, unable to tolerate her persistent pleading any longer, afraid that he would be foolish enough to tell her about his hands, Ollie shoved her away from him. The back of her knees caught the bed, and she sat down hard, surprised by his sudden anger.

She said no more, and their relationship returned to an easier pitch. But everything had changed.

Since she couldn't nag him about learning the con game, she had time to think. Late in the evening, she said, "I had my last fix days ago, but I don't feel any need for drugs. I haven't been this long without the crap in at least five years."

Ollie held his guilty hands out to his sides to indicate his own puzzlement.

"Did you throw away my tools, the skag?"

He nodded.

A while later, she said, "The reason I don't need dope . . . is it you, something you did? Did you hypnotize me and make me not want it?" When he nodded, she said, "The same way you made the clerk see the twenty-dollar bill?"

He agreed, using his fingers and eyes to do a comic imitation of a stage hypnotist hamming it up for an audience.

"Not hypnotism at all," she said, fixing him with her piercing eyes, seeing through his facade as no one had done in years. "ESP?"

What's that? he asked with gestures.

"You know," Annie said. "You know."

She was a more observant girl, a much brighter girl than he had thought.

She began to nag again, but not about the con game any longer. "Come on! Really, what's it like? How long have you had it, this power, this gift? Don't be ashamed of it! It's wonderful! You should be proud! You have the world on a string!"

And so on.

Sometime during the long night—later, Ollie could never recall the precise moment or understand what single telling argument she used to finally break him down—he agreed to show her what he could do. He was nervous, wiping his magical hands on his shirt. He was excited about showing her his abilities, felt like a young boy trying to impress his first date—but he also feared the consequences.

First he handed her a nonexistent twenty-dollar bill, made her see it, and then made it disappear. Then, with a dramatic wave of his hand, he levitated a coffee cup (empty), a coffee cup (filled), the straight-backed chair, a lamp, the bed (empty), the bed (with Annie in it), and finally himself, floating off the floor as though he were an Indian fakir. The girl whooped and hollered with delight. She persuaded him to give her a ride around the room on a broomstick of air. She hugged him, kissed him, asked for more tricks. He turned on the water in the sink without touching the faucet, divided the stream into two streams that fell on both sides of the drain. He let her throw a cup of water at him and diverted it in a hundred different sprays, keeping himself dry.

"Hey," she said, more flushed and excited than he had ever seen her, "no one is going to tramp on us again, not ever. No one!" She stood on her toes and hugged him. He was grinning so hard that his jaws ached. She said, "You're fabulous!"

He knew, with sweet anticipation and awful dread, that one day soon they would be ready to share a bed. Soon. From that moment his life would be changed. She still did not fully understand what his talent meant, what a wall between them his hands might soon become.

She said, "I still don't understand why you hide your—talent."

Eager that she understand, he forced himself to confront hideous memories of childhood that he had long suppressed. He tried to tell her, first with words that wouldn't come and then with gestures, why he hid his abilities.

Somehow she got the gist of it. "They hurt you."

He nodded. *Yes. Very much.*

The talent came upon him without warning when he was twelve, as if it were a secondary sex characteristic accompanying puberty, manifested in modest ways at first, then increasingly strong and demanding. It was the sort of thing a boy knew must be concealed from adults. For months he even hid it from other children, from his friends, confused and frightened by his own hands, in which the power seemed to be focused. Slowly, however, he revealed himself, did tricks for his friends, performed, became their secret from the grown-up world. But it wasn't long until they rejected him—subtly at first, then with increasing vigor until they beat and kicked him, knocked him in the mud, forced him to drink filthy water, all because of his talent. He could have used his power to protect himself from one of them, perhaps from two, but even he could not protect himself from a gang. For a time he hid his powers again, even from himself. But as the years passed, he learned that he could not conceal and deny the talent without causing himself physical and psychological damage. The urge to use the power was a need stronger than the need for food, for sex, for the breath of life itself. To refuse it was to refuse to live; he lost weight, grew nervous and ill. He was forced to use the power then, but refrained from exhibiting it in front of others. He began to understand that he would always be alone as long as he had the power—not from choice, from necessity. Like athletic agility or a cleverness with words, it could not be successfully hidden in company: It flowered unexpectedly, startling friends. And whenever he was found out, friends were lost, and the consequences were more dangerous than he cared to face. The only sensible life for him was that of a hermit. In the city he naturally gravitated to the life of a vagrant, one of the invisible men of the concrete jungle—unnoticed, friendless, safe.

"I can understand people being jealous or afraid of you," she said. "Some of them . . . but not everyone. I think you're great."

With gestures, he explained what little he could. Twice he grunted, trying words, without success.

"You read their minds," she interpreted. "So? I guess everyone has secrets. But to hurt you for it . . ." She shook her head sadly. "Well, you don't have to run away from it any longer. Together, we can turn it into a blessing. Us against the world."

He nodded. But he was deeply sorry to have misled her, for at that moment the *mesh* occurred. Just like that: *Flick!* And he knew that this time would be no different from others. When she learned about the mesh, she would panic.

In the past it had happened only when a relationship had progressed to intimacy. But Annie was special, and this time the mesh occurred even before they made love.

The next day, Annie spent hours making plans for their future, while he listened. All day he enjoyed planning with her, for he knew that soon there would be no more joy to share, none at all, nothing. The mesh made joy impossible.

After dinner, as they lay on the bed holding hands, the trouble began just as he had known it would. She was quiet, thinking, and then she said, "Have you been reading my mind today?"

It was useless to lie. He nodded.

"Very much?"

Yes.

She said, "You know everything before I say it."

He waited—cold and frightened.

"Have you been reading my mind *all day long?*"

He nodded.

She frowned and spoke firmly this time: "I want you to stop it. Have you stopped?"

Yes.

She sat up, let go of his hand, and looked closely at him. "But you haven't. I can almost *feel* you inside there, watching me."

He dared not respond.

She took his hand again. "Don't you understand? I feel silly, rambling on about things you've already seen in my head. I feel like an idiot hanging out with a genius."

He tried to calm her and to change the subject. He croaked at her like a magic frog with pretensions to princeship but then resorted again to gestures.

She said, "If we both had the gift ... But this one-way thing makes me feel ... inadequate. Worse than that. I don't much like it." She waited. Then: "Have you stopped?"

Yes.

"You're lying, aren't you? I feel ... yeah ... I'm sure I can feel you. ..." Then the terrible realization came to her, and she drew away from him. *"Can* you stop reading my mind?"

He couldn't explain the mesh: how, when he had come to care for her deeply enough, their minds had blended in some mystical fashion. He didn't fully understand it himself—though it had happened to him before. He couldn't explain that she was now almost an extension of him, forever a part of him. He could only nod in acknowledgment of the dreadful truth: *I can't stop reading your mind, Annie. It comes to me like air into my lungs.*

Thoughtfully, she said, "No secrets, surprises, nothing I can keep from you."

Minutes passed.

Then she said, "Do you begin to run my life, make my decisions, push me this way or that, without me knowing? Or have you already begun to do that?"

Such control was beyond his power, although she would never be convinced of that. Breathing rapidly, she succumbed to that naked fear that he'd seen often before in others.

She said, "I'll leave right now . . . if you'll let me."

Sadly, he put one trembling hand to her head and gave her deep but temporary darkness.

That night, while she slept, he sensed into her mind and erased certain memories. He kept the wine jug at his feet and drank while he worked. Before dawn, he was done.

The streets were bleak and empty when he carried her back to the alley where he'd found her, put her down, and placed her purse beneath her. She was still purged of all desire for drugs, and in possession of a new self-confidence and a profound sense of her value as a person that might help her make a new life. His gifts to her.

Ollie returned home without taking a last look at her clear, perfect face.

He opened a jug of wine. Hours later, drunk, he unaccountably remembered what a childhood "friend" had said when he first displayed his power: "Ollie, you can rule the world! You're a superman!"

He laughed out loud, now, spitting wine. Rule the world! He couldn't even rule himself. Superman! In a world of ordinary men, a superman was no king, not even a romantic fugitive. He was simply *alone.* And alone, he could accomplish nothing.

He thought of Annie, of dreams and love unshared, of futures destroyed. He continued to drink.

After midnight of that day, he returned to Staznik's Restaurant to check the garbage for discarded tableware. At least that was what he intended to do. Instead, he spent the night walking swiftly down a succession of dark, twisting alleyways and side streets, his hands held out before him, a blind man trying to find his way. As far as Annie was concerned, he'd never existed.

Never.

SNATCHER

BILLY NEEKS HAD A FLEXIBLE PHILOSOPHY REGARDING PROPERTY rights. He believed in the proletarian ideal of shared wealth—as long as the wealth belonged to someone else. On the other hand, if the property belonged to him, Billy was prepared to defend it to the death. This was a simple, workable philosophy for a thief—which Billy was.

Billy Neeks's occupation was reflected in his grooming: He looked slippery. His thick black hair was slicked back with enough scented oil to fill a crankcase. His coarse skin was perpetually pinguid, as if he suffered continuously from malaria. He moved cat quick on well-lubricated joints, and his hands had the buttery grace of a magician's hands. His eyes resembled twin pools of Texas crude, wet and black and deep—and utterly untouched by any human warmth or feeling. If the route to Hell were an inclined ramp requiring a hideous grease to facilitate descent, Billy Neeks would be the devil's choice to pass eternity in the application of that noxious, oleaginous substance.

In action, Billy could bump into an unsuspecting woman, separate her from her purse, and be ten yards away and moving fast by the time she realized that she'd been victimized. Single-strap purses, double-strap purses, clutch purses, purses carried over the shoulder, purses carried in the hand—all meant easy money to Billy Neeks. Whether his target was cautious or careless was of no consequence. Virtually no precautions could foil him.

That Wednesday in April, pretending to be drunk, he jostled a well-dressed elderly woman on Broad Street, just past Bartram's Department Store. As she recoiled in disgust from that oily contact, Billy slipped her purse off her shoulder, down her arm, and into the plastic shopping bag that he carried. He reeled away from her and took six or eight steps in an exaggerated stagger before she realized that the collision had not been as accidental as it seemed. Even as the victim shrieked, "police," Billy had begun to run, and by the time she added, "help, police, help," Billy was nearly out of earshot.

He raced through a series of alleyways, dodged around garbage cans and Dumpsters, and leaped across the splayed legs of a sleeping wino. He sprinted across a parking lot and fled into another alley.

Blocks from Bartram's, Billy slowed to a walk. He was breathing only slightly harder than usual. Grinning.

Stepping out of the alley onto Forty-sixth Street, he spotted a young mother carrying a baby, a shopping bag, *and* a purse. She looked so defenseless that Billy couldn't resist the opportunity, so he flicked open his switchblade and, in a wink, cut the thin straps on her bag, a stylish blue-leather number. Then he dashed off again, across the street, where drivers braked sharply and blew their horns at him, into another network of alleyways, all familiar to him.

As he ran, he giggled. His giggle was neither shrill nor engaging, but more like the sound of ointment squirting from a tube.

When he slid on spilled garbage—orange peels, rotting lettuce, mounds of molding and soggy bread—he was not tripped up or even slowed down. The disgusting muck seemed to facilitate his flight, and he came out of the slide moving faster than he had gone into it.

He slowed to a normal pace when he reached Prospect Boulevard. The switchblade was in his pocket again. Both stolen purses were concealed in the plastic shopping bag. He projected what he believed to be an air of nonchalance, and although his calculated expression of innocence was actually a dismal failure, it was the best that he could do.

He strolled to his car, which he had parked at a meter along Prospect. The Pontiac, unwashed for at least two years, left oil drippings wherever it went, just as a wolf in the wilds marked its territory with dribbles of urine. Billy put the stolen purses in the trunk of the car and, whistling happily, drove away from that part

of the city, toward yet untouched prowling grounds in other neighbor-
hoods.

Of the several reasons for his success as a purse snatcher, mobility
was perhaps the most important. Many snatchers were kids seeking
a few fast bucks, young hoods without wheels. Billy Neeks was
twenty-five, no kid, and possessed reliable transportation. He usually
robbed two or three women in one neighborhood and then quickly
moved on to another territory where no one was looking for him
and where more business waited to be done.

To him, this was not small-time thievery committed either by
impulse or out of desperation. Instead, Billy saw it as a business,
and he was a businessman, and like other businessmen he planned
his work carefully, weighed the risks and benefits of any opportunity,
and acted only as a result of careful, responsible analysis.

Other snatchers—amateurs and punks, every one of them—
paused on the street or in an alley to hastily search purses for
valuables, risking arrest because of their inadvisable delays, at the
very least creating a host of additional witnesses to their crimes.
Billy, on the other hand, stashed the stolen purses in the trunk of
his car to be retrieved later for more leisurely inspection in the
privacy of his home.

He prided himself on his methodicalness and caution.

That cloudy and humid Wednesday in late April, he crossed and
recrossed the city, visiting three widely separated districts and
snatching six purses in addition to those that he had taken from the
elderly woman outside Bartram's and from the young mother on
Forty-sixth Street. The last of the eight also came from an old woman.
At first he thought that it was going to be an easy hit, and then he
thought that it was going to get messy, and finally it just turned out
to be weird.

When Billy spotted her, she was coming out of a butcher's shop
on Westend Avenue, clutching a package of meat to her breast. She
was *old*. Her brittle white hair stirred in the spring breeze, and Billy
had the curious notion that he could hear those dry locks rustling
against one another. Her crumpled-parchment face, her slumped
shoulders, her pale withered hands, and her shuffling step combined
to convey the impression not only of extreme age but of frailty and
vulnerability—which drew Billy Neeks as if he were an iron filing

and she a magnet. Her purse was big, almost a satchel, and the weight of it—in addition to the package of meat—seemed to bother her, because she was shrugging the straps farther up on her shoulder and wincing in pain, as if suffering from a flare-up of arthritis.

Although it was spring, she was dressed in black: black shoes, black stockings, black skirt, dark gray blouse, even a heavy black cardigan sweater unsuited to the mild day.

Billy looked up and down the street, saw no one else nearby, and quickly made his move. He did his drunk trick: staggering, jostling the old biddy. But as he pulled the purse down her arm, she dropped the package of meat, seized the bag with both hands, and for a moment they were locked in an unexpectedly fierce struggle. Ancient as she was, she possessed surprising strength. He tugged at the purse, wrenched and twisted it, desperately attempted to rock her backward off her feet, but she stood her ground and held on with the tenacity of a deeply rooted tree resisting a storm wind.

He said, "Give it up, you stupid old bitch, or I'll bust your face."

And then a strange thing happened:

She *changed* before Billy's eyes. She no longer appeared frail but steely, no longer weak but darkly energized. Her bony, arthritic hands suddenly looked like the dangerous talons of a powerful bird of prey. That singular face—pale yet jaundiced, nearly fleshless, all wrinkles and sharp pointy lines—was still ancient, but it no longer seemed quite *human* to Billy Neeks. And her eyes. God, her eyes. At first glance, Billy saw only the watery, myopic gaze of a doddering crone, but abruptly they were eyes of tremendous power, eyes of fire and ice, simultaneously boiling his blood and freezing his heart, eyes that saw into him and through him, not the eyes of a helpless old granny but those of a murderous beast that had the desire and ability to devour him alive.

He gasped in fear, and he almost let go of the purse, almost ran. In a blink, however, she was transformed into a defenseless old woman again. Abruptly she capitulated. Like pop beads, the swollen knuckles of her twisted hands seemed to come apart, and her finger joints went slack. She lost her grip, releasing the purse with a small cry of despair.

Emitting a menacing snarl that served not only to frighten the old woman but also to chase away Billy's own irrational terror, he shoved her backward into a curbside trash container, and he bolted past her

with the satchel-size purse under his arm. He glanced back after
several steps, half expecting to see that she had fully assumed the
form of a great dark bird of prey, flying at him, eyes aflame, teeth
bared, talon-hands spread and hooked to tear him to bits. But she
was clutching at the trash container to keep her balance, as age-
broken and helpless as she had been when he had first seen her.

The only odd thing: She was looking after him with a smile. No
mistaking it. A wide, stained-tooth smile. Almost a lunatic grin.

Senile old fool, Billy thought. *Has to be senile if she finds anything
funny about having her purse snatched.*

He could not imagine why he had ever been afraid of her.

He ran, dodging from one alleyway to another, down side streets,
across a sun-splashed parking lot, along a shadowy service passage
between two tenements, and onto a street far removed from the
scene of his latest theft. At a stroll, he returned to his parked car
and put the old woman's black purse in the trunk with the others
taken elsewhere in the city. At last, a hard day's work behind him,
he drove home, looking forward to counting his take, having a few
icy beers, and watching some TV.

Once, stopped at a red traffic light, Billy thought he heard something moving in the car trunk. A few hollow thumps. A brief but
curious scraping. When he cocked his head and listened closer,
however, he heard nothing more, and he decided that the noise had
only been the pile of stolen purses shifting under their own weight.

⊲ ⋀ ⊳

Billy Neeks lived in a ramshackle four-room bungalow between
a vacant lot and a transmission shop, two blocks from the river. The
place had belonged to his mother, and it had been clean and in good
repair when she had lived there. Two years ago, Billy had convinced
her to transfer ownership to him "for tax reasons," then had shipped
her off to a nursing home to be tended at the expense of the state.
He supposed she was still there; he didn't know for sure because
he never visited.

That evening in April, Billy arranged the eight purses side by side
in two rows on the kitchen table and stared at them for a while in

sweet anticipation of the treasure hunt to come. He popped the tab on a Budweiser. He tore open a bag of Doritos. He pulled up a chair, sat down, and sighed contentedly.

Finally, he opened the purse that he had taken off the woman outside Bartram's and began to calculate his "earnings." She had looked well-to-do, and the contents of her wallet did not disappoint Billy Neeks: four hundred and nine dollars in folding money, plus another three dollars and ten cents in change. She also carried a stack of credit cards, which Billy would be able to fence through Jake Barcelli, the pawnshop owner, who would also give him a few bucks for whatever other worthwhile loot he found in the purses. In the first bag, those miscellaneous fenceable items included a gold-plated Tiffany pen, a matching gold-plated Tiffany compact and lipstick tube, and a fine though not extraordinarily expensive opal ring.

The young mother's purse contained only eleven dollars and forty-two cents. Nothing else of value. Billy had expected as much, but this meager profit did not diminish the thrill he got from going through the contents of the bag. He regarded snatching as a business, yes, and thought of himself as a good businessman, but he also took considerable pleasure simply from examining and *touching* his victims' possessions. The violation of a woman's personal property was a violation of her too, and when his quick hands explored the young mother's purse, it was almost as if he were exploring her body. Sometimes, Billy took unfenceable items—cheap compacts, inexpensive tubes of lipstick, eyeglasses—and put them on the floor and stomped them, because crushing them beneath his heel was curiously almost like crushing the woman herself. Easy money made his work worthwhile, but he was equally motivated by the tremendous sense of power that he got from the job; it stimulated him, it really did, stimulated and satisfied.

By the time he'd gone slowly through seven of the eight purses, savoring their contents, it was seven-fifteen in the evening, and Billy was euphoric. He breathed fast and occasionally shuddered ecstatically. His oily hair looked oilier than usual, for it was damp with sweat and hung in clumps and tangles. Perspiration glimmered on his face. During his exploration of the purses, he knocked the open Doritos off the kitchen table but didn't notice. He opened a second beer, but he never took a taste of it; now it stood warm and forgotten. His world had shrunk to the dimensions of a woman's purse.

Billy had saved the crazy old woman's bag for last because he had a hunch that it was going to provide the greatest treasure of the day.

The hag's purse was big, almost a satchel, made of supple black leather, with long straps and with a single main compartment that was zippered shut. He pulled it in front of him and stared at it for a while, letting sweet anticipation build.

He remembered how the crone had resisted him, holding fast to the bag until he thought that he might have to flick open his switchblade and cut her. He had cut a few women before, not many but enough to know that he *liked* cutting them.

That was the problem. Billy was smart enough to realize that, liking knife play so much, he must deny himself the pure pleasure of cutting people, resorting to violence only when absolutely necessary. If he used the knife too often, he would be unable to stop using it, would be compelled to use it—and then he would be lost. Although the police expended no energy in the search for mere purse snatchers, they would be a lot more aggressive and relentless in the pursuit of a slasher.

Still, he had not cut anyone for several months, and by such admirable self-control, he should have earned the right to have some fun. He would have taken enormous pleasure in separating the old woman's withered meat from her bones. Now he wondered why he had not ripped her up the moment that she had given him trouble.

He had virtually forgotten how she'd briefly terrified him, how she'd looked less human than avian, how her bony hands had seemed to metamorphose into wicked talons, and how her eyes had blazed. Deeply confirmed in his macho self-image, he had no capacity for any memory that had the potential for humiliation.

With a growing certainty that he was about to find a surprising treasure, he put his hands on the purse and lightly squeezed. It was crammed full, straining at the seams, the mother of all purses, and Billy told himself that the forms he felt through the leather were wads of money, banded stacks of hundred-dollar bills.

His heart thumped with excitement.

He pulled open the zipper, looked in, and frowned.

The inside of the purse was . . . dark.

Billy peered closer.

Very dark.

Impossibly *dark.*

Squinting, he could see nothing in there at all: not a wallet or a compact or a comb or a packet of Kleenex, not even the lining of the purse itself, only a flawless and deep darkness, as if he were peering into a well. "Deep" was the word, all right, for he had a sense that he was staring down into unplumbable and mysterious depths, as if the bottom of the purse were not just a few inches away but thousands of feet down—even farther—countless miles below him. Suddenly he realized that the glow from the overhead fluorescents fell into the open purse but illuminated nothing; the bag seemed to swallow every ray of light and digest it.

Billy Neeks's warm sweat of quasi-erotic pleasure turned icy, and his skin dimpled with gooseflesh. He knew that he should pull the zipper shut, cautiously carry the purse blocks away from his own house, and dispose of it in someone else's trash bin. But he saw his right hand slipping toward the gaping maw of the bag. When he tried to pull his hand back, he could not, as though it were a stranger's hand over which he had no control. His fingers disappeared into the darkness, and the rest of his hand followed. He shook his head—no, no—but still he could not stop himself. He was *compelled* to reach into the bag. And now his hand was in all the way to the wrist, and he felt nothing in there, nothing but a terrible cold that made his teeth chatter, and still he reached in and down until his arm was shoved all the way in to the elbow. He should have felt the bottom of the purse long before this, but there was just a vast emptiness in it, so he reached down farther, until he was in almost to his shoulder, feeling around with splayed fingers, searching in that impossible void for something, anything.

That was when something found *him.*

Down deep in the bag, something brushed his hand.

Billy jerked in surprise.

Something bit him.

Billy screamed and finally found the will to resist the siren call of the darkness in the purse. He tore his hand out and leaped to his feet, knocking over his chair. He stared in astonishment at the bloody punctures on the meaty portion of his palm. Tooth marks. Five small holes, neat and round, welling blood.

At first numb with shock, he at last let out a wail and grabbed for the zipper on the purse to close it. Even as Billy's blood-slick fingers touched the pull tab, the creature climbed out of the bag, ascending from a lightless place, and Billy snatched his hand back in terror.

The beast was small, only about a foot tall, not too big to crawl out through the open mouth of the purse. It was gnarly and darkish, like a man in form—two arms, two legs—but not like a man in any other way at all. If its tissues had not once been inanimate lumps of stinking sewage, then they had been a sludge of mysterious though equally noxious origins. Its muscles and sinews appeared to be formed from human waste, all tangled with human hair and decaying human entrails and desiccated human veins. Its feet were twice as large as they should have been and terminated in razor-edged black claws that put as much fear into Billy Neeks as his own switchblade had put into others. A hooked and pointed spur curved up from the back of each heel. The arms were proportionately as long as those of an ape, with six or maybe seven fingers—Billy could not be sure how many because the thing kept working its hands ceaselessly as it crawled out of the purse and stood up on the table—and each finger ended in an ebony claw.

As the creature rose to its feet and emitted a fierce hiss, Billy stumbled backward until he came up against the refrigerator. Over the sink was a window, locked and covered with greasy curtains. The door to the dining room was on the other side of the kitchen table. To get to another door that opened onto the back porch, he would have to go past the table as well. He was effectively trapped.

The thing's head was asymmetrical, lumpy, pocked, as if crudely modeled by a sculptor with an imperfect sense of human form, crafted from sewage and scraps of rotten tissue, as was its body. A pair of eyes were set high on that portion of the face that would have been the forehead, and a second pair blinked below them. Two more eyes, making six in all, were located at the sides of the skull, where ears should have been, and all these organs of vision were entirely white, without iris or pupil, so the beast appeared to be blinded by cataracts.

But it could see. Most definitely, it could see, for it was looking straight at Billy.

Trembling violently, making strangled sounds of fear, Billy

reached to one side with his bitten right hand, and he pulled open a drawer in the cabinet next to the refrigerator. Never taking his eyes off the thing that had come out of the purse, he fumbled for the knives that he knew were there, found them, and extracted the butcher's knife.

On the table, the six-eyed demon opened its ragged mouth, revealing rows of pointed yellow teeth. It hissed again.

"Oh, G-G-God," Billy said, pronouncing the second word as if it were in a foreign language, its meaning not quite clear to him.

Twisting its deformed mouth into what might have been a grin, the demon kicked the open can of beer off the table and let out a hideous dry sound halfway between a snarl and a giggle.

Suddenly lunging forward and swinging the big butcher's knife as if it were a mighty Samurai sword, Billy slashed at the creature, intending to lop off its head, chop it in half. The blade connected with its disgusting flesh, sank less than an inch into its darkly glistening torso, above its knobby hips, but would not go any deeper, certainly not all the way through. Billy felt as if he had taken a hack at a slab of steel, for the aborted power of the blow coursed back through the handle of the knife and shivered painfully through his hands and arms like the vibrations that would have rebounded upon him if he had grabbed a crowbar and, with all his strength, slammed it into a solid iron post.

In that same instant, one of the creature's hands moved flash-quick, slashed Billy, revealing two of his knuckle bones.

With a cry of surprise and pain, Billy let go of the weapon. He staggered back against the refrigerator, holding his gouged hand.

The creature on the table stood unfazed, the knife embedded in its side, neither bleeding nor exhibiting any signs of pain. With its small black gnarled hands, the beast gripped the handle and pulled the weapon from its flesh. Turning six scintillant, milky eyes on Billy, it raised the knife, which was nearly as big as the beast itself, and snapped it in two. It threw the blade in one direction and the handle in another.

Billy ran.

He had to go around the table, past the creature, too close, but he did not care, did not hesitate, because his only alternative was to stand at the refrigerator and be torn to bits. Dashing out of the kitchen into the bungalow's dining room, he heard a thump behind him as the demon leaped off the table. Worse: He heard the *click-tick-clack* of its chitinous feet and horny claws as it scrambled across the linoleum, hurrying after him.

As a purse snatcher, Billy had to keep in shape and had to be able to run as fast as a deer. Now, his conditioning was the only advantage he had.

Was it possible to outrun the devil?

He bounded out of the dining room, jumped over a footstool in the living room, and fled toward the front door. His bungalow was isolated between an empty lot and a transmission repair shop that was closed at this hour of the evening. A few houses stood across the street, however, and at the corner was a 7-Eleven market that was usually busy. He figured that he would be safe if he was with other people, even strangers. He sensed that the demon would not want to be seen by anyone else.

Expecting the beast to leap on him and sink its teeth into his neck, Billy tore open the front door and almost plunged out of the house—then stopped abruptly when he saw what lay outside. Nothing. No front walk. No lawn, no trees. No street. No other houses across the way, no 7-Eleven on the corner. Nothing, nothing. No light whatsoever. The night beyond the house was unnaturally dark, as utterly lightless as the bottom of a mine shaft—or as the inside of the old hag's purse, from which the beast had clambered. Although it should have been a warm late-April evening, the velvet-black night was icy, bone-numbingly cold, just as the inside of the big black leather purse had been.

Billy stood on the threshold, swaying, breathless, shaken by his jackhammer heart, and he was seized by the mad idea that his entire bungalow was now inside the crazy old woman's purse. Which made no sense. The bottomless purse was back there in the kitchen, on the table. The purse could not be inside the house at the same time that the house was inside the purse. Could it?

He felt dizzy, confused, nauseous.

He had always known everything worth knowing. Or thought he did. Now he knew better.

He didn't dare venture out of the bungalow into the unremitting blackness. He sensed no haven within that coaly gloom. And he knew instinctively that, if he took one step into the frigid darkness, he would not be able to turn back. One step, and he would fall into the same terrible void that he had felt within the hag's purse: down and down, forever down.

A hiss.

The beast was behind him.

Whimpering wordlessly, Billy Neeks turned from the horrifying emptiness beyond his house, looked back into the living room, where the demon was waiting for him, and cried out when he saw that it had grown bigger than it had been a moment ago. Much bigger. Three feet tall instead of one. Broader in the shoulders. More muscular arms. Thicker legs. Bigger hands and longer claws. The repulsive creature was not as close as he had expected, not on top of him, but standing in the middle of the small living room, watching him with predatory interest, grinning, taunting him merely by choosing not to end the confrontation quickly.

The disparity between the warm air in the house and the freezing air outside generated a draft that sucked the door shut behind Billy. It closed with a bang.

Hissing, the demon took a step forward. When it moved, Billy could hear its gnarly skeleton and oozing flesh work one against the other like the parts of a grease-clogged machine in ill repair.

He backed away from it, heading around the room toward the short hall that led to the bedroom.

The repugnant apparition followed, casting a hellish shadow that was somehow even more grotesque than it should have been, as if it were thrown not by the monster's malformed body but by its more hideously malformed soul. Perhaps aware that its shadow was wrong, perhaps unwilling to consider the meaning of its twisted silhouette, the beast purposefully knocked over the floor lamp as it stalked Billy, and in the influx of shadows, it proceeded more confidently and more eagerly, as if darkness greased its way.

At the entrance to the hallway, Billy stopped edging sideways, bolted flat-out for his bedroom, reached it, and slammed the door behind him. He twisted the latch with no illusions of having found sanctuary. The creature would smash through that flimsy barrier with no difficulty. Billy only hoped to reach the nightstand where he kept a Smith & Wesson .357 Magnum, and indeed he got it with time to spare.

The gun was smaller than he remembered. He told himself that it seemed inadequate only because the enemy was so formidable.

The weapon would prove plenty big enough when he squeezed the trigger. But it still seemed small. Virtually a toy.

With the loaded .357 held in both hands and aimed at the door, he wondered if he should fire through the barrier or wait until the beast burst inside.

The demon resolved the issue by *exploding* through the locked door in a shower of splinters and mangled hinges.

It was bigger still, more than six feet tall, bigger than Billy, a gigantic and loathsome creature that, more than ever, appeared to be constructed of filth, wads of mucus, tangled hair, fungus, and the putrescent bits and pieces of cadavers. Redolent of rotten eggs, with its multiplicitous white eyes now as radiant as incandescent bulbs, it lurched inexorably toward Billy, not even hesitating when he pulled the trigger of the .357 and pumped six rounds into it.

Who or what had that old crone been, for God's sake? She was no ordinary senior citizen, living on Social Security, paying a visit to her butcher's shop, looking forward to bingo on Saturday night. Hell no. No way. What kind of crazy woman carried such a strange purse and kept such a thing as this at her command? What kind of bitch, what kind of bitch? A witch?

Of course, a witch.

At last, backed into a corner, with the creature looming over him, the empty gun still clutched in his left hand, the scratches and bites burning in his right hand, Billy really *knew* for the first time what it meant to be a defenseless victim. When the hulking, unnameable entity put its massive saber-clawed hands upon him—one on his shoulder, one on his chest—Billy peed in his pants and was at once reduced to the pitiable condition of a weak, helpless, and frightened child.

He was sure that the demon was going to tear him apart, crack his spine, decapitate him, and suck the marrow out of his bones, but instead it lowered its malformed face to his throat and put its gummy lips against his throbbing carotid artery. For one wild moment, Billy thought it was kissing him. Then he felt its cold tongue lick his throat from collarbone to jawline, and he felt as if he'd been stung by a hundred needles. Sudden and complete paralysis ensued.

The creature lifted its head and studied his face. Its breath stank worse than the graveyard odor exuded by its repellent flesh. Unable to close his eyes, in the grip of a paralysis so complete that he could not even blink, Billy stared into the demon's maw and saw its moon-white, prickled tongue.

The beast stepped back. Unsupported, Billy dropped limply to the floor. Though he strained, he could not move a single finger.

Grabbing a handful of Billy's well-oiled hair, the beast began to drag him out of the bedroom. He could not resist. He could not even protest, because his voice was as frozen as the rest of him.

He could see nothing but what moved past his fixed gaze, for he could neither turn his head nor roll his eyes. He had glimpses of furniture past which he was dragged, and he could see the walls and the ceiling above, over which shadows cavorted. When he rolled onto his stomach, he felt no pain in his cruelly twisted hair, and thereafter he could see only the floor in front of his face and the demon's clawed black feet as it trod heavily toward the kitchen, where the chase had begun.

Billy's vision blurred, cleared, blurred again, and he thought his failing sight was related to his paralysis. Then he understood that copious but unfelt tears were pouring from his eyes, streaming down his face. In all his mean and hateful life, he had no memory of having wept before.

He knew what was going to happen to him.

In his racing, fear-swollen heart, he *knew.*

The stinking, oozing beast dragged him rudely through the dining room, banging him against the table and chairs. It took him into the kitchen, pulling him through spilled beer, over a carpet of scattered Doritos. The thing plucked the old woman's huge black purse from the table and put it on the floor within Billy's view. The unzippered mouth of the bag yawned wide.

The demon was noticeably smaller now, at least in its legs and torso and head, although the arm—with which it held fast to Billy—remained enormous and powerful. With horror and amazement, but not with much surprise, Billy watched the creature crawl into the purse, shrinking as it went. Then it pulled him in after it.

He didn't feel himself shrinking, but he must have grown smaller in order to fit through the mouth of the purse. Still paralyzed and still held by his hair, Billy looked back under his own arm and saw the kitchen light beyond the purse, saw his own hips balanced on the edge of the bag above him, tried to resist, saw his thighs coming in, then his knees, the bag was swallowing him, oh God, he could do nothing about it, the bag was swallowing him, and now only his feet were still outside, and he tried to dig his toes in, tried to resist, but could not.

Billy Neeks had never believed in the existence of the soul, but now he knew that he possessed one—and that it had just been claimed.

His feet were in the purse now.

All of him was in the purse.

Still looking back under his arm as he was dragged down by his hair, Billy stared desperately at the oval of light above and behind him. It was growing smaller, smaller, not because the zipper was being drawn shut up there, but because the hateful beast was dragging him a long way down into the bag, which made the open end appear to dwindle the same way that the mouth of a turnpike tunnel dwindled in the rearview mirror as one drove toward the other end.

The other end.

Billy could not bear to think about what might be waiting for him at the other end, at the infinitely deep bottom of the purse and beyond it.

He wished that he could go mad. Madness would be a welcome escape from the dread that filled him. Madness would provide sweet relief. But evidently part of his fate was that he should remain totally sane and *acutely* aware.

The light above had shrunk to the size of a small, pale, oblate moon riding high in a night sky.

It was like being born, Billy realized—except that, this time, he was being born out of light and into darkness.

The albescent moonform above shrank to the size of a small and distant star. The star winked out.

In the perfect blackness, many strange voices hissed a welcome to Billy Neeks.

◁ ∧ ▷

That night in late April, the bungalow was filled with distant, echoey screams of terror from so far away that, although carrying through every room of the small house, they did not reach the quiet street beyond the walls and did not draw any attention from nearby residents. The screams continued for a few hours, faded gradually, and were replaced by licking-gnawing-chewing sounds of satisfied consumption.

Then silence.

Silence held dominion for many hours, until the middle of the following afternoon, when the stillness was broken by the sound of an opening door and footsteps.

"Ah," the old woman said happily as she stepped through the kitchen door and saw her purse standing open on the floor. With arthritic slowness, she bent, picked up the bag, and stared into it for a moment.

Smiling, she pulled the zipper shut.

TRAPPED

1

On the night that it happened, a blizzard swept the entire Northeast. Creatures that preferred to venture out only after sunset were, therefore, doubly cloaked by darkness and the storm.

Snow began to fall at twilight, as Meg Lassiter drove home from the doctor's office with Tommy. Powdery flakes sifted out of an iron-gray sky and at first fell straight down through the cold, still air. By the time she had covered eight miles, a hard wind had blasted in from the southwest and harried the snow at a slant through the headlights of the Jeep station wagon.

Behind her, sitting sideways on the rear seat to accommodate his cast-encumbered leg, Tommy sighed. "I'm going to miss a lot of sledding, skiing—ice skating too."

"It's early in the season," Meg said. "You ought to heal up in time to have some fun before spring."

"Yeah, well, maybe." He had broken his leg two weeks ago, and during the follow-up visit to Dr. Jacklin a short while ago, they had learned that he'd be in a cast another six weeks. The fracture was splintered—"minor but complicating comminution"—impacted as well, and it would knit more slowly than a simple break. "But, Mom, there's only so many winters in a life. I hate to waste one."

Meg smiled and glanced at the rearview mirror, in which she could see him. "You're only ten years old, honey. In your case the winters ahead are countless—or darn close to it."

"No way, Mom. Soon it'll be college, which'll mean a lot more studying, not so much time to have fun—"

"That's eight years away!"

"You always say time goes faster the older you get. And after college I'll have a job, and then a family to support."

"Trust me, buckaroo, life doesn't speed up till you're thirty."

Though he was as fun-loving as any ten-year-old, he was also occasionally a strangely serious boy. He'd been that way even as a toddler, but he had become increasingly solemn after his father's death two years ago.

Meg braked for the last stoplight at the north end of town, still seven miles from their farm. She switched on the wipers, which swept the fine dry snow from the windshield.

"How old are you, Mom?"

"Thirty-five."

"Wow, really?"

"You make it sound as if I'm ancient."

"Did they have *cars* when you were ten?"

His laugh was musical. Meg loved the sound of his laughter, perhaps because she had heard so little of it during the past two years.

On the right-hand corner, two cars and a pickup were filling up at the Shell station pumps. A six-foot pine tree was angled across the bed of the truck. Christmas was only eight days away.

On the left-hand corner was Haddenbeck's Tavern, standing before a backdrop of hundred-foot spruces. In the burnt-out gray twilight, the falling snow was like cascading ashes descending from an unseen celestial blaze, though in the amber light of the roadhouse windows, the flakes resembled not ashes but gold dust.

"Come to think of it," Tommy said from the rear seat, "how could there have been cars when you were ten? I mean, gee, they didn't invent the wheel till you were eleven."

"Tonight for dinner—worm cakes and beetle soup."

"You're the meanest mother in the world."

She glanced at the mirror again and saw that in spite of his bantering tone, the boy was not smiling any longer. He was staring grimly at the tavern.

Slightly more than two years ago, a drunk named Deke Slater had left Haddenbeck's Tavern at the same time that Jim Lassiter had been driving toward town to chair a fund-raising committee at St. Paul's Church. Traveling at high speed on Black Oak Road, Slater's

Buick ran head-on into Jim's car. Jim died instantly, and Slater was paralyzed from the neck down.

Often, when they passed Haddenbeck's—and when they rounded the curve where Jim had been killed—Tommy tried to conceal his enduring anguish by involving Meg in a jokey conversation. Not today. He had already run out of one-liners.

"Light's green, Mom."

She went through the intersection and across the township line. Main Street became a two-lane county route: Black Oak Road.

Tommy had adjusted intellectually—for the most part emotionally as well—to the loss of his father. During the year following the tragedy, Meg had often come upon the boy as he sat quietly at a window, lost in thought, tears slipping down his face. She hadn't caught him weeping for ten months. Reluctantly he had accepted his father's death. He would be okay.

Nevertheless, that didn't mean he was *whole*. Still—and perhaps for a long time to come—there was an emptiness in Tommy. Jim had been a wonderful husband but an even better father, so devoted to his son that they essentially had been a part of each other. Jim's death left a hole in Tommy as real as any that a bullet might have made, although it would not scar over as fast as a gunshot wound.

Meg knew that only time could knit him completely.

Snow began to fall faster and dusk surrendered to night, reducing visibility, so she slowed the Jeep wagon. Hunching over the wheel, she could see ahead only twenty yards.

"Getting bad," Tommy said tensely from the rear seat.

"Seen worse."

"Where? The Yukon?"

"Yep. Exactly right. Middle of the Gold Rush, winter of 1849. You forgetting how old I am? I was mushing Yukon dog sleds before they'd invented *dogs.*"

Tommy laughed but only dutifully.

Meg could not see the broad meadows on either side, or the frozen silver ribbon of Seeger's Creek off to the right, although she could make out the gnarled trunks and jagged, winter-stripped limbs of the looming oaks that flanked that portion of the county road. The trees were a landmark by which she judged that she was a quarter mile from the blind curve where Jim had died.

Tommy settled into silence.

Then, when they were seconds from the curve, he said, "I don't really miss sledding and skating so much. It's just . . . I feel so helpless in this cast, so . . . so trapped."

His use of the word "trapped" wrenched Meg because it meant that his uneasiness about being immobilized was closely linked to memories of his dad's death. Jim's Chevy had been so mangled by the impact that the police and coroner's men had required more than three hours to extract his corpse from the overturned car; ensnared by tangled metal, his body had to be cut loose with acetylene torches. At the time, she had tried to protect Tommy from the worst details of the accident, but when eventually he returned to his third-grade class, his schoolmates shared the grisly facts with him, motivated by a morbid curiosity about death and by an innocent cruelty peculiar to some children.

"You're not trapped in the cast," Meg said, as she piloted the Jeep into the long, snow-swept curve. "Hampered, yeah, but not trapped. I'm here to help."

Tommy had come home early from his first day of school after the funeral, bawling: "Daddy was trapped in the car, couldn't move, all tangled up in the twisted metal, they had to cut him loose, he was *trapped.*" Meg soothed him and explained that Jim had been killed on impact, in an instant, and had not suffered: "Honey, it was only his body, his poor empty shell, that was trapped. His mind and soul, your *real* daddy, had already gone up to Heaven."

Now Meg braked as she approached the midpoint of the curve, *that* curve, which would always be a frightening place no matter how often they navigated it.

Tommy had come to accept Meg's assurances that his father had not suffered. Nevertheless, he was still haunted by the image of his dad's body in the clutch of mangled metal.

Suddenly, oncoming headlights seared Meg's eyes. A car rushed at them, moving too fast for road conditions, not out of control but not stable either. It started to fishtail, straddling the double line down the center of the road. Meg pulled the steering wheel to the right, swinging onto the hard shoulder, pumping the brakes, afraid of putting two wheels in a ditch and rolling the station wagon. She held it all the way around the curve, however, with the tires churning up gravel that rattled against the undercarriage. The oncoming car skinned past with no more than an inch to spare, vanishing in the night and snow.

"Idiot," she said angrily.

When she had driven around the bend into a straightaway, she pulled to the side of the road and stopped.

"You okay?" she asked.

Tommy was huddled in one corner of the backseat, with his head pulled turtlelike into the collar of his heavy winter coat. Pale and trembling, he nodded. "Y-yeah. Okay."

The night seemed strangely still in spite of the softly idling Jeep, the thump of windshield wipers, and the wind.

"I'd like to get my hands on that irresponsible jerk." She struck the dashboard with the flat side of her fist.

"It was a Biolomech car," Tommy said, referring to the large research firm located on a hundred acres half a mile south of their farm. "I saw the name on the side. 'Biolomech.' "

She took several deep breaths. "You okay?"

"Yeah. I'm all right. I just . . . want to get home."

The storm intensified. They were beneath the snowy equivalent of a waterfall, flakes pouring over them in churning currents.

Back on Black Oak Road, they crawled along at twenty-five miles an hour. Weather conditions wouldn't permit greater speed.

Two miles farther, at Biolomech Labs, the night was shot full of light. Beyond the nine-foot-high, chain-link fence that ringed the place, sodium-vapor security lamps glowed eerily atop twenty-foot poles, the light diffused by thickly falling snow.

Although the lamps were set at hundred-foot intervals across the expansive grounds that surrounded the single-story offices and research laboratories, they were rarely switched on. Meg had seen them burning on only one other night in the past four years.

The buildings were set back from the road, beyond a screen of trees. Even in good weather and daylight, they were difficult to see, cloistered and mysterious. Currently they were invisible in spite of the hundred or more pools of yellow light that surrounded them.

Pairs of men in heavy coats moved along the perimeter of the property, sweeping flashlights over the fence as if expecting to find a breach, focusing especially on the snow-mantled ground along the chain link.

"Somebody must've tried to break in," Tommy said.

Biolomech cars and vans were clustered around the main gate. Sputtering red emergency flares flickered and smoked along both shoulders of Black Oak Road, leading to a roadblock at which three men held powerful flashlights. Three other men were armed with shotguns.

"Wow!" Tommy said. "Door-buster riot guns! Something really big must've happened."

Meg braked, stopped, and rolled down her window. Cold wind knifed into the car.

She expected one of the men to approach her. Instead, a guard in boots, gray uniform pants, and a black coat with the Biolomech logo moved toward the Jeep from the other side, carrying a long pole at the base of which were attached a pair of angled mirrors and a light. He was accompanied by a much taller man, similarly dressed, who had a shotgun. The shorter guard thrust the lighted mirrors beneath the Jeep and squinted at the reflection of the undercarriage that the first mirror threw onto the second.

"They're looking for bombs!" Tommy said from the rear seat.

"Bombs?" Meg said disbelievingly. "Hardly."

The man with the mirror moved slowly around the Jeep wagon, and his armed companion stayed close at his side. Even in the obscuring snow, Meg could see that their faces were lined with anxiety.

When the pair had circled the Jeep, the armed guard waved an all-clear to the other four at the roadblock, and at last one man approached the driver's window. He wore jeans and a bulky, brown leather flight jacket with sheepskin lining, without a Biolomech patch. A dark blue toboggan cap caked with snow was pulled half over his ears.

He leaned down to the open window. "I'm real sorry for the inconvenience, ma'am."

He was handsome, with an appealing—but false—smile. His gray-green eyes were disturbingly direct.

"What's going on?" she asked.

"Just a security alert," he said, the words steaming from him in the icy air. "Could I see your driver's license, please?"

He was evidently a Biolomech employee, not a police officer, but Meg saw no reason to decline to cooperate.

As the man was holding her wallet, studying the license, Tommy said, "Spies try to sneak in there tonight?"

That same insincere smile accompanied the man's response: "Most likely just a short circuit in the alarm system, son. Nothing here that spies would be interested in."

Biolomech was involved in recombinant-DNA research and the application of their discoveries to commercial enterprises. Meg knew that in recent years genetic engineering had produced a man-made virus that threw off pure insulin as a waste product, a multitude of wonder drugs, and other blessings. She also knew that the same science could engender biological weapons—new diseases as deadly as nuclear bombs—but she always avoided pondering the frightening possibility that Biolomech, half a mile overland from their house, might be engaged in such dangerous work. In fact, a few years ago rumors had surfaced that Biolomech had landed a major defense contract, but the company had assured the county that it would never perform research related to bacteriological warfare. Yet their fence and security system seemed more formidable than necessary for a commercial facility limited to benign projects.

Blinking snow off his lashes, the man in the sheepskin-lined jacket said, "You live near here, Mrs. Lassiter?"

"Cascade Farm," she said. "About a mile down the road."

He passed her wallet back through the window.

From the backseat, Tommy said, "Mister, do you think terrorists with bombs are maybe gonna drive in there and blow the place up or something?"

"Bombs? Whatever gave you that idea, son?"

"The mirrors on the pole," Tommy said.

"Ah! Well, that's just part of our standard procedure in a security alert. Like I said, it's probably a false alarm. Short circuit, something like that." To Meg he said, "Sorry for the trouble, Mrs. Lassiter."

As the man stepped back from the station wagon, Meg glanced past him at the guards with shotguns and at more distant figures combing the eerily lighted grounds. These men did not believe that they were investigating a false alarm. Their anxiety and tension were visible not only in the faces of those nearby but in the way that all of them stood and moved in the blizzard-shot night.

She rolled up the window and put the car in gear.

As she pulled forward, Tommy said, "You think he was lying?"

"It's none of our business, honey."

"Terrorists or spies," Tommy said with the enthusiasm for a good crisis that only young boys could muster.

They passed the northernmost end of Biolomech's land. The sodium-vapor security lights receded into the gloom behind them, while the night and snow closed in from all sides.

More leafless oaks thrust spiky arms over the lane. Among their thick trunks, the Jeep headlights stirred brief-lived, leaping shadows.

Two minutes later, Meg turned left off the county route into their quarter-mile driveway. She was relieved to be home.

Cascade Farm—named after three generations of the Cascade family who once lived there—was a ten-acre spread in semirural Connecticut. It was not a working farm any more. She and Jim had bought the place four years ago, after he had sold his share in the New York ad agency that he'd founded with two partners. The farm was to have been the start of a new life, where he could pursue his dream of being a writer of more than ad copy, and where Meg could enjoy an art studio more spacious and in a more serene environment than anything she could have had in the city.

Before he died, Jim had written two moderately successful suspense novels at Cascade Farm. There also, Meg found new directions for her art: first a brighter tone than she previously had employed; then after Jim's death, a style so brooding and grim that the gallery handling her work in New York had suggested a return to the brighter style if she hoped to continue to sell.

The two-story fieldstone house stood a hundred yards in front of the barn. It had eight rooms plus a spacious kitchen with modern appliances, two baths, two fireplaces, and front and back porches for sitting and rocking on summer evenings.

Even in this stormy darkness, its scalloped eaves bedecked with ice, battered by wind, and lashed by whips of snow, with not a single front window warmed by a lamp's glow, the house looked cozy and welcoming in the headlights.

"Home," she said with relief. "Spaghetti for dinner?"

"Make a lot so I can have cold leftovers for breakfast."

"Yuck."

"Cold spaghetti makes a *great* breakfast."

"You're a demented child." She pulled alongside the house, stopped next to the rear porch, and helped him out of the wagon.

"Leave your crutches. Lean on me," she said over the whistling-hooting wind. The crutches would be of no use on snow-covered ground. "I'll bring them in after I put the Jeep in the garage."

If the heavy cast had not encased his right leg from toes to above the knee, she might have been able to carry him. Instead he leaned on her and hopped on his good leg.

She had left a light in the kitchen for Doofus, their four-year-old black Labrador. The frost-rimed windows shimmered with that amber glow, and the porch was vaguely illuminated by it.

At the door, Tommy rested against the wall of the house while Meg disengaged the lock. When she stepped into the kitchen, the big dog did not rush at her, wagging his tail with excitement, as she expected. Instead he slunk forward with his tail between his legs, his head down, clearly happy to see her but rolling his eyes warily as if expecting an angry cat to streak at him suddenly from one corner or another.

She pushed the door shut behind them and helped Tommy to a chair at the kitchen table. Then she took off her boots and stood them on a rag rug in the corner by the door.

Doofus was shivering, as though cold. But the oil furnace was on, and the place was warm. The dog made an odd, mewling sound.

"What's the matter, Doofus?" she asked. "What've you been up to? Knock over a lamp? Huh? Chew up a sofa cushion?"

"Ah, he's a good pooch," Tommy said. "If he knocked over a lamp, he'll pay for it. Won't you, Doofus?"

The dog wagged his tail but only tentatively. He glanced nervously at Meg, then looked back toward the dining room—as if someone lurked there, someone he feared too much to confront.

Sudden apprehension clutched Meg.

2

BEN PARNELL LEFT THE ROADBLOCK NEAR THE MAIN GATE AND DROVE his Chevy Blazer to lab number three, the building deepest in the Biolomech complex. Snow melted off his toboggan cap and trickled under the collar of his sheepskin-lined flight jacket.

All across the grounds, anxious searchers moved cautiously through the sulfur-yellow glow of the security lamps. In deference to the stinging wind, they hunched their shoulders and held their heads low, which made them appear less than human, demonic.

In a strange way he was glad that the crisis had arisen. If he hadn't been there, he would have been at home, alone, pretending to read, or pretending to watch television, but brooding about Melissa, his much-loved daughter, who was gone, lost to cancer. And if he could have avoided brooding about Melissa, he would have brooded instead about Leah, his wife, who had also been lost to . . .

Lost to what?

He still did not fully understand why their marriage had ended after the ordeal with Melissa was over. As far as Ben could see, the only thing that had come between him and Leah had been her grief, which had been so great and dark and heavy that she had no longer been capable of harboring any other emotion, not even love for him. Maybe the seeds of divorce had been there for a long time, sprouting only after Melissa succumbed, but he had loved Leah; he still loved her, not passionately any more, but in the melancholy way that a man could love a dream of happiness even knowing that the dream could never come true. That's what Leah had become during the past year: not even a memory, painful or otherwise, but a dream, and not even a dream of what might be but of what could never be.

He parked the Blazer in front of lab three, a windowless single-story structure that resembled a bunker. He went to the steel door, inserted his plastic ID card in the slot, reclaimed the card when the light above the entrance changed from red to green, and stepped past that barrier as it slid open with a hiss.

He was in a vestibule that resembled the air lock of a spaceship. The outer door hissed shut behind him, and he stood before the inner door, stripping off his gloves while he was scanned by a security camera. A foot-square wall panel slid open, revealing a lighted screen painted with the blue outline of a right hand. Ben matched his hand to the outline, and the computer scanned his fingerprints. Seconds later, when his identity was confirmed, the inner door slid open, and he went into the main hall, off which led other halls, labs, and offices.

Minutes ago Dr. John Acuff, head of Project Blackberry, had returned to Biolomech in response to the crisis. Now Ben located Acuff in the east-wing corridor where he was conferring urgently with three researchers, two men and a woman, who were working on Blackberry.

As Ben approached, he saw that Acuff was half sick with fear. The director of the project—stocky, balding, with a salt-and-pepper beard—was neither absentminded nor coldly analytic, in no way a stereotypical man of science, and in fact he possessed a splendid sense of humor. There was usually a merry, positively Clausian twinkle in his eyes. No twinkle tonight, however. And no smile.

"Ben! Have you found our rats?"

"Not a trace. I want to talk to you, get some idea where they might go."

Acuff put one hand against his forehead as if checking for a fever. "We've *got* to get them, Ben. And quick. If we don't recover them tonight . . . Jesus, the possible consequences . . . it's the end of everything."

3

THE DOG TRIED TO GROWL AT WHOEVER WAS IN THE DARKNESS BEYOND the archway, but the growl softened into another whine.

Meg moved reluctantly yet boldly to the dining room, fumbling along the wall for the light switch. Clicked it. The eight chairs were spaced evenly around the Queen Anne table; plates gleamed softly behind the beveled panes of the big china cabinet; nothing was out of place. She had expected to find an intruder.

Doofus remained in the kitchen, trembling. He was not an easily frightened dog, yet something had spooked him. Badly.

"Mom?"

"Stay there," she said.

"What's wrong?"

Turning on lamps as she went, Meg searched the living room and the book-lined den. She looked in closets and behind large pieces of furniture. She kept a gun upstairs but didn't want to get it until she was sure that no one was downstairs with Tommy.

Since Jim's death, Meg had been paranoid about Tommy's health and safety. She knew it, admitted it, but could do nothing about her attitude. Every time he got a cold, she was sure it would become pneumonia. When he cut himself, no matter how small the wound, she feared the bleeding, as if the loss of a mere teaspoon of his blood would be the death of him. When, at play, he had fallen out of a tree and broken his leg, she'd nearly fainted at the sight of his twisted limb. If she lost Tommy, whom she loved with all her heart, she would not only be losing her son but the last living part of Jim, as well. More than her own death, Meg Lassiter had learned to fear the deaths of those she loved.

She had been afraid that Tommy would succumb to disease or accident—but, although she'd bought a gun for protection, she had not given much thought to the possibility that her boy might fall victim to foul play. *Foul play.* That sounded so melodramatic, ridiculous. After all, this was the country, uninfected by the violence that had been such a part of life in New York City.

But something had shaken the usually boisterous Labrador, a breed prized for gameness and courage. If not an intruder—what?

She stepped into the front hall and peered up the dark stairs. She flicked a wall switch, turning on the second-floor lights.

Her own courage was draining away. She had stormed through the first-floor rooms, driven by fear for Tommy's welfare, giving no consideration to her safety. Now she began to wonder what she would do if she actually encountered an intruder.

No sound descended from the second floor. She could hear only the keening and susurrant wind. Yet she was overcome by a prescient feeling that she should not venture into the upper rooms.

Perhaps the wisest course would be to return with Tommy to the station wagon and drive to the nearest neighbors, who lived more than a quarter mile north on Black Oak. From there she could call the sheriff's office and ask them to check out the house from attic to basement.

On the other hand, in a rapidly escalating blizzard, travel could be hazardous even in a four-wheel-drive Jeep.

Surely if an intruder was upstairs, Doofus would be barking furiously. The dog was somewhat clumsy, but he was no coward.

Maybe his behavior had not been indicative of fear. Maybe she had misinterpreted his symptoms. His tucked tail, hung head, and trembling flanks could have been signs of illness.

"Don't be such a *wimp*," she said angrily, and she hurriedly climbed the stairs.

The second-floor hall was deserted.

She went to her room and took the 12-gauge, piston-grip, short-barreled Mossberg shotgun from under the bed. It was an ideal weapon for home protection: compact yet plenty powerful enough to deter an assailant. To use it, she didn't have to be a marksman, for the spread pattern of the pellets guaranteed a hit if only she aimed in the general direction of an attacker. Furthermore, by using lightly loaded shells, she could deter an aggressor without having to destroy him. She didn't want to kill anyone.

In fact, hating guns, she might never have acquired the Mossberg if she'd not had Tommy to worry about.

She checked her son's room. No one there.

The two bedrooms at the back of the house had been connected with a wide archway to make one studio. Her drawing board, easels, and white-enameled art-supply cabinets were as she had left them.

No one lurked in either of the bathrooms.

Jim's office, the last place she searched, was deserted too. Evidently she *had* misinterpreted the Labrador's behavior, and she felt a bit sheepish about her overreaction.

She lowered the shotgun and stood in Jim's office, composing herself. After his death, Meg had left the room untouched, so she could use his computer to write letters and do bookkeeping. In fact, she also had sentimental reasons for leaving his things undisturbed. The room helped her to recall how happy Jim had been with a novel under way. He'd had a charmingly boyish aspect that was never more visible than when he was excited about a story, elaborating on a kernel of an idea. Since his funeral, she sometimes came to this room to sit and remember him.

Often she felt trapped by Jim's death, as if a door had slammed shut and locked after him when he had stepped out of her life, as if she were now in a tiny room behind that door, with no key to free herself, with no window by which she could escape.

How could she build a new life, find happiness, after losing a man she had loved so deeply? What she'd had with Jim had been perfection. Could any future relationship equal it?

She sighed, turned off the light, and closed the door on her way out. She returned the shotgun to her own room.

In the hall, as she approached the head of the stairs, she had the peculiar feeling that someone was watching her. This uncanny awareness of being under observation was so powerful that she turned to look back up the hall.

Empty.

Besides, she had searched everywhere. She was certain that she and Tommy were alone.

You're just jumpy because of that maniac jerk on Black Oak Road, driving as if he's guaranteed to live forever.

When she returned to the kitchen, Tommy was sitting in the chair where she'd left him. "What's wrong?" he asked worriedly.

"Nothing, honey. The way Doofus was acting, I thought maybe we had a burglar, but no one's been here."

"Did old Doofus break something?"

"Not that either," she said. "Not that I noticed."

The Labrador was no longer slinking about with his head held low. He wasn't trembling either. He was sitting on the floor beside Tommy's chair when Meg entered the room, but he got up, padded to her, grinned, and nuzzled her hand when she offered it. Then he went to the door and scratched at it lightly with one paw, which was his way of indicating that he needed to go outside to relieve himself.

"I'll put the Jeep away. Take off your coat and gloves," she told Tommy, "but don't you get out of that chair until I come back with your crutches."

She pulled her boots on again and went outside, taking the dog with her, into a storm that had grown more fierce. The snowflakes were smaller and harder, almost sandlike; they made millions of tiny, ticking sounds as they struck the porch roof.

Undaunted by the storm, Doofus dashed into the yard.

Meg parked the station wagon in the barn, which served as a garage. When she got out of the Jeep, she glanced up at half-seen rafters in the gloom above; they creaked as gusts of wind slammed into the roof. The place smelled of oil drippings and grease, but the underlying sweet scent of hay and livestock had not entirely dissipated even after all these years.

As she took Tommy's crutches out of the wagon, she again felt that creepy prickling at the back of her neck—an awareness of being watched. She surveyed the dim interior of the old barn, which was illuminated only by the inadequate bulb on the automatic door opener. Someone could have been lurking behind one of the board dividers that separated the area along the south wall into horse stalls. Someone might be crouching in the loft above. But she saw no evidence of an intruder to justify her suspicion.

"Meg, you've been reading too many mysteries lately," she said aloud, seeking reassurance from the sound of her own voice.

Carrying Tommy's crutches, she stepped outside, pushed the automatic door button, and watched the segmented metal panels roll down until they met the concrete sill with a solid *clunk*.

When she reached the middle of the yard, she stopped, struck by the beauty of the winter nightscape. The scene was revealed primarily by the ghostly radiance of the snow on the ground, a luminescence akin to moonlight but more ethereal and, in spite of the ferocity of the storm, more serene. Marking the northern end of the yard were five leafless maples, stark black branches spearing the night; wind-hammered snow had begun to plate the rough bark.

By morning she and Tommy might be snowbound. A couple of times every winter, Black Oak Road was closed for a day or two by drifts. Being cut off from civilization for short periods wasn't particularly inconvenient and, in fact, had a certain appeal.

Though strangely lovely, the night was also hard. The tiny pellets of snow stung her face.

When she called Doofus, he appeared around the side of the house, half seen in the dimness, more a phantom than a dog. He seemed to be *gliding* over the ground, as if he were not a living creature but a dark revenant. He was panting, wagging his tail, unbothered by the weather, invigorated.

Meg opened the kitchen door. Tommy was still sitting at the table. Behind her, Doofus had halted on the top porch step.

"Come on, pooch, it's cold out here."

The Labrador whined, as if afraid to return to the house.

"Come on, come on. It's suppertime."

He climbed the last step and hesitantly crossed the porch. He put his head in the open door and studied the kitchen with suspicion. He sniffed the warm air—and shuddered.

Meg playfully bumped one boot against the dog's bottom.

He looked at her reproachfully and did not move.

"Come on, boy. You going to leave us in here unprotected?" Tommy asked from his chair by the table.

As if he understood that his reputation was at stake, the dog reluctantly slunk across the threshold.

Meg entered the house and locked the door behind them.

Taking the dog's towel off a wall hook, she said, "Don't you dare shake your coat till I've dried you, pooch."

Doofus shook his coat vigorously as Meg bent to towel his fur, spraying melted snow in her face and over nearby cabinets.

Tommy laughed, so the dog looked at him quizzically, which made Tommy laugh harder, and Meg had to laugh too, and the dog was buoyed by all the merriment. He straightened up from his meek crouch, dared to wag his tail, and went to Tommy.

When she and Tommy had first come home, perhaps they had been tense and frightened because of the crash they'd narrowly avoided at the blind curve on Black Oak Road, and maybe their residual fear had been communicated to Doofus, just as their laughter now lifted his spirits. Dogs were sensitive to human moods, and Meg saw no other explanation for Doofus's behavior.

4

THE WINDOWS WERE FROSTED OVER, AND THE WIND WAS WAILING outside as if it would abrade the whole planet down to the size of a moon, then an asteroid, then a speck of dust. The house seemed all the cozier by contrast.

Meg and Tommy ate spaghetti at the kitchen table.

Doofus wasn't acting as strangely as he had earlier, but he was not himself. More than usual, he sought companionship, even to the extent that he didn't want to eat by himself. Meg watched with surprise and amusement as the dog pushed his dish of Alpo across the floor with his nose, to a spot beside Tommy's chair.

"Next thing you know," Tommy said, "he's going to want to sit in a chair and have his plate on the table."

"First," Meg said, "he'll have to learn to hold a fork properly. I hate it when he holds a fork backward."

"We'll send him to charm school," Tommy said, twirling long strands of spaghetti onto his fork. "And maybe he can learn to stand on his hind feet and walk like a real person."

"Once he can stand erect, he'll want to learn to dance."

"He'll cut a fine figure on the ballroom floor."

They grinned at each other across the dinner table, and Meg relished the special closeness that came only from being silly together. In the past two years Tommy had too seldom been in the mood for frivolity.

Lying on the floor by his dish, Doofus ate his Alpo but didn't gobble it as usual. He nibbled daintily, frequently lifting his head and raising his floppy ears to listen to the wind moaning at the windows.

Later, as Meg was washing the dinner dishes and as Tommy was sitting at the table reading an adventure novel, Doofus suddenly let out a low *woof* of alarm and sprang to his feet. He stood rigidly, staring at the cabinets on the other side of the room, those between the refrigerator and the cellar door.

As she was about to say something to soothe the dog, Meg heard what had alarmed him: a rustling inside the cabinets.

"Mice?" Tommy said hopefully, for he loathed rats.

"Sounds too big for mice."

They'd had rats before. After all, they lived on a farm that had once been attractive to rodents because of the livestock feed stored in the barn. Although the barn housed only a Jeep now, and though the rats had sought better scavenging elsewhere, they returned once every winter, as if the long-ago status of Cascade Farm as a rat haven still stirred in the racial memory of each new generation.

From within the closed cabinet came the frenzied scratching of claws on wood, then a thump as something was knocked over, then the unmistakable sound of a rat-thick, sinuous body slipping along one of the shelves, rattling the stacks of canned goods as it passed between them.

"*Really* big," Tommy said, wide-eyed.

Instead of barking, Doofus whined and padded to the other end of the kitchen, as far from the rat-inhabited cabinet as he could get. At other times he had been eager to pursue rats, although he was not especially successful at catching them.

As she dried her hands on the dishtowel, Meg wondered again about the dog's loss of spirit. She went to the cabinet. There were three sets of doors, top to bottom, and she put her head against the middle set, listening. Nothing.

"It's gone," she said after a long silence.

"You're not going to *open* that, are you?" Tommy asked when she put her hand on one of the door handles.

"Well, of course I am. I have to see how it got in, if maybe it's chewed a hole in the cabinet backing."

"But what if it's still in there?" the boy asked.

"It's not, honey. Anyway, it's disgusting and filthy, but it's not dangerous. Nothing's more cowardly than a rat."

She thumped the cabinet with one fist to be sure she scared off the foul thing if in fact it was in there. She opened the middle doors, saw everything was in order, got on her hands and knees, and opened the lower doors. A few cans were knocked over. A new box of Saltines was chewed open, the contents plundered.

Doofus whimpered.

She reached into the lower cupboard and pushed some of the canned goods aside. She removed several boxes of macaroni and put them on the floor beside her, trying to get a look at the back wall of the cabinet. Just enough light from the kitchen seeped into that secluded space to reveal a ragged-edged hole in the plywood backing, where the rat had chewed through from the wall behind. A vague, cool draft was flowing out of the hole.

She got up, dusting her hands together. "Yep, it's definitely not Mickey Mouse stopping by for a visit. This is a genuine capital R, capital A, capital T. Better get the traps."

As Meg stepped to the cellar door, Tommy said, "You're not leaving me alone?"

"Just till I get the traps, honey."

"But . . . but what if the rat comes around while you're gone?"

"It won't. They like to stay where it's dark."

The boy was blushing, embarrassed by his fear. "It's just . . . with this leg . . . I couldn't get away if it came after me."

Sympathetic but aware that coddling him would encourage his irrational fear, she said, "It won't come after you, skipper. It's more scared of us than we are of it."

She switched on the cellar lights and went down the stairs, leaving him with Doofus. The shadowy basement was lighted by two bulbs dimmed by dust. She found six heavy-duty traps on the utility shelves, rat breakers with steel hammers, not flimsy mousetraps—and a box of warfarin-poisoned food pellets—and she took them upstairs without seeing or hearing the unwelcome houseguest.

Tommy sighed with relief when she returned. "There's something weird about these rats."

"There's probably only one," she said as she put the traps down on the counter by the sink. "What do you mean—weird?"

"They've got Doofus jumpy, like he was when we came home, so it must've been rats that spooked him then too. He doesn't spook easy, so what is it about these rats that have him so nervous?"

"Not rats, plural," Meg corrected. "There's probably just the one. And I don't know what's gotten under that pooch's skin. He's just being silly. Remember how he used to be scared witless by the vacuum cleaner?"

"He was just a puppy then."

"No, he was scared of it until he was almost three," she said as she took from the refrigerator a packet of Buddig dried beef, with which she intended to bait the traps.

Sitting on the floor beside his young master's chair, the dog rolled his eyes at Meg and whined softly.

In truth she was as unnerved by the Labrador's behavior as Tommy was, but by saying so she would only feed the boy's anxiety.

After filling two dishes with the poisoned pellets, she put one in the cupboard under the sink and the other in the cabinet with the Saltines. She left the ravaged crackers as they were, hoping the rat would return for more and take the warfarin instead.

She baited four traps with beef. She put one in the cabinet under the sink. The second went in the cabinet with the Saltines and the dish of warfarin, but on a different shelf from the poison. She placed the third trap in the walk-in pantry and the fourth in the basement.

When she returned to the kitchen, she said, "Let me finish washing the dishes, then we'll move into the living room. We might nail it tonight, but certainly by tomorrow morning."

Ten minutes later, on leaving the kitchen, Meg turned off the lights behind them, hoping that the darkness would lure the rat out of hiding and into a trap before she retired for the night. She and Tommy would sleep better knowing that the thing was dead.

While Meg built a fire in the living-room fireplace, Doofus settled in front of the hearth. Tommy sat in an armchair, put his crutches nearby, propped his castbound leg on a footstool, and opened his adventure novel. Meg programmed the compact-disc player with some easy-listening music and settled into her own chair with a new novel by Mary Higgins Clark.

The wind sounded cold and sharp, but the living room was cozy. In half an hour Meg was involved in the novel when, in a lull between songs, she heard a hard *snap!* from the kitchen.

Doofus lifted his head.

Tommy's eyes met Meg's.

Then a second sound: *Snap!*

"Two," the boy said. "We caught two at the same time!"

Meg put her book aside and armed herself with an iron poker from the fireplace in case the prey needed to be struck to finish them off. She *hated* this part of rat catching.

She went to the kitchen, switched on the lights, and looked first in the cabinet beneath the sink. In the dish, the poisoned food was almost gone. The beef was gone from the big trap too; the steel bar had been sprung, but no rat had been caught.

Nevertheless, the trap wasn't empty. Caught under the bar was a six-inch-long stick of wood, as if it had been used to spring the trap so the bait could be taken safely.

No. That was ridiculous.

Meg took the trap from the cupboard to have a closer look. The stick was stained dark on one side, natural on the other: a strip of plywood. Like the plywood backing in all the cabinets, through which the rat had chewed to get at the Saltines.

A shiver shook her, but she remained reluctant to consider the frightening possibility that had given rise to her tremors.

In the cupboard by the refrigerator, the poisoned bait had been taken from the other dish. The second trap had been sprung too. With another stick of plywood. The bait had been stolen.

What rat was smart enough . . . ?

She rose from her knees and eased open the middle doors of the cabinet. The canned goods, the packages of Jell-O, the boxes of raisins, and the boxes of cereal looked undisturbed at first.

Then she noticed the brown, pea-size pellet on the shelf in front of an open box of All-Bran: a piece of warfarin bait. But she had not put any bait on the shelf with the cereal; all of it had been in the dish below or under the kitchen sink. So a rat had carried a piece of it onto the higher shelf.

If she hadn't been alerted by the pellet, she might not have noticed the scratch marks and small punctures on the package of All-Bran. She stared at the box for a long time before she took it off the shelf and carried it to the sink.

She put the poker on the counter and, with trembling hands, opened the cereal box. She poured some into the sink. Mixed in with the All-Bran were scores of poison pellets. She emptied the entire box into the sink. All the missing bait from both plastic dishes had been transferred to the cereal.

Her heart was racing, pounding so hard that she could feel the throb of her own pulse in her temples.

What the hell is going on here?

Something screeched behind her. A strange, angry sound.

She turned and saw the rat. A hideous white rat.

It was on the shelf where the All-Bran had been, standing on its hind quarters. The shelf was fifteen inches high, and the rat was not entirely erect because it was about eighteen inches long, six inches longer than an average rat, exclusive of its tail. But its size wasn't what iced her blood. The scary thing was its head: twice the size of an ordinary rat's head, as big as a baseball, out of proportion to its body—and oddly shaped, bulging toward the top of the skull, eyes and nose and mouth squeezed in the lower half.

It stared at her and made clawing motions with its upraised fore-paws. It bared its teeth and hissed—actually *hissed* as though it were a cat—then shrieked again, and there was such hostility in its shrill cry and in its demeanor that she snatched up the fireplace poker again.

Though its eyes were beady and red like any rat's, there was a difference about them that she could not immediately identify. The way it stared at her so boldly was intimidating. She looked at its enlarged skull—the bigger the skull, the bigger the brain—and sud-denly realized that its scarlet eyes revealed an unthinkably high, unratlike degree of intelligence.

It shrieked again, challengingly.

Wild rats weren't white.

Lab rats were white.

She knew now what they had been hunting for at the roadblock at Biolomech. She didn't know *why* their researchers would have wanted to create such a beast as this, and though she was a well-educated woman and had a layman's knowledge of genetic engi-neering, she didn't know *how* they had created it, but she knew beyond a doubt that they *had* created it, for there was no place else on earth from which it could have come.

Clearly, it had not ridden on the undercarriage of their car. Even as Biolomech's security men had been searching for it, this rat had been here, out of the cold, setting up house.

On the shelf behind it and on the three shelves below it, other rats pushed through cans, bottles, and boxes. They were repulsively large and pale like the mutant that still challenged her from the cereal shelf.

Behind her, claws clicked on the floor.

More of them.

Meg did not even look back, and she didn't delude herself into thinking that she could handle them with the poker. She threw that useless weapon aside and ran for her shotgun upstairs.

5

BEN PARNELL AND DR. ACUFF CROUCHED IN FRONT OF THE CAGE THAT stood in one corner of the windowless room. It was a six-foot cube with a sheet-metal floor that had been softened with a deep layer of silky yellow-brown grass. The food and water dispensers could be filled from outside but were operable from within, so the occupants could obtain nourishment as they desired it. One third of the pen was equipped with miniature wooden ladders and climbing bars for exercise and play.

The cage door was open.

"Here, see?" Acuff said. "It locks automatically every time the door is shut. Can't be left unlocked by mistake. And once shut, it can only be opened with a key. Seemed safe to us. I mean, we didn't think they'd be smart enough to pick a lock!"

"But surely they didn't. How could they—without hands?"

"You ever take a close look at their feet? A rat's feet aren't like hands, but they're more than just paws. There's an articulation of digits that lets them grasp things. It's true of most rodents. Squirrels, for instance: You've seen them sitting up, holding a piece of fruit in their forepaws."

"Yes, but without an opposable thumb—"

"Of course," Acuff said, "they don't have great dexterity, nothing like we have, but these aren't ordinary rats. Remember, these creatures have been genetically engineered. Except for the shape and size of their craniums, they aren't physically much different from other rats, but they're *smarter*. A lot smarter."

Acuff was involved in intelligence-enhancement experiments, seeking to discover if lower species, like rats, could be genetically altered to breed future generations with drastically increased brain power, in hope that success with lab animals might lead to procedures that would enhance human intelligence. His research was labeled

Project Blackberry in honor of the brave, intelligent rabbit of the same name in Richard Adams's *Watership Down.*

At John Acuff's suggestion, Ben had read and immensely enjoyed Adams's book, but he had not yet quite decided whether he approved or disapproved of Project Blackberry.

"Anyway," Acuff said, "whether they could have picked the cage lock is debatable. And maybe they didn't. Because there's *this* to consider." He pointed to the slot in the frame of the cage door where the stubby brass bolt was supposed to fit when engaged. The slot was packed full of a grainy brown substance. "Food pellets. They chewed up food pellets, then filled the slot with the paste, so the bolt couldn't automatically engage."

"But the door had to be open for them to do that."

"It must have happened during a maze run."

"A what?"

"Well, there's this flexible maze we constantly reconfigure, half as big as this whole room. It's made of clear plastic tubes with difficult obstacles. We attach it to the front of the cage, then just open their door, so they go straight from the cage into the maze. We were doing that yesterday, so the cage was open a long time. If some of them paused at the door before entering the maze, if they sniffed around the lock slot for a few seconds, we might not have noticed. We were more interested in what they did *after* they entered the maze."

Ben rose from a crouch. "I've already seen how they got out of the room itself. Have you?"

"Yeah."

They went to the far end of the long room. Near floor level, something had tampered with an eighteen-inch-square intake duct to the building's ventilation system. The grille had been held in place only by light tension clamps, and it had been torn away from the opening behind it.

Acuff said, "Have you looked in the exchange chamber?"

Because of the nature of the work done in lab number three, all air was chemically decontaminated before being vented to the outside. It was forced under pressure through multiple chemical baths in a five-tiered exchange chamber as big as a pickup truck.

"They couldn't get through the exchange chamber alive," Acuff said hopefully. "Might be eight dead rats in those chemical baths."

Ben shook his head. "There aren't. We checked. And we can't find vent grilles disturbed in other rooms, where they might have left the ducts—"

"You don't think they're still in the ventilation system?"

"No, they must've gotten out at some point, into the walls."

"But how? PVC pipe is used for the ductwork, pressure sealed with a high-temperature bonding agent at all joints."

Ben nodded. "We think they chewed up the adhesive at one of the joints, loosened two sections of pipe enough to squeeze out. We've found rat droppings in the crawl-space attic . . . and a place where they gnawed through the subroof and the overlying shingles. Once on the roof, they could get off the building by gutters and downspouts."

John Acuff's face had grown whiter than the salt part of his salt-and-pepper beard. "Listen, we've got to get them back tonight, no matter what. *Tonight.*"

"We'll try."

"Just trying isn't good enough. We've *got* to do it. Ben, there are three males and five females in that pack. And they're fertile. If we don't get them back, if they breed in the wild . . . ultimately they'll drive ordinary rats into extinction, and we'll be faced with a menace unlike anything we've known. Think about it: *smart* rats that recognize and elude traps, quick to detect poison bait, virtually ineradicable. Already, the world loses a large portion of its food supply to rats, ten or fifteen percent in developed countries like ours, fifty percent in many third-world countries. Ben, we lose that much to *dumb* rats. What'll we lose to these? We might eventually see famine even in the United States—and in less advanced countries, there could be starvation beyond imagination."

Frowning, Ben said, "You're overstating the danger."

"Absolutely not! Rats are parasitical. They're competitors, and these will be competing far more vigorously and aggressively than any rats we've ever known."

The lab seemed as cold as the winter night outside. "Just because they're a bit smarter than ordinary rats—"

"More than a bit. Scores of times smarter."

"But not as smart as we are, for heaven's sake."

"Maybe half as smart as the average man," Acuff said.

Ben blinked in surprise.

"Maybe even smarter than that," Acuff said, fear evident in his lined face and eyes. "Combine that level of intellect with their natural cunning, size advantage—"

"Size advantage? But we're much bigger—"

Acuff shook his head. "Small can be better. Because they're smaller, they're faster than we are. And they can vanish through a chink in the wall, down a drainpipe. They're bigger than the average rat, about eighteen inches long instead of twelve, but they can move unseen through the shadows because they're still relatively small. And size isn't their only advantage, however. *They can also see at night as well as in daylight.*"

"Doc, you're starting to scare me."

"You better be scared half to death. Because these rats we've made, this new species we've engineered, is hostile to us."

Finally Ben was forming an opinion of Project Blackberry. It wasn't favorable. Not sure he wanted to know the answer to his own question, he said, "What exactly do you mean by that?"

Turning away from the wall vent, walking to the center of the room, planting both hands on the marble lab bench, leaning forward with his head hung down and his eyes closed, Acuff said, "We don't know why they're hostile. They just are. Is it some quirk of their genetics? Or have we made them just intelligent enough so they can understand that we're their masters—and resent it? Whatever the reason, they're aggressive, fierce. A few researchers were badly bitten. Sooner or later someone would've been killed if we hadn't taken extreme precautions. We handled them with heavy bite-proof gloves, wearing Plexiglas face masks, suited in specially made Kevlar coveralls with high, rolled collars. *Kevlar!* That's the stuff they make bulletproof vests out of, for God's sake, and we needed something that tough because these little bastards were determined to hurt us."

Astonished, Ben said, "But why didn't you destroy them?"

"We couldn't destroy a success," Acuff said.

Ben was baffled. "Success?"

"From a scientific point of view, their hostility wasn't important because they were also *smart*. What we were trying to create was smart rats, and we succeeded. Given time, we figured to identify the cause of the hostility and deal with it. That's why we put them all in one pen—'cause we thought their isolation in individual cages might be to blame for their hostility, that they were intelligent enough to need a communal environment, that housing them together might—mellow them."

"Instead it only facilitated their escape."

Acuff nodded. "And now they're loose."

6

HURRYING ALONG THE HALL, MEG PASSED THE WIDE ARCHWAY TO THE living room and saw Tommy struggling up from his chair, groping for his crutches. Doofus was whining, agitated. Tommy called to Meg, but she didn't pause to answer because every second counted.

Turning at the newel post, starting up the stairs, she glanced back and could see no rats following her. The light wasn't on in the hallway itself, however, so something could have been scurrying through the shadows along the baseboard.

She climbed the steps two at a time and was breathing hard when she reached the second floor. In her room, she took the shotgun from under the bed and chambered the first of the five rounds in the magazine.

A vivid image of rats swarming through the cabinet flickered across her mind, and she realized that she might need additional ammo. She kept a box of fifty shells in her clothes closet, so she slid open that door—and cried out in surprise when two large, white rats scuttled across the closet floor. They clambered over her shoes and disappeared through a hole in the wall, moving too fast for her to take a shot at them even if she had thought to do so.

She had kept the box of shells on the closet floor, and the rats had found it. They had chewed open the cardboard carton and stolen the shells one at a time, carrying them away through the hole in the wall.

Only four rounds were left. She scooped them up and stuffed them into the pockets of her jeans.

If the rats had succeeded in making off with all the shells, would they then have tried subsequently to find a way to remove the last five rounds from the shotgun's magazine as well, leaving her defenseless? Just how smart *were* they?

Tommy was calling her, and Doofus was barking angrily.

Meg left the bedroom at a run. She descended the steps so fast that she risked twisting an ankle.

The Labrador was in the first-floor hall, his sturdy legs planted wide, his blocky head lowered, his ears flattened against his skull. He was staring intently toward the kitchen, no longer barking but growling menacingly, even though he was also trembling with fear.

Meg found Tommy in the living room, standing with the aid of his crutches, and she let out a wordless cry of relief when she saw that no rats were swarming over him.

"Mom, what is it? What's wrong?"

"The rats . . . I think . . . I *know* they're from Biolomech. That's what the roadblock was all about. That's what those men were looking for with their spotlights, with the angled mirrors they poked under the car." She swept the room with her gaze, looking for furtive movement along the walls and beside the furniture.

"How do you know?" the boy asked.

"I've seen them. You'll know it too, if you see them."

Doofus remained in the hall, but Meg took small comfort from the warning growl he directed toward the kitchen. She realized the dog was no match for these rats. They'd trick or overpower him without difficulty, as soon as they were ready to attack.

They *were* going to attack. Besides being genetically altered, with large skulls and brains, they *behaved* differently from other rats. By nature rats were scavengers, not hunters, and they thrived because they skulked through shadows, living secretively in walls and sewers; they never dared to assault a human being unless he was helpless— an unconscious wino, a baby in a crib. But the Biolomech were bold and hostile, hunters as well as scavengers. Their scheme to steal her shotgun shells and disarm her was clear preparation for an attack.

His voice shaky, Tommy said, "But if they aren't like ordinary rats, what *are* they like?"

She remembered the hideously enlarged skull, the scarlet eyes informed with malevolent intelligence, the pale and plump and somehow obscene white body. She said, "I'll tell you later. Come on, honey, we're getting out of here."

They could have gone out the front door, around the house, and across the rear yard to the barn in which the Jeep was parked, but that was a long way through driving snow for a boy on crutches. Meg decided they would have to go through the kitchen and out the back. Besides, their coats were drying on the rack by the rear door, and her car keys were in her coat.

Doofus bravely led them along the hall to the kitchen, though he was not happy about it.

Meg stayed close to Tommy, holding the pistol-grip, pump-action 12-gauge ready in both hands. Five shells in the gun, four in her pockets. Was that enough? How many rats had escaped Biolomech? Six? Ten? Twenty? She would have to avoid shooting them one at a time, save her ammunition until she could take them out in twos or threes. Yes, but what if they didn't attack in a pack? What if they rushed at her singly, from several different directions, forcing her to swivel left and right and left again, blasting at them one at a time until her ammunition was all gone? She *had* to stop them before they reached her or Tommy, even if they came singly, because once they were on her or climbing the boy, the shotgun would be useless; then she and Tommy would have to defend themselves with bare hands against sharp teeth and claws. They'd be no match for even half a dozen large, fearless—and smart—rats intent on tearing out their throats.

But for the wind outside and the tick of granular snow striking the windows, the kitchen was silent. The cupboard stood open, as she had left it, but no rats crouched on the shelves.

This was *crazy!* For two years she had worried about raising Tommy without Jim's help. She'd been concerned about instilling in him the right values and principles. His injuries and illnesses had scared her. She had worried about how she would handle unexpected crises if they arose, but she had never contemplated anything as unexpected as *this*. Sometimes she had taken comfort in the thought that she and Tommy lived in the country, where crime was not a concern, because if they had still lived in the city, she would have had even more to worry about; but now bucolic Cascade Farm, at the hayseed end of Black Oak Road, had proved to be as dangerous as any crime-riddled metropolis.

"Put on your coat," she told Tommy.

Doofus's ears pricked. He sniffed the air. He turned his head side to side, surveying the base of the cupboards, the refrigerator, the unlit open cabinet under the sink.

Holding the Mossberg in her right hand, Meg speared her own coat off the rack with her left, struggled until she got her arm into it, took the shotgun in her left hand, shrugged her right arm into the second sleeve. She used just one hand to pull on her boots, refusing to put down the weapon.

Tommy was staring at the rat trap that she had left on the counter, the one that she had taken from under the sink. The stick that the rats had used to trip the mechanism was still wedged between the anvil and the hammer bar. Tommy frowned at it.

Before he could ask questions or have more time to think, Meg said, "You can do without a boot on your good foot. And leave your crutches here. They're no good outside. You'll have to lean on me."

Doofus twitched and went rigid.

Meg brought up the gun and scanned the kitchen.

The Labrador growled deep in his throat, but there was no sign of the rats.

Meg pulled open the back door, letting in the frigid wind. "Let's move, let's go, now."

Tommy lurched outside, holding on to the door frame, then balancing against the porch wall. The dog slipped out after him. Meg followed, closing the door behind them.

Holding the Mossberg in her right hand, using her left arm to support Tommy, she helped the boy across the porch, down the snow-covered steps, and into the yard. With the windchill factor, the temperature must have been below zero. Her eyes teared, and her face went numb. She hadn't paused to put on gloves, and the cold sliced through to the bones of her hands. Still, she felt better outside than in the house, safer. She didn't think that the rats would come after them, for the storm was a far greater obstacle to those small creatures than it was to her and Tommy.

Conversation was impossible because the wind keened across the open land, whistled under the eaves of the house, and clattered the bare branches of the maples against one another. She and Tommy progressed silently, and Doofus stayed at their side.

Though they slipped several times and almost fell, they reached the barn quicker than she had expected, and she hit the switch to put up the electric door. They ducked under the rising barrier before it was entirely out of their way. In the weak light of the lone bulb, they went directly to the station wagon.

She fished her keys out of her coat pocket, opened the door on the passenger side, slid the seat back all the way on its tracks, and helped Tommy into the front of the car because she wanted him beside her now, close, not in the backseat, even if he would have been more comfortable there. When she looked around for the dog, she saw that he was standing outside the barn, at the threshold, unwilling to follow them inside.

"Doofus, here, quick now," she said.

The Labrador whined. Surveying the shadows in the barn, he let the whine deepen into a growl.

Remembering the feeling of being watched when she had parked the Jeep in the barn earlier, Meg also scanned the murky corners and the tenebrous reaches of the loft, but she saw neither pale, slinking figures nor the telltale red glimmer of rodent eyes.

The Labrador was probably excessively cautious. His condition was understandable, but they had to get moving. More forcefully, Meg said, "Doofus, get in here, right now."

He entered the barn hesitantly, sniffing the air and floor, came to her with a sudden urgency, and jumped into the backseat of the station wagon.

She closed the door, went around to the other side, and got in behind the wheel. "We'll drive back to Biolomech," she said. "We'll tell them we've found what they're looking for."

"What's wrong with Doofus?"

In the backseat, the dog was moving from one side window to the other, peering out at the barn, making thin, anxious sounds.

"He's just being Doofus," Meg said.

Huddled in his seat, angled awkwardly to accommodate his cast, Tommy appeared to be younger than ten, so frightened and vulnerable.

"It's okay," Meg said. "We're out of here."

She thrust the key in the ignition, turned it. Nothing. She tried again. The Jeep would not start.

7

AT THE HIGH FENCE ALONG THE NORTHEAST FLANK OF THE BIOLOMECH property, Ben Parnell crouched to examine the rat-size tunnel in the half-frozen earth. Several of his men gathered around him, and one directed the beam of a powerful flashlight on the patch of ground in question. Luckily the hole was in a place where the wind scoured most of the snow away instead of piling it in drifts, but the searchers had still not spotted it until they'd made a second circuit of the perimeter.

Steve Harding raised his voice to compete with the wind: "Think they're in there, curled up in a burrow?"

"No," Ben said, his breath smoking in the arctic air. If he'd thought that the rats were in a burrow at the end of this entrance tunnel, he would not have been crouched in front of the hole, where one of them might fly out at him, straight at his face.

Hostile, John Acuff had said. Exceedingly hostile.

Ben said, "No, they weren't digging a permanent burrow. They came up somewhere on the other side of this fence, and they're long gone now."

A tall, lanky young man in a county sheriff's department coat joined the group. "One of you named Parnell?"

"That's me," Ben said.

"I'm Joe Hockner." He was half shouting to be heard above the skirling wind. "Sheriff's office. I brought the bloodhound you asked for."

"Terrific."

"What's happenin' here?"

"In a minute," Ben said, returning his attention to the tunnel that went under the fence.

"How do we know it was them that dug here?" asked George Yancy, another of Ben's men. "Could've been some other animal."

"Bring that light closer," Ben said.

Steve Harding shone the beam directly into the five-inch-diameter tunnel.

Squinting, leaning closer, Ben saw what appeared to be snippets of white thread adhering to the moist earth just far enough inside the hole to be undisturbed by the wind. He took off his right glove, reached carefully into the mouth of the tunnel, and plucked up two of the threads. White hairs.

8

TOMMY AND THE DOG STAYED IN THE STATION WAGON WHILE MEG GOT out with the shotgun—and with a flashlight from the glove compartment—to open the hood. The light revealed a mess of torn and tangled wires inside the engine compartment; all the lines from the spark plugs to the distributor cap were severed. Holes had been gnawed in the hoses; oil and coolants dripped onto the barn floor under the Jeep.

She was no longer just scared. She was flat-out terrified. Yet she had to conceal her fear to avoid panicking Tommy.

She closed the hood, went around to the passenger's side, and opened the door. "I don't know what's wrong, but it's dead."

"It was all right a while ago, when we came home."

"Yes, well, but it's dead now. Come on, let's go."

He allowed her to help him out of the car, and when they were face to face, he said, "The rats got to it, didn't they?"

"Rats? The rats are in the house, yes, and they're ugly things, like I said, but—"

Interrupting her before she could lie to him, the boy said, "You're trying not to show it, but you're afraid of them, really afraid, which must mean they're not just a little different from ordinary rats but a whole lot different, because you don't scare easy, not you. You were scared when Dad died, I know you were, but not for long, you took charge real quick, you made me feel safe, and if Dad's dying couldn't make you fall to pieces, then I guess pretty much nothing can. But these rats from Biolomech, whatever they are, *they* scare you more than anything ever has."

She hugged him tight, loving him so hard that it almost hurt—though she did not let go of the shotgun.

He said, "Mom, I saw the trap with the stick in it, and I saw the cereal in the sink all mixed up with the poison pellets, and I've been thinking. I guess one thing about these rats is . . . they're awful smart, maybe because of something that was done to them at the lab, smarter than rats should ever be, and now they somehow zapped the Jeep."

"They're not smart enough. Not smart enough for us, skipper."

"What're we going to do?" he whispered.

She also whispered, though she had seen no rats in the barn and was not sure that they had remained after disabling the station wagon. Even if they were nearby, watching, she was certain that they could not understand English. Surely there were limits to what the people at Biolomech had done to these creatures. But she whispered anyway, "We'll go back to the house—"

"But maybe that's what they want us to do."

"Maybe. But I've got to try to use the telephone."

"They'll have thought of the phone," he said.

"Maybe but probably not. I mean how smart can they *be?*"

"Smart enough to think of the Jeep."

9

BEYOND THE FENCE WAS A MEADOW APPROXIMATELY A HUNDRED YARDS across, and at the end of the meadow were woods.

The chance of finding the rats now was slim. The men fanned out across the field in teams of two and three, not sure what signs of their quarry could have survived the storm. Even in good weather, on a dry and sunny day, it would be virtually impossible to track animals as small as rats across open ground.

Ben Parnell took four men directly to the far side of the meadow, where they began searching the perimeter of the forest with the aid of the bloodhound. The dog's name was Max. He was built low and broad, with huge ears and a comical face, but there was nothing funny about his approach to the case at hand: He was eager, serious. Max's handler, Deputy Joe Hockner, had given the dog a whiff of the rats' spoor from a jarful of grass and droppings that had been taken from their cage, and the hound hadn't liked what he smelled. But the scent was apparently so intense and unusual that it was easy to follow, and Max was a game tracker, willing to give his best in spite of wind and snow.

Within two minutes the hound caught the scent in a clump of winter-dried brush. Straining at his leash, he pulled Hockner into the woods. Ben and his men followed.

10

MEG LET DOOFUS OUT OF THE STATION WAGON, AND THE THREE OF THEM headed toward the big open door of the barn, past which the storm wind drove whirling columns of snow like ghosts late for a haunting. The blizzard had accelerated, raising a noisy clatter on the roof as it tore off a few shingles and spun them away in the night. The rafters creaked, and the loft door chattered on loose hinges.

"Tommy, you'll stay out on the porch, and I'll go into the kitchen as far as the phone. If it's out of order . . . we'll walk the driveway to the county road and flag down a car."

"No one's going to be out in this storm."

"Someone will be. A county snowplow or a cinder truck."

He halted at the threshold of the open barn door. "Mom, it's three quarters of a mile to Black Oak Road. I'm not sure I can walk that far with this cast, in this storm, not even with you helping. I'm already tired, and my good leg keeps buckling. Even if I can do it, it'll take a long, long time."

"We'll make it," she said, "and it doesn't matter how long we take. I'm sure they won't pursue us outside. We're safe in the storm— safe from *them*, at least." Then she remembered the sled. "I can pull you to the county road!"

"What? Pull me?"

She risked leaving Tommy with Doofus long enough to run back into the barn, to the north wall, where the boy's sled—*Midnight Flyer* was the legend in script across the seat—hung on the wall beside a shovel, a hoe, and a leaf rake. Without putting down the Mossberg, she quickly unhooked the sled and carried it in one hand to the open door where Tommy waited.

"But, Mom, I'm too heavy to pull."

"Haven't I pulled you back and forth over this farm on at least a hundred snowy days?"

"Yeah, but that was years ago, when I was little."

"You're not so huge now, buckaroo. Come on."

She was pleased that she had remembered the sled. She had one great advantage over this high-tech Hamlin plague: She was a mother with a child to protect, and that made her a force with which even Biolomech's nightmares would find it hard to reckon.

She took the sled outside and helped him onto it.

He sat with his shoe-clad left foot braced against the guide bar. His right foot was covered with the cast except for his toes, and both his toes and the lower part of the cast were sheathed in a thick woolen sock that was now wet and half frozen; nevertheless, he managed to wedge even that foot into the space in front of the guide bar. When he held on to the sides of the sled with both hands, he was in no danger of falling off.

Doofus circled them anxiously as they got Tommy settled on the sled. Several times he barked at the barn behind them, but each time that Meg looked back, she saw nothing.

Picking up the sturdy nylon towrope, Meg prayed that when they got to the house the phone would work, that she would be able to call for help. She dragged Tommy across the long backyard. In some places the runners cut through the thin layer of snow, digging into frozen ground beneath, and the going was tough. In other places, however, where the snow was deeper or the ground icy, the sled glided smoothly enough to give her hope that, if they had to, they would be able to reach the county road before the relentless gales hammered her to her knees in exhaustion.

11

THE BRUSH ON THE FOREST FLOOR WAS NOT TOO DENSE, AND THE RATS evidently took advantage of deer trails to make greater speed, for the bloodhound plunged relentlessly forward, leading the searchers where the creatures had gone. Fortunately the interlaced evergreens kept most of the snow from sifting under the trees, which made their job easier and was a boon to the stumpy-legged dog. Ben expected Max to bay, for he had seen all the old jailbreak movies in which Cagney or Bogart had been pursued by baying hounds, but Max made a lot of chuffing and snuffling sounds, barked once, and did not bay at all.

They had gone a quarter of a mile from the Biolomech fence, stumbling on the uneven ground, frequently spooked by the bizarre shadows stirred by the bobbling beams of the flashlights, when Ben realized that the rats had not burrowed into the forest floor. If that had been their intention, they could have tunneled into the ground shortly after entering the cover of the trees. But they had raced on, searching for something better than a wild home, which made sense because they were *not* wild, far from it. They had been bred from generations of tame lab rats and lived all their lives in a cage, with food and water constantly available. They would be at a loss in the woods, even as smart as they were, so they would try to press ahead in hope of finding a human habitation to share, travel as far as possible before exhaustion and the deepening cold stopped them.

Cascade Farm.

Ben remembered the attractive woman in the Jeep wagon: chestnut hair, almond-brown eyes, an appealing spatter of freckles. The boy in the backseat, his leg in a cast, had been nine or ten and had reminded Ben of his own daughter, Melissa, who had been nine when she had lost her hard-fought war with cancer. The boy had that look of innocence and vulnerability that Melissa had possessed and that had made it so hard for Ben to watch her decline. Peering at mother and son through the open car window, Ben had envied them the normal life he imagined they led, the love and sharing of a family unscathed by the whims of fate.

Now, crashing through the woods behind Deputy Hockner and the dog, Ben was seized by the horrible certainty that the rats— having escaped from Biolomech hours before the snow began to fall—had made it to Cascade Farm, the nearest human habitat, and that the family he had envied was in mortal danger. Lassiter. That was their name. With a surety almost psychic in intensity, Ben knew that the rats had taken up residence with the Lassiters.

Hostile, Acuff had said. Exceedingly hostile. Mindlessly, unrelentingly, demonically hostile.

"Hold up! Wait! Hold up!" he shouted.

Deputy Hockner reined in Max, and the search party came to a halt in a clearing encircled by wind-shaken pines. Explosive clouds of crystallized breath plumed from the nostrils and mouths of the men, and they all turned to look questioningly at Ben.

He said, "Steve, go back to the main gate. Load up a truck with men and get down to Cascade Farm. You know it?"

"Yeah, it's the next place along Black Oak Road."

"God help those people, but I'm sure the rats have gone there. It's the only warm place near enough. If they didn't stumble on Cascade Farm and take refuge there, then they'll die in this storm— and I don't think we're lucky enough to count on the weather having done them in."

"I'm on my way," Steve said, turning back.

To Deputy Hockner, Ben said, "All right, let's go. And let's hope to God I'm wrong."

Hockner relaxed the tension on Max's leash. This time the hound bayed once, long and low, when he caught the rats' scent.

12

BY THE TIME MEG DREW THE SLED ACROSS THE LONG YARD TO THE FOOT of the porch steps, her heart was thudding almost painfully, and her throat was raw from the frigid air. She was far less sanguine than she first had been about her ability to haul Tommy all the way out to the county road. The task might have been relatively easy after the storm had passed; however, now she was not just fighting the boy's weight but the vicious wind as well. Furthermore, the sled's runners had not been sanded, oil polished, and soaped in preparation for the season, so the rust on them created friction.

Doofus stayed close to the sled, but he was beginning to suffer from the effects of the blizzard. He shuddered uncontrollably. His coat was matted with snow. In the vague amber light that radiated from the kitchen windows to the yard at the bottom of the porch steps, Meg could see tiny glistening icicles hanging from the ruff on the Labrador's throat.

Tommy was in better shape than the dog. He had pulled up the hood on his coat and had bent forward, keeping his face out of the punishing wind. But neither he nor Meg wore insulated underwear, and they were both dressed in jeans rather than heavy outdoor pants. On the longer trek from the house to Black Oak Road, the wind would leach a lot of heat from them.

Again she prayed that the telephone would work.

Looking up at her, Tommy was bleak faced within the cowl of his coat. All but shouting against the cacophonous babble of the storm, she told him to wait there (as if he could do anything else), told him that she would be back in a minute (although they both knew that something terrible could happen to her in the house).

Carrying the 12-gauge Mossberg, she went up the porch steps and cautiously opened the back door. The kitchen was a mess. Packages of food had been dragged out of the cabinets, torn open, and the contents scattered across the floor. Several kinds of cereal, sugar, flour, cornstarch, cornmeal, crackers, cookies, macaroni, and spaghetti were mixed with the shattered glass and wet contents of a score of broken jars of spaghetti sauce, applesauce, cherries, olives, and pickles.

The destruction was unnerving because it was so unmistakably an expression of mindless rage. The rats had not torn these packages to obtain food. The creatures seemed so inimical to humankind that they destroyed people's property for the joy of it, reveling in the ruin and waste in much the way that gremlins of age-old myth were supposed to delight in the trouble that they caused.

These monsters, of course, were man-made. What kind of world had it become when men created their own goblins? Or had that always been the case?

She could see no signs of the rats that had caused the ruin in the kitchen, no furtive movement in the shadowy cupboards, no sinuous forms slinking along the walls or through the rubble. Cautiously she stepped across the threshold into the house.

The icy wind came with her, exploding through the door, as if it were water under high pressure. White clouds of flour and sparkling miniature tornadoes of sugar granules were spun across the room, and some of the heavier debris—Cheerios and broken bits of spaghetti—took flight as well.

Garbage and shattered glass crunched underfoot as she edged warily to the telephone, which hung on the wall on the far side of the room, near the refrigerator.

Three times she saw movement from the corner of her eye and was sure it was purposeful—the rats—and she swung the muzzle of the shotgun to bear on it. But it was always just an empty raisin box or the torn wrapper from a package of cookies stirring in the invasive wind.

She reached the phone and lifted the handset. No dial tone. The line was dead, either because of the storm or the rats.

As Meg regretfully returned the handset to its cradle, the wind subsided. In the suddenly still air, she smelled fumes. Natural gas. No, not natural gas. Something else. More like . . . gasoline.

Heating oil.

All her internal alarm bells began to clang.

Now that cold wind was no longer sweeping through the room, Meg realized that the house reeked of heating-oil fumes, which must be rising from the basement where the lines between the big oil tank and the furnace had been breached. She had walked into a trap. These ratlike gremlins were so hostile, so demonic, that they were willing to destroy the house that provided them with shelter if, in leveling it, they could kill one human being.

She stepped away from the telephone, toward the door.

Through the ventilation duct she heard the soft, hollow, echoey, familiar *thump-click-whoosh* of the electronic pilot light on the basement furnace: the sparking of an electric arc to ignite the heating coils.

A fraction of a second later, before she could even take a second step, the house exploded.

13

FOLLOWING THE BLOODHOUND AND DEPUTY HOCKNER, FOLLOWED IN turn by three of his own men, Ben Parnell reached the northern perimeter of the woods and saw the faint lights of the house at Cascade Farm, dimly visible through the heavily falling snow, perhaps two hundred yards away across a sloping field.

"I *knew* it," he said. "That's where they've gone."

He thought of the woman and the boy in the station wagon, and he was overcome by a powerful sense of responsibility for them that went beyond his duties at Biolomech. For two years he'd felt that he had failed his own child, Melissa, by not saving her from cancer, which was irrational, of course, because he was not a doctor and did not have the knowledge to cure her. But his profound feeling of failure couldn't be assuaged. He'd always had an unusually strong sense of responsibility to and for others, a virtue that sometimes could be a curse. Now, as he looked down on Cascade Farm, he was gripped by a powerful and urgent need to ensure the safety of that woman, her boy, and whatever other members of their family shared the farmhouse.

"Let's move," he said to his men.

Deputy Hockner was unfolding a lightweight blanket made from one of those space-age materials with high insulation. "You go ahead," he said, dropping to his knees and wrapping Max in the blanket. "My dog has to warm up. He isn't built for prolonged exposure to this kind of weather. Soon as he's thawed out a bit, we'll follow you."

Ben nodded, turned, and took only two steps when, out on the lowlands, the farmhouse exploded. A yellow-orange flash of light was followed by a shock wave, a low and ominous *wham* that was felt as much as heard. Flames leaped from the shattered windows and raced up the walls.

14

THE FLOOR BUCKED, THROWING MEG OFF HER FEET; THEN IT FELL INTO place, and she fell with it, facedown in the torn packages, scattered food, and glass. The breath was knocked out of her, and she was temporarily deafened by the blast. But she was not so disoriented that she was unaware of the fire, which licked up the walls and spread across the floor with frightening speed, as though it were alive and intent upon cutting her off from the door.

As she pushed onto her knees, she saw that blood slicked her hand. She had been cut by the broken glass. It wasn't life-threatening, just a gash across the meaty part of her left palm, but deep enough to hurt. She felt no pain, probably because she was in a state of shock.

Still holding the shotgun tightly in her right hand, she rose to her feet. Her legs were shaky, but she stumbled toward the door as fire seethed over all four walls, across the ceiling.

She made it through the door just as the kitchen floor began to crack apart behind her. The porch was badly damaged by the blast, and the roof sagged toward the middle. When she moved off the bottom step into the yard, one of the corner posts snapped from the strain of dislocation. The porch collapsed in her wake, as if her passage had been sufficient to disturb its delicate balance, and her temporary deafness ended with that crash.

Tommy had been thrown off the sled by the shock wave of the explosion, and he had either rolled or crawled about twenty feet farther from the burning house. He was sprawled in the snow, and the Labrador was attending him solicitously. Meg raced to him, certain that he had been hurt, though nothing had fallen on him, and though he was beyond the reach of the fire. He was all right—frightened, crying, but all right.

She said, "It's okay, everything's going to be fine, baby," but she doubted that he could hear her reassurances above the howling of the wind and the roar of the flames that consumed the house.

Hugging him, feeling him alive against her, Meg was relieved and grateful—and furious. Furious with the rats and with the men who had made those gremlins.

She had once thought that her career as an artist was the most important thing in her life. Then for a while, when she and Jim were first married and struggling to build the ad agency into a thriving business, financial success seemed ever so important. But long ago she had realized that the most important thing in life was family, the caring relationships between husbands and wives, parents and children. In this world beneath Heaven and above Hell, it seemed that irresistible forces were bent on the destruction of the family; disease and death tore loved ones apart; war, bigotry, and poverty dissolved families in the corrosive acids of violence, hatred, want; and sometimes families brought themselves to ruin through base emotions—envy, jealousy, lust. She had lost Jim, half her family, but she had held on to Tommy and to the house that had harbored the memory of Jim. Now the house had been taken from her by those rat-form, man-made gremlins. But she was not going to let them take Tommy, and she was determined to make them pay dearly for what they had already stolen.

She helped Tommy move farther away from the house, into the open where the full force of the wind and cold would probably protect him from the rats. Then she set out alone for the barn at the back of the yard.

The rats would be there. She was certain that they had not immolated themselves. They had left the house after tampering with the furnace and setting the trap for her. She knew that they would not huddle in the open, which left only the barn. She figured that they had constructed a tunnel between the two structures. They must have arrived in midafternoon, which gave them time to scout the property and to dig the long, connecting, subterranean passage; they were big, stronger than ordinary rats, so the tunnel would not have been a major project. While she and Tommy had struggled from house to barn to house again, the rats had scampered easily back and forth through the ground beneath them.

Meg went to the barn not just to blast away at the rats out of a need for vengeance. More important, it was the only place where she and Tommy had a hope of surviving the night. With the cut in her left hand, she was limited to one arm with which to pull the sled. She was also in mild shock, and shock was draining. Previously she had realized that pulling the sled out to Black Oak Road in sixty-mile-per-hour winds and subzero cold, then waiting hours until a road crew came by, was a task at the extremity of her endurance; in her current condition, she would not make it, and neither would Tommy. The house was gone, which left only the barn as a shelter, so she would have to take it back from the rats, kill all of them and reclaim her property, if she and her son were to live.

She had no hope that anyone would see the glow of the fire from afar and come inquiring as to the cause. Cascade Farm was relatively isolated, and the cloaking effect of the blizzard would prevent the flames from being seen at much of a distance.

At the open barn door, she hesitated. The lone bulb still burned inside, but the shadows seemed deeper than before. Then, with the wind and the orange light of her burning home at her back, she entered the gremlins' lair.

15

BEN PARNELL DISCOVERED THAT THE SLOPING MEADOW WAS CUT BY A series of natural, angled drainage channels that made progress difficult. In the nearly blinding tempest of snow, the ground was dangerous, for he often realized that a ditch lay ahead only when he fell into it. Rapid progress across the field was sure to result in a sprained ankle or broken leg, so he and his three men maintained a cautious pace, although the sight of the burning house terrified him.

He knew that the rats had caused the fire. He did not know how or why they had done it, but the timely eruption of the flames could not be a coincidence. Through his mind passed disturbing images of the woman and the boy, their rat-gnawed bodies aflame in the middle of the house.

16

SHE WAS SCARED. IT WAS AN ODD FEAR THAT DID NOT WEAKEN HER BUT contributed to her strength and determination. A cornered rat would freeze up in panic, but a cornered woman was not always easy prey. It depended on the woman.

Meg walked to the middle of the barn, in front of the Jeep. She looked around at the shadowy stalls along the south wall, at the open loft suspended from the front wall—and at the large, empty, and long-unused feed bin in the northeast corner.

She sensed that the rats were present and watching her.

They were not going to reveal themselves while she was armed with the shotgun, yet she had to lure them into the open to shoot them. They were too smart to be enticed with food. So . . . if she could not lure them, perhaps she could force them into the open with a few well-placed rounds from the 12-gauge.

She walked slowly down the center of the barn, to the end farthest from the door. As she passed the stalls that had once housed livestock, she peered intently into the shadows, seeking the telltale gleam of small red eyes. At least one or two gremlins must be crouched in those pools of darkness.

Although she saw none of the enemy, she began to fire into the stalls as she moved again toward the front of the barn—*blam, blam, blam*—three rounds in three of those narrow spaces, a yard-long flare spurting from the muzzle with each hard explosion, the thunderous gunfire echoing off the barn walls. When she fired the third shot, a squealing pair of rats burst from the fourth stall into the better-lighted center of the barn, sprinting toward the cover offered by the disabled Jeep. She pumped two rounds into them, and both were hit, killed, tossed end over end as if they were rags in a typhoon.

She had emptied the Mossberg. Wincing, she dug in her pockets with her injured hand and extracted the four shells, reloading fast. As she jammed the last of the rounds into the magazine, she heard several high shrieks behind her. She turned. Six large, white rats with misshapen skulls were charging her.

Four of the creatures realized that they were not going to reach her fast enough; they peeled off from the pack and disappeared under the car. Unnerved by the swiftness with which the last two closed the gap, she fired twice, decisively eliminating them.

She hurried around the Jeep in time to see the other four scurry out from under the vehicle and across the floor toward the old feed bin. She fired once, twice, as they vanished into the shadows at the base of that big storage box.

She was out of ammunition. She pumped the Mossberg anyway, as if by that act she could make another shell appear magically in the chamber, but the *clackety-clack* of the gun's action had a distinctly different sound when the magazine was empty.

Either because they knew what that sound meant as well as she did or because they knew that she had been left with only nine rounds—the five in the shotgun and the four they had not managed to steal from the carton in her bedroom closet—the rats that had vanished under the bin now reappeared. Four pale forms slunk into the wan light from the single, dusty bulb overhead.

Meg reversed her hold on the shotgun, gripping it by the barrel, making a club of it. Trying to ignore the pain in her left palm, she raised the gun over her head.

The rats continued to approach slowly . . . then more boldly.

She glanced behind, half expecting to see a dozen other rats encircling her, but evidently there were no more. Just these four. They might as well have numbered a thousand, however, for she knew that she wouldn't be able to club more than one of them before they reached her and crawled up her legs. When they were on her, biting and clawing at her throat and face, she would not be able to deal with even three of them, not with her bare hands.

She glanced at the big open door, but she knew that if she threw the gun down and ran for the safety of the mean winter night, she would not make it before the rats were on her.

As if sensing her terrible vulnerability, the four creatures began to make a queer keening sound of triumph. They lifted their grotesque, malformed heads and sniffed at the air, lashed their thick tails across the floor, and in unison let out a short shriek more shrill than any that Meg had heard from them before.

Then they streaked toward her.

Although she knew that she could never make the door in time, she had to try. If the rats killed her, Tommy would be helpless out there in the snow, with his broken leg. He would freeze to death by morning . . . if the rats didn't risk the fury of the storm to go after him.

She turned from the advancing pack, dashed toward the exit, and was startled to see a man silhouetted in the fading but still bright glow of the burning house. He was holding a revolver, and he said, "Get out of the way!"

Meg flung herself to one side, and the stranger squeezed off four quick shots. He hit only one of the rats, because they made small targets for a handgun. The remaining three vanished again into the shadows at the base of the feed bin.

The man hurried to Meg, and she saw that he wasn't a stranger, after all. He had spoken to her at the roadblock. He was still wearing his sheepskin-lined jacket and snow-crusted toboggan cap.

"Are you all right, Mrs. Lassiter?"

"How many of them are there? I killed four, and you killed one, so how many are left?"

"Eight escaped."

"So just those three are left?"

"Yes. Hey, your hand's bleeding. Are you sure you're—"

"I think maybe they've got a tunnel between the barn and the house," she said urgently. "And I've got a hunch the opening to it is around the bottom of that feed bin." She was speaking through clenched teeth and with a fury that surprised her. "They're foul, disgusting, and I want to finish them, all of them, make them pay for taking my home from me, for threatening Tommy, but how can we get at them if they're down there in the ground?"

He pointed to a large truck that had just pulled into the driveway. "We figured when we found the rats, we might have to go after them in a burrow, so among a lot of other things, we have the necessary equipment to pump gas down in their holes."

"I want them dead," she said, frightened by the purity of the anger in her own voice.

Men were pouring out of the back of the big truck, coming toward the barn. Snow—and wind-borne ashes from the collapsing house—slanted through their flashlight beams.

"We'll need the gas," the man in the toboggan cap shouted.

One of the other men answered him.

Shaking with anger and with the fear to which she had not dared give herself until now, Meg went outside to find her son.

17

SHE AND TOMMY AND DOOFUS SHARED THE WARMTH AND SAFETY OF the truck cab while the men from Biolomech attempted to eradicate the last of the vermin. The boy huddled against her, trembling even after the warm air from the heater had surely chased the chill from his bones.

Doofus was blessed with the greater emotional resilience that arose from being a member of a playful and less intelligent species that lacked a dark imagination, so eventually he slept.

Though they did not think that the rats would follow the tunnel back to the ruined house, some of the Biolomech security men established a cordon around that still-burning structure, prepared to kill any creature that appeared from out of the conflagration. Likewise, a cordon was thrown up around the barn to prevent any escape from that building.

Several times Ben Parnell came to the truck. Meg put down the window, and he stood on the short running board to report on their progress.

Wearing respirators to protect themselves, they pumped a lethal gas into the mouth of the rats' tunnel, which had indeed been located by the feed bin. "We gave 'em a generous dose," Parnell said during one visit. "Enough to saturate a burrow ten times larger than any they've had time to dig. Now we've got to excavate the tunnel until we find the bodies. Shouldn't be too difficult. They won't have gone deep while boring out a passage between the house and the barn, because going deep would've been wasted effort. So we'll start stripping the surface off the ground, the top few inches, digging backwards from the barn wall, across the yard, shearing the top off the tunnel, you see, until we turn them up."

"And if you don't turn them up?" she asked.

"We will. I'm sure we will."

Meg wanted to hate all these men, and she especially wanted to hate Parnell because he was in charge of the search and, therefore, the only authority figure on whom she could vent her anger. But speaking harshly to him—and maintaining her rage in the face of his obvious concern for her and Tommy—was difficult, because she realized that these were not the men responsible for the creation of the rats or for letting them escape. This was just the cleanup crew, ordinary citizens, just like all the ordinary citizens who, down through all the centuries, had been called in to clean up when the big shots screwed up. It was the ordinary citizen who always made the world safe for peace by fighting the current war to the bitter end, always the ordinary citizen whose taxes and labors and sacrifices paved the way for those advancements of civilization for which the politicians stole the credit.

Furthermore, she was touched by the genuine sympathy and understanding that Parnell showed when he learned that her husband had died and that she and Tommy were alone. He spoke of loss and loneliness and longing as if he had known his share of them.

"I heard of this woman once," he said rather enigmatically, leaning in the open truck window, "who lost her only daughter to cancer, and she was so crushed by grief that she had to change her entire life, move on to totally new horizons. She couldn't bear to look at her own husband any more, even though he loved her, because they *shared* the experience of their daughter, you see, and every time she looked at him . . . well, she saw her little daughter again, and was reminded again of the girl's suffering. See, that shared experience, that shared tragedy, was like a trap their relationship just couldn't escape. So . . . divorce, a new city, new state . . . that was the only solution for her, drastic as it was. But you seem to've handled grief better than that, Mrs. Lassiter. I know how hard it must've been for you these past couple years, but maybe you can take some heart in the fact that, for certain people who don't have your strength, life can be harder."

At ten minutes past eleven that night, two thirds of the way across the yard from the barn to the ruined house, they scraped off another couple of feet from the top of the tunnel and found the three dead rats. They put the bodies side by side on the barn floor, next to the other five that had been shot.

Ben Parnell came to the truck. "I thought maybe you'd want to see them—that we've got all eight of them, I mean."

"I would," she said. "Yes. I'll feel safer."

Meg and Tommy got out of the truck.

"Yeah," the boy said, "I want to see them. They thought they trapped us, but it was the other way around." He looked at Meg. "As long as we've got each other, we can get out of any scrape, huh?"

"Bet on it," she said.

Parnell scooped up the weary boy in his arms to carry him to the barn.

As the raw wind nipped at Meg, she jammed her hands into her coat pockets. She was relieved. At least for the moment, not all of the burden was hers.

Looking over his shoulder, Tommy said, "You and me, Mom."

"Bet on it," she repeated. And she smiled. She felt as if the door to a cage, of which she'd been only dimly aware, had opened now, giving them access to a new freedom.

BRUNO

1

I WAS SLEEPING OFF HALF A BOTTLE OF GOOD SCOTCH AND A BLONDE named Sylvia, who hadn't been so bad herself. But no one can sneak up on me, no matter how bushed I am. You have to be a light sleeper to last long in this business. I heard the thump near the foot of my bed, and I was reaching under the pillow for my Colt .38 in the next instant.

If I hadn't been out celebrating the successful conclusion of a case, the blinds and drapes wouldn't have been drawn. But I had been, and they were, so I didn't see anything.

I thought I heard footsteps in the hallway to the living room, but I couldn't be sure. I slid out of bed, stared intently around the room. Brown gloom, no intruder. I padded into the hall, looked both ways. No one.

In the front room, I distinctly heard the rod of the police-special lock pull out of its floor groove. The door opened, closed, and footsteps pounded in the outside hall, then down the apartment-house steps.

I ran into the living room and almost into the corridor before I remembered I was in my skivvies. It's not a building where anyone would care—or maybe even notice—a guy in his briefs, but I like to think I have higher standards than some of the weird creeps I call neighbors.

Turning on the lights, I saw that the police lock had been disengaged. I slid the bolt back in place.

I carefully searched the apartment from the john to the linen closet.

There weren't any bombs or other dirty work, at least as far as I could see. I checked the bedroom twice, since that was where I first heard him, but it was clean.

I brewed some coffee. The first sip was so bad that I poured half the mug in the sink, wondering if the old plumbing could take it, and then laced what was left with some good brandy. Better. My kind of breakfast.

So there I stood in my shorts on the cold kitchen floor, warming my gut with liquor and wondering who had broken in and why.

Then I had a bad thought. When the intruder left, he'd pulled the rod of the special lock out of its nest in the floor. Which meant he'd entered the apartment through a window or that, when he'd first come through the door, he had replaced the police rod. The last idea was stupid. No dude is going to make it hard for himself to get out if the job goes sour.

I went around checking all the windows. They were locked as always. I even checked the bathroom window, though it has no lock, is barred, and is set in a blank wall eight floors above the street. No one had come in any of the windows.

I slapped my head a few times, as if I might knock some smarts into myself and figure this out. No smarter, I decided to take a shower and get on with the day.

It must have been hallucinations. I'd never had what the two-hundred-dollar-an-hour shrinks call postcoital depression. Maybe this was what it was supposed to be like. After all, no one walks into your apartment after achieving the near impossible of silently throwing a police lock, then sneaks into your bedroom, just to look you over and leave. And none of my enemies would send a killer who would chicken out after he got that far.

I finished the shower at four-thirty and did my exercises until five. Then I showered again—cold, this time—toweled hard enough to raise blisters, combed my mop into a semblance of order, and dressed.

By five-thirty, I was sliding into a booth down at the Ace-Spot, and Dorothy, the waitress, was plopping a Scotch and water in front of me before the smell of the place was properly in my nose.

"What'll it be, Jake?" she asked. She has a voice like glass dropped into a porcelain basin.

I ordered steak and eggs with a double helping of french fries, then topped it off with a question: "Anybody been asking around about me, Dory?"

She wrote half the question down on the order pad before she realized that I had stopped ordering. Dory was supposed to have been a fine-looking street girl in her day, but no one ever said she had many smarts.

"Not me," she said. "I'll ask Benny."

Benny was the bartender. He was smarter than Dory. Some days, he was capable of winning a debate with a carrot.

I don't know why I tend to hang around with so many chumps, saps, and blockheads. Maybe it makes me feel superior. A guy who's dumb enough to be trying to make a living as an old-fashioned shamus in the late twentieth century, in the age of computers and space-age eavesdropping equipment and drug thugs who'd kill their grandmothers for a nickel—hell, he needs *some* reason to feel good about himself.

When Dory came back, she brought a negative from Benny, plus the food. I took it down in large bites, thinking about the stranger who had walked through the wall into my bedroom.

After two more big Scotches, I went home to look the place over again.

Just as I reached my apartment door and thrust the key toward the lock, this dude opened it from the inside and started coming out.

"Hold it right there, creepo," I said, leveling my .38 on his big belly. I pushed him back into the living room, closed the door behind us, and turned on the light.

"What do you want?" he asked.

"What do *I* want? Look, buster, these are my digs, see? I live here. And the last time I looked, you didn't."

He was dressed like something out of a Bogart film, and I might have laughed except that I was angry enough to chew up a little bunny rabbit and spit out good-luck charms. He had a huge hat pulled down over half his face. The overcoat might have been tailored for Siamese twins. It hung to his knees, and after that there were wide, sloppy trousers and big—I mean BIG—scuffy tennis shoes. The tennis shoes didn't fit Bogart, but the air of mystery was there.

For size, this guy reminded me of that actor from the old movies, Sidney Greenstreet, though with a serious gland condition.

"I don't want to harm you," he said. His voice was about a

thousand registers below Dory's, but it had that same harsh sound of something breaking.

"You the same dude who was here earlier?" I asked.

He hunched his head and said, "I never been here before."

"Let's see what you look like."

I reached for his hat. He tried to pull away, discovered I was faster than he was, tried to slug me in the chest. But I got the hat off and managed to take the clip on the shoulder instead of over the heart where he had aimed it.

Then I smiled and looked up at his face and stopped smiling and said, "Good God!"

"That kicks it!" His face contorted, and his big square teeth thrust over his black lip.

I was backed up against the door. And though I was terrified for the first time in years, I wasn't about to let him out. If my threats didn't keep him where he was, a hot kiss from the .38 would manage just fine—I hoped.

"Who . . . what are you?" I asked.

"You were right the first time. Who."

"Answer it, then."

"Can we sit down? I'm awful tired."

I let him sit, but I stayed on my feet to be able to move fast, and while he walked to the sofa and collapsed as if he were on his last legs, I looked him over good. He was a bear. A bruin. He was a big one too, no little Teddy, six feet four. His shoulders were broad, and under those baggy clothes he probably had a barrel chest and legs like tree trunks. His face was a block of granite that some artist had tried to sculpt with a butter knife, a straight pin, and a blunt screwdriver. All sharp planes, eyes set under a shelf of bone, a jaw better than Schwarzenegger's. Over all that: fur.

If I hadn't been used to watching afternoon TV talk shows when business was slow, all those programs featuring husbands-who-cheat-with-their-wives'-mothers and transvestite-dentists-who-have-been-abducted-by-aliens, then sure as hell the sight of a talking bruin would have crumpled me like an old paper cup. But even being a couch potato in the nineties and facing up to what's creeping around on our city streets is enough to make you tougher than Sam Spade and Philip Marlowe combined.

"Spill it," I said.

"My name is Bruno," he said.

"And?"

"You only asked who I was."

"Don't get cute with me."

"Then you weren't being literal?"

"Say what?"

"By asking who I was, you were actually asking for a general accounting, a broader spectrum of data."

"I could blow your head off for that," I told him.

He seemed surprised and shifted uneasily on the sofa, making the springs sing. "For what?"

"Talking like a damn accountant."

He considered for a moment. "Okay. Why not? What do I have to lose? I'm after Graham Stone, the first man you heard in here a few hours ago. He's wanted for some crimes."

"What crimes?"

"You wouldn't understand them."

"Do I look like I was raised in a nunnery, don't understand sin? Nothing any sleazeball would do could surprise me. So how did this Stone character get in here? And you?"

I waved the .38 at him when he hesitated.

"I guess there's no concealing it," Bruno said. "He and I came through from another probability."

"Huh?" It was hard to make even that sound with my mouth hanging open as if I were a stoned fan at a Grateful Dead concert.

"Another probability. Another time line. Graham Stone is from a counter-Earth, one of the infinity of possible worlds that exist parallel to one another. I come from a different world than Stone's. You've become a focal point for cross-time energies. If this is the first time it's happened to you, then your talent must be a new one. Besides, you're not mapped—no record of you in the guidebook. If it were an old talent—"

I made a number of wordless grunts until he got the idea to shut his yap. I made him go pour me half a glass of Scotch and drank most of it before I said anything. "Explain this . . . ability I've acquired. I don't scan it."

"It's possible to travel across the probabilities, from one Earth to another. But the only portals are those generated around living beings who somehow absorb cross-time energy and dissipate it without the rudeness of an explosion."

"Rudeness."

"Yes. That can be messy."

"How messy? Very."

"Anyway, you're one of those talented people who don't explode."

"Good for me."

"You broadcast a portal like—well, sort of like a spiritual aura—in a twenty-foot radius, in all directions."

"Is that so?" I said numbly.

"Not all possible worlds have such talented creatures on them, and therefore the infinity of possibilities is not really completely open to us."

I finished the Scotch and wanted to lick the glass. "And there is a . . . a counter-Earth where intelligent bears have taken over?" I couldn't any longer blame this business on my hot night with Sylvia. Not even the most persuasive shrink in the world would ever convince me that postcoital depression could be like this.

"Not exactly taken over," Bruno said. "But on my probability line, there was a nuclear war of distressing dimensions shortly after the close of World War Two. In the aftermath, science survived, but not a great many people did. In order to survive as a race, they had to learn to stimulate intelligence in lesser species, master genetic engineering to create animals with human intelligence and dexterity."

He held up his hands, which were graced with stubby fingers rather than paws. He wiggled them at me and showed all his square teeth in a broad, silly grin.

"If I can somehow get us an appointment with Steven Spielberg," I said, "we're both going to be filthy rich."

He frowned. "Steven Spielberg? The father of space travel?"

"Huh? No, the movie director."

"Not on my world."

"On your world, Spielberg is the father of space travel?"

"He invented frozen yogurt too."

"Really?"

"And antigravity boots and microwave popcorn. He's the richest man in history."

"I see."

"And the architect of world peace," Bruno said reverently.

I sat down as the implications of what he had told me began to work their way through my thick head. "Do you mean that weird characters from a thousand different worlds are going to be popping up around me all the time?"

"Not really," he said. "First of all, there just isn't that much reason to visit your probability—or any other, for that matter. There are too many alternate realities for cross-time traffic to get heavy in any one of them. Unless it's such a weird Earth as to be a tourist area. But your Earth looks bland and ordinary, judging from this apartment."

I ignored that and said, "But suppose I had been walking down the street when you popped through? That's going to cause some excitement when it happens!"

"Funny thing about that," Bruno said. "When one of us first pops through, not even you can see us. We gradually come into your perception, like someone seen out of the corner of your eye, and it doesn't look magical at all."

I made him go and get me more Scotch. After a third of that, I felt more cheerful. "You said you were a cop."

"Did I?"

"Just as much. You said this Stone is wanted for some crime or other. Unless you're an average citizen with more than his share of humanitarianism, then you're a cop."

He took a curious-looking silver circle out of his overcoat pocket and held it up: PROBABILITY POLICE. When he ran his thumb down its surface, the words disappeared under a picture of him. "Now, I really must be going. Graham Stone is too dangerous a man to be permitted freedom here."

Beside me were the controls for the CD player. I selected a disc and turned up the volume while he rose and pulled on his absurd hat. When the Butterfield Blues Band blared in at top volume, I put a slug in the couch beside him, incidentally tearing a hole through his overcoat.

He sat down.

I lowered the volume.

"What do you want?" he asked. I had to admit that he was cool about it. He didn't even check out his coat to see how close the round had actually been.

I already had my angle. "You're going to need help. I know this urban dump. You don't."

"I have my own devices," he said.

"Devices? You're not Sherlock Holmes in Victorian England, buster. This is America in the nineties, the big city—they eat bears like you for breakfast."

He looked worried. "I'm not particularly familiar with this reality—"

"So you need me," I said, keeping the Colt aimed in his general direction.

"Go on," he said gruffly. If he could have gotten to me, I'm sure he would have shown me how fast those blocky fists could move.

"It just so happens that I'm a private investigator. I never have much liked the badge-carrying kind of police—like you. But I'm never against working with them if there's a profit in it."

He seemed about to reject the proposal, then paused to give it some thought. "How much?"

"Let's say two thousand for the whole caper."

"Two thousand dollars."

"Or two pair of Spielberg gravity boots, if you've got 'em."

He shook his head. "Can't introduce revolutionary technology across the probability lines. Bad things happen."

"Like what?"

"Little girls spontaneously combusting in New Jersey."

"Don't play me for a fool."

"I'm serious." He *looked* serious, all right—bearishly dour, bearishly grim. "The effects are unpredictable and often weird. The universe is a mysterious place, you know."

"I hadn't noticed. So do we have a deal for two thousand bucks?"

"You use the gun well," he said. "Okay. Agreed."

He had accepted the figure too smoothly. "Better make that *three* thousand," I said.

He grinned. "Agreed."

I realized that money meant nothing to him—not the money of this probability line. I could have asked for anything. But I could not squeeze more out of him. It would be a matter of principle now.

"In advance," I said.

"You have any money on you?" he asked. "I'll need it to see what sort of bills you have."

I took two hundred out of my wallet and flopped it on the coffee table in front of him.

He lined up the fifties and twenties on the coffee table, then produced what appeared to be a thin camera from his overcoat. He photographed the bills, and a moment later duplicates slid out of the developing slit in the device's side. He handed them across and waited for my reaction.

They were perfect bills.

"But they're counterfeit," I complained.

"True. But no one will ever catch them. Counterfeiters get caught because they make a couple of thousand bills with the same serial numbers. You only have two bills of each. If you have more cash around, I'll copy that."

I dug out my cash reserves, which were hidden in a lockbox in the false bottom of the kitchen cabinet. I had my three thousand within a few minutes. When I had put everything back under the kitchen cabinet, with the original two hundred in my pocket, I said, "Now let's find Stone."

2

BY TWILIGHT, WHEN SNOW BEGAN TO FALL AND THE TRAIL STARTED TO get hot, we were in an alley two miles from my apartment.

Bruno checked the silver wafer that had been his ID badge but that obviously served other purposes. He grunted approval at the shimmering orange color. It measured, he said, the residual time energy that Stone radiated, and it changed colors the closer we got to the quarry.

"Neat gadget," I said.

"Spielberg invented it."

Yellow when we had left the apartment, the disc was now turning a steadily deeper shade of orange.

"Getting closer," Bruno said. He examined the rim, where the color changes began, and snorted his satisfaction. "Let's try this alley."

"Not the best part of town."

"Dangerous."

"Probably not for a seven-foot bear with futuristic weapons."

"Good." Hunching to minimize his height, huddling in the big coat and enormous hat, striving to pass for a big bearded human being, he put his head down and plodded forward. I followed him, bent against the brisk wind and the driving snow.

The alley led into a street lined with auto yards, industrial-equipment companies, warehouses, and a few other businesses that didn't look so obviously like mafia front operations. One of the warehouses was an abandoned heap of cinder block and corrugated aluminum; its two windows, high above the street, were shattered.

Bruno checked his disc and looked at the warehouse. "There," he said. The wafer was glowing soft red.

We crossed the street, leaving black tracks in the undisturbed skiff of white. There were two ground-floor entrances: one a man-size door, the other a roll-up large enough to admit trucks. Both were firmly locked.

"I could blast the sucker open," I said, indicating the lock on the smaller door.

"He's upstairs anyway," Bruno said, checking the wafer again. "Let's try the second-story door."

We climbed the fire escape, gripping the icy iron railing because the stairs were treacherous. The door at the top had been forced open and was bowed outward on flimsy hinges. We went inside and stood in the quiet darkness, listening.

Finally I switched on a flashlight when I realized that Bruno could probably see in the dark and I definitely couldn't. We were standing in a wide gallery that encircled an open well to the ground floor of the warehouse.

A hundred feet to the left, a rattling sound arose, like a sack of bones being shaken. When we tracked it down it was only a wooden ladder, still vibrating after someone had descended it.

I peered over the edge, but Stone was gone. We had not heard either of the lower doors open, so we went down after him.

Ten minutes later, we had checked out all the empty crates and broken pieces of machinery, all the blind spots in the row of empty offices along the rear wall. We hadn't found a trace of this Stone joker. The front doors were still locked from the inside.

Neither of us put away his gun. I had replaced the expended shell in the Smith & Wesson and now had a full clip.

Bruno's weapon wasn't anything like I'd seen before, but he assured me it was deadly. "It's a Disney .780 Death Hose."

"Disney?"

"Walt Disney. Best armament manufacturers in the world."

"Really?"

"You don't have them here?"

"Mine's a Smith and Wesson," I said.

"The hamburger people?"

I frowned. "What?"

"You know—the Smith and Wesson golden arches?"

I dropped the subject. There are some pretty weird alternate realities out there.

I heard faint strains of heavy-metal music that seemed to emanate from the thin air around us, but when I looked carefully along the walls, I found an old door that we had missed, painted to match the walls. I opened it cautiously and stared into black depths. Thrashing guitars, a keyboard synthesizer, drums. I went down the steps, and Bruno followed.

"Where's the music coming from?" my bruin friend asked.

I didn't like his hot breath storming down my neck, but I didn't complain. As long as he was behind me, nobody was going to sneak up on me unawares. "Looks like maybe there's a cellar in this place or in some connecting building where they're playing."

"Who?"

"The band."

"What band?"

"How should I know what band?"

He said, "I like bands."

"Good for you."

"I like to dance," said the bear.

"In the circus?" I asked.

"Where?"

Then I realized that maybe I was on the verge of insulting him. After all, he was an intelligent mutant, a probability cop, not one of our bears. He was no more likely to have performed a dance routine in a circus than he was to have worn a tutu and ridden a unicycle.

"We're getting closer," Bruno informed me as we continued down the stairs, "but Stone isn't here."

The wafer still was not a bright crimson.

"This way," I said as we reached the bottom of the stairs and arrived at the damp, fetid, trash-heaped basement of the abandoned warehouse. The place smelled of urine and dead meat, and it was most likely the breeding ground of the virus that will eventually wipe out humanity.

I followed the siren strains of the head-banger music from one cold stone room to another, scaring rats and spiders and God knows what else. Even Jimmy Hoffa might have been down there. Or Elvis—but a strange, walking-dead Elvis with lots of sharp teeth, red eyes, and an uncharacteristically bad attitude.

In the dankest, most stench-filled room of all, I came to an old timbered door with iron hinges. It was locked.

"Stand back," I said.

"What're you doing?"

"Renovation," I said, and blew the lock out of the door.

When that hellacious roar finished bouncing around the cellar, Bruno said, "I have subtler devices that accomplish the same thing."

"To hell with them," I said.

I opened the door—only to discover another door behind it. Steel. Relatively new. There was no handle or lock on our side. The double-door arrangement was meant to seal off this building from the next, so it was impossible to get from one to the other without people acting in concert on both sides.

Stepping forward into the beam of my flashlight, Bruno said, "Allow me."

From a pocket of his voluminous coat, he produced a four-inch-long rod of green crystal and shook it as if it were a thermometer.

I could hear the instrument begin to ring, way up on the scale where it would soon become inaudible to human beings but bother the hell out of dogs. Weirdly, I could feel the vibrations of the damn thing in my tongue.

"My tongue's vibrating," I said.

"Of course."

He touched the crystal rod to the steel door, and the locks—more than one—popped open with a hard *clack-clack-clack*.

My tongue stopped vibrating, Bruno returned the crystal rod to his pocket, and I pushed open the steel door.

We were in a washroom, alone. Two stalls with the doors half open, two urinals that some of the stoned customers evidently found too stationary to hit with any regularity, a sink so filthy that it looked as if Bobo the Dog Boy regularly took baths in it, and a stained mirror that showed us grimacing like a pair of old maids in a bordello.

"What's that music?" Bruno shouted. It was necessary to shout, because the heavy-metal band was nearby now.

"Metallica!"

"Not very danceable," he complained.

"Depends on how old you are."

"I'm not that old."

"Yeah, but you're a bear."

I sort of like heavy metal. It clears out my sinuses and makes me feel immortal. If I listened to too much of it, I'd start eating live cats and shooting people whose names annoyed me. I needed my jazz and blues. But a little was always good, and the band at this club wasn't half bad.

"Now what?" Bruno shouted.

"Sounds like a bar or club or something," I said. "We'll go out and look for him."

"Not me. I mean, it's okay to be out on the streets, especially at night, at a distance from people where they can't quite get a look at me unless I let them, but this would be close quarters. Stone shouldn't be mingling either. He looks human mostly—but someone might get suspicious. He should never have tried jaunting into an unexplored time line in the first place. It was desperation when he knew I almost had him."

"What then?" I asked.

"I'll stay here, in one of the stalls. You check the place out. If he isn't there, we'll go back into the warehouse and up into the street where we can pick up the trail."

"Earning my money, eh?" I asked.

While I adjusted my tie in the mirror, Bruno went into a toilet stall and closed the door.

From in there, he said, "Lord Almighty."

"What's wrong."

"Do people on this world have *any* respect for cleanliness?"

"Some of us have standards."

"This is disgusting."

"Try the other stall," I advised.

"What might be in *there?*" he grumbled.

"I won't be long," I promised, and I left the reeking washroom in search of Graham Stone.

3

I HAD TO BULL MY WAY OUT OF THE WASHROOM, BECAUSE THERE WERE so many people in the place that they were stacked like cordwood on end, wall to wall. I had seen Graham Stone's picture on that changing badge of Bruno's, and I knew what to look for: six feet tall, pale face, jet-black hair, eyes that were crystal blue and looked as empty as a tax collector's heart, thin lips—an image of cruelty. I checked out those around me, rejected them, and worked my way deeper into the mob of head-bangers who were swilling beer, smoking medicinal herbs, feeling up their girls, feeling up their guys, jumping to the music, and looking me over as if I might hand them copies of *Watchtower* magazine and try to convince them that Jesus was their savior.

It wasn't easy finding one face out of that crowd. Things kept distracting me. There were strobe lights winking every few minutes, and when they were on, I had to stop and wait before moving on again. When the strobes were off, there were shimmering film clips from horror movies projected on the walls and ceiling, and on the patrons as well. About ten minutes after I had started across the floor, through the scattered dancers, past the bar and bandstand, I spotted Graham Stone working his way to the lighted doorway in the far right corner.

A sign above the door claimed OFFICE, and another on the door itself insisted EMPLOYEES ONLY. It was half open, and I walked through as though I belonged there, keeping a hand in my jacket pocket where I had the pistol.

There were several rooms back here, all leading off a short hall, all the doors closed. I rapped on the first one, and when a woman said, "Yes?" I opened it and checked out the room.

She was a stacked redhead in a leotard, doing ballet steps in front of a mirror to the sounds—now—of Megadeth. Ten chairs were lined up against the walls around the room, and in each chair sat a different ventriloquist dummy. Some held bananas in their wooden hands.

I didn't want to know any more about it.

"Sorry," I said. "Wrong room."

I closed the door and went to the one across the hall.

Graham Stone was there. He stood by the desk, watching me with those cold eyes. I stepped inside, closed the door, and took the Smith & Wesson out of my pocket to be certain that he understood the situation. "Stand real still," I said.

He didn't move, and he didn't answer me. When I started toward him, however, he sidestepped. I cocked the .38, but it didn't grab his attention like it should have. He watched disinterestedly.

I walked forward again, and he moved again. I'd had the word from Bruno that a bring-him-back-alive clause was not a condition of my employment contract. In fact, the bear had implied that any display of mercy on my part would be met with all the savagery of a Hare Krishna panhandler on a megadose of PCP. Well, he hadn't put it quite that way, but I got the message. So I shot Graham Stone in the chest, pointblank, because I had no way of knowing what he might be able to do to me.

The bullet ripped through him, and he sagged, folded onto the desk, fell to the floor, and deflated. Inside of six seconds, he was nothing more than a pile of tissue paper painted to look like a man. A three-dimensional snakeskin that, shed, was still convincingly real. I examined the remains. No blood. No bones. Just ashes.

I looked at the Smith & Wesson. It was my familiar gun. Not a Disney .780 Death Hose. Which meant that this hadn't been the real Graham Stone but—something else, an amazing construct of some kind that was every bit as convincing as it was flimsy. Before I had too much time to think about that, I beat it back into the corridor. No one had heard the shot. The thrashmasters on the bandstand were doing a fair imitation of Megadeth—a bitchin' number from *Youthanasia*—and providing perfect cover.

Now what?

I cautiously checked the other two rooms that opened off the hallway, and I found Graham Stone in both. He crumpled between my fingers in the first room, as solid in appearance as any face on Mount Rushmore but was, in actuality, as insubstantial as any current politician's image. In the second room, I shredded him with a well-placed kick to the crotch.

By the time I reached the dance floor again, I was furious. When you blew a guy away, you expected him to go down like bricks and stay down. That was how the game was played. I didn't like this cheap trick.

In the washroom, I rapped on Bruno's stall door, and he came out with his hat still pulled way down and his collar still turned up. Face wrinkled in disgust, he said, "If you people don't bother flushing, why even put the lever on the toilet to begin with?"

"There's trouble," I said. I told him about the three extra Graham Stones and demanded some explanation.

"I didn't want to have to tell you this." He looked sheepish. "I was afraid it would scare you, affect your efficiency."

"What? Tell me what?" I asked.

He shrugged his burly shoulders. "Well, Graham Stone isn't a human being."

I almost laughed. "Neither are you."

He looked hurt, and I felt like a blockhead.

"I am a little bit human," he said. "Certain borrowed genetic material . . . But forget that. What I should have said is that Graham Stone doesn't really come from any alternate Earth. He's an alien. From another star system."

I went to the sink and splashed a lot of cold water on my face. It didn't do much good.

"Tell me," I said.

"Not the whole story," he said. "That would take too much time. Stone is an alien. Humanoid except when you're close enough to see that he doesn't have any pores. And if you look closely at his hands, you'll see where he's had his sixth fingers amputated to pass for human."

"Sixth-finger-amputation scar—always a sure indicator of the alien among us," I said sarcastically.

"Yes, exactly. There was a shipload of these creatures that crashed on one of the probability lines seven months ago. We've never been able to communicate with them. They're extremely hostile and very strange. The general feeling is that we've met a species of megalomaniacs. All have been terminated except Graham Stone. He's escaped us thus far."

"If he's an alien, why the British-sounding name?"

"That's the first name he went by when he started to pass for human. There have been others since. Apparently even aliens seem to feel that being British has a certain connotation of class and style. It's also a constant on eighty percent of the time lines. Although there are a couple of realities wherein being from the island-nation of Tonga is the epitome of class."

"And what the hell has this alien done to deserve death?" I asked. "Maybe if a greater attempt was made to understand him—"

"An attempt was made. One morning, when the doctors arrived at the labs for a continuation of the study, they found the entire night crew dead. A spiderweb fungus was growing out of their mouths, nostrils, eye sockets. . . . You get the picture? He hasn't done it since. But we don't think he has lost the capacity."

I went back to the sink and looked at myself in the mirror. Someone came in to use the urinal, and Bruno leaped backward into the toilet stall and slammed the door. "Oh, yuck!" he growled, but the newcomer didn't seem to find anything strange about the bearish voice.

I had three minutes to study my precious kisser in the mirror until the head-banger left. Then Bruno came out again, grimacing worse than ever.

"Listen," I said, "suppose Stone was within twenty feet of me, back there in the offices while I was playing around with those paper decoys or whatever the hell they were. He could have tripped right out of this probability by now."

"No," Bruno said. "You're a receiver, not a transmitter. He'll have to locate someone with the reverse talent of yours before he can get out of this time line."

"Are there others?"

"I detect two within the city," Bruno said.

"We could just stake those two out and wait for him!"

"Hardly," the bruin said. "He would just as soon settle down here and take over a world line for himself. That would give him a better base with which to strike out against the other continuums."

"He has that kind of power?"

"I said he was dangerous."

"Let's move it," I said, turning to the steel door from the adjacent warehouse basement.

"You're marvelous," Bruno said.

I turned and looked at him, trying to find sarcasm in that crazy face of his. I couldn't tell what he was thinking. "Marvelous? I'm marvelous? Listen, one guy doesn't tell another guy he's marvelous—especially not when the two of them are in a bathroom."

"Why?"

"Never mind why," I said, starting to burn.

"Anyway, I'm not a guy. I'm a bear."

"You're a guy bear, aren't you?"

"Well, yes."

"So can it with this 'marvelous' crap."

"All I meant was, in the space of a few short hours, you have accepted the existence of probability worlds, an intelligent bear, and an alien from another world. And you don't seem shaken at all."

I set him straight: "Yesterday, I got good and drunk. I spent six active hours in bed with a great blonde named Sylvia. I ate two steaks, half a dozen eggs, and piles of fried potatoes. I sweated out every drop of tension from the last job I took on. I'm a purged man. I can take anything tonight. Nobody has ever thrown anything at me that I can't take, and it isn't going to start with this. Besides, I have three thousand bucks at stake—to say nothing about a little thing called 'pride.' Now, let's get the hell out of here."

We went through the steel door and the wood door beyond it, into the basement of the abandoned warehouse.

4

WHEN WE GOT BACK ON THE STREET AGAIN, WE DISCOVERED THAT AN inch of snow had fallen since we'd gone into the warehouse and the storm had cranked up two notches. Hard snow whipped about us, pasted our clothes, stung our faces. I cursed but Bruno just accepted it and said nothing.

What seemed like a millennium later and some ten million miles from the metal bar where I had almost cornered Stone, using the color-changing disc as our guide, we found some of the shifty alien's handiwork. Five teenage boys were lying in an alleyway, all with a white, gossamer fungus growing out of their mouths, eyes, nostrils—even their rectums, for all I knew.

"I was afraid of this," Bruno said, genuine anguish in his voice.

"Don't sweat it," I said, bending to look more closely at the corpses. They weren't pretty. "They're thugs. Delinquents. Members of some street gang. They'd just as soon shoot your sister as eat a doughnut. It's a new gang to me. See the cobra each one has tattooed on his hand? They probably tried to mug Graham and had the old proverbial tables turned on them. For once, Graham did something worthwhile. They won't be snatching welfare money from old ladies and beating grandfathers up to steal pocket watches."

"Just the same," he said, "we have to dispose of the bodies. We can't allow these to be found. There'll be a lot of questions about what killed them, and this probability line is not yet ready to be taken into the world travel societies."

"Why's that?"

"Credit problems."

"So . . . what do you propose?" I asked.

He took that strange pistol out of his pocket, changed the setting on the regulator dial on the butt, then ashed all the dead gang-bangers. He was right about the Disney .780 Death Hose—it was the mother of all ray guns.

As we stirred the gray residue around with our feet and let the wind blow it away, I didn't feel so good. I kept reminding myself about the three thousand bucks. And Sylvia. And the taste of good Scotch. And how I would lose all those things if I once let my nerve crack. Because, see, once a private richard backs down, his career is finished. Either his career or his life.

After the snowplows had passed, we walked in the middle of the street where we didn't have to fight the drifting snow. At first, the tracking disc was little more than amber, but it soon began to change to a brilliant orange. As redness crept in around its edges, our spirits rose again.

We eventually had to leave the street for the river park, where the untouched snow soaked my socks and trouser cuffs.

As the wafer in Bruno's hand grew brighter red than it had been all evening, we topped a knoll and saw Graham Stone. He was at the end of a pier at the yacht basin. He scrambled onto the deck of a sleek boat, ran for the wheelhouse door, swung up the steps, and disappeared inside. The running lights popped on along the length of the boat, and the engines coughed and stuttered to life.

I ran down the hill, my pistol in my right hand, while I thrust my other arm forward to break any fall I might make on the slippery ground.

Behind me, Bruno was shouting something. I didn't listen to it. He shouted it again, then started running after me. I could tell he was running, even without looking, for I could hear his big feet slamming the ground.

When I reached the end of the pier, Stone had reversed the boat and was taking it out into the dark river. As I ran the last few yards, I judged the distance to the deck of the receding craft at maybe twelve feet. I leaped, fell over the rail of the boat in a tangle of arms and legs, smacked the polished deck with my shoulder, and watched the pretty stars for a moment.

Behind me, I heard a bellow of frustration, then a huge splash. Bruno hadn't made it.

From where I lay, I could look up into the wheelhouse windows. Graham Stone stood up there, staring down at me—maybe the real creature or maybe just another of his shed skins. I pushed to my feet, shook those stars out of my head, and looked for my gun.

It was gone.

I glanced back toward the pier. There was no sign of Bruno.

And somewhere in the intervening stretch of dark water, my .38 lay in river muck, useless.

I didn't feel so good. I wished that I had never left the Ace-Spot this morning, had never met Bruno. Then I shook off all the negative thoughts and started looking around for something I could use as a weapon.

If you start wishing things were different from what they are, the next step is depression, then inactivity, and finally vegetation. No matter what the state of the world, you have got to move. Move.

I found a length of pipe in a tool chest that was bolted to the deck against the far railing. I could cave in a skull very nicely if I put the proper swing behind it. I felt better.

Stone was still in the wheelhouse, still watching me. The blue eyes gleamed with the reflection of the ship lights. He seemed too confident as I walked along the deck to the steps. I swung inside, crouching low. I kept the pipe extended, and he didn't even bother to turn and look at me.

I approached carefully, using mincing little steps because I hated to commit myself to more than a few inches at a time. I kept thinking of the five young thugs lying back there with the cobweb fungus growing out of their bodies.

When I was close enough, I swung the pipe in a short, vicious arc. It slammed into his head—and on down through his neck and chest and stomach and thighs.

Another snakeskin. The lousy simulacrum collapsed, seemed to dissolve, and was a little pile of wrinkled useless tissue at my feet. Damn him!

Or should I say *it?*

When I looked through the bridge window, I could see that we were more than halfway across the river toward the West Shore district of the city. The boat was on automatic pilot. I couldn't make anything of the controls, and though I worked them at random, safeguards must have kept anything from changing. More wary than I had been, I left the wheelhouse in search of Stone.

I found him by the toolbox where I had found the piece of pipe. He gripped the railing with both hands and stared longingly at the approaching shore where we would surely run aground.

I sneaked up behind him, and I let him have it. Hard.

It was another tissue-paper construction.

I wished I knew how the bastard made those things. It was a handy talent.

We were two thirds of the way to shore now, and if I didn't find him soon, he might escape us again. And Bruno had explained that a few days in any one probability will dissipate the residual energy of cross-time travel—rendering the tracking disc useless.

Stone had to be below deck. I could see all of the planking above the waterline, and I knew the wheelhouse was empty. So I found the hatch and the stairs to the lower cabins. I went down like any good private richard learns to do—carefully.

In the galley was another simulacrum, which I heroically crumpled with my trusty pipe. I felt like an idiot, but I was not about to take it easy with one of them—and then discover that it was the real and deadly thing.

I found another paper demon in the first of the double-bunk sleeping quarters and dispatched him quickly. The second sleeping cabin was empty, containing neither a scarecrow Graham Stone nor the real one.

Which left the bathroom. The door was closed but not locked. I twisted the lever, yanked it open, and found him.

For a moment, I was disoriented. Before me was the real Graham Stone, *and* a false shell separating from him. It looked like I had double vision, with the two images overlapping slightly. Then he snarled and smashed the simulacrum away as it separated from him. On his hands, ugly brown bubbles of flesh rose up, burst free, and spun at me like biological missiles.

I stepped backward, swung the pipe, and broke open one of the spinning . . . seeds, spores, whatever the hell they were. Instantly, the end of the pipe was sheathed in writhing white fibers. The fungus spread inexorably down toward my hand, and I had to drop the pipe. The second bubble had struck the doorjamb; a colony of cobweb fungus wriggled along the wood and aluminum, anchoring itself, spreading outward in all directions.

"Hold it right there!" I said, pretending that I was tough.

His hands came up again. I could see the spores forming. The skin turned brown, bulged, leaped away from him.

One of them burst on the wall next to me and sent climbing white tendrils toward the ceiling and the floor. Cracks appeared in the fiberboard as the stuff ate its way into the core of the ship.

The second spore struck my sports-coat sleeve, exploded with a bubbling froth of white growth. Never before or since have I stripped off a coat that fast, not even when a delectable blonde was waiting for me and cooing sweet things; I nearly strangled myself in the damn thing, but I got rid of it. By the time the coat hit the floor, the albino fronds were trembling like the hairs on the back of my neck.

Stone stepped out of the bathroom into the companionway, raising those hands at me again, and I turned and ran like hell.

Once before, I said that a private detective is finished when his nerve cracks, that the first time he backs down is the point at which his career begins to terminate. Well, I stand by that. I wasn't turning chicken. I was just using my head for once. Those who fight and run away—live to fight another day. So I ran. There are times when you know it isn't sensible to take on a tank with a target pistol, because you'll be standing there holding your target pistol and looking at the twelve-inch hole they just put in your gut.

Besides, this creepy Stone character wasn't playing the same game I was. He didn't know the rules. Even the crummiest two-bit punk will give you half a chance. He'll use a rod or a knife or even a jar full of sulfuric acid. But nothing this tricky. Stone didn't have *any* respect for tradition.

Topside, I ran to the bow of the craft and checked the onrushing bank of the river. It seemed no more than two hundred feet away now. It was the most welcome sight of my life. On the rail next to me, a pod of fibrous death split and wrapped spidery tentacles around the iron, bored into the metal, and began to greedily devour it. I was struck with the notion that these pods were more virulent than those that had killed the gang-bangers in the alleyway.

I dove to the right, behind an exhaust housing. Cautiously, I peered over the top and saw Stone standing by the wheelhouse steps, his bright eyes flashing, his palms flattened in my direction.

The boat rushed closer to the shore.

But not fast enough to suit me.

Two pods spun over my head, landed on the deck behind, and ate down through the planking. Before long, the yacht was going to be honeycombed with the white tentacles, each as thin as a thread but as strong, surely, as a steel wire.

A whining sound arose, the sound of tortured metal. The deck of the boat shuddered, and we seemed almost to come to a stop. Then there was a jolt, and we sped forward again. The bottom had dragged over a shoreline rock formation, but we had not been grounded.

And then we were.

The boat hit the second reef, tore out its bottom, and settled into four feet of water, most of its bulk still high and dry.

I rolled back across the deck, grabbed the rail, heaved myself over the side. I struck shallow water and went under, striking my jaw on a hunk of smooth driftwood. My mouth sagged open, and I swallowed water. *So this is what it's like to drown*, I thought. Then I closed my stupid kisser and struggled to the surface again. I broke water, flailed my arms, pushed up, and staggered toward that blessed beach, sputtering and coughing and trying not to pass out.

I may not have a number of qualities that modern society considers admirable—like refined tastes and finesse. But there's one thing I do have, damn it. Grit.

I was five short steps from dry ground when the pods of fungus erupted before me. Two. Then two more. A wild tangle of white snakes rose up to block my escape. I turned and looked back. Graham Stone, alien Anglophile, looking like an evil Cary Grant, had left the ship too. He was splashing toward me.

I turned to my right. Two spores fell there. The pale snakes twisted out of the water, seeking, wriggling toward me.

On my left, two more.

No respect for tradition at all.

The water was only halfway up my calves, not deep enough for me to go beneath the surface and swim away. Besides, if the fungus was going to take me, I'd rather it happened up here, where I could see what those filaments were doing.

Graham Stone came relentlessly onward, holding his fire now. He knew he had me.

We were on a dark stretch of shore. No one to whom I could call for help.

Then from the left arose the furious whine of a small powerboat driven to the limits of its performance. A whooping siren wailed to life, one of those ooga horns from ancient automobiles. Out of the gloom and the falling snow, Bruno appeared. He was standing in a two-seat twelve-footer, holding on to the wheel for all he was worth. The craft was hitting better than fifty miles an hour.

It skimmed the water, the bow in the air. Since the boat sat higher in the water than the yacht, it passed over the rock formations and kept coming.

"Bruno!" I shouted.

He was a textbook example of a man—or a bear—in the grip of an anxiety attack. His big eyes rolled wildly, and he braced for the worst.

The little boat hit the beach, the screws churning frantically. It slammed forward through the sand at twenty miles an hour for ten feet or so, struck a rock, stopped dead, and pitched the bruin over the windshield, across the bow, and onto the beach, flat on his enormous back.

And he got up. He looked dizzy, and he was covered with sand, but he had survived.

I started jumping up and down in the water yelling, "Get him, Bruno! Get him now!"

Those white tentacles were threading their way closer to me, even though Graham Stone had stopped approaching.

The bear raised his head, looked at me, felt for his floppy hat, then shrugged when he couldn't find it.

"Get him, Bruno, get him!" I bellowed.

He took out that silly-looking pistol of his, and while Stone tried to hit him with a spore of fungus, my friend the bear burned the sonofabitch on the spot with the Disney .780 Death Hose. The only thing left was some ashes, which floated away.

I knew I was going to have to get one of those. Maybe Mickey Mouse sold them out of a secret shop in Tomorrow Land.

"You killed him!" I shouted as Bruno burned down the white forest of fungus on all other sides of me.

Then I must have had an attack of low blood sugar or something, because I passed out. I'm sure I didn't faint.

5

WE HAD TO DISPOSE OF THE YACHT. IN ABOUT FIFTEEN SECONDS, WHEN Bruno was done with it, it was only a dusting of ashes slowly washing away on the water. No fire, really. Just *whoosh*—and it was nothing but dust. He destroyed the powerboat too, every trace of what had taken place here this evening.

We walked the dark shore for about a mile, until we found a waterside club where we could call a cab, and went back to my place. The driver kept wanting to know if Bruno had won the prize at the costume party, but we didn't answer him.

At home, we cleaned up, ate every steak in my refrigerator, every egg, every slice of cheese, every—well, everything. Then we finished off three bottles of Scotch between us—though I have to admit that he drank most of it himself.

We didn't talk about Graham Stone once. We talked a lot about being a cop—both the private and the badge-carrying kind. We talked about the types of punks at work out there—and discovered that they don't vary much from probability to probability. He explained why my Earth is not civilized enough to be welcomed into the probability societies—besides that credit thing. Strangely, he said that it won't be quite good enough until my type has all but vanished from the face of the Earth. Yet he liked me. I'm sure of that. Strange.

Shortly before dawn, he gave himself an injection that sobered him instantly. We shook hands (or at least he reached down and shook mine) and parted company. He went off to find a transmitting point to return to his own probability. And I went to sleep.

I never saw Bruno again.

But there have been other odd characters. Stranger than all the crooks I've known in this city. Stranger than Benny "the Ostrich" Deekelbaker and Sam "the Plunger" Sullivan. Stranger than Hunchback Hagerty, the deformed hired killer. Stranger, in fact, than either Graham Stone or Bruno. I'll tell you about them some-time. Right now, I've got a date with the cutest redhead you ever saw. Her name's Lorella, she can dance like a dream, and aside from a weird interest in ventriloquist dummies, she's got her head on straight.

WE THREE

1

JONATHAN, JESSICA, AND I ROLLED OUR FATHER THROUGH THE DINING room and across the fancy Olde English kitchen. We had some trouble getting Father through the back door, because he was rather rigid. This is no comment on his bearing or temperament, though he could be a chilly bastard when he wanted. Now he was stiff quite simply because rigor mortis had tightened his muscles and hardened his flesh. We were not, however, to be deterred. We kicked at him until he bent in the middle and popped through the door frame. We dragged him across the porch and down the six steps to the lawn.

"He weighs a ton!" Jonathan said, mopping his sweat-streaked brow, huffing and puffing.

"Not a ton," Jessica said. "Less than two hundred pounds."

Although we are triplets and are surprisingly similar in many ways, we differ from one another in a host of minor details. For example, Jessica is by far the most pragmatic of us, while Jonathan likes to exaggerate, fantasize, and daydream. I am somewhere between their two extremes. A pragmatic daydreamer?

"What now?" Jonathan asked, wrinkling his face in disgust and nodding toward the corpse on the grass.

"Burn him," Jessica said. Her pretty lips made a thin pencil line on her face. Her long yellow hair caught the morning sun and glimmered. The day was perfect, and she was the most beautiful part of it. "Burn him all up."

"Shouldn't we drag Mother out and burn the two of them at the same time?" Jonathan asked. "It would save work."

"If we make a big pyre, the flames might dance too high," she said. "And we don't want a stray spark to catch the house on fire."

"We have our choice of all the houses in the world!" Jonathan said, spreading his arms to indicate the beach resort around us, Massachusetts beyond the resort, the nation past the state's perimeters—the world.

Jessica only glared at him.

"Aren't I right, Jerry?" Jonathan asked me. "Don't we have the whole world to live in? Isn't it silly to worry about this one old house?"

"You're right," I said.

"I *like* this house," Jessica said.

Because Jessica liked *this* house, we stood fifteen feet back from the sprawled corpse and stared at it and thought of flames and ignited it in an instant. Fire burst out of nowhere and wrapped Father in a red-orange blanket. He burned well, blackened, popped, sizzled, and fell into ashes.

"I feel as if I ought to be sad," Jonathan said.

Jessica grimaced.

"Well, he *was* our father," Jonathan said.

"We're above cheap sentimentality." Jessica stared hard at each of us to be certain we understood this. "We're a new race with new emotions and new attitudes."

"I guess so." But Jonathan was not fully convinced.

"Now, let's get Mother," Jessica said.

Although she is only ten years old—six minutes younger than Jonathan and three minutes younger than I—Jessica is the most forceful of us. She usually has her way.

We went back into the house and got Mother.

2

THE GOVERNMENT HAD ASSIGNED A CONTINGENT OF TWELVE MARINES and eight plainclothes operatives to our house. Supposedly, these men were to guard us and keep us from harm. Actually, they were there only to be sure that we remained prisoners. When we were finished with Mother, we dragged these other bodies onto the lawn and cremated them one at a time.

Jonathan was exhausted. He sat down between two smoldering skeletons and wiped sweat and ashes from his face. "Maybe we made a big mistake."

"Mistake?" Jessica asked. She was immediately defensive.

"Maybe we shouldn't have killed *all* of them," Jonathan said.

Jessica stamped one foot. Her golden ringlets of hair bounced prettily. "You're a stupid bastard, Jonathan! You *know* what they were going to do to us. When they discovered just how far-ranging our powers were and just how fast we were acquiring new powers, they finally understood the danger we posed. They were going to kill *us.*"

"We could have killed just a few of them to make our point," Jonathan said. "Did we really have to finish them all?"

Jessica sighed. "Look, they were like Neanderthals compared to us. We're a new race with new powers, new emotions, new attitudes. We are the most precocious children of all time—but they *did* have a certain brute strength, remember. Our only chance was to act without warning. And we did."

Jonathan looked around at the black patches of grass. "It's going to be so much work! It's taken us all morning to dispense with these few. We'll never get the whole world cleaned up."

"Before long, we'll learn how to levitate the bodies," Jessica said. "I feel a smidgen of that power already. Maybe we'll even learn how to teleport them from one place to another. Things will be easier then. Besides, we aren't going to clean up the whole world—just the parts of it we'll want to use for the next few years. By that time, the weather and the rats will have done the rest of the job for us."

"I guess you're right," Jonathan said.

But I knew he remained doubtful, and I shared some of his doubt. Certainly, we three are higher on the ladder of evolution than anyone who came before us. We are fledgling mind readers, fortune tellers, capable of out-of-body experiences whenever we desire them. We have that trick with the fire, converting thought energy into a genuine physical holocaust. Jonathan can control the flow of small streams of water, a talent he finds most amusing whenever I try to urinate; though he is one of the new race, he is still strangely enchanted by childish pranks. Jessica can accurately predict the weather. I have a special empathy with animals; dogs come to me, as do cats and birds and all manner of offal-dropping creatures. And, of course, we can put a stop to the life of any plant or animal just by *thinking* death at it. Like we thought death at all the rest of humanity. Perhaps, considering Darwin's theories, we were *destined* to destroy these new Neanderthals once we developed the ability. But I cannot rid myself of the nagging doubt. I feel that, somehow, we will suffer for the destruction of the old race.

"That's backward thinking," Jessica said. She had read my mind, of course. Her telepathic talents are stronger and more developed than either Jonathan's or mine. "Their deaths meant nothing. We cannot feel remorse. We are the new ones, with new emotions and new hopes and new dreams and new *rules."*

"Sure," I said. "You're right."

3

WEDNESDAY, WE WENT DOWN TO THE BEACH AND BURNED THE CORPSES of the dead sunbathers. We all like the sea, and we do not want to be without a stretch of unpolluted sand. Putrefying bodies make for a very messy beach.

When we finished the job, Jonathan and I were weary. But Jessica wanted to do the nasty.

"Children our age shouldn't be capable of that," Jonathan said.

"But we are capable," Jessica said. "We were meant to do it. And I want to. Now."

So we did the nasty. Jonathan and her. Then me and her. She wanted more, but neither of us cared to oblige.

Jessica stretched out on the beach. Her shapeless, slender body was white against the white sand. "We'll wait," she said.

"For what?" Jonathan asked.

"For the two of you to be ready again."

4

FOUR WEEKS AFTER THE END OF THE WORLD, JONATHAN AND I WERE alone on the beach, soaking up the sun. He was oddly silent for a while, almost as if he was afraid to speak.

At last he said, "Do you think it's normal for a girl her age to be always . . . wanting like that? Even if she is one of the new race?"

"No."

"She seems . . . driven."

"Yes."

"There's a purpose we don't grasp."

He was right. I sensed it too.

"Trouble," he said.

"Maybe."

"Trouble coming."

"Maybe. But what trouble can there be *after* the end of the world?"

5

TWO MONTHS AFTER THE END OF THE WORLD AND THE BURNING OF OUR parents, when Jonathan and I were getting bored with the house and wanted to strike out for more exotic places, Jessica let us in on the big news. "We can't leave here just yet," she said. Her voice was especially forceful. "We can't leave for several more months. I'm pregnant."

6

WE BECAME AWARE OF THAT FOURTH CONSCIOUSNESS WHEN JESSICA was in her fifth month of pregnancy. We all woke in the middle of the night, drenched with sweat, nauseated, sensing this new person.

"It's the baby," Jonathan said. "A boy."

"Yes," I said, wincing at the psychic impact of the new being. "And although he's inside of you, Jessica, he's aware. He's unborn but completely *aware.*"

Jessica was racked with pain. She whimpered helplessly.

7

"THE BABY WILL BE OUR EQUAL, NOT OUR SUPERIOR," JESSICA INSISTED. "And I won't listen to any more of this nonsense of yours, Jonathan."

She was only a child herself, yet she was swollen with child. She was getting to be more grotesque with each passing day.

"How can you *know* he isn't our superior?" Jonathan asked. "None of us can read his mind. None of us can—"

"New species don't evolve that fast," she said.

"What about *us?*"

"Besides, he's safe—he came from us," she said. Apparently, she thought that this truth made Jonathan's theory even more the lie.

"We came from our parents," Jonathan said. "And where are they? Suppose we *aren't* the new race. Suppose we're a brief, intermediate step—the cocoon stage between caterpillar and butterfly. Maybe the baby is—"

"We have nothing to fear from the baby," she insisted, patting her revolting stomach with both hands. "Even if what you say is true, he needs us. For reproduction."

"He needs you," Jonathan said. "He doesn't need us."

I sat and listened to the argument, not knowing what to think. In truth, I found it all a bit amusing even as it frightened me. I tried to make them see the humor: "Maybe we have this wrong. Maybe the baby is the Second Coming—the one Yeats wrote about in his poem, the beast slouching toward Bethlehem to be born."

Neither of them thought that was funny.

"I never could stand Yeats," Jonathan said.

"Yes," Jessica said, "such a gloomy ass, he was. Anyway, we're above superstitions like that. We're the new race with new emotions and new dreams and new hopes and new rules."

"This is a serious threat, Jerry," Jonathan said. "It's not anything to joke about."

And they were at it again, screaming at each other—quite like Mother and Father used to do when they couldn't make the household budget work. Some things never change.

8

THE BABY WOKE US REPEATEDLY EVERY NIGHT, AS THOUGH IT ENJOYED disturbing our rest. In Jessica's seventh month of pregnancy, toward dawn, we all were jolted awake by a thunder of thought energy that poured from the womb-wrapped being-to-be.

"I think I was wrong," Jonathan said.

"About what?" I asked. I could barely see him in the dark bedroom.

"It's a girl, not a boy," he said.

I probed out with my mind and tried to get a picture of the creature inside Jessica's belly. It resisted me successfully, for the most part, just as it resisted Jonathan's and Jessica's psychic proddings. But I was sure it was male, not female. I said so.

Jessica sat up in bed, her back against the headboard, both hands on her moving stomach. "You're wrong, both of you. I think it's a boy *and* girl. Or maybe neither one."

Jonathan turned on the bedside lamp in the house by the sea and looked at her. "What is that supposed to mean?"

She winced as the child within her struck out hard against her. "I'm in closer contact with it than either of you. I *sense* into it. It isn't like us."

"Then I was right," Jonathan said.

Jessica said nothing.

"If it's both sexes, or neither, it doesn't need *any* of us," he said. He turned off the light again. There was nothing else to do.

"Maybe we could kill it," I said.

"We couldn't," Jessica said. "It's too powerful."

"Jesus!" Jonathan said. "We can't even read its mind! If it can hold off all three of us like that, it can protect itself for sure. Jesus!"

In the darkness, as the blasphemy echoed in the room, Jessica said, "Don't use that word, Jonathan. It's beneath us. We're above those old superstitions. We're the new breed. We have new emotions, new beliefs, new rules."

"For another month or so," I said.

HARDSHELL

1

ARTERIES OF LIGHT PULSED THROUGH THE BLACK SKY. IN THAT stroboscopic blaze, millions of cold raindrops appeared to have halted in midfall. The glistening street reflected the celestial fire and seemed to be paved with broken mirrors. Then the lightning-scored sky went black again, and the rain resumed. The pavement was dark. Once more the flesh of the night pressed close on all sides.

Clenching his teeth, striving to ignore the pain in his right side, squinting in the gloom, Detective Frank Shaw gripped the Smith & Wesson .38 Chief's Special in both hands. He assumed a shooter's stance and squeezed off two rounds.

Ahead of Frank, Karl Skagg sprinted around the corner of the nearest warehouse just in time to save himself. The first slug bored a hole in the empty air behind him, and the second clipped the corner of the building.

The relentless roar of the rain on metal warehouse roofs and on the pavement, combined with rumbling thunder, effectively muffled the shots. Even if private security guards were at work in the immediate area, they probably had not heard anything, so Frank could not expect assistance.

He would have welcomed assistance. Skagg was big, powerful, a serial killer who had committed at least twenty-two murders. The guy was incredibly dangerous even in his best moments, and right now he was about as approachable as a whirling buzzsaw. This was definitely not a job for one cop.

Frank considered returning to his car and putting in a call for backup, but he knew that Skagg would slip away before the area could be cordoned off. No cop would call off a chase merely out of concern for his own welfare—especially not Frank Shaw.

Splashing across the puddled serviceway between two of the huge warehouses, Frank took the corner wide, in case Skagg was waiting for him just around the bend. But Skagg was gone.

Unlike the front of the warehouse, where concrete loading ramps sloped to the enormous roll-up garage doors, this side was mostly blank. Two hundred feet away, below a dimly glowing bulb in a wire security cage, was a man-size metal door. It was half open but falling shut.

Wincing at the pain in his side, Frank hurried to the entrance. He was surprised to see that the handle was torn off and that the lock was shattered, as if Skagg had used a crowbar or sledgehammer. Had he found a tool leaning against the warehouse wall, and had he used it to batter his way inside? He had been out of sight for mere seconds, no more than half a minute, which surely wasn't enough time to break through a steel door.

Why hadn't the burglar alarm sounded? Surely the warehouse was protected by a security system. And clearly Skagg had not entered with sufficient finesse to circumvent an alarm.

Thoroughly soaked, Frank shivered involuntarily when he put his back to the cold wall beside the door. He gritted his teeth, willed himself to stop shaking, and listened intently.

He heard only the hollow drumming of rain on metal roofs and walls. The sizzle of rain dancing on the wet pavement. The gurgle and slurp and chuckle of rain in gutters and downspouts.

Wind bleating. Wind hissing.

Frank broke the cylinder out of his revolver, tipped the two unused cartridges into his hand, dropped them in a pocket, and used a speedloader to put him back in business, fully stocked.

His right side throbbed. Minutes ago Skagg had taken him by surprise, stepping out of shadows with a length of rebar picked up at a construction site, swinging it as Mickey Mantle might have swung a baseball bat. Frank felt as if chunks of broken glass were working against one another in his deep muscles and bones; the pain sharpened slightly each time he drew a breath. Maybe he had a broken rib or two. Probably not . . . but maybe. He was wet, cold, and weary.

He was also having fun.

2

TO OTHER HOMICIDE DETECTIVES, FRANK WAS KNOWN AS HARDSHELL Shaw. That was also what his buddies had called him during Marine Corps basic training more than twenty-five years ago, for he was stoical, tough, and could not be cracked. The name had followed him when he left the service and joined the Los Angeles Police Department. He never encouraged anyone to use the sobriquet, but they used it anyway because it was apt.

Frank was tall, wide in the shoulders, narrow in the waist and hips, with a rock-solid body. His enormous hands, when curled into fists, were so formidable that he usually needed only to brandish them to assure an adversary's cooperation. His broad face appeared to have been carved out of granite—and with some difficulty, with much breaking of chisels and snapping of hammers.

His colleagues in the homicide division of the LAPD sometimes claimed that Frank had only two basic expressions: mean and meaner.

His pale-blue eyes, clear as rainwater, regarded the world with icy suspicion. When thinking, he frequently sat or stood perfectly still for long periods during which the quickness and alertness of his blue eyes, contrasted with his immobility, gave the impression that he was peering out from within a shell.

He had a damn hard shell, so his friends claimed. But that was only half of what they said about him.

Now, finished reloading his revolver, he stepped in front of the damaged door to the warehouse. He kicked it open. Crouched, head down, holding the .38 in front of him, he went in fast, looking left and right, expecting Skagg to rush at him with a crowbar, hammer, or whatever tool the scumbag had used to get into the building.

To Frank's left was a twenty-foot-high wall of metal shelving filled with thousands of small boxes. To his right were large wooden crates stacked in rows, towering thirty feet overhead, extending half the length of the building, alternating with avenues wide enough to admit forklifts.

The banks of overhead fluorescents suspended from the fifty-foot-high warehouse ceiling were switched off. Only a few security lamps in conical tin shades shed a wan glow over the stored goods below, leaving most of the place sheathed in shadows.

Frank moved cautiously and silently. His soggy shoes squished, but that sound was barely audible over the pounding rain on the roof. With water dripping off his brow, his jawline, and the barrel of his gun, he eased from one row of crates to another, peering into each passageway.

Skagg was at the far end of the third aisle, about a hundred and fifty feet away, half in shadow, half in milk-pale light, waiting to see if Frank had followed him. He could have kept out of the light, could have crouched entirely in the gloom against the crates, where he might not have been visible; by waiting in plain sight, he seemed to be taunting Frank. Skagg hesitated as if to be sure that he had been spotted, and then he disappeared around the corner.

For five minutes they played hide-and-seek, moving stealthily through the maze of cartons and crates. Three times, Skagg allowed himself to be seen, although he never let Frank get close.

He's having fun too, Frank thought.

That made him angry.

High on the walls, under the cobweb-festooned eaves, were slit windows that helped illuminate the cavernous building during the day. Now, only the flicker of lightning revealed the existence of those narrow panes. Although that inconstant pulse did not brighten the warehouse, it occasionally caused shadows to leap disconcertingly, and twice Frank nearly shot one of those harmless phantoms.

Easing along another avenue, scanning the gloom on both sides, Frank heard a noise, a hard scraping. He knew at once what it was: a crate sliding on a crate.

He looked up. In the grayness high above, a sofa-size box—visible only as a black silhouette—teetered on the edge of the crate beneath it. Then it tipped over and plummeted straight toward him.

Wile E. Coyote time.

Frank threw himself forward, hit the floor, and rolled just as the crate exploded against the concrete where he had been standing. He averted his face as wood disintegrated into hundreds of splintery shards of shrapnel. The box had contained plumbing fixtures; bright, chrome-plated faucets and shower heads bounced along the floor, and a couple thumped off Frank's back and thighs.

Hot tears of agony burned in his eyes, for the pain in his right side flared brighter. Further abused by all of this activity, his battered ribs now seemed not merely broken but pulverized.

Overhead, Skagg let out a sound that was one part a cry of rage, one part an animalistic ululation celebrating the thrill of the hunt, and one part insane laughter.

With some sixth sense, Frank was suddenly aware of a murderous, descending weight. He rolled to his right, flat up against the same wall of crates atop which Skagg stood. Behind him, a second huge box crashed to the warehouse floor.

"You alive?" Skagg called.

Frank did not respond.

"Yeah, you must be down there, because I didn't hear you scream. You're a quick bastard, aren't you?"

That laugh again. It was like atonal music played on an out-of-tune flute: a cold, metallic sound. Inhuman. Frank Shaw shivered.

Surprise was Frank's favorite strategy. During a pursuit, he tried to do what his prey would least expect. Now, taking advantage of the masking roar of the rain on the corrugated steel roof, he stood up in the darkness beside the wall of crates, holstered his revolver, blinked tears of pain out of his eyes, and began to climb.

"Don't cower in the shadows like a rat," Skagg shouted. "Come out and try to take a shot at me. You've got a gun. I don't. It'll be your bullets against whatever I can throw at you. What better odds do you want, you chickenshit cop?"

Twenty feet up the thirty-foot-high wall of wooden boxes, with his chilled fingers hooked into meager niches, with the toes of his shoes pressed hard against narrow ledges, Frank paused. The pain in his right side tightened as if it were a lasso, and it threatened to pull him backward into the aisle almost two stories below. He clung to his precarious position and squeezed his eyes tightly shut, willing the pain to go away.

"Hey, asshole," Skagg shouted.

Yeah?

"You know who I am?"

Big man on the psycho circuit, aren't you?
"I'm the one the newspapers call the Night Slasher."
Yeah, I know, I know, you drooling degenerate.
"This whole damn city lays awake at night, worrying about me, wondering where I am," Skagg shouted.
Not the whole city, man. Personally, I haven't lost any sleep over you.

Gradually the hot, grinding pain in his ribs subsided. It did not disappear altogether, but now it was a dull throb.

Among friends in the marines and on the police force, Frank had a reputation for persevering and triumphing in spite of wounds that would have incapacitated anyone else. In Nam he had taken two bullets from a Vietcong machine gun, one in the left shoulder and one through his left side directly above the kidney, but he had kept on going and had wasted the gunner with a grenade. Bleeding profusely, he had nevertheless used his good arm to drag his badly wounded buddy three hundred yards to a place of concealment, where they were safe from enemy snipers while the medevac chopper had sought and found them. As the medics loaded him into the helicopter, he had said, "War is hell, all right, but it's also sure exhilarating!"

His friends said he was iron hard, nail tough. But that was only part of what they said about him.

Overhead, Karl Skagg hurried along the tops of the boxes. Frank was close enough to hear the heavy footsteps above the ceaseless rumble of the rain.

Even if he had heard nothing, he would have known that Skagg was on the move. The two-crate-thick wall trembled with the killer's passage—though not violently enough to shake Frank off his perch.

He started to climb again, feeling cautiously for handholds in the darkness, inching along the pile of plumbing supplies. He got a few splinters in his fingers, but it was easy to screen out those small, stabbing pains.

From his new position atop the wall, Skagg shouted into another shadowy section of the warehouse to which he apparently thought Frank had moved, "Hey, chickenshit!"
You called?
"I have something for you, chickenshit."
I didn't know we were exchanging gifts.

"I got something sharp for you."
I'd prefer a TV set.
"I got the same thing for you that I used on all the others."
Forget the TV. I'll settle for a nice bottle of cologne.
"Come and get your guts ripped out, you chickenshit!"
I'm coming, I'm coming.

Frank reached the top, raised his head above the edge of the wall, looked left, then right, and saw Skagg about thirty feet away. The killer had his back to Frank and was peering intently down into another aisle.

"Hey, cop, look at me, standing right up here in the light. You can hit me with no trouble. All you have to do is step out and line up a shot. What's the matter? Don't you even have the nerve for that, you yellow bastard?"

Frank waited for a peal of thunder. When it came, he levered himself over the edge, on top of the stack of crates, where he rose to a crouch. The pounding rain was even louder up here, and combined with the thunder it was enough to cover any noise he made.

"Hey, down there! You know who I am, cop?"
You're repeating yourself. Boring, boring.
"I'm a real prize, the kind of trophy a cop dreams of!"
Yeah, your head would look good on my den wall.
"Big career boost if you brought me down, promotions and medals, you chickenshit."

The ceiling lights were only ten feet above their heads, and at such short range even the dim bulbs in the security lamps cast enough of a glow to illuminate half the crates on which they stood. Skagg was in the brightest spot, posturing for the one-man audience that he believed was below him.

Drawing his .38, Frank stepped forward, out of a shadowy area into a fall of amber light.

Skagg shouted, "If you won't come for me, you chickenshit, I'll come for you."

"Who're you calling chickenshit?" Frank asked.

Startled, Skagg spun toward him and, for an instant, teetered on the edge of the boxes. He windmilled his arms to keep from falling backward into the aisle below.

Holding his revolver in both hands, Frank said, "Spread your arms, drop to your knees, then lay flat on your belly."

Karl Skagg had none of that heavy-browed, slab-jawed, cement-faced look that most people associated with homicidal maniacs. He was handsome. Movie-star handsome. His was a broad, well-sculpted face with masculine yet sensitive features. His eyes were not like the eyes of a snake or a lizard or some other wild thing; they were brown, clear, and appealing.

"Flat on your belly," Frank repeated.

Skagg did not move. But he grinned. The grin ruined his movie-star looks because it had no charm. It was the humorless leer of a crocodile.

The guy was big, even bigger than Frank. He was six five, maybe even six and a half feet. Judging by the solid look of him, he was a dedicated, lifelong weight lifter. In spite of the chilly November night, he wore only running shoes, jeans, and a blue cotton shirt. Damp with rain and sweat, the shirt molded to his muscular chest and arms.

He said, "So how're you going to get me down from here, cop? Do you think I'll let you cuff me and then just lay up here while you go for backup? No way, pig face."

"Listen and believe me: I'll blow you away without the slightest hesitation."

"Yeah? Well, I'll take that gun off you quicker than you think. Then I'll rip your head off and shove it up your ass."

With unconcealed distaste, Frank said, "Is it really necessary to be so vulgar?"

Grinning more broadly, Skagg moved toward him.

Frank shot him pointblank in the chest.

The hard report echoed off the metal walls, and Skagg was thrown backward. Screaming, he pitched off the crates and plummeted into the aisle below. He landed with a *thunk* that cut off his scream.

Skagg's violent departure caused the crates to rock, and for a moment the unmortared wall of boxes swayed dangerously, creaking and grinding. Frank fell to his hands and knees.

Waiting for the stacks to steady under him, he thought about all the paperwork involved in a shooting, the many forms required to appease the bleeding hearts who were always certain that every victim of police gunfire was as innocent as Mother Teresa. He wished that Skagg had not forced the issue so soon. He wished that the killer had been more clever, had managed a more involved game of cat and mouse before the climactic scene. Thus far the chase had not provided half enough fun to compensate for the mountain of paperwork ahead.

The crates quickly steadied, and Frank got to his feet. He moved to the edge of the wall, to the place where Skagg had been flung into empty space by the impact of the slug. He looked down into the aisle. The concrete floor was silvery in the glow of the security lamp.

Skagg was not there.

Storm light flickered at the windows in the warehouse eaves. At his side, Frank's shadow leaped, shrank back, leaped, and shrank again, as though it belonged to Alice in one of her potion-swilling fits beyond the looking glass.

Thunder pummeled the night sky, and an even harder fall of rain dissolved against the roof.

Frank shook his head, squinted into the aisle below, and blinked in disbelief.

Skagg was still not there.

3

HAVING DESCENDED THE CRATES WITH CAUTION, FRANK SHAW LOOKED left and right along the deserted aisle. He studied the shadows intently, then crouched beside the spots and smears of blood where Karl Skagg had hit the floor. At least a liter of blood marked the point of impact, so fresh that a portion had still not soaked into the porous concrete but glistened in small, red, shallow puddles.

No man could take a .38 hollow-point in the chest at pointblank range, get up immediately, and walk away. No man could fall three stories onto concrete and spring straight to his feet.

Yet that seemed to be what Skagg had done.

A trail of gore indicated the man's route. With his .38 tightly in hand, Frank traced the psycho to an intersection, turned left into a new aisle, and moved stealthily through alternating pools of shadow and light for a hundred and fifty feet. There, he came to the end of the blood trail, which simply stopped in the middle of the passage.

Frank peered up at the piled crates on both sides, but Skagg was not clinging to either partition. No offshoot passageways between the boxes and no convenient niches provided a good hiding place.

Although badly hurt and hurrying to get out of his pursuer's reach, Skagg appeared to have carefully bound his grievous wounds to control the bleeding, had literally bound them on the run. But with what? Had he torn his shirt into strips to make tourniquets, bandages?

Damn it, Skagg had a mortal chest wound. Frank had seen the terrible impact of bullet in flesh, had seen Skagg hurled backward, had seen blood. The man's breastbone was shattered, splinters driven inward through vital organs. Arteries and veins were severed. The slug itself surely passed through Skagg's heart. Neither tourniquets nor bandages could stanch that flow or induce mangled cardiac muscles to resume rhythmic contractions.

Frank listened to the night.

Rain, wind, thunder. Otherwise silence.

Dead men don't bleed, Frank thought.

Maybe that was why the blood trail ended where it did—because Skagg died after going that far. But if he had died, death had not stopped him. He had kept right on going.

And now what am I chasing? A dead man who won't give up?

Most cops would have laughed off such a thought, embarrassed by it. Not Frank. Being tough, hard, and unbreakable did not mean that he had to be inflexible as well. He had the utmost respect for the mysterious complexity of the universe.

A walking dead man? Unlikely. But if that *was* the case, then the situation was certainly interesting. Fascinating. Suddenly Frank was more thoroughly involved in his work than he had been in weeks.

4

THE WAREHOUSE WAS VAST BUT, OF COURSE, FINITE. As FRANK explored the gloom-filled place, however, the chilly interior seemed to be larger than the space enclosed by its walls, as if portions of the building extended into another dimension, or as if the actual size of the structure changed magically and constantly to conform to his exaggerated perception of its immensity.

He searched for Skagg in aisles formed by crates and along other aisles between towering metal shelves filled with cardboard cartons. He stopped repeatedly to test the lids of crates, suspecting that Skagg had hidden in an empty one, but he found no makeshift coffin belonging to the walking dead man.

Twice he briefly suspended the search to take time to stay in touch with the throbbing pain in his side. Intrigued by the mystery of Skagg's disappearance, he had forgotten that he'd been hammered with a length of steel rebar. His extraordinary ability to block pain contributed to his hard-boiled reputation. A good buddy in the department once said that Hardshell Shaw's pain threshold was between that of a rhinoceros and a wooden fence post. But there were times when experiencing pain to the fullest was desirable. For one thing, pain sharpened his senses and kept him alert. Pain was humbling as well; it encouraged a man to keep his perspective, helped him to remember that life was precious. He was no masochist, but he knew that pain was a vital part of the human condition.

Fifteen minutes after having shot Skagg, Frank still hadn't found him. Nevertheless, he remained convinced that the killer was in the warehouse, dead or alive, and had not fled into the rainy night. His conviction was based on more than a hunch; he possessed the reliable intuition that distinguished great cops from good cops.

A moment later, when his intuition proved unnervingly accurate, Frank was exploring a corner of the building where twenty forklifts of various sizes were parked beside a dozen electric carts. Because of their knobby hydraulic joints and blunt tines, the lifts resembled enormous insects, and in the smoky yellow glow of the overhead lamp, they cast praying-mantis silhouettes across other machinery.

Frank was moving quietly through those spiky shadows when Karl Skagg spoke behind him:

"You looking for me?"

Frank turned, bringing up his gun.

Skagg was about twelve feet away.

"See me?" the killer asked.

His chest was intact, unwounded.

"See me?"

His three-story fall had resulted in no shattered bones, no crushed flesh. His blue cotton shirt was stained with blood, but the source of those stains was not visible.

"See me?"

"I see you," Frank said.

Skagg grinned. "You know *what* you're seeing?"

"A piece of shit."

"Can your small mind possibly conceive of my true nature?"

"Sure. You're a dog turd."

"You can't offend me," Skagg said.

"I can try."

"Your petty opinions are of no interest or concern to me."

"God forbid that I should bore you."

"You're getting tiresome."

"And you're nuts."

Skagg cracked a humorless smile of the sort that earlier had reminded Frank of a crocodile's grin. "I'm so far superior to you and to all of your kind that you're incapable of judging me."

"Oh, then forgive me for my presumption, great lord."

Skagg's grin faded into a vicious grimace, and his eyes widened. They no longer seemed like ordinary brown eyes. In their dark depths was a hungry, chilling reptilian watchfulness that made Frank feel as if he were but a fieldmouse staring into the mesmeric eyes of a blacksnake.

Skagg took one step forward.

Frank took one step backward.

"Your kind have only one use—you're interesting prey."

Frank said, "Well, I'm glad to hear we're interesting."

Skagg took another step forward, and a mantis shadow rippled across his face.

Frank stepped backward.

"Your kind are born to die."

Always interested in the workings of a criminally insane mind, just as a surgeon is always interested in the nature of the cancers that he excises from his patients' bodies, Frank said, "My kind, huh? What kind is that exactly?"

"Humankind."

"Ah."

"Humankind," Skagg repeated, speaking the word as if it were the vilest epithet.

"You're not human? Is that it?"

"That's it," Skagg agreed.

"What are you then?"

Skagg's insane laughter was as affecting as hard arctic wind.

Feeling as if bits of ice had begun to form in his bloodstream, Frank shivered. "All right, enough of this. Drop to your knees, then flat on your face."

"You're so slow-witted," Skagg said.

"Now *you're* boring *me*. Lie down and spread your arms and legs, you son of a bitch."

Skagg reached out with his right hand in such a way that for one disconcerting moment it seemed to Frank that the killer was going to change tactics and begin pleading for his life.

Then the hand began to change. The palm grew longer, broader. The fingers lengthened by two inches. The knuckles became thicker, gnarled. The hand darkened until it was singularly unhealthy, mottled brown-black-yellow. Coarse hairs sprouted from the skin. The fingernails extended into wickedly sharp claws.

"So tough you were. Imitation Clint Eastwood. But you're afraid now, aren't you, little man? Afraid at last, aren't you?"

Only the hand changed. No alterations occurred in Skagg's face or body or even in his other hand. He obviously had complete control of his metamorphosis.

"Werewolf," Frank said in astonishment.

With another peal of lunatic laughter that rebounded tinnily from the warehouse walls, Skagg worked his new hand, curling and extending and recurling his monstrous fingers.

"No. Not a werewolf," he whispered fiercely. "Something far more adaptable. Something infinitely stranger and more interesting. Are you afraid now? Have you wet your pants yet, you chickenshit cop?"

Skagg's hand began to change again. Coarse hairs receded into the flesh that had sprouted them. The mottled skin grew darker still, the many colors blending into green-black, and scales appeared. The fingertips thickened and grew broader, and suction pads formed on them. Webs spun into existence between fingers. The claws subtly changed shape, but they were no shorter or less sharp than the lupine claws had been.

Skagg peered at Frank through those hideous spread fingers and over the half-moon curves of the opaque webs. Then he lowered his hand slightly and grinned. His mouth had also changed. His lips were thin, black, and pebbled. He revealed pointed teeth and two hooked fangs. A thin, glistening, fork-tipped tongue flickered across those teeth, licked the pebbled lips.

At the sight of Frank's horrified astonishment, Skagg laughed. His mouth once more assumed the appearance of a human mouth.

But the hand underwent yet another metamorphosis. The scales were transformed into a hard-looking, smooth, purple-black, chitinous substance, and the fingers, as if wax brought before a flame, melted together until Skagg's wrist terminated in a serrated, razor-sharp pincer.

"You see? No need of a knife for this Night Slasher," whispered Skagg. "Within my hands are an infinite variety of blades."

Frank kept his .38 revolver pointed at his adversary, though by now he knew that even a .357 Magnum loaded with magnum cartridges with Teflon tips would provide him with no protection.

Outside, the sky was split by an ax of lightning. The flash of the electric blade sliced through the narrow windows high above the warehouse floor. A flurry of rafter shadows fell upon Frank and Skagg.

As thunder crashed across the night, Frank said, "What the hell are you?"

Skagg did not answer right away. He stared at Frank for a long moment and seemed perplexed. When he spoke, his voice had a double-honed edge: curiosity and anger. "Your species is soft. Your kind has no nerve, no guts. Faced with the unknown, your kind react as sheep react to the scent of a wolf. I despise your weakling breed. The strongest men break after what I've revealed. They scream like children, flee in panic, or stand paralyzed and speechless with fear. But not you. What makes you different? What makes you so brave? Are you simply thickheaded? Don't you realize you're a dead man? Are you foolish enough to think you'll get out of this place alive? Look at you—your gun hand isn't even trembling."

"I've had more frightening experiences than this," Frank said tightly. "I've been through two tax audits."

Skagg did not laugh. He clearly needed a terrified reaction from an intended victim. Murder was not sufficiently satisfying; evidently he also required the complete humiliation and abasement of his prey.

Well, you bastard, you're not going to get what you need from me, Frank thought.

He repeated, "What the hell are you?"

Clacking the halves of his deadly pincers, slowly taking a step forward, Karl Skagg said, "Maybe I'm the spawn of Hell. Do you think that could be the explanation? Hmmmm?"

"Stay back," Frank warned.

Skagg took another step toward him. "Am I a demon perhaps, risen from some sulfurous pit? Do you feel a certain coldness in your soul; do you sense the nearness of something satanic?"

Frank bumped against one of the forklifts, stepped around the obstruction, and continued to retreat.

Advancing, Skagg said, "Or am I something from another world, a creature alien to this one, conceived under a different moon, born under another sun?"

As he spoke, his right eye receded into his skull, dwindled, vanished. The socket closed up as the surface of a pond would close around the hole made by a pebble; only smooth skin lay where the eye had been.

"Alien? Is that something of which you could conceive?" Skagg pressed. "Have you sufficient wit to accept that I came to this world across an immense sea of space, carried on galactic tides?"

Frank no longer wondered how Skagg had battered open the door of the warehouse; he would have made hornlike hammers of his hands—or ironlike pry bars. No doubt he had also slipped incredibly thin extensions of his fingertips into the alarm switch, deactivating it.

The skin of Skagg's left cheek dimpled, and a hole formed in it. The lost right eye flowered into existence within the hole, directly under his left eye. In two winks both eyes re-formed: They were no longer human but insectoid, bulging and multifaceted.

As if changes were taking place in his throat too, Skagg's voice lowered and became gravelly. "Demon, alien . . . or maybe I'm the result of some genetic experiment gone terribly wrong. Hmmmm? What do you think?"

That laugh again. Frank *hated* that laugh.

"What do you think?" Skagg insisted as he approached.

Retreating, Frank said, "You're probably none of those things. Like you said . . . you're stranger and more interesting than that."

Both of Skagg's hands had become pincers now. The metamorphosis continued up his muscular arms as his human form gave way to a more crustacean anatomy. The seams of his shirt sleeves split; then the shoulder seams also tore as the transformation continued into his upper body. Chitinous accretions altered the size and shape of his chest, and his shirt buttons popped loose.

Though Frank knew he was wasting ammunition, he fired three shots as rapidly as he could squeeze the trigger. One round took Skagg in the stomach, one in the chest, one in the throat. Flesh tore, bones cracked, blood flew. The shapechanger staggered backward but did not go down.

Frank saw the bullet holes and knew that a man would die instantly of those wounds. Skagg merely swayed. Even as he regained his balance, his flesh began to knit up again. In half a minute the wounds had vanished.

With a wet cracking noise, Skagg's skull swelled to twice its previous size, though the change had nothing to do with the revolver fire that the shapechanger had absorbed. His face seemed to *implode,* all the features collapsing inward, but almost at once a mass of tissue bulged outward and began to form queer insectoid features.

Frank did not wait to see the grotesque details of Skagg's new countenance. He fired two more rounds at the alarmingly plastic face, then ran, leaped over an electric cart, dodged around a big forklift, sprinted into an aisle between tall metal shelves, and tried *not* to feel pain in his side as he ran back through the long warehouse.

When that morning had begun, dreary and rain-swept, with traffic moving through the city's puddled streets at a crawl, with the palm trees dripping, with the buildings somber in the gray storm light, Frank had thought that the spirit of the day was going to be as soggy and grim as the weather—uneventful, boring, perhaps even depressing. Surprise. Instead the day had turned out to be exciting, interesting, even exhilarating. He just never knew what fate had in store for him next, which was what made life fun and worth living.

Frank's friends said that in spite of his hard shell, he had an appetite for life and fun. But that was only part of what they said about him.

Skagg let out a bleat of rage that sounded utterly inhuman. In whatever shape he had settled upon, he was coming after Frank, and he was coming fast.

5

FRANK CLIMBED SWIFTLY AND UNHESITATINGLY IN SPITE OF THE PAIN IN his ribs. He heaved himself onto the top of another three-story-high wall of crates—machine tools, transmission gears, ball bearings— and rose to his feet.

Six other crates, which were not part of the wall itself, were stacked at random points along the otherwise flat top of those wooden palisades. He pushed one box to the edge. According to the printing on the side, it was filled with twenty-four portable compact-disc players, the kind that was carried by antisocial young men who used the volume of their favorite unlistenable music as a weapon with which to assault innocent passersby on the street. He had no idea what the damn things were doing among the stacks of machine tools and bearings; but the box weighed only about two hundred pounds, and he was able to slide it.

In the aisle below, something issued a shrill, piercing cry that was part rage, part challenge.

Frank leaned out past the box that he had brought to the brink, squinted down, and saw that Karl Skagg had now assumed a repulsive insectoid form that was not quite that of a two-hundred-fifty-pound cockroach and not quite a praying mantis but something between.

Suddenly the thing's chitin-capped head swiveled. Its antennae quivered. Multifaceted, luminous amber eyes gazed up at Frank.

He shoved the box over the edge. Unbalanced, he nearly plummeted with it. Wrenching himself back from the brink, he tottered and fell on his butt.

The carton of portable compact-disc players met the floor with thunderous impact. Twenty-four arrogant punks with bad taste in music but with a strong desire for high-tech fidelity would be disappointed this Christmas.

Frank crawled quickly to the edge on his hands and knees, looked down, and saw Skagg's squirming insectoid form struggling free of the burst carton that had briefly pinned him to the floor. Getting to his feet, Frank began to shift his weight rapidly back and forth, rocking the heavy crate under him. Soon half the wall was rocking too, and the column of boxes beneath Frank swayed dangerously. He put more effort into his frantic dance of destruction, then jumped off the toppling column just as it began to tilt out of the wall. He landed on an adjacent crate that was also wobbling but more stable, and he fell to his hands and knees; several formidable splinters gouged deep into his palms, but at the same time he heard at least half a dozen heavy crates crashing into the aisle behind him, so his cry was one of triumph rather than pain.

He turned and, flat on his belly this time, eased to the brink.

On the floor below, Skagg could not be seen beneath the ton of debris. However, the shapechanger was not dead; his inhuman screams of rage attested to his survival. The wreckage was moving as Skagg pushed and clawed his way out of it.

Satisfied that he had at least gained more time, Frank got up, ran the length of the wall of boxes, and descended at the end. He hurried into another part of the warehouse.

Along his randomly chosen route, he passed the half-broken door by which he and Skagg had entered the building. Skagg had closed it and stacked several apparently heavy crates against it to prevent Frank from making an easy, silent exit. No doubt the shapechanger also had damaged the controls for the electric garage doors at the front of the warehouse and had taken measures to block other exits.

You needn't have bothered, Frank thought.

He was not going to cut and run. As a police officer, he was duty-bound to deal with Karl Skagg, for Skagg was an extreme threat to the peace and safety of the community. Frank believed strongly in duty and responsibility. And he was an ex-marine. And . . . well, though he would never have admitted as much, he enjoyed being called Hardshell, and he took pleasure in the reputation that went with the nickname; he would never fail to live up to that reputation.

Besides, though he was beginning to tire of the game, he was still having fun.

6

IRON STEPS ALONG THE SOUTH WALL LED UP TO A HIGH BALCONY WITH a metal-grid floor. Off the balcony were four offices in which the warehouse's managerial, secretarial, and clerical staffs worked.

Large, sliding glass doors connected each office with the balcony, and through the doors Frank could see the darkish forms of desks, chairs, and business equipment. No lamps were on in any of the rooms, but each had outside windows that admitted the yellow glow of nearby streetlamps and the occasional flash of lightning.

The sound of rain was loud, for the curved ceiling was only ten feet above. When thunder rolled through the night, it reverberated in that corrugated metal.

At the midpoint of the balcony, Frank stood at the iron railing and looked across the immense storage room below. He could see into some aisles but by no means into all or even a majority. He saw the shadowy ranks of forklifts and electric carts among which he had encountered Skagg and where he had first discovered his adversary's tremendous recuperative powers and talent for changing shape. He also could see part of the collapsed wall of crates where he had buried Skagg under machine tools, transmission gears, and CD players.

Nothing moved.

He drew his revolver and reloaded. Even if he fired six rounds pointblank into Skagg's chest, he would succeed only in delaying the shapechanger's attack for a minute or less while the bastard healed. A minute. Just about long enough to reload. He had more cartridges, although not an endless supply. The gun was useless, but he intended to play the game as long as possible, and the gun was definitely part of the game.

He no longer allowed himself to feel the pain in his side. The showdown was approaching, and he could not afford the luxury of pain. He had to live up to his reputation and become Hardshell Shaw, had to blank out everything that might distract him from dealing with Skagg.

He scanned the warehouse again.

Nothing moved, but all the shadows in the enormous room, wall to wall, seemed to shimmer darkly with pent-up energy, as if they were alive and, though unmoving now, were prepared to spring at him if he turned his back on them.

Lightning cast its nervous, dazzling reflection into the office behind Frank, and a bright reflection of the reflection flickered through the sliding glass doors onto the balcony. He realized that he was revealed by the sputtering, third-hand electric glow, but he did not move away from the railing to a less conspicuous position. He was not trying to hide from Karl Skagg. After all, the warehouse was their Samarra, and their appointment was drawing near.

However, Frank thought confidently, *Skagg is sure going to be surprised to discover that the role of Death in this Samarra belongs not to him but to me.*

Again lightning flashed, its image entering the warehouse not only by way of the offices behind Frank but through the narrow panes high in the eaves. Ghostly flurries of storm light fluttered across the curve of the metal ceiling, which was usually dark above the shaded security lamps. In those pulses of queer luminosity, Skagg was disclosed at the highest point of the ceiling, creeping along upside down, as if he were a spider with no need to be concerned about the law of gravity. Although Skagg was visible only briefly and not in much detail, he currently seemed to have cloaked himself in a form that was actually less like a spider than like a lizard.

Holding his .38 in both hands, Frank waited for the storm's next bright performance. During the dark intermission between acts, he estimated the distance Skagg would have traveled, slowly tracking the unseen enemy with his revolver. When again the eave windows glowed like lamps and the spectral light glimmered across the ceiling, his gunsights were aimed straight at the shapechanger. He fired three times and was certain that at least two rounds hit the target.

Jolted by the shots, Skagg shrieked, lost his grip, and fell off the ceiling. But he did not drop stone-swift to the warehouse floor. Instead, healing and undergoing metamorphosis even as he fell, he relinquished his spider-lizard form, reverted to his human shape, but sprouted batlike wings that carried him, with a cold leathery flapping sound, through the air, across the railing, and onto the metal-grid balcony only twenty feet from Frank. His clothes—even his shoes—having split at the seams during one change or another, had fallen away from him, and he was naked.

Now the wings transformed into arms, one of which Skagg raised to point at Frank. "You can't escape me."

"I know, I know," Frank said. "You're like a cocktail-party bore—descended from a leech."

The fingers of Skagg's right hand abruptly telescoped out to a length of ten inches and hardened from flesh into solid bone. They tapered into knifelike points with edges as sharp as razor blades. At the base of each murderous fingertip was a barbed spur, the better to rip and tear.

Frank squeezed off the last three shots in the revolver.

Hit, Karl Skagg stumbled and fell backward on the balcony floor.

Frank reloaded. Even as he snapped shut the cylinder, he saw that Skagg already had risen.

With an ugly burst of maniacal laughter, Karl Skagg came forward. Both hands now terminated in long, bony, barbed claws. Apparently for the sheer pleasure of frightening his prey, Skagg exhibited the startling control he possessed over the form and function of his flesh. Five eyes opened at random points on his chest, and all fixed unblinking on Frank. A gaping mouth full of rapier teeth cracked open in Skagg's belly, and a disgusting yellowish fluid dripped from the points of the upper fangs.

Frank fired four shots that knocked Skagg down again, then fired the two remaining rounds into him as he lay on the balcony floor.

While Frank reloaded with his last cartridges, Skagg rose again and approached.

"Are you ready? Are you ready to die, you chickenshit cop?"

"Not really. I only have one more car payment to make, and for once I'd sure like to know what it's like to really *own* one of the damn things."

"In the end you'll bleed like all the others."

"Will I?"

"You'll scream like all the others."

"If it's always the same, don't you get tired of it? Wouldn't you like me to bleed and scream differently, just for some variety?"

Skagg scuttled forward.

Frank emptied the gun into him.

Skagg went down, got up, and spewed forth a noxious stream of shrill laughter.

Frank threw aside the empty revolver.

The eyes and mouth vanished from the shapechanger's chest and belly. In their place he sprouted four small, segmented, crablike arms with fingers that ended in pincers.

Retreating along the metal-grid balcony, past glass office doors that flared with reflected lightning, Frank said, "You know what your trouble is, Skagg? You're too flamboyant. You might be a lot more frightening if you were more subtle. All these changes, this frenzied discarding of one form after another—it's just too dazzling. The mind has difficulty comprehending, so the result is more awesome than terrifying. Know what I mean?"

If Skagg understood, he either disagreed or did not care, for he caused curved, bony spikes to burst forth from his chest, and he said, "I'll pull you close and impale you, then suck the eyes out of your skull." To fulfill the second half of his threat, he rearranged his face yet again, creating a protruding tubular orifice where his mouth had been; fine, sharp teeth rimmed the edge of it, and it made a disgustingly wet, vacuuming sound.

"That's exactly what I mean by flamboyant," Frank said as he backed up against the railing at the end of the balcony.

Skagg was only ten feet away now.

Regretting that the game was over, Frank released his body from the human pattern that he had imposed upon it. His bones dissolved. Fingernails, hair, internal organs, fat, muscle, and all other forms of tissue became as one, undifferentiated. His body was entirely amorphous. The darksome, jellied, throbbing mass flowed out of his suit through the bottoms of his sleeves.

With a rustle, his clothes collapsed in a soft heap on the metal-grid floor of the balcony.

Beside his empty suit, Frank reassumed his human form, standing naked before his would-be assailant. *"That* is the way to transform yourself without destroying your clothes in the process. Considering your impetuosity, I'm surprised you have any wardrobe left at all."

Shocked, Skagg abandoned his monstrous appearance and put on his human cloak. "You're one of my kind!"

"No," Frank said. "One of your species, but certainly not one of your demented kind. I live in peace with ordinary men, as most of our people have for thousands of years. You, on the other hand, are a repulsive degenerate, mad with your own power, driven by the insane need to dominate."

"Live in *peace* with them?" Skagg said scornfully. "But they're born to die, and we're immortal. They're weak, we're strong. They've no purpose but to provide us with pleasure of one kind or another, to titillate us with their death agonies."

"On the contrary," Frank said, "they're valuable because their lives are a continuing reminder to us that existence without self-control is only chaos. I spend nearly all of my time locked within this human form, and with but rare exception I force myself to suffer human pain, to endure both the anguish and joy of human existence."

"You're the one who's mad."

Frank shook his head. "Through police work I serve humankind, and therefore my existence has meaning. They so terribly need us to help them along, you see."

"Need us?"

As a roar of thunder was followed by a downpour more vigorous than at any previous moment of the storm, Frank searched for the words that might evoke understanding even in Skagg's diseased mind. "The human condition is unspeakably sad. Think of it: Their bodies are fragile; their lives are brief, each like the sputtering decline of a short candle; measured against the age of the earth itself, their deepest relationships with friends and family are of the most transitory nature, mere incandescent flashes of love and kindness that do nothing to light the great, endless, dark, flowing river of time. Yet they seldom surrender to the cruelty of their condition, seldom lose faith in themselves. Their hopes are rarely fulfilled, but they go on anyway, struggling against the darkness. Their determined striving in the face of their mortality is the very definition of courage, the essence of nobility."

Skagg stared at him in silence for a long moment, then let loose another peal of insane laughter. "They're prey, you fool. Toys for us to play with. Nothing more. What nonsense is this about our lives requiring purpose, struggle, self-control? Chaos isn't to be feared or disparaged. Chaos is to be *embraced*. Chaos, beautiful chaos, is the base condition of the universe, where the titanic forces of stars and galaxies clash without purpose or meaning."

"Chaos can't coexist with love," Frank said. "Love is a force for stability and order."

"Then what need is there for love?" Skagg asked, and he spoke the final word of that sentence in a particularly scornful tone.

Frank sighed. "Well, I have an appreciation of the need for love. I've been enlightened by my contact with the human species."

"Enlightened? 'Corrupted' is the better word."

Nodding, Frank said, "Of course, you would see it that way. The sad thing is that for love, in the defense of love, I'll have to kill you."

Skagg was darkly amused. "Kill me? What sort of joke is this? You can't kill me any more than I can kill you. We're both immortal, you and I."

"You're young," Frank said. "Even by human standards, you're only a young man, and by *our* standards you're an infant. I'd say I'm at least three hundred years older than you."

"So?"

"So there are talents we acquire only with great age."

"What talents?"

"Tonight I've watched you flaunt your genetic plasticity. I've seen you assume many fantastic forms. But I haven't seen you achieve the ultimate in cellular control."

"Which is?"

"The complete breakdown into an amorphous mass that in spite of utter shapelessness remains a coherent being. The feat I performed when I shucked off my clothes. It requires iron control, because it takes you to the brink of chaos, where you must retain your identity while on the trembling edge of dissolution. You haven't acquired that degree of control, for if total amorphousness had been in your power, you'd have tried to terrify me with an exhibition of it. But your shapechanging is so energetic that it's frenzied. You transform yourself at a whim, assuming whatever shape momentarily seizes your fancy, with a childish lack of discipline."

"So what?" Skagg remained unafraid, blissfully sure of himself, arrogant. "Your greater skill in no way changes the fact that I'm immortal, invincible. For me, all wounds heal regardless of how bad they may be. Poisons flush from my system without effect. No degree of heat, no arctic cold, no explosion less violent than a nuclear blast, no acid can shorten my life by so much as one second."

"But you're a living creature with a metabolic system," Frank said, "and by one means or another—by lungs in your human form, by other organs when in other forms—you must respire. You must have oxygen to maintain life."

Skagg stared at him, not comprehending the threat.

In an instant Frank surrendered human form, assumed a totally amorphous state, spread himself as if he were a giant manta ray in the depths of the sea, and flew forward, wrapping himself tightly around Skagg. His flesh conformed to every fold and crease, every concavity and convexity, of Skagg's body. He enveloped his startled adversary, sheathing every millimeter of Skagg, stoppering his nose and ears, coating every hair, denying him access to oxygen.

Within that jellied cocoon, Skagg sprouted claws and horns and bony, barbed spikes from various portions of his anatomy, attempting to gouge and tear through the suffocating tissue that bound him. But Frank's flesh couldn't be torn or punctured; even as his cells parted before a razor claw, they flowed together and knitted instantly in the wake of that cutting edge.

Skagg formed half a dozen mouths at various places on his body. Some were filled with needle-tipped fangs and some with double rows of shark's teeth, and all of them tore ravenously at his adversary's flesh. But Frank's amorphous tissue flowed into the orifices instead of retreating from them—*This is my body; taste of it*—clogging them to prevent biting and swallowing, coating the teeth and thus dulling the edges.

Skagg assumed a repulsive insectoid shape.

Frank conformed.

Skagg sprouted wings and sought escape in flight.

Frank conformed, weighed him down, and denied him the freedom of the air.

Outside, the night was ruled by the chaos of the storm. In the warehouse, where the aisles were neatly arranged, where the humidity and temperature of the air were controlled, order ruled everywhere except in the person of Karl Skagg. But Skagg's chaos was now firmly contained within the impenetrable envelope of Frank Shaw.

The inescapable embrace with which Frank enfolded Skagg was not merely that of an executioner but that of a brother and a priest; he was gently conveying Skagg out of this life, and he was doing so with some measure of the regret with which he watched ordinary men suffer and expire from accident and disease. Death was the unwelcome son of chaos in a universe woefully in need of order.

For the next hour, with diminishing energy, Skagg writhed and thrashed and struggled. A man could not have endured for so long without oxygen, but Skagg was not a man; he was both more and less than human.

Frank was patient. Hundreds of years of self-enforced adaptation to the limits of the human condition had taught him extreme patience. He held fast to Skagg a full half hour after the last detectable sign of life ebbed from the mad creature, and Skagg was as encapsulated as an object dipped in preserving bronze or eternally frozen in a cube of amber.

Then Frank returned to human form.

Karl Skagg's corpse was in human form as well, for that was the final metamorphosis that he had undergone in the last seconds of his agonizing suffocation. In death he looked as pathetic and fragile as any man.

When he had dressed, Frank carefully wrapped Skagg's body in a tarp that he found in a corner of the warehouse. This was one corpse that could not be permitted to fall into the hands of a pathologist, for the profound mysteries of its flesh would alert humankind to the existence of the secret race that lived among them. He carried the dead shapechanger outside, through the rainy night to his Chevy.

Gently he lowered Skagg into the car trunk and closed the lid.

Before dawn, in the dark scrub-covered hills along the perimeter of the Angeles National Forest, with the yellow-pink metropolitan glow of Los Angeles filling the lowlands south and west of him, Frank dug a deep hole and slipped Skagg's corpse into the ground. As he filled the grave, he wept.

From that wild burial ground he went directly home to his cozy five-room bungalow. Murphy, his Irish setter, was at the door to greet him with much sniffling and tail wagging. Seuss, his cat, held back at first with typical feline aloofness, but at last the Siamese rushed to him as well, purring noisily and wanting to be stroked.

Though the night had been filled with strenuous activity, Frank did not go to bed, for he never required sleep. Instead, he got out of his wet clothes, put on pajamas and a robe, made a large bowl of popcorn, opened a beer, and settled down on the sofa with Seuss and Murphy to watch an old Frank Capra movie that he had seen at least twenty times before but that he never failed to enjoy: Jimmy Stewart and Donna Reed in *It's a Wonderful Life*.

All of Frank Shaw's friends said that he had a hard shell, but that was only part of what they said. They also said that inside his hard shell beat a heart as soft as any.

KITTENS

T HE COOL GREEN WATER SLIPPED ALONG THE STREAMBED, BUB-
bling around smooth brown stones, reflecting the melancholy willows
that lined the bank. Marnie sat on the grass, tossing stones into a
deep pool, watching the ripples spread in ever-widening circles and
lap at the muddy banks. She was thinking about the kittens. This
year's kittens, not last year's. A year ago, her parents had told her
that the kittens had gone to Heaven. Pinkie's litter had disappeared
the third day after their squealing birth.

Marnie's father had said, "God took them away to Heaven to live
with Him."

She didn't exactly doubt her father. After all, he was a religious
man. He taught Sunday school every week and was an officer or
something in the church, whose duty it was to count collection
money and mark it down in a little red book. He was always picked
to give the sermon on Laymen's Sunday. And every evening, he
read passages to them from the Bible. She had been late for the
reading last night and had been spanked. "Spare the rod and spoil
the child," her father always said. No, she didn't actually doubt her
father, for if anyone would know about God and kittens, it was he.

But she continued to wonder. Why, when there were hundreds
upon thousands of kittens in the world, did God have to take all
four of hers? Was God selfish?

This was the first that she had thought of those kittens for some
time. In the past twelve months, much had happened to make her
forget. There was her first year in school, the furor of getting ready

for the first day—the buying of paper, pencils, and books. And the first few weeks had been interesting, meeting Mr. Alphabet and Mr. Numbers. When school began to bore her, Christmas rushed in on polished runners and glistening ice: the shopping, the green and yellow and red and blue lights, the Santa Claus on the corner who staggered when he walked, the candlelit church on Christmas Eve when she had had to go to the bathroom and her father had made her wait until the service was over. When things began to lose momentum again in March, her mother had given birth to twins. Marnie had been surprised at how small they were and at how slowly they seemed to grow in the following weeks.

Here it was June again. The twins were three months old, finally beginning to grow a great deal heavier; school was out, and Christmas was an eternity away, and everything was getting dull again. Therefore, when she heard her father telling her mother that Pinkie was going to have another litter, she grasped at the news and wrenched every drop of excitement from it. She busied herself in the kitchen, preparing rags and cotton for the birth and a fancy box for the kittens' home when they arrived.

As events ran their natural course, Pinkie slunk away and had the kittens during the night in a dark corner of the barn. There was no need for sterilized rags or cotton, but the box came in handy. There were six in this litter, all gray with black spots that looked like ink hastily blotted.

She liked the kittens, and she was worried about them. What if God was watching again like last year?

"What are you doing, Marnie?"

She didn't have to look; she knew who was behind her. She turned anyway, out of deference, and saw her father glaring down at her, dark irregular splotches of perspiration discoloring the underarms of his faded blue work coveralls, dirt smeared on his chin and caked to the beard on his left cheek.

"Throwing stones," she answered quietly.

"At the fish?"

"Oh, no, sir. Just throwing stones."

"Do we remember who was the victim of stone throwing?" He smiled a patronizing smile.

"Saint Stephen," she answered.

"Very good." The smile faded. "Supper's ready."

⊲ ∧ ⊳

She sat ramrod stiff in the old maroon easy chair, looking attentive as her father read to them from the ancient family Bible that was bound in black leather, all scuffed and with several torn pages. Her mother sat next to her father on the dark blue corduroy couch, hands folded in her lap, an isn't-it-wonderful-what-God-has-given-us smile painted on her plain but pretty face.

"Suffer the little children to come to me, and forbid them not; for such is the kingdom of God." Her father closed the book with a gentle slap that seemed to leap into the stale air and hang there, holding up a thick curtain of silence. No one spoke for several minutes. Then: "What chapter of what book did we just read, Marnie?"

"Saint Mark, chapter ten," she said dutifully.

"Fine," he said. Turning to his wife, whose smile had changed to a we've-done-what-a Christian-family-should-do expression, he said, "Mary, how about coffee for us and a glass of milk for Marnie?"

"Right," said her mother, getting up and pacing into the kitchen.

Her father sat there, examining the inside covers of the old holy book, running his fingers along the cracks in the yellow paper, scrutinizing the ghostly stains embedded forever in the title page where some great-uncle had accidentally spilled wine a million-billion years ago.

"Father," she said tentatively.

He looked up from the book, not smiling, not frowning.

"What about the kittens?"

"What about them?" he countered.

"Will God take them again this year?"

The half-smile that had crept onto his face evaporated into the thick air of the living room. "Perhaps," was all that he said.

"He can't," she almost sobbed.

"Are you saying what God can and cannot do, young lady?"

"No, sir."

"God can do anything."

"Yes, sir." She fidgeted in her chair, pushing herself deeper into its rough, worn folds. "But why would he want my kittens again? Why always mine?"

"I've had quite enough of this, Marnie. Now be quiet."

"But why mine?" she persisted.

He stood suddenly, crossed to the chair, and slapped her delicate face. A thin trickle of blood slipped from the corner of her mouth. She wiped it away with the palm of her hand.

"You must not doubt God's motives!" her father insisted. "You are far too young to doubt." The saliva glistened on his lips. He grabbed her by the arm and brought her to her feet. "Now you get up those stairs and into bed."

She didn't argue. On the way to the staircase, she wiped away the re-forming stream of blood. She walked slowly up the steps, allowing her hand to run along the smooth, polished wood railing.

"Here's the milk," she heard her mother saying below.

"We won't be needing it," her father answered curtly.

In her room, she lay in the semidarkness that came when the full moon shone through her window, its orange-yellow light glinting from a row of religious plaques that lined one wall. In her parents' room, her mother was cooing to the twins, changing their diapers. "God's little angels," she heard her mother say. Her father was tickling them, and she could hear the "angels" chuckling—a deep gurgle that rippled from down in their fat throats.

Neither her father nor her mother came to say good night. She was being punished.

⚊ ⋀ ⋎

Marnie was sitting in the barn, petting one of the gray kittens, postponing an errand her mother had sent her on ten minutes earlier. The rich smell of dry, golden hay filled the air. Straw covered the floor and crackled underfoot. In the far end of the building, the cows were lowing to each other—only two of them, whose legs had been sliced by barbed wire and who were being made to convalesce. The kitten mewed and pawed the air below her chin.

"Where's Marnie?" her father's voice boomed from somewhere in the yard between the house and the barn.

She was about to answer when she heard her mother call from the house: "I sent her to Brown's for a recipe of Helen's. She'll be gone another twenty minutes."

"That's plenty of time," her father answered. The crunch of his heavy shoes on the cinder path echoed in military rhythm.

Marnie knew that something was wrong; something was happening that she was not supposed to see. Quickly, she put the kitten back in the red and gold box and sprawled behind a pile of straw to watch.

Her father entered, drew a bucket of water from the wall tap, and placed it in front of the kittens. Pinkie hissed and arched her back. The man picked her up and shut her in an empty oat bin from which her anguished squeals boomed in a ridiculously loud echo that belonged on the African veldt and not on an American farm. Marnie almost laughed, but remembered her father and suppressed the levity.

He turned again to the box of kittens. Carefully, he lifted one by the scruff of the neck, petted it twice, and thrust its head under the water in the bucket! There was a violent thrashing from within the bucket, and sparkling droplets of water sprayed into the air. Her father grimaced and shoved the entire body under the smothering pool. In time, the thrashing ceased. Marnie found that her fingers were digging into the concrete floor, hurting her.

Why? Why-why-why?

Her father lifted the limp body from the bucket. Something pink and bloody hung from the animal's mouth. She couldn't tell whether it was the tongue or whether the precious thing had spewed its entrails into the water in a last attempt to escape the heavy, horrible death of suffocation.

Soon six kittens were dead. Soon six silent fur balls were dropped in a burlap sack. The top was twisted shut. He let Pinkie out of the bin. The shivering cat followed him out of the barn, mewing softly, hissing when he turned to look at her.

Marnie lay very still for a long time, thinking of nothing but the execution and trying desperately to understand. Had God sent her father? Was it God who told him to kill the kittens—to take them away from her? If it was, she didn't see how she could ever again stand before that gold and white altar, accepting communion. She stood and walked toward the house, blood dripping from her fingers, blood and cement.

"Did you get the recipe?" asked her mother as Marnie slammed the kitchen door.

"Mrs. Brown couldn't find it. She'll send it over tomorrow." She lied so well that she surprised herself. "Did God take my kittens?" she blurted suddenly.

Her mother looked confused. "Yes," was all that she could say.

"I'll get even with God! He can't do that! He can't!" She ran out of the kitchen toward the staircase.

Her mother watched but didn't try to stop her.

Marnie Caufield walked slowly up the stairs, letting her hand run along the smooth, polished wood railing.

⊲ ⋀ ⊳

At noon, when Walter Caufield came in from the field, he heard a loud crash and the tinkling of china and the shattering of glass. He rushed into the living room to see his wife lying at the foot of the stairs. A novelty table was overturned, statuettes broken and cracked.

"Mary, Mary. Are you hurt?" He bent quickly to her side.

She looked up at him out of eyes that were far away in distant mists. "Walt! My Good God, Walt—our precious angels. The bathtub—our precious angels!"

THE NIGHT OF THE STORM

H E WAS A ROBOT MORE THAN A HUNDRED YEARS OLD, BUILT BY OTHER robots in an automated factory that had been continuously engaged in the production of robots for many centuries.

His name was Curanov, and as was the custom of his kind, he roamed the earth in search of interesting things to do. Curanov had climbed the highest mountains in the world, with the aid of special body attachments (spikes in his metal feet, tiny but strong hooks on the ends of his twelve fingers, an emergency grappling rope coiled inside his chest-area storage compartment and ready for a swift ejection if he should fall); his small, antigravity flight motors were removed to make the climb as dangerous and, therefore, as interesting as possible. Having submitted to heavy-duty component-sealing procedures, Curanov had once spent eighteen months under water, exploring a large portion of the Pacific Ocean, until he was bored even by the mating of whales and by the ever-shifting beauty of the sea bottom. Curanov had crossed deserts, explored the Arctic Circle on foot, gone spelunking in countless different subterranean systems. He had been caught in a blizzard, in a major flood, in a hurricane, and in the middle of an earthquake that would have registered nine on the Richter scale, if the Richter scale had still been in use. Once, specially insulated, he had descended halfway to the center of the earth, there to bask in pockets of glowing gases, between pools of molten stone, scalded by eruptions of magma, feeling nothing. Eventually, he grew weary of even that colorful spectacle, and he surfaced again.

Having lived only one of his two assigned centuries, he wondered if he could last through another hundred years of such tedium.

Curanov's private counselor, a robot named Bikermien, assured him that this boredom was only temporary and easily alleviated. If one was clever, Bikermien said, one could find limitless excitement as well as innumerable, valuable situations for data collection about both one's environment and one's mechanical aptitude and heritage. Bikermien, in the last half of his second century, had developed such an enormous and complex data vault that he was assigned stationary duty as a counselor, attached to a mother computer, utterly immobile. By now, extremely adept at finding excitement even through secondhand experience, Bikermien did not mourn the loss of his mobility; he was, after all, a spiritual superior to most robots, inwardly directed. Therefore, when Bikermien advised, Curanov listened, however skeptical he might be.

Curanov's problem, according to Bikermien, was that he had started out in life, from the moment he'd left the factory, to pit himself against the greatest of forces—the wildest sea, the coldest cold, the highest temperatures, the greatest pressures—and now, having conquered these things, he could see no interesting challenges beyond them. Yet, the counselor said that Curanov had overlooked some of the most fascinating explorations. The quality of any challenge was directly related to one's ability to meet it; the less adequate one felt, the better the experience, the richer the contest, and the more handsome the data reward.

Does this suggest anything to you? Bikermien inquired, without speaking, the telebeam open between them.

Nothing.

So Bikermien explained it:

Hand-to-hand combat with a full-grown male ape might seem like an uninteresting, easy challenge at first glance; a robot was the mental and physical superior of any ape. However, one could always modify oneself in order to even the odds of what might appear to be a sure thing. If a robot couldn't fly, couldn't see as well at night as in the daylight, couldn't communicate except vocally, couldn't run faster than an antelope, couldn't hear a whisper at a thousand yards—in short, if all of his standard abilities were dulled, except for his thinking capacity, might not a robot find that a hand-to-hand battle with an ape was a supremely exciting event?

I see your point, Curanov admitted. *To understand the grandeur of simple things, one must humble himself.*

Exactly.

And so it was that, on the following day, Curanov boarded the express train north to Montana, where he was scheduled to do some hunting in the company of four other robots, all of whom had been stripped to their essentials.

Ordinarily they would have flown under their own power. Now none had that ability.

Ordinarily they would have used telebeams for communication. Now they were forced to talk to one another in that curious, clicking language that had been designed especially for machines but that robots had been able to do without for more than six hundred years.

Ordinarily, the thought of going north to hunt deer and wolves would have profoundly bored them. Now, however, each of them felt a curious tingle of anticipation, as if this were a more important ordeal than any he had faced before.

◁ ∧ ▷

A brisk, efficient robot named Janus met the group at the small station house just outside of Walker's Watch, toward the northernmost border of Montana. To Curanov, it was clear that Janus had spent several months in this uneventful duty assignment, and that he might be near the end of his obligatory two years' service to the Central Agency. He was actually *too* brisk and efficient. He spoke rapidly, and he behaved altogether as if he must keep moving and doing in order not to have time to contemplate the uneventful and unexciting days that he had spent in Walker's Watch. He was one of those robots too eager for excitement; one day, he would tackle a challenge that he had not been prepared for, and he would end himself.

Curanov looked at Tuttle, another robot who, on the train north, had begun an interesting if silly argument about the development of the robot personality. He contended that until quite recently, in terms of centuries, robots hadn't possessed individual personalities. Each, Tuttle claimed, had been like the other, cold and sterile, with no private dreams. A patently ridiculous theory. Tuttle had been unable to explain how this could have been, but he'd refused to back down from his position.

Now, watching Janus chatter at them in a nervous staccato, Curanov was incapable of envisioning an era when the Central Agency would have dispatched mindless robots from the factories. The whole purpose of life was to explore, to carefully store data collected from an individual viewpoint, even if it was repetitive data. How could mindless robots ever function in the necessary manner?

As Steffan, another of their group, had said, such theories were on a par with belief in Second Awareness. (Some believed, without evidence, that the Central Agency occasionally made a mistake and, when a robot's allotted life span was up, only partially erased his accumulated memory before refitting him and sending him out of the factory again. These robots—or so the superstitious claimed— had an advantage and were among those who matured fast enough to be elevated to duty as counselors and, sometimes, even to service in the Central Agency itself.)

Tuttle had been angered to hear his views on robot personality equated with wild tales of Second Awareness. To egg him on, Steffan also suggested that Tuttle believed in that ultimate of hobgoblins, the "human being." Disgusted, Tuttle settled into a grumpy silence while the others enjoyed the jest.

"And now," Janus said, calling Curanov back from his reverie, "I'll issue your supplies and see you on your way."

Curanov, Tuttle, Steffan, Leeke, and Skowski crowded forward, eager to begin the adventure.

Each of the five was given: binoculars of rather antique design, a pair of snowshoes that clipped and bolted to their feet, a survival pack of tools and greases with which to repair themselves in the event of some unforeseen emergency, an electric hand torch, maps, and a drug rifle complete with an extra clip of one thousand darts.

"This is all, then?" Leeke asked. He had seen as much danger as Curanov, perhaps even more, but now he sounded frightened.

"What else would you need?" Janus asked impatiently.

Leeke said, "Well, as you know, certain modifications have been made to us. For one thing, our eyes aren't what they were, and—"

"You've a torch for darkness," Janus said.

"And then, our ears—" Leeke began.

"Listen cautiously, walk quietly," Janus suggested.

"We've had a power reduction to our legs," Leeke said. "If we should have to run—"

"Be stealthy. Creep up on your game before it knows you're there, and you'll not need to chase it."

"But," Leeke persisted, "weakened as we are, if we should have to run from something—"

"You're only after deer and wolves," Janus reminded him. "The deer won't give chase—and a wolf hasn't any taste for steel flesh."

Skowski, who had thus far been exceptionally quiet, not even joining the good-natured roasting the others had given Tuttle on the train, now stepped forward. "I've read that this part of Montana has an unusual number of . . . unexplained reports."

"Reports of what?" Janus asked.

Skowski swept the others with his yellow visual receptors, then looked back at Janus. "Well . . . reports of footprints similar to our own but not those of any robot, and reports of robotlike forms seen in the woods."

"Oh," Janus said, waving a glittering hand as if to brush away Skowski's suggestion like a fluff of dust, "we get a dozen reports each month about 'human beings' sighted in wilder regions northwest of here."

"Where we're going?" Curanov asked.

"Yes," Janus said. "But I wouldn't worry. In every case, those who make the reports are robots like yourselves: They've had their perceptions decreased in order to make the hunt a greater challenge for them. Undoubtedly, what they've seen has a rational explanation. If they had seen these things with their full range of perceptions, they would not have come back with these crazy tales."

"Does anyone besides stripped-down robots go there?" Skowski asked.

"No," Janus said.

Skowski shook his head. "This isn't anything at all like I thought it would be. I feel so weak, so . . ." He dropped his supplies at his feet. "I don't believe I want to continue with this."

The others were surprised.

"Afraid of goblins?" Steffan asked. He was the teaser in the group.

"No," Skowski said. "But I don't like being a cripple, no matter how much excitement it adds to the adventure."

"Very well," Janus said. "There will be only four of you."

Leeke said, "Don't we get any weapons besides the drug rifle?"

"You'll need nothing else," Janus said.

Leeke's query had been a strange one, Curanov thought. The prime directive in every robot's personality—installed in the factory—forbade the taking of any life that could not be restored. Yet, Curanov sympathized with Leeke, shared Leeke's foreboding. He supposed that, with a crippling of their perceptions, there was an inevitable clouding of the thought processes as well, for nothing else explained their intense and irrational fear.

"Now," Janus said, "the only thing you need to know is that a storm is predicted for northern Montana early tomorrow night. By then you should be to the lodge that will serve as your base of operations, and the snow will pose no trouble. Questions?"

They had none they cared to ask.

"Good luck to you," Janus said. "And may many weeks pass before you lose interest in the challenge." That was a traditional send-off, yet Janus appeared to mean it. He would, Curanov guessed, prefer to be hunting deer and wolves under severely restricted perceptions rather than to continue clerking at the station house in Walker's Watch.

They thanked him, consulted their maps, left the station house, and were finally on their way.

Skowski watched them go and, when they looked back at him, waved one shiny arm in a stiff-fingered salute.

◁ ∧ ▷

They walked all that day, through the evening, and on into the long night, requiring no rest. Though the power supply to their legs had been reduced and a governor put on their walking speed, they did not become weary. They could appreciate the limitations put on their senses, but they could not actually grow tired. Even when the drifts were deep enough for them to break out their wire-webbed snowshoes and bolt those in place, they maintained a steady pace.

Passing across broad plains where the snow was swept into eerie peaks and twisting configurations, walking beneath the dense roof of crossed pine boughs in the virgin forests, Curanov felt a tingle of anticipation that had been missing from his exploits for some years now. Because his perceptions were so much less acute than usual, he sensed danger in every shadow, imagined obstacles and complications around every turn. It was positively exhilarating to be here.

Before dawn, a light snow began to fall, clinging to their cold steel skin. Two hours later, by the day's first light, they crested a small ridge and looked out across an expanse of pine woods to the lodge on the other side of a shallow valley. The place was made of a burnished, bluish metal: oval windows, Quonset walls, functional.

"We'll be able to get some hunting in today," Steffan said.

"Let's go," Tuttle said.

Single file, they went down into the valley, crossed it, and came out almost at the doorstep of the lodge.

◁ ∧ ▷

Curanov pulled the trigger.

The magnificent buck, decorated with a twelve-point rack of antlers, reared up onto its hind legs, pawing at the air, breathing steam.

"A hit!" Leeke cried.

Curanov fired again.

The buck went down onto all four legs.

The other deer, behind it in the woods, turned and galloped back along the well-trampled trail.

The buck shook its huge head, staggered forward as if to follow its companions, stopped abruptly, and then settled onto its haunches. After one last valiant effort to regain its footing, it fell sideways into the snow.

"Congratulations!" Steffan said.

The four robots rose from the drift where they'd concealed themselves when the deer had come into sight, and they crossed the small open field to the sleeping buck.

Curanov bent and felt the creature's sedated heartbeat, watched its grainy black nostrils quiver as it took a shallow breath.

Tuttle, Steffan, and Leeke crowded in, squatting around the creature, touching it, marveling at the perfect musculature, the powerful shoulders, and the hard-packed thighs. They agreed that bringing down such a brute, when one's senses were drastically damped, was indeed a challenge. Then, one by one, they got up and walked away, leaving Curanov alone to more fully appreciate his triumph and to carefully collect and record his own emotional reactions to the event in the microtapes of his data vault.

Curanov was nearly finished with his evaluation of the challenge and of the resultant confrontation—and the buck was beginning to regain its senses—when Tuttle cried out as if his systems had been accidentally overloaded.

"Here! Look here!"

Tuttle stood two hundred yards away, near the dark trees, waving his arms. Steffan and Leeke were already moving toward him.

At Curanov's feet, the buck snorted and tried to stand, failed to manage that yet, and blinked its gummed eyelids. With nothing more to record in his data vault, Curanov rose and left the beast, walked toward his three companions.

"What is it?" he asked when he arrived.

They stared at him with glowing amber visual receptors that seemed especially bright in the gray light of late afternoon.

"There," Tuttle said, pointing at the ground before them.

"Footprints," Curanov said.

Leeke said, "They don't belong to any of us."

"So?" Curanov asked.

"And they're not robot prints," Tuttle said.

"Of course they are."

Tuttle said, "Look closer."

Curanov bent down and realized that his eyes, with half their power gone, had at first deceived him in the weak light. These weren't robot prints in anything but shape. A robot's feet were crosshatched with rubber tread; these prints showed none of that. A robot's feet were bottomed with two holes that acted as vents for the antigrav system when the unit was in flight; these prints showed no holes.

Curanov said, "I didn't know there were any apes in the north."

"There aren't," Tuttle said.

"Then—"

"These," Tuttle said, "are the prints . . . of a man."

"Preposterous!" Steffan said.

"How else do you explain them?" Tuttle asked. He didn't sound happy with his explanation, but he was prepared to stick with it until someone offered an acceptable alternative.

"A hoax," Steffan said.

"Perpetrated by whom?" Tuttle asked.

"One of us."

They looked at one another, as if the guilt would be evident in their identical metal faces.

Then Leeke said, "That's no good. We've been together. These tracks were made recently, or they'd be covered over with snow. None of us has had a chance, all afternoon, to sneak off and form them."

"I still say it's a hoax," Steffan insisted. "Perhaps someone was sent out by the Central Agency to leave these for us to find."

"Why would Central bother?" Tuttle asked.

"Maybe it's part of our therapy," Steffan said. "Maybe this is to sharpen the challenge for us, add excitement to the hunt." He gestured vaguely at the prints, as if he hoped they'd vanish. "Maybe Central does this for everyone who's troubled by boredom, to restore the sense of wonder that—"

"That's highly unlikely," Tuttle said. "You know that it's the responsibility of each individual to engineer his own adventures and to generate his own storable responses. The Central Agency never interferes. It is merely a judge. After that fact, it evaluates us and gives promotions to those whose data vaults have matured."

By way of cutting the argument short, Curanov said, "Where do these prints lead?"

Leeke indicated the marks with a shiny finger. "It looks as if the creature came out of the woods and stood here for a while—perhaps watching us as we stalked the buck. Then he turned and went back the way he came."

The four robots followed the footprints into the first of the pine trees, but they hesitated to go into the deeper regions of the forest.

"Darkness is coming," Leeke said. "The storm's almost on us, as Janus predicted. With our senses as restricted as they are, we should be getting back to the lodge while we've still enough light to see by."

Curanov wondered if their surprising cowardice was as evident to the others as it was to him. They all professed not to believe in the monsters of myth, and yet they rebelled at following these footprints. Curanov had to admit, however, that when he tried to envision the beast that might have made these tracks—a "man"—he was more anxious than ever to reach the sanctity of the lodge.

◁ ∧ ▷

The lodge had only one room, which was all that they required. Since each of the four was physically identical to the others, no one felt a need for geographical privacy. Each could obtain a more rewarding isolation merely by tuning out all exterior events in one of the lodge's inactivation nooks, thereby dwelling strictly within his mind, recycling old data and searching for previously overlooked juxtapositions of seemingly unrelated information. Therefore, no one was discomfited by the single, gray-walled, nearly featureless room where they would spend as much as several weeks together, barring any complications or any lessening of their interest in the challenge of the hunt.

They racked their drug rifles on a metal shelf that ran the length of one wall, and they unbolted their other supplies that, until now, they had clipped to various portions of their body shells.

As they stood at the largest window, watching the snow sheet past them in a blinding white fury, Tuttle said, "If the myths are true, think what would be done to modern philosophy."

"What myths?" Curanov asked.

"About human beings."

Steffan, as rigid as ever, was quick to counter the thrust of Tuttle's undeveloped line of thought. He said, "I've seen nothing to make me believe in myths."

Tuttle was wise enough, just then, to avoid an argument about the footprints in the snow. But he was not prepared to drop the conversation altogether. "We've always thought that intelligence was a manifestation solely of the mechanized mind. If we should find that a fleshy creature could—"

"But none can," Steffan interrupted.

Curanov thought that Steffan must be rather young, no more than thirty or forty years out of the factory. Otherwise, he would not be so quick to reject anything that even slightly threatened the status quo that the Central Agency had outlined and established. With the decades, Curanov knew, one learned that what had once been impossible was now considered only commonplace.

"There are myths about human beings," Tuttle said, "which say that robots sprang from them."

"From flesh?" Steffan asked, incredulous.

"I know it sounds odd," Tuttle said, "but at various times in my life, I have seen the oddest things prove true."

"You've been all over the earth, in more corners than I have been. In all your travels, you must have seen tens of thousands of fleshy species, animals of all descriptions." Steffan paused, for effect. "Have you ever encountered a single fleshy creature with even rudimentary intelligence in the manner of the robot?"

"Never," Tuttle admitted.

"Flesh was not designed for high-level sentience," Steffan said. They were quiet.

The snow fell, pulling the gray sky closer to the land.

None would admit the private fear he nurtured.

"Many things fascinate me," Tuttle said, surprising Curanov, who had thought that the other robot was done with his postulating. "For one—where did the Central Agency come from? What were its origins?"

Steffan waved a hand disparagingly. "There has *always* been a Central Agency."

"But that's no answer," Tuttle said.

"Why isn't it?" Steffan asked. "For all intents and purposes, we accept that there has *always* been a universe, stars and planets and everything in between."

"Suppose," Tuttle said, "just for the sake of argument, that there has *not* always been a Central Agency. The Agency is constantly doing research into its own nature, redesigning itself. Vast stores of data are transferred into increasingly sophisticated repositories every fifty to a hundred years. Isn't it possible that occasionally the Agency loses bits and pieces, accidentally destroys some of its memory in the move?"

"Impossible," Steffan said. "There are any number of safeguards taken against such an eventuality."

Curanov, aware of many of the Central Agency's bungles over

the past hundred years, was not so sure. He was intrigued by Tuttle's theory.

Tuttle said, "If the Central Agency somehow lost most of its early stores of data, its knowledge of human beings might have vanished along with countless other bits and pieces."

Steffan was disgusted. "Earlier, you ranted against the idea of Second Awareness—but now you can believe *this*. You amuse me, Tuttle. Your data vault must be a trove of silly information, contradictory beliefs, and useless theorizing. If you believe in these human beings—then do you also believe in all the attendant myths? Do you think they can only be killed with an instrument of wood? Do you think they sleep at night in dark rooms? Sleep like beasts? And do you think that, though they're made of flesh, they cannot be dispatched but that they pop up somewhere else in a new body?"

Confronted with these obviously insupportable superstitions, Tuttle backed down from his entire point. He turned his amber visual receptors on the snow beyond the window. "I was only supposing. I was just spinning a little fantasy to help pass the time."

Triumphant, Steffan said, "However, fantasy doesn't contribute to a maturation of one's data vault."

"And I suppose that you're eager to mature enough to gain a promotion from the Agency," Tuttle said.

"Of course," Steffan said. "We're only allotted two hundred years. And besides, what else is the purpose of life?"

Perhaps to have an opportunity to mull over his strange theories, Tuttle soon retired to an inactivation nook in the wall beneath the metal shelf on which the guns lay. He slid in feet first and pulled the hatch shut behind his head, leaving the others to their own devices.

Fifteen minutes later, Leeke said, "I believe I'll follow Tuttle's example. I need time to consider my responses to this afternoon's hunt."

Curanov knew that Leeke was only making excuses to be gone. He was not a particularly gregarious robot and seemed most comfortable when he was ignored and left to himself.

Alone with Steffan in the lodge, Curanov was in an unpleasantly delicate position. He felt that he, too, needed time to think inside a deactivation nook. However, he did not want to hurt Steffan's feelings, did not want to give him the impression that they were all anxious to be away from him. For the most part, Curanov liked the young robot; Steffan was fresh, energetic, obviously a first-line mentality. The only thing he found grating about the youth was his innocence, his undisciplined drive to be accepted and to achieve. Time, of course, would mellow Steffan and hone his mind, so he did not deserve to be hurt. How then to excuse oneself without slighting Steffan in any way?

The younger robot solved the problem by suggesting that he, too, needed time in a nook. When Steffan was safely shut away, Curanov went to the fourth of the five wall slots, slid into it, pulled the hatch shut, and felt all of his senses drain away from him, so that he was only a mind, floating in darkness, contemplating the wealth of ideas in his data vault.

Adrift in nothingness, Curanov considers the superstition that has begun to be the center of this adventure: the human being, the man:

1. *Though of flesh, the man thinks and knows.*
2. *He sleeps by night, like an animal.*
3. *He devours other flesh, as does the beast.*
4. *He defecates.*
5. *He dies and rots, is susceptible to disease and corruption.*
6. *He spawns his young in a terrifyingly unmechanical way, and yet his young are also sentient.*
7. *He kills.*
8. *He can overpower a robot.*
9. *He dismantles robots, though none but other men know what he does with their parts.*
10. *He is the antithesis of the robot. If the robot represents the proper way of life, man is the improper.*
11. *Man stalks in safety, registering to the robot's senses, unless clearly seen, as only another harmless animal—until it is too late.*
12. *He can be permanently killed only with a wooden implement. Wood is the product of an organic lifeform, yet it lasts as metal does; halfway between flesh and metal, it can destroy human flesh.*
13. *If killed in any other way, by any means other than wood, the man will only appear to be dead. In reality, the moment that he drops before his assailant, he at once springs to life elsewhere, unharmed, in a new body.*

Although the list goes on, Curanov abandons that avenue of thought, for it disturbs him deeply. Tuttle's fantasy can be nothing more than that—conjecture, supposition, imagination. If the human being actually existed, how could one believe the Central Agency's prime rule: that the universe is, in every way, entirely logical and rational?

◁ ∧ ▷

"The rifles are gone," Tuttle said when Curanov slid out of the deactivation nook and got to his feet. "Gone. All of them. That's why I re-called you."

"Gone?" Curanov asked, looking at the shelf where the weapons had been. "Gone where?"

"Leeke's taken them," Steffan said. He stood by the window, his long, bluish arms beaded with cold droplets of water precipitated out of the air.

"Is Leeke gone too?" Curanov asked.

"Yes."

He thought about this, then said, "But where would he go in the storm? And why would he need *all* the rifles?"

"I'm sure it's nothing to be concerned about," Steffan said. "He must have had a good reason, and he can tell us all about it when he comes back."

Tuttle said, *"If* he comes back."

Curanov said, "Tuttle, you sound as if you think he might be in danger."

"In light of what's happened recently—those prints we found— I'd say that could be a possibility."

Steffan scoffed at this.

"Whatever's happening," Tuttle said, "you must admit it's odd." He turned to Curanov. "I wish we hadn't submitted to the operations before we came out here. I'd do anything to have my full senses again." He hesitated. "I think we have to find Leeke."

"He'll be back," Steffan argued. "He'll return when he wants to return."

"I'm still in favor of initiating a search," Tuttle said.

Curanov went to the window and stood next to Steffan, gazing out at the driving snow. The ground was covered with at least twelve inches of new powder; the proud trees had been bowed under the white weight; and snow continued to fall faster than Curanov had ever seen it in all his many journeys.

"Well?" Tuttle asked again.

"I concur," Curanov said. "We should look for him, but we should do it together. With our lessened perceptions, we might easily get separated and lost out there. If one of us became damaged in a fall, he might experience a complete battery depletion before anyone found him."

"You're right." Tuttle said. He turned to Steffan. "And you?"

"Oh, all right," Steffan said crossly. "I'll come along."

◁ ▲ ▷

Their torches cut bright wounds in the darkness but did little to melt through the curtain of wind-driven snow. They walked abreast around the lodge, continuing a circle search. Each time that they completed another turn about the building, they widened their search pattern. They decided to cover all the open land, but they would not enter the forest even if they hadn't located Leeke elsewhere. They agreed to this limitation, though none—not even Steffan—admitted that half the reason for ignoring the woods was a purely irrational fear of what might live among the trees.

In the end, however, it was not necessary to enter the woods, for they found Leeke less than twenty yards away from the lodge. He was lying on his side in the snow.

"He's been terminated," Steffan said.

The others didn't need to be told.

Both of Leeke's legs were missing.

"Who could have done something like this?" Steffan asked.

Neither Tuttle nor Curanov answered him.

Leeke's head hung limply on his neck, because several of the links in his ring cable had been bent out of alignment. His visual receptors had been smashed, and the mechanism behind them ripped out through the shattered sockets.

When Curanov bent closer, he saw that someone had poked a sharp object into Leeke's data vaults, through his eye tubes, and scrambled his tapes into a useless mess. He hoped that poor Leeke had been dead by then.

"Horrible," Steffan said. He turned away from the grisly scene, began to walk back to the lodge, but stopped abruptly as he realized that he should not be out of the other robots' company. He shuddered mentally.

"What should we do with him?" Tuttle asked.

"Leave him," Curanov said.

"Here to rust?"

"He'll sense nothing more."

"Still—"

"We should be getting back," Curanov said, shining his light around the snowy scene. "We shouldn't expose ourselves."

Keeping close to one another, they returned to the lodge.

As they walked, Curanov reviewed certain disturbing data: *9. He dismantles robots, though none but other men know what he does with their parts. . . .*

◁ ʌ ▷

"As I see it," Curanov told them when they were once again in the lodge, "Leeke did not take the rifles. Someone—or something—entered the lodge to steal them. Leeke must have come out of his inactivation nook just as the culprits were leaving. Without pausing to wake us, he gave chase."

"Or was forced to go with them," Tuttle said.

"I doubt that he was taken out by force," Curanov said. "In the lodge, with enough light to see by and enough space to maneuver in, even with lessened perceptions, Leeke could have kept himself from being hurt or forced to leave. However, once he was outside, in the storm, he was at their mercy."

The wind screamed across the peaked roof of the lodge, rattled the windows in their metal frames.

The three remaining robots stood still, listening until the gust died away, as though the noise were made not by the wind but by some enormous beast that had reared up over the building and was intent on tearing it to pieces.

Curanov went on: "When I examined Leeke, I found that he was felled by a sharp blow to the ring cable, just under the head— the kind of blow that would have had to come suddenly from behind and without warning. In a room as well lighted as this, nothing could have gotten behind Leeke without his knowing it was there."

Steffan turned away from the window and said, "Do you think that Leeke was already terminated when . . ." His voice trailed away, but in a moment he had found the discipline to go on: "Was he terminated when they dismantled his legs?"

"We can only hope that he was," Curanov said.

Steffan said, "Who could have done such a thing?"

"A man," Tuttle said.

"Or men," Curanov amended.

"No," Steffan said. But his denial was not as adamant as it had been before. "What would they have done with his legs?"

"No one knows what they do with what they take," Curanov said.

Steffan said, "You sound as if Tuttle's convinced you, as if you believe in these creatures."

"Until I have a better answer to the question of who terminated Leeke, I think it's safest to believe in human beings," Curanov explained.

For a time, they were silent.

Then Curanov said, "I think we should start back to Walker's Watch in the morning, first thing."

"They'll think we're immature," Steffan said, "if we come back with wild tales about men prowling around the lodge in the darkness. You saw how disdainful Janus was of others who had made similar reports."

"We have poor, dead Leeke as proof," Tuttle said.

"Or," Curanov said, "we can say Leeke was terminated in an accident and we're returning because we're bored with the challenge."

"You mean, we wouldn't even have to mention—human beings?" Steffan asked.

"Possibly," Curanov said.

"That would be the best way to handle it, by far," Steffan said.

"Then no second-hand reports of our temporary irrationality would get back to the Agency. We could spend much time in the inactivation nooks, until we finally were able to perceive the *real* explanation of Leeke's termination, which somehow now eludes us. If we meditate long enough, a proper solution is bound to arise. Then, by the time of our next data-vault audits by the Agency, we'll have covered all traces of this illogical reaction from which we now suffer."

"However," Tuttle said, "we might already know the *real* story of Leeke's death. After all, we've seen the footprints in the snow, and we've seen the dismantled body. . . . Could it be that men—human beings—really are behind it?"

"No," Steffan said. "That's superstitious nonsense. That's irrational."

"At dawn," Curanov said, "we'll set out for Walker's Watch, no matter how bad the storm is by then."

As he finished speaking, the distant hum of the lodge generator—which was a comforting background noise that never abated—abruptly cut out. They were plunged into darkness.

With snow crusted on their chilled metal skins, they focused three electric torches on the compact generator in its niche behind the lodge. The top of the machine casing had been removed, exposing the complex inner works to the elements.

"Someone's removed the power core," Curanov said.

"But who?" Steffan asked.

Curanov directed the beam of his torch to the ground.

The others did likewise.

Mingled with their own footprints were other prints similar to but not made by any robot: those same, strange tracks that they had seen near the trees in the late afternoon. The same tracks that profusely marked the snow all around Leeke's body.

"No," Steffan said. "No, no, no."

"I think it's best that we set out for Walker's Watch tonight," Curanov said. "I don't think it would any longer be wise to wait until morning." He looked at Tuttle, to whom clung snow in icy clumps. "What do you think?"

"Agreed," Tuttle said. "But I suspect it's not going to be an easy journey. I wish I had all my senses up to full power."

"We can still move fast," Curanov said. "And we don't need

to rest, as fleshy creatures must. If we're pursued, we have the advantage."

"In theory," Tuttle said.

"We'll have to be satisfied with that."

Curanov considered certain aspects of the myth: *7. He kills; 8. He can overpower a robot.*

⊀ ∧ ⊁

In the lodge, by the eerie light of their hand torches, they bolted on their snowshoes, attached their emergency repair kits, and picked up their maps. The beams of their lamps preceding them, they went outside again, staying together.

The wind beat upon their broad backs while the snow worked hard to coat them in hard-packed, icy suits.

They crossed the clearing, half by dead reckoning and half by the few landmarks that the torches revealed, each wishing to himself that he had his full powers of sight and his radar back in operation again. Soon, they came to the opening in the trees that led down the side of the valley and back toward Walker's Watch. They stopped there, staring into the dark tunnel formed by sheltering pines, and they seemed reluctant to go any farther.

"There are so many shadows," Tuttle said.

"Shadows can't hurt us," Curanov said.

Throughout their association, from the moment they had met one another on the train coming north, Curanov had known that he was the leader among them. He had exercised his leadership sparingly, but now he must take full command. He started forward, into the trees, between the shadows, moving down the snowy slope.

Reluctantly, Steffan followed.

Tuttle came last.

Halfway down toward the valley floor, the tunnel between the trees narrowed drastically. The trees loomed closer, spread their boughs lower. And it was here, in these tight quarters, in the deepest shadows, that they were attacked.

Something howled in triumph, its mad voice echoing above the constant whine of the wind.

Curanov whirled, not certain from which direction the sound had come, lancing the trees with torchlight.

Behind, Tuttle cried out.

Curanov turned as Steffan did, and their torches illuminated the struggling robot.

"It can't *be!*" Steffan said.

Tuttle had fallen back under the relentless attack of a two-legged creature that moved almost as a robot might move, though it was clearly an animal. It was dressed in furs, its feet booted, and it wielded a metal ax.

It drove the blunted blade at Tuttle's ring cable.

Tuttle raised an arm, threw back the weapon, saved himself—at the cost of a severely damaged elbow joint.

Curanov started forward to help but was stopped as a second of the fleshy beasts delivered a blow from behind. The weapon struck the center of Curanov's back and drove him to his knees.

Curanov fell sideways, rolled, got to his feet in one well-coordinated maneuver. He turned quickly to confront his assailant.

A fleshy face stared back at him from a dozen feet away, blowing steam in the cold air. It was framed in a fur-lined hood: a grotesque parody of a robot face. Its eyes were too small for visual receptors, and they did not glow. Its face was not perfectly symmetrical as it should have been; it was out of proportion, also puffed and mottled from the cold. It did not even shine in the torchlight, and yet . . .

. . . yet . . . obvious intelligence abided there. No doubt malevolent intelligence. Perhaps even maniacal. But intelligence nonetheless.

Surprisingly, the monster spoke to Curanov. Its voice was deep, its language full of rounded, softened syllables, not at all like the clattering language the robots spoke to one another.

Abruptly, the beast leaped forward, crying out, and swung a length of metal pipe at Curanov's neck.

The robot danced backward out of range.

The demon came forward.

Curanov glanced at the others and saw that the first demon had backed Tuttle almost into the woods. A third had attacked Steffan, who was barely managing to hold his own.

Screaming, the man before Curanov charged, plowed the end of the pipe into Curanov's chest.

The robot fell hard.

The man came in close, raising his bludgeon.

Man thinks, though he's of flesh . . . sleeps as an animal sleeps, devours other flesh, defecates, rots, dies. . . . He spawns his young in an unmechanical manner, although his young are sentient. . . . He kills . . . he kills . . . he overpowers robots, dismantles them, and does monstrous things (what?) with their parts. . . . He can be killed, permanently, only with a wooden implement . . . and if killed in any other manner, he does not die a true death, but at once springs up elsewhere in a new body. . . .

As the monster swung his club, Curanov rolled, rose, and struck out with his long-fingered hand.

The man's face tore, gave blood.

The demon stepped back, bewildered.

Curanov's terror had changed into rage. He stepped forward and struck out again. And again. Flailing with all his reduced strength, he broke the demon's body, temporarily killed it, leaving the snow spattered with blood.

Turning from his own assailant, he moved on the beast that was after Steffan. Clubbing it from behind, he broke its neck with one blow of his steel hand.

By the time Curanov reached Tuttle and dispatched the third demon, Tuttle had sustained one totally demolished arm, another smashed hand, and damage to the ring cable that, luckily, had not terminated him. With any luck, the three robots would survive.

"I thought I was finished," Tuttle said.

Dazed, Steffan said to Curanov, "You killed all three of them!"

"They would have terminated us," Curanov said. Inside, where they could not see, he was in turmoil.

Steffan said, "But the prime directive from the Central Agency forbids the taking of life—"

"Not quite," Curanov disagreed. "It forbids the taking of life which cannot be restored. *Which cannot be restored.*"

"These lives will be restored?" Steffan asked, looking at the hideous corpses, unable to understand.

"You've seen human beings now," Curanov said. "Do you believe the myths—or do you still scoff?"

"How can I scoff?"

"Then," Curanov said, "if you believe that such demons exist, you must believe what else is said of them." He quoted his own store of data on the subject: "If killed in any other way, by any means other than wood, the man will only appear to be dead. In reality, the moment he drops before his assailant, he springs at once to life elsewhere, unharmed, in a new body."

Steffan nodded, unwilling to argue the point.

Tuttle said, "What now?"

"We continue back to Walker's Watch," Curanov said.

"And tell them what we found?"

"No."

"But," Tuttle said, "we can lead them back here, show them these carcasses."

"Look around you," Curanov said. "Other demons are watching from the trees."

A dozen hateful white faces could be seen, leering.

Curanov said, "I don't think they'll attack us again. They've seen what we can do, how we have learned that, with them, the prime directive does not apply. But they're sure to remove and bury the bodies when we've gone."

"We can take a carcass along with us," Tuttle said.

Curanov said, "No. Both of your hands are useless. Steffan's right arm is uncontrollable. I couldn't carry one of those bodies all by myself as far as Walker's Watch, not with my power as reduced as it is."

"Then," Tuttle said, "we still won't tell anyone about what we've seen up here?"

"We can't afford to, if we ever want to be promoted," Curanov said. "Our only hope is to spend a long time in some inactivation nook, contemplating until we've learned to cope with what we've witnessed."

They picked their torches out of the snow and, staying close to one another, started down toward the valley once more.

"Walk slowly and show no fear," Curanov warned.

They walked slowly, but each was certain that his fear was evident to the unearthly creatures crouching in the shadows beneath the pine trees.

They walked all that long night and most of the following day before they reached the station house at Walker's Watch. In that time, the storm died out. The landscape was serene, white, peaceful. Surveying the rolling snowfields, one felt sure that the universe was rational. But Curanov was haunted by one icy realization: If he must believe in specters and other worldly beings like men, then he would never again be able to think of the universe in rational terms.

TWILIGHT OF THE DAWN

"SOMETIMES YOU CAN BE THE BIGGEST JACKASS WHO EVER LIVED," MY wife said the night that I took Santa Claus away from my son.

We were in bed, but she was clearly not in the mood for either sleep or romance.

Her voice was sharp, scornful. "What a terrible thing to do to a little boy."

"He's seven years old—"

"He's a little boy," Ellen said harshly, though we rarely spoke to each other in anger. For the most part ours was a happy, peaceful marriage.

We lay in silence. The drapes were drawn back from the French doors that opened onto the second-floor balcony, so the bedroom was limned by ash-pale moonlight. Even in that dim glow, even though Ellen was cloaked in blankets, her anger was apparent in the tense, angular position in which she pretended to seek sleep.

Finally she said, "Pete, you used a sledgehammer to shatter a little boy's fragile fantasy, a *harmless* fantasy, all because of your obsession with—"

"It wasn't harmless," I said patiently. "And I don't have an obsession."

"Yes, you do," she insisted.

"I simply believe in rational—"

"Oh, shut up."

"Won't you even talk to me about it?"

"No. It's pointless."

I sighed. "I love you, Ellen."

She was silent a long while.

Wind soughed in the eaves, an ancient voice.

In the boughs of one of the backyard cherry trees, an owl hooted.

At last Ellen said, "I love you too, but sometimes I want to kick your ass."

I was angry with her because I felt that she was not being fair, that she was allowing her least admirable emotions to overrule her reason. Now, many years later, I would give anything to hear her say that she wanted to kick my ass, and I'd bend over with a smile.

⊲ ∧ ⊳

From the cradle, my son, Benny, was taught that God did not exist under any name or in any form, and that religion was the refuge of weak-minded people who did not have the courage to face the universe on its own terms. I would not permit Benny to be baptized, for in my view that ceremony was a primitive initiation rite by which the child would be inducted into a cult of ignorance and irrationality.

Ellen—my wife, Benny's mother—had been raised as a Methodist and still was stained (as I saw it) by lingering traces of faith. She called herself an agnostic, unable to go further and join me in the camp of the atheists. I loved her so much that I was able to tolerate her equivocation on the subject. Nevertheless, I had nothing but scorn for others who could not face the fact that the universe was godless and that human existence was nothing more than a biological accident.

I despised all who bent their knees to humble themselves before an imaginary lord of creation: all the Methodists and Lutherans and Catholics and Baptists and Mormons and Jews and others. They claimed many labels but in essence shared the same sick delusion.

My greatest loathing was reserved, however, for those who had once been clean of the disease of religion, rational men and women, like me, who had slipped off the path of reason and fallen into the chasm of superstition. They were surrendering their most precious possessions—their independent spirit, self-reliance, intellectual integrity—in return for half-baked, dreamy promises of an afterlife with togas and harp music. I was more disgusted by the rejection of their previously treasured secular enlightenment than I would have been to hear some old friend confess that he had suddenly developed an all-consuming obsession for canine sex and had divorced his wife in favor of a German-shepherd bitch.

Hal Sheen, my partner with whom I had founded Fallon and Sheen Design, had been proud of his atheism too. In college we were best friends, and together we were a formidable team of debaters whenever the subject of religion arose; inevitably, anyone harboring a belief in a supreme being, anyone daring to disagree with our view of the universe as a place of uncaring forces, any of *that* ilk was sorry to have met us, for we stripped away his pretensions to adulthood and revealed him for the idiot child that he was. Indeed, we often didn't even wait for the subject of religion to arise but skillfully baited fellow students who, to our certain knowledge, were believers.

Later, with degrees in architecture, neither of us wished to work with anyone but each other, so we formed a company. We dreamed of creating brawny yet elegant, functional yet beautiful buildings that would delight and astonish, that would win the admiration of not only our fellow professionals but the world. And with brains, talent, and dogged determination, we began to attain some of our goals while we were still very young men. Fallon and Sheen Design, a wunderkind company, was the focus of a revolution in design that excited university students as well as longtime professionals.

The most important aspect of our tremendous success was that our atheism lay at the core of it, for we consciously set out to create a new architecture that owed nothing to religious inspiration. Most laymen are not aware that virtually all the structures around them, including those resulting from modern schools of design, incorporate architectural details originally developed to subtly reinforce the rule of God and the place of religion in life. For instance, vaulted ceilings, first used in churches and cathedrals, were originally intended to draw the gaze upward and to induce, by indirection, contemplation of Heaven and its rewards. Underpitch vaults, barrel vaults, grain vaults, fan vaults, quadripartite and sexpartite and tierceron vaults are more than mere arches; they were conceived as agents of religion, quiet advertisements for Him and for His higher authority. From the start, Hal and I were determined that no vaulted ceilings, no spires, no arched windows or doors, no slightest design element born of religion would be incorporated into a Fallon and Sheen building. In reaction we strove to direct the eye earthward and, by a thousand devices, to remind those who passed through our structures that they were born of the earth, not children of any God but merely more intellectually advanced cousins of apes.

Hal's reconversion to the Roman Catholicism of his childhood was, therefore, a shock to me. At thirty-seven, when he was at the top of his profession, when by his singular success he had proven the supremacy of unoppressed, rational man over imagined divinities, he returned with apparent joy to the confessional, humbled himself at the communion rail, dampened his forehead and breast with so-called holy water, and thereby rejected the intellectual foundation on which his entire adult life, to that point, had been based.

The horror of it chilled my heart, my marrow.

For taking Hal Sheen from me, I despised religion more than ever. I redoubled my efforts to eliminate any wisp of religious thought or superstition from my son's life, and I was fiercely determined that Benny would never be stolen from me by incense-burning, bell-ringing, hymn-singing, self-deluded, mush-brained fools. When he proved to be a voracious reader from an early age, I carefully chose books for him, directing him away from works that even indirectly portrayed religion as an acceptable part of life, firmly steering him to strictly secular material that would not encourage unhealthy fantasies. When I saw that he was fascinated by vampires, ghosts, and the entire panoply of traditional monsters that seem to intrigue all children, I strenuously discouraged that interest, mocked it, and taught him the virtue and pleasure of rising above such childish things. Oh, I did not deny him the enjoyment of a good scare, because there's nothing essentially religious in that. Benny was permitted to savor the fear induced by books about killer robots, movies about the Frankenstein monster, and other threats that were the work of man. It was only monsters of Satanic and spiritual origins that I censored from his books and films, because belief in things Satanic is merely another facet of religion, the flip side of God worship.

I allowed him Santa Claus until he was seven, though I had a lot of misgivings about that indulgence. The Santa Claus legend includes a Christian element, of course. Good *Saint* Nick and all that. But Ellen was insistent that Benny would not be denied that fantasy. I reluctantly agreed that it was probably harmless, but only as long as we scrupulously observed the holiday as a purely secular event having nothing to do with the birth of Jesus. To us, Christmas was a celebration of the family and a healthy indulgence in materialism.

In the backyard of our big house in Bucks County, Pennsylvania, grew a pair of enormous, long-lived cherry trees, under the branches of which Benny and I often sat in milder seasons, playing checkers or card games. Beneath those boughs, which already had lost most of their leaves to the tugging hands of autumn, on an unusually warm day in early October of his seventh year, as we were playing Uncle Wiggly, Benny asked if I thought Santa was going to bring him lots of stuff that year. I said it was too early to be thinking about Santa, and he said that *all* the kids were thinking about Santa and were starting to compose want lists already. Then he said, "Daddy, how's Santa *know* we've been good or bad? He can't watch all us kids all the time, can he? Do our guardian angels talk to him and tattle on us, or what?"

"Guardian angels?" I said, startled and displeased. "What do you know about guardian angels?"

"Well, they're supposed to watch over us, help us when we're in trouble, right? So I thought maybe they also talk to Santa Claus."

Only months after Benny was born, I had joined with like-minded parents in our community to establish a private school guided by the principles of secular humanism, where even the slightest religious thought would be kept out of the curriculum. In fact, our intention was to ensure that, as our children matured, they would be taught history, literature, sociology, and ethics from an anticlerical viewpoint. Benny had attended our preschool and, by that October of which I write, was in second grade of the elementary division, where his classmates came from families guided by the same rational principles as our own. I was surprised to hear that in such an environment he was still subjected to religious propagandizing.

"Who told you about guardian angels?"

"Some kids."

"They believe in these angels?"

"Sure. I guess."

"Do they believe in the tooth fairy?"

"Sheesh, no."

"Then why do they believe in guardian angels?"

"They saw it on TV."

"They did, huh?"

"It was a show you won't let me watch."

"And just because they saw it on TV, they think it's true?"

Benny shrugged and moved his game piece five spaces along the Uncle Wiggly board.

I believed then that popular culture—especially television—was the bane of all men and women of reason and goodwill, not least of all because it promoted a wide variety of religious superstitions and, by its saturation of every aspect of our lives, was inescapable and powerfully influential. Books and movies like *The Exorcist* and television programs about guardian angels could frustrate even the most diligent parent's attempts to raise his child in an atmosphere of untainted rationality.

The unseasonably warm October breeze was not strong enough to disturb the game cards, but it gently ruffled Benny's fine brown hair. Wind mussed, sitting on a pillow on his redwood chair in order to be at table level, he looked so small and vulnerable. Loving him, wanting the best possible life for him, I grew angrier by the second; my anger was directed not at Benny but at those who, intellectually and emotionally stunted by their twisted philosophy, would attempt to propagandize an innocent child.

"Benny," I said, "listen, there are no guardian angels. They don't exist. It's all an ugly lie told by people who want to make you believe that you aren't responsible for your own successes in life. They want you to believe that the bad things in life are the result of your sins and *are* your fault, but that all the good things come from the grace of God. It's a way to control you. That's what all religion is—a tool to control and oppress you."

He blinked at me. "Grace who?"

It was my turn to blink. "What?"

"Who's Grace? You mean Mrs. Grace Keever at the toy shop? What tool will she use to press me?" He giggled. "Will I be all mashed flat and on a hanger when she's done pressing me? Daddy, you sure are silly."

He was only a seven-year-old boy, after all, and I was solemnly discussing the oppressive nature of religious belief as if we were two intellectuals drinking espresso in a coffeehouse. Blushing at the realization of my own capacity for foolishness, I pushed aside the Uncle Wiggly board and struggled harder to make him understand why believing in such nonsense as guardian angels was not merely innocent fun but was a step toward intellectual and emotional enslavement of a particularly pernicious sort. When he seemed alternately bored, confused, embarrassed, and utterly baffled—but never for a moment enlightened—I grew frustrated, and at last (I am now ashamed to admit this) I made my point by taking Santa Claus away from him.

Suddenly it seemed clear to me that by allowing him to indulge in the Santa myth, I'd laid the groundwork for the very irrationality that I was determined to prevent him from adopting. How could I have been so misguided as to believe that Christmas could be celebrated entirely in a secular spirit, without risk of giving credence to the religious tradition that was, after all, the genesis of the holiday. Now I saw that erecting a Christmas tree in our home and exchanging gifts, by association with such other Christmas paraphernalia as manger scenes on church lawns and trumpet-tooting plastic angels in department-store decorations, had generated in Benny an assumption that the spiritual aspect of the celebration had as much validity as the materialistic aspect, which made him fertile ground for tales of guardian angels and all the other rot about sin and salvation.

Under the boughs of the cherry trees, in an October breeze that was blowing us slowly toward another Christmas, I told Benny the truth about Santa Claus, explained that the gifts came from his mother and me. He protested that he had evidence of Santa's reality: the cookies and milk that he always left out for the jolly fat man and that were unfailingly consumed. I convinced him that Santa's sweet tooth was in fact my own and that the milk—which I don't like—was always poured down the drain. Methodically, relentlessly—but with what I thought was kindness and love—I stripped from him all of the so-called magic of Christmas and left him in no doubt that the Santa stuff had been a well-meant but mistaken deception.

He listened with no further protest, and when I was finished he claimed to be sleepy and in need of a nap. He rubbed his eyes and yawned elaborately. He had no more interest in Uncle Wiggly and went straight into the house and up to his room.

The last thing that I said to him beneath the cherry trees was that strong, well-balanced people have no need for imaginary friends like Santa and guardian angels. "All we can count on is ourselves, our friends, and our families, Benny. If we want something in life, we can't get it by asking Santa Claus and certainly not by praying for it. We get it only by earning it—or by benefiting from the generosity of friends or relatives. There's no reason ever to *wish* for or pray for anything."

Three years later, when Benny was in the hospital and dying of bone cancer, I understood for the first time why other people felt a need to believe in God and seek comfort in prayer. Our lives are touched by some tragedies so enormous and so difficult to bear that the temptation to seek mystical answers to the cruelty of the world is powerful indeed.

Even if we can accept that our own deaths are final and that no souls survive the decomposition of our flesh, we often can't endure the idea that our *children*, when stricken in youth, are also doomed to pass from this world into no other. Children are special, so how can it be that they too will be wiped out as completely as if they had never existed? I've seen atheists, though despising religion and incapable of praying for themselves, nevertheless invoke the name of God on behalf of their seriously ill children—only to realize, sometimes with embarrassment but often with deep regret, that their philosophy denies them the foolishness of petitioning for divine intercession.

When Benny was afflicted with bone cancer, I was not shaken from my convictions; not once during the ordeal did I put principles aside and blubber at God. I was stalwart, steadfast, stoical, determined to bear the burden by myself, though there were times when the weight bowed my head and when the very bones of my shoulders felt as if they would splinter and collapse under a mountain of grief.

That day in October of Benny's seventh year, as I sat beneath the cherry trees and watched him return to the house to nap, I did not know how severely my principles and self-reliance would be tested in days to come. I was proud of having freed my son of his Christmas-related fantasies about Santa Claus, and I was pompously certain that the time would come when Benny, grown to adulthood, would eventually thank me for the rigorously rational upbringing that he had received.

⊀ ⋏ ⊱

When Hal Sheen told me that he had returned to the fold of the Catholic Church, I thought he was setting me up for a joke. We were having an after-work cocktail at a hotel bar near our offices, and I was under the impression that the purpose of our meeting was to celebrate some grand commission that Hal had won for us. "I've got news for you," he had said cryptically that morning. "Let's meet at the Regency for a drink at six o'clock." But instead of telling me that we had been chosen to design a building that would add another chapter to the legend of Fallon and Sheen, he told me that after more than a year of quiet debate with himself, he had shed his atheism as if it were a moldy cocoon and had flown forth into the realm of faith once more. I laughed, waiting for the punch line, and he smiled, and in his smile there was something—perhaps pity for me—that instantly convinced me that he was serious.

I argued quietly, then not so quietly. I scorned his claim to have rediscovered God, and I tried to shame him for his surrender of intellectual dignity.

"I've decided a man can be both an intellectual and a practicing Christian, Jew, or Buddhist," Hal said with annoying self-possession.

"Impossible!" I struck our table with one fist to emphasize my rejection of that muddle-headed contention. Our cocktail glasses rattled, and an unused ashtray nearly fell to the floor, which caused other patrons to look our way.

"Look at Malcolm Muggeridge," Hal said. "Or C. S. Lewis. Isaac Singer. Christians and a Jew—*and* indisputably intellectuals."

"Listen to you!" I said, appalled. "On how many occasions have other people raised those names—and other names—when you and I were arguing the intellectual supremacy of atheism, and you joined me in proving what fools the Muggeridges, Lewises, and Singers of this world really are."

He shrugged. "I was wrong."

"Just like that?"

"No, not just like that. Give me some credit, Pete. I've spent a year reading, thinking. I've actively resisted the urge to return to the faith, and yet I've been won over."

"By whom? What propagandizing priest or—"

"No *person* won me over. It's been entirely an interior debate, Pete. No one but me has known I've been wavering on this tightrope."

"Then what started you wavering?"

"Well, for a couple of years now, my life has been empty. . . ."

"Empty? You're young and healthy. You're married to a smart and beautiful woman. You're at the top of your profession, admired by one and all for the freshness and vigor of your architectural vision, and you're wealthy! You call that an empty life?"

He nodded. "Empty. But I couldn't figure out why. Just like you, I added up all that I've got, and it seemed like I should be the most fulfilled man on the face of the earth. But I felt hollow, and each new project we approached had less interest for me. Gradually I realized that all I'd built and that all I might build in the days to come was not going to satisfy me because the achievements were not lasting. Oh, sure, one of our buildings might stand for two hundred years, but a couple of centuries are but a grain of sand falling in the hourglass of time. Structures of stone and steel and glass are not enduring monuments. They're not, as we once thought, testimonies to the singular genius of mankind. Rather the opposite: They're reminders that even our mightiest structures are fragile, that our greatest achievements can be quickly erased by earthquakes, wars, tidal waves, or simply by the slow gnawing of a thousand years of sun and wind and rain. So what's the point?"

"The point," I reminded him angrily, "is that by erecting those structures, by creating better and more beautiful buildings, we are improving the lives of our fellow men and encouraging others to reach toward higher goals of their own—and then together all of us are making a better future for the whole human species."

"Yes, but to what end?" he pressed. "If there's no afterlife, if each individual's existence ends entirely in the grave, then the *collective* fate of the species is precisely that of the individual: death, emptiness, blackness, nothingness. Nothing can come from nothing. You can't claim a noble, higher purpose for the species as a whole when you allow no higher purpose for the individual spirit." He raised one hand to halt my response. "I know, I know. You've arguments against that statement. I've supported you in them through countless debates on the subject. But I can't support you any more, Pete. I think there *is* some purpose to life besides just living. And if I didn't think so, then I would leave the business and spend the rest of my life having fun, enjoying the precious finite number of days left to me. However, now that I believe there is something called a soul and that it survives the body, I can go on working at Fallon and Sheen because it's my destiny to do so, which means the achievements can be meaningful. I hope you'll be able to accept this. I'm not going to proselytize. This is the first and last time you'll hear me mention my religion, because I'll respect your right *not* to believe. I'm sure we can go on as before."

But we could not.

I felt that religion was a hateful degenerative sickness of the mind, and I was thereafter uncomfortable in Hal's presence. I still pretended that we were close, that nothing had changed between us, but I felt that he was not the same man as he had been.

Besides, Hal's new faith inevitably began to infect his fine architectural vision. Vaulted ceilings and arched windows began to appear in his designs, and everywhere his new buildings encouraged the eye and mind to look up and regard the heavens. This change of direction was welcomed by certain clients and even praised by critics in prestigious journals, but I could not abide it because I knew he was regressing from the man-centered architecture that had been our claim to originality. Fourteen months after his embrace of the Roman Catholic Church, I sold out my share of the company to him and set up my own organization, free of his influence.

"Hal," I told him the last time that I saw him, "even when you claimed to be an atheist, you evidently never understood that the nothingness at the end of life isn't to be feared or raged against. Either accept it regretfully as a fact of life . . . or welcome it."

Personally, I welcomed it, because not having to concern myself about my fate in the afterlife was liberating. Being a nonbeliever, I could concentrate entirely on winning the rewards of *this* world, the one and only world.

◁ ▲ ▷

The night of the day that I took Santa Claus away from Benny, the night that Ellen told me that she wanted to kick me in the ass, as we lay in our moonlit bedroom on opposite sides of the large four-poster bed, she also said, "Pete, you've told me all about your childhood, and of course I've met your folks, so I have a pretty good idea what it must have been like to be raised in that crackpot atmosphere. I can understand why you'd react against their religious fanaticism by embracing atheism. But sometimes . . . you get carried away. You aren't happy merely to *be* an atheist; you're so damn eager to impose your philosophy on everyone else, no matter the cost, that sometimes you behave very much like your own parents . . . except instead of selling God, you're selling godlessness."

I raised myself on the bed and looked at her blanket-shrouded form. I couldn't see her face; she was turned away from me. "That's just plain nasty, Ellen."

"It's true."

"I'm nothing like my parents. Nothing like them. I don't *beat* atheism into Benny the way they tried to beat God into me."

"What you did to him today was as bad as beating him."

"Ellen, all kids learn the truth about Santa Claus eventually, some of them even sooner than Benny did."

She turned toward me, and suddenly I could see her face just well enough to discern the anger in it but, unfortunately, not well enough to glimpse the love that I knew was also there.

"Sure," she said, "they all learn the truth about Santa Claus, but they don't have the fantasy ripped away from them by their own fathers, damn it!"

"I didn't *rip* it away. I reasoned him out of it."

"He's not a college boy on a debating team," she said. "You can't reason with a seven-year-old. They're all emotion at that age, all heart. Pete, he came into the house today after you were done with him, and he went up to his room, and an hour later when I went up there, he was still crying."

"Okay, okay," I said.

"Crying."

"Okay, I feel like a shit."

"Good. You should."

"And I'll admit that I could have handled it better, been more tactful about it."

She turned away from me again and said nothing.

"But I didn't do anything wrong," I said. "I mean, it was a real mistake to think we could celebrate Christmas in a strictly secular way. Innocent fantasies can lead to some that aren't so innocent."

"Oh, shut up," she said again. "Shut up and go to sleep before I forget I love you."

⊲ ∧ ⊳

The trucker who killed Ellen was trying to make more money to buy a boat. He was a fisherman whose passion was trolling; to afford the boat, he had to take on more work. He was using amphetamines to stay awake. The truck was a Peterbilt, the biggest model they make. Ellen was driving her blue BMW. They hit head-on, and though she apparently tried to take evasive action, she never had a chance.

Benny was devastated. I put all work aside and stayed home with him the entire month of July. He needed a lot of hugging, reassuring, and some gentle guidance toward acceptance of the tragedy. I was in bad shape too, for Ellen had been more than my wife and lover: She had been my toughest critic, my greatest champion, my best friend, and my only confidant. At night, alone in the bedroom we had shared, I put my face against the pillow upon which she had slept, breathed in the faintly lingering scent of her, and wept; I couldn't bear to wash the pillowcase for weeks. But in front of Benny, I managed for the most part to maintain control of myself and to provide him with the example of strength that he so terribly needed.

I allowed no funeral. Ellen was cremated, and her ashes were dispersed at sea.

A month later, on the first Sunday in August, when we had begun to move grudgingly and sadly toward acceptance, forty or fifty friends and relatives came to the house, and we held a quiet memorial service for Ellen, a purely secular service with not the slightest thread of religious content. We gathered on the patio near the pool, and half a dozen friends stepped forward to tell amusing stories about Ellen and to explain what an impact she'd had on their lives.

I kept Benny at my side throughout that service, for I wanted him to see that his mother had been loved by others too, and that her existence had made a difference in more lives than his and mine. He was only eight years old, but he seemed to take from the service the very comfort that I had hoped it would give him. Hearing his mother praised, he was unable to hold back his tears, but now there was something more than grief in his face and eyes; now he was also proud of her, amused by some of the practical jokes that she had played on friends and that they now recounted, and intrigued to hear about aspects of her that had theretofore been unknown to him. In time these new emotions were certain to dilute his grief and help him adjust to his loss.

The day following the memorial service, I rose late. When I went looking for Benny, I found him beneath one of the cherry trees in the backyard. He sat with his knees drawn up against his chest and his arms around his legs, staring at the far side of the broad valley on one slope of which we lived, but he seemed to be looking at something still more distant.

I sat beside him. "How're you doin'?"

"Okay," he said.

For a while neither of us spoke. Overhead the leaves of the tree rustled softly. The dazzling white-pink blossoms of spring were long gone, of course, and the branches were bedecked with fruit not yet quite ripe. The day was hot, but the tree threw plentiful, cool shade.

At last he said, "Daddy?"

"Hmmmm?"

"If it's all right with you . . ."

"What?"

"I know what you say. . . ."

"What I say about what?"

"About there being no Heaven or angels or anything like that."

"It's not just what I say, Benny. It's true."

"Well . . . just the same, if it's all right with you, I'm going to picture Mommy in Heaven, wings and everything."

He was still in a fragile emotional condition even a month after her death and would need many more months if not years to regain his full equilibrium, so I didn't rush to respond with one of my usual arguments about the foolishness of religious faith. I was silent for a moment, then said, "Well, let me think about that for a couple of minutes, okay?"

We sat side by side, staring across the valley, and I knew that neither of us was seeing the landscape before us. I was seeing Ellen as she had been on the Fourth of July the previous summer: wearing white shorts and a yellow blouse, tossing a Frisbee with me and Benny, radiant, laughing, laughing. I don't know what poor Benny was seeing, though I suspect his mind was brimming with gaudy images of Heaven complete with haloed angels and golden steps spiraling up to a golden throne.

"She can't just end," he said after a while. "She was too nice to just end. She's got to be . . . somewhere."

"But that's just it, Benny. She *is* somewhere. Your mother goes on in you. You've got her genes, for one thing. You don't know what genes are, but you've got them: her hair, her eyes. . . . And because she was a good person who taught you the right values, you'll grow up to be a good person as well, and you'll have kids of your own someday, and your mother will go on in them and in *their* children. Your mother still lives in our memories, too, and in the memories of her friends. Because she was kind to so many people, those people were shaped to some small degree by her kindness. They'll now and then remember her, and because of her they might be kinder to people, and that kindness goes on and on."

He listened solemnly, although I suspected that the concepts of immortality through bloodline and impersonal immortality through one's moral relationships with other people were beyond his grasp. I tried to think of a way to restate it so a child could understand.

But he said, "Nope. Not good enough. It's nice that lots of people are gonna remember her. But it's not good enough. *She* has to be somewhere. Not just her memory. *She* has to go on. So if it's all right with you, I'm gonna figure she's in Heaven."

"No, it's not all right, Benny." I put my arm around him. "The healthy thing to do, son, is to face up to unpleasant truths—"

He shook his head. "She's all right, Daddy. She didn't just end. She's somewhere now. I know she is. And she's happy."

"Benny—"

He stood, peered up into the trees, and said, "We'll have cherries to eat soon?"

"Benny, let's not change the subject. We—"

"Can we drive into town for lunch at Mrs. Foster's restaurant—burgers and fries and Cokes and then a cherry sundae?"

"Benny—"

"Can we, can we?"

"All right. But—"

"I get to drive!" he shouted and ran off toward the garage, giggling at his joke.

⋆ ⋀ ⋆

During the next year, Benny's stubborn refusal to let his mother go was at first frustrating, then annoying, and finally intensely aggravating. He talked to her nearly every night as he lay in bed, waiting for sleep to come, and he seemed confident that she could hear him. Often, after I tucked him in and kissed him good night and left the room, he slipped out from under the covers, knelt beside the bed, and prayed that his mother was happy and safe where she had gone.

Twice I accidentally heard him. On other occasions I stood quietly in the hall after leaving his room, and when he thought I had gone downstairs, he humbled himself before God, although he could know nothing more of God than what he had illicitly learned from television shows or other pop culture that I had been unable to monitor.

I was determined to wait him out, certain that his childish faith would expire naturally when he realized that God would never answer him. As the days passed without a miraculous sign assuring him that his mother's soul had survived death, Benny would begin to understand that all he had been taught about religion was true, and he eventually would return quietly to the realm of reason where I had made—and was patiently saving—a place for him. I did not want to tell him that I knew of his praying, did not want to force the issue, because I knew that in reaction to a too heavy-handed exercise of parental authority, he might cling even longer to his irrational dream of life everlasting.

But after four months, when his nightly conversations with his dead mother and with God did not cease, I could no longer tolerate even whispered prayers in my house, for though I seldom heard them, I *knew* they were being said, and knowing was somehow as maddening as hearing every word of them. I confronted him. I reasoned with him at great length on many occasions. I argued, pleaded. I tried the classic carrot-and-stick approach: I punished him for the expression of any religious sentiment; and I rewarded him for the slightest antireligious statement, even if he made it unthinkingly or if it was only my *interpretation* of what he'd said that made his statement antireligious. He received few rewards and much punishment.

I did not spank him or in any way physically abuse him. That much, at least, is to my credit. I did not attempt to beat God out of him the way my parents had tried to beat Him *into* me.

I took Benny to Dr. Gerton, a psychiatrist, when everything else had failed. "He's having difficulty accepting his mother's death," I told Gerton. "He's just not . . . coping. I'm worried about him."

After three sessions with Benny over a period of two weeks, Dr. Gerton called to say he no longer needed to see Benny. "He's going to be all right, Mr. Fallon. You've no need to worry about him."

"But you're wrong," I insisted. "He needs analysis. He's still not . . . coping."

"Mr. Fallon, you've said that before, but I've never been able to get a clear explanation of what behavior strikes you as evidence of his inability to cope. What's he *doing* that worries you so?"

"He's praying," I said. "He prays to God to keep his mother safe and happy. And he talks to his mother as if he's sure she hears him, talks to her *every* night."

"Oh, Mr. Fallon, if that's all that's been bothering you, I can assure you there's no need to worry. Talking to his mother, praying for her, all that's perfectly ordinary and—"

"Every night!" I repeated.

"Ten times a day would be all right. Really, there's nothing unhealthy about it. Talking to God about his mother and talking to his mother in Heaven . . . it's just a psychological mechanism by which he can slowly adjust to the fact that she's no longer actually here on earth with him. It's perfectly ordinary."

I'm afraid I shouted: "It's not perfectly ordinary in *this* house, Dr. Gerton. We're atheists!"

He was silent, then sighed. "Mr. Fallon, you've got to remember that your son is more than your son—he's a person in his own right. A *little* person but a person nonetheless. You can't think of him as property or as an unformed mind to be molded—"

"I have the utmost respect for the individual, Dr. Gerton. Much more respect than do the hymn singers who value their fellow men less than they do their imaginary master in the sky."

His silence lasted longer than before. Finally he said, "All right. Then surely you realize there's no guarantee the son will be the same person in every respect as the father. He'll have ideas and desires of his own. And ideas about religion might be one area in which the disagreement between the two of you will widen over the years rather than narrow. This might not be *only* a psychological mechanism that he's using to adapt to his mother's death. It might also turn out to be the start of lifelong faith. At least you have to be prepared for the possibility."

"I won't have it," I said firmly.

His third silence was the longest of all. Then: "Mr. Fallon, I have no need to see Benny again. There's nothing I can do for him because there's nothing he really needs from me. But perhaps you should consider some counseling for yourself."

I hung up on him.

⊲ ⋀ ⊳

For the next six months Benny infuriated and frustrated me by clinging to his fantasy of Heaven. Perhaps he no longer spoke to his mother every evening, and perhaps sometimes he even forgot to say his prayers, but his stubborn faith could not be shaken. When I spoke of atheism, when I made a scornful joke about God, whenever I tried to reason with him, he would only say, "No, Daddy, you're wrong," or, "No, Daddy, that's not the way it is," and he would either walk away from me or try to change the subject. Or he would do something even more infuriating: He would say, "No, Daddy, you're wrong," and then he would throw his small arms around me, hug me very tight, and tell me that he loved me, and at these moments there was a too apparent sadness about him that included an element of pity, as if he was afraid for me and felt that *I* needed guidance and reassurance. Nothing made me angrier than that. He was nine years old, not an ancient guru!

As punishment for his willful disregard of my wishes, I took away his television privileges for days—and sometimes weeks—at a time. I forbade him to have dessert after dinner, and once I refused to allow him to play with his friends for an entire month. Nothing worked.

Religion, the disease that had turned my parents into stern and solemn strangers, the disease that had made my childhood a nightmare, the very sickness that had stolen my best friend, Hal Sheen, from me when I least expected to lose him, *religion* had now wormed its way into my house again. It had contaminated my son, the only important person left in my life. No, it wasn't any particular religion that had a grip on Benny. He didn't have any formal theological education, so his concepts of God and Heaven were thoroughly nondenominational, vaguely Christian, yes, but only vaguely. It was religion without structure, without dogma or doctrine, religion based entirely on childish sentiment; therefore, some might say that it was not really religion at all, and that I should not have worried about it. But I knew that Dr. Gerton's observation was true: This childish faith might be the seed from which a true religious conviction would grow in later years. The virus of religion was loose in my house, rampant, and I was dismayed, distraught, and perhaps even somewhat deranged by my failure to find a cure for it.

To me, this was the essence of horror. It wasn't the acute horror of a bomb blast or plane crash, mercifully brief, but a chronic horror that went on day after day, week after week.

I was sure that the worst of all possible troubles had befallen me and that I was in the darkest time of my life.

Then Benny got bone cancer.

⊲ ∧ ⊳

Nearly two years after his mother died, on a blustery day late in February, we were in the park by the river, flying a kite. When

Benny ran with the control stick, paying out string, he fell down. Not just once. Not twice. Repeatedly. When I asked what was wrong, he said that he had a sore muscle in his right leg: "Must've twisted it when the guys and I were climbing trees yesterday."

He favored the leg for a few days, and when I suggested that he ought to see a doctor, he said that he was feeling better.

A week later he was in the hospital, undergoing tests, and in another two days, the diagnosis was confirmed: bone cancer. It was too widespread for surgery. His physicians instituted an immediate program of radium treatments and chemotherapy.

Benny lost his hair, lost weight. He grew so pale that each morning I was afraid to look at him because I had the crazy idea that if he got any paler he would begin to turn transparent and, when he was finally as clear as glass, would shatter in front of my eyes.

After five weeks he took a sudden turn for the better and was, though not in remission, at least well enough to come home. The radiation and chemotherapy continued on an outpatient basis. I think now that he improved not due to the radiation or cytotoxic agents or drugs but simply because he wanted to see the cherry trees in bloom one last time. His temporary turn for the better was an act of sheer will, a triumph of mind over body.

Except for one day when a sprinkle of rain fell, he sat in a chair under the blossom-laden boughs, enjoying the spring greening of the valley and delighting in the antics of the squirrels that came out of the nearby woods to frolic on our lawn. He sat not in one of the redwood lawn chairs but in a big, comfortably padded easy chair that I brought out from the house, his legs propped on a hassock, because he was thin and fragile; a harder chair would have bruised him horribly.

We played card games and Chinese checkers, but usually he was too tired to concentrate on a game for long, so mostly we just sat there, relaxing. We talked of days past, of the many good times he'd had in his ten short years, and of his mother. But we sat in silence a lot too. Ours was never an awkward silence; sometimes melancholy, yes, but never awkward.

Neither of us spoke of God or guardian angels or Heaven. I knew that he hadn't lost his belief that his mother had survived the death of her body in some form and that she had gone on to a better place. But he said nothing more of that and didn't discuss his hopes for his own place in the afterlife. I believe he avoided the subject out of respect for me and because he wanted no friction between us during those last days.

I will always be grateful to him for not putting me to the test. I am afraid that I'd have tried to force him to embrace rationalism even in his last days, thereby making a bigger jackass of myself than usual.

After only nine days at home, he suffered a relapse and returned to the hospital. I booked him into a semiprivate room with two beds; he took one, and I took the other.

Cancer cells had migrated to his liver, and a tumor was found there. After surgery, he improved for a few days, was almost buoyant, but then sank again.

Cancer was found in his lymphatic system, in his spleen, tumors everywhere.

His condition improved, declined, improved, and declined again. Each improvement, however, was less encouraging than the one before it, while each decline was steeper.

I was rich, intelligent, and talented. I was famous in my field. But I could do nothing to save my son. I had never felt so small, so powerless.

At least I could be strong for Benny. In his presence, I tried to be cheerful. I did not let him see me cry, but I wept quietly at night, curled in the fetal position, reduced to the helplessness of a child, while he lay in troubled, drug-induced slumber on the other side of the room. During the day, when he was away for therapy or tests or surgery, I sat at the window, staring out, seeing nothing.

As if some alchemical spell had been cast, the world became gray, entirely gray. I was aware of no color in anything; I might have been living in an old black-and-white movie. Shadows became more stark and sharp edged. The air itself seemed gray, as though contaminated by a toxic mist so fine that it could not be seen, only sensed. Voices were fuzzy, the aural equivalent of gray. The few times that I switched on the TV or the radio, the music seemed to have no melody that I could discern. My interior world was as gray as the physical world around me, and the unseen but acutely sensed mist that fouled the outer world had penetrated to my core.

Even in the depths of that despair, I did not step off the path of reason, did not turn to God for help or condemn God for torturing an innocent child. I didn't consider seeking the counsel of clergymen or the help of faith healers.

I endured.

If I had slipped and sought solace in superstition, no one could have blamed me. In little more than two years, I'd had a falling out with my only close friend, had lost my wife in a traffic accident, and had seen my son succumb to cancer. Occasionally you hear about people with runs of bad luck like that, or you read about them in the papers, and strangely enough they usually talk about how they were brought to God by their suffering and how they found peace in faith. Reading about them always makes you sad and stirs your compassion, and you can even forgive them their witless religious sentimentality. Of course, you always quickly put them out of your mind because you know that a similar chain of tragedies could befall you, and such a realization does not bear contemplation. Now I not only had to contemplate it but *live* it, and in the living I did not bend my principles.

I faced the void and accepted it.

After putting up a surprisingly long, valiant, painful struggle against the virulent cancer that was eating him alive, Benny finally died on a night in August. They had rushed him into the intensive-care unit two days before, and I had been permitted to sit with him only fifteen minutes every second hour. On that last night, however, they allowed me to come in from the ICU lounge and stay beside his bed for several hours, because they knew that he didn't have long.

An intravenous drip pierced his left arm. An aspirator was inserted in his nose. He was hooked up to an EKG machine that traced his heart activity in green light on a bedside monitor, and each beat was marked by a soft beep. The lines and the beeps frequently became erratic for as much as three or four minutes at a time.

I held his hand. I smoothed the sweat-damp hair from his brow. I pulled the covers up to his neck when he was seized by chills and lowered them when the chills gave way to fevers.

Benny slipped in and out of consciousness. Even when awake he was not always alert or coherent.

"Daddy?"

"Yes, Benny?"

"Is that you?"

"It's me."

"Where am I?"

"In bed. Safe. I'm here, Benny."

"Is supper ready?"

"Not yet."

"I'd like burgers and fries."

"That's what we're having."

"Where're my shoes?"

"You don't need shoes tonight, Benny."

"Thought we were going for a walk."

"Not tonight."

"Oh."

Then he sighed and slipped away again.

Rain was falling outside. Drops pattered against the ICU window and streamed down the panes. The storm contributed to the gray mood that had claimed the world.

Once, near midnight, Benny woke and was lucid. He knew exactly where he was, who I was, and what was happening. He turned his head toward me and smiled. He tried to rise up on one arm, but he was too weak even to lift his head.

I got out of my chair, stood at the side of his bed, held his hand, and said, "All these wires . . . I think they're going to replace a few of your parts with robot stuff."

"I'll be okay," he said in a faint, tremulous voice that was strangely, movingly confident.

"You want a chip of ice to suck on?"

"No. What I want . . ."

"What? Anything you want, Benny."

"I'm scared, Daddy."

My throat grew tight, and I was afraid that I was going to lose the composure that I had strived so hard to hold on to during the long weeks of his illness. I swallowed and said, "Don't be scared, Benny. I'm with you. Don't—"

"No," he said, interrupting me. "I'm not scared . . . for me. I'm afraid . . . for you."

I thought that he was delirious again, and I didn't know what to say.

But he was not delirious, and with his next few words he made himself painfully clear: "I want us all . . . to be together again . . . like we were before Mommy died . . . together again someday. But I'm afraid that you . . . won't . . . find us."

The rest is agonizing to recall. I was indeed so obsessed with holding fast to my atheism that I could not bring myself to tell my son a harmless lie that would make his last minutes easier. If only I had promised to believe, had told him that I would seek him in the next world, he would have gone to his rest more happily. Ellen was right when she called it an obsession. I merely held Benny's hand tighter, blinked back tears, and smiled at him.

He said, "If you don't believe you can find us . . . then maybe you *won't* find us."

"It's all right, Benny," I said soothingly. I kissed him on the forehead, on his left cheek, and for a moment I put my face against his and held him as best I could, trying to compensate with affection for the promise of faith that I refused to give.

"Daddy . . . if only . . . you'd look for us?"

"You'll be okay, Benny."

". . . just please *look* for us . . ."

"I love you, Benny. I love you with all my heart."

". . . if you look for us . . . you'll find us . . ."

"I love you, I love you, Benny."

". . . don't look . . . won't find . . ."

"Benny, Benny . . ."

The gray ICU light fell on the gray sheets and on the gray face of my son.

The gray rain streamed down the gray window.

He died while I held him.

Abruptly color came back into the world. Far too much color, too intense, overwhelming. The light brown of Benny's staring, sightless eyes was the purest, most penetrating, most beautiful brown that I had ever seen. The ICU walls were a pale blue that made me feel as if they were made not of plaster but of water, and as if I were about to drown in a turbulent sea. The sour-apple green of the EKG monitor blazed bright, searing my eyes. The watery blue walls flowed toward me. I heard running footsteps as nurses and interns responded to the lack of telemetry data from their small patient, but before they arrived I was swept away by a blue tide, carried into deep blue currents.

◁ ∧ ▷

I shut down my company. I withdrew from negotiations for new commissions. I arranged for those commissions already undertaken to be transferred as quickly as possible to other design firms of which I approved and with which my clients felt comfortable. I pink-slipped my employees, though with generous severance pay, and helped them to find new jobs where possible.

I put my wealth into treasury certificates and conservative savings instruments—investment requiring little or no monitoring. The temptation to sell the house was great, but after considerable thought I merely closed it and hired a part-time caretaker to look after it in my absence.

Years later than Hal Sheen, I had reached his conclusion that no monuments of man were worth the effort required to erect them. Even the greatest edifices of stone and steel were pathetic vanities, of no consequence in the long run. When viewed in the context of the vast, cold universe in which trillions of stars blazed down on tens of trillions of planets, even the pyramids were as fragile as origami sculptures. In the dark light of death and entropy, even heroic effort and acts of genius appeared foolish.

Yet relationships with family and friends were no more enduring than humanity's fragile monuments of stone. I had once told Benny that we lived on in memory, in the genetic trace, in the kindness that our own kindnesses encouraged in others. But those things now seemed as insubstantial as shapes of smoke in a brisk wind.

Unlike Hal Sheen, however, I did not seek comfort in religion. No blows were hard enough to crack my obsession.

I had thought that religious mania was the worst horror of all, but now I had found one that was worse: the horror of an atheist who, unable to believe in God, is suddenly also unable to believe in the value of human struggle and courage, and is therefore unable to find meaning in anything whatsoever, neither in beauty nor in pleasure, nor in the smallest act of kindness.

I spent that autumn in Bermuda. I bought a Cheoy Lee sixty-six-foot sport yacht, a sleek and powerful boat, and learned how to handle it. Alone, I ran the Caribbean, sampling island after island. Sometimes I dawdled along at quarter throttle for days at a time, in sync with the lazy rhythms of Caribbean life. Then suddenly I would be overcome with the frantic need to move, to stop wasting time, and I would press forward, engines screaming, slamming across the waves with reckless abandon, as if it mattered whether I got anywhere by any particular time.

When I tired of the Caribbean, I went to Brazil, but Rio held interest for only a few days. I became a rich drifter, moving from one first-class hotel to another in one far-flung city after another: Hong Kong, Singapore, Istanbul, Paris, Athens, Cairo, New York, Las Vegas, Acapulco, Tokyo, San Francisco. I was looking for something that would give meaning to life, though the search was conducted with the certain knowledge that I would not find what I sought.

For a few days I thought I could devote my life to gambling. In the random fall of cards, in the spin of roulette wheels, I glimpsed the strange, wild shape of fate. By committing myself to swimming in that deep river of randomness, I thought I might be in harmony with the pointlessness and disorder of the universe and, therefore, at peace. In less than a week I won and lost fortunes, and at last I walked away from the gaming tables a hundred thousand dollars out of pocket. That was only a tiny fraction of the millions on which I could draw, but in those few days I learned that even immersion in the chaos of random chance provided no escape from an awareness of the finite nature of life and of all things human.

In the spring I went home to die. I'm not sure if I meant to kill myself. Or, having lost the will to live, perhaps I believed that I could just lie down in a familiar place and succumb to death without needing to lift my hand against myself. But, although I did not know how death would be attained, I was certain that death was my goal.

The house in Bucks County was filled with painful memories of Ellen and Benny, and when I went into the kitchen and looked out the window at the cherry trees in the backyard, my heart ached as if pinched in a vise. The trees were ablaze with thousands of pink and white blossoms.

Benny had loved the cherry trees when they were at their radiant best, and the sight of their blossoms sharpened my memories of Benny so well that I felt I had been stabbed. For a while I leaned against the kitchen counter, unable to breathe, then gasped painfully for breath, then wept.

In time I went out and stood beneath the trees, looking up at the beautifully decorated branches. Benny had been dead almost nine months, but the trees he had loved were still thriving, and in some way that I could not quite grasp, their continued existence meant that at least a part of Benny was still alive. I struggled to understand this crazy idea—

—and suddenly the cherry blossoms fell. Not just a few. Not just hundreds. Within one minute every blossom on both trees dropped to the ground. I turned around, around, startled and confused, and the whirling white flowers were as thick as snowflakes in a blizzard. I had never seen anything like it. Cherry blossoms just don't fall by the thousands, simultaneously, on a windless day.

When the phenomenon ended, I plucked blossoms off my shoulders and out of my hair. I examined them closely. They were not withered or seared or marked by any sign of disease.

I looked up at the branches.

Not one blossom remained on either tree.

My heart was hammering.

Around my feet, drifts of cherry blossoms began to stir in a mild breeze that sprang up from the west.

"No," I said, so frightened that I could not even admit to myself what I was saying no *to*.

I turned from the trees and ran to the house. As I went, the last of the cherry blossoms blew off my hair and clothes.

In the library, however, as I took a bottle of Jack Daniel's from the bar cabinet, I realized that I was still clutching blossoms in my hand. I threw them down on the floor and scrubbed my palm on my pants as though I had been handling something foul.

I went to the bedroom with the Jack Daniel's and drank myself unconscious, refusing to face up to the reason why I needed to drink at all. I told myself that it had nothing to do with the cherry trees, that I was drinking only because I needed to escape the misery of the past few years.

Mine was a diamond-hard obsession.

◁ ʌ ▷

I slept for eleven hours and woke with a hangover. I took two aspirin, stood in the shower under scalding water for fifteen minutes, under a cold spray for one minute, toweled vigorously, took two more aspirin, and went into the kitchen to make coffee.

Through the window above the sink, I saw the cherry trees ablaze with pink and white blossoms.

Hallucination, I thought with relief. Yesterday's blizzard of blossoms was just hallucination.

I ran outside for a closer look at the trees. I saw that only a few pink-white petals were scattered on the lush grass beneath the boughs, no more than would have blown off in the mild spring breeze.

Relieved but also curiously disappointed, I returned to the kitchen. The coffee had brewed. As I poured a cupful, I remembered the blossoms that I had cast aside in the library.

I drank two cups of fine Colombian before I had the nerve to go to the library. The blossoms were there: a wad of crushed petals that had yellowed and acquired brown edges overnight. I picked them up, closed my hand around them.

All right, I told myself shakily, you don't have to believe in Christ or in God the Father or in some bodiless Holy Spirit.

Religion is a disease.

No, no, you don't have to believe in any of the silly rituals, in dogma and doctrine. In fact you don't have to believe in *God* to believe in an afterlife.

Irrational, unreasonable.

No, wait, think about it: Isn't it possible that life after death is perfectly natural, not a divine gift but a simple fact of nature? The caterpillar lives one life, then transforms itself to live again as a butterfly. So, damn it, isn't it conceivable that our bodies are the caterpillar stage and that our spirits take flight into another existence when our bodies are no longer of use to us? The human metamorphosis may just be a transformation of a higher order than that of the caterpillar.

Slowly, with dread and yet hope, I walked through the house, out the back door, up the sloped yard to the cherry trees. I stood beneath the flowery boughs and opened my hand to reveal the blossoms that I had saved from yesterday.

"Benny?" I said wonderingly.

The blossomfall began again. From both trees, the pink and white petals dropped in profusion, spinning lazily to the grass, catching in my hair and on my clothes.

I turned, breathless, gasping. "Benny? Benny?"

In a minute the ground was covered with a white mantle, and again not one small bloom remained on the trees.

I laughed. It was a nervous laugh that might degenerate into a mad cackle. I was not in control of myself.

Not quite sure why I was speaking aloud, I said, "I'm scared. Oh, shit, am I scared."

The blossoms began to drift up from the ground. Not just a few of them. All of them. They rose back toward the branches that had shed them only moments ago. It was a blizzard in reverse. The soft petals brushed against my face.

I was laughing again, laughing uncontrollably, but my fear was fading rapidly, and this was good laughter.

Within another minute, the trees were cloaked in pink and white as before, and all was still.

I sensed that Benny was not within the tree. This phenomenon did not conform to pagan belief any more than it did to traditional Christianity. But he was *somewhere*. He was not gone forever. He was out there somewhere, and when my time came to go where he and Ellen had gone, I only needed to believe that they could be found, and then I would surely find them.

The sound of an obsession cracking could probably be heard all the way to China.

A scrap of writing by H. G. Wells came into my mind. I had long admired Wells's work, but nothing he had written had ever seemed so true as that which I recalled while standing under the cherry trees: "The past is but the beginning of a beginning, and all that is and has been is but the twilight of the dawn."

He had been writing about history, of course, and about the long future that awaited humanity, but those words seemed to apply as well to death and to the mysterious rebirth that followed it. A man might live a hundred years, yet his long life will be but the twilight of the dawn.

"Benny," I said. "Oh, Benny."

But no more blossoms fell, and through the years that followed I received no more signs. Nor did I need them.

From that day forward, I knew that death was not the end and that I would be rejoined with Ellen and Benny on the other side.

And what of God? Does He exist? I don't know. Although I have believed in an afterlife of some kind for ten years now, I have not become a churchgoer. But if, upon my death, I cross into that other plane and find Him waiting for me, I will not be entirely surprised, and I will return to His arms as gratefully and happily as I will return to Ellen's and to Benny's.

CHASE

1

1971.

Bruce Springsteen wasn't famous in 1971. Neither was Tom Cruise, a mere schoolboy. Julia Roberts haunted no young men's dreams. Robin Williams, Steve Martin, Arnold Schwarzenegger—their fortunes were as yet unmade.

Richard Milhous Nixon was President of the United States. The war in Vietnam raged. In Wilmington, North Carolina, January was a time of violence against black citizens—arson, bombings, shootings. At the Attica Correctional Facility in New York State, the bloodiest prison riot in U.S. history claimed forty-three lives.

The best-seller list of *The New York Times* included *The Winds of War* by Herman Wouk and *Another Roadside Attraction* by Tom Robbins.

The movies: *The French Connection, A Clockwork Orange, Klute, Carnal Knowledge, The Last Picture Show.*

The music: Carole King, John Denver, John Lennon on his own, Led Zeppelin, Elton John just beginning.

Cigarette sales in the United States topped five hundred and forty-seven *billion.* J. C. Penney died at the age of ninety-five. As many as five hundred thousand Soviet citizens perished in the Gulags during those twelve months—evidence of government restraint.

It was a different time. A different world.

The term "serial killer" was unknown. And "sociopath."

2

At seven o'clock, seated on the platform as the guest of honor, Ben Chase was served a bad roast-beef dinner while dignitaries talked at him from both sides, breathing over his salad and his half-eaten fruit cup.

At eight o'clock the mayor rose to deliver a boring panegyric to the city's most famous Vietnam War hero. Half an hour after he began, he finally presented Chase with a special scroll detailing his supposed accomplishments and restating the city's pride in him.

Chase was also given the keys to a new Mustang convertible, which he had not been expecting. It was a gift from the Merchants' Association.

By nine-thirty Benjamin Chase was escorted from the Iron Kettle Restaurant to the parking lot where his new car waited. It was an eight-cylinder job with a sports package that included automatic transmission with a floor shift, bucket seats, side mirrors, white-wall tires—and a wickedly sparkling black paint job that contrasted nicely with the crimson racing stripes over the trunk and hood.

At ten minutes after ten, having posed for newspaper photographs with the mayor and the officers of the Merchants' Association, having expressed his gratitude to everyone present, Chase drove away in his reward.

At twenty minutes past ten he passed through the suburban development known as Ashside, doing slightly more than one hundred miles an hour in a forty-mile-an-hour zone. He crossed three-lane Galasio Boulevard against the light, turned a corner at such speed that he briefly lost control, and sheared off a traffic sign.

At ten-thirty he started up the long slope of Kanackaway Ridge Road, trying to see if he could hold the speed at one hundred all the way to the summit. It was a dangerous bit of play, but he did not care if he killed himself.

Perhaps because the car had not yet been broken in, or perhaps because it simply had not been designed for that kind of driving, it wouldn't perform as he wished. Although he held the accelerator to the floor, the speedometer registered only eighty miles per hour by the time that he was two thirds of the way up the winding road; it fell to seventy when he crested the rise.

He took his foot off the accelerator—the fire of anger having burned out of him for the moment—and let the sleek machine glide along the flat stretch of two-lane blacktop along the ridge above the city.

Below lay a panorama of lights to stir the hearts of lovers. Though the left side of the road lay against a sheer rock wall, the right was maintained as a park. Fifty yards of grassy verge, dotted with shrubs, separated the street from an iron and concrete railing near the brink of the cliff. Beyond the railing, the streets of the city far below seemed like a miniature electric map, with special concentrations of light toward the downtown area and out near the Gateway Mall shopping center.

Lovers, mostly teenagers, parked here, separated by stands of pine and rows of brambles. Their appreciation for the dazzling city view turned—in almost every case and dozens of times each night—to an appreciation of the flesh.

Once, it had even been that way for Chase.

He pulled the car to the shoulder of the road, braked, and cut the engine. The stillness of the night seemed complete and deep. Then he heard crickets, the cry of an owl somewhere close, and the occasional laughter of young people muffled by closed car windows.

Until he heard the laughter, it did not occur to Chase to wonder why he had come here. He felt oppressed by the mayor, the Merchants' Association, and the rest of them. He had not really wanted the banquet, certainly not the car, and he had gone only because he could find no gracious way to decline them. Confronted with their homespun patriotism and their sugar-glazed vision of the war, he felt burdened with an indefinable load, smothered. Perhaps it was the past on his shoulders—the realization that he'd once shared their innocence. At any rate, free of them, he had struck out for that one place in the city that represented remembered pleasure, the much-joked-about lovers' lane atop Kanackaway.

Now, however, the comparative silence only gave his thoughts a chance to build toward a scream. And the pleasure? None of that, either, for he had no girl with him—and would have been no better off with one at his side.

Along the shadowed length of the park, half a dozen cars were slotted against walls of shrubbery. Moonlight glinted on the bumpers and windows. If he had not known the purpose of this retreat, he would have thought that all the vehicles were abandoned. But the mist on the inside of the windows gave the game away.

Occasionally a shadow moved inside one of the cars, distorted by the steamed glass. Those silhouettes and the rustle of leaves as the wind swept down from the top of the ridge were all that moved.

Then something dropped from a low point on the rock wall to the left and scurried across the blacktop toward the darkness beneath a huge weeping willow tree a hundred feet in front of Chase's car. Though bent and moving with the frantic grace of a frightened animal, the new arrival was clearly a man.

In Vietnam, Chase had developed an uncanny sense of imminent danger. His inner alarm was clanging.

The one thing that did not belong in a lovers' lane at night was a man alone, on foot. A teenager's car was a mobile bed, such a necessity of seduction, such an extension of the seducer, that no modern Casanova could be successful without one.

It was possible, of course, that the interloper was engaging in some bird-dogging: spotting parkers for his own amusement and to their embarrassment. Chase had been the victim of that game a few times in his high-school years. That was, however, a pastime usually associated with the immature or the socially outcast, those kids who hadn't the opportunity to be *inside* the cars where the real action was. It was not, as far as Chase knew, something that adults enjoyed. And this man creeping through the shadows was easily six feet tall; he had the carriage of an adult, no youthful awkwardness. Besides, bird-dogging was a sport most often played in groups as protection against a beating from one of the surprised lovers.

Trouble.

The guy came out from beneath the willow, still doubled over and running. He stopped against a bramble row and studied a three-year-old Chevrolet parked at the end, near the cliff railing.

Not sure what was happening or what he should do, Chase turned in his car seat and worked the cover off the dome light. He unscrewed the tiny bulb and dropped it into a pocket of his suit jacket. When he turned front again, he saw that the bird-dogger had not moved: The guy was still watching the Chevrolet, leaning into the brambles as if unfazed by the thorns.

A girl laughed, the sound of her voice clear in the night air. Some of the lovers must have found it too warm for closed windows.

The man by the brambles moved again, closing in on the Chevrolet.

Quietly, because the stalker was no more than a hundred fifty feet from him, Chase got out of the Mustang. He left the door open, because he was sure that the sound of it would alert the intruder. He went around the car and across the grass, which had recently been mown and was slightly damp and slippery underfoot.

Ahead, a light came on in the Chevrolet, diffused by the steamed windows. Someone shouted, and a young girl screamed. She screamed again.

Chase had been walking. Now he ran as the sounds of a fight rose ahead. When he came up on the Chevrolet, he saw that the door on the driver's side was open and that the intruder was halfway into the front seat, flailing away at someone. Shadows bobbled, dipped, and pitched against the frosted glass.

"Hold it!" Chase shouted, directly behind the man now.

As the stranger pulled back out of the car, Chase saw the knife. The bird-dogger held it in his right hand, raised high. His hand and the weapon were covered with blood.

Chase raced forward the last few feet, slammed the stalker against the Chevy's window post. He slipped his arm around the guy's neck and tried to get a hammerlock on him.

The girl was still screaming.

The stranger swung his arm down and back, trying to catch Chase's thigh with the blade. He was an amateur.

Chase twisted out of the arc of the weapon. Simultaneously he drew his arm more tightly across the other's windpipe.

Around them, cars started. Trouble in lovers' lane aroused all the repressed sexual guilt in every teenager nearby. No one wanted to stay to see what the problem was.

"Drop it," Chase said.

Although the stranger must have been desperate for breath, he stabbed backward again and missed again.

Suddenly furious, Chase jerked his adversary onto his toes and applied the last effort necessary to choke him unconscious.

In the same instant, the wet grass betrayed him. His feet slipped, and he went down with the stranger on top.

This time the knife took Chase in the meaty part of his thigh, just below the hip. But it was torn from the assailant's hand as Chase bucked and tossed him aside.

The stalker rolled and scrambled to his feet. He took a few steps toward Chase, seeking the knife, but then he seemed to realize the formidable nature of his opponent. He ran.

"Stop him!" Chase shouted.

But most of the cars had gone. Those still parked along the cliff reacted to this latest uproar just as the more timid parkers had reacted to the first cries: lights flicked on, engines started, tires squealed. In a moment the only cars in lovers' lane were the Chevrolet and Chase's Mustang.

The pain in his leg was bad, though not any worse than a hundred others he had endured. In the light from the Chevrolet, he could see that he was bleeding slowly from a shallow wound—not the fearsome spurt of a torn artery. When he tried, he was able to stand and walk with little trouble.

He went to the car, peered in, and then wished that he hadn't been curious. The body of a young man, perhaps nineteen or twenty, was sprawled half on the seat and half on the floor. Blood-soaked. Mouth open. Eyes glazed.

Beyond the victim, curled in the corner by the far door, a petite brunette, a year or two younger than her murdered lover, was moaning softly. Her hands gripped her knees so tightly that they resembled claws latched around a piece of game. She wore a pink miniskirt but no blouse or bra. Her small breasts were spotted with blood, and her nipples were erect.

Chase wondered why this last detail registered more vividly with him than anything else about the grisly scene.

He expected better of himself. Or at least—there had been a time when he had expected better.

"Stay there," Chase said from the driver's door. "I'll come around for you."

She did not respond, though she continued to moan.

Chase almost closed the door, then realized that he would be shutting off the light and leaving the brunette alone in the car with the corpse. He walked around the Chevy, leaning on it to favor his right leg, and he opened her door.

Apparently these kids had not believed in locks. That was, he supposed, part of their generation's optimism, part and parcel with their theories on free love, mutual trust, and brotherhood. Theirs was the same generation that was supposed to live life so fully that they all but denied the existence of death.

Their generation. Chase was only a few years older than they were. But he did not consider himself to be part of their generation or any other. He was alone in the flow of time.

"Where's your blouse?" he asked.

She was no longer fixated on the corpse, but she was not looking at Chase either. She stared at her knees, at her white knuckles, and she mumbled.

Chase groped around on the floor under her legs and found the balled-up garment. "You better put this on."

She wouldn't take it. She continued murmuring wordlessly to herself.

"Come on, now," he said as gently as he could.

The killer might not have gone very far.

She spoke more urgently now, coherently, although her voice was lower than before. When he bent closer to listen, he discovered that she was saying, "Please don't hurt me, please don't hurt me."

"I won't hurt you," Chase assured her, straightening up. "I didn't do that to your boyfriend. But the man who did it might still be hanging around. My car's back there. Will you please come with me?"

She blinked, nodded, and got out of the car. He handed the blouse to her. She unrolled it, shook it out, but could not seem to get it on. She was still in a state of shock.

"You can dress in my car," Chase said. "It's safer there."

The shadows under the trees were deeper than they had been.

He put his arm around her and half carried her back to the Mustang. The door on the passenger's side was locked. By the time he got her to the other door and followed her inside, she seemed to have recovered her senses. She slipped one arm into the blouse, then the other, and slowly buttoned it.

When he closed his door and started the engine, she said, "Who are you?"

"Passerby. I saw the bastard and thought something was wrong."

"He killed Mike," she said hollowly.

"Your boyfriend?"

She didn't respond but leaned back against the seat, chewing her lip and wiping absentmindedly at the few spots of blood on her face.

"We'll get to a phone—or a police station. You all right? You need a hospital?"

"No."

Chase swung the car around and drove down Kanackaway Ridge Road as fast as he had driven up. He took the turn at the bottom so hard that the girl was thrown against the door.

"Buckle your seat belt," he advised.

She did as directed, but she appeared to be in a daze, staring straight ahead at the streets that unrolled before them.

"Who was he?" Chase asked as he reached the intersection at Galasio Boulevard and crossed it with the light this time.

"Mike," she said.

"Not your boyfriend."

"What?"

"The other one."

"I don't know," she said.

"Did you see his face?"

She frowned. "His face?"

"Yes.

"Face." As if the word were meaningless to her.

"Have you been doing anything?" he asked.

"Anything?"

"Drugs?"

"A little grass. Earlier."

Maybe more than a little, he decided.

He tried again: "Did you see his face? Did you recognize him?"

"Face? No. Yes. Not really. A little."

"I thought it might be an old lover, rejected suitor, something like that."

She said nothing.

Her reluctance to talk about it gave Chase time to consider the situation. As he recalled the killer's approach from the top of the ridge, he began to wonder whether the man had known which car he was after or whether any car would have done, whether this was an act of revenge directed against Mike specifically or only the work of a madman. Even before he had been sent overseas, the papers

had been filled with stories of meaningless slaughter. He had not read any papers since his discharge, but he suspected that the same brand of senseless murder still flourished.

The possibility of random, unmotivated homicide unnerved him. The similarity to Nam, to Operation Jules Verne and his part in it, stirred bad memories.

Fifteen minutes after they had left the ridge, Chase parked in front of the divisional police headquarters on Kensington Avenue.

"Are you feeling well enough to talk with them?" Chase asked.

"Cops?"

"Yeah."

She shrugged. "I guess so."

She had recovered remarkably fast. She even had the presence of mind to take Chase's pocket comb and run it through her dark hair. "How do I look?"

"Fine."

Maybe it was better to be without a woman than to die and leave behind one who grieved so briefly as this.

"Let's go," she said. She opened her door and stepped out, her lovely, trim legs flashing in a rustle of brief cloth.

◁ ⋀ ▷

The door of the small gray room opened, admitting a small gray man. His face was lined, and his eyes were sunken as if he had not slept in a day or two. His light-brown hair was uncombed and in need of a trim. He crossed to the table behind which Chase and the girl sat, and he took the only chair left. He folded into it as if he would never get up again. "I'm Detective Wallace."

"Glad to meet you," Chase said, though he was not glad at all.

The girl was quiet, examining her nails.

"Now, what's this all about?" Wallace asked, folding his hands on the scarred table and regarding them wearily, as if he'd already heard their story countless times.

"I already told the desk sergeant most of it," Chase said.

"He isn't in homicide. I am," Wallace said.

"Someone should be on the way out there. The body—"

"A car's been despatched. Your report's being checked out. That's what we do. Maybe not always well, but we do it. So you say someone was murdered."

"Her boyfriend, stabbed," Chase told him.

Wallace studied the girl as she studied her nails. "Can't she speak?"

"She's in shock maybe."

"These days?" Wallace joked, exhibiting a disregard for the girl's feelings that Chase found disconcerting.

The girl said, "Yeah, I can speak."

"What's your name?" Wallace asked.

"Louise."

"Louise what?"

"Allenby. Louise Allenby."

Wallace said, "You live in the city?"

"In Ashside."

"How old?"

Anger flared in her, but then she damped it and turned her gaze back to her nails. "Seventeen."

"In high school?"

"I graduated in June," she said. "I'm going to college in the fall. Penn State."

Wallace said, "Who was the boy?"

"Mike."

"That's it?"

"That's what?"

"Just Mike? Like Liberace. Like Picasso? One name?"

"Michael Karnes," she said.

"Just a boyfriend, or you engaged?"

"Boyfriend. We'd been going together for about a year, kind of steady."

"What were you doing on Kanackaway Ridge Road?" Wallace asked.

She looked boldly at him. "What do you think?"

Though Wallace's bored tone was disconcerting, Chase found the girl's detachment so unnerving that he wanted to be away from her as quickly as possible. "Look, Detective Wallace," he interjected, "is this really necessary? The girl wasn't involved in it. I think the guy might've gone for her next if I hadn't stopped him."

Wallace said, "How'd you happen to be there in the first place?"

"Just out driving," Chase said.

A light of interest switched on in the detective's eyes. "What's your name?"

"Benjamin Chase."

"I *thought* I'd seen you before." His manner softened and his energy level rose. "Your picture was in the papers today."

Chase nodded.

"That was really something you did over there," Wallace said. "That really took guts."

"It wasn't as much as they make out," Chase said.

"I'll *bet* it wasn't!" Wallace said, though it was clear that he thought Chase's actions in Vietnam must have been even more heroic than the papers had portrayed them.

The girl had taken a new interest in Chase and was studying him openly.

Wallace's tone toward her changed too. He said, "You want to tell me about it, just how it happened?"

She told him, losing some of her eerie composure in the process. Twice Chase thought that she was going to cry, and he wished that she would. Her cold manner, so soon after all the blood, gave him the creeps. Maybe she *was* still in denial. She repressed the tears, and by the time she had finished her story, she was calm again.

"You saw his face?" Wallace asked.

"Just a glimpse," she said.

"Can you describe him?"

"Not really."

"Try."

"He had brown eyes, I think."

"No mustache or beard?"

"I don't think so."

"Long sideburns or short?"

"Short, I think."

"Any scars?"

"No."

"Anything at all memorable about him?"

"No."

"The shape of his face—"

"No."

"No what?"

"It was just a face, any shape."

"His hair receding or full?"

"I can't remember," she said.

Chase said, "When I got to her, she was in a state of shock. I doubt she was registering anything."

Instead of a grateful agreement, Louise scowled at him.

He realized, too late, that the worst embarrassment for someone Louise's age was to lose her cool, to fail to cope. He had betrayed her momentary lapse to, of all people, a cop. She would have little gratitude for him now, even though he had saved her life.

Wallace got up. "Come on," he said.

"Where?" Chase asked.

"We'll go out there."

"Is that really necessary? For me, anyway?" Chase asked.

"Well, I have to take statements from both of you, in more detail than this. It would help, Mr. Chase, to be on the scene when you're describing it again. It'll only take a short while. We'll need the girl longer than we'll need you."

⊲ ⋀ ⊳

Chase was sitting in the rear of Wallace's squad car, thirty feet from the scene of the murder, answering questions, when the staff car from the *Press-Dispatch* arrived. Two photographers and a reporter got out.

For the first time, Chase realized that there would be local newspaper and television coverage. They would make a reluctant hero of him. Again.

"Please," he said to Wallace, "can we keep the reporters from learning who helped the girl?"

"Why?"

"I'm tired of reporters," Chase said.

Wallace said, "But you did save her life. You ought to be proud of that."

"I don't want to talk to them," Chase said.

"That's up to you. But they'll have to know who interrupted the killer. It'll be in the report."

Later, when Wallace was finished and Chase was getting out of the car to join another officer who would take him back to town, he felt the girl put a hand on his shoulder. He turned, and she said, "Thank you."

Maybe he was imagining it, but he thought that her touch had the quality of a caress and that her hand lingered. Even the possibility sickened him.

He met her eyes. Looked away at once.

At the same instant, a photographer snapped a picture. The flashbulb sprayed light. The light was brief—but the photograph would haunt him forever.

In the car, on the way back to town, the uniformed officer behind the wheel said that his name was Don Jones, that he had read about Chase, and that he would like to have Chase's autograph for his kids. Chase signed his name on the back of a blank homicide report, and at Jones's urging, he prefaced it with "To Rick and Judy Jones." The officer asked a lot of questions about Nam, which Chase answered as curtly as courtesy would allow.

In his prize Mustang, he drove more sedately than he had before. There was no anger in him now, only infinite weariness.

At a quarter past one in the morning, he parked in front of Mrs. Fielding's house, relieved to see that no lights were on. He unlocked the front door as quietly as the ancient deadbolt would permit, stepped knowingly around most of the loose boards in the staircase, and made his way to his attic apartment: one large room that served as a kitchen, bedroom, and living room, plus one walk-in closet and a private bath.

He locked his door.

He felt safe now.

Of course, he knew that he would never be safe again. No one ever was. Safety was an illusion.

This night at least, he hadn't been required to make polite conversation with Mrs. Fielding as she posed coyly in one of her half-unbuttoned housedresses, revealing the fish-belly-white curves of her breasts. He never understood why she chose to be so casually immodest at her age.

He undressed. He washed his face and hands. In fact, he washed his hands three times. He washed his hands a lot lately.

He studied the shallow knife wound in his thigh. It was already clotted and beginning to scab. He washed it, flushed it with alcohol, swabbed it with Merthiolate, and bandaged it.

In the main room, he completed the medication by pouring a glass of Jack Daniel's over two ice cubes. He sank onto the bed with the whiskey. He usually consumed half a bottle a day, minimum. This day, because of the damn banquet, he'd tried to stay sober. No longer.

Drinking, he felt clean again. Alone with a bottle of good liquor—that was the *only* time he felt clean.

He was pouring his second glassful when the telephone rang.

When he had first moved into the apartment, he hadn't wanted a telephone. No one would ever call. And he had no desire to make contact with anyone.

Mrs. Fielding had not believed that he could live without a phone. Envisioning herself becoming a messenger service for him, she had insisted that he have a telephone hooked up as a condition of occupancy.

That had been long before she knew that he was a war hero. It was even before *he* knew it.

For months the phone went unused except when she called from downstairs to tell him that mail had been delivered or to invite him to dinner.

Since the announcement by the White House, however, since all the excitement about the medal, he received calls every day, most of them from perfect strangers who offered congratulations that he did not deserve or sought interviews for publications that he had never read. He cut most of them short. Thus far, no one had ever had gall enough to ring him up this late at night, but he supposed he could never regain the solitude to which he had grown accustomed in those first months after his discharge.

He considered ignoring the phone and concentrating on his Jack Daniel's. But when it had rung for the sixteenth time, he realized that the caller was too persistent to be ignored, and he answered it.

"Hello?"

"Chase?"

"Yes."

"Do you know me?"

"No," he said, unable to place the voice. The man sounded tired—but aside from that one clue, he might have been anywhere between twenty and sixty years old, fat or thin, tall or short.

"How's your leg, Chase?" His voice contained a hint of humor, though the reason for it escaped Chase.

"Good enough," Chase said. "Fine."

"You're very good with your hands."

Chase said nothing, could not bring himself to speak, for now he understood what the call was about.

"Very good with your hands," the bird-dogger repeated. "I guess you learned that in the army."

"Yes," Chase said.

"I guess you learned a lot of things in the army, and I guess you think you can take care of yourself pretty well."

Chase said, "Is this *you?*"

The man laughed, momentarily shaking off his dispirited tone. "Yes, it's me. I am me. Exactly right. I've got a badly bruised throat, Chase, and I know my voice will be just awful by morning. Otherwise, I got away about as lightly as you did."

With a clarity reserved for moments of danger, Chase recalled the struggle with the killer on the grass by the Chevrolet. He tried to get a clear picture of the man's face but could do no better for his own sake than he had for the police. "How did you know I was the one who stopped you?"

"I saw your picture in the paper. You're a war hero. Your picture was everywhere. When you were lying on your back, beside the knife, I recognized you and got out of there fast."

"Who are you?"

"Do you really expect me to say?"

Chase had forgotten his drink altogether. The alarms, the goddamn alarms in his head, were ringing at peak volume. "What do you want?"

The stranger was silent for so long that Chase almost asked the question again. Suddenly, the amusement gone from his voice, the killer said, "You messed in where you had no right messing. You don't know the trouble I went to, picking the proper targets out of all those young fornicators, the ones who most deserved to die. I planned it for weeks, Chase, and I had given that young sinner his just punishment. The slut was left, and you saved her before I could perform my duty, saved a whore like that who had no right to be spared. This is not a good thing."

"You're not well." Chase realized the absurd inadequacy of that statement, but the killer—like all else in the modern world—had reduced him to clichés.

The killer either did not hear or pretended not to hear what Chase had said. "I just wanted to tell you, Mr. Chase, that it doesn't end here. You are not a facilitator of justice."

"What do you mean?"

"I'll deal with you, Chase, once I've researched your background and have weighed a proper judgment on you. Then, when you've been made to pay, I'll deal with the whore, that girl."

"Deal with?" Chase asked.

The euphemism reminded him of the similar evasions of vocabulary to which he had grown accustomed in Nam. He felt much older than he was, more tired than he had been a moment earlier.

"I'm going to kill you, Chase. I'm going to punish you for whatever sins are on your record, because you've interfered with the intended pattern. You are not a facilitator of justice." He was silent. Then: "Do you understand?"

"As much as I understand anything."

"That's all you have to say?"

"What more?" Chase wondered.

"I'll be talking to you again."

"What's the point of this?"

"Facilitation," the killer said—and disconnected.

Chase hung up and leaned back against the headboard of the bed. He felt something cold in his hand, looked down, and was surprised to see the glass of whiskey. He raised it to his lips and took a taste. It was slightly bitter.

He closed his eyes.

So easy not to care.

Or maybe not so easy. If it had been as easy as he wanted it to be, he could have put the whiskey aside and gone to sleep. Or, instead of waiting for the bird-dogger to come after him, he could have blown out his own brains.

Too easy to care. He opened his eyes.

He had to decide what to do about the call.

The police would be interested, of course, because it was a solid lead to the man who had killed Michael Karnes. They would probably want to monitor the telephone line in hope that the killer would call again—especially since he had said that Chase would be hearing from him. They might even station an officer in Chase's room, and they might put a tail on him both for his own protection and to try to nab the murderer.

Yet he hesitated to call Detective Wallace.

The past few weeks, since the news about the Medal of Honor, Chase's daily routine had been destroyed. He loathed the change.

He had been accustomed to deep solitude, disturbed only by his need to talk to store clerks and to Mrs. Fielding, his landlady. In the mornings he went downtown and had breakfast at Woolworth's. He bought a paperback, occasionally a magazine—but never a news-paper—picked up what incidentals he required, stopped twice a week at the liquor store, spent the noon hour in the park watching the girls in their short skirts as they walked to and from their jobs, then went home and passed the rest of the day in his room. He read during the long afternoons, and he drank. By evening he could not clearly see the print on the pages of his book, and he turned on the small television to watch old movies that he had memorized virtually scene by scene. Around eleven o'clock, he finished the day's bottle or portion thereof, after having eaten little or nothing for dinner—and then he slept as long as he could.

It was not much of a life, certainly not what he had once expected, but it was bearable. Because it was simple, it was also solid, safe, empty of doubt and uncertainty, lacking in choices and decisions that might bring about another breakdown.

Then, after the AP and UPI had carried the story of the Vietnam hero who had declined to attend a White House ceremony for the awarding of the Congressional Medal of Honor (though he had not declined the medal itself, since he felt that would bring more publicity than he could handle), there had been no hope of simplicity.

He had weathered the uproar, granting as few interviews as possi-ble, talking in monosyllables on the phone. The only thing for which he had been required to leave his room was the banquet, and he had been able to cope with that only because he knew that once it was over, he could return to his attic apartment and resume the uneventful life that had been wrenched from him.

The incident in lovers' lane had changed his plans, postponed a return to stability. The papers would carry the Medal of Honor story again, with pictures, along with the report of his latest act of foolish interference. There would be more calls, congratulations, interviewers to be turned down.

Then it would die out. In a week or two—if he could tolerate the spotlight that long—things would be as they had once been, quiet and manageable.

He took another swallow of whiskey. It tasted better than it had a short while ago.

There were limits to what he could endure. Two more weeks of newspaper stories, phone calls, job offers, and marriage proposals would take him to the end of his meager resources. During that same time, if he had to share his room with an officer of the law and be followed everywhere he went, he would not hold up.

Already he felt the same vague emptiness arising in him that had filled him so completely in the hospital. It was that profound lack of purpose that he must stave off at all costs. Even if it meant withholding information from the authorities.

He wouldn't tell the police about the call.

He drank more Jack Daniel's.

Good people down there in Tennessee, distilling Jack Daniel's for the solace of the world. Good product. Better than fame or praise or love. And cheaper.

He went to the cupboard and refreshed the glass with another two ounces from the dark bottle.

He worried that he was keeping a lead from the police, but the cops were clever. They would find the man without Chase's assistance. They would find fingerprints on the door handle of the Chevrolet and on the murder weapon. He knew that they had already issued a statement to the effect that the killer would be suffering from a badly bruised throat and resultant laryngitis.

What Chase was keeping from them would do little to speed up their efficient law-enforcement machine.

He knew he was lying to himself.

It wasn't the first time.

He finished his drink. It went down quickly, smoothly.

He poured more whiskey, returned to bed, slid beneath the covers, and stared at the blank eye of the television.

In a few days everything would be back to normal. As normal as this world could ever be. He could settle into old routines, living comfortably on his disability pension and the moderate inheritance from his parents' estate.

He had no need to get a job or to talk to anyone or to make decisions. His only task was to consume enough whiskey to be able to sleep despite the nightmares.

He wasn't lonely: He communed with Jack Daniel's.

He watched the blank television.

Sometimes he felt that the TV was watching him too.

Time passed. It always did.

He slept.

3

CHASE ROSE EARLY THE NEXT MORNING, FRIGHTENED AWAKE BY DEAD men talking to him through mouths full of graveyard soil. After that the day deteriorated.

His mistake was in trying to go on with his day as if the events of the previous night had never happened. He rose, bathed, shaved, dressed, and went downstairs to see if there was any mail on the hall table. There was none, but Mrs. Fielding heard him and hurried out of the perpetually gloomy living room to show him the first edition of the *Press-Dispatch*. His picture was on the front page: He was turning toward Louise Allenby as she got out of a squad car. The girl appeared to be crying, gripping his arm with one hand, looking far more grief stricken than she had actually been.

"I'm so proud of you," Mrs. Fielding said.

She sounded as though she were his mother. Indeed, she was old enough for the post—though whatever mothering instinct she showed always seemed strained and false. Her hair was tightly curled and bleached blond. The excessive rouge and bright lipstick made her seem older than she actually was.

"It wasn't anything like they said, not as exciting as that," Chase told her.

"How do you know? You haven't read it."

"They always exaggerate. Reporters."

"Oh, you're just too modest," Mrs. Fielding said.

She was wearing a blue and yellow housedress with the two top buttons undone. Chase could see the pallid bulge of her breasts and the edge of a lacy yellow brassiere.

Though he was much stronger and much younger than Mrs. Fielding, she frightened him. Perhaps because he could not figure out what she wanted from him.

She seemed to want something more than the rent. More than some companionship. There was a desperation in her—maybe because she herself didn't know what she wanted.

She said, "I bet this brings twice the job offers that the last article brought!"

Mrs. Fielding was much more interested in Chase's eventual employment than was Chase himself. At first he'd thought that she was afraid he would fall in arrears on the rent, but he'd eventually decided that her concern went deeper than that.

She said, "As I've often told you, you're young and strong, and you have a lifetime ahead of you. The thing for a fellow like you is work, hard work, a chance to make something of yourself. Not that you haven't done all right so far. Don't misunderstand me. But this lounging around, not working—it hasn't been good for you. You must have lost fifteen pounds since you first moved in."

Chase did not respond.

Mrs. Fielding moved closer to him and took the morning paper out of his hands. She stared at the picture in the center of the front page and sighed.

"I have to be going," Chase said.

She looked up from the paper. "I *saw* your car."

"Yes."

"Do you like it?"

"It's a car."

"It tells about the car in the paper."

"I suppose it does."

"Wasn't that nice of them?"

"Yes. Very nice."

"They hardly ever do anything for the boys who serve and don't make a big protest of it. You read all about the bad ones, but no one ever lifts a hand for good boys like you. It's about time, and I hope you enjoy the car."

"Thank you," he said, opening the front door and stepping outside, trying not to look as though he were fleeing.

He drove to Woolworth's for breakfast.

The novelty of the car had worn off. He would have preferred to walk. There were too many decisions to make while driving a car. Walking was simpler. Walking, it was easier to shut the mind off and just drift along.

Ordinarily, the lunch counter at Woolworth's was a guarantee of privacy, even when every stool was taken. Businessmen reading the financial pages, secretaries drinking coffee and doing crossword puzzles, laborers hunched over plates of eggs and bacon—all wanted a moment of solitude before the daily hubbub began. Strangely, the elbow-to-elbow proximity fostered a respect for privacy. That Tuesday morning, however, halfway through his meal, Chase discovered that most of the other customers were watching him with only poorly disguised interest.

The ubiquitous newspaper with the front-page photograph had betrayed him.

He stopped eating, left a tip, paid his check, and got out of there. His hands were shaking, and the backs of his knees quivered as if his legs would fail him.

He didn't like being watched. He didn't even like being smiled at by a waitress or a clerk. His preference was to go through life as one of those nondescript men whom people looked *through*.

When he went to the newsstand around the corner from Woolworth's to purchase a paperback, he was confronted with so many images of his face in the newspaper racks that he turned away at the door without going in.

At the nearby liquor store, for the first time in months, the clerk commented on the size of the whiskey purchase. Clearly, he felt that a man like Chase shouldn't be buying so much booze. Unless, of course, the whiskey was for a party.

"Giving a party?" the clerk asked.

"Yeah."

Anxious for the barren confines of his little attic room, Chase walked two blocks toward home before he remembered that he now owned a car. He walked back to it, embarrassed that someone might have seen his confusion.

When he settled behind the wheel, he felt too tightly wound to risk driving. He sat for fifteen minutes, paging through the service manual and the ownership papers before finally starting the engine and pulling away from the curb.

He didn't go to the park to watch the girls on their lunch hour, because he feared recognition. If someone tried to strike up a conversation, he would not know what to say.

In his room, he poured a glass of whiskey over two ice cubes and stirred it with his finger.

He turned on the television and found an old movie starring Wallace Beery and Marie Dressler. He'd seen it at least half a dozen times, but he kept it on just the same. The repetition, the dependable order of the sequential scenes—through thousands of showings in movie theaters and on television—gave him a sense of stability and soothed his nerves. He watched Wallace Beery's clumsy romantic pass at Marie Dressler, and the familiarity of Beery's antics, seen so often before and in that same exact detail, was like a balm on his troubled mind.

At five minutes past eleven the telephone rang.

He finally answered it, declined to do a press interview, and hung up.

At eleven-twenty-six it rang again.

This time it was the insurance agent with whom the Merchants' Association had taken out a year's policy on the Mustang. He wanted to know if the coverage was adequate or whether Chase would like to increase it for a nominal sum. He was chatty at first but less so when Chase said that the coverage was adequate.

At eleven-fifty the phone rang a third time. When Chase answered, the killer said, "Hello, how has your morning been?" His voice was hoarse, hardly louder than a whisper.

"Not good."

"Did you see the papers?"

"One."

454 STRANGE HIGHWAYS

"Lovely coverage."
Chase said nothing.
The man said, "Most people want fame."
"Not me."
"Some people would kill for it."
"You?"
"I'm not after fame," said the killer.
"What are you after?"
"Meaning, purpose."
"There is none."
The killer was silent. Then: "You're a strange egg, Mr. Chase."
Chase relied on silence.
"Be by your phone at six o'clock this evening, Mr. Chase. It's important."
"I'm tired of this."
"*You're* tired? *I'm* doing all the work here. I've spent the morning researching your background, and I have similar plans for the afternoon. At six I'll tell you what I've found."
Chase said, "Why?"
"I can't very well pass judgment on you until I know what sort of transgressions you're guilty of, can I?" Under the pervading wheeze of protesting vocal cords lay a trace of the amusement that Chase had previously noticed. "You see, I didn't randomly select which fornicators I would punish up on Kanackaway."
"You didn't?"
"No, I researched the situation. I went up there every night for two weeks and copied license-plate numbers. Then I matched them until I found the one most often repeated."
"Why?"
"To discover the most deserving sinners," the stranger said. "In this state, for two dollars, the Bureau of Motor Vehicles will trace a license number for you. I had that done and learned the identity of the boy who owned the car. From there it was a simple matter to investigate his background and to learn the name of his partner in these activities." The formality of his speech led him into odd locutions—or evasions. "She wasn't the only young woman he entertained on Kanackaway, even though she thought he was seeing no one else. She had her own promiscuous affairs too. I followed her

twice when other boys picked her up, and one of those times she gave herself to the date."

"Why don't you just stay home and watch old movies?" Chase wondered.

"What?"

"Or seek counseling."

"I'm not in need of counseling. This sick *world* is in need of counseling. The *world*, not me." His anger sent him into another coughing fit. Then: "They were both sluts, the boy as well as the girl. They deserved what they got—except she didn't get hers, thanks to you."

Chase waited.

The man said, "You see, I must research you as thoroughly as I did those two. Otherwise, I would never be sure if you deserved the judgment of death or whether I'd eliminated you simply because you'd interfered with my plans and I wanted revenge. In short, I'm not killing people. I'm executing those who deserve it."

Chase said, "I don't want you calling here again."

"Yes, you do."

Chase didn't reply.

"I'm your motivation," said the killer.

"My motivation?"

"There's a destiny here."

"My motivation to do what?"

"That," said the killer, "is for you to decide."

"I'll have the line bugged."

"That won't stop me," the stranger said, again amused. "I'll simply place the phone calls from various booths around the city, and I'll keep them too short to trace."

"If I refuse to answer my phone?"

"You'll answer it. Six o'clock this evening," he reminded Chase, and he hung up.

Chase dropped the receiver, uneasily aware that the killer knew him better than he knew himself. He would answer every time, of course. And for the same reasons that he had answered all the nuisance calls of the last few weeks rather than obtain an unlisted number. The only problem was that he didn't know just what those reasons were.

Impulsively, he lifted the receiver and placed a call to the police headquarters downtown. It was the first time in ten and a half months that he had initiated a call.

When the desk sergeant answered, Chase asked for Detective Wallace.

Wallace came on the line a moment later. "Yes, Mr. Chase, can I help you?"

Chase didn't mention the calls from the killer—which had been why he thought he'd phoned Wallace. Instead he asked, "How's the investigation coming along?"

Wallace was not averse to talking shop. "Slowly but surely. We found prints on the knife. If he's ever been arrested for a serious crime or worked for any branch of government, we'll have him soon."

"And if he's never been printed?"

Wallace said, "We'll get him anyway. We found a man's ring in the Chevy. It didn't belong to the dead boy, and it looks as if it would be too small for your fingers by a size or three. Didn't lose a ring, did you?"

"No," Chase said.

"I thought so. Should have called you on it, but I was pretty sure about it. It's his, right enough."

"Anything else besides the prints and ring?"

"We're keeping a constant watch on the girl and her parents, though I'd appreciate it if you didn't say anything about that to anyone."

"You think he might try for her?"

"Maybe. If he thinks she can identify him. You know, it's occurred to me that we wouldn't be far off if we gave you a tail as well. Have you thought of that?"

Alarmed out of proportion by the suggestion, Chase said, "No. I don't see what value that would have."

"Well, the story was in the papers this morning. He probably doesn't fear you identifying him as much as he does the girl, but he might bear a grudge against you."

"Grudge? He'd have to be nuts."

Wallace laughed. "Well, if not nuts, what *is* he?"

"You mean you've found no motives from questioning the girl, no old lovers who might have—"

"No," Wallace said. "Right now we're operating on the assumption there's no rational motive, that he's psychotic."

"I see."

"Well," Wallace said, "I'm sorry there isn't more solid news."

"And I'm sorry to have bothered you," Chase said.

He hung up without telling Wallace about the calls that he had received from the killer, though he had intended to spill it all. A twenty-four-hour guard on the girl. They would do the same to him, if they knew that he'd been contacted.

The walls seemed to sway, alternately closing in like the jaws of an immense vise and swinging away from him as if they were flat gray gates. The floor rose and fell—or seemed to.

A sense of extreme instability overcame him, a sense that the world was not a solid place but as fluid as a shimmering mirage: the very thing that had landed him in the hospital and had eventually led to his seventy-five-percent disability pension. He could not let it grip him again, and he knew that the best way to fight it was to constrict the perimeters of his world, take solace from solitude. He got another drink.

The telephone woke him from his nap just as the dead men touched him with soft, white, corrupted hands.

He sat straight up in bed and cried out, his arms held before him to ward off their cold touch.

When he saw where he was and that he was alone, he sank back, exhausted, and listened to the phone. After thirty rings, he had no choice but to pick it up.

"Yes."

"I was about to come check on you," Mrs. Fielding said. "Are you all right?"

"I'm okay,"

"It took you so long to answer."

"I was asleep."

She hesitated, as if framing what she was about to say. "I'm having Swiss steak, mushrooms, baked corn, and mashed potatoes for supper. Would you like to come down? There's more than I can use."

"I don't think—"

"A strapping boy like you needs his regular meals."

"I've already eaten."

She was silent. Then she said, "All right. But I wish you'd waited, 'cause I got all this food."

"I'm sorry, but I'm stuffed," he said.

"Tomorrow night, maybe."

"Maybe," he said. He rang off before she could suggest a late-night snack together.

The ice melted in his glass, diluting what whiskey he had not drunk. He emptied the watered booze into the bathroom sink, got new ice and a new shot of liquor. It tasted as sour as a bite of lemon rind. He drank it anyway. The cupboard and refrigerator contained nothing else but a bag of Winesap apples.

He turned on the small black-and-white television again and slowly cycled through all the local channels. Nothing but news, news, news, and a cartoon program. He watched the cartoons.

None was amusing.

After the cartoons, he watched an old movie.

Except for the telephone call he'd been told to expect at six o'clock, he had the whole evening ahead of him.

At six o'clock on the nose, the phone rang.

"Hello?"

"Good evening, Chase," the killer said. His voice was still rough.

Chase sat on the bed.

"How are you tonight?" the killer asked.

"Okay."

"You know what I've been up to all day?"

"Research."

"That's right."

"Tell me what you found," Chase said, as if it would be news to him even though he was the subject. And maybe it *would* be.

"First, you were born here a little over twenty-four years ago on June eleventh, 1947, in Mercy Hospital. Your parents died in an auto accident a couple of years ago. You went to school at State and graduated in a three-year accelerated program, having majored in business administration. You did well in all subjects except a few required courses, chiefly Basic Physical Sciences, Biology One and Two, Chemistry One, and Basic Composition." The killer whispered on for two or three minutes, reciting biographical facts that Chase had thought private. Courthouse records, college files, newspaper morgues, and half a dozen other sources had provided the killer with far more information about Chase's life than could have been gleaned merely from the recent articles in the *Press-Dispatch.*

"I think I've been on the line too long," the killer said. "It's time I went to another booth. Is your phone tapped, Chase?"

"No."

"Just the same, I'll hang up now and call you back in a few minutes." The line went dead.

Five minutes later the killer called again.

"What I gave you before was just so much dry grass, Chase. But let me add a few more things and do some speculating. Let's see if I can add a match to it."

"Whatever you have to do."

"For one thing," the man said, "you inherited a lot of money, but you haven't spent much of it."

"Not a lot."

"Forty thousand after taxes, but you live frugally."

"How would you know that?"

"I drove by your house today and discovered that you live in a furnished apartment on the third floor. When I saw you coming home, it was apparent that you don't spend much on clothes. Until that pretty new Mustang, you didn't have a car. It follows, then, that you must have a great deal of your inheritance left, what with the monthly disability pension from the government to pay most or all of your bills."

"I want you to stop checking on me."

The man laughed. "Can't stop. Remember the necessity to evaluate your moral content before passing judgment, Mr. Chase."

Chase hung up this time. Having taken the initiative cheered him a little. When the phone began to ring again, he summoned the will not to answer it. After thirty rings, it stopped.

When the ringing began again, ten minutes later, he finally picked it up and said hello.

The killer was furious, straining his damaged throat to the limit. "If you ever do that to me again, then I'll make sure it isn't a quick, clean kill. I'll see to that. You understand me?"

Chase was silent.

"Mr. Chase?" A beat. "What's *wrong* with you?"

"Wish I knew," Chase said.

The stranger decided to let his anger go, and he fell into his previous tone of forced irony: "That 'wounded in action' bit excites me, Mr. Chase. That part of your biography. Because you don't appear disabled enough to deserve a pension, and you more than held your own in our fight. That gives me ideas, makes me think your most serious wounds aren't physical at all."

"Whose are?"

"I think you had psychological problems that put you in that army hospital and got you a discharge."

Chase said nothing.

"And you tell *me* that I need counseling. I'll have to take more time to check in to this. Very interesting. Well, rest easy tonight, Mr. Chase. You're not scheduled to die yet."

"Wait."

"Yes?"

"I have to have a name for you. I can't go on thinking of you in totally impersonal terms like 'the man' and 'the stranger' and 'the killer.' Do you see how that is?"

"Yes," the man admitted.

"A name?"

He considered. Then he said, "You can call me Judge."

"Judge?"

"Yes, as in 'judge, jury, and executioner.'" He laughed until he coughed, and then he hung up as if he were just an anonymous prankster who had phoned to ask if Chase had Prince Albert in a can.

Chase went to the refrigerator and got an apple. He peeled it and cut it into eight sections, chewing each thoroughly. It wasn't much of a dinner. But there were a lot of energy-giving calories in a glass of whiskey, so he poured a few ounces over ice, for dessert.

He washed his hands, which had become sticky with apple juice. He would have washed them even if they hadn't been sticky. He washed his hands frequently. Ever since Nam. Sometimes he washed them so often in a single day that they became red and chapped.

With another drink, he went to the bed and watched a movie on TV. He tried not to think about anything except the satisfying daily routines to which he was accustomed: breakfast at Woolworth's, paperback novels, old movies on television, the forty thousand of go-to-hell money in his savings account, his pension check, and the good folks in Tennessee who made Jack Daniel's. Those were the things that counted, that made his small world satisfying and safe.

Again, he refrained from calling the police.

4

THE NIGHTMARES WERE SO BAD THAT CHASE SLEPT FITFULLY, WAKING repeatedly at the penultimate moment of horror, as he was surrounded by the tight circle of dead men, as their silent accusations began, as they closed in on him with their hands outstretched.

He rose early, abandoning any hope of rest. He bathed, shaved, and washed his hands with special attention to the dirt under his fingernails.

He sat at the table and peeled an apple for breakfast. He did not want to face the regular customers at Woolworth's lunch counter now that he was more than just another face to them, yet he couldn't think of any place where he might go unrecognized.

It was nine-thirty-five, much too early to begin drinking. He observed few rules, but never drinking before lunch was one of them. He seldom broke that one. Afternoons and evenings were for drinking. Mornings were for remorse, regret, and silent repentance.

But what could he do with the long hours until noon? Filling time without drinking was increasingly difficult.

He turned on the television but couldn't find any old movies. Turned it off.

At last, with nothing to do, he began to recall the details of the nightmare that had awakened him, and that was no good. That was dangerous.

He picked up the phone and placed another call.

It rang three times before a pert young woman answered. She said, "Dr. Fauvel's office, Miss Pringle speaking, can I help you?"

Chase said, "I'd like to see the doctor."

"Are you a regular patient?"

"Yes. My name's Ben Chase."

"Oh, yes!" Miss Pringle gasped, as though it was a small joy to be hearing from him. "Good morning, Mr. Chase." She rattled the pages of an appointment book. "Your regularly scheduled visit is this Friday afternoon at three."

"I have to see Dr. Fauvel before that."

"Tomorrow morning we have half an hour—"

Chase interrupted her. "Today."

"I beg your pardon?" Miss Pringle's pleasure at hearing his voice seemed to have diminished appreciably.

"I want an appointment today," Chase repeated.

Miss Pringle informed him of the heavy workload that the doctor carried and of the numerous extra hours in each day that the doctor required to study case histories of new patients.

"Please call Dr. Fauvel himself," Chase said, "and see if he can find time for me."

"Dr. Fauvel is in the middle of an appointment—"

"I'll hold."

"But it's impossible to—"

"I'll wait."

With a sigh of exasperation, she put him on hold. A minute later, chagrined, Miss Pringle returned to the phone to tell Chase that he had an appointment at four o'clock this afternoon. Clearly, she was perturbed that the rules should be broken for him. She must have known that the government paid the tab and that Fauvel received less compensation than he would have received from one of the wealthy neurotics on his patient list.

If one had to be psychologically disturbed, it helped to have a *unique* disturbance that intrigued the doctor—and a measure of fame or infamy to ensure special treatment.

⊰ ∧ ⊱

At eleven-thirty, while Chase was dressing to go out for lunch, Judge called again. His voice sounded better, although still far from normal. "How are you feeling this morning, Mr. Chase?"

Chase waited.

"Be expecting a call at six this evening," Judge said.

"From whom?"

"Very funny. At six o'clock sharp, Mr. Chase." Judge spoke with the smooth authority of a man accustomed to being obeyed. "I will have several interesting points to discuss with you, I'm sure. Have a good day now."

⊲ ⋏ ⊳

The inner office of Fauvel's suite on the eighth floor of the Kaine Building, in the center of the city, did not resemble the standard psychiatrist's therapy room as portrayed in countless films and books. For one thing, it was not small and intimate, not at all reminiscent of the womb. It was a pleasantly large space, perhaps thirty feet by thirty-five, with a high shadow-shrouded ceiling. Two walls held bookshelves floor to ceiling; one wall was dressed with paintings of tranquil country scenes, and the fourth was all windows. The bookshelves contained a handful of expensively bound volumes— and perhaps three hundred glass dogs, none larger than the palm of a man's hand and most a good deal smaller. Collecting glass dogs was Dr. Fauvel's hobby.

Just as the decor of the room—battered desk, heavily padded armchairs, foot-scarred coffee table—didn't match its function, Dr. Fauvel was unlike any stereotypical image of a psychiatrist, whether by intent or by nature. He was a small but solidly built man, athletic-looking, with hair that spilled over his collar in a manner that suggested carelessness rather than style. He always always wore a blue suit cut too long in the trousers and in need of a hot iron.

"Sit down, Ben," Fauvel said. "Like something to drink—coffee, tea, a Coke?"

"No, thank you," Chase said.

No couch was provided. The doctor did not believe in pampering his patients. Chase sat in an armchair.

Fauvel settled into the chair to Chase's right and propped his feet on the coffee table. He urged Chase to follow suit. When they were in a pose of relaxation, he said, "No preliminaries, then?"

"Not today," Chase said.

"You're tense, Ben."

"Yes."

"Something's happened."

"Yes."

"But that's life. Something always happens. We don't live in stasis, frozen in amber."

"This is more than the usual something," Chase said.

"Tell me about it."

Chase was silent.

"You came here to tell me, didn't you?" Fauvel urged.

"Yeah. But. . . . talking about a problem sometimes makes it worse."

"That's never true."

"Maybe not for you."

"Not for anyone."

"To talk about it, I have to think about it, and thinking about it makes me nervous. I like things calm. Still and calm."

"Want to play some word association?"

Chase hesitated, then nodded, dreading the game that they often used to loosen his tongue. He frequently exposed more of himself in his answers than he wished to reveal. And Fauvel did not play the game according to established rules, but with a swift and vicious directness that cut to the heart of the matter. Nevertheless, Chase said, "Go on."

Fauvel said, "Mother."

"Dead."

"Father."

"Dead."

Fauvel steepled his fingers as if he were a child playing the see-the-church game. "Love."

"Woman."

"Love."

"Woman," Chase repeated.

Fauvel did not look at him but stared studiously at the blue glass terrier on the bookshelf nearest him. "Don't repeat yourself, please."

Chase apologized, aware that it was expected. The first time that Fauvel had expected an apology in these circumstances, Chase had been surprised. They were therapist and patient, after all, and it seemed odd for the therapist to foster a dependent relationship in which the patient was encouraged to feel guilty for evasive answers.

Session by session, however, he was less surprised at anything that Fauvel might suggest.

The doctor again said, "Love."

"Woman."

"Love."

"Woman."

"I asked you not to repeat yourself."

"I'm not a latent homosexual, if that's what you're after."

Fauvel said, "But the simple 'woman' is an evasion."

"Everything is an evasion."

That observation appeared to surprise the doctor, but not enough to jar him out of the stubborn, wearying routine that he had begun. "Yes, everything is an evasion. But in this case it's an egregious evasion, because there *is* no woman. You won't allow one into your life. So, more honesty, if you will. Love."

Already Chase was perspiring, and he did not know why.

"Love," Fauvel insisted.

"Is a many splendored thing."

"Unacceptable childishness."

"Sorry."

"Love."

Chase finally said, "Myself."

"But that's a lie, isn't it?"

"Yes."

"Because you don't love yourself."

"No."

"Very good," Fauvel said. Now the interchange of words went faster, one barked close after the other, as if speed counted in the scoring. Fauvel said, "Hate."

"You."

"Funny."

"Thanks."

"Hate."

"Self-destructive."

"Another evasion. Hate."

"Army."

"Hate."

"Vietnam."

"Hate."

"Guns."

"Hate."

"Zacharia," Chase said, although he had often sworn never to mention that name again or to remember the man attached to it or, indeed, to recall the events that the man had perpetrated.

"Hate," Fauvel persisted.

"Another word, please."

"No. Hate."

"Lieutenant Zacharia."

"It goes deeper than Zacharia."

"I know."

"Hate."

"Me," Chase said.

"And that's the truth, isn't it?"

"Yes."

After a silence, the doctor said, "Okay, let's back up from you to Zacharia. Do you remember what Lieutenant Zacharia ordered you to do, Benjamin?"

"Yes, sir."

"What were those orders?"

"We'd sealed off two back entrances to a Cong tunnel system."

"And?"

"Lieutenant Zacharia ordered me to clear the last entrance."

"How did you accomplish that?"

"With a grenade, sir."

"And?"

"And then before the air around the tunnel face could clear, I went forward."

"And?"

"And used a machine gun."

"Good."

"Not so good, sir."

"Good that you can at least talk about it."

Chase was silent.

"What happened then, Benjamin?"

"Then we went down, sir."

"We?"

"Lieutenant Zacharia, Sergeant Coombs, Privates Halsey and Wade, a couple of other men."

"And you."

"Yeah. Me."

"Then?"

"In the tunnel, we found four dead men and parts of men lying in the foyer of the complex. Lieutenant Zacharia ordered a cautious advance. A hundred fifty yards along, we came to a bamboo gate."

"Blocking the way.

"Yeah. Villagers behind it."

"Tell me about the villagers."

"Mostly women."

"How many women, Ben?"

"Maybe twenty."

"Children?" Fauvel asked.

Silence was a refuge.

"Were there children?"

Chase sank down in the heavy padding of the armchair, shoulders drawn up as if he wished to hide between them. "A few."

"They were imprisoned there?"

"No. The bamboo was an obstacle. The Cong tunnels ran a lot deeper than that, a lot farther. We hadn't even reached the weapons cache. The villagers were assisting the Vietcong, collaborating with them, obstructing us."

"Do you think they were forced to obstruct you, forced by the Vietcong . . . or were they willing agents of the enemy?"

Chase was silent.

"I'm waiting for an answer," Fauvel said sternly.

Chase didn't reply.

"*You* are waiting for an answer," Fauvel told him, "whether you realize it or not. Were these villagers being forced to obstruct your advance, forced at gunpoint by the Cong in the tunnels behind them, or were they there at their own choice?"

"Hard to say."

"Is it?"

"Hard for me, anyway."

"In those situations you could never be sure."

"Right."

"They might have been collaborationists—or they might have been innocent."

"Right."

"Okay. Then what happened?"

"We tried to open the gate, but the women were holding it shut with a system of ropes."

"Women."

"They used women as a shield. Or sometimes the women were the worst killers of all, cut you down with a smile."

"So you ordered them out of the way?" Fauvel asked.

"They wouldn't move. The lieutenant said it might be a trap designed to contain us at that point, delay us long enough for the Cong to somehow get behind us."

"Could that have been true?"

"Could have been."

"Likely?"

"Yes."

"Go on."

"It was dark. There was a smell in that tunnel I can't explain, made up of sweat and urine and rotting vegetables, as heavy as if it had substance. Lieutenant Zacharia ordered us to open fire and clear the way."

"Did you comply?"

Chase was silent.

"Did you comply?"

"Not immediately."

"But eventually?"

"The stench . . . the darkness . . ."

"You complied."

"So claustrophobic down there, Cong probably coming around behind us through a secret tunnel."

"So you complied with the order?"

"Yes."

"You personally—or the squad?"

"The squad and me. Everyone did."

"You shot them."

"Cleared the way."

"Shot them."

"We could have died there."

"Shot them."

"Yeah."

Fauvel gave him a rest. Half a minute. Then: "Later, when the tunnel had been cleared, searched, the weapons cache destroyed, then you ran into the ambush that earned you the Medal of Honor."

"Yes. That was above ground."

Fauvel said, "You crawled across the field of fire for nearly two hundred yards and brought back a wounded sergeant named Coombs."

"Samuel Coombs."

"You received two minor but painful wounds in the thigh and calf of your right leg, but you didn't stop crawling until you had reached shelter. Then you secured Coombs behind a stand of scrub, and having reached a point on the enemy's flank by means of your heroic crossing of the open field—what happened?"

"I killed some of the bastards."

"Enemy soldiers."

"Yeah."

"How many?"

"Eighteen."

"Eighteen Vietcong soldiers?"

"Yeah."

"So you not only saved Sergeant Coombs's life but contributed substantially to the well-being of your entire unit." He had only slightly paraphrased the wording on the scroll that Chase had received in the mail from the president himself.

Chase said nothing.

"You see where this heroism came from, Ben?"

"We've talked about it before."

"So you know the answer."

"It came from guilt."

"That's right."

"Because I wanted to die. Subconsciously wanted to be killed, so I rushed onto the field of fire, hoping to be shot down."

"Do you believe that analysis, or do you think maybe it's just something I made up to degrade your medal?"

Chase said, "I believe it. I never wanted the medal in the first place."

"Now," Fauvel said, unsteepling his fingers, "let's extend that analysis just a bit. Though you hoped to be shot and killed in that ambush, although you took absurd risks to ensure your death, you lived. And became a national hero."

"Life's funny, huh?"

"When you learned Lieutenant Zacharia had submitted your name for consideration for the Medal of Honor, you suffered a nervous breakdown that hospitalized you and eventually led to your honorable discharge."

"I was just burnt out."

"No, the breakdown was an attempt to punish yourself, once you'd failed to get yourself killed. Punish yourself and escape from your guilt. But the breakdown failed too, because you pulled out of it. Well regarded, honorably discharged, much too strong not to recover psychologically, you still had to carry your burden of guilt."

Chase was silent again.

Fauvel continued: "Perhaps when you chanced upon that scene in the park on Kanackaway, you recognized another opportunity to punish yourself. You must have realized that there was a strong possibility you'd be hurt or killed, and you must have subconsciously anticipated your death agreeably enough."

"You're wrong," Chase said.

Fauvel was silent.

"You're wrong," Chase repeated.

"Probably not," Fauvel said with a hint of impatience, and he used a direct stare to try to make Chase uncomfortable.

"It wasn't like that at all. I had thirty pounds on him, and I knew what I was doing. He was an amateur. He had no hope of really hurting me."

Fauvel said nothing.

Finally Chase said, "Sorry."

Fauvel smiled. "Well, you aren't a psychiatrist, so we can't expect you to see into it so clearly. You aren't detached from it like I am." He cleared his throat, looked back at the blue terrier. "Now that we've come this far—why did you solicit this extra session, Ben?"

Once he began, Chase found the telling easy. In ten minutes he had related the events of the previous day and repeated, almost word for word, the conversations that he'd had with Judge.

When Chase finished, Fauvel asked, "So. What do you want from me, then?"

"I want to know how to handle it, some advice."

"I don't advise. I guide and interpret."

"Some guidance then. When Judge calls, it's more than just the threats that upset me. It's—this feeling I have of being detached, separated from everything."

"Another breakdown?"

"I feel the edge," Chase said.

Fauvel said, "Ignore him."

"Judge?"

"Ignore him."

"But don't I have a responsibility to—"

"Ignore him."

"I can't."

"You must," Fauvel said.

"What if he's serious?"

"He's not."

"What if he's really going to kill me?"

"He won't."

"How can you be sure?" Chase was perspiring heavily. Great dark circles stained the underarms of his shirt and plastered the cotton to his back.

Fauvel smiled at the blue terrier and shifted his gaze to a glass greyhound blown in amber. The smug, self-assured look was back. "I can be so sure of that, because Judge does not exist."

Chase did not immediately understand the reply. When he grasped the import of it, he didn't like it. "You're saying what—that this Judge isn't real?"

"Is that what you're saying, Chase?"

"No."

"You're the one who said it."

"I didn't hallucinate him. None of this. The part about the murder and the girl are in the papers."

"Oh, that was real enough," Fauvel said. "But these phone calls . . . I don't know. What do you think, Chase?"

Chase was silent.

"Were they real phone calls?"

"Yes."

"Or imagination?"

"No."

"Delusions of—"

"No."

Fauvel said, "I've noticed for some time that you have begun to shake off this unnatural desire for privacy and that you're gradually facing the world more squarely, week by week."

"I haven't noticed that."

"Oh, yes. Subtly, perhaps, but you've grown curious about the rest of the world. You're beginning to be restless about getting on with life."

Chase didn't feel restless.

He felt cornered.

"Perhaps you're even beginning to experience a reawakening of your sex drive, though not much yet. Guilt overwhelmed you, because you hadn't been punished for the things that happened in that tunnel, and you didn't want to lead a normal life until you felt that you'd suffered enough."

Chase disliked the doctor's smug self-assurance. Right now all he wanted was to get out of there, to get home and close the door and open the bottle.

Fauvel said, "You couldn't accept the fact that you wanted to taste the good things of life again, and you invented Judge because he represented the remaining possibility of punishment. You had to make some excuses for being forced into life again, and Judge worked well in this respect too. You would, sooner or later, have to take the initiative to stop him. You could pretend that you still wanted seclusion in which to mourn but were no longer being permitted that indulgence."

"All wrong," Chase said. "Judge is real."

"Oh, I think not." Fauvel smiled at the amber greyhound. "If you really and truly thought this man was real, that these calls to you were real—then why wouldn't you go to the police rather than to your psychiatrist?"

Chase had no answer. "You're twisting things."

"No. Just showing you the straight truth."

"He's real."

Fauvel stood and stretched. "I recommend you go home and forget Judge. You don't need an excuse to live like a normal human being. You *have* suffered enough, Ben, more than enough. You made a terrible mistake. All right. But in that tunnel, you were in an incredibly stressful situation, under unendurable pressures. It was a *mistake,* not a calculated savagery. For the lives you took, you saved others. Remember that."

Chase stood, bewildered, no longer perfectly sure that he did know what was real and what was not.

Fauvel put his arm around Chase's shoulders and walked him to the door. "Friday at three," the doctor said. "Let's see how far out of your hole you've come by then. I think you're going to make it, Ben. Don't despair."

Miss Pringle escorted him to the outer door of the waiting room and closed it after him, leaving him alone in the hallway.

"Judge is real," Chase said to no one at all. "Isn't he?"

5

AT SIX O'CLOCK, CHASE WAS SITTING ON THE EDGE OF HIS BED BY THE nightstand and telephone, sipping Jack Daniel's. He put the drink down, wiped his sweaty hands on his slacks, cleared his throat so that his voice wouldn't catch when he tried to speak.

At five minutes past six he began to feel uneasy. He thought of going downstairs to ask Mrs. Fielding what time her clocks showed, in the event that his own was not functioning properly. He refrained from doing so only because he was afraid of missing the call while downstairs.

At six-fifteen he washed his hands.

At six-thirty he went to the cupboard, took down his whiskey bottle of the day—which he'd barely touched—and poured a glassful. He did not put it away again. He read the label, which he had studied a hundred times before, then carried his drink back to the bed.

By seven o'clock he was feeling the liquor. He settled back against the headboard and finally considered what Fauvel had said: that there was no Judge, that he had been illusory, a psychological mechanism for rationalizing the gradual diminishment of Chase's guilt complex. He tried to think about that, to study the meaning of it, but he could not be sure if this was a good or a bad development.

In the bathroom, he drew a tub of warm water and tested it until it was just right. He folded a damp washcloth on the wide porcelain rim of the tub and placed his drink on that. The whiskey, the water, and the rising steam conspired to make him feel as though he were floating up into soft clouds. He leaned back until his head touched the wall, closed his eyes, and tried not to think about anything— especially blocking all thoughts of Judge and the Medal of Honor and the nine months that he had spent on active duty in Nam.

Unfortunately, he began to think of Louise Allenby, the girl whose life he had saved, and in his mind's eye he saw her small, trembling, bare breasts, which had looked so inviting in the weak light of the car in lovers' lane. The thought, though pleasant enough, was unfortunate because it contributed to his first erection in nearly a year. That development was perhaps desirable; he wasn't sure. But it seemed inappropriate, given the hideous circumstances in which he'd seen the girl half undressed. He was reminded of the blood in the car—and the blood reminded him of the reasons for his recent inability to function as a man. Those reasons were still so formidable that he couldn't face them alone. The erection was short-lived, and when it was gone, he wasn't certain if it indicated an eventual end to his psychological impotency or whether it had resulted only from the warm water.

He got out of the water when his whiskey glass was empty. He was toweling himself when the telephone rang.

The electric clock showed two minutes past eight.

Naked, he sat on the bed and answered the phone.

"Sorry I'm late," Judge said.

Dr. Fauvel had been wrong.

"I thought you weren't going to call," Chase said.

"I required a little more time than I'd expected to locate some information on you."

"What information?"

Judge ignored the question, intent on proceeding in his own fashion. "So you see a psychiatrist once a week, do you?"

Chase did not reply.

"That alone is fairly good proof that the accusation I made yesterday is true—that your disability pension is for mental, not physical, injuries."

Chase wished that he had a drink with him, but he could not ask Judge to hold on while he poured one. For reasons that he could not explain, he didn't want Judge to know that he drank heavily.

Chase said, "How did you find out?"

"Followed you this afternoon," Judge said.

"Bold."

"The righteous can afford to be bold."

"Of course."

Judge laughed as if delighted with himself. "I saw you going into the Kaine Building, and I got into the lobby fast enough to see which elevator you took and which floor you got off at. On the eighth floor, besides Dr. Fauvel's offices, there are two dentists and three insurance companies. It was simple enough to look in the waiting rooms of those other places and inquire after you, like a friend, with the secretaries and receptionists. I left the shrink's place for last, because I just *knew* that's where you were. When no one knew you in the other offices, I didn't have to risk glancing in Fauvel's waiting room. I knew."

Chase said, "So what?"

He hoped that he sounded more nonchalant than he felt, for it was somehow important to make the right impression on Judge. He was sweating again. He would need to take another bath by the time this conversation was concluded. And he would need a drink, a cold drink.

"As soon as I knew you were in the psychiatrist's office," Judge said, "I decided I had to obtain copies of his personal files on you. I remained in the building, out of sight in a maintenance closet, until all the offices were closed and the employees went home."

"I don't believe you," Chase said, aware of what was coming, dreading to hear it.

"You don't *want* to believe me, but you do." Judge took a long, slow breath before he continued: "The eighth floor was clear by six o'clock. By six-thirty I got the door open to Dr. Fauvel's suite. I know a little about such things, and I was very careful. I didn't damage the lock, and I didn't trip any alarms because there were none. I required an additional half an hour to locate his files and to secure your records, which I copied on his photocopier."

"Breaking and entering—then theft," Chase said.

"But it hardly matters on top of murder, does it?"

"You admit that what you've done is murder."

"No. Judgment. But the authorities don't understand. They call it murder. They're part of the problem. They're not good facilitators."

Chase said nothing.

"You'll receive in the mail, probably the day after tomorrow, complete copies of Dr. Fauvel's notes on you, along with copies of several articles he's written for various medical journals. You're mentioned in all these and are, in some of them, the sole subject of discussion. Not by name. 'Patient C,' he calls you. But it's clearly you."

Chase said, "I didn't know he'd done that."

"They're interesting articles, Chase. They'll give you some idea of what he thinks of you." Judge's tone changed, became more contemptuous. "Reading those records, Chase, I found more than enough to permit me to pass judgment on you."

"Oh?"

"I read all about how you got your Medal of Honor."

Chase waited.

"And I read about the tunnels and what you did in them—and how you failed to expose Lieutenant Zacharia when he destroyed the evidence and falsified the report. Do you think the Congress would have voted you the Medal of Honor if they knew you killed civilians, Chase?"

"Stop."

"You killed women, didn't you?"

"Maybe."

"You killed women and children, Chase, noncombatants."

"I'm not sure if I killed anyone," Chase said more to himself than to Judge. "I pulled the trigger . . . but I was . . . firing wildly at the walls . . . I don't know."

"Noncombatants."

"You don't know what it was like."

"Children, Chase."

"You know nothing about me."

"You killed children. What kind of animal are you, Chase?"

"Fuck you!" Chase had come to his feet as if something had exploded close behind him. "What would you know about it? Were you ever over there, did you ever have to serve in that stinking country?"

"Some patriotic paean to duty won't change my mind, Chase. We all love this country, but most of us realize there are limits to—"

"Bullshit," Chase said.

He could not remember having been this angry in all the time since his breakdown. Now and then he had been irritated by something or someone, but he had never allowed himself to feel extremes of emotion.

"Chase—"

"I bet you were all for the war. I'll bet you're one of the people that made it possible for me to be there in the first place. It's easy to set standards of performance, select limits of right and wrong, when you never get closer than ten thousand miles to the place where it's all coming down."

Judge tried to speak, but Chase talked him down:

"I didn't even *want* to be there. I didn't believe in it, and I was scared shitless the whole time. All I thought about was staying alive. In that tunnel, I couldn't think of anything else. I wasn't *me*. I was a textbook case of paranoia, living in blind terror, just trying to get through."

He had never spoken about the experience so directly or at such length to anyone, not even to Fauvel, who had pried his story from him in single words and sentence fragments.

"You're eaten with guilt," Judge said.

"That doesn't matter."

"I think it does. It proves you know you did wrong and you—"

"It *doesn't* matter, because regardless of how guilty I feel, you haven't the right to pass judgment on me. You're sitting there with your little list of commandments, but you've never been anywhere that made a list seem pointless, anywhere that circumstances forced you to act in a way you loathed."

Chase was amazed to realize that he was crying. He had not cried in a long time.

"You're rationalizing," Judge began, trying to regain control of the conversation. "You're a despicable, murdering—"

Chase said, "You've not exactly followed that commandment yourself. You killed Michael Karnes."

"There was a difference," Judge said. Some of the hoarseness had returned to his voice.

"Oh?"

"Yes," Judge said defensively. "I studied his situation carefully, collected evidence against him, and only then passed judgment. You didn't do any of that, Chase. You killed perfect strangers, and you very likely murdered innocents who had no black marks on their souls."

Chase hung up.

When the phone rang at four different times during the following hour, he was able to ignore it completely. His anger remained sharp, the strongest emotion that he had experienced in long months of near catatonia.

He drank three more glasses of whiskey before be began to feel mellow again. The tremors in his hands gradually subsided.

At ten o'clock he dialed the number of police headquarters and asked for Detective Wallace, who at that moment was out.

He tried again at ten-forty. This time Wallace was in and willing to speak to him.

"Nothing's going as well as we hoped," Wallace said. "This guy doesn't seem to have been printed. At least, he's not among the most obvious profile group of felons. We still might find him in another group—military files or something."

"What about the ring?"

"Turns out to be a cheap accessory that sells at under fifteen bucks retail in about every store in the state. Impossible to keep track of where and when and to whom a particular ring might have been sold."

Chase committed himself reluctantly. "Then I have something for you," he said. In a few short sentences, he told the detective about Judge's calls.

Wallace was angry, though he made an effort not to shout. "Why in the hell didn't you let us know about this before?"

"I thought, with the prints, you'd be sure to get him."

"Prints hardly ever make a difference in a situation like this," Wallace said. There was still a bite in his voice, though it was softer now. He had evidently remembered that his informant was a war hero.

"Besides," Chase said, "the killer realized the chance of the line being tapped. He's been calling from pay phones and keeping the calls under five minutes."

"Just the same, I'd like to hear him. I'll be over with a man in fifteen minutes."

"Just one man?"

Wallace said, "We'll try not to upset your routine too much."
Chase almost laughed at that.

⟡ ⋀ ⟡

From his third-floor window, Chase watched for the police. He
met them at the front door to avoid Mrs. Fielding's involvement.
Wallace introduced the plainclothes officer who came with him:
James Tuppinger. Tuppinger was six inches taller than Wallace—
and not drab-looking. He wore his blond hair in such a short crew
cut that he appeared almost bald from a distance. His eyes were
blue and moved from one object to another with the swift, penetrating
glance of an accountant itemizing an inventory. He carried a large
suitcase.

Mrs. Fielding watched from the living room, where she pretended
to be engrossed in a television program, but she did not come out
to see what was happening. Chase got the two men upstairs before
she could learn who they were.

"Cozy little place you have," Wallace said.

"It's enough for me," Chase said.

Tuppinger's gaze flicked about, catching the unmade bed, the dirty
whiskey glasses on the counter, and the half-empty bottle of liquor.
He did not say anything. He took his suitcase full of tools to the
phone, put it down, and began examining the lead-in wires that came
through the wall near the base of the single window.

While Tuppinger worked, Wallace questioned Chase. "What did
he sound like on the phone?"

"Hard to say."

"Old? Young?"

"In between."

"Accent?"

"No."

"Speech impediment?"

"No. Just hoarse—apparently from the struggle we had."

Wallace said, "Can you remember what he said, each time he
called?"

"Approximately."

"Tell me." He slumped down in the only easy chair in the room and crossed his legs. He looked as if he had fallen asleep, though he was alert.

Chase told Wallace everything that he could remember about the strange conversations with Judge. The detective had a few questions that stirred a few additional details from Chase's memory.

"He sounds like a religious psychotic," Wallace said. "All this stuff about fornication and sin and passing judgments."

"Maybe. But I wouldn't look for him at tent meetings. I think it's more of a moral excuse to kill than a genuine belief."

"Maybe," Wallace said. "Then again, we get his sort every once in a while."

Jim Tuppinger finished his work. He outlined the workings of his listening and recording equipment and further explained the trace equipment that the telephone company would use to seek Judge when he called.

"Well," Wallace said, "tonight, for once, I intend to go home when my shift ends." Just the thought of eight hours' sleep made his lids droop over his weary, bloodshot eyes.

"One thing," Chase said.

"Yeah?"

"If this leads to something—do you have to tell the press about my part in it?"

"Why?" Wallace asked.

"It's just that I'm tired of being a celebrity, of having people bother me at all hours of the day and night."

"It has to come out in the trial, if we nab him," Wallace said.

"But not before?"

"I guess not."

"I'd appreciate it," Chase said. "In any case, I'll have to appear at the trial, won't I?"

"Probably."

"If the press didn't have to know until then, it would cut down on the news coverage by half."

"You really *are* modest, aren't you?" Wallace asked. Before Chase could respond to that, the detective smiled, clapped him on the shoulder, and left.

"Would you like a drink?" Chase asked Tuppinger.

"Not on duty."

"Mind if I—?"

"No. Go ahead."

Chase noticed that Tuppinger watched him with interest as he got new ice cubes and poured a large dose of whiskey. It wasn't as large as usual. He supposed he'd have to restrain his thirst with the cop around.

When Chase sat on the bed, Tuppinger said, "I read all about your exploits over there."

"Oh?"

"Really something," Tuppinger said.

"Not really."

"Oh, yes, really," Tuppinger insisted. He was sitting in the easy chair, which he had moved close to his equipment. "It had to be hard over there, worse than anybody at home could ever know."

Chase nodded.

"I'd imagine the medals don't mean much. I mean, considering everything you had to go through to earn them, they must seem kind of insignificant."

Chase looked up from his drink, surprised at the insight. "You're right. They don't mean anything."

Tuppinger said, "And it must be hard to come back from a place like that and settle into a normal life. Memories couldn't fade that quickly."

Chase started to respond, then saw Tuppinger glance meaningfully at the glass of whiskey in his hand. He closed his mouth, bit off his response. Then, hating Tuppinger as badly as he hated Judge, he lifted the drink and took a large swallow.

He said, "I'll have another, I think. Sure you don't want one?"

"Positive," Tuppinger said.

When Chase returned to the bed with another glassful, Tuppinger cautioned him against answering the phone without first waiting for the tape to be started. Then he went into the bathroom, where he remained almost ten minutes.

When the cop returned, Chase asked, "How late do we have to stay up?"

"Has he ever called this late—except that first night?"

"No," Chase said.

"Then I'll turn in now," Tuppinger said, flopping in the easy chair. "See you in the morning."

⊲ ⋀ ⊳

In the morning, the whispers of the dead men woke Chase, but they proved to be nothing more than the sound of water running in the bathroom sink. Having risen first, Tuppinger was shaving.

When the cop opened the door and came into the main room of the tiny efficiency apartment a few minutes later, he looked refreshed. "All yours!" He seemed remarkably energetic for having spent the night in the armchair.

Chase took his time bathing and shaving, because the longer he remained in the bathroom, the less he would have to talk to the cop. When he was finally finished, it was quarter to ten. Judge had not yet called.

"What have you got for breakfast?" Tuppinger asked.

"Sorry. There isn't anything here."

"Oh, you've got to have something. Doesn't have to be breakfast food. I'm not particular in the morning. I'll eat a cheese sandwich as happily as bacon and eggs."

Chase opened the refrigerator and took out the bag of Winesap apples. "Only these."

Tuppinger stared at the apples and into the empty refrigerator. He glanced at the whiskey bottle on the counter. He didn't say anything.

"They'll do fine," Tuppinger said enthusiastically, taking the clear plastic bag of apples from Chase. "Want one?"

"No."

"You ought to eat breakfast," Tuppinger said. "Even something small. Gets the stomach working, sharpens you for the day ahead."

"No, thanks."

Tuppinger carefully peeled two apples, sectioned them, and ate them slowly, chewing well.

By ten-thirty Chase was worried. Suppose Judge did not call today? The idea of having Tuppinger here for the afternoon and the evening, of waking up again to the sound of Tuppinger in the bath-room shaving, was all but intolerable.

"Do you have a relief man?" Chase asked.

"Unless it gets too protracted," Tuppinger said, "I'll stick with it myself."

"How long might that be?"

"Oh," Tuppinger said, "if we don't have it wrapped up in forty-eight hours, I'll call in my relief."

Though another forty-eight hours with Tuppinger was in no way an attractive prospect, it was probably no worse—perhaps better—than it would have been with another cop. Tuppinger was too obser-vant for comfort, but he didn't talk much. Let him look. And let him think whatever he wanted to think. As long as he could keep his mouth shut, they wouldn't have any problems.

At noon Tuppinger ate two more apples and cajoled Chase into eating most of one. They decided that Chase would go for take-out fried chicken, fries, and slaw at dinnertime.

At twelve-thirty Chase had his first Jack Daniel's of the day.

Tuppinger watched, but he didn't say anything.

Chase didn't offer him a drink this time.

At three in the afternoon the telephone rang. Although this was what they had been waiting for since the night before, Chase didn't want to answer it. Because Tuppinger was there, urging him to pick it up while he adjusted his own earphones, he finally lifted the receiver.

"Hello?" His voice sounded cracked, strained.

"Mr. Chase?"

"Yes," he said, immediately recognizing the voice. It was not Judge.

"This is Miss Pringle, calling for Dr. Fauvel, to remind you of your appointment tomorrow at three. You have a fifty-minute session scheduled, as usual."

"Thank you." This double check was a strict routine with Miss Pringle, although Chase had forgotten about it.

"Tomorrow at three," she repeated, then hung up.

◁ ▲ ▷

At ten minutes before five, Tuppinger complained of hunger and of a deep reluctance to consume a fifth Winesap apple.

Chase didn't object to an early dinner, accepted Tuppinger's money, and went out to buy the chicken, French fries, and slaw. He purchased a large Coca-Cola for Tuppinger but nothing for himself. He would drink his usual.

They ate at a quarter past five, without dinner conversation, watching an old movie on television.

Less than two hours later Wallace arrived, looking thoroughly weary although he had only come on duty at six. He said, "Mr. Chase, do you think I might have a word alone with Jim?"

"Sure," Chase said.

He stepped into the bathroom, closed the door, and turned on the water in the sink, which made a sound like dead men whispering. The noise put him on edge.

He lowered the lid of the commode and sat facing the empty tub, realizing that it needed to be scrubbed. He wondered if Tuppinger had noticed.

Less than five minutes passed before Wallace knocked on the door. "Sorry to push you out of your own place like that. Police business."

"We haven't been lucky, as Mr. Tuppinger probably told you."

Wallace nodded. He looked peculiarly sheepish, and for the first time he could not meet Chase's gaze. "I've heard."

"It's the longest he's gone without calling."

Wallace nodded. "It's possible, you know, that he won't be calling at all, any more."

"You mean, since he passed judgment on me?"

Chase saw that Tuppinger was disconnecting wires and packing his equipment into the suitcase.

Wallace said, "I'm afraid you're right, Mr. Chase. The killer has passed his judgment—or lost interest in you, one or the other—and he isn't going to try to contact you again. We don't want to keep a man tied up here."

"You're leaving?" Chase asked.

"Well, yeah, it seems best."

"But another few hours might—"

"Might produce nothing," Wallace said. "What we're going to do, Mr. Chase, is we're going to rely on you to tell us what Judge says if, as seems unlikely now, he should call again." He smiled at Chase.

In that smile was all the explanation that Chase required. He said, "When Tuppinger sent me out for dinner, he called you, didn't he?" Not waiting for a response, he went on: "And he told you about the call from Dr. Fauvel's secretary—the word 'session' probably alarmed him. And now you've talked to the good doctor."

Tuppinger finished packing the equipment. He hefted the case and looked quickly around the room to be sure that he had not left anything behind.

"Judge is real," Chase told Wallace.

"I'm sure that he is," Wallace said. "That's why I want you to report any calls he might make to you." But his tone was that of an adult humoring a child.

"You stupid bastard, he *is* real!"

Wallace flushed with anger. When he spoke, there was tension in his voice, and his controlled tone was achieved with obvious effort. "Mr. Chase, you saved the girl. You deserve to be praised for that. But the fact remains, no one has called here in nearly twenty-four hours. And if you believed such a man as Judge existed, you surely would've contacted us before this, when he first called. It would've been natural for you to rush to us—especially a duty-conscious young man like yourself. All these things, examined in the light of your psychiatric record and Dr. Fauvel's explanations, make it clear that the expenditure of one of our best men isn't required. Tuppinger has other duties."

Chase saw how overwhelmingly the evidence seemed to point to Fauvel's thesis, just as he saw how his own behavior hadn't helped him. His fondness for whiskey in front of Tuppinger. His inability to carry on a simple conversation. Worst of all, his anxiety about publicity might have appeared to be the insincere protestations of a man who, in fact, wanted attention. Still, with his fists balled at his sides, he said, "Get out."

"Take it easy, son," Wallace said.

"Get out right now."

Wallace looked around the room and let his attention come to rest on the bottle of whiskey. "Tuppinger tells me you haven't any food on hand, but that there are five bottles in that cupboard." He did not look at Chase. He seemed to be embarrassed by Tuppinger's obvious spying. "You look thirty pounds underweight, son."

"Get out," Chase repeated.

Wallace was not ready to leave yet. He was searching for some way to soften the accusation implicit in their departure. But then he sighed and said, "Son, no matter what happened to you over there in Vietnam, you aren't going to forget about it with whiskey."

Before Chase, infuriated at the homespun psychoanalysis, could order him out again, Wallace finally left with Jim Tuppinger at his heels.

Chase closed the door after them. Quietly.

He locked it.

He poured a drink.

He was alone again. But he was accustomed to being alone.

6

THURSDAY EVENING AT SEVEN-THIRTY, HAVING SUCCESSFULLY EVADED Mrs. Fielding on his way out of the house, Chase drove his Mustang to Kanackaway Ridge Road, aware and yet unaware of his destination. He stayed within the speed limits through Ashside and the outlying districts, but floored the accelerator at the bottom of the mountain road, taking the wide curves on the far outside. The white guardrails slipped past so quickly and so close on the right that they blurred into a continuous wall of pale planking, the cables between them like black scrawls on the phantom boards.

On the top of the ridge, he parked where he had pulled off the road Monday night, killed the engine. He slouched in his seat, listening to the whispering breeze.

He should never have stopped, should have kept moving at all costs. As long as he was moving, he did not have to wonder what to do next. Stopped, he was perplexed, frustrated, restless.

He got out of the car, uncertain of what he expected to find here that would be of any help to him. A good hour of daylight remained in which to search the area where the Chevy had been parked. But, of course, the police would have combed and recombed it far more thoroughly than he ever could.

He strolled along the edge of the park to the bramble row where the Chevy had been. The sod was well trampled, littered with half-smoked cigarette butts, candy wrappers, and balled-up pages from a reporter's notepad. He kicked at the debris and scanned the mashed grass, feeling ridiculous. Too many morbid curiosity seekers had been here. He wouldn't find a clue in all this mess.

Next he went to the railing at the edge of the cliff, leaned against it, and stared down the wall of rock to the tangled patch of brambles and locust trees far below. When he raised his head, he could see the entire city spread along the valley. In the late-afternoon light, the green copper dome of the courthouse was like a structure out of a fairy tale.

He was still gazing at that corroded curve of metal when he heard a sharp whine. And again. The steel handrail shivered under his hands. An old war sound: a bullet slapping metal, ricocheting.

With a quickness honed in combat, he dropped to the ground, surveyed the park, and decided that the nearest row of shrubs was the best cover. He rolled toward that hedgerow and came up against the thorns so hard that he tore his cheek and forehead.

He lay motionless. Waiting.

A minute passed. Another. No sound but the wind.

Chase crawled on his stomach to the far end of the bramble row, which paralleled the highway. He eased into the open, looked to his right, and saw that the park appeared to be deserted.

He started to get up and turn toward the highway, then fell back again. Instinct. Where he'd been, the grass flew into the air, torn loose by a bullet. Judge had a pistol fitted with a sound suppressor.

No one in civilian life could have legal access to a silencer. Evidently, Judge had black-market resources.

Chase scrambled back along the shrubs, the way he had come, to the middle of the hedgerow. Swiftly he took off his shirt, tore it in two pieces, and wrapped his hands with the cloth. Lying on his stomach, he pressed the thorny vines apart until he opened a chink through which he could survey the land immediately beyond.

He saw Judge at once. The man was huddled by the front fender of Chase's Mustang, down on one knee, the pistol held at arm's length as he waited for his prey to appear. Two hundred feet away, in the weak light of the dusk, he was well shielded from Chase, little more than a dark figure; his face was but a blur in veils of shadow.

Chase let go of the brambles and stripped the cloth from his hands. He had minor nicks on the tips of three fingers, but he was for the most part unscathed.

To his right, no more than four feet away, a bullet snapped through the brambles, spraying chopped leaves. Another passed at the level of Chase's head, no more than two feet to his left, and then another still farther to the left.

Judge did not have the nerves of a professional killer. Tired of waiting, he had begun to fire blindly, wasting ammunition, hoping for a lucky hit.

Chase crawled back toward the right end of the row.

He peered out cautiously and saw Judge leaning against the car, attempting to reload his pistol. His head was bent over the gun, and although it should have been a simple task, he was fumbling nervously with the clip.

Chase went for the bastard.

He had covered only a third of the distance between them when Judge heard him coming. The killer looked up, still a cipher in the waning light, twisted around the end of the car, and sprinted along the highway.

Chase was underweight and out of shape, but he was gaining.

The road crested a rise and sloped so sharply that Chase was forced to put less effort into his pursuit lest he pitch forward and lose his balance.

Ahead, a red Volkswagen was parked along the shoulder of the highway. Judge reached the car, got behind the wheel, and swung the door shut. He had left the engine running. The Volkswagen instantly pulled away. Its tires hit the asphalt, spun briefly, shrieking and kicking up thick smoke; then the car shot down Kanackaway Ridge Road.

Chase didn't have a chance to catch even part of the license-plate number, because he was startled by an air horn frighteningly close behind.

He leaped sideways off the road, tripped, rolled on the gravel verge, hugging himself for protection from the stones.

Brakes barked just once, like the cry of a wounded man. A large

moving van—with dark letters against its orange side: U-HAUL—
boomed past, moving much too fast on the steep incline of Kanackaway Ridge Road, swaying slightly as its load shifted.
Then both the car and truck were out of sight.

7

A TWO-INCH SCRATCH ON HIS FOREHEAD AND A SMALLER SCRATCH ON
his cheek, inflicted by the thorns in the bramble row, were already
crusted with dried blood. The tips of three fingers also were scarred
by the brambles, but with all his other pains, he didn't even feel
these minor wounds. His ribs ached from the roll he'd taken on the
gravel shoulder of Kanackaway Ridge Road—although none seemed
broken when he pressed on them—and his chest, back, and arms
were bruised where the largest stones had dug in as he tumbled over
them. Both his knees were skinned. He had lost his shirt, of course,
when he ripped it in two as protection from the thorns, and his
trousers were fit only for the trash can.

He sat in the Mustang by the edge of the park, assessing the
damage, and he was so angry that he wanted to strike at something,
anything. Instead, he waited, cooled off, settled down.

Already, in the early darkness, a few cars had arrived at lovers'
lane, driving over the sod to the hedges. Chase was amazed that all
these young lovers were returning unfazed to the scene of the murder,
apparently unconcerned that the man who had knifed Michael Karnes
was still on the loose. He wondered if they would bother to lock
their car doors.

Since police patrols might be out along Kanackaway, hoping for
the killer to return to the scene as well, a man sitting alone in a car
would be highly suspicious. Chase started the engine and headed
back into the city.

As he drove, he tried to recall everything that he had seen, so no
clue to Judge's identity would slip by. The guy owned a silencer-
equipped pistol and a red Volkswagen. He was a bad shot, but a
good driver. And that was about the sum of it.

What next? The police?

No. To hell with the cops. He had sought help from Fauvel and received nothing but bad advice. The cops had been even less help.

He would have to handle the whole business himself. Track Judge down before Judge killed him.

◁ ʌ ▷

Mrs. Fielding met him at the door but stepped backward in surprise when she saw his condition. "What happened to you?"

"I fell down," Chase said. "It's nothing."

"But there's blood on your face. You're all skinned up!"

"Really, Mrs. Fielding, I'm perfectly all right now. I had a little accident, but I'm on my feet and breathing."

She looked him over more carefully. "Have you been drinking, Mr. Chase?" Her tone had gone swiftly from concern to disapproval.

"No drinks at all," Chase said.

"You know I don't approve."

"I know." He went past her, heading for the stairs. They appeared to be a long way off.

"You didn't wreck your car?" she called after him.

"No."

He climbed the stairs, looking anxiously ahead toward the turn at the landing—blessed escape. Strangely, he did not feel nearly as oppressed by Mrs. Fielding as usual.

"That's good news," she said. "As long as you have your car, you'll be able to look for jobs better than before."

After a glass of whiskey over ice, he drew a tub of water as hot as he could tolerate it, and he settled in as though he were an old man with arthritis. Water slopped over his open wounds and made him sigh with both pleasure and pain.

Later, he dressed the worst abrasions with Merthiolate, then put on lightweight slacks, a sports shirt, socks, and loafers. With a second glass of whiskey, he sat in the easy chair to contemplate his next move.

He looked forward to action with a mixture of excitement and apprehension.

First, he should speak with Louise Allenby, the girl who had been with Michael Karnes the night he was killed. She and Chase had been questioned separately by the police, but brooding on the event together, they might be able to remember something useful.

The telephone book listed eighteen Allenbys, but Chase recalled Louise telling Detective Wallace that her father was dead and that her mother had not remarried. Only one of the Allenbys in the book was listed as a woman: Cleta Allenby on Pine Street, an address in the Ashside district.

He dialed the number and waited through ten rings before Louise answered. Her voice was recognizable, although more womanly than he remembered.

"This is Ben Chase, Louise. Do you remember me?"

"Of course," she said. She sounded genuinely pleased to hear from him. "How are you?"

"Coping."

"What's wrong? Is there anything I can do to help?"

"I'd like to talk to you, if possible," Chase said. "About what happened Monday night."

"Well, sure, all right."

"It won't upset you?"

"Why should it?" Her hardness continued to amaze him. "Can you come over now?"

"If it's convenient."

"Fine," she said. "It's ten o'clock now—in half an hour, at ten-thirty? Will that be all right?"

"Just right," Chase said.

"I'll be expecting you."

She put the phone down so gently that for seconds Chase did not realize that she had hung up.

He was beginning to stiffen from his injuries. He stood and stretched, found his car keys, and quickly finished his drink.

When it was time to go, he did not want to begin. Suddenly he realized how completely this assumption of responsibility would destroy the simple routines by which he had survived in the months since his discharge from the army and the hospital. He would have no more leisurely mornings in town, no more afternoons watching old movies on television, no more evenings reading and drinking until he could sleep—at least not until this mess was straightened out. If he just stayed here in his room, however, if he took his chances, he might remain alive until Judge was caught in a few weeks or, at most, in a few months.

Then again, Judge might not miss the next time.

He cursed everyone who had forced him out of his comfortable niche—the local press, the Merchants' Association, Judge, Fauvel, Wallace, Tuppinger—yet he knew that he had no choice but to get on with it. His sole consolation was the hope that their victory was only a temporary one: When this was all finished, he would come back to his room, close the door, and settle once more into the quiet and unchallenging life that he had established for himself during the past year.

Mrs. Fielding did not bother him on his way out of the house, and he chose to see this as a good omen.

⌐ ⋀ ⌐

The Allenbys, mother and daughter, lived in a two-story neo-Colonial brick home on a small lot in middle-class Ashside. Two matched maples were featured at the head of the short flagstone walk and two matched pines at the end of it. Two steps rose to a white door with a brass knocker.

Louise answered the door herself. She was wearing white shorts and a thin white halter top, and she looked as if she had spent the past thirty minutes putting on makeup and brushing her long hair.

"Come in," she said.

The living room was more or less what he had expected: matched Colonial furniture, a color television in a huge console cabinet, knotted rugs over polished pine floors. The house was not dirty but carelessly kept: magazines spilling out of a rack, a dried water ring on the coffee table, traces of dust here and there.

"Sit down," Louise said. "The sofa's comfortable, and so's that big chair with the flowered print."

He chose the sofa. "I'm sorry to bother you like this, so late at night—"

"Don't worry about that," she interrupted breezily. "You're no bother, never could be."

He hardly recognized her as the shaken, whimpering girl in Michael Karnes's car on Monday night.

She said, "Since I'm finished with school, I only go to bed when I feel like it, usually around three in the morning. College in the fall. Big girl now." She grinned as if she'd never had a boyfriend knifed to death in front of her. "Can I get you a drink?"

"No, thanks."

"Mind if I have something?"

"Go ahead."

He stared at her trim legs as she went to the wet bar in the wall of bookcases. "Sicilian Stinger. Sure you wouldn't like one? They're delicious."

"I'm fine."

As she mixed the drink with professional expertise, she stood with her back to him, her hips artfully canted, her round butt thrust toward him. It might have been the unconscious stance of a girl not yet fully aware of her womanliness, with only a partial understanding of the effect her pneumatic body could have on men. Or it might have been completely contrived.

When she returned to the sofa with her drink, Chase said, "Are you old enough to drink?"

"Seventeen," she said. "Almost eighteen. No longer a child, right? Maybe I'm not of legal age yet, but this is my own home, so who's going to stop me?"

"Of course."

Only seven years ago, when he'd been her age, seventeen-year-old girls *seemed* seventeen. They grew up faster now—or thought that they did.

Sipping her drink, she leaned back against the couch and crossed her bare legs.

He saw the hard tips of her breasts against the thin halter.

He said, "It's just occurred to me that your mother may be in bed, if she gets up early for work. I didn't mean—"

"Mother's working now," Louise said. She looked at him coyly, her lashes lowered and her head tilted to one side. "She's a cocktail waitress. She goes on duty at seven, off at three, home about three-thirty in the morning."

"I see."

"Are you frightened?"

"Excuse me?"

She smiled mischievously. "Of being here alone with me?"

"No."

"Good. So . . . where do we begin?" With another coy look, she tried to make the question seductive.

For the following half hour, he guided her through her memories of Monday night, augmenting them with his own, questioning her on details, urging her to question him, looking for some small thing that might be the key. They remembered nothing new, however, though the girl genuinely tried to help him. She was able to talk about Mike Karnes's murder with complete detachment, as though she had not been there when it happened but had only read about it in the papers.

"Mind if I have another one?" she asked, raising her glass.

"Go ahead."

"I'm feeling good. Want one this time?"

"No, thank you," he said, recognizing the need to keep his head clear.

She stood at the wet bar in the same provocative pose as before, and when she returned to the couch, she sat much closer to him than she had previously. "One thing I just thought of—he was wearing a special ring."

"Special in what way?"

"Silver, squarish, with a double lightning bolt. A guy Mom dated for a while wore one. I asked him about it once, and he told me it was a brotherhood ring, from this club he belonged to."

"What club?"

"Just for white guys. No blacks, Japs, Jews, or anybody else welcome, just white guys."

Chase waited as she sipped her drink.

"Bunch of guys who're willing to stand up for themselves, if it ever comes to that, guys who aren't going to let the nappy-heads or the Jew bankers or anybody else push them around and take what they have." She clearly approved of any such organization. Then she frowned. "Did I just screw up my chances?"

"Chances?"

"Are you maybe a Jew?"

"No."

"You don't look like a Jew."

"I'm not."

"Listen, even if you were a Jew, it wouldn't matter much to me. I find you real attractive. You know?"

"So the killer might be a white supremacist?"

"They're just guys who won't take any crap the way everyone else will. That's all. You have to admire that."

"This guy who dated your mother—did he tell you the name of this club?"

"The Aryan Alliance."

"You remember his name?"

"Vic. Victor. Don't remember his last name."

"Could you ask your mom for me?"

"Okay. When she gets home. Listen, you're absolutely sure you're not a Jew?"

"I'm sure."

"Because ever since I said it, you've been looking at me sort of funny."

As he might have looked at something pale and squirming that he'd discovered under an overturned rock.

He said, "Did you tell Wallace about this?"

"No, I just now thought of it. You loosened me up, and it just came back to me in a flash."

Chase imagined nothing more gratifying than establishing a body of information about Judge—working from this essential bit of data—and then presenting it to the detective.

"It may be helpful," he said.

She slid next to him with the oiled smoothness of a machine made for seduction, all sleek lines and golden tan. "Do you think so, Ben?"

He nodded, trying to decide how best to excuse himself without hurting her feelings. He had to keep on the good side of her until she got that name from her mother.

Her thigh was pressed against his. She put her drink down and turned to him, expecting to be embraced.

Chase stood abruptly. "I ought to be going. This has given me something concrete to consider, more than I had hoped for."

She rose too, remaining close to him. "It's early. Not even midnight. Mom won't be home for hours."

She smelled of soap, shampoo, a pleasant perfume. It was such a clean smell—but he knew now that she was corrupted in her heart.

He was fiercely aroused—and sickened by his arousal. This cheap, cold-hearted, hate-filled girl reached him in a way that no woman had reached him in longer than a year, and he despised himself for wanting her so intensely. At that moment, of course, virtually any attractive woman might have affected him the same way. Perhaps the pent-up sexual energy of many lonely months had become too great to repress, and perhaps the reawakening of sexual desire was the result of being forced out of his self-imposed isolation. Once he admitted to a healthy survival instinct, once he decided not to stand still and be a target for Judge, he was able to admit to all the desires and needs that were the essence of life. Nevertheless, he despised himself.

"No," he said, edging away from her. "I have other people to see."

"At this hour?"

"One or two other people."

She pressed against him, pulled his face down to hers, and licked his lips. No kiss. Just the maddeningly quick flicking of her warm tongue—an exquisitely erotic promise.

"We've got the house for several hours yet," she said. "We don't even have to use the couch. I've got a great big white bed with a white canopy."

"You're something else," he said, meaning something other than what she thought he meant.

"You don't know the half of it," she said.

"But I can't. I really can't, because these people are waiting for me."

She was experienced enough to know when the moment for seduction had passed. She stepped back and smiled. "But I do want to thank you. For saving my life. That deserves a big reward."

"You don't owe me anything," he said.

"I *do*. Some other night, when you don't have plans?"

He kissed her, telling himself that he did so only to remain in her good graces. "Definitely some other night."

"Mmmmm. And we'll be good together."

She was all polish, fast and easy, no jagged edges to get hung up on.

He said, "If Detective Wallace questions you again, do you think you could sort of . . . forget about the ring?"

"Sure. I don't like cops. They're the ones who put the guns to our heads, make us kiss the asses of the nappy-heads and the Jews and all of them. They're part of the problem. But why are you carrying on with this by yourself? I never did ask."

"Personal," he said. "For personal reasons."

⊲ ⋀ ⊳

At home again, he undressed and went directly to bed. The darkness was heavy and warm and, for the first time in longer than he could remember, comforting.

Alone, he began to wonder if he had been a fool not to respond to Louise Allenby's offer. He had been a long time without a woman, without even a desire for one.

He had told himself that he'd rejected Louise because he'd found her as personally repulsive as she was physically attractive. But he wondered if, instead, he'd retreated from the prospect because he feared it would draw him even further into the world, further away from his precious routines. A relationship with a woman, regardless of how transitory, would be one more crack in his carefully mortared walls.

On the edge of sleep, he realized that something had happened that was far more important than either his strong physical response to Louise or his rejection of her. For the first time in longer than Chase could recall, he hadn't needed whiskey before bed. A natural sleep claimed him—although it was still populated by the grasping dead.

8

WHEN HE WOKE IN THE MORNING, CHASE WAS RACKED WITH PAIN FROM the fall that he had taken the previous evening on Kanackaway Ridge Road. Each contusion and laceration throbbed. His eyes felt sunken, and his headache was as intense as if he'd been fitted with an exotic torture device—an iron helmet—that would be slowly tightened until his skull imploded. When he tried to get out of bed, his muscles cramped and spasmed.

In the bathroom, when he leaned toward the mirror above the sink, he saw that he was drawn and pale. His chest and back were spotted with bruises, most about as large as a thumbprint, from the gravel over which he'd rolled to avoid the hurtling truck.

A hot bath didn't soothe him, so he forced himself to do a couple of dozen situps, pushups, and deep knee bends until he was dizzy. The exercises proved more therapeutic than the bath.

The only cure for his misery was activity—which, he supposed, was a prescription for his emotional and spiritual miseries as well.

Wincing at the pain in his legs, he went downstairs.

"Mail for you," said Mrs. Fielding as she shuffled out of the game-show-audience laughter in the living room. She took a plain brown envelope from the table in the hall and gave it to him. "As you can see, there's no return address."

"Probably advertisements," Chase said. He took a step toward the front door, hoping that she wouldn't notice his stiffness and inquire about his health.

He need not have worried, because she was more interested in the contents of the envelope than in him. "It can't be an ad in a plain envelope. The only things that come in plain envelopes without return addresses are wedding invitations—which this isn't—and dirty literature." Her expression was uncharacteristically stern. "I won't tolerate dirty literature in my house."

"And I don't blame you," Chase said.

"Then it isn't?"

"No." He opened the envelope and withdrew the psychiatric file and journal articles that Judge had promised to send to him. "I'm interested in psychology, and this friend of mine sometimes sends me particularly interesting articles on the subject when he comes across them."

"Oh." Mrs. Fielding was obviously surprised that Chase harbored such intellectual and hitherto unknown interests. "Well . . . I hope I didn't embarrass you—"

"Not at all."

"—but I couldn't tolerate having pornography in my home."

Barely refraining from commenting on the half-undone bodice of her housedress, he said, "I understand."

He went out to his car and drove three blocks before pulling to the curb. Letting the engine idle, he examined the Xeroxes.

The extensive handwritten notes that Dr. Fauvel had made during their sessions were so difficult to read that Chase passed over them for the time being, but he studied the five articles—three in the form of magazine tearsheets, two in typescript. In all five pieces, Fauvel's high self-esteem was evident, his egotism unrelenting. The doctor referred to the subject as "Patient C"; however, Chase recognized himself—even though he was portrayed through a radically distorting lens. Every symptom that he suffered had been exaggerated to make its eventual amelioration appear to be a greater achievement on Fauvel's part. All the clumsy probes that Fauvel had initiated were never mentioned, and he claimed to have succeeded with strategies of therapy that he had never employed but that he'd apparently developed through hindsight. Chase was, according to Fauvel: *one of those young men who go to war with no well-formed moral beliefs and who, therefore, are clay in the hands of manipulative superiors, capable of being induced to commit any atrocities without questioning their orders.* Elsewhere, he observed that Patient C: *came to me from a military hospital, where he had recovered sufficiently from a total nervous breakdown to attempt social reintegration. The cause of his breakdown had been not a sense of guilt but extreme terror at the prospect of his own death, not a concern for others but a crippling recognition—and fear—of his own mortality.*

"You bastard," Chase said.

Guilt had been his constant companion, whether he was awake or asleep. Recognition of his mortality had not been a source of fear, for God's sake; instead, it had been his only consolation, and for a long time he had hoped for nothing more than the strength to end his own life.

Fauvel had written: *He still suffered nightmares and impotence, which he felt were his only afflictions and were a result of his fear. I recognized, however, that the real problem for Patient C was an underlying lack of moral values. He could never heal himself psychologically until he made peace with his horrific past, and he could not make peace with his past until he fully understood and acknowledged the gravity of the crimes that he had committed, even if in war.*

Understood and acknowledged! As if Chase had blithely pulled the trigger, waded through the blood of his victims, and then had gone in search of a good shoeshine boy to buff the stains off his boots. Jesus.

Dr. G. Sloan Fauvel—psychiatrist extraordinaire, confessor, and tower of moral rectitude—had therefore: *at last commenced the long, difficult process of inculcating in Patient C, by diverse and subtle means, an understanding of the concept of morality and a capacity for guilt. If he could develop a sincere sense of guilt about what he had done, then the guilt subsequently could be relieved through classic therapy. A cure might then be possible.*

Chase returned the material to the plain brown envelope. He tucked the envelope under the passenger seat.

He was shaken by the realization that he had spent so much time in the care of a physician who neither understood him nor possessed the capacity to understand. For too long, Chase had trusted in others to save him, but the only salvation was to be found in God and in himself. And after his experiences in Southeast Asia, he still was not entirely sure of God.

◁ ∧ ▷

In the Metropolitan Bureau of Vital Statistics, in the basement of the courthouse, three women hammered away at typewriters with a rhythmic swiftness that seemed to have been arranged and conducted with all the care of a symphony-orchestra performance.

Chase stood at the reception counter, waiting for service.

The stoutest and oldest of the three women—her desk plate read NANCY ONUFER, *Manager*—typed to the end of a page, pulled the page from her typewriter, and placed it in a clear-plastic tray full of similar forms. "May I help you?"

He had already figured what tact Judge must have used when asking to search the files here, and he said, "I'm doing a family history, and I was wondering if I could be permitted to look up a few things in the city records."

"Certainly," said Nancy Onufer. She popped up from her chair, came to the gate at the end of the service counter, and opened it for him.

The other two women continued to type with machine-gun rapidity. There was a high degree of efficiency in the Bureau of Statistics that was unusual for any government office, no doubt because Nancy Onufer would accept no less. Her brisk but not unfriendly manner reminded Chase of the better drill sergeants whom he had known in the service.

He followed her through the office area behind the counter, past desks and worktables, and through a fire door into a large concrete-walled chamber lined with metal filing cabinets. More cabinets stood in rows down the center of the room, and to one side was a scarred worktable with three hard chairs.

"The cabinets are all labeled," Nancy Onufer said crisply. "The section to the right contains birth certificates, death certificates there, then health-department records over there, bar and restaurant licenses in that corner. Against the far wall we keep carbons of the draft-board records, then the minutes and budgets of the city council going back thirty years. You get the idea. Depending on the contents, each drawer is primarily organized either alphabetically or by date. Whatever you remove from the files must be left on this table. Do not attempt to replace the material yourself. That's my job, and I do it far more accurately than you would. No offense."

"None taken."

"You may not remove anything from this room. For a nominal fee, one of my assistants will provide photocopies of documents that interest you. If anything should be removed from this room, you will be subjected to a five-thousand-dollar fine and two years in prison."

"Ouch."

"We enforce it too."

"I've no doubt. Thanks for your help."

"And no smoking," she added.

"I don't."

"Good."

She left the room, closing the door behind her.

It had been this easy for Judge too. Chase had hoped that the city would require a sign-in procedure by which those who wanted to use the files were identified. Considering Nancy Onufer's efficiency and the law against removing documents, Chase was surprised that she didn't keep a meticulous log of visitors.

He looked up his own birth certificate and also found the minutes of the city-council meeting during which a vote had been taken to hold an awards dinner in his honor. In the carbons of the selective-service records, he located the pertinent facts regarding his past eligibility for the draft and the document calling him for service in the United States Army.

Easy. Too easy.

When he left the storage vault, Nancy Onufer said, "Find what you were looking for?"

"Yes, thank you."

"No trouble, Mr. Chase," she said, immediately turning back to her work.

Her reply stopped him. "You know me?"

She glanced up and flashed a smile. "Who doesn't?"

He crossed the open office area to her desk. "If you hadn't known who I was, would you have asked for a name and ID before I went into the file room?"

"Certainly. No one's ever taken any records in the twelve years I've been here, but I still keep a log of visitors." She tapped a notebook on the edge of her desk. "I just put your name down."

"This may sound like an odd request, but could you tell me who was here this past Tuesday?" When Mrs. Onufer hesitated, he said, "I'm being bothered a lot by reporters, and I don't care for all the publicity. They've said everything about me there is to be said, after all. It's getting to be overkill. I've heard there's a local man working on a series for a national magazine, against my wishes, and I was wondering if he'd been here Tuesday."

He thought that the lie was transparent, but she trusted him. He was a war hero, after all. "It must be a pain in the butt. But journalists—they can never leave anyone alone. Anyway, I don't see the harm in telling you who was here. There's nothing confidential about the visitors' log." She consulted the notebook. "Only nine people came around all Tuesday. These two are from an architectural firm, checking some power-and-water easements on properties they're developing. I know them. These four were women, and you're looking for a man, so we can rule them out. That leaves three—here, here, and here."

As she showed him the names, Chase tried to commit them to memory. "No . . . I guess . . . none of them is him."

"Anything else?"

"Do you ordinarily just take names—or ask for ID?"

"Always ID, unless I know the person."

"Well, thanks for your help."

Acutely conscious of all the work on her desk, Nancy Onufer shut the notebook, dismissed Chase with a quick smile, and returned to her typing.

When he left the courthouse, it was a quarter till noon, and he was starving. He went to a drive-in restaurant—Diamond Dell—that had been a favorite hangout when he'd been in high school.

He was surprised by his appetite. Sitting in the car, he ate two cheeseburgers, a large order of fries, and cole slaw, washing it all down with a Pepsi. That was more than he had eaten in any *three* meals during the past year.

After lunch, at a nearby service station, he used the phone-booth directory to find numbers for the men who were possibles in Nancy Onufer's log. When he called the first, he got the guy's wife; she gave him a work number for her husband. Chase dialed it and spoke to the suspect—who sounded nothing whatsoever like Judge. The second man was at home, and he sounded even less like Judge than the first.

The directory had no number for the third man—Howard Devore—which might only mean that his telephone was unlisted. Or it might mean that the name was phony. Of course, Mrs. Onufer always asked for ID, so if Judge was using a phony name, he also must have access to a source of false identification.

Because he didn't trust himself to remember every clue and to notice links between them, Chase went to a drugstore and purchased a small ring-bound notebook and a Bic pen. Inspired by Mrs. Onufer's efficiency, he made a neat list:

Alias—Judge
Alias—Howard Devore (possible)
Aryan Alliance
No criminal record (prints not on file)
Can pick locks (Fauvel's office)
May own a red Volkswagen
Owns a pistol with sound suppressor

Sitting in his car in the drugstore parking lot, he studied the list for a while, then added another item:

Unemployed or on vacation

He could think of no other way to explain how Judge could call him at any hour, follow him in the middle of the afternoon, and spend two days researching his life. The killer neither sounded nor acted old enough to be retired. Unemployed, on vacation—or on a leave of absence from his work.

But how could that information be useful in finding the bastard? It narrowed the field of suspects but not significantly. The local economy was bad; therefore, more than a few people were out of work. And it was summer, vacation season.

He closed the notebook and started the car. He was dead serious about tracking down Judge, but he felt less like Sam Spade than like Nancy Drew.

◀ ▲ ▶

Glenda Kleaver, the young blonde in charge of the *Press-Dispatch* morgue room, was about five feet eleven, only two inches shorter than Chase. In spite of her size, her voice was as soft as the July breeze that lazily stirred maple-leaf shadows across the sun-gilded windows. She moved with natural grace, and Chase was instantly fascinated with her, not solely because of her quiet beauty but because she seemed to calm the world around her by her very presence.

She demonstrated the use of microfilm viewers to Chase and explained that all editions prior to January first, 1968, were now stored on film to conserve space. She explained the procedure for ordering the proper spools and for obtaining the editions that had not yet been transferred to film.

Two reporters were sitting at the machines, twisting the controls, staring into the viewers, jotting on notepads beside them.

Chase said, "Do you get many outsiders here?"

"A newspaper morgue is chiefly for the use of the staff. But we keep it open to the public without charge. We get maybe a dozen people a week."

"What are outsiders looking for here?"

"What are *you* looking for?" she asked.

He hesitated, then gave her the same story that he had first given Mrs. Onufer at the Metropolitan Bureau of Vital Statistics. "I'm gathering facts for a family history."

"That's what most outsiders come here for. Personally, I haven't the least bit of curiosity about dead relatives. I don't even like the living relatives very much."

He laughed, surprised to discover acidic humor in someone so gentle-looking and so soft-spoken. She was a study in contrasts. "No sense of pride in your lineage?"

"None," she said. "It's more mutt than thoroughbred."

"Nothing wrong with that."

"Go back far enough in my family tree," she said, "and I bet you'll find some ancestors hanging from the limbs by their necks."

"Descended from horse thieves, huh?"

"At best."

Chase was more at ease with her than he had been in the presence of any woman since Jules Verne, the underground operation in Nam. But when it came to small talk, he was long out of practice, and as much as he would have liked to make a stronger connection with her, he was unable to think of anything to say except: "Well . . . do I have to sign anything to use the files?"

"No. But I have to get everything for you, and you have to return it to me before you leave. What do you need?"

Chase had come there not to conduct research but only to ask about any outsiders who had used the morgue this past Tuesday, but no convenient cover story came to mind. He could not spin the same tale that he'd used with Mrs. Onufer, the lie about the nosy reporter— not here of all places.

Furthermore, though he had been prepared to make up any story that circumstances seemed to require, he discovered that he didn't want to lie to this woman. Her blue-gray eyes were direct, and in them he saw a forthrightness and honesty that he was compelled to respect.

On the other hand, if he told her the truth about Judge and the attempt on his life, and if she didn't believe him, he would feel like a prize ass. Oddly enough, although he had only just met her, he didn't want to embarrass himself in front of her.

Besides, one of the reporters working in the morgue might overhear too much. Then Chase's picture would be on the front page again. They might treat the story either straight or tongue-in-cheek (probably the latter, if they talked to the police), but either way the publicity would be an intolerable development.

"Sir?" Glenda said. "How can I help you? What editions would you like to see first?"

Before Chase could respond, a reporter at one of the microfilm machines looked up from his work. "Glenda, dear, could I have all the dailies between May fifteenth, 1952, and September that same year?"

"In a moment. This gentleman was first."

"That's okay," Chase said, grasping the opportunity. "I've got plenty of time."

"You sure?" she asked.

"Yeah. Get him what he needs."

"I'll be back in five minutes," she said.

As she walked the length of the small room and through the wide arch into the filing room, both Chase and the reporter watched her. She was tall but not awkward, moving with a feline grace that actually made her seem fragile.

When she had gone, the reporter said, "Thanks for waiting."

"Sure."

"I've got an eleven o'clock deadline on this piece, and I haven't even begun to get my sources together." He turned back to his viewer, so engrossed in his work that he apparently had not recognized Chase.

Chase returned to his Mustang, opened his notebook, and studied his list, but he had absolutely nothing to add to it, and he could not see any pertinent connections between the familiar eight items. He closed the book, started the car, and drove out into the traffic on John F. Kennedy Throughway.

Fifteen minutes later he was on the four-lane interstate beyond the city limits, doing a steady seventy miles an hour, wind whistling at the open windows and ruffling his hair. As he drove, he thought about Glenda Kleaver, and he hardly noticed the miles going by.

◁ ∧ ▷

After high school, Chase had gone to State because it was just forty miles from home, so he could see his mom and dad more often, still get back to visit old friends from high school and to see a girl who had mattered to him then, before Vietnam changed everything.

Now, as he parked in front of the administration building, the campus seemed to be a strange place, as if he had not spent nearly four years in these classrooms, on these flagstone paths, under these canopies of willows and elms. This part of his life was all but lost to him because it was from the far side of the war. To recapture the mood and feeling of that time, to connect emotionally with these old haunts, he would have to cross through the river of war memories to the shores of the past—and that was a journey that he chose not to make.

In the Student Records Office, as the manager approached him, Chase decided that this time the simple truth would get the best response. "I'm curious to know who may have been here, asking about me, within the past week. I'm having some problems with a researcher who's . . . well, been more or less harassing me."

The manager was a small, pale, nervous man with a neatly clipped mustache. He ceaselessly picked up items around him, put them down, picked them up again: pencils, pens, a notepad, a pamphlet about the university's tuition schedules and scholarship programs. He said that his name was Franklin Brown and that he was pleased to meet such a distinguished alumnus. "But there must've been dozens of inquiries about you in recent months, Mr. Chase, ever since the Medal of Honor was announced."

"Do you have the names and addresses of everyone requesting records?"

"Oh, yes, of course. And as you may know, we provide those records only to prospective employers—and even then, only if you signed an automatic authorization when you graduated."

"This man may have passed himself off as a prospective employer. He's very convincing. Could you check your records and tell me who might have stopped in last Tuesday?"

"He could have requested the records by mail. Most of the inquiries we receive are by mail. Few people actually come in."

"No. He didn't have time to do it by mail."

"Just a moment then," Brown said. He brought a ledger to the counter and thumbed through it. "There was just the one gentleman that day."

"Who was he?"

As he read it, Brown showed the entry to Chase. "Eric Blentz, Gateway Mall Tavern. It's in the city."

"I know exactly where it's at," Chase said.

Picking up a fountain pen, twisting it in his fingers, putting it down again, Brown asked, "Is he legitimate? Is he someone you're seeking a position with?"

"No. It's probably this reporter I mentioned, and he just made up the name Blentz. Do you remember what he looked like?"

"Certainly," Brown said. "Nearly your height, though not robust at all, very thin, in fact, and with a stoop to his shoulders."

"How old?"

"Thirty-eight, forty."

"His face? Do you remember that?"

"Very ascetic features," Brown said. "Very quick eyes. He kept looking from one of my girls here to the other, then at me, as if he didn't trust us. His cheeks were drawn, an unhealthy complexion. A large thin nose, so thin the nostrils were very elliptical."

"Hair?"

"Blond. He was quite sharp with me, impatient, self-important.

Dressed very neatly, a high polish to his shoes. I don't think there was a hair out of place on his head. And when I asked for his name and business address, he took the pen right out of my hand, turned the ledger around, and wrote it down himself because, as he said, everyone always spelled his name wrong, and he wanted it right this time."

Chase said, "How is it that you remember him in such detail?"

Brown smiled, picked up the pen, put it down, and toyed with the ledger as he said, "Evenings and weekends during the summer, my wife and I run The Footlight. It's a legitimate theater in town— you might even have attended a play there when you were in school. Anyway, I take a role in most of our productions, so I'm always studying people to pick up expressions, mannerisms."

"You must be very good on stage by now," Chase said.

Brown blushed. "Not particularly. But that kind of thing gets in your blood. We don't make much money on the theater, but as long as it breaks even, I can indulge myself."

Returning to his car, Chase tried to picture Franklin Brown on stage, before an audience, his hands trembling, his face paler than ever; his compulsion to handle things might be exacerbated by being in the spotlight. Perhaps it was no mystery why The Footlight didn't show much profit.

In the Mustang, Chase opened his notebook and looked over the list that he'd made earlier, trying to find something that indicated that Judge might actually be Eric Blentz, a saloon owner. No good. Didn't anyone who applied for a liquor license have to be fingerprinted as a matter of routine? And a man who owned a thriving business like the Gateway Mall Tavern probably wouldn't drive a Volkswagen.

There was one way to find out for sure. He started the car and drove back toward the city, wondering what sort of reception he would get at the Gateway Mall Tavern.

9

THE TAVERN DECOR WAS SUPPOSED TO BE REMINISCENT OF AN ALPINE inn: low beamed ceilings, rough white plaster walls, a brick floor, heavy dark-pine furniture. The six windows that faced onto the mall promenade were leaded glass the color of burgundy, only slightly translucent. Around the walls were upholstered booths. Chase sat in one of the smaller booths toward the rear of the place, facing the bar and the front entrance.

A cheerful apple-cheeked blonde in a short brown skirt and low-cut white peasant blouse lit the lantern on his table, then took his order for a whiskey sour.

The bar was not especially busy at six o'clock; only seven other patrons shared the place, three couples and a lone woman who sat at the bar. None of the customers fit the description that Brown had given Chase, and he disregarded them. The bartender was the only other man in the place, aging and bald, with a potbelly, but quick and expert with the bottles and obviously a favorite with barmaids.

Blentz might not frequent his own tavern, of course, though he would be an exception to the rule if that was the case. This was largely a cash business, and most saloon owners liked to keep a watch on the till.

Chase realized that he was tense, leaning away from the back of the booth, his hands curled into fists on the table. He settled back and forced himself to relax, since he might have to wait hours for Blentz.

After the second whiskey sour, he asked for a menu and ordered a veal chop and a baked potato, surprised to be hungry after the meal that he'd had at the drive-in joint earlier.

After dinner, shortly after nine o'clock, Chase finally asked the waitress if Mr. Blentz would be in this evening.

She looked across the now-crowded room and pointed at a heavy-set man on a stool at the bar. "That's him."

The guy was about fifty, weighed well over two hundred and fifty pounds, and was four or five inches shorter than the man in Franklin Brown's description.

"Blentz?" Chase asked. "You're sure?"

"I've worked for him two years," the waitress said.

"I was told he was tall, thin. Blond hair, sharp dresser."

"Maybe twenty years ago he was thin and a sharp dresser," she said. "But he couldn't ever have been tall or blond."

"I guess not," Chase said. "I guess I must be looking for another Blentz. Could I have the bill, please?"

He felt like Nancy Drew again, rather than Sam Spade. Of course, Nancy Drew *did* solve every case—and generally, if not always, before anyone was killed.

When he went outside, the mall parking lot was deserted but for the cars in front of the tavern. The stores had closed twenty minutes before.

The night air was sultry after the air-conditioned tavern. It seemed to press Chase to the blacktop, so each step that he took was flat-footed, loud, as though he were walking on a planet with greater gravity than that of earth.

As he was wiping sweat from his forehead, stepping around the front of the Mustang, he heard an engine roar behind him and was pinned by headlights. He didn't turn to look, but vaulted out of the way and onto the hood of his car.

An instant later a Pontiac scraped noisily along the side of the Mustang. Showers of sparks briefly brightened the night, leaving behind a faint smell of hot metal and scorched paint. Although the car rocked hard when it was struck, Chase held fast by curling his fingers into the trough that housed the recessed windshield wipers. If he fell off, the Pontiac sure as hell would swing around or back up to run him down before he could scramble away again.

Chase stood on the hood of the Mustang and stared after the retreating Pontiac, trying to see the license number. Even if he had been close enough to read the dark numerals, he couldn't have done so, because Judge had twisted a large piece of burlap sacking over the plate.

The Pontiac reached the exit lane from the mall lot, took the turn too hard, and appeared in danger of shooting across the sidewalk and striking one of the mercury arc lights. But then Judge regained control, accelerated, went through the amber traffic light at the inter-section, and swung right onto the main highway toward the heart of the city. In seconds, the Pontiac passed over the brow of a hill and was out of sight.

Chase looked around to see if anyone had witnessed the short, violent confrontation. He was alone.

He got down from the hood and walked the length of the Mus-tang, examining the damage. The front fender was jammed back toward the driver's door, though it hadn't been crushed against the tire and wouldn't prevent the car from being driven. The entire flank of the vehicle was scraped and crumpled. He doubted that there was any serious structural or mechanical damage—although the body work would cost several hundred bucks to repair.

He didn't care. Money was the least of his worries.

He opened the driver's door, which protested with only a thin shriek, sat behind the wheel, closed the door, opened his notebook, and reread his list. His hand trembled when he added the ninth, tenth, and eleventh items:

Third alias—Eric Blentz
Given to rash action in the face of previous failures
Pontiac, second car (stolen just to make the hit?)

He sat in the car, staring at the empty lot, until his hands stopped shaking. Weary, he drove home, wondering where Judge would be waiting for him the next time.

⊀ ⋀ ⊁

The telephone woke him Saturday morning.

Rising from a darkness full of accusatory corpses, Chase put a hand on the receiver—then realized who might be calling. Judge hadn't phoned since early Wednesday night. He was overdue.

"Hello?"
"Ben?"
"Yes?"
"Dr. Fauvel here."

It was the first time that Chase had ever heard the psychiatrist on the phone. Except during their office sessions, all communications were through Miss Pringle.

"What do you want?" Chase asked. The name had fully awakened him and chased off his lingering nightmares.

"I wondered why you hadn't kept your Friday appointment."

"Didn't need it."

Fauvel hesitated. Then: "Listen, if it was because I talked to the police so frankly, you must understand that I wasn't violating a doctor-patient relationship. They weren't accusing you of any crime, and I thought it was in your best interest to tell them the truth before they wasted more time on this Judge."

Chase said nothing.

Fauvel said, "Should we get together this afternoon and talk about it, all of it?"

"No."

"I think you would benefit from a session right now, Ben."

"I'm not coming in again."

"That would be unwise," Fauvel said.

"Psychiatric care was not a condition of my hospital discharge, only a benefit I could avail myself of."

"And you still *can* avail yourself of it, Ben. I'm here, waiting to see you—"

"It's no longer a benefit," Chase said. He was beginning to enjoy this. For the first time, he had Fauvel on the defensive for more than a brief moment; the new balance of power was gratifying.

"Ben, you *are* angry about what I said to the police. That is the whole thing, isn't it?"

"Partly," Chase said. "But there are other reasons."

"What?"

Chase said, "Let's play the word-association game."

"Word association? Ben, don't be—"

"Publish."

"Ben, I'm ready to see you anytime that—"

"Publish," Chase interrupted.

"This doesn't help—"

"Publish," Chase insisted.

Fauvel was silent. Then he sighed, decided to play along, and said, "I guess . . . books."

"Magazines."

"I don't know where you want me to go, Ben."

"Magazines."

"Well . . . newspapers."

"Magazines."

"New word, please," Fauvel said.

"Contents."

"Oh. Articles?"

"Five."

"Five articles?"

"Psychiatry."

Puzzled, Fauvel said, "You're not managing this correctly. Word association has to be—"

"Patient C."

Fauvel was stunned into silence.

"Patient C," Chase repeated.

"How did you get hold of—"

"One word."

"Ben, we can't discuss this in one-word exchanges. I'm sure you're upset, but—"

"Play the game with me, Doctor, and maybe—just maybe—I won't make a public response to your five articles and won't subject you to professional ridicule."

The silence on the other end of the line was as deep as any Chase had ever heard.

"Patient C," Chase said.

"Valued."

"Bullshit."

"Valued," Fauvel insisted.

"Exploited."

"Mistake," Fauvel admitted.

"Correction?"

"Necessary."

"Next?"

"Session."

"Next?"

"Session."

"Please don't repeat your answers," Chase admonished. "New word. Psychiatrist."

"Healer."

"Psychiatrist."

"Me."

"Sonofabitch."

"That's childish, Ben."

"Egomaniac."

Fauvel only sighed.

"Asshole," Ben said, and he hung up.

He hadn't felt so good in years.

Later, as he was exercising the stiffness out of his battered muscles, he realized that making the break with his psychiatrist was a stronger rejection of his recent despair than anything else that he had done. He'd been telling himself that when Judge was located and dealt with, he could then resume his sheltered existence on the third floor of Mrs. Fielding's house. But that was no longer possible. By discontinuing all psychiatric treatment, he was admitting that he had changed forever and that his burden of guilt was growing distinctly less heavy.

Chase's pleasure in Fauvel's humiliation was tempered by the daunting prospect of having to *live* again. If he forsook the solace of solitude—what would replace it?

A new, quiet, but profound anxiety overcame him. Embracing the possibility of hope was far riskier and more frightening than walking boldly through enemy gunfire.

◁ ⋀ ▷

Once Chase had shaved and bathed, he realized that he had no leads to follow in his investigation. He had been everywhere that Judge had been, and yet he had gained nothing for his trouble except a description of the man, which would do him no good unless he could connect a name with it.

While eating a late breakfast at a pancake house on Galasio Boulevard, he decided to return to the Gateway Mall Tavern and talk to the real Eric Blentz to see if the man could put a name to Judge's description. It seemed likely that Judge had not just chosen Blentz's name out of the phone book when he'd used it in the Student Records

Office at State. Perhaps he knew Blentz. And even if Blentz could provide no new lead, Chase could go back to Glenda Kleaver at the newspaper morgue and question her about anyone who had come into her office on Tuesday—which he hadn't done previously, for fear of making a fool of himself or pricking the interest of the reporters in the room.

From a phone booth outside the restaurant, he called the newspaper morgue, but it wasn't open for business on Saturday. In the directory he found a listing for Glenda Kleaver.

She answered on the fourth ring. He had forgotten how like music her voice was.

He said, "Miss Kleaver, you probably don't remember me. I was in your office yesterday. My name's Chase. I had to leave while you were out of the room getting information for one of your reporters."

"Sure. I remember you."

He hesitated, not certain how to proceed. Then he blurted out a request or an invitation; he wasn't sure which it was. "My name's Chase, Benjamin Chase, and I'd like to see you again, see you today, if that's at all possible."

"See me?"

"Yes, that's right."

After a hesitation, she said, "Mr. Chase . . . are you asking me for a date?"

He was so out of practice—and so surprised to discover that he did, indeed, want to see her again for reasons that had nothing to do with Judge—that he was as awkward as a schoolboy. "Well, yes, more or less, I suppose, yeah, a date, if that's okay."

"You have an interesting approach," she said.

"I guess so." He was afraid that she would turn him down—and was simultaneously frightened that she would accept.

"What time?" she asked.

"Well, actually, I was thinking today, this evening, dinner."

She was silent.

"But now," he said, "I realize that isn't much notice—"

"It's fine."

"Really?" His throat was tight, and his voice rose toward an adolescent pitch. He amazed himself.

"One problem, though," she said.

"What's that?"

"I've already started marinating a lovely sea bass for dinner. Started preparing other dishes too. I don't like wasting any of this. Could you come here for supper?"

"Okay," he said.

She gave him the address. "Dress casually, please. And I'll see you at seven."

"At seven."

When the connection was broken, Chase stood for a while in the booth, trembling. Into his mind's eye came vivid memories of Operation Jules Verne: the narrow tunnel, the descent, the awful darkness, the fear, the bamboo gate, the women, the guns . . . the blood. His knees felt weak, and his heart beat rabbit-fast, as it had done in that subterranean battleground. Shaking violently, he leaned against the Plexiglas wall of the booth and closed his eyes.

Making a date with Glenda Kleaver was in no way a rejection of his responsibility in the deaths of those Vietnamese women. A long time had passed, after all, and a great deal of penitence had been suffered. And suffered alone.

Nevertheless, he still felt that making a date with her was wrong. Callous and selfish and wrong.

He left the booth.

The day was hot and humid. His damp shirt clung to him nearly as tenaciously as guilt.

◁ ∧ ▷

At the shopping mall, Chase browsed in the bookstore until shortly after noon, then walked up the carpeted slope of the main promenade to the tavern. The bartender said that Blentz was expected at one o'clock. Chase sat on a stool at the bar, watching the door, and nursed a beer while he waited.

When Eric Blentz arrived, wearing a rumpled white linen suit and a pale-yellow shirt, looking even heavier than he had appeared the previous night, he was friendly and willing to chat.

"I'm looking for a guy who used to come here," Chase said.

Blentz overwhelmed a bar stool and ordered a beer. He listened to the description but claimed that he didn't know anyone who fit it.

"He might not have been a customer. Maybe an employee."

"Not here, he wasn't. What do you want him for, anyway? He owe you some money?"

"Just the opposite," Chase said. "I owe him."

"Yeah? How much?"

"Two hundred bucks," Chase lied. "You still don't know him?"

"Nope. Sorry."

Disappointed, Chase got up. "Thanks anyway."

Blentz turned on his stool. "How did you go about borrowing two hundred bucks from a guy without learning his name?"

Chase said, "We were both drunk. If I'd been half sober, I'd have remembered it."

Blentz smiled. "And if he'd been half sober, he wouldn't have made the loan."

"Probably not."

Blentz raised his glass and took a swallow of beer. Light sparkled on the polished edges of his silver ring. A double lightning bolt.

As Chase walked across the tavern and out the door into the mall, he knew that Eric Blentz was still twisted away from the bar, watching.

Aryan Alliance. Some sort of club, like the Elks Club or the Moose Lodge, for God's sake, but for a bunch of white supremacists who had perhaps grown tired of running around the countryside in hooded white sheets and were looking for a more modern, urban image.

But why the hell would they want to kill a high-school boy like Michael Karnes? Why would one of these fanatics—Judge—be engaged in a campaign against promiscuous teenagers, ranting on the phone about sin and judgment? What did that have to do with making the world safe for the white race? Michael Karnes had been a white-bread boy—not a natural target for something like the Aryan Alliance but a potential recruit.

The blacktop in the parking lot was soft in places.

The summer sky was gas-flame blue. And as blind as a dead television screen, offering no answers.

Chase started the car and drove home.

No one shot at him.

In his room, he turned on the television, watched it for fifteen minutes, and turned it off before the program was finished. He opened a paperback book, but he couldn't concentrate on the story.

He paced, instinctively staying away from his window.

◁ ∧ ▷

At six o'clock he left the house to keep his date with Glenda Kleaver.

To avoid leading Judge to the woman and perhaps endangering her, Chase drove aimlessly for half an hour, turning at random from street to street, watching his rearview mirror. But no tail stayed with him along his circuitous route.

Glenda lived in an inexpensive but well-kept garden-apartment complex on St. John's Circle, on the third floor of a three-floor building. There was a peephole in her door, and she took the time to use it before answering his knock. She was wearing white shorts and a dark blue blouse.

"You're punctual," she said. "Come in. Can I get you something to drink?"

As he stepped inside, he said, "What're you having?"

"Iced tea. But I've got beer, wine, gin, vodka."

"Iced tea sounds good."

"Be right back."

He watched her as she crossed the room and disappeared down a short corridor that evidently led to the dining room and kitchen. She moved like sunlight on water.

The living room was sparely furnished but cozy. Four armchairs, a coffee table, a couple of end tables with lamps. No sofa. There were no paintings because all the walls without windows were covered with bookshelves, and every shelf was crammed full of paperbacks and book-club hardbacks.

He was reading the titles on the spines of the books when she returned with two glasses of iced tea. "You're a reader," he said.

"I confess."

"Me too."

"See any shared interests?"

"Quite a few," he said, accepting the tea. He pulled a volume off one shelf. "What did you think of this?"

"It reeked."

"Didn't it?"

"All the publicity, but it's empty."

He returned the book to the shelf, and they adjourned to two of the armchairs.

"I like people," Glenda said, which seemed an odd comment until she added, "but I like them more in books than in real life."

"Why's that?"

"I'm sure you know," she said.

And he did. "In a book, even the real bastards can't hurt you."

"And you can never lose a friend you make in a book."

"When you get to a sad part, no one's there to see you cry."

"Or wonder why you don't cry when you should," she said.

"I don't mind living secondhand. Through books."

"It has big advantages," she agreed.

He wondered who had hurt her, how often, and how badly. Beyond doubt, she had suffered. He could sense a depth of pain in her that was disturbingly familiar to him.

Yet there was nothing melancholy about her. She had a sweet, gentle smile, and she virtually radiated a quiet happiness that made him more comfortable in her living room than he had been anywhere since he'd left home for college seven years ago.

"When I returned to the reference desk at the morgue and you'd gone," she said, "I thought you were angry about being made to wait."

"Not at all. I just remembered . . . an appointment I'd forgotten."

"I'll be back on duty Monday if you want to stop around."

"You like working there?"

"It's nice and quiet. Some of the reporters can be too flirty, but that's the worst of it."

He smiled. "You can handle them."

"Reporters all think they're persistent and tough," she said. "But they're no match for a newspaper-morgue librarian."

"At least not for this one."

"Where do you work?" she asked.

"Nowhere right now."

"Waiting," she said, instead of anything that anyone else might have said. "Sometimes waiting is the hardest thing."

"But it's all you can do."

She sipped her iced tea. "One day there'll be a door like any other door, but when you open it, right in front of you will be just the thing you need."

"It's nice to think so," he said.

"Then you forget the pain of waiting."

Chase had never been party to a conversation half as strange as this—yet it made more sense than any conversation that he'd ever had in his life.

"Have you found that door?" he asked.

"There's not just one. A series of them. With spells of waiting in between."

Dinner was delicious: tossed salad, potatoes and pasta layered with spinach and basil and feta cheese, zucchini with slivers of red pepper, and marinated sea bass lightly grilled. For dessert, fresh orange slices sprinkled with coconut.

When they weren't talking in that strange shorthand that came naturally to them, they fell into silences that were never awkward.

After dinner in the dining area off the kitchen, she suggested that they adjourn to the small balcony off the living room, but Chase said, "What about the dishes?"

"I'll take care of them later."

"I'll help, and we'll get them done twice as fast."

"A man who offers to wash dishes."

"I thought maybe I could *dry.*"

After the dishes, they sat on a pair of lawn chairs on the balcony in the warm July darkness. The garden courtyard was below. Voices drifted to them from other balconies, and city crickets made a sound as lonely as any made by their country cousins.

When at last it was time to leave, he said, "Is this a magical apartment—or do you make it peaceful wherever you go?"

"You don't have to make the world peaceful," she said. "It is to begin with. You just have to learn not to disturb things."

"I could stay here forever."

"Stay if you want."

The balcony had no lamp, only fireflies in the night beyond the railing. In such deep shadows, Chase couldn't read her face.

He thought of dead women in a tunnel, half a world away, and the weight of guilt in his heart was immeasurable.

He found himself apologizing to Glenda for what she might have thought was a pass. "I'm sorry. I had no right, I didn't mean—"

"I know," she said softly.

"I don't want—"

"I know. Hush."

They were silent for a while.

Then she said, "Being alone can be good. It's easy to find peace alone. But sometimes . . . being alone is a kind of death."

He could add nothing more to what she'd said.

Later she said, "I only have one bedroom, one bed. But the armchairs in the living room were all bought secondhand, here and there, and one of them is a lounger that pretty much folds into a bed."

"Thank you," he said.

Later still, as he sat in the lounger, reading a book from her shelves, she reappeared, dressed for bed in a T-shirt and panties. She leaned down, kissed his cheek, and said, "Good night, Ben."

He put down his book and took her hand in both of his. "I'm not sure what's happening here."

"Do you find it strange?"

"I should."

"But?"

"I don't."

"All that happened is—we both found the same doorway from different sides."

"And now?"

"We give it time, enough time, and see if this is what we need," she said.

"You're special."

"And you're not?"

"I know I'm not," he said.

"You're wrong."

She kissed him again and went to bed.

And later still, after he had converted the chair into its fullest reclining position, turned off the lamp on the end table, and settled down, she returned in the darkness and sat across from him. He did not hear her coming as much as feel the serenity that she brought with her.

"Ben?" she said.

"Yes?"

"Everyone is damaged."

"Not everyone," he said.

"Yes. Everyone. Not just you, not just me."

He knew why she had waited for darkness. Some things were not easily said in the light.

"I don't know if I can ever . . . be with a woman again," he said. "The war. What happened. No one knows. I have this guilt. . . ."

"Of course you do. Good men wear chains of guilt all their lives. They feel."

"This is . . . this is worse than what other men have done."

"We learn, we change, or we die," she said quietly.

He couldn't speak.

From the darkness, she said, "When I was a little girl, I had to give what I never wanted to give, day after day, week after week, year after year, to a father who didn't know the meaning of guilt."

"I'm so sorry."

"You needn't be. That's long ago," she said. "Many doors away from where I am now."

"I should never touch you."

"Hush. You will touch me one day, and I'll be happy for your touch. Maybe next week. Next month. Maybe a year from now or even longer. Whenever you're ready. Everyone is damaged, Ben, but the heart can be repaired."

When she rose from her chair and returned to the bedroom, she left a place of peace behind her, and Ben found a sleep without nightmares.

⤢ ⋀ ⤡

Sunday morning, Glenda was still sleeping soundly when Ben went to her bedroom to check on her. He stood in the doorway for a long while, listening to her slow, steady breathing, which seemed to him to have all the subtle power of a gentle tide breaking on a beach.

He left her a note in the kitchen: *I've got some business to take care of. Will call soon. Love, Ben.*

The morning sun was already fiercely hot. The sky was gas-flame blue, as it had been the previous day, but it no longer seemed like a flat, blind vault. It was a deep sky now, with places beyond.

He returned to his apartment, where he encountered Mrs. Fielding in the front hall.

"Been out all night?" she asked, eyeing the rumpled clothes in which he'd slept. "You didn't have an accident, did you?"

"No," he said, climbing the stairs, "and I wasn't bar hopping the topless joints either."

He was surprised that he had been able to be brusque with her, and she was so startled that she had no reply.

After a shower and a shave, he sat with his notebook of clues, trying to decide what his next step should be.

When the telephone rang, he hoped it was Glenda, but Judge said, "So you've found yourself a bitch in heat, have you?"

Ben *knew* that he hadn't been followed to Glenda's apartment.

Judge could be aware of nothing more than that he'd been out all night; the bastard was just assuming that he'd been with a woman.

"Killer and fornicator," Judge accused.

"I know what you look like," Ben said. "About my height, blond, with a long thin nose. You walk with your shoulders hunched. You're a neat dresser."

Judge was amused. "With that and the entire U.S. Army to help you search, you might find me in time, Chase."

"You're part of the brotherhood."

The killer was silent. This was a nervous silence and therefore different from his usual judgmental silences.

"The Aryan Alliance," Ben said. "You and Eric Blentz. You and a lot of other moronic assholes who think you're the master race."

"You don't want to cross certain people, Mr. Chase."

"You don't scare me. I've been dead for years anyway. You've got a dead man looking for you, Judge, and we dead men never stop."

With sudden anger hotter than the July morning, Judge said, "You don't know anything about me, Chase, not anything that matters— and you're not going to get a chance to learn anything more."

"Whoa, easy, easy," Ben said, enjoying being on the delivery end of the needle for a change. "You master-race guys, you come from a lot of inbreeding, cousins lying with cousins, sisters with brothers, makes you a little unstable sometimes."

Judge was silent again, and when he finally spoke, he sounded as if he was shaking with the effort to control his anger. "Do you like your new bitch, Chase? Isn't that the name of the good witch in the land of Oz? Glenda the good witch?"

Ben's heart felt as if it had turned over. He tried to fake bafflement: "Who? What're you talking about?"

"Glenda, tall and golden."

There was *no way* that he had been followed to her apartment.

"Works in a morgue," said Judge.

He couldn't know.

"Dead newspapers. I think I'll send the fornicating bitch to another kind of morgue, Chase, a morgue where the dead have some real *meat* on them."

Judge hung up.

He couldn't know.

But he did.

Suddenly Chase felt pursued by a supernatural avenger. Justice had come for him at last. Out of those faraway, long-ago tunnels.

10

GLENDA ANSWERED BEN'S KNOCK, READ THE ANXIETY IN HIS EYES, AND said, "What's wrong?"

Once inside, he closed the front door and engaged both the latch and the deadbolt.

"Ben?" She was wearing a pink T-shirt, white shorts, and tennis shoes. Her golden hair was pulled back in a pair of ponytails, one behind each ear, and even as tall as she was, she still seemed like a little girl. In spite of what she'd told him in the darkness last night, she was the personification of innocence.

"Do you own a gun?" he asked.

"No."

"Neither do I. Didn't want to see a gun after the war. Now nothing would make me happier than to have one in my hand."

In the dining area off the kitchen, at the table where they'd had dinner the previous night, he told her about Judge, everything since the murder of Michael Karnes. "Now . . . because of me . . . you're part of it."

She reached across the small table and took his hand. "No. That's the wrong way to look at it. Now, because we met, we're in it together—and you're no longer alone."

"I want to call Detective Wallace, ask him to provide you with protection."

"Why should he believe you any more now than he did before?" she asked.

"The damage to my car, when the guy sideswiped it out at the mall, trying to run me down."

"He won't believe that's how it happened. You don't have any witnesses. He'll say you were drinking."

Ben knew that she was right. "We need to get help *somewhere.*"

"You were handling it on your own, tracking him down on your own. So why not the two of us now?"

He shook his head. "That was all right when it was only my life on the line. But now—"

"People in books," she said.

"What?"

"We can trust people in books. But here, right now—we can't trust anyone but ourselves."

He was scared as he had not been in a long time. Not scared only for her. Scared for himself. Because at last he had something to lose.

"But how do we find the creep?" he wondered.

"We do whatever you were going to do on your own. First, call Louise Allenby. Find out if she got the name of the guy who dated her mother, the guy with the Aryan Alliance ring."

"He won't be Judge. Louise would have recognized him."

"But he might be a link to Judge."

"That would be too neat."

"Sometimes life *is* neat."

Ben called the Allenby house, and Louise answered. When she heard who it was, her voice dropped into a seductive purr. She had the name he wanted, but she wouldn't give it to him on the telephone.

"You'll have to come around and see me," she said coquettishly. "My mom's away for the weekend with this guy. Got the place all to myself."

◁ ⋀ ▷

When Louise answered the bell, she was wearing a yellow bikini, and she smelled of coconut tanning lotion. Opening the door, she said, "I knew you'd be back to get the reward—"

When she saw Glenda, she fell silent.

"May we come in?" Ben asked.

Louise stepped back, confused, and closed the door behind them.

Ben introduced Glenda as a close friend, and Louise's face soured into a pout.

Heading to the living room, rolling her hips to show off her tight butt, the girl said, "Will you have a drink this time?"

"Early, isn't it?"

"Noon."

"No, thanks," Ben said. "We've only got a couple of questions, and we'll be going."

At the wet bar, Louise stood with her right hip cocked, mixing her drink.

Ben and Glenda sat on the sofa, and Louise carried her drink to an armchair opposite them. The girl slouched in the chair, with her legs spread. The crotch of her skimpy swimsuit conformed to the folds of flesh that it was supposed to conceal, leaving nothing to the imagination.

Chase felt uncomfortable, but Glenda seemed as serene as ever.

"The name you wanted," Louise said, "is Tom Deekin. The guy who dated my mom, the guy with the ring. He sells insurance. Has an office over on Canby Street by the firehouse. But he isn't the guy who knifed Mike."

"I know. Still . . . he might be able to give us the names of other people in the brotherhood."

"Fat chance." She was holding her drink in one hand and lightly caressing one well-tanned thigh with the other, trying to make her self-appreciation seem unconscious but being too blatant by half. "These guys are committed to something, you know, they have ideals—and you're an outsider. Why're they going to tell you anything?"

"They might."

She smiled and shook her head. "You think maybe you can squeeze a few names out of Tom Deekin? Listen, these guys have steel balls. They have to be tough, getting ready to defend against the nappy-heads and the kikes and the rest of them."

Ben supposed that some members of the Aryan Alliance might be dangerous—but most of them were probably playing at this master-race stuff, drinking beer and gassing about racial Armageddon instead of watching football games on the tube.

Glenda said, "Louise, as I understand it, you'd gone with Mike for a year before . . ."

"Before that fruitcake gutted him?" Louise said, as if to prove that she was as tough as anyone. Or maybe the coldness in her was as real as it seemed. "A year—yeah, that's about right. Why?"

"Did you ever notice anyone following you—as if they were keeping a watch on you?"

"No."

Ben knew what Glenda was after. Judge researched his potential victims to discover their sins, to attempt to justify his murderous urges as righteous judgments. He had followed Mike and Louise; he'd told Ben as much; therefore, they might have noticed him.

"You answered too fast, without thinking," Ben said. "Glenda doesn't mean was someone following you recently. Maybe it was even weeks ago, even months ago."

Louise hesitated, sipping her drink. Her free hand slid from her thigh to the crotch of her bikini. Her fingertips moved in slow circles over the yellow fabric.

Though she stared mostly at Ben, the girl occasionally glanced assessingly at Glenda. She clearly felt that they were engaged in a competition.

Glenda, in her serenity, had won all the necessary races years ago—and had never run against anyone but herself.

Louise said, "The beginning of the year, about February and March, there was something like that. Some creep hanging around—but it never amounted to anything. It turned out not to be any mysterious stranger."

"Not a stranger? Then who?"

"Well, when Mike first said he was following us, I just laughed, you know? Mike was like that, always off on one fantasy or another. He was going to be an artist, did you know? First he was going to work in a garret and become world famous. Jesus. Then he was going to be a paperback-book illustrator. Then a film director, paint with the camera. He never could decide—but he knew whatever it was he would be famous and rich. A dreamer."

"And he thought someone was watching you together?" Ben asked.

"It was this guy in a Volkswagen. A red Volkswagen. After a week or so I saw it wasn't another fantasy. There really was this guy in the VW."

"What did he look like?" Ben asked.

"I never saw him. He stayed far enough away. But he wasn't dangerous. Mike knew him."

Ben felt as if the top of his head were coming off, and he wanted to shake the rest of the story out of her without having to go through this question-and-answer routine. Calmly he said, "Who was the guy?"

"I don't know," she said. "Mike wouldn't tell me."

"And you weren't curious?" he asked.

"Sure I was. But when Mike made up his mind about something, he wouldn't change it. One night, when we went to the Diamond Dell—that's a drive-in hamburger joint on Galasio—he got out of the car and went back and talked to the guy in the VW. When he came back, he said he knew him and that we wouldn't have any more trouble with him. And he was right. The guy drove away, and he didn't follow us any more. I never knew what it was about, and I forgot about it till you asked."

"But you must have had some idea," Ben insisted. "You can't have let it drop without having found out something more concrete."

She put down her drink. "Mike didn't want to talk about it, and I thought I knew why. He never said directly, but I think maybe the weasel in the VW made a pass at him once."

"A pass?" Ben said.

"I only think so," she said. "Couldn't prove it. Anyway, it couldn't be the same guy that killed him, the guy with the ring."

"Why not?" Glenda asked.

"These Aryan Alliance guys, they hate fags every bit as much as they hate all the coloreds. No way they're ever going to let some pansy-ass wear the ring."

"One more thing," Ben said. "I'd really like a list of Mike's friends, five or six guys his own age that he was close to. Someone he might have told about this guy in the red Volkswagen."

"Five or six—you're wasting your time. Mike wasn't close to very many people. Fact is, Marty Cable was his one best friend."

"Then we'll need to talk to Cable."

"He's probably at Hanover Park. Summers, he works as a lifeguard at the municipal pool." She looked more directly at Glenda than she had since they'd entered the house. "You think Ben here is ever going to screw me?"

"Probably not," Glenda said, evincing no surprise whatsoever at the question.

"Am I a package or not?" Louise asked.

Glenda said, "You are a package, all right."

"Then he must be nuts."

"Oh, he's okay," Glenda said.

"You think so?" the girl asked.

"Yeah," Glenda said. "He's a good guy."

"If you say so, then he must be."

The two women smiled at each other.

Then Louise took her hand from her crotch, looked at Ben, and sighed. "Too bad."

In the car, driving away from the house, Ben said, "Is the world going to hell or what?"

"You mean Louise?"

"Are girls like that now?"

"Some. But there have always been some like her. She's nothing new. She's just a child."

"She's almost eighteen, going to college in the fall, old enough to have some sense."

"No, that's not what I mean. She's *just* a child, and she always will be. Perpetually immature, always needing to be the center of attention. Don't waste your time disliking her, Ben. What she needs is sympathy, and lots of it, because she's going to have a bad life, a load of pain. When her looks eventually start to go, she won't know what to be."

"She liked you, even if she didn't want to," he said.

"A little, yeah."

"You liked her?"

"No. But we're all God's children, right? None of us deserve what life's going to dish out to her."

They drove along a street lined with enormous trees. Sunlight and shadow flickered across the windshield. Light and shadow. Hope and despair. Yesterday and tomorrow. Flickering.

After a while, he said, "She's a perpetual child, but you've been grown up forever."

"In spite of everything," she said, "I'm the lucky one."

◁ ∧ ▷

Under the trees in Hanover Park, every patch of shade had been claimed by families with picnic hampers. Sunbathers lounged on big beach towels on the lawns, and games of volleyball were under way.

The Olympic-size municipal pool was full of screaming, splashing children. A lifeguard was posted at each end, on a raised chair, and half a dozen admiring teenage girls were gathered at each station, hoping to be noticed.

Ben led Glenda through the flesh market and introduced himself to Martin Cable.

The lifeguard was lean and muscular. He had a lot of long dark hair, but his face was as beardless as that of a much younger boy.

"Sure, me and Mike were buddies," he said when Ben asked him about Karnes. "What's it to you?"

"I don't think the cops are doing enough to nail the killer, and I don't like the idea of some lunatic running around with a grudge against me."

"Why should I care?"

"Your friend was killed."

"Everybody dies. Don't you watch the evening news?"

Because Cable was wearing mirror sunglasses, Ben couldn't see the teenager's eyes. He found it unnerving to watch his twin reflections in those silvered lenses and be unable to tell for sure whether Cable's attention was focused on him, on the parade of girls, or on the swimmers in the pool.

"I wasn't there when it happened," Cable said, "so how could I know anything that would help?"

Glenda said, "Don't you want Mike's killer to be caught?"

Because Cable didn't move a fraction of an inch or even tilt his head one degree to answer her, it was obvious that behind his mirror glasses, his attention was already on Glenda. "Whatever happens," he said cryptically.

"We talked to Louise Allenby," Chase said.

"Entertaining, huh?"

"You know her?"

"Pretty much."

"She said maybe Mike had some trouble with a guy a while ago."

Cable didn't reply.

Ben said, "She thinks this guy made a pass at him."

Cable frowned. "Mike, he was your fundamental pussy hound."

"I don't doubt that."

"Man, he didn't even get laid till he was halfway through his junior year, and then once it happened, he just went nuts for it. Couldn't keep his mind on anything else."

Ben looked around uneasily at the teenage girls vying for the lifeguard's attention. Some were as young as fourteen or fifteen. He wanted to tell Cable to watch his language—but that would mean the end of their conversation.

"You know his parents," Cable said, "you can see why Mike would go off the deep end over something—pussy, drugs, booze, something just to prove he was alive."

"I've never met his folks," Ben said.

"Ma and Pa Tightass. He just sort of broke loose, all at once. After that, his grades dropped. He wanted to get into State, but he wasn't going to make it if he didn't pull up his grade-point average. No college deferral. Hello, Vietnam."

Screams rose from the pool. They could have been the shrieks of a hyperkinetic child at play or the frantic cries of a drowner. Marty Cable didn't turn to see which. He still seemed to be focused on Glenda.

"Physics was his worst subject. He had to get a tutor Saturdays. The guy was a sleaze."

"This was who made the pass at him?" Glenda asked. "The tutor?"

"Tried to convince Mike there was nothing wrong with swinging both ways. Mike got another tutor, but this guy kept calling him."

"You remember the name?"

"No."

"Not even the first name?"

"No. Mike, he got another tutor, passed physics. But you stop and think about it, what was all the trouble for? He's never going to go to State after all, is he? He might've been better off just forgetting about physics and screwing his brains out. Better use of what time he had left."

"With that attitude, then what's the point of doing *anything?*" Glenda asked.

"Is no point," Cable said, as if he thought she was agreeing with him. "We're all meat." To Chase, he said, "You know how things really are—you were in Nam," as if he himself understood the horrors of the war thanks to his monthly subscription to *Rolling Stone.* "Hey, you know how many nuclear bombs the Russians have aimed at us?"

"A lot," Chase said, impatient with the boy's cynicism.

"Twenty thousand," Cable said. "Enough to kill every one of us five times over."

"I'm not too worried until it's six times."

"Cool," Cable said with a small laugh, impervious to sarcasm. "Me neither. Not worried about a damn thing. Take what you can get and hope you wake up in the morning—that's the smart way to look at it."

As a pair of squabbling crows flew low overhead, the lifeguard tilted his face toward the sky. The sun was a ferocious white fire on his mirror glasses.

◁ ∧ ▷

Lora Karnes apparently didn't believe in makeup. Her hair was cut short and carelessly combed. Even in the July heat, she wore loose khaki slacks and a long-sleeve blouse. Although she must have been in her early forties, she seemed at least fifteen years older. She perched on the edge of her chair with her knees together, her hands folded in her lap, hunched forward like a gargoyle that was queerly disturbing yet insufficiently grotesque to be used on a cathedral parapet.

The house was as drab and quiet as the woman. The living-room furniture was heavy and dark. The drapes were shut against the July glare, and two lamps shed a peculiar gray light. On the television, an evangelist was gesticulating furiously, but the sound was muted, so he seemed like a crazed and poorly trained mime.

Framed and hung on the walls were needlepoint samplers with quotations from the Bible. Mrs. Karnes evidently had made them herself. Curiously, the quotations were obscure and enigmatic, perhaps taken out of context. Ben couldn't make much sense of them or quite grasp what spiritual guidance they were supposed to offer:

> I WILL LAY MINE HAND
> UPON MY MOUTH
> > —*Job, xl, 4*
>
> PUT THEM IN MIND . . .
> TO OBEY MAGISTRATES
> > —*Titus, iii, 1*
>
> BLESSED IS HE,
> WHOSOEVER SHALL NOT
> BE OFFENDED IN ME
> > —*Luke, vii, 23*

AND JACOB SOD POTTAGE
—*Genesis, xxv, 29*

The walls also featured framed portraits of religious leaders, but the gallery was an eclectic mix: the pope, Oral Roberts, Billy Graham, a couple of faces that Chase recognized as those of tackier television evangelists with more interest in contributions than in salvation. There seemed to be a wealth of religious feeling in the Karnes house—but no clear-cut faith.

Harry Karnes was as drab as his wife and the room: short, only perhaps ten years older than Lora but so thin and prematurely aged as to be on the verge of frailty. His hands shook when they were not resting on the arms of his Barcalounger. He could not look directly at Ben but gazed over his head when speaking to him.

On the sofa beside Glenda, Ben figured that visitors to the Karnes house were rare indeed. One day, someone would realize they hadn't heard from Lora or Harry in a while and, upon investigation, would find the couple sitting as they were now, but shriveled and shrunken and long mummified, dead a decade before anyone noticed.

"He was a good boy," said Harry Karnes.

"Let's not lie to Mr. Chase," Lora admonished.

"He did well in school, and he was going to college too," Harry said.

"Now, Dad, we know that isn't truthful," Lora said. "He went wild."

"Later, yes. But before that, Mother, he was a good boy," said Harry.

"He went wild, and you'd not have thought he was the same boy from one year to the next. Running around. Always out later than he should be. How could it end any way but what it did?"

The longer that Chase remained in the warm, stuffy house, the chillier he became. "I'm primarily interested in this physics tutor he had back in the beginning of the year."

Lora Karnes frowned. "Like I said, the second teacher's name was Bandoff, but I don't remember the first. Do you, Dad?"

"It's in the back of my mind, Mother, but I can't quite see it," said Harry Karnes, and he turned his attention to the silently ranting preacher on the television.

"Didn't you have to pay the man?" Glenda asked.

"Well, but it was in cash. Never wrote out a check," said Lora Karnes. She glanced disapprovingly at Glenda's bare legs, then looked quickly away, as though embarrassed. "Besides, he only tutored for a couple of weeks. Michael couldn't learn from him, and we had to get Mr. Bandoff."

"How did you find the first tutor?"

"Michael found him through the school. Both were through the school."

"The high school where Mike attended classes?"

"Yes, but this teacher didn't work there. He taught at George Washington High, on the other side of town, but he was on the list of recommended tutors."

"Michael was a smart boy," Harry said.

"Smart is never smart enough," his wife said.

"He could have been something someday."

"Not with just being smart," his wife corrected.

The Karneses made Ben nervous. He couldn't figure them out. They were fanatics of some sort, but they seemed to have gone down their own strange little trail in the wilderness of disorganized— as opposed to organized—religion.

"If he hadn't gone wild like he did," Lora said, "he might've made something of himself. But he couldn't control himself. And then how could it end any way but how it did?"

Glenda said, "Do you remember anything at all about the first tutor—where he lived? Didn't Mike go there for the lessons?"

"Yes," said Lora Karnes. "I think it was in that nice little neighborhood over on the west side, with all the bungalows."

"Crescent Heights?" Glenda suggested.

"That's it."

Turning away from the television, looking over his wife's head, Harry said, "Mother, wasn't the fella's name Lupinski, Lepenski— something like that?"

"Dad, you're right. Linski. That was his name. Linski."

"Richard?" Harry suggested.

"Exactly, Dad. Richard Linski."

"But he wasn't any good," Harry told the wall past Ben's left shoulder. "So we got the second tutor, and then Michael's grades improved. He was a good boy."

"Once, he was, Dad. And you know, I don't blame him for it all. Plenty of blame for us to share in it."

Ben felt their weird gloom sucking him down as surely as if he'd been caught in a whirlpool in a dark sea.

Glenda said, "Can you spell that last name for me."

"L-i-n-s-k-i," said Lora.

Richard Linski.

"Michael didn't like him," Lora said.

"Michael was a good boy, Mother." Harry had tears in his eyes.

Seeing her husband's condition, Lora Karnes said, "Let's not blame the boy too much, Dad. I agree. He wasn't wicked."

"Can't blame a child for all its faults, Mother."

"You have to go back to the parents, Dad. If Michael wasn't so perfect, then it's because we weren't perfect ourselves."

As if speaking to the muted evangelist on the television, Harry Karnes said, "You can't raise a godly child when you've done wicked things yourself."

Afraid that the couple was about to descend into a series of teary confessions that would make no more sense than the words on the needlepoint samplers, Ben abruptly got to his feet and took Glenda's hand as she rose beside him. "Sorry to have brought this all back into your minds again."

"Not at all," Lora Karnes said. "Memory chastens."

One of the quotations on the wall caught Ben's eye:

SEVEN THUNDERS UTTERED THEIR VOICES
—Revelation, x, 3

"Mrs. Karnes," Ben said, "did you make the samplers yourself?"

"Yes. Needlepoint helps keep my hands to the Lord's work."

"They're lovely. But I was wondering . . . what does that one mean exactly?"

"Seven thunders all at once," she said quietly, without fervor—in fact, with an unnervingly calm authority that made it seem as if what she said must surely make sense. "That's how it will be. And then we'll know why we've always got to do our best. Then we'll wish we'd done better, much better, when the seven thunders roll all at once."

At the front door, as Ben and Glenda were leaving, Mrs. Karnes said, "Does God work through you, Mr. Chase?"

"Doesn't He work through all of us?" Ben asked.

"No. Some aren't strong enough. But you—are you His hand, Mr. Chase?"

He had no idea what answer she wanted. "I don't think so, Mrs. Karnes."

She followed them onto the front walk. "I think you are."

"Then God works in even more mysterious ways than anyone ever knew before."

"I think you are God's hand."

The scorching, late-afternoon sun was oppressive, but Lora Karnes still chilled Ben. He turned from her without another word.

The woman was still standing in the doorway, watching, as they drove away in the battered Mustang.

◁ ∧ ▷

All day, from Glenda's apartment to the Allenby house to Hanover Park to the Karnes's house, Ben had driven evasively, and both he and Glenda had looked for a tail. No one had followed them at any point in their rambling journey.

No one followed them from the Karnes's house either. They drove until they found a service station with a pay phone.

On the floor of the booth, an army of ants was busy moving the carcass of a dead beetle.

Glenda stood at the open door while Ben searched for Richard Linski in the directory. He found a number. In Crescent Heights.

With change from Glenda's purse, Ben made the call.

It rang twice. Then: "Hello?"

Ben said nothing.

"Hello?" Richard Linski said. "Is anyone there?"

Quietly, Ben hung up.

"Well?" Glenda asked.

"It's him. Judge's real name is Richard Linski."

11

THE MOTEL ROOM WAS SMALL, FILLED WITH THE RUMBLE OF THE WINdow-mounted air-conditioner.

Ben closed the door and checked the dead-bolt lock to be sure that it worked properly. He tested the security chain; it was well fitted.

"You're safe enough if you stay here," he said. "Linksi can't know where you are."

To avoid giving Judge a chance to find them, they hadn't gone back to her apartment to pack a bag for her. They had checked in without luggage. If everything went well, they wouldn't be staying the whole night anyway. This was just a way station between the loneliness of the past and whatever future fate might grant them.

Sitting on the edge of the bed, still childlike in her pink socks and twin ponytails, she said, "I should go with you."

"I have combat training. You don't. It's that simple."

She didn't ask him why he hadn't called the police. With what they had learned, even Detective Wallace would at least question Linski—and if Linski was the killer, then the evidence would fall into place. Anyone else would have asked him that tough question— but she was not like anyone else.

Night had fallen.

"I better go," he said.

She got off the edge of the bed and came into his arms. For a while he held her.

By unspoken mutual consent, they didn't kiss. A kiss would have been a promise. In spite of his combat training, however, he might not leave Linski's house alive. He didn't want to make a promise to her that he might be unable to fulfill.

He unlocked the door, took the chain off, and stepped outside onto the concrete promenade. He waited for her to close the door and engage the deadbolt.

The night was warm and humid. The sky was bottomless.
He left the motel in his Mustang.

◁ ᴧ ▷

At ten o'clock, Ben parked two blocks from Richard Linski's
house and put on a pair of gardening gloves that he had purchased
earlier. He made the rest of the journey on foot, staying on the
opposite side of the street from the house.

The well-kept house was the second from the corner: white brick
with emerald-green trim and dark-green slate roof. It was set on two
well-landscaped lots, and the entire property was ringed with waist-
high hedges that were so even they might have been trimmed with
the aid of a quality micrometer.

Some windows glowed. Linski was apparently at home.

Ben walked the street that ran perpendicular to the one on which
the bungalow faced. He entered a narrow, deserted alleyway that
led behind the property.

A wrought-iron gate punctuated the wall of hedges. It wasn't
locked. He opened it and went into Linski's backyard.

The rear porch was not so deep as the one at the front. It was
bracketed by large lilac bushes. The boards didn't creak under his
feet.

Lights were on in the kitchen, filtered through red-and-whitecheck-
ered curtains.

He waited a few minutes in the lilac-scented darkness, not thinking
about anything, geared down and idling, preparing himself for confrontation as he had learned to do in Nam.

The back door was locked when he quietly tried it. But both
kitchen windows were open to admit the night breeze.

Deeper in the house, a radio was playing big-band music. Benny
Goodman. *One O'clock Jump.*

Stooping low, he brought his face to the window and peered between
the half-drawn curtains, which stirred in the gentle breeze. He saw a
pine table and chairs, a straw basket full of apples in the center of the
table, a refrigerator, and double ovens. Cannisters for flour and sugar

and coffee. A utensil rack holding scoops and ladles and big spoons and cooking forks. A blender plugged into a wall outlet.

No Judge. Linski was elsewhere in the house.

Glenn Miller. *String of Pearls.*

Ben examined the window screen and found that it was held in place by simple pressure clips. He removed the screen and set it aside.

The table was just beyond the window. He had to climb onto it as he went inside, careful not to knock over the basket of apples. From the table he eased himself silently to the vinyl-tile floor.

The music on the radio covered what small noises he made.

Acutely aware that he was without a weapon, he considered trying the drawers in the cupboard by the sink and securing a sharp knife, but he quickly dismissed that idea. A knife would bring events to an unnerving point, full circle, except that now he himself would be the slasher—and would be forced to confront directly the issue of not Linski's sanity but his own.

He paused at the archway between the kitchen and the dining room, because there were no lights in that intervening space except what spilled into it from the kitchen and living room. He didn't dare risk stumbling over anything in the dark.

When his eyes adjusted to the shadows, he edged across the room. Here, a deep-pile carpet absorbed his footsteps.

He stood at the threshold of the front room, letting his eyes adjust to the brighter light.

Someone coughed. A man.

In Nam, when a mission was especially tense, Ben had been able to devote his mind to its completion with a singleness of purpose that he had never achieved before or since. He wanted to be as brisk and clean and quick about this as he had been about those wartime operations, but he was bothered by thoughts of Glenda waiting alone and surely wondering if the motel-room door would be one of those *special* doors beyond which lay the thing that she needed.

He flexed his gloved hands and drew a slow breath. Preparing himself.

The smart thing to do was to turn around right now, cross the darkened dining room as quietly as possible, cross the kitchen, leave by the back door, and call the police.

But they would be real police. Not like the police in books. Perhaps reliable. Perhaps not.

He stepped into the living room.

In a large armchair near the fireplace sat a man with an open newspaper on his lap. He wore tortoiseshell reading glasses pushed far down on his thin, straight nose, and he was humming along with Glenn Miller's tune while reading the comics.

Briefly, Ben thought that he had made a grave mistake, because he couldn't quite believe that a psychotic killer, like anyone else, could become happily engrossed in the latest exploits of Snoopy and Charlie Brown and Broom Hilda. Then the man looked up, surprised, and he fit Judge's description: tall, blond, ascetic.

"Richard Linski?" Ben asked.

The man in the chair seemed frozen in place, perhaps a mannequin propped there to distract Ben while the real Judge, the real Richard Linski, crept up on him from behind. The illusion was so complete that Ben almost turned to see if his fear was warranted.

"You," Linski whispered.

He wadded the comic pages in his hands and threw them aside as he exploded out of the armchair.

All fear left Ben, and he was unnaturally calm.

"What are *you* doing here?" Linski asked, and his voice was without doubt the voice of Judge.

He backed away from the chair, toward the fireplace. His hands were feeling behind him for something. The fireplace poker.

"Don't try it," Chase said.

Instead of making a grab for the brass poker, Linski snatched something off the mantel, from beside an ormolu clock: a silencer-fitted pistol.

The clock had hidden it.

Ben stepped forward as Linski brought the weapon up, but he did not move quite fast enough. The bullet took him in the left shoulder and twisted him sideways, off balance, and into the floor lamp.

He fell, taking the lamp with him. Both bulbs smashed when they struck the floor, plunging the room into near-total darkness that was relieved only by the weak light from distant streetlamps outside and the faint glow from the kitchen.

"Fornicator," Judge whispered.

Ben's shoulder felt as if a nail had been driven into it, and his arm was half numb. He lay still, playing dead in the dark.

"Chase?"

Ben waited.

Linski stepped away from the mantel, bent forward as he tried to make out Ben's body in the jumble of shadows and furniture. Ben couldn't be certain, but he thought the killer was holding the pistol straight out in front of him, like a teacher holding a pointer toward a chalkboard.

"Chase?"

Weak, trembling, cold, sweating, Ben knew that shock accounted for his sudden weakness more than the wound did. He could overcome shock.

"How's our hero now?" Judge asked.

Chase launched himself at Linski, ignoring the flash of pain in his shoulder.

The pistol fired—the *whoosh* of the silencer was clearly audible in such close quarters—but Ben was under the weapon by then, and the round passed over him, shattering glass at the other end of the room.

He dragged Linski down, past the fireplace, into the television, which toppled off its stand. It struck the wall and then the floor with two solid thumps, though the screen did not shatter.

The pistol flew from Linski's hand and clattered into the gloom.

Ben bore Linski all the way down onto the floor and drove a knee into his crotch.

With a dry and nearly silent scream of pain, Linski tried to throw Ben off, but he couldn't manage more than a weak shudder of protest.

Ben's wounded shoulder seemed afire. In spite of the pain, he throttled Linski with both hands, unerringly finding the right pressure points with his thumbs, as he'd been trained, applying as little pressure as possible but enough to put Linski out.

Getting to his feet, swaying like a drunk, Ben fumbled in the darkness until he found a lamp that hadn't been knocked over.

Linski was on the floor, unconscious, his arms out like wings at his sides, as if he were a bird that had fallen from the sky and broken its back on a thrust of rock.

Ben wiped his face with one gloved hand. His stomach, knotted with fear, now loosened too quickly, and he felt as if he might be sick.

Outside, a car full of shouting teenagers went by, screeched at the corner, sounded its horn, and peeled off with a squeal of rubber.

Ben stepped across Richard Linski and looked out the window. There was no one in sight. The lawn was dark. The sounds of the struggle had not carried any distance.

He turned from the window and listened to Linski's breathing. Shallow but steady.

A quick examination of his shoulder indicated that the bullet probably had passed straight through. He wasn't bleeding much, but he'd have to take a closer look at the wound as soon as possible.

In the half bath off the kitchen, he found two rolls of first-aid adhesive tape, enough to securely bind Linski. He dragged the killer into the kitchen and bound him to one of the breakfast chairs.

In the master bathroom, Chase took off his gloves and set them aside to avoid getting them bloody. He stripped out of his blood-soaked shirt and dropped it into the sink.

He took a bottle of rubbing alcohol from the medicine cabinet. When he poured it into the wound, he nearly passed out in agony. For a while he bent over the sink, paralyzed by the pain.

When he could move again, he packed the wound with wads of paper towels until the bleeding slowed even further. He slapped a washcloth over the wound and then wound wide adhesive tape over the entire mess. It wasn't a professional bandage, but it would ensure that he didn't get blood over everything.

In the bedroom, he took one of Linski's shirts from the closet and struggled into it. He was stiffening fast from the wound.

In the kitchen again, he found a box of large plastic garbage bags and brought one to the master bathroom. He dropped his bloody shirt into it. He used paper towels to wipe his blood off the sink and the mirror, and threw those in the garbage bag when he was done. Standing in the doorway, pulling on his gardening gloves, he studied the bathroom, decided that there was no trace of what he had done, turned off the light, and closed the door.

On his way downstairs, he stumbled and had to grab the railing for support. A spell of vertigo pulled a spinning darkness into the edges of his vision—but then it passed.

Judge's second shot had missed Chase, but it had thoroughly smashed a three-foot-square ornamental mirror that had hung on the wall above the bar at the far end of the living room. All the glass had fallen out of the ornate bronze frame, and fragments were scattered over a six-foot radius. In five minutes he had picked up all the major shards, but hundreds of slivers still sparkled in the nap of the carpet and in the upholstery of nearby chairs.

He was considering this problem when Richard Linski awoke and called out.

Ben went to the chair in the kitchen. Linski's wrists were taped to the arms, each ankle to a chair leg. He twisted and tried to break free, but stopped when he realized that he wouldn't be able to pull loose.

Ben said, "Where is your vacuum sweeper?"

"What?" Linski was still groggy.

"Vacuum."

"What do you want that for?"

Ben threatened to backhand him.

"In the cellarway," Linski said.

Ben took the vacuum to the living room and swept up every piece of shattered mirror that caught his attention. Fifteen minutes later, satisfied with the job that he'd done, he put the sweeper away again, just as he had found it.

He secreted the damaged mirror frame in a corner of the garage, behind a stack of other junk.

"What are you doing?" Judge asked.

Ben didn't answer him.

In the living room again, he replaced the television on its stand, plugged it in, switched it on. A situation comedy was playing, one of those in which the father is always an idiot and the mother is little better. The kids are cute monsters.

Afraid that his spells of dizziness were soon going to progress to disorientation, Ben righted the overturned floor lamp and examined the metal shade. It was dented, but there was no way to tell that the dent was new. He unscrewed the damaged lightbulbs; along with the larger scraps of the broken mirror, he threw them into the plastic garbage bag on top of the bloody shirt and paper towels. He used the pages of a magazine to scoop up the smaller pieces, and threw those and the magazine into the garbage bag.

Returning to the kitchen, Ben said, "Where do you keep spare lightbulbs?"

"Go to hell."

Ben noticed that there were no red marks on the skin over Linski's carotid arteries. The pressure had been pinpoint and too briefly applied to produce bruises.

Without Linski's help, Ben required almost five minutes to find the spare lightbulbs in the back of a kitchen cabinet. He screwed two new 60-watt bulbs into the living-room lamp. The lamp lit when he switched it on.

In the kitchen again, he got a bucket of water, soap, ammoniated cleanser, and a carton of milk—his mother's favorite spot remover—from the refrigerator. Back in the living room, with several rags and a sponge, he worked on the few small smears of his blood that marred the carpet. When he was done, the faint stubborn stains that remained were all but invisible in the long dark-brown nap. The room wouldn't have to pass a full forensic investigation, anyway. As long as it appeared that nothing had happened there, the police wouldn't take a closer look.

He put the cleaning materials away. He threw the rags into the garbage bag with the other items.

After that, he stood in the center of the room and slowly searched it for traces of the fight. The only thing that might draw anyone's suspicion was the pale, soot-ringed square where the ornate mirror had hung.

Ben pulled the two picture hangers out of the wall; they left small nail holes behind. He used a handful of paper towels to wipe away most of the dirty ring, successfully feathering the dirt to blend the lighter and darker portions of the wall. It was still obvious that something had hung there, though one might now think that it had been removed several months ago.

After locating the pistol that had flown out of Linski's hand, Ben returned to the kitchen. "I have some questions to ask you."

"Fuck you," Linski said.

Ben put the muzzle of the pistol against the bridge of his captive's nose.

Linski stared. Then: "You wouldn't."

"Remember my war record."

Linski paled but still glared at him.

"The silencer's homemade. Is this something the average physics teacher does for a hobby?"

"It's part of what we learn in the Alliance. Survival skills."

"Real Boy Scouts, huh?"

"It may be funny to you, but someday you'll be glad we taught ourselves good defense. Guns, explosives, lock picking—everything we'll need for the day when the cities burn and we have to fight for our race."

"What does the Aryan Alliance have to do with this, anyway?"

Linski's manner changed. He grew less arrogant and nervously licked his lips.

"I've got to understand what's going on. I have to know if they're going to come after me," Ben said, "this whole crazy group. And if they are—why? What did I step into the middle of when I pulled you out of that car on lovers' lane?"

When Linski didn't reply, Ben put the muzzle of the pistol against his right eye, so he could look directly into the barrel.

Linski sagged in the chair. A sudden despair seized him. "It goes back a way."

"What does?"

"The Aryan Alliance."

"Tell me."

"We were in our twenties then."

"We?"

"Lora, Harry. Me."

"Karnes? His parents?"

"That's how we met. Through the Alliance."

The connection so surprised Ben that he wondered if he were hallucinating the conversation. The pain in his shoulder had spread to his neck and up the back of his skull.

"They fell on hard times. Harry out of work. Lora was ill. But they had . . . the boy."

"Mike."

"He was a beautiful child."

Ben knew, didn't want to hear, had no choice but to listen.

"An exquisitely beautiful child," said Linski, clearly seeing the boy in his mind's eye. "Three, almost four years old."

Ben no longer pressed the pistol to Linski's eye. Now that he had started, the killer would need no encouragement to continue. His entire demeanor had changed—and he almost seemed relieved to be forced to this confession. He was unburdening himself for his own sake more than Ben's.

"I had some money, a trust fund. Lora and Harry needed money . . . and I needed what they had."

"They sold him to you."

"They set a high price for a night now and then," Linski said.

"His own parents," Ben said, remembering Lora and Harry Karnes and the enigmatic needlepoint quotations on their living-room walls.

"A high price in more ways than one."

"How long did that go on?" Ben asked.

"Less than a year. Then . . . remorse, you know."

"You realized it was wrong?"

"Them." Linski's voice, gray with despair, was briefly enlivened by sarcasm: "They had the money they needed, they were out of their financial trouble . . . so they were in a better position to find their misplaced scruples. They denied me the boy and told me to stay away forever. He was such a little angel. Forever, they said. It was so difficult. They threatened to tell others in the Alliance that I'd molested Mikey without their knowledge. There are some members who would take me out in the woods and shoot me in the back of the head if they knew what I am. I couldn't risk exposure."

"And all these years . . ."

"I watched Mikey from a distance," Linski said. "Watched him as he grew up. He was never again as beautiful as when he'd been so young, so innocent. But I was growing older and *hated* growing older. Year by year, I became more aware that I'd never have . . . never have anyone . . . anything as beautiful as Mikey again. He was always there to remind me of the best time of my life, the brief best time of my life."

"How did you manage to get the tutoring job? Why would he come to you of all people?"

"He didn't remember me."

"You're sure?"

"Yes. That was a terrible realization . . . knowing that every kindness I'd shown him was forgotten . . . every tenderness forgotten. I think he forgot not just me but *everything* that happened . . . being touched, being adored . . . when he was four."

Ben didn't know if his worsening nausea was a result of his wound or of Linski's strange characterization of the molestation.

The killer sighed with regret. "What do any of us remember from that far back? Time steals everything from us. Anyway, when he needed a tutor, he came to me because I was on the list the school gave him. Maybe it was a subconscious recollection of my name that made him choose me. I'd like to think he still held *some* memory of me even if he wasn't aware of it. However, I think it was really just pure chance. Fate."

"So you told him what you'd done to him when he was little?"

"No. No, no. But I tried . . . to reawaken his desire."

"It was focused on girls by then."

"He shunned me," Linski said, not with anger, not in a cold mad voice, but with deep sadness. "And then he told his parents, and they threatened me again. My hope was raised, you see . . . raised and then shattered forever. It was so unfair to have it raised and then . . . nothing. It hurt."

"Lora and Harry . . . they must have suspected you killed him."

"Who're they to point a finger?" Linski said.

"They gave me your name."

Ben thought of the way in which they had directed him toward Linski: Harry pretending to recall the tutor's name only with effort, getting it only half right, and Lora correcting him. Too gutless to violate the sixth commandment and seek the vengeance they wanted, they had contrived to see in Ben the hand of God and had deviously pointed him toward this man.

"I should have passed judgment on Harry and Lora too," Linski said but without anger. "For letting the boy become what he became."

"It had nothing to do with what the boy had become. You killed him because you couldn't have him."

In a still, solemn voice, Linski said, "No. That isn't it at all. Don't you see? He was a fornicator. Don't you understand? I couldn't bear to see what Mikey had become over the years. Once so innocent . . . and then just as filthy as anyone, as filthy as all of us, a filthy and callow fornicator. Seeing what he became . . . in a way that soiled me, soiled the memories of what we'd once had. You can understand that."

"No."

"It soiled me," Linski repeated, his voice gradually growing softer. He seemed lost and far away. "Soiled me."

"And what you did with him . . . that wasn't sin, wasn't filthy?"

"No."

"Then what?"

"Love."

War was waged to make peace. Abuse was love. Welcome to the funhouse, where strange mirrors reflect the faces of Hell.

Ben said, "Would you have killed the girl with him?"

"Yes. If I'd had time. But you interrupted. And then . . . I just didn't care about her so much any more."

"She was a witness. If she'd seen anything . . ."

Linski shrugged.

"All your anger turned toward me."

"You being a hero," Judge said cryptically.

"What?"

"You being the war hero . . . what did that make me?"

"I don't know. What did it make you?"

"The villain, the monster," he said, and tears welled in his eyes. "Until you showed up, I was clean. I was judgment. Just passing judgment. But you're the big hero . . . and every hero has to have a monster to slay. So they made me the monster."

Ben said nothing.

"I was only trying to preserve the memory of Mikey the way he was so long ago. The pure innocence that he was. Preserve it. Is that so bad?"

Finally, Linski sobbed.

Ben could not bear the weeping.

The killer huddled pathetically in the chair, trying to lift his taped hands so that he could bury his face in them.

The trial. The press. Unending publicity. Back into the attic room to escape. And Linski, huddled and pathetic, would never spend time in a prison. A mental hospital, yes, but not prison. Innocent by reason of insanity.

He put one hand on Linski's head, smoothed his hair.

Linski leaned into the comforting touch.

"Everybody's damaged," Chase said.

Linski looked up at him through tears.

"Some are just damaged too much. Far too much."

"I'm sorry," Linski said.

"It's okay."

"I'm sorry."

"Open wide for me."

Linski knew what was coming. He opened his mouth.

Ben put the muzzle between Linski's teeth and pulled the trigger.

He dropped the gun and turned away from the dead man, walked into the hall, and opened the bathroom door. He put up the lid of the toilet bowl, dropped to his knees, and vomited. He remained on his knees for a long time before he could control the spasms that racked him. He flushed the toilet three times. He put the lid down and sat on it, blotting the cold sweat on his face with his gloved hands.

Having won the Congressional Medal of Honor, the most sacred and jealously guarded award his country bestowed, he had wanted nothing more than to return to the attic room in Mrs. Fielding's house and resume his penitence.

Then he met Glenda, and things changed. There was no question about living as a hermit any more, sealed off from experience. All that he wanted now was quietude, a chance for their love to develop, a life. Fauvel, the police, the press, and Richard Linski had not allowed him even that.

Chase rose and went to the sink. He rinsed his mouth out until the bad taste was gone.

He no longer had to be a hero.

He left the bathroom.

In the front room, he unwound the tape from Richard Linski's wrists and ankles. He let the body slide out of the chair and sprawl onto the floor.

When he considered the pistol, he realized that there would be three slugs missing from the clip. In the den he found a gun cabinet and drawers of ammunition. He reloaded the clip, leaving out only one round. In the kitchen, he put the gun on the floor, near the dead man's right hand.

In the living room, he searched for the two slugs that Judge had expended earlier. He found the one that had passed through his shoulder; it was embedded in the baseboard, and he dug it out without leaving a particularly noticeable mark. The other was on the floor behind the portable bar, where it had fallen after striking the bronze frame of the shattered bar mirror.

It was a quarter of twelve when he reached the Mustang and put the garbage bag and the cotton gloves into the trunk.

He drove past Linski's bungalow. The lights were on. They would burn all night.

◁ ∧ ▷

Ben knocked twice, and Glenda let him into the motel room. They held each other for a while.

"You're hurt." When she realized the nature of the wound, she said, "I'd better get you back to my place. You'll stay with me. I'll have to nurse you through this. We can't risk infection. Doctors have to report gunshot wounds to the police."

She drove the Mustang.

He slumped in the passenger seat. A great weariness overcame him—not merely a result of the experiences of the past couple of hours but a weariness of years.

Heroes need monsters to slay, and they can always find them—within if not without.

"You haven't asked," he said as they rolled through the night.

"I never will."

"He's dead."

She said nothing.

"I think it was the right thing."

"It was a door you had to go through, whether you wanted to or not," she said.

"Only the Karneses can connect me to him, and they're never going to talk. The cops can't nail me for it."

"Anyway," she said, "you'll make your own punishment."

A full moon rode the night sky. He stared at its cratered face, trying to read the future in the destruction of the past.

NOTES TO THE READER

1

WHEN I WAS EIGHT YEARS OLD, I WROTE SHORT STORIES ON TABLET paper, drew colorful covers, stapled the left margin of each story, put electrician's tape over the staples for the sake of neatness, and tried to peddle these "books" to relatives and neighbors. Each of my productions sold for a nickel, which was extremely competitive pricing—or would have been if any other obsessive-compulsive writers of grade-school age had been busily exercising their imaginations in my neighborhood. Other children, however, were engaged in such traditional, character-building, healthful activities as baseball, football, basketball, tearing the wings off flies, terrorizing and beating smaller kids, and experimenting with ways to make explosives out of ordinary household products such as laundry detergent, rubbing alcohol, and Spam. I sold my stories with such relentless enthusiasm that I must have been a colossal pest—like a pint-size Hare Krishna panhandler in a caffeine frenzy.

I had no special use for the pittance that I earned from this activity, no dreams of unlimited wealth. After all, I had taken in no more than two dollars before savvy relatives and neighbors conducted a secret and highly illegal meeting to agree that they wouldn't any longer permit trafficking in hand-printed fiction by eight-year-olds. This, of course, was at least restraint of trade, if not a serious abridgment of my First Amendment rights. If anyone in the United States Department of Justice is interested, I think some of these co-conspirators are still around and available for prison.

Although I had no intention of either investing the nickels in a playground loan-sharking operation or squandering them on Twinkie binges, I knew instinctively that I must charge *something* for my stories if I wanted people to take them seriously. (If Henry Ford had launched the automotive industry by *giving* cars away, people would have filled them with dirt and used them for planters. Today there would *still* be no federal highway system, no drive-in burger joints, a gajillion fewer chase movies than Hollywood has thus far churned out, and none of those aesthetically pleasing wobbly-headed dog statues with which so many of us accessorize the ledge between the backseat and the rear window.) Nevertheless, when the local fiction-consumer cartel tried to close me down at the age of eight, I continued to produce stories and gave them away without charge.

Later, as an adult (or as close as I have gotten to being one), I began to write stories that were published by real publishers in New York City, who didn't bind them with staples and electrician's tape and who actually produced more than a single copy of each tale. They paid me more than nickels too—although, at first, not a lot more. In fact, for years, I wasn't convinced that it was possible to make a living as a writer without a second source of income. Aware that second occupations for writers need to be colorful in order to make good biographical copy, I considered bomb disposal and hijacking airliners for ransom. Fortunately, my wonderful wife's earning capacity, frugality, and awesome common sense prevented me from becoming either a resident of a federal penitentiary or a pile of unidentifiable remains.

Eventually, as my books became best-sellers, the nickels piled up, and one day I was offered a substantial four-book deal that was as lucrative as any airliner hijacking in history. Though writing those four books was hard work, at least I didn't have to wear Kevlar body armor, carry heavy bandoliers of spare ammunition, or work with associates named Mad Dog.

When word of my good fortune got around, some people—including a number of writers—said to me, "Wow, when you finish this contract, you'll never have to write again!" I expected to deliver all four novels before I turned forty-two. What was I then supposed to do? Start frequenting bars that feature dwarf-tossing contests? That is *exactly* the kind of aberrant and socially unacceptable activity that guys like me are liable to slide into if we don't keep busy.

More to the point, I had written most of my life, undeterred when the pay was poor, unfazed when writing didn't even pay nickels, so I was unlikely to stop when, at last, I found an audience that liked my work. It isn't the money that motivates: It's the love of the process itself, the storytelling, the creation of characters who live and breathe, the joy of struggling to take words and make a kind of music with them as best I can.

Writing fiction can be grueling when I'm on, say, the twenty-sixth draft of a page (some go through fewer than twenty-six, some more, depending on the daily fluctuation in my insanity quotient). After endlessly fussing with syntax and word choice, after having been at the computer ten hours, there are times when I'd much rather be working as a stock clerk in a supermarket warehouse or washing dishes in a steam-filled institutional kitchen—jobs that I've held, though as briefly as possible. In my worst moments, I'd even rather be gutting halibut in the reeking hold of an Alaskan fishing trawler or, God help me, assisting space aliens with those proctological examinations that they seem intent on giving to hapless, abducted Americans from every walk of life.

But understand: Writing fiction is also intellectually and emotionally satisfying—and great *fun*. If a writer *isn't* having fun when he's working, the stories that he produces are never going to be a pleasure to read. No one will buy them, and his public career, at least, will soon end.

For me, that is the secret to a successful, prolific career as a writer: Have fun, entertain yourself with your work, make yourself laugh and cry with your own stories, make yourself shiver in suspense along with your characters. If you can do that, then you will most likely find a large audience; but even if a large audience is never found, you'll have a happy life. I don't measure success by the number of copies sold but by the delight that I get from the process and the finished work.

Oh, yes, from time to time, a rare disturbed individual with a public forum *does* measure my success by what I earn—and gets really *steamed* about it. The fact that people take pleasure in my work becomes an intolerable personal affront to this odd duck, and he (or she) periodically produces long paragraphs of execrable syntax in support of the proposition that the world is going to hell simply because I am in it and doing all right for myself. (I'm not talking here of genuine critics; critics are a different group, and ninety percent of them like what I do; the other ten percent manage to dislike it without implying either that I have deadly body odor or that I'm an undiscovered serial killer.) Although the work of brilliant medical researchers is routinely reported on page twenty-three, if at all, and although millions of acts of courage and gratuitous kindness go unreported every day, one of these crusaders nevertheless fills astounding amounts of newspaper space with claims, ipse dixit, that I am the literary Antichrist.

I'm not the only target of such stuff, of course; *every* successful writer is stalked by such weird fauna on occasion. In our house, being a charitable bunch, we kindly refer to these folks as "spiteful malcontents" or "humorless scum." (In more enlightened centuries than ours, they were correctly seen as being possessed by demons and were dealt with accordingly.)

My point—have faith; one exists—is that writing for the sheer *love* of it is even a defense against unprovoked assaults by the spawn of Satan. What these occasional ink-stained stalkers never understand is that even if they were to get their wish, even if no publisher on earth would issue my work, I'd be compelled to write, to make my little books with staples and electrician's tape if necessary—and *give* them copies to annoy them. There is no escape from me. Be afraid. Be very afraid.

2

MOST LITERARY AGENTS ADVISE YOUNG WRITERS TO AVOID WRITING short stories. Spending time on short fiction is widely considered dumb, unproductive, self-destructive, the sure sign of a hopeless amateur, and a reliable indicator that the writer is the progeny of a marriage between first cousins.

This prejudice arises from the hard fact that there are very few markets for short stories. Most magazines do not use them, and annually only a handful of anthologies are published with all-new material. If Edgar Allan Poe were alive today, his agent would be constantly slapping him upside the head with tightly rolled copies of his brilliant short stories and novelettes, yelling, "Full-length novels, you moron! Pay attention! What's the matter with you—are you shooting heroin or something? Write for the market! No more of this midlength 'Fall of the House of Usher' crap!"

Furthermore, existing markets for short fiction don't pay well. Generally, a short story will earn only a few hundred dollars. If the writer manages to place the piece with *Playboy*, he might actually make a few *thousand* bucks for it—and for the extra compensation, he will happily delude himself into believing that at least one of the magazine's millions of oglers will, in fact, read it. Nevertheless, a short story can take two or three weeks—or two months!—to write, so even with an occasional *Playboy* sale, any author concentrating on short fiction will eat a lot of rice and beans—and even, from time to time, less costly food like hay. After mercilessly pummeling poor troubled Poe with the manuscript of "The Tell-Tale Heart," his agent would no doubt shriek at him, "Novels! Novels, novels, you moron! Writing novels is where the money is, Eddie! Listen, take that weird 'Masque of the Red Death' thing, shorten the title to something punchier like 'Red Death,' pump it up to at least three hundred thousand words, make a doorstop out of it, and then you'll *have* something! We might even get a film sale! And will you write in a role for Jim Carrey, for God's sake? Couldn't this Red Death character be a little less *solemn*, Eddie? Couldn't he be a little *goofy?*"

In spite of the risk of being pummeled by our agents and being seen as fools-dreamers-amateurs-geeks by other writers smart enough not to waste their time on short fiction, some of us still manage to squeeze in a short story or a novelette from time to time. That's because ideas come to us that simply will not fly at a hundred and fifty thousand words or more but that haunt us, won't let go of us, *demand* to be written. So we get out our tablets, our staplers, our rolls of electrician's tape....

This book contains fourteen pieces of fiction shorter than my usual novels. Many of you would probably prefer to have another novel, and one is coming along later in the year (remember, there is no escape from me), but in the meantime, I think you'll enjoy this collection. Actually, a lot of you have been asking for it. Anyway, I had as much fun writing the stories herein as I have writing a novel, so if my aforementioned theory is correct, you'll have fun reading them. I sure hope so. You are the reason that I have a career, and when you lay your money down, you have a right to expect some fun in return. Besides, I don't want any of you to feel that you have to smack me upside the head with this volume; it must weigh a couple of pounds, and if I'm smacked with it too often, I'm going to wind up writing even stranger stories than I already do.

3

OF THE STORIES HEREIN, TWO ACTUALLY *ARE* NOVELS, SINCE A "NOVEL-length" work is usually defined as anything at least fifty thousand words long. The first of those—the title story, "Strange Highways"—appears for the first time here. It's one of my rare ventures into supernatural fiction: At novel length, the list of supernatural tales on my resumé includes only *Darkfall, The Funhouse, The Mask, Hideaway,* and maybe *The Servants of Twilight.* Although as a reader I love such stories, I tend not to write about vampires, werewolves, haunted houses, or house pets that die and then return from the Other Side with a maniacal determination to wreak vengeance for having been forced to eat out of a bowl on the floor all those years instead of at the table with the rest of the family. "Strange Highways" was an idea I couldn't shake, however, and I've got to admit that a certain inherent power in stories of the supernatural makes them terrific fun to write.

The other novel-length piece included here is "Chase." A version of this story was published by Random House, under the pen name K. R. Dwyer, when I was just a puppy. As Dwyer, I also wrote *Shattered*, which has been available under my real name for years. When I reread "Chase" for possible inclusion in this collection, I blushed and groaned nonstop because it had "beginner" written all over it—also "meandering" and "sloppy"—although it had been well reviewed in many places at the time of publication. The character of Ben Chase still intrigued me, however, and the basic story still had power. So, before packing it up and sending it off to Warner

Books, I revised it. The revision resulted in the cutting of at least twenty-five percent of the original text, the addition of new scenes, and a thorough cleanup of the prose and dialogue. As always happens when I revisit a work from early in my career, I was tempted to change the entire intent of the story, the style, the characters, the plot—and turn it into a piece that would read exactly as if I had written it today. That isn't the point of collecting previous work, of course; a book like *Strange Highways* is *supposed* to show the author's range of interests and various approaches over the years. Consequently, I restrained myself. "Chase" is straight psychological suspense, with no hint of the supernatural; it's also character driven, relying almost entirely on the character of Benjamin Chase for its effect, so if he doesn't intrigue you, I'm in deep trouble. One warning: This is a fairly dark piece, and some of Ben Chase's moral choices may startle you, Gentle Reader—though they're virtually the only ones he could have made.

I won't write notes on each story in *Strange Highways*. If you want to be bored by literary analysis, you can always take a college course. A few pieces, however, require a word or two:

"Kittens" is the first short story that I ever sold. It was written while I was in college, won a prize in an annual fiction competition for college students sponsored by the *Atlantic Monthly*, and then earned me fifty dollars when it was bought by a magazine called *Readers & Writers*. As I recall, *Readers & Writers* went belly up soon thereafter. Over the years, I have had books released by the following publishers that *also* went out of business: Atheneum, Dial Press, Bobbs-Merrill, J. P. Lippincott, Lancer, and Paperback Library. I informed Warner Books of this unsettling fact, but brave souls that they are, they accepted *Strange Highways* with enthusiasm.

"Bruno," a science-fiction parody of a private-eye story (!) is just meant to be a hoot. I revised and updated it from the original text and had a darn good time with it. As you know, virtually all my novels since *Watchers* have included substantial comic elements. Since most of the stories in this book do *not* have comic elements, I was itching to balance the tone with some flat-out silliness, and "Bruno" seemed to do the trick.

"Twilight of the Dawn" is my personal favorite of all the short fiction that I have written—and the piece that has generated the most mail in spite of appearing in a relatively obscure anthology. I think it appeals to people because it is about faith and hope—but is not in the least sentimental. The narrator is a cold fish for most of the story, and when he is eventually humanized through personal suffering and tragedy, his grudging admission that life may have meaning is effective. At least it was for me when I was writing the piece.

Finally, "Trapped" originally appeared in an anthology titled *Stalkers*, with an introduction that some readers say they enjoyed a great deal. So here's what I said about it then:

A major national magazine, which shall remain nameless, asked my agent if I would be willing to write a two-part novella dealing with genetic engineering, scary but not too bloody, incorporating a few of the elements of *Watchers* (my novel that dealt with the same subject). They offered excellent pay; furthermore, the appearance of the piece in two successive issues would reach many millions of readers, providing considerable exposure. I'd long had the idea for "Trapped." In fact, it predated *Watchers*, and after writing that novel, I figured that I'd never do the novella because of the similarities. Now someone wanted the piece precisely *because* of those similarities.

Well, hey, kismet. I seemed destined to write the story. It would be a nice break between long novels. Nothing could be easier, huh?

Every writer is an optimist at heart. Even if his work trades in cynicism and despair, even if he is genuinely weary of the world and cold in his soul, a writer is always sure that the end of the rainbow will inevitably be found on the publication date of his next novel. "Life is crap," he will say, and seem to mean it, and a moment later will be caught dreamily ruminating on his pending elevation by critics to the pantheon of American writers *and* to the top of the *New York Times* best-seller list.

The aforementioned magazine had certain requirements for the novella. It had to be between twenty-two and twenty-three thousand words. It had to divide naturally into two parts, slightly past the midpoint. No problem. I set to work, and in time I delivered to specifications, without having to strain or contort the tale.

The editors loved the piece. Couldn't wait to publish it. They virtually pinched my cheeks with pleasure, the way your grandma does when she hears that you received a good report card and that you are not into satanic rock 'n' roll or human sacrifices, the way that other eight-year-olds are.

Then a few weeks passed, and they came back and said, "Listen, we like this so much that we don't want the impact of it to be diluted by spreading it over two issues. It should appear in a single issue. But we don't have *room* for quite this much fiction in one issue, so you'll have to cut it." Cut it? How much? "In half."

Having been commissioned to produce a two-parter of a certain length, I might have been justified if I had responded to this suggestion with anger and a sullen refusal to discuss the matter further. Instead, I banged my head against the top of my desk, as hard as I could, for . . . oh, for about half an hour. Maybe forty minutes. Well, maybe even forty-five minutes, but surely no longer. Then, slightly dazed and with oak splinters from the desk embedded in my forehead, I called my agent and suggested an alternative. If I put in another week or so on the piece, with much effort, I might be able to pare it down as far as eighteen to nineteen thousand words, but that would be all I could do if I was to hold fast to the story values that made me want to write "Trapped" in the first place.

The magazine editors considered my proposal and decided that if the story could be printed in slightly smaller type than they usually employed, the new length would fit within their space limitations. I sat down at my word processor again. A week later the work was done—but I had even more oak splinters in my head, and the top of the desk looked like hell.

When the new version was finished—and just as it was being submitted—the editors decided that eighteen to nineteen thousand words were still too many, that the solution offered by a smaller than usual type size was too problematic, and that about four or five thousand *more* words would have to come out. "Not to worry," I was assured, "we'll cut it for you."

Fifteen minutes later, my desk collapsed from the additional pounding (and to this day, it is necessary for me to apply lemon-oil polish to my forehead once a week, because the ratio of wood content to flesh is now so high that the upper portion of my facial structure is classified as furniture by federal law).

Apparently, major magazines often fiddle with writers' prose, and writers don't care much. But I sure care, and I can't bear to relinquish authorial control to anyone. Therefore, I asked that the script be returned, told them that they could keep their money, and put "Trapped" on the shelf, telling myself that I had not really *wasted* weeks and weeks of my time but had, in fact, come out of the affair with a valuable lesson: *Nota bene*—never write for a major national magazine, on commission, unless you are able to hold the editor's favorite child hostage through publication date of the issue that contains your work.

Shortly thereafter, a fine suspense writer named Ed Gorman called to say that he was editing an anthology of stories about stalkers and people being stalked. "Trapped" came instantly to my mind.

Kismet.

Maybe it makes sense to be an eternal optimist.

Anyway, that's how "Trapped" came to be written, that's why it contains elements familiar to readers of *Watchers,* and that's why, if you see me some day, you'll notice that my forehead has a lovely oaken luster.